Browne und Nolan

The Irish Ecclesiastical Record

Volume II.

Browne und Nolan

The Irish Ecclesiastical Record
Volume II.

ISBN/EAN: 9783742802415

Manufactured in Europe, USA, Canada, Australia, Japa

Cover: Foto ©Andreas Hilbeck / pixelio.de

Manufactured and distributed by brebook publishing software
(www.brebook.com)

Browne und Nolan

The Irish Ecclesiastical Record

THE IRISH
ECCLESIASTICAL RECORD

THE IRISH
ECCLESIASTICAL RECORD

A Monthly Journal, under Episcopal Sanction

VOLUME II.

JULY to DECEMBER, 1897

Fourth Series

DUBLIN
BROWNE & NOLAN, LIMITED, NASSAU-STREET
1897

Nihil Obstat.

GIRALDUS MOLLOY, S.T.D.,

CENSOR DEP.

Imprimatur.

✠ GULIELMUS,

Archiep. Dublin., Hiberniae Primas.

TABLE OF CONTENTS

FIRST NUMBER OF NEW VOLUME.

"Ut Christiani ita et Romani sitis."   "As you are children of Christ, so be you children of Rome."
Ex Dictis S. Patricii, In Libro Armacana, fol. 9.

The Irish Ecclesiastical Record

A Monthly Journal, under Episcopal Sanction.

Thirtieth Year]
No. 355.

JULY, 1897.

[Fourth Series
Vol. II.

Nihil Obstat.
GERALDUS MOLLOY, S.T.D.
Censor Dep.

Imprimatur.
✠ GULIELMUS,
Archiep. Dublin.,
Hiberniae Primas.

BROWNE & NOLAN, Limited

Publishers and Printers, 24 & 25

NASSAU STREET, DUBLIN.

THE IRISH ECCLESIASTICAL RECORD

A · Monthly Journal · under Episcopal Sanction

THE LIBRARY OF THE VATICAN

AMIDST the confusion, rush, and unrest of the present time, it is a pleasant thing, and refreshing to the spirit, to turn aside for a while from the current of life around us, into the serenity of a past that is linked to the present by the golden chain of the arts and literature. 'Whatever,' wrote Dr. Johnson, 'withdraws us from the power of our senses, whatever make the past, the distant, or the future predominate over the present, advances us in the dignity of human beings.'

Few things fulfil these conditions more effectually than those store-houses of the world's literature, and the mind's food, represented by great and famous libraries.

All minds in the world's history [wrote a French Archbishop of the sixteenth century] find their focal point in a library. This is that pinnacle from which we might see all the kingdoms of the earth and the glory of them. My library shelves are the avenues of time. Cities and empires are put into a corner. Ages have wrought, generations have grown, and all the blossoms are cast down here. It is the garden of immortal fruits, without dog, or dragon.

Amongst the famous libraries of the world, it cannot be doubted that the most historically interesting, is the Bibliotheca Apostolica Vaticana, the Apostolic library of the Vatican at Rome. As regards the antiquity of its origin, the length of time it has existed, the preciousness of its contents, the number and greatness of the names of those who helped to form it, it claims the first place amongst the historic libraries of the world. The most celebrated antiquarian and archæologist of modern times, the Cavaliere de Rossi, has left us an exhaustive history, in three volumes, on the origin of the library of the Vatican. He reminds us in the opening sentences of this work, that the learned Oriental scholar, Assemani, himself chief custodian of the Vatican Library during the early part of the eighteenth century, ascribed the first origin of a Christian library at Rome to the Gospel of St. Mark, the amanuensis of St. Peter, and to the parchments that St. Paul when a prisoner at Rome, ordered St. Timothy to bring with him from Troas. There is abundant evidence to show that the first Christians were most careful as to the safe custody of their cherished documents, which were necessarily chiefly of a religious and sacred character. It is generally allowed that the earliest collections of books made by the Christians, consisted of those used in the Church services.

In the Acts of Minutius Felix, at the end of the second, and beginning of the third century, it is related that the magistrates made a raid upon the meeting-place of the Christians to seize their books, and how they found there nothing but empty book-cases, the books having been concealed by the Christians in their houses. Signor Lanciani, the present learned Professor of Archæology at the Roman University, in a most interesting work on Ancient Rome, recently translated into English, states that the first libraries of the first three centuries of Christendom were at Rome.

Such [he writes] was the importance attributed to books in these early days of our faith, that in basilicas or places of worship, they were kept in the place of honour, next to the episcopal chair. Many of these basilicas which we discovered from time to time, especially in the Campagna, have the apse *trichora*, that is, subdivided into three smaller hemicycles. The reason and the meaning of this peculiar form of apse was long sought in vain ; but a recent discovery made at Hispalis, proves that of the three hemicycles in those apses, the central one contained the tribunal or episcopal chair, the one on the right the sacred implements, the one on the left the sacred books.

However, the first record that we have of a building

raised for the special and exclusive purpose of a library in Christian times, is that of the building erected by Pope St. Damasus, who occupied the Chair of St. Peter from 366 to 384. He selected as a site the stables or barracks of the Green Squadron of the Charioteers of the Circus Maximus, hard by the theatre of Pompey, and there he raised a basilica, or basilical hall, surrounded by a square portico. This hall he dedicated to St. Lawrence, and the two original dedication-inscriptions have been discovered in a MS., formerly at Heidelberg, and now in the Vatican.

In the front of the building, over the main entrance, this inscription was set up in Latin hexameters :—' I have erected this structure for the archives of the Roman Church; I have surrounded it with porticoes on either side; and I have given it my name, which I hope will be remembered for centuries.' Around the apse of the inner hall there was another inscription which ran as follows :—' With the help of St. Lawrence the martyr, I have raised to Thee, Christ God, this hall, in thine honour.' The wishes of the Pope have been splendidly realized, for the building which now occupies that site has been known for centuries, and is still known, as the church of ' San Lorenzo in Damaso.' St. Jerome, who was once the secretary of Pope St. Damasus, and who afterwards sent to him from the East many valuable MSS., calls this collection of documents so housed by St. Damasus, the ' Chartarium Ecclesiæ Romanæ,' and asserts that the epistles, encyclicals, decrees, and constitutions of the Popes, the *Regesta Pontificum*, as they were called in later ages, were shown to everybody, and could be copied on application to the keeper-in-chief.

The Acts of the martyrs formed a considerable portion of the literature of the early Christians, which they guarded with jealous care. These acts were drawn up, as regards Rome, by the notaries, who occupied a most important and responsible office. They were at first seven in number, and afterwards fourteen. They were called regionary notaries, as they each had a special region of the city allotted to them. They have left their name to this day in the Notaries Apostolic, who are dignitaries of the Papal Court. A still

larger collection of documents consisted of the 'Epistolæ
Salutatoriæ,' which were what we should call letters of
introduction, given to pilgrims and travellers from one bishop
to another.   The lectors or readers, who constitute one of
the minor orders of the clergy, had the duty of safe-guarding
all these documents; and the place where they were kept
was called Archivum, or, as we should say, the Archives.
In the Archives of the present Vatican Library to-day, there
are no less than two thousand and sixteen volumes of
such documents, although the complete collection of the
letters of the early Popes collected by St. Damasus, has been
lost since the reign of Honorius III., who died in 1227, and
who is the last Pope who mentions having seen these documents, and who frequently refers to them.

The next step in the history of the origin of the Vatican
Library, after the times of Pope St. Damasus, takes us to
the seventh century, when the Papal Archives and books
were removed to the Lateran Basilica.   The building erected
by Pope St. Damasus in the fourth century survived, with
various alterations and disfigurements, till towards the end
of the fifteenth century, when in 1468 Cardinal Raphael
Riario, nephew of Sixtus IV., had it levelled to the ground,
and a new church built, about two hundred feet east of the
Basilica Damasiana, in conjunction with his magnificent
Palace of the Cancelleria.   'Those,' writes Lanciani, 'who
have visited Rome, or are otherwise acquainted with its
prominent buildings, will recollect, I am sure, the wonderful
courtyard of the Palazzo Cancelleria, the *chef-d'œuvre* of
Bramante, resting, as by a miracle of art, on a double tier of
light columns of red Egyptian granite.   These are the very
columns which Pope Damasus carried from Pompey's
theatre to his library, and which Cardinal Riario, in 1486,
removed from the library to his palace.'   The seventh
century is more remarkable for the dispersion of books from
the Papal library than for their collection.

In 601 Pope St. Gregory the Great sent to St. Augustine,
who was then preaching the Gospel to the Anglo-Saxons,
'plurimos codices,' 'very many books,' of which, unfortunately, only two, as far as it is at present known, have

come down to us. One is in the Bodleian Library, and the other is at Cambridge, both of which are considered by antiquarians as exceedingly fine specimens of sixth century palæography. They are both books of the Gospels— 'Evangeliaria.' Demands for books, from the Gallic, Spanish, and Alexandrian Churches, were not only taken into consideration at Rome, but granted as liberally as the resources of the Archives and library of the Holy See would permit. Missionaries to the northern regions of Europe were especially frequent in their demand for books. In 649 Amandus, Bishop of Trajectum, sent a message to Pope Martin I. to obtain duplicates from the Pontifical library. The answer of the Pope was, 'Our library is absolutely exhausted, and we could not give your messenger a single duplicate. We authorized him, however, to translate and copy some of them himself, but he left Rome in a hurry.' It is generally supposed that the reason why no duplicates could then be obtained, was because all the available copies of theological books had been distributed amongst the bishops who were assembled in that year, 649, at the great Roman Council, to help them in their inquiries about the heresy of the Monothelites.

During the seventh century, the founders of monasteries in England were especially distinguished as book-hunters, and St. Bede relates how one of them, St. Bennet Biscop, made no less than five journeys to Rome, between the years 653 and 684, for the express purpose of increasing the literary supply of his abbey. As a result of one of these journeys, he tells us, that he increased his collection with (and these are his own words) 'an innumerable quantity of books in literature.' On his death-bed, the last words of this saintly Abbot were words of exhortation to his successor to preserve and enlarge his 'copiosissima et nobilissima bibliotheca,' nearly the whole of which had been brought from Rome. The successor of St. Bennet Biscop shared his passion for books. He brought over from Rome a 'pandect' of the sacred text, of which he ordered three copies to be made; and when he was far advanced in years, he set out again for Rome, taking with him the fairest of the three copies as a present to the Papal library. The volume still exists, having ultimately found its way into the Medicean library at Florence.

By the eighth century the bulk of the collection contained in the 'Archivum' of Pope St. Damasus had been housed at the Lateran, and there it remained undisturbed until the tenth century, in the course of which the most precious documents were transferred to a stronghold, especially built for the purpose, in the ' Turris Cartularia, a massive tower built alongside the Arch of Titus, by the Via Sacra, and to which the Arch of Titus served as a buttress. A portion of the foundations of this muniment tower, which was only pulled down at the beginning of the present century, can still be seen. It is known that this tower fell into the hands of the Imperial troops in their invasion of Rome, in 1244, and it is supposed that it was then that the complete collection of the Regesta Pontificum collected by Pope St. Damasus was lost or destroyed. During the residence of the Papal Court at Avignon, we have no record of special interest concerning the Papal library ; but in 1443 after the Popes had left Avignon and returned again to Rome, Eugenius IV. had a catalogue made of the books that had been sent back to the Papal library at Rome, from Avignon, in which catalogue three hundred and forty books are enumerated.

We have now reached the period of the Renaissance, and find ourselves in the very centre of that fascinating and wonderful movement. It was on the 6th March, 1447, that Tommaso Parentucelli was elected Pope, and took to himself the name of Nicholas V. To him it is that we owe the foundation of the Vatican library, as it at present exists. Than this man, perhaps, no greater patron of the arts and literature ever lived. The son of a country doctor, after a brief course of studies· at the University of Bologna, he obtained the post of tutor in the noble family of the Strozzi, at Florence. Then for twenty years as a priest, he was Major Domo to the household of the Archbishop of Florence. He was afterwards elected Bishop of Bologna, and rewarded with a Cardinal's hat in 1446. Alike as

Bishop, Cardinal, and Pope, he was so kind to all-comers that no one went away unassisted. A signal proof of his benevolence is furnished in the foundation of the great Papal Almshouse near the church of the German Campo Santo, where on Mondays and Fridays about two thousand poor people received bread and wine, and every day a dinner was given to thirteen. When he was still a young man and poor he used to say, that if ever he had wealth he would spend it on two things—books and buildings. He was a genuine book collector, most keen in his search for new works, ransacking the libraries wherever he went, looking for fresh treasures. The future founder of the Vatican library gradually became one of the first connoisseurs of his day in books, and was looked upon as a great authority among bibliographers and book collectors. Æneas Sylvius Piccolomini, afterwards Pope Pius II., wrote of him :—' From his youth he has been initiated into all liberal arts ; he is acquainted with all philosophers, historians, poets, cosmographers, and theologians ; and is no stranger to civil and canon law, or even to medicine.'

Such then being the character of the man, it is not to be wondered at that during the pontificate of Nicholas V., Rome should have been transformed into a huge building yard, and immense workshop, and studio, as well as a vast literary laboratory. ' All the scholars of the world,' wrote Vespasiano Bisticci, ' came to Rome in the time of Pope Nicholas, partly of their own accord, and partly at his request, because he desired to have them there.' Besides scholars, a great number of famous architects and artists were employed by Nicholas. He it was who brought his dear friend, Fra Angelico da Fiesole, from the convent of St. Mark at Florence, to Rome, and caused him to decorate the Vatican palace with those sublime frescoes the remnants of which we still can gaze upon in that little shrine of Christian Art, known as the chapel of Nicholas V. But the crowning glory of the pontificate of Nicholas was to be the formation of the most noble library in the world. For this purpose he had agents at work in almost every country in Europe. No expense was to be spared—armies of transcribers, many of whom were French and German, were employed on the work of transcription of the precious manuscripts he had collected.

Nearly all the manuscripts were copied on parchment, and bound in a sumptuous manner in red velvet, with silver mountings, and silver clasps. The library was intended by the Pope to have been a public institution, accessible to the whole learned world. The zeal displayed by Nicholas in the prosecution of his undertaking was unexampled. During the eight years of his short pontificate, he had got together from all parts of the world a collection of five thousand volumes of rare and costly books, a very large proportion of which consisted of manuscripts of the Greek and Latin classics. The Latin MSS. in the library of Nicholas V., were contained in eight chests, or armaria, arranged after the manner of the ancient Roman libraries, in which the books were not placed in an upright position, as now, but laid lengthways, and piled up, one on the other, a wooden panel enclosing them on the outside of the case.

It was [writes Voigt, the historian of humanism] the greatest joy of Nicholas, to walk about his library, arranging the books, and glancing through their pages, admiring the handsome bindings, and taking pleasure in contemplating his own arms stamped on those that had been dedicated to him, and dwelling in thought on the gratitude that further generations of scholars, would entertain towards him, their benefactor. Thus he is to be seen depicted in one of the halls of the Vatican Library, employed in settling his books.

May it not with truth be said, that the hearts of every generation of the lovers of literature and artistic culture will go out in grateful and enthusiastic greeting, to that beautiful, serene, and noble character, whose only earthly ambition was to benefit mankind, by leaving to posterity, the most splendid collection of literature in the world ? 'Don't refuse,' he once said to one who hastened to receive a gift at his hands, ' don't refuse, you may not find another Nicholas.' So we might say now to all the lovers of learning and literature, 'don't refuse your meed of praise and gratitude to Tommaso Parentucelli, for his glorious, immortal gift, for you may not find another Nicholas.'

This noble Pope [wrote Gregorovius] might have been well represented with a cornucopia in his hand, showering gold on scholars and artists. In the eight years of his pontificate he filled Rome with books and parchments : he was another Ptolemy Philadelphus. Few men have had ampler experience of the happiness of giving towards worthy ends.

Here we should do well to recall two remarkable events of the time that helped to revive knowledge of the ancient Greek literature. These two events were, the temporary re-union of the Latin and Greek Churches, at the Council of Florence, and the taking of Constantinople by the Turks. Both these events brought the East into closer contact with the West than had existed for many centuries, but especially the fall of Constantinople, which resulted in the wholesale immigration of multitudes of the educated and cultured class to Italy, who brought with them treasures, far more precious than the silver and gold of which their conquerors had robbed them.

In the shipwreck of the Byzantine libraries [writes Gibbon] each fugitive seized a fragment of treasure, a copy of some author, who without his industry might have perished. The transcripts were multiplied by an assiduous, and sometimes an elegant pen ; and the text was corrected and explained by their own comments or those of the elder scholiasts. The sense, though not the spirit of the Greek classics was interpreted to the Latin world.

Many valuable Greek MSS. from the libraries of Constantinople found their way into the Vatican Library during the pontificate of Callixtus III., who succeeded Nicholas V. Crowds of Greek refugees found literary employment at Rome, Florence, and throughout Italy. It would be hardly possible to exaggerate the immense impetus given to the study of literature in the West, by the fall of the capital of the Eastern Empire.

The next great landmark in the history of the Vatican Library is the pontificate of Sixtus IV., who has left his great monument in the celebrated Sistine Chapel. The large hall constructed by this Pope, under the chapel, was

added to the library built by Nicholas V. It was
Sixtus IV. who appointed the celebrated Platina, the
author of the lives of the Popes, as chief librarian. William
Roscoe, by his *Life and Pontificate of Leo X.*, has made all
English-speaking people more or less familiar with the
splendid artistic and literary efforts of that Pope. Learned
and experienced men were frequently dispatched by him to
every country in Europe, and often to remote and barbarous
nations, for the sole purpose of rescuing the precious literary
remains of antiquity from destruction, by having them
brought to Rome, and placed in the Papal library. He
frequently sought the assistance of the other sovereigns of
Europe, earnestly entreating them to aid him by every
means in their power in his search for literary treasure.
Some of the letters of Leo X., written to various sovereigns
for this purpose yet remain. Those efforts of the Pope were
crowned with success, and the library was very considerably
increased under his pontificate.

In 1527, during the pontificate of Clement VII., Rome
was sacked by the Spanish and German mercenaries under
the Constable of Bourbon, and the library suffered much
from the general plunder and pillage that then took place
throughout the city, many valuable works there deposited
being destroyed or stolen. Under the succeeding pontificate
of the Farnese Pope, Paul III., the library began to recover
from its great losses, and to regain its former splendour. It
was Paul III. who first decreed that the office of chief
librarian of the Vatican should always be held by a
Cardinal.

We now come to the pontificate of the greatest of the
building Popes of the Renaissance period, Sixtus V. In five
years he had so thoroughly transformed the appearance of
the city, that the intelligent and cultivated Abbot of the
Benedictines of Mantua, Dom Angelo Grilli, could write,
shortly after the Pope's death :—

I am now in *Rome* after an absence of ten years, and do not
recognise it, so new does all appear to me to be : monuments,
streets, piazzas, fountains, aqueducts, obelisks, and other
wonders, all the work of Sixtus V. If I were a poet I would say

that to the imperious sound of the trumpet of that magnanimous Pope the wakened limbs of that half-buried and gigantic body which spreads over the Latin Campagna have replied—and that, thanks to that fervent and exuberant spirit, a new Rome has risen from its ashes.

Among the noble buildings put up by Sixtus V., the great hall of the Vatican library will always hold a foremost place. One thousand two hundred feet in length, covered with a dazzling brilliancy of colour, from its frescoed vaulting and wall panels, to its inlaid marble floor, it stands unique, in its long drawn perspective, as the noblest hall devoted to literature in the world, an immortal monument of Sixtus V. and his architect, Domenico Fontana.

Throughout the rest of Europe at this epoch, outside Italy, with the exception of those in some of the great monasteries, there can hardly be said to have existed any-thing worthy of being called a great library. No sooner did the influence of the Renaissance begin to make itself felt in the North than the religious troubles of the sixteenth century arose, and such brilliant and remarkable patrons of the new learning as Sir Thomas More and Cardinal Fisher in England, together with the fascinating and interesting Erasmus of Rotterdam, found themselves embroiled in that vast polemical wrangle which put an end for a time, in a large measure, to the study of humanities and literature in Northern Europe.

The dispersion and wholesale devastation of MSS. belonging to the monasteries and to the two Universities in England under Henry VIII. and Edward VI. was lamentable.

The invention of printing was by no means popular in Italy, and particularly at Rome, the chief reason being that it was looked upon as a mechanical and inartistic contri-vance, that threatened to put an end to the means of livelihood of a large number of persons who lived by copying and transcribing MSS. From an artistic point of view, there is much to be said for the prejudice against printing; for who would not say that a really beautiful MS. of the Middle Ages is not a finer thing as a work of art than the finest

printed book? However, printing was introduced very
early into Italy, and the first Italian printing-press was set
up in the Benedictine Abbey of St. Scholastica at Subiaco
in 1465, sixty years before Caxton set up the first English
printing-press in the Benedictine Abbey of St. Peter at
Westminster. The Vatican printing-press was set up soon
after that of Subiaco. The specimens of printing produced
at the Vatican press surpass in clearness of type and firmness of impression even the best productions of the Plantin
press at Antwerp.

In the sixteenth century two remarkable additions were
made to the library—one the library of the Elector Palatine
at Heidelberg, presented by Maximilian of Bavaria, to
Gregory XV., and the other the library of Urbino, which
was acquired by Alexander VII., together with a large
number of MSS. from the ancient monastery of Bobbio,
originally founded by the Irish monk, St. Columbanus, in
the Appenines. In 1689, Alexander VIII. placed one
thousand nine hundred MSS. in the library, which had
been left to his family by Queen Christina of Sweden.
During the eighteenth century almost every pontificate
made very considerable additions to the library. Two
celebrated collections of books were obtained for it by
Benedict XIV. in 1740, and Clement XIII. in 1748;
Clement XIV. in 1769, and Pius VI. in 1775, were important benefactors. Great damage was done by the French
in 1798, who carried off to Paris some of the most precious
treasures of the library, but nearly all of them were restored
in 1815. Pius VII., Leo XII., and Gregory XVI. each
added notable additions. Pius IX. was able to crown the
work of his predecessors by placing in the library the magnificent collection of forty thousand volumes that had belonged
to Cardinal Angelo Maii.

The printed books kept in the Borgia apartment are the
only ones in open cases in which the books are visible. All
the MSS. are in closed cases. The whole interior of
the library is covered with fresco paintings by celebrated
artists, representing scenes in Church history connected
with literature and art.

There are at present in the Vatican library 220,000 printed volumes, 25,000 of which are fifteenth century editions, and 5,000 Aldines. It contains 25,000 MSS., of which 19,641 are Latin, 3,613 Greek, 609 Hebrew, 900 Arabic, 460 Syriac, and 79 Coptic.

The Vatican collection of MSS. is the largest and most valuable of any in existence. The *Codex Vaticanus*, comprising the greater part of the New Testament, is the oldest yet known version of Holy Scripture, dating from the early part of the fourth century. The Virgil and Terence of the Vatican library are respectively the earliest known versions of those authors.

An interesting work might well be written on the famous librarians of the Vatican library, from Tortello, appointed by Nicholas V., to the learned Benedictine Cardinal Pitra, who held the office during the early years of the present pontificate. However, this paper cannot be concluded without a passing notice of one of those librarians to whom the world is indebted for the discovery of the palimpsest literature. Cardinal Angelo Maii, after holding the post of curator at the Ambrosian library at Milan for six years, was appointed sub-librarian of the Vatican in 1819, and soon afterwards librarian-in-chief. Whilst at Milan he had commenced a series of literary discoveries, which raised him to the very highest place among the students of palæography. In 1814 he discovered a palimpsest, written over by another MS., of some orations of Cicero. In 1815 he published the hitherto unedited works of the Emperor Marcus Aurelius. As librarian of the Vatican, his most signal discovery was the six books of Cicero, *De Republica*, of which only fragments had been previously known. This MS. was a palimpsest three times written over. The remainder of his life was spent in a series of discoveries which are of immense value to the literary world. He likewise was the first to publish the *Codex Vaticanus*, towards the end of his life. He died on the 9th September, 1854.

And now, having passed in rapid review through the well-nigh nineteen centuries of the history of the Papal library, it is time to finish this paper with a description of

the public reading-rooms, and consultation library of the
Vatican, which has been thrown open to the students of all
nations by Leo XIII. The description is written by one
who is himself a constant reader at the British Museum,
and who visited Rome last winter to consult documents in
the Vatican Archives :—

Dr. Salvatori's kindness [he writes] obtained for me access
to the Vatican Library without need of delay or further explanations. The first thing that struck me was the number of
workers. In Rome there are half a dozen libraries each with
manuscripts counted by thousands ; in London there is (Lambeth
apart, which is inconsiderable) only one collection, yet the
'Students' room (as it is called) at the Museum is, as a rule, I
am happy to say, comfortably empty ; the room at the Vaticana,
which is of about the same size, is packed with workers, our own
countrymen, by the way, being singularly distinguished by their
absence. I am told that at the Archives things are worse,
or (as we may look at it, if we please), better still. The
liberality of Pope Leo XIII. has, in this matter, been practically appreciated, except by our liberal and practical nation.
But then, we have better things to do, most of us, than to busy
ourselves over dusty parchments.

At the Vatican there is further liberality in the opening of
what is called the 'Consultation Library,' of printed books. We
descend a marble staircase which (in the surroundings here) may
be termed mean, to enter a series of noble halls some three or
four hundred feet long perhaps, bright and light, and decorated
with painting and guilding. It may be that the details do not
admit of being closely examined, but such surroundings have at
least this effect, that they enable the mind to address itself in the
happiest external conditions to tasks in themselves sufficiently
laborious and wearisome. Those who know by experience in
Bloomsbury, the effort that it demands, independently of the
work itself, to resist and conquer the adverse influences of gloom
without the building, and dinginess within, will feel grateful for
the brightness of that Roman library ; and turning to its shelves,
we are more grateful still. It is formed with the single and
special view to illustrate the twenty or five-and-twenty thousand
Vatican manuscripts, and enable those who work on them, to do
so with the utmost ease and profit. We are pleased, and justly
pleased, with the twenty-two or twenty-three thousand volumes
on the shelves of the Reading Room at the British Museum,
a collection covering every department of human knowledge and
inquiry ; here there must be more than double, or perhaps
treble that number of printed books, but restricted to a
special class of subjects : Biblical texts, Orientalia, patristics,

ecclesiastical history, the history of the Papacy, that is, the history of every European country, together with such necessary supplements as dictionaries, and a capital collection of catalogues of manuscripts of the libraries of Europe ; and all is at the freest disposal of the inquirer. This liberty, without restriction, is delightful ; there is nothing like it elsewhere ; and, happily, the various Governments, our own included, have understood its value, and have, by sending many official publications as presents, seconded worthily the intentions of the Pope.

But in walking through these halls, and using the good things thus freely placed at our disposal, the thought suggests itself—how long will our age admit of such generous treatment? Will it not be abused ? The warning has already come in the shameless mutilation of priceless manuscripts, a misfortune which, along with the *désagrémens* it entailed, brought about a calamity worse still, in the death of the late amiable and active prefect of the library, Monsignor Carini.

Here I must conclude this very inadequate and imperfect sketch of the formation of a famous library : a formation that began with the first Christian records, and, keeping pace with the progress of the ages, became in time, and still remains, the most glorious literary monument of all the Christian centuries, and the most splendid shrine of artistic and literary treasure in the world.

In endeavouring to put before you a brief epitome of the history of the formation of the Vatican Library, I have had to take you, as by a flying journey, from the beginning of the second century to the closing years of the nineteenth. I will only trust that, during the journey, you have not felt too badly the want of a sleeping-car.

W. H. KIRWAN.

BOOKS AND READING

CATHOLICS in general, and Irish Catholics in particular, hail with pleasure any work from the pen of that great father of the spiritual life—the illustrious St. Alphonsus. No saint has written a more imperishable name in the theological and ascetic literature of the Church than the Bishop of Agatha. There are two things which give man an abiding place in the remembrance of his fellow-men: piety and learning; and both of these St. Alphonsus possessed in a very remarkable degree even among the saints. No one can study his theological works without being astonished at the vastness and profundity of his erudition, and no one can read his ascetic and popular writings without being struck with the passion, so to speak, for holiness which breathes and glows through every page. And yet withal no saint was more in sympathy and touch with our poor fallen humanity.

Humility, self-abasement, is the dominant note and predominant virtue in the interior life of this truly great man, and compassion for the sinner the grand characteristic of all his dealings with his fellow-men. Hence Catholics all the world over, love his name, revere his memory, and like his books. His sons who have inherited the spirit of their great founder hold a high place in the hearts of the Irish people who are never slow to appreciate true zeal for the salvation of souls. Nor do we see any signs that the enthusiasm with which those good men are greeted and the reverence in which they are held, is likely to grow less with time. On the contrary, time which changes so much, seems to give them a higher and firmer place in the affections of the people. For these reasons we can, we think, bespeak for the popular works of St. Alphonsus ably edited by a distinguished member of his congregation, and admirably produced by Messrs. Duffy & Son, a speedy sale and a large circulation.

Those books which are amongst the best of the popular writings of St. Alphonsus, consist of eight numbers, each of which costs one penny. Each little book is complete in itself, and the seven are so connected as to form a complete whole and a beautiful chaplet of devotion. No subtlety of thought nor loftiness of words will be found in these works, but they are full of solid learning, of practical devotion, and like all his popular writings are replete with unction. They are adapted to every capacity and calculated to excite piety in every heart. Who can read his little treatise on Divine love, or the Passion of our Lord, or on prayer, whether mental or oral, without having his 'heart stirred within him' and yearning for better things—in fact, experiencing somewhat of the feeling which the Apostles felt on their way to Emmaus?

The writings of St. Alphonsus are especially suited for popular reading. United with a fervour and vehemence of devotion which is peculiar to himself, his works show in an equal degree acquaintance with the interior life, and that clear and perspicacious knowledge of the human heart by which its secrets are discovered, its vices laid bare, remed'es are discovered, and courage st'mulated. Those little looks come to us with every human safeguard and the highest sanction. They bear the *nihil obstat* of an able theolog'an, the *imprimatur* of the distinguished Archbishop of Dublin, and they come to us with the hearty approval of our present illustrious Holy Father. In his letter to the translators of the saint's works into French, Leo XIII. says :—

Although the writings of the Holy Doctor, St. Alphonsus Maria Liguori, have already reached the ends of the earth, to the greatest advantage of Christianity, it is nevertheless to be desired that they be propagated more and more, and put into the hands of everyone. For he has most learnedly accommodated the truths of faith to the intelligence of all; he has laid down the rules of morality for all; he has excited in a wonderful manner piety in the hearts of all; and to those wandering in the dense darkness of the world he shows the way by which, delivered from the powers of darkness, they can pass to the light of God and to His kingdom.

What the great Pontiff so ardently desires, and has so

beautifully expressed, the present editor has done. He has translated into English some of the select works of the saint, which will soon be followed by others, and has spared no labour nor cost to place them within reach of all. The work of the translator is not an easy one; and Father Magnier is to be congratulated in having done a difficult work in an admirable manner. Whilst conscientiously faithful to the original, he has executed the translation with a beauty of style and force of diction worthy of all praise. St. Alphonsus is fortunate in having found a translator with the loyalty and love of a true son. We cannot forbear writing that those works come to us with an especial appropriateness—we might almost say with a divine opportuneness —in these our days. For if ever there was a period which called for the unsleeping vigilance, the prudent foresight, the self-sacrificing zeal of the ministers of Christ, and some antidote against the great evils of the day, that period is the present. It requires no depth of thought, nor acumen of judgment, nor close acquaintance with the current events of the several nations, to observe that the Christian world, at the present day, presents an alarming spectacle. It is no longer, as of old, a single heresy or an eccentric fanaticism, the denial of some revealed truth or the excesses of some extravagant error, that trouble or devastate some portion of the Church of Christ, but it is a well-digested and well-organized system of unbelief, suited to every capacity, and reaching every intellect, adorned with all the embellishments of taste and eloquence by genius seduced by its suggestions, planned and planted by hired miscreants in every land, that corrupts and desolates the whole moral world.

It is no longer a controversy and a conflict between different forms of Christian beliefs, but a stand-up fight and a fierce struggle, and in the near future the struggle will be fiercer still between faith and infidelity. A spurious philosophy has prevailed under one name or another in every age, from the days of Democritus down to our own ; but it has received of late years an immense impetus from the audacious teachings of modern Materialists, call them scientists if you like. Emboldened by their successes in research, the professors of this Materialistic school have attempted to lift the mysterious veil of nature and have challenged the truths of Revelation on the very fundamental principles of the Christian creed. The inanities of Democritus which for so many centuries did duty as arguments to bolster up Materialism have, especially of late years, been re-inforced by a long line of sophistries, call them arguments if you will, taken from the whole field of the physical sciences. In fact, the Materialistic theories of to-day which deify reason and eternize matter—and recognise in it the principle and perfection of every form of life, are only the teachings of a school of Pagan philosophers who, from Democritus to Thales, and from Thales to Socrates, delivered themselves up to speculations concerning the nature and origin of the physical world. In language as sublime as it is truthful the divinely-inspired author of the Book of Wisdom, whilst he predicts their teachings with the accuracy of a listener, holds up to eternal reprobation the guilty delirium of their philosophy.

According to them, as according to their latest disciples, man is but a streak of morning cloud, destined to melt into the infinite azure of the past. ' We are born of nothing,' thus does the sacred writer describe the doctrine of those so-called scientists, and ' after this we shall be as if we had not been ; for the breath in our nostrils is smoke, and speech a spark to move our hearts, which being put out, our body shall be ashes, and our spirit poured abroad as soft air, and our life shall pass away as the trace of a cloud, and shall be dispersed as a mist which is driven away by the beams of the sun and overpowered by the heat thereof ' (Wisdom 2). Such was the doctrine of the old time Pagan philosophers, and such is the doctrine of modern Materialists. It does not matter that against such degrading theories human reason itself, unaided by Revelation, indignantly revolted—that six hundred years before the Christian era—when Christ's coming was only dimly foreshadowed, these degrading doctrines were broached in the school of Athens, to be spurned by the greatest intellects of Greece, to be refuted by the lofty intelligence of Plato, to be annihilated by the acute intellect of Aristotle.   In this thing of infidelity, want of novelty is, it seems, no reproach, nor the repetition of blasphemy any shame.

Nor does it matter that the modern Apostles of evil, no more than their old masters, have established nothing by their wild and conflicting doctrines but their own incapacity to offer anything to man instead of that of which they would ruthlessly rob him.   We may well say to these friends of humanity, as Job said to his consolers, ' Miserable comforters are ye all.'   Nor does it matter that such degrading doctrines have filled the earth with crime, and made the lives of their votaries a very inferno; their pernicious influence has been stealing over men's minds all the same till it has come to pass that such teaching has shaken to its centre the whole fabric of social life in our day almost in every country in Europe in succession.   And there is this difference between the old times and the present, that whereas formerly these wild and unsettling theories were confined to the schools, they are now scattered broadcast by means of the Press all over the world.   There is no medium for their diffusion from the philosophic essay to the work of fiction and the daily print to which the apostleship of infidelity has not had recourse.   Nor is the danger which is great abroad much less in our day at home.

Let us not live in a fool's paradise.   The bad literature which has wrought and is working such havoc—such whole-sale slaughter of souls on the continents of Europe and America, and nearer home across the Channel, has invaded our country, and is beginning, I regret to be obliged to write, to do much mischief in our midst.   Many of the irreligious works of the European continent have been translated into the English language—circulated in every variety of form, from the most ornate to the cheapest and most accessible, and, I bitterly lament to state, are occasionally to be seen even in the precincts of the domestic circle where nothing defiling should be permitted to enter.   Nor are works of a similar spirit and tendency wanting in our own literature. And these works are adapted to every class of reader and to

every grade of intellect—reviving the old errors and fertile in
the production of new ones—flattering the pride of the
understanding and stimulating the passions of the heart—
diffusing their moral poison in every department of learning
and through every form of publication by which the popular
mind can be reached.

An evil Press too, largely circulated and read by many
who suspect no evil, is slowly but surely sapping the foundations of the faith of our people. Charged in an especial
manner with the guardianship of the faith, placed as
sentinels on the watch-towers of Israel, the Irish bishops
have spoken on this subject with no uncertain sound, and we
hope their paternal counsel and charitable warning will have
the effect, if not of changing the heart and chastening the
pen of these unholy scribes, at least of opening the eyes of
an unwary public to see the abyss into which such uncatholic
reading will inevitably lead them. It is our sincere belief
that there never was a period in the history of our Irish
Church, which is the glory of Christendom, in which so
many and such various agencies were at work to undermine
and injure it, as are at present in active and unscrupulous
motion ; and, consequently, never before was it more needful
to watch, to warn, to implore, and to inculcate, in order to
prevent the weak, the simple-minded, and the credulous
from being poisoned by bad literature and being seduced
from their allegiance to religion and its ministers by evil
men, who under the guise of politics, and in the name of
patriotism, are aiming a deadly blow at faith and morality.
Shall we yield to the wicked in zeal ? Shall we who share
the priesthood of a good Master give a monopoly of activity
to infidels and atheists—to secularists and other enemies of
our faith ? From all sacerdotal lips methinks I hear the
thunderous No.

But what antidote can we offer against the desperate and
widespread evils of the day ? We can offer a very effectual
one—the dissemination of good books—such books as those
of St. Alphonsus. Would that the blessed spirit of that
truly good and great man lived and thrived and throbbed in
our poor hearts ! what a change would be made on the face

of society—what countless souls would be won to God!
The great Pontiff who rules the destinies of the Church, and
who presents in his own personality in its highest form the
happy union of piety and Letters, tells us that religious
indifference is the curse of the age.   In a letter addressed to
all the Bishops, while lamenting the suffering state of the
Church on earth and the present condition of society, the
evil days upon which they are fallen, Leo XIII. pointed
out in clear and unmistakable language the source and
fountain-head of the evils of the world. 'The great wound,'
said the Pope, 'is religious indifference—indifference about
everything supernatural, indifference about everything that
was not "of the earth, earthy." It was a poison eating
its way into the heart of society, acting as a fraud upon
the intellect of men, tearing to pieces all religion and every
hope of everlasting life.'

Surely the noble priesthood of Ireland, who have a
record second to none in Christendom, shall not be indifferent
to the interests of their great Master and the salvation of
souls. Let us then be up and doing, let us step into the
breach and to stem the tide of bad literature and infamous
pictures which is beginning to flood the land, let us bring
good books to the doors of our good and faithful people,
but who, alas! are easily led astray. If needs, be let us as
the apostles of evil do in other lands, put them into their
hands.   Any trouble, any cost, any sacrifice is not too great
to preserve the priceless jewel of faith—that faith for which
our fathers made sacrifices that have no parallel in the
history of any other nation.   That morality and religion
mainly depend on the nature of the books that are disseminated among men is an assertion that needs no proof.
Yet it may be well to recall what a pleasure and power is
reading—what a fascinating influence books have in every
age exercised over the minds of men.

The man who reads lives in all ages is the contemporary of all mankind. For such a one the boundaries of
time seem to be at once removed. Nothing is past, for
everything lives as it were before him. The thoughts of
beings who had trod the most distant soil in the most distant

periods arise again in his mind with the same warmth and freshness as when they first awoke to life in the bosoms of their authors. 'Books,' says Plato, ' are immortal children that immortalize and deify their fathers.'

Give a man [says Sir John Herschel] a taste for reading and a means of gratifying it, and you can hardly fail of making him a happy man, unless indeed you put into his hands a most perverse selection of books. You place him in contact with the best society in every period of history; with the wisest, the wittiest, with the tenderest, the bravest, and purest characters who have adorned humanity; you make him a denizen of all nations, a contemporary of all ages. The world has been created for him.

And what a power is reading! If we look attentively around us, if we pause and consider how men's minds are swayed, from what source their opinions have sprung, how they have been nurtured and how matured, we shall invariably find that reading has exercised a powerful influence over them, either for good or evil. By it good and bad doctrines are alike disseminated ; virtue and vice held up to our admiration or contempt ; political opinions diffused and debated ; yea, what is more, the passions of the multitude not unfrequently aroused by it to such a pitch that we see mighty thrones totter and fall ; religion and order swept away, and the hideous monster of anarchy and revolution reigning in their stead.

We have often heard it said that music hath charms to soften savage breasts. Reading, like music, exercises a magic spell over mind and heart. We see it every day. People who turn away in scorn from the piteous appeal of a famishing old man or woman who cries begging at their door, are moved to tears in secret over an imaginary evil, depicted by a master-hand in some work of fiction. And thus reading, like music, and more than music, plays on the chords of the finest instrument in creation—the heart of man. It is admitted, even by the most depraved, that virtue ennobles man.

And does not reading make us acquainted with the heroes of humanity, with the best types of moral and Christian virtues; unfold to us their hard struggles, their noble

sacrifices, their heroic and generous deeds? 'That man,' it
has been beautifully observed, 'is little to be envied whose
patriotism would not be inflamed on the plains of Marathon,
or whose piety would not grow warm midst the ruins of
Iona;' and it may also well be added : or who can view
unmoved the ruined aisles where our forefathers prayed,
the mountain caverns where, despite the persecutions of
tyrants, they circled round His lowly altars, and preserved
unquenched the hallowed fire of a nation's faith. In like
manner, base indeed would be the man who could read the
lives of the saints, and not feel some touch of his better
nature. Very depraved and utterly demoralized must be
he on whom such examples would not have, at least, some
salutary effect. And thus reading, like virtue, ennobles
man; it raises him above his lowly self, what our poor
fallen humanity so sadly needs :—

> Unless above himself he can
> Erect himself, how base is man.

It has been truly said that the pen is mightier than the
sword ; and does not reading produce effects greater even
than the sword ? We see empires rise and fall by the power
of arms ; but where is the power that can crush the effects
produced by the reading of a single book ? The sword can
only add to or take from our worldly prosperity, or at most
destroy the body ; but reading, like an angel of light or
darkness, transforms man into a saint, a hero, or a fiend.

History has made memorable the words ' Tolle, lege '—
words addressed by a heavenly monitor to the gifted and
cultured apostle of Manicheism, at a supreme moment in his
life, at the end of a long and terrible struggle against grace.
Augustine took and read. He read in the Book of books
the passage of St. Paul's Epistle beginning with the words:
' Let us, therefore, cast off the works of darkness, and put
on the armour of light; let us walk honestly, as in the
day.' The reading of that book won for the Church her
greatest champion, for philosophy her most profound and
eloquent expounder, and for the empire of letters one of her
greatest monarchs. And does not the same illustrious

authority tell us that by reading the life of St. Antony of the Desert, which they happened to meet on their way, two courtiers of the Emperor Valentian the Younger were so touched by the wonders of that wondrous life, and so convinced of the vanity of mere human services, though these services be given to an earthly potentate, that they and the ladies whom they were to wed abandoned the world, and consecrated their lives to God.

We know too the story of the brave Spanish soldier who was wounded at the siege of Pampeluna. His energies had hitherto been enlisted on the world's side. He had dreamt of glory, of fame, of, perhaps, transmitting to posterity a name enriched with daring deeds of valour and renown. Such was the man at the siege, 'seeking the bubble reputation even in the cannon's mouth.' Behold now the effects of a good book. Stretched on his bed of pain, he asked for a book to beguile the weary hours. He did not want anything serious. No, some light amusing story would have answered his purpose, some romantic love tale would suit him best. However, by God's providence there were none to be had, and he was handed the Lives of the Saints. Need I recount the result? How the gay cavalier became from that moment the zealous and indefatigable servant of God ; how the aspirant to worldly honours and fame from that moment courted humiliations, thirsted for ignominy and reproach. Look too at the heroic band of spiritual soldiers he has formed, fighting so nobly, so generously, and so frequently at the sacrifice of their lives, the battle of Christ and His Church, shedding a lustre of learning, virtue, and sanctity, which three centuries of persecution and calumny have in vain sought to dim. You may trace the conversion of an Ignatius Loyola to the reading of a good book. The Church is indebted after God, to a half hour's good reading for the foundation of a religious Order which is one of her strongest pillars and her brightest ornaments, and whose history can find no parallel in human records, except that of the Church herself. These are only a few out of many instances of conversions brought about, and marvels wrought on the

lives of men by the reading of good books. And if we look
into the annals of military fame, we shall find that the
desire of emulating great men, conceived by the reading of
their exploits, has inflamed many a breast, and made many
a hero. The poet Cowper understood it well when he
wrote these beautiful lines :—

> And when recording history displays
> Feats of renown, though wrought in ancient days,
> Tells of a few stout hearts that fought and died,
> Where duty placed them, at their country's side,
> The man that is not moved with what he reads,
> That takes not fire at their heroic deeds,
> Unworthy of the blessings of the brave,
> Is base in kind, and born to be a slave.

And so we find Charles XII. of Sweden, while only
yet a child, fired by the love of conquest, at reading the
exploits of Alexander the Great. Being asked one day
what he thought of that hero, he replied, 'I should like to
resemble him.' 'But,' said his master, 'he only attained
the age of thirty-two.' 'Ah!' exclaimed he, 'is it not enough
when one has conquered kingdoms?' And do we not find
the career of that extraordinary man—the most extraordinary
perhaps that has ever been on earth, according to one of his
biographers, exactly corresponding to the ideas he then
conceived? Do we not see him at the early age of eighteen,
fighting at the head of his army three great kings, who
wanting to take advantage of his youth came to attack him ;
defeating them in turn, and routing with eight thousand
Swedes, a powerful army of eighty thousand Muscovites?
As Dr. Johnson says :—

> A frame of adamant, a soul of fire,
> No dangers fright him, no labours tire ;
> War sounds the trump, he rushes to the field.
> Behold surrounding kings their powers combine,
> And one capitulates, and one resign.
> He left a name at which the world grew pale,
> To point a moral or adorn a tale.

Charles XII. was a hero and a great warrior, no
doubt; but he was far from being a great man. Pride and
obstinate rashness caused his ruin. It is to be regretted

that the lives of some good and great men, such as the Emperor Antoninus Pius, were not also presented to the study of his youthful mind; it is very probable he would also have taken them for his models. Then, indeed, he would have become not only a great warrior, but also a great man, and handed down to posterity a name not unworthy to be remembered and cherished as a blessing to humanity.

Too great attention cannot be paid to this. The mind of youth is impressionable—the bias which it receives then, it retains just like primal tincture, ever after. We are told that Lamartine, when a child, was thought by his grandmother to spell and read out of the Bible, and if we turn over the pages of that great man's poetry, we shall find them replete with the beautiful lessons of Holy Writ he then imbibed. Such were the effects of Lamartine's early reading. How different might it have been had he not so good an instructor. Books are mighty things for good or for evil. ' They are dead but sceptred sovereigns, who still rule our spirits by their works.'

We have glanced at their agency for good, and what shall we say of their agency for evil ? Unfortunately there exists in our nature a propensity to evil. It is one of the results of the sad fall of our great progenitor. Whatever flatters our passions or vicious inclinations, we, as a rule, are readier to follow than what is good and virtuous. And hence we find that bad books are more generally read than good ones, and that newspapers wherein religion and morality are outraged, have a very wide circulation. If anything more than bad example tends ¡to propagate vice, I think I am right in saying it is bad reading. Vice is in itself odious, but when decked out in all the false colouring of a cleverly-written book it becomes enticing. Young inquisitive people (and young people are generally inquisitive) are tempted. After perusing such a book their horror of vice is very much lessened ; they take up another; and so, by degrees, their ideas become perverted. Alas ! they did not perceive the poison till they had drunk of it to the very dregs ; they did not see the hidden serpent till they were caught in its coils.

But they should be forewarned, and to be forewarned is to be forearmed. Revelation proclaims that ' those who love the danger shall perish in it '—' that we should incessantly watch and pray lest we enter into temptation ;' and that ' we carry the treasure of Divine Grace in earthen vessels :' in fine, the whole tenor of its teaching is to inculcate the humility and self-distrust that fly the occasions of sin, not the pride and self-sufficiency that court them. Hence all shall be studiously on their guard against the daring curiosity or intellectual pride that would spurn a restraint which the Church in every age has deemed so necessary for the moral government of the faithful ; and hence the rigorous obligation of every pastor, parent, and guardian, to save, as far as is in their power, those under their charge from the demoralizing influence of those impious and licentious works. Even the poet, who wrote—

> Vice is a monster of so frightful a mien,
> As to be hated needs but to be seen ;

wrote also these lines—

> Yet seen too oft, familiar with his face,
> We first endure, then pity, then embrace.

The truth of the last two quoted lines is painfully obvious to all who have studied city life. Nearly all men agree, that it is familiarity with vice which develops all the immoral and vicious propensities of human nature, and it is this familiarity with the face of vice which is so contagious, and draws so many souls into such an abyss of crime in large cities, and it is the absence of that familiarity with the face of vice which keeps country life so pure and untarnished. Applying this principle to our subject, we are not surprised that we sometimes hear or read of terrible falls of persons, who acting in direct opposition to the warning of God's word, have fallen away from the faith, and even into the dark depths of unbelief. If we now and then come across a young man who scoffs at religion, and cries down morality by word and example, we are to trace his sad state to the same cause. Let us not imagine that he was bred and born in the poisoned atmosphere of infidelity. He may have been blessed with one of the greatest of all blessings—with good and virtuous parents. A time was when he was a dutiful son, a good Christian, and an exemplary young man ; but in an evil hour a companion whom he could not influence by his example slipped into his hand a bad book. He read, and the reading of that book has done its work.' What a work of ruin ! What a fall of virtue into vice, deep, dark, and obdurate. It is like the fall of Lucifer from the heights of heaven into the abyss of hell. Many a good Christian mother is at a loss to know what has brought about the awful change she deplores in her son. She little suspects it is due to the reading of a bad book. While recently conducting a retreat in a certain city of this country, the writer of the present essay came across several young men and women, who from such reading had lost all faith. Oh, what an evil is a bad book ! Evil men, evil lives, evil examples spread a moral pestilence openly and powerfully, but nothing spreads falsehood and evil more surely and deeply than a bad book. For a bad book is falsehood, and sin in a permanent and impersonal form, and all the more dangerous, because disguised and tenacious in its action upon the soul. Some books are to be found in our literature, and I regret to say many of them are written by men and women of the English nation, every page of which panders to the grossest passions, every page of which is filled with blasphemies against Christ, His Church, and His sacred ministers.

And I do not know which is the more dangerous— the books that are written professedly against Christ, His Church, and His laws, or the furtive and stealthy serpentine literature which is penetrated through and through with unbelief and passion, false principles, immoral whispers, and inflaming imaginations. These books could scarcely be worse were they penned in hell, and I firmly believe that the devil suggests the thoughts, and directs the pen of their authors. To read such books is a moral contagion—it is to imbibe poison—it is certain death.

It is, indeed, a melancholy reflection, that any such books should be extant among us. It is sad to think that

any of the human species should have so far lost all sense of
shame, all feelings of conscience, as to sit down deliberately,
and compile a work entirely in the cause of vice and
immorality, which for aught they know, may serve to pollute
the minds of millions, and propagate contagion and iniquity
through generations yet unborn—living and spreading its
baneful effects long after the unhappy hand which wrote it
is mouldered into dust ; but perhaps not so long as the
unhappy mind which composed it is paying the due punishment for its offence in the doleful regions of futurity.   If
the authors of such writings could feel this reflection—if
they would consider the numberless youths whose minds
may be blasted by their evil efforts ; if they would consider
that works of this kind, once made public, are impossible to
be recalled ; that, however they may themselves repent of
the evil—if aught of repentance can touch such obdurate
hearts—it is yet of such a nature as can never be repaired,
for which no restitution can be made.   If men would a
moment attend to this reflection, certainly we should hear
no more of such contaminating works ; certainly some of
those who have taken the devil's office, and turned corrupter
of our youth in the present day, would pause in their work
of defilement and destruction.   It is a striking observation
made by one of the fathers of the Church, that " as the
authors of good books may hope to find their future crown
in glory, brightened by the degree of wisdom and virtue
which their writings impart through successive generations ;
so the writers of bad ones may well dread an increase of
punishment in the future world proportionate to the pollution
which they spread, and the ill effects which their writings
shall produce as long as they continue to be read."   Writing
on this subject, Addison says :—

Writers of great talents who employ their parts in propagating
immorality and seasoning vicious sentiments with wit and humour,
are to be looked upon as the pests of society and the enemies of
mankind. They leave books behind them as it is said of those who
die in distempers which breed an ill-will towards their own
species, to scatter infection and destroy their prosperity.   They
act the counterpart of a Confucius or a Socrates; and seem, as it

were, sent into the world to deprave human nature, and sink it into the condition of brutality.[1]

And Dr. Young, whose poetic pen has been so well employed in the cause of truth and virtue, speaks with an noble resentment against this prostitution of genius :—

> The flowers of eloquence profusely pour'd
> O'er spotted vice, fill half the letter'd world,
> Art, cursed art! wipes off the indebted blush
> From Nature's cheek, and bronzes every shame.
> Man smiles in ruin, glories in his guilt ;
> And Infamy stands candidate for praise.[2]

We all know the immediate cause of the so-called Reformation ; we all know by whose instrumentality it was chiefly effected. Every school can recount its history. Protestants are taught to revere Luther's name. Catholics hold that name in execration. Whatever may be said on the one side or the other, there is no doubt—history bears unmistakable testimony, that passion, pride, and lust were the springs which set in motion the fierce, reckless, and daring spirit of that apostate friar. But how are we to account for his amazing success ? What was the immediate cause of that great religious revolt of the sixteenth century ? On this aspect of the case there seems not to be such a clear understanding. Much is due, no doubt, to the untiring energies of the man, to his powerful patrons, to his voluminous and scurrilous writings. More is due still to his salvation-made-easy kind of doctrines, which by favouring the passions made thousands of proselytes—which made faith alone the sheet-anchor of salvation—the passport to heaven. But other men in other times, with spirits no less daring, and abilities by no means inferior, endeavoured to sow dissensions in the Catholic Church and failed, miserably failed. Their pernicious doctrines were nipped in their very bud; their sects dwindled away and their names became as by-words. How then is it that the leader of the Reformation met with such

---

unparalled success?   I find the answer in the words of the
great poet :—

> The evil that men do lives after them,
> The good is oft interred with their bones.

A century before Luther's time, the first seeds of that
great revolt, so evil in its design and so disastrous in its
consequences, were sown by Bocaccio's writings. By degrees
his famous *Decameron* found its way among the masses of
the people, and at length pervaded every rank of society.
His ' satire ' not only tended to shake the confidence of the
faithful in their pastors, but to undermine their very faith.
And when Luther appeared, the people's minds were
prepared, the ground was ready, the mine was laid, and it
only required the touch of a daring hand to make it spring.
In 1517 Lutheranism was but a spark ; in the following
year it burst forth into a mighty conflagration, the embers
of which are still smouldering over the ruins of morality in
every land where it gained a foothold. And as the writings
of Bocaccio prepared the way for the so-called Reformation,
so we find later on a great but very depraved man preparing
the way in like manner to another revolution.   So well did
Voltaire and his impious followers know the power of the
Press and the influence of reading, that they entered into an
unholy alliance—a sacrilegious combination to write down,
as they flattered themselves they might, the Christian
religion.   While they endeavoured by the sophistry of a
spurious philosophy to sap the principles of faith, they sought
by works of fiction to inflame the passions and corrupt the
heart, especially of the young—to deprive vice of its deformity
and the stigma of dishonour attached to it—to increase the
appetite for pleasure—to clothe immorality in an amiable
and seductive form, and thus to create a hatred to the sacred
restraints of religion, whose holy and inviolable laws can
never tolerate defilement or unlawful pleasures.   To that
infidel philosopher, Frederick, called the Great, one day said,
' In twenty years you will bury the Church and write its
epitaph.'
     Poor day dreams !   Did they forget that the Eternal and

Infallible Truth hath said: 'Tu es Petrus et super hanc petram aedificabo Ecclesiam meam, et portae inferni non praevalebunt adversus eam.' If then, the arch-fiend with his countless legions cannot loosen one stone of that indestructible edifice, what canst thou do, poor feeble man, with all thy ingenuity. You may sneer and scoff. You may issue your ribald pamphlets, and cry out Down with priests, down with the Church; you may arm the passions of the multitude; you may gather your mighty armies, and hurdle your destructive engines against it: that Church will outlive your rage and fury. Like those adamantine rocks which encircle our island home, and which withstand the tempest's shock and the ocean's storm, so will that Church founded, on the rock of Peter, withstand the storms of persecutions, which the powers of darkness raise against it. And as we behold when the tempests have ceased, and the waters have subsided, those rocks erect in all their stupendous grandeur, so when the persecutions and raging storms of men's unbridled passions have died away, and those men that raised them are mouldering to dust, will that Church stand forth in all its majestic beauty and grandeur, with the Eternal Sun of Justice shining upon it. Many a twenty years have passed away since Frederick the Great uttered that foolish and impious blasphemy; and he is dead and gone, and the Church which his infidel friend and philosopher in his presumption sought to crush, is towering over his mouldering ashes. But it is a well-known fact, that Voltaire and his clique, the authors of the infamous Encyclopædia, had created by their writings, a resolution in the minds of the people before that terrible Revolution broke out, which deluged France with the blood of some of her best sons, swept away order and religion for a time, and stained the scaffold with the innocent blood of a martyred king and his virtuous queen. And long before that event which plunged France into an abyss of confusion and anarchy, unprecedented in the annals of the world, the minds of the French people had been prepared to imbibe the impious spirit which then seemed to take possession of them by the writings of the Jansenists which had been widely circulated before the appearance of Voltaire, Rousseau, and the other monsters. So it is an indisputable historic fact, that pernicious books, and the principles of infidelity propagated by them, were notoriously the chief cause at the close of the last century of that Revolution in France, the horrors of which will ever remain inscribed in the pages of history in characters of blood. And what shall I say of the events which immediately followed? The Revolution alluded to, terminated in the wars of Napoleon, which for well-nigh ten years overturned so many thrones, covered Europe with the ruins of so many dynasties, dethroned the Supreme Pontiff—banished him from his see, and sent him into exile in a foreign land.

That wholesale slaughter, and that atheism, which for so long a period bathed Europe in a sea of tears and blood, was the result of Voltaire's immoral and impious writings, and of his followers, who by the same agency raised the standard of revolt and anarchy in every country of Europe in which they found a footing. And coming down to our own times, have we not still fresh in our memories the frightful crimes which have been perpetrated in that very same country. Who will deny that the infidel writings of the day had any hand in them? What interest couldt he Commune have in massacring their illustrious Archbishop and gifted priests—holy, self-sacrificing, and noble-hearted men? None whatever. But they burned with a fierce hatred of religion and priests, and they longed to give it vent. And whence did that diabolical hatred arise? They were not born such fiends. I answer out of the infidel and immoral writings of the day. Less than twenty years before that terrible massacre we have been just contemplating, an official report, addressed to the Minister of the Interior, declared that of the nine millions of works which book-hawkers scattered broadcast among the people of France, eight-ninths, that is to say, eight millions were books more or less immoral. The evil grew with years, till it culminated in the horrible massacre of the Commune, and

---

[1] *Moniteur*, April 8th, 1853.

deluged the fair Capital of France with the blood of her best and most sacred sons.

In England too, immoral and infidel literature is a widespread evil; it is one of her most deadly plagues, and unfortunately it is a plague which has spread its infection to other lands; in fact, England, like another Babylon, has sent forth emissaries of evil to every land. We are told on undisputed authority, that the issue of immoral publications in that country amounts annually to more than thirty millions, of purely infidel publications to more than twelve millions, and of avowed atheism to more than one million.

We are informed by persons of unimpeached integrity, that "there are twelve thousand women in London only, to whom the crime of child-murder may be attributed.' In other words, that one in every thirty women (I presume between fifteen and forty-five) is a murderess; and that 'the metropolitan canal boats are impeded in their course by the number of drowned infants with which they come in contact, and that the land is becoming defiled with the blood of her innocents.'[1]

According to recent statistics, there are thousands in Great Britain who seem to have no more elevated notion of the God by whom they were created than the heathen flat-head of the prairie or the wild Zealander in the Bush. The great majority of the working-classes are said to attend no place of worship whatever. In one populous provincial city there are upon an average thirty thousand habitual drunkards on the Lord's day. In short, it is calculated that 33 per cent. of the English population live and die like beasts, in the utter neglect of all religion. Indeed, it would not be going too far to apply to this modern Babylon Osee's description of Israel's wickedness: 'There is no truth, and there is no mercy, and there is no knowledge of God in the land. Cursing, and lying, and killing, and theft, and adultery, have overflowed, and blood hath touched blood; therefore shall the land mourn' (Osee, iv. 3). Nor is the evil unabated. To-day our imagination is horrified

---

[1] *Infanticide : Its causes and Cure*, by Henry Humble.

by the thought of three living fellow-creatures being suddenly
sent, and at the same time and place, before their Maker,
at the hands of the common hangman. To-morrow, the
same awful picture rises up before our mental vision.[1]
Day after day chronicles a calendar of crime—a sum of sin
in that country—of brutal and cold-blooded murder, of which
no less than twelve within the past twelve months were
murders committed by children—of outrages on females,
bestial passion, utter lawlessness varied by suicide
committed in the most distressing circumstances, not to
speak of lesser crimes without number, which suggests a
very inferno, and which shows that England is a very
Sodom of iniquity.

What is the cause of this dreadful state of things—a
state of things which would disgrace the society of even the
pagan world? The cause is to be found in the literature of
the day. That literature, light and popular, stately and
philosophical alike, teems with immorality and infidelity.
It displays itself in every form of poetry and prose, in
lectures, essays, histories, and to an appalling extent in
the latest form of biblical criticism. There it stands out
palpable, like Milton's Death, black as night, and terrible as
hell, obstructing the light of heaven, and overshadowing
God's fair creation. The Press is a Catholic institution ;
a Catholic invented it ; a Catholic first printed books ;
the Catholic Church fostered its infancy. Pope Nicholas'
letter, dated 1455, is the first publication having a date ;
and the first book of any magnitude that was printed,
was probably the Latin Bible, which according to Hallam[2]
appeared in the same year. Seventeen years before Luther's
rebellion, over two hundred cities in Europe had printing
presses, and it is also a well ascertained fact, that during
the seventy-five years intervening between the first issue of
the press and the publication of Luther's German Bible in
1530, more than seventy different editions of the Bible had
been published in the various vernacular tongues of Europe.
At the Council of Lateran, Pope Leo X. declared printing

[1] Triple execution at Old Bailey and Winchester.
[2] *Introduction to the History of Literature in Europe.*

invented for the glory of God, for the propagation of our
holy faith, and for the advancement of knowledge. But·
the enemies of Catholicity have seized this powerful
weapon, and turned it into an engine of destruction to faith
and morals. The abuse of the art of printing cannot be
better described than in the words of another illustrious
Pontiff, who at the end of three hundred years, during
which period Protestantism arrogated to itself unchecked
power over the press, thus describes the result : ' We are
filled with horror in seeing what monstrous doctrines, or
rather what prodigies of error, we are inundated, with,
through that deluge of books, of pamphlets, and of works of
all kinds, the lamentable inroad of which has spread a curse
upon the face of the earth.' [1]

If the children of Ireland are a religious, good-living
and moral people—if they surpass in that respect every
nation of the earth, I think it may be attributed in no
small degree to the fact, that there exist less infidel and
immoral writings in this country than in any other. And if
Ireland is to preserve her unspotted character of holiness,
she must be guarded from such dangerous and disastrous
influences. Unhappily of late years, bad books are fast
creeping in among us, and in some portions of the country
are doing their deadly work.

I feel it a duty to bear my testimony against another
species of corruption, eminently fatal to the minds of our
people in general, and of our youth in particular. I refer
to the loose and obscene prints and pictures, which to the
great scandal of good morals, and detriment of religion, are
not only engraved but publicly sold in some of our cities,
and in several parts of our country. It becomes all who
have at heart the morality of our noble people, especially
those who are placed as sentinels on the outposts, to watch,
to warn—to prevent by every means in their power, such
deadly agencies from gaining the ascendancy in our country.
This we can do by disseminating good books, by preaching and
speaking on the necessity and importance of good reading,

---

[1] Gregory XVI., Encyclical, *Miravi vos.*

and to encourage such a beneficent work, by establishing lending libraries. There is no parish, no matter how small or poor, in which a lending library that could be made self-supporting, may not be established. Such has been done with no little success in England, and in many parts of our own country. Why not in all ?

In this way we would help to feed our flocks with the word of life. It is not my especial purpose to treat in this paper of the importance of spiritual reading which ' is intended to perfect the will by means of pious affections, and to spur it on to put these affections into practical shape; '[1] but I may be pardoned for adding this one word on this subject, that experience, which is a mighty preceptor, teaches us that for the most part the spiritual life is not a living reality where the taste for spiritual reading is not fostered. At all events, all the fathers and doctors of the Church tell us that what is true of meditation is also true of spiritual reading—that the habit of sin and of spiritual reading cannot co-exist—where spiritual reading is practised, there sin has no abiding abode.   Spiritual reading so arouses men to the great realities of their being—it so frees them from that sleep of death and indifference in which sin had placed them —it so transmutes them into other beings, indeed we may say into such new creations, that the habit of sin is abandoned, and a new life is at once begun. No doubt, it may be said that our people hear sermons on Sundays. But we all know how little impression from one cause or another, sermons make on the mass of hearers ; and even if they do, we know how quickly in the din and strife of life these impressions are effaced.   The affairs of the world—its success or its failure—its cares and anxieties are so often telegraphed in upon the soul that the recollections of religion are soon banished from the minds of even the best intentioned.

The newspapers of the day teem with scandals which absorb the thoughts or arouse the passions. Such reading familiarizes the young with the details of vice, and their

---

[1] Scaramelli, *Direttorio Mistico*, sect. i., art. 4.

better nature is overshadowed by the vicious existences
depicted, while moral strength to resist temptation is slowly
but surely weakened.   Then there is that inward strife and
struggle—that warring of the passions, from which no one
is free—that tendency to evil which seeks to cast off the
salutary restraints of religion, and which, alas! has carried
down with the current of innate corruption the great mass
of mankind.   All these things are borne in upon the soul,
day by day, and year by year, as though life were to last for
ever, and we cannot shut our eyes to the sad fact that they
inordinately wed men to a world that perisheth.   Besides
how many thousands of Catholics are there especially in our
large cities who never hear a sermon.   From choice or
through necessity they frequent the early Masses where
the word of God is not preached.   The better disposed may
indeed go to evening devotions where the want is supplied;
but the great bulk are never fed with the word of life.   How
can they fight the great fight?   How can they have the
bloom and freshness of health upon their soul?   They are
indeed in a sad, sad state—in the state of spiritual starvation
and death.   How many too, who hear the word of God,
leave the confessional with the best intentions and the
strongest resolutions for a new life, but quickly fall away
under the pressure of temptation, because they have no
spiritual book at hand wherewith to feed their souls day by
day, and strengthen their good resolutions?

   We all know how little we can trust ourselves, and
how evanescent are oftentimes the best resolutions unless
constantly supported and sustained by spiritual aids.   In
this age men talk much of enlightment, progress, insight,
wisdom; and these things are good in their way; but what
our age sadly needs is illumination from God, and that
illumination is to be found in spiritual books which teach us
about Him and His mercies, and teach us also that greatest
of all sciences; and I may add, the most difficult—the science
of knowing ourselves.   Many even of those who fear God
and serve Him, do not understand how bright a light and
how clear a vision of Divine things await them in that
treasure-house of holiness—spiritual reading.   Grace is

mighty and essential—it is superior to every endowment of
nature or the most brilliant talents ; to every intoxication of
pleasure, glory, or power, to the possession of the whole
world ; it is a participation of the light and love, and even of
the nature of God.   It is the God-like life commenced in
time to be consummated in eternity.   And yet grace is for
the most part made operative through spiritual reading;
since, to adopt the words of a learned living author (Bishop
Hedley), 'as grace does not work miracles (as a rule),
it will not put ideas into our heads, or pictures into
our imagination.'   The sacraments contain and convey
treasures of enlightenment and strength ; but why do these
mighty channels of grace so often produce so little fruit ?
It is because their recipients are barren of ideas—are devoid
of fixed purposes and generous aims to act as intercepters,
and transmute these great forces into heat and action.
'And is not mental prayer itself too frequently feeble,
intermittent, and cold, simply because our mind and memory
are empty, and we have no store of thought to set our
devotion working?   It is spiritual reading which supplies
ideas, motives, views, interesting information, touching histories, useful explanation, fertile developments of doctrines,
wide generalizations on God, the Church, and eternity;
and this great store of material only requires prayer and
grace to be turned into the precious stones which form the
walls of the heavenly Sion.'

It need not be said that of all books the Bible is the
highest and holiest, and therefore the best and most profit-
able.   The reason of this is, not merely the sublimity of the
thought, the beauty of the diction, and the eloquence of the
writers, although in this respect the Bible is above and
beyond all other books—(man could not compose it); but
the force and illuminating power of the Divine Inspiration.
By it we are admitted into the presence of the Living God,
who becomes our very preceptor, and the mysteries of the
Inner Temple are disclosed to our view.   The Holy Scripture
was intended by its Divine Author to illuminate our minds
with the light of heavenly wisdom, and to draw us to Himself.   And what God intends that He effects.   He says that

His word is 'effectual,' that 'it never returns void,' that it is
'a fire,' that it is 'a lamp,' and 'a light;' that 'it converts
souls,' and 'gives wisdom to little ones;' that it rejoices the
heart and enlightens the soul; 'that it is an infinite treasure
to men.' But from the very greatness and holiness of the
treasure arises the necessity of reading it with reverence.
The Catholic Church which has never forbidden the reading
of the approved edition of the Bible in the vernacular,
commands and exhorts her children to read it with obedience
to her teaching, with desire for their own spiritual profit,
with the fear and consciousness of God; and so not to read
it to gratify vain curiosity, to take from it every 'wind of
doctrine,' and 'wrest it' as the Apostle says to their own
destruction.' Before concluding this phase of the subject, I
cannot forbear stating that the manner of reading is no less
important than the matter. And as Fr. Faber tells us, if
there be one thing upon which the masters of the spiritual
life are agreed, it is that the books used for spiritual reading,
should be read slowly, and a little at a time. Hence it has
been recommended that the works chosen should be those
which are not too attractive to the intellect; nay, according
to Fr. Consolini, a great master of the spiritual life, and the
first novice master of the Oratorians, 'they should not be
even read quite through, in order to lose the intellectual
interest which completeness might give.' Nourishment of
the spirit, not instruction of the mind, is the primary end—
though, of course, both ends may be attained—for which
spiritual books should be written and read. It is for this
precise reason that the works of St. Alphonsus are so
strikingly adapted for spiritual reading, and why they have
produced, wherever they are known, such beneficent results
among the children of the Catholic Church.

To sum up what I have been saying. It is our duty as
ministers of the Lord to teach our people the importance
and necessity of good reading, and the dangerous and
disastrous consequences of bad reading. What we want to
do, is to create and cultivate a conscience among our people
for sound, healthy reading, especially spiritual reading. I
say to create and cultivate. For our people, as a people, do

not read, least of all have they a taste for spiritual reading. This taste by a little labour and sacrifice, we can create and foster among our faithful people who are ever ready to receive the light, provided it be put before them clearly and constantly.   In the material world, the science of light is advancing with the strides of an intellectual Colossus.   Would that we could say the same of the higher realm of light— the course of sacred truth!   The Cathode ray of potent, irresistible truth, is needed now as it was never needed before.   While the allied banners of atheism and Free- masonry fret the air on the European Continent, the forces of infidelity and indifferentism are doing their deadly work nearer home.   The spirit of revolt, born of corruption and bred of disease, has swept across the Channel, and has, alas! found a resting-place in our land.   The enemy has laid hold of the Press, and is everywhere outside our own country, and to some extent within it—utilizing it for the destruction of morality and the perversion of truth.   The wells of know- ledge and the fountains of truth are being daily and hourly poisoned by means of the Press and current literature.   A spiritual pestilence is passing over the earth—the souls of millions are perishing through such foul agencies.   And shall we who stand for the cause of God, and morality, and truth, fold our arms, and say we have done our duty by bewailing in private the public pest of a poisonous literature?   Most emphatically no; our resistance must be active, not merely passive.   If God has not given us wealth of ability and strength of mind, and richness of opportunity to engage in the intellectual combat which is being fought everywhere around us, we may, the very least of us, do a great work for a good Master by opposing to the tide of infidelity and indifferentism which is sweeping over the nations, and which is beginning to creep in on our own, the barrier of good books and sound Catholic reading.   We need only look around us to see that the great opportunity for Catholicism is at hand everywhere.   A marvellous transformation has come over the spirit of the great body of the English people. The mists are lifting out of that land, and her people have at last begun to look at the Catholic Church through her openly proclaimed doctrines, through her magnificent works in building up the mighty fabric of the social world and her lofty ideals of humanity, as shown in her priests and religious. Secularism in education is confessing its failure at home and abroad. The toiling masses are turning to the Church for the solution of the vexed problem of labour. The creeds are falling to pieces from want of unity, cohesive principle and authority. Thousands are flocking back to the old Church in sheer weariness of spirit. The thousands would quickly swell into millions if we were up and active in the dissemination of goods books, and did our part in the wide domain of letters. Let us avail of the opportunity. Let us remember the spreading of the light in Scott's romance. It was by the speeding of the fiery cross from hand to hand. The Catholic book, the Catholic magazine, and the Catholic newspaper are the fiery cross by which we are to dissipate the darkness of the enemy. If we do not utilize the means at our disposal to stamp out the lie and spread the light, we shall most certainly fail in our duty; for God has said ' He that is not with Me, is against Me.'

W. J. MULCAHY.

SERMON OR HOMILY?
II.

THE 'homily' was the method of preaching, we remarked
in a former paper,[1] followed by the fathers of the Church
in the early ages. These homilies were for the most part
wonderfully simple and earnestness breathes in every phrase·
Though so simple the profoundest theology has been drawn
from them. What was their secret? Like the Apostolic
men they spoke the sense of God and not their own; and
that divine sense they obtained by meditating on the Holy
Scriptures and the traditions of their fathers. In illustration
of this we enlarged on the example of St. John Chrysostom.
We saw that this great Christian orator explained the Gospel
of the day in its entirety, and then drew moral and practical consequences. But the homily can take other forms.
Frequently the Gospel of the day can be reduced to a regular
division, and then the homily resembles in form the sermon;
thus in the Gospel of the Prodigal Son one may show—(1) the
misfortune of the sinner who abandons God; (2) the sentiments
with which he should return to God; and (3) the goodness
of God towards the sinner who is converted. Another manner
of commenting on the Scripture which is the homily is when
the preacher takes two or three salient points relative to a
virtue or to a vice and treats them one after the other though
they are not capable of falling into a regular division; and
finally, one may explain all the sentences in the Gospel, and
draw from each according as he proceeds the moral and
affecting lessons which they suggest; thus changing the
subject-matter at almost every verse there is an opportunity
offered for attacking many vices, teaching many virtues, and
recommending many useful practices. Through this variety
each one finds in the instruction a help in his difficulties and
a remedy for his failings. If, on account of the length of
the ceremonies or from any other obstacle, a long instruction

---

[1] See I. E. RECORD for May (Fourth Series), vol. i., p. 448.

cannot be given on certain Sundays, one can very briefly
expound the Gospel, and draw from it for the five or six
minutes a few interesting reflections. If these are enunciated
clearly and with unction the faithful will listen with
attention, and often profit more by them than by a long
discourse.[1]

Allied to the homily is the ' prone,' which word was, in
the first ages, applied to the instruction given to both catechumens and Christians assembled in the nave of the Church:
it is now generally employed to signify any simple and short
instruction given at the parochial mass.   The ' prone ' differs
from the ' homily ' in this that it is not concerned with the
paraphrase of Scripture, and is at great liberty in the choice
of the subject-matter.   It differs from the sermon in this
that it is not subservient to the rules which rhetoric
gives for oratorical discourses.   It is the simple language of
a father to his children where the artifice of rhetoric is what
is farthest from the thoughts.

The ' prone ' is generally more useful than the sermon
inasmuch as it is of a simpler kind, is more within the grasp
of the artisan, the poor, and the ignorant, and much more
adapted to spread instruction amongst the people.   It is often
more useful than the 'homily,' because it does not divide the
attention on many objects and thus is capable of throwing
a better and fuller light on the detached subject which it
explains ; of deducing consequences ; and of making practical
applications : for the disadvantage of the ' homily ' is that in
endeavouring to treat many subjects none is profoundly dealt
with, and it is thus difficult to make a deep impression or
move the affections.

To obtain these happy results of this method of preaching,
the ambassador of God's word must prepare his ' prone ' many
days in advance. · It is an illusion to believe that clearness
in the instruction, description of manners, or the unction
of piety can be improvised.

Preaching without preparation does not exonerate the
conscience of the pastor because far from possessing that

---

[1] *Traité de la prédication*, M. Hamon.

interest, power, and clearness by which he is enabled to instruct and touch, he does but disgust his flock with the word of God.

The matter of the 'prone' embraces every duty of the Christian life and every essential point of religion, and it does not require text, peroration, or preamble; one simply commences one's subject after the reading of the Gospel. Abstruse reasonings are out of place ; proofs simple yet solid, many comparisons and a variety of examples are necessary. Substitute clear explanations and urgent exhortations for grand oratorical movements ; a flowing natural style which conveys the truth with perspicuity, so that the ignorant cannot but understand, for a brilliant one : choose a popular though dignified eloquence rather than magnificent oratory ; but with equal care avoid a negligent and trivial method of expression. For the conclusion of the *prone* certain practices of piety are indicated and acts of virtue for the sanctification of the week. The 'prone' is the food distributed to the flock for the week that they may nourish themselves from it daily.

In saying that the 'prone' does not propose a paraphrase of Scripture, we by no means insinuate that a knowledge of the Inspired Word is not necessary to this simple style of evangelical eloquence ; on the contrary, it is the soul, the 'form' of the *prone*, though the material words are not the words of the holy books. And as the 'form' gives life and character to matter, so the Word of God living in the preacher's heart vivifies and characterizes every style of preaching. St. Augustine assures us of this in his profound work, *De doctrina Christiana*, when he says that the preacher excels in the ministry of the Word in proportion that he is skilful in the science of Scripture. The *word* has in ordinary language different significations. We have the *word* conceived in the heart ; we have the *word* produced on the lips, and the *word* written on paper. As conceived in the soul it is a thought ; produced by the lips it is a sound, written with the pen a sign. Thought dwells in the mind ; sounds strike the ear ; signs remain in a book. The Word of God reposes eternally in the bosom of the Father and is called thought or interior word. He manifested Himself to the world without quitting the right hand of the Father and is called the Word. Finally, we have the Truth or Word of God in the Holy Scriptures.

But what is of importance to the preacher is how he may incorporate the Divine truth which he is commissioned to preach to every creature. Now, the great principle is that he puts himself by prayer in direct relation with God. ' I would wish,' says St. Gregory the Great, ' that pity should make the preacher descend to the level of each, and that contemplation raise him above all. In this manner he will not forget the infirmities of men when scaling the heavens, nor will he quit the celestial regions when condescending to the weakness of his brethren.' In the second place it is necessary to give one's attention to the teaching of the Doctors in order to know the Word of God always living in the Church. ' For,' says St. Jerome, ' it is not precisely the Doctors of the Church who instruct us, but God in them' (Ps. lxxxi.). These different schools of the Word of Truth complete one another. Interior illumination if left to itself would lead men to religious fanaticism. Teaching without prayer would become a tinkling cymbal. Scripture to be rightly understood demands the light of contemplation and the *magisterium* of the Doctors of the Church.

' Thus,' as Bossuet profoundly remarks, ' the evangelical preacher is he who makes Jesus Christ to speak : but he does not make Him speak the language of men ; *he fears to give a strange body to the Eternal Truth.*' Indeed preaching contains two natures ; one divine, the other human; therefore it has in its outward expression a movable side, while the other remains unchangeable.

The particular education of the orator, the taste of the audience, the necessity of the circumstances will effect differences in the beauty of the instructions. The spoken word must make itself all to all to gain all to Jesus Christ. Sometimes the Christian orator, wishing to give truth a more tangible form will recount the history of the Church and the lives of the saints : sometimes on the occasion of a festival or religious ceremony he will explain the visible symbols of

a dogma ; again he will, in presence of a cultured audience
bring out in relief the philosophy of our faith.   If he attacks
the enemies of our belief, he will choose the setting of the
sermon ; if in a simple manner he expounds the Gospel he
will prefer the ' homily.'   Ought he not to vary his style as
he addresses priests, religious, or the simple faithful !   Will
he not modify his language as he exalts the happiness of the
saints or weeps over the dead ! And yet notwithstanding
these differences of style the Sacred Word has an unalterable
character and one altogether peculiar.   The Fathers have
marked the limits which we cannot exceed; they may be
summed up in a few words.

Divine wisdom and human eloquence ought, as far as
possible, be found united on the lips of the preacher.
Standing alone, wisdom can suffice of itself, but eloquence
unaided often produces evil and scarcely ever any good.
Nevertheless, the ideal of Christian preaching, according to
St. Augustine, consists in the happy union of wisdom and
eloquence.   Hence, there is for the priest a double obligation of studying the Scriptures, as well as the great principles
of natural eloquence.   Therefore, although the Scriptures
and the fathers furnish us with the theory and practice of
all preaching, it is by no means useless to read the books
composed by rhetoricians, and to work carefully the discourse to be pronounced before an assembly.   St. Augustine
and St. Chrysostom give this advice.   What place, then,
does eloquence hold in preaching?   Bossuet will answer in
his celebrated sermon, ' Sur la parole de Dieu.' ' If you
should ask what place eloquence may have in the Christian
discourse, St. Augustine will tell you that it is not permitted her to appear but in the train of wisdom.   There is
here an order to be observed : Divine wisdom precedes as
the mistress, eloquence follows after as the handmaid.' This
principle condemns those orators who employ the flattering
words of human wisdom to gain applause and evacuate the
influence of the Cross.   Moreover, wisdom not only should
dominate eloquence, but this latter should present herself
without being called.   ' But,' adds Bossuet, ' remark the
circumspection of St. Augustine, who says that eloquence

should follow without being called. He means that eloquence in order to be worthy to take a place in the Christian discourse, ought not to be sought after with too much study. She should come of herself, attracted by the grandeur of the subjects, and to serve as an interpreter of the wisdom which speaks. But what is this wisdom which ought to speak in the pulpit, if not our Lord Jesus Christ, who is the Wisdom of the Father? Thus the evangelical preacher draws everything from Scripture, borrows even its sacred terms not only to fortify, but to embellish his discourse.'[1] In one word, the preacher, to announce worthily the Divine Word, ought to employ the venerable style of the Holy Spirit who speaks in the Holy Scriptures and the Fathers of the Church. This truth then being so essential, I will conclude in quoting a few of the earnest and weighty words of the greatest saints and Doctors.

Our Divine Master on one occasion said to the Jews, while teaching in the Temple, 'My doctrine is not of Me, but of Him who sent Me' (John vii. 14). St. Paul wrote likewise to the faithful of Corinth: 'The Spirit of God has been revealed to us, and this is what we teach you, not with the flattering words of human wisdom, but with the doctrine of the Spirit.' Thus also, all the fathers of the Church cry out to us with one voice, with our Saviour, 'Preach the Gospel,' or with the Apostle, 'Preach the Word.' St. Jerome impresses on the priest Nepotien the importance of incessant study of Scripture in these words: 'Read the Scriptures frequently, or, rather, let not the holy books ever leave your hands. Let the speech of the priest be seasoned with the Holy Scriptures. Take care that you descend not to declamation, wordiness, or that which is not useful.'[2] Let us listen to the immortal Bossuet, who with great majesty, resumes the pith of this patristic doctrine :—

You ought now to be convinced that the preacher of the Gospel does not enter the pulpit to pronounce vain discourses, which are listened to as a recreation. God forbid that we believe it ! They enter it in the same spirit that they go to the altar,

---

[1] *Ibid.*   [2] Epis. lii. 8.

there to celebrate a mystery, and a mystery like to that of the Eucharist. For the Body of Jesus Christ is not more really in the adorable Sacrament than the truth of Jesus Christ is in evangelical preaching. In the mystery of the Eucharist the species which we see are signs, but what is contained under them is the Body of Jesus Christ, and in the sacred discourse the words which you hear are signs, but the thought which produces them, and what they bear into your minds, is the doctrine of the Son of God. But consider, my brethren, how great is the audacity of those who expect and even exact from the preacher anything but the Gospel! who wish that the Christian truths be toned down, or that they be made agreeable by mingling with them the product of the human mind. They could with as much reason wish to see the sanctity of the altar violated by falsifying the mysteries.

Therefore, according to Bossuet, who borrows his doctrine from St. Augustine, the preacher and his audience should feel, as it were, under the signs of the words, the presence and truth of Jesus Christ; and in this regard preaching merits the same respect as the Eucharist, for Truth is God also. As the Apostle says, the Holy Scripture fulfils every end of preaching, let the object be either the teaching of dogma or of the mysteries, or the development of moral subjects or the attacking of vice : ‘ Omnis scriptura divinitus inspirata utilis est ad docendum, ad arguendum, ad corripiendum, ad erudiendum in justitia ut perfectus sit homo Dei, ad omne opus bonum instructus ’ (2 Tim. iii. 16, 17).

JEROME O'CONNELL, O.D.C.

A NOTE IN THE 'LEABHAR IMUIN' ON ALLELUIA'S LITURGICAL ORIGIN AND IMPORT

IN the course of an article entitled 'Alleluia's Story,' in the current number of *The Dublin Review*, at the conclusion of some remarks touching the question as to when this form of acclamation, which now heads the principal psalms of praise, was first introduced into the Hebrew liturgy, I said :—' Besides reasons proper to the very text of the Psalter, or drawn from a purely philological consideration of the word itself, data both of Christian and Jewish tradition, it seems to me, all point to the conclusion that it belonged to the Hebrew liturgy from the beginning.'

As adverse to that conclusion, as distinctly forbidding it from the side of Christian tradition, a learned friend referred me to a passage from Gerebrard's *Commentaries*, a work which he had reason to know I greatly esteemed. The passage referred to may be seen in Migne's *Scripturæ Sacræ Cursus Completus*, at the head of page 1416. Commenting on Alleluia's first appearance in the Psalter, and thereupon turning to the question of its introduction into the liturgy, Gerebrard observes :—' Ejus canendi usum in Ecclesia ex Aggeo propheta manare, qui primus illud cecinerit cum novam structuram templi vidit, testatur Epiphanius, *de vitis Prophet.* idque secundum Tobiae prophetiam. Tob. xiii. 35.'

Upon that passage, I would first remark that there is in it no declaration of tradition, either Jewish or Christian, eastern or western. It simply endorses a *dictum* of Epiphanius, and that itself (*idque*) is not given as a traditional saying, but as a personal conclusion drawn from a text of Scripture, the prophetic words of Tobias in reference to the rebuilding of the Temple, which, as a matter of fact, was completed during the lifetime, and, no doubt, to some extent, owing to the exhortations of the Prophet Aggeus. It is quite natural to suppose that, ' seeing the building,' at the foundation or dedication, of the second Temple, Aggeus should have raised the cry of Halleluiah! It is also natural to suppose that, in fulfilment of the prophecy of Tobias, the assembled multitudes should have taken up the sacred acclamation; that, in the vivid language of the prophecy, 'the streets of Jerusalem should sing it.' But it is also natural to suppose that they did so, and that Tobias prophesied they should do so, because it was already the consecrated cry of joy for the people of God. Was it already such, or did it only then become such? That is the question. Epiphanius, reasoning, it would seem, from the text of Tobias, states it only then became so, and Gerebrard approvingly quotes the statement as made by him. More recent writers repeat it as being 'said,' without giving reason or authority for the 'saying.' At the commencement of the remarks which I made on the question, I noticed this. Having remarked that it is at present impossible to *ascertain* when as a form of acclamation Alleluia was introduced into the liturgy of the Temple, I said :—' Some rather positively assert it was by the Prophet Aggeus on the occasion of laying the foundation-stone of the second Temple, or at its dedication, and that in accordance with the prophecy of Tobias, &c.' I then gave my reason, an exegetical reason, for not adopting that opinion, and subsequently gave reasons of the same order for not adopting the other opinions which I noticed further on.

But now, I would direct the attention of the readers of the I. E. RECORD to a reason in the order of tradition, of what it seems to me may be called Irish Catholic tradition, certainly of ancient Irish Catholic opinion, in favour of the conclusion which, in the article of *The Dublin Review*, I observed I felt disposed to adopt. This—to say no more—distinct expression of ancient Irish Catholic opinion may be read in a glossa on the refrain of St. Cummain's Alleluiatic Hymn,[1] in the Trinity College codex of the *Leabhar Imuin*,

---

[1] See I. E. RECORD, Fourth Series, vol. i., p. 441. In the course of that article, comparing the T. C. Codex with the one preserved in the Franciscan library of this city, at page 443, I observed :—' The Trinity College copy is abundantly annotated, seemingly by the original copyist: the Franciscan one not at all.' That referred only to this hymn, of which I was then writing, and of which I wrote immediately after as—' the only one for which I collated the two copies.'

or, as it is now more commonly called, the *Liber Hymnorum*. That glossa, or marginal note, is admitted to have been written by the same hand which copied the hymn ; consequently, in the ninth or tenth century, according to Dr. Todd and O'Donovan, in the eleventh century according to others. It was written, in either case, many hundred years before Gerebrard penned his Commentary, and may well have been copied from a note written shortly after the composition of the hymn itself, which would bring it near the time of Epiphanius.

The beginning and the end of the note 'have been cut off'—Dr. Todd says—' by the binder.' All that now remains legible is as follows . . . 'ebraice interpretatur *Laudate Dominum* vel *Laus tibi Domine* vel *Salvum me fac Domine*. Moises primus usus est Alleluia decantans contra Amalech in deserto, extensis manibus ad cœlum a mane usque ad vesperam et sic deletus Amalech a filiis Israel, et postea (David) decantavit apud Ebreos Alleluia causa timoris videns bestiam in Tabor et Hermon, et iterum propter timorem Absolon filii sui cantavit.' . . . There stops what remains legible of the glossa. The old writer, it will be observed, assigns no reason for its statements. To all appearance he only voices the tradition or received opinion of his time and country, or at least of his own community. In that light I am not concerned with appreciating its doctrinal or historic value. I simply notice, and, doing so, would accentuate it merely as an expression of ancient Irish Catholic tradition or opinion on Alleluia's liturgical origin and import.

Thus regarded, whatever may be the precise force of the word *primus* in the text, this ancient glossa clearly assumes that Moses used the mystic word as a form of prayerful acclamation, as a formula of great spiritual power—*usus est Alleluia decantans contra Amalech in Deserto extensis manibus ad cœlum*, &c. Now, Moses may assuredly be taken as the father of the Hebrew liturgy, and so, using the word the way he is supposed to have done, may naturally be supposed to have introduced it into the liturgy which he formed for his people. At any rate, that passage from our *Liber Hymnorum* may well be put against the one

I have quoted from Migne's *Cursus Completus*, and, as against it, against those who so positively assert that Alleluia was first used as a sacred acclamation by the Prophet Aggeus—*cum novam structuram Templi vidit*. Our ancient Irish scholiast, whoever he was, quite as positively asserts that the father of the builder of the first Temple, 'sang it'—*decantavit apud ebreos Alleluia*, as before him Moses 'used it'—*usus est Alleluia decantans contra Amalech in Deserto*.

Finally, analyzing this ancient glossa as a current exposition of Alleluia's import, what most strikes us is the triple form of interpretation it gives for the word: first, as being that of a kind of rallying call among the Lord's own, crying to one another—'*Laudate Dominum !*' then, that of a cheer or glory-giving cry direct to the Lord Himself—'*Laus tibi Domine;*' then, that of a general appeal for succour—'*Salvum me fac Domine;*' rallying call, cheer, cry for relief—the three constituents of the sense of universal acclamation. Last year, in an article in the *Catholic World* on 'Alleluia's traditional import,' I had occasion to remark: 'A vivid sense of its acclamatory character with *trine* signification is most apparent in those Alleluiatic services which form such a striking feature in the liturgical literature of the early part of the middle ages. They exhibit a constant effort after some triple evolution of the word's fundamental thought while retaining its form of universal acclaim.' Those words, it will be seen, exactly describe the Alleluiatic exposition of the ancient glossa I have analyzed. It may, indeed, be said that the old writer of that glossa had no scientific certainty as to Alleluia's etymological meaning, and accordingly what may be called its first literal sense. But he had the real sense, the spirit, the truth of it as a form of universal prayer and praise and self-strengthening cry, as that of his race's traditional aspiration, that appealing 'Glory be to God !' which so naturally rises to Irish-Catholic lips in all life's solemn crises. So was the word to him what it has ever been to God's own, in the desert, in the temple, in the Cenaculum, in the first Christian Church of Jerusalem; what it is in the Church of the world to-day, what it is in God's kingdom for ever—*the Divine acclamation*.

A thoroughly Catholic application of that view of it may be read in the yet unpublished MS. of our ancient *Book of Dimma*, one of the MSS. treasures preserved' in' the library of Trinity College, Dublin. This *Book of Dimma* is so called from the scribe's name, which is thus given on the final page of the volume: ' Fiuit, amen—Dimma Mac Nathi.' It is held to have been written about the middle of the seventh century. In Gilbert's *Facsimiles* it is marked *circa* 650, while O'Curry in his MS. Materials marks it *circa* 620. It contains four Gospels in Latin with what is said to be a ritual for the visitation of the sick. The latter portion of it may be regarded as one of the most ancient bits of local Celtic ritual existing among our national MSS. Now, the 'thoroughly Catholic' Alleluiatic passage I have alluded to is to be found in this liturgical portion, among the versicles having reference to the Blessed Eucharist, those that are like ejaculations for thanksgiving after Communion. It may thus serve for appropriate expression of the spirit of this festive midsummer season, of the parting spirit of Paschal time, passing through June's fervent festivities, from Whitsuntide through Corpus Christi's octave, into the glowing month of the Precious Blood. It is : ' *Alleluia. Refecti Christi corpore et sanguine, tibi (Domine) semper dicamus, Alleluia.*'

A similar ritual for visitation of the sick *pro infirmis*) is found in our ancient *Book of Mulling* (Trinity College), in the *Stowe Missal*, in the *Benchor Antiphonarium*, and in the Scotch *Book of Deer.* Each of these gives the Alleluiatic versicle or antiphon I have noticed in the *Book of Dimma*, but with ' Domine ' expressed. The three first mentioned have: ' Refecti Christi corpore et sanguine, tibi semper Domine dicamus Alleluia,' while the *Book of Deer* gives the latter part as: ' tibi semper dicamus Domine alleluia, alleluia.' In each case, it will be noticed, the Antiphon gives ' tibi semper;' gives that which is the term-thought of St. Cummain's hymn, of our ancient scholiast's note on its refrain, and of the Alleluiatic services of the middle ages; the thought that this Paschal cry of the people of God is eternal life's acclamation.

T. J. O'MAHONY, D.D.

DR. EVERARD, ARCHBISHOP OF CASHEL.

IN that galaxy of illustrious and saintly bishops, who have occupied the sees of Ireland from the days of St. Patrick to the present time, there are not a few whose lives, had they been spent in other less favoured countries, would have been stored and storied in the annals of celebrated men. As a rule, the perils and persecutions a nation has to endure, its privations and struggles, bring to the fore, if they do not produce, men of sound calibre, of noble endeavour, of exceptional ability, and of heroic virtue. The piping times of peace did not beget the Hildebrands, the Beckets, or the O'Connells. The poet, for want of a theme or a tragedy, wasting his muse goes and sings to the fields and woods; the orator is buried in the obscurity of a rural parish; the man capable of achieving great successes reads of the deeds of other men by his lonely fireside.

Thus, the troubled history of poverty-stricken Ireland, even in the recent period of the last hundred years, contains the names and the works of many men who are known throughout the world of learning. But there are others, around whose unwritten career the episodes of romance and of fidelity cluster, whose strength lay more in action and foresight than in the pen ; who deserve to be chronicled with such lights as Troy or Plunkett, Crolly, O'Hanlon, or Neville. Such a one was Dr. Patrick Everard, Archbishop of Cashel, President of Maynooth College, master of a once famous school in England, superior of a college in France, Vicar-General of a great diocese there during the Revolution, and a worthy member of a noble and ancient family in Ireland.

He was a lineal descendant of Sir John Everard, Knight, who possessed not only the town of Fethard ' for ever,' but also several 'castles, towns, and lands,' viz., 'Knockelly, Leagharry, Barretstowne, Rathcowle, Kilbrydy, Longbridge, &c.' in the County of Tipperary, and who had a ' licence to hold

Courts Leet and Barron' in the same county.[1] Sir John's
eldest son and heir, Nicholas, married a daughter of
James Lord Dunboyne. This Nicholas is described in the
Office of Arms in Dublin Castle, as 'Viscount Mount
Everard and Baron of Fethard.' Sir John had two other
sons, Richard and Gabriel. Gabriel, from whom the Archbishop was descended, was created 'Barronett' in 1622, and
lived·at Burncourt Castle near Clogheen. He was one of
the twenty-four sentenced by Ireton to be hanged at Limerick
in 1651.[2] A grandson of Gabriel, viz., also a Sir John
Everard, fought as a cavalry officer at the battle of the
Boyne, and was killed at the battle of Aughrim in 1691.[3]
Sons and grandsons of Nicholas and Richard married
daughters of Viscount Fermoy, the Duke of Ormond, and
Lord Cahir.

The arms of the Everards, to attempt a diffident blazoning
of them, are: a lion langued, armed, rampant, combatant on
dexter chief sable; a mullet among a triangle of three
crescents of the first sable on sinister chief gules; base
fourteen pellets in four lines on field argent. These arms
may still be seen on the silver plate which belonged to the
Archbishop, or in the Office of Arms at Dublin Castle. The
exact house in which Dr. Patrick Everard, Archbishop of
Cashel, first saw the light of day, is perhaps a matter of little
importance, but is also one of much dispute. Some affirm
that he was born at the country-seat of his family, a short
distance out of Fethard, in the lovely County of Tipperary;
others that he was born in the town-house in Fethard itself.
To speak of a town-house in that little rural city of only one
street worthy of the name, where a few cattle may generally
be seen loitering, which is flooded with the sweet air of
heaven at all times, and where the fields, woods, and mountains can be seen from every gap or corner, may seem
somewhat extravagant. Nevertheless, Fethard is an important little town in its own quiet way, and is the birth-place

---

[1] See D'Arcy M'Gee's *Hist. of Ireland*, vol. ii., p. 84, seq.: also Haverty,
p. 502.
[2] See M'Gee, *ib.*, p. 46, and Hav., *ib*, p. 592.
[3] See *Records of Ireland*, p. 384.

of more than one illustrious person. It is one of the few
ancient strongholds whose fortifications remain almost
intact at the present moment. Fethard is a walled city.
And those walls, like most of the walls of Ireland, have stood
amidst, if not withstood, the missiles of the cruel invaders
of her peaceful homes.

It may not, perchance, be tedious, or out of place, to
recall here the *ruse de guerre*, which the inhabitants of
Fethard are said to have made use of, when Cromwell with
his heaven-sent butchers came creeping over the lower slopes
of Slievnamon, to besiege the place in 1650. All the farmers
of the town and district brought in their largest milk-cans
and placed them with the mouths facing the enemy, like so
many pieces of heavy ordnance, upon the walls. Then the
'Sovereign,' or Mayor of Fethard, who was, on that memorable
occasion, James Everard, a direct ancestor of the Archbishop,
together with the leading men of the town, went forth to
the hostile camp to discuss the terms of capitulation. This
may or may not be true. However, we are informed by
Mr. Prendergast,[1] that ' the terms of truce with Fethard
were the best obtained by any town in Ireland,' if that be
anything to boast of. It would seem that Ireland has never
sent out from her primeval fields anything more formidable
than milk and butter, saints and scholars. This is surely
good for evil.

However this may be, it is quite certain that Dr. Everard
was born in or near that most picturesque city of Fethard,
about the year 1752. There, in the wide market-place
stands the large quaint and ancient mansion of the Everards,
and looks now as able to outlast the vicissitudes of men as
ever. It is a huge house of but two storeys with dormers in
the roof, and in the long front facing the street there are
two rows of ten windows each, the lower row being divided
in the middle by the main door with a pillar at each side.
On the right of this door, and in the wall, there is still a large
square stone slab, bearing the arms of the Everards carved
upon it. The charge, as far as can be distinguished, is a

---

[1] See his *Cromwellian Settlement*.

lion rampant, with its tail not bending as usual over the
back, but hanging behind, and having many branches, each
terminating in a shamrock. Possibly this greatly feathered
tail is a playful allusion to the English sound of the name
Fethard. The fine old mansion, once the home of culture,
virtue, and peace, is now a garrison; for the Everards are
dispersed and impoverished, and their seat is the seat of war,
or rather of a barracks of British soldiers. Not even secluded
Fethard is impregnable to the onward step of 'civilization.'
Now it is a town of glorious ruins and dismantled towers
and churches and schools. Everywhere you go you light
upon the wreck of former plenty, peace, and prosperity,
temporal and spiritual. To the English visitor, unaccus-
tomed to seeing such places, Fethard is full of a sort of sad
romantic charm and interest. Here, may still be seen a
noble battered 'gate,' over which stands a strong watch-
tower, with barbacan and bastion almost complete ; there,
a massive castle-like piece of masonry rises up at the very
edge of the river; now, lovely flower-gardens are met with
enclosed by the ancient fortifications, against which are
reared the choicest fruit trees ; then, a once substantial
church or abbey, or castle handed over to the ivy, the jack-
daws, and the elements. The town is bounded on two sides
by a natural moat of the dark-flowing Suir, and on the other
two sides by walls, which are only about five feet thick.
Until quite recent days, a strong embattled tower stood on
each side of a drawbridge which formed the sole entrance to
the town from the West. Several times each day troops of
horses from the quondam mansion of the Everards may be
seen scampering headlong up the broad street of Fethard
after their watering at the river. At other times that street
of irregular, old and pretty houses is quiet enough. An
occasional donkey with its tiny cart dozes and blinks near
the shop door, undisturbed by a gang of noisy geese, and
seeming glad to wait for his gossiping master or mistress
within. They do not race time in Ireland ; it is, there, the
slave, not the master.

We have dwelt for a considerable time upon Fethard,
because not only was Patrick Everard born there, but

because the names of Fethard and Everard are almost
synonymous words ; with the interests, the history, and the
fate of that little city the noble family of the Everards were
for ages part and parcel. Here too the future Archbishop's
childhood and early youth were spent. His elementary and
classical education were, for the most part, acquired at home
and at the Grammar School of Fethard. Providence having
endowed him with a gentle and saintly disposition, he was
irresistibly led on to the vocation of the priesthood. Almost
every family has a member a priest in that country, which is
the modern tribe of Levi among the nations of the English
tongue. Accordingly, when this young Levite had learnt
all that his native town could teach him, his father sent him
across the seas to the distant, celebrated schools of Salamanca,
in Spain. One can imagine the handsome figure of that
noble youth, dressed in his knee breeches, silk stockings and
white cravat, stepping out of his father's house for the last
time and into the stage-coach. It was a long journey in
those days, through Clonmel to Waterford, and thence by
ship to Oporto, or Bilbao, for Salamanca. That was a
pathetic event in his life. He would not be able to return
home at Christmas and midsummer, as youths do now ; nay,
more than twenty summers would come and go before he
returned, if even then he did.

It is not improbable that young Everard called at
Bordeaux, on this his first voyage, to visit a friend and
former neighbour of his own family, a certain Mr. Barton.
This gentleman owned extensive vineyards there and also
the ¦Grove estate, Co. Tipperary, which Mr. Everard, the
father of Patrick, was agent for, in the absence of its owner.

With what assiduity Patrick pursued his studies of
philosophy and theology in the Irish College at Salamanca,
for to that College he proceeded, can only be gathered from
his subsequent brilliant career and the splendid success which
crowned his labours wherever he went and whatever he
undertook. In the home and atmosphere of that famous
school of theology, the Salmanticenses, the devoted young
Irish student was sure to take full advantage of the fine
opportunities he had of becoming a theologian of the first

rank. It is a noteworthy fact, that he had among his companions at the Irish College in Salamanca, three other future Archbishops of Ireland. The four metropolitans, Dr. Murray of Dublin, Dr. Kelly of Tuam, Dr. Laffan and Dr. Everard, both of Cashel, studied, prayed, played, slept, and ate together when boys under the same roof at Salamanca. We do not know the precise year in which he entered Salamanca, but we know that he was certainly there in 1776, when he was twenty-four years of age. We also are certain that he was raised to the dignity of priesthood in the year 1783, at Salamanca, when he was thirty-one. To some this may seem a somewhat mature age at which to be ordained, and might perhaps argue a want of talent in the candidate for Holy Orders. But such was not the case. The course of studies at that great university was long and difficult. We, in England, are accustomed to see young men admitted to the sacred priesthood at the age of about twenty-five and after a substantial, but comparatively meagre curriculum. It was not so in those former times at Salamanca, the Louvain of the South. Taking the degree of S.T.D. there was no trivial affair. There is not the least doubt that Patrick Everard was made a Doctor of Divinity at the great University of Salamanca. When he left his Spanish *Alma Mater* upon his ordination he was styled ' Dr. Everard,' a title he ever afterwards went by. M. L'Abbé Bertrand informs us that Patrick Everard occupied the chair of Doctor of Theology at Bordeaux.[1] To this day, at Ulverston which we shall have occasion to speak of by-and-bye, and where his memory is still green, the people always mention him as ' Dr. Everard,' though he was not raised to the episcopate until his long sojourn in that town was practically over. But, let us now follow him from Salamanca to Bordeaux, where the first years of his fruitful priesthood were spent.

It was the custom of the sons of gentlemen in those days, as soon as they had completed their education, to make a tour through the various places of interest in Europe. With

---

[1] See his *Histoire des Séminaires de Bordeaux*, t. i., p. 381.

this intention the newly-made priest and Doctor of Theology
left his college at Salamanca, intending also, as soon as his
well-earned vacation was at an end, to return to his native
land and place himself at the disposal of his own bishop.
But man proposes and God disposes.

Naturally enough, on leaving Spain he bent his steps
towards Bordeaux, where an intimate friend of his family
lived in affluence, where he would hear the latest news from
Tipperary, and where he could communicate more speedily
with his parents. There was also the Irish College at
Bordeaux, where he would, doubtless, meet some of his old
acquaintance. Little did he dream that his proposed visit
of pleasure to Bordeaux was to develop into a delay of more
than ten years in that city. Yet so it was to be. How
different was the actual, eventful course, which awaited the
bright young ecclesiastic from the one he had planned out
for himself in his own simple unassuming mind! An exile
for many years in a distant land, a voluntary prisoner in the
halls of learning, he now yearned to go back to the pleasant
meadows and the clear streams of 'the Golden Vale of
Tipperary.' What a joy it would be for him to revisit dear
old Fethard, and to share in the joy of his father and mother
and their tenants; at meeting once again their beloved boy,
now grown into a priest and a Doctor of Divinity! His own
ambition, if that it can be called, was no more than to
administer to the spiritual wants of a rustic flock, to visit
and cheer the dwellers in the white-washed cottages of his
own native county, where, from almost any point, he could
turn and see the venerable and revered Rock of Cashel with
its hoary, mysterious, and hallowed cluster of buildings
sublimely noble, nay, unique. '*Has inter 'epulas, ut juvat
pastas oves videre properantes domum!*' But, alas! that
happy dream was never to be realized.

Dr. Glynn, Rector of the Irish College at Bordeaux, old
and infirm when Dr. Everard arrived from Spain, was not
slow to appreciate the abilities of the young Salamancan
Doctor, nor to avail himself of the opportunity thus afforded
him of resigning the arduous duties of a superior. There
was an accomplished priest, an Irishman and a nobleman,

in the prime of life, abounding in zeal, knowledge, and energy, educated and ordained on his own patrimony, and therefore under no obligation of serving any particular bishop. It was no slight temptation to the old man. He yielded to it, and who can blame him ? But Dr. Glynn was too prudent to rely upon his own influence in accomplishing his plan. There was one, however, whose influence and authority would carry all before it. This was Monseigneur de Ceci, the Archbishop of Bordeaux. He himself had not been insensible to the attractions of the elegant and gifted ecclesiastic now in their midst. He probably might not succeed in affiliating Dr. Everard to his diocese, did he desire to do so ; but he might at least by persuasion retain him in the city as a valuable and useful ornament. To the Archbishop, then, Dr. Glynn betook himself, to unfold his scheme, and secure the co-operation he so coveted. Needless to say, he succeeded. The Doctor was summoned to the palace of the Archbishop, and, in the course of an interview, was prevailed upon to accept the reins of rectorship of the Irish College.[1] The Venerable Dr. Glynn then retired into a well-merited and honourable seclusion.

It would have been well for the old man had he then sought his peaceful native shore of Ireland, well—if it be well to escape the crown of martyrdom and a cruel, sanguinary death. Yet who could then foresee that the 'Eldest Daughter of the Church,' France, flourishing, opulent, and basking in the rays of her own effete splendour, would, before long, be torn by insane frenzy, be disgraced and drenched with the blood of her own population ; her religion, her laws, her wealth, art, honour, all swallowed up and drowned in a diluvian outburst of infamy ?

Dr. Everard presided over the destinies of the Irish College at Bordeaux for ten years. Each of those years he sent over to Ireland a little batch of priests, trained under his own eyes, and schooled in that deep theology of which he was a thorough master ; but, above all, in those great virtues, lofty principles, and unsurpassed refinement, for which he was always so remarkable.

---

[1] See *Archives of the Diocese of Bordeaux*, t. 3.

Indeed, the Irish theologian's reputation for sanctity,
learning, and prudence became so great in Bordeaux, that
the Archbishop Monseigneur de Ceci could afford to pass
over the native clergy, and make Dr. Everard Vicar-General
of that immense diocese.[1] This singular distinction speaks
volumes in praise of Dr. Everard, and is the more wonderful
when we remember that he was at the time only a young
man between thirty and forty years of age. It was an
honour which reminds us of that obtained by Henrietta
Maria for the English exiled poet and priest, Crashaw,
in his being made a Canon of Loretto.

Then that Revolution of France came. As if possessed
by the evil spirit, the rabble concentrated their hatred and
cruelty upon the priests of the Church. For a short while
the Irish clergy seem to have been protected by a sort of
fragile immunity. But the French clergy had to flee, and
their Archbishop Monseigneur de Ceci with them. Before
taking his departure, however, the Archbishop gave
Dr. Everard a still greater proof of his confidence and
esteem. He made him sole administrator of the diocese
of Bordeaux. Throughout many months of that fearful
upheaval of iniquity, the fearless Irish Vicar-General,
Patrick Everard, of Fethard, kept those bloodhounds at
bay. He carried his life in his hands. But God was with
him, and there is a limit even to the wickedness of a French
revolution. He remained at the helm, and faithfully steered
the bark committed to his charge as long as only his life
was spared. Nothing short of the guillotine could make
him leave his post ; and would not the guillotine make him
leave it, besides give the foes of religion a fiendish triumph ?
How he escaped that dreadful death was an undoubted
miracle, as we shall soon see.

The poor old man, Dr. Glynn, then verging on the grave,
tottering, bent, and feeble, was dragged out of his house in
his soutane, and goaded along to the place of public execution, amidst the shouts of the abandoned mob. A Mr. Roche,
of Cork, at that time in Bordeaux, has handed down this

---

[1] See *Hist. des Seminaires de Bordeaux*, t. i., p. 381.

fact, and says he saw with his own eyes the appalling tragedy. Still, the good shepherd, although he had heard of the fate of his venerable old friend, did not flee. We have the authority of the same Mr. Roche for stating that Dr. Everard did not attempt to escape until an armed band broke into his house, seized upon him, and were about to drag him away, when, the string of his gown breaking, he fled, and, like Joseph' left his cloak in the very hands of his would-be murderers.

Where Monseigneur de Ceci had gone to nobody knew, not even his heroic vicar-general, for, when life itself was not respected, how could correspondence be? A touching episode, yet to be related in chronological order, will reveal the Archbishop's harbour of refuge, and also the unbounded filial devotion of his adopted son and heir. Dr. Everard himself made good his miraculous escape, crossed over into Spain, and thence sailed to England. In passing through London in his flight from the Revolution in 1794, he was introduced to Edmund Burke, who, to quote from an authentic letter, 'was so fascinated with Dr. Everard's courtly manner and conversation, that he became ever after his attached friend, and introduced him to the leading statesmen and principal Catholic families of England.

We now come to what may be called the third epoch in Dr. Everard's changeful career. Hidden away in a remote and charming valley of Furness, surrounded on three sides by green lofty terraces of noble hills and on the fourth by the estuary of meeting rivers from the English lakes, reposing in a serene solitude all its own, lies the old picturesque market town of Ulverston. Here we next find Dr. Everard. In this town the faith has had a little nook of some sort almost since the days of the so-called Reformation. And Ulverston has been unusually fortunate in having had, in the past, several illustrious priests as its rectors. 'That celebrated historian, Father Thomas (Daniel) West, S.J.,' to quote from the 'Records' of this Society—' who wrote that scholarly and classical work, *The Antiquities of Furness*,[1] was a predecessor

[1] Twenty-three Dukes and Lords; twenty-two Baronets; forty-nine Protestant Clergymen; eighteen Professors of the Universities of Oxford and Cambridge, and nearly all the Catholic gentry of England and Scotland were subscribers to this work. He also was the first to write a *Guide to the Lakes*.

of Dr. Everard at Ulverston. Fathers Sewall, Cobb, and
Weld, the great pioneer of the Gospel, all three subsequent
provincials of the same Society, were Dr. Everard's successors.[1]

The once famous school kept at Ulverston by Dr. Everard
is not, perhaps, as well known as it deserves to be. Ulverston,
in those days especially, was an ideal situation for an advanced
school for the sons of the aristocracy. The open sea and
lakes Windermere and Coniston are close at hand; hard by
is the noble ruin of Furness Abbey, noble, if ruins can be:
every outlet from the town leads into the most charming
scenery of mountain, ravine, wood, and stream; the hills
abound in grouse and other game, the brooks and rivers in
trout and salmon; no railway then disturbed or disfigured
the vicinity, no factories polluted its salubrious atmosphere: in short, it was a choice home for study, piety, and
recreation. Dr. Everard obtained his lucrative appointment
to Ulverston through the instrumentality of Edmund Burke.
No place could better afford a peaceful abode to the refugee
from the jaws of death, a home congenial to the scholar
and professor, than Ulverston.

The Most Rev. Dr. Healy, in his *Centenary History of
Maynooth College*, says: 'Dr. Everard bought from the
Jesuit fathers their school at Ulverstone in Lancashire,
which he conducted with great success for many years.'[2] In
the official *Record* of Maynooth, Dr. Everard is described as
'formerly Superior of the Irish community at Bordeaux and
Vicar-General of that diocese, Principal of a lay Academy at
Ulverstone.'

It would seem, therefore, that Dr. Everard was not the
original founder of the school. It is quite possible that it
owed its first establishment to Father West, S.J., who was
as renowned all over England for learning as Dr. Everard
afterwards became. But there is no mention of a Jesuit
school, previous to Dr. Everard's time, in the *Collectanea* of
that Society, which, however, do mention that Dr. Everard
'kept a school there, besides serving the mission.' They

---

[1] See *Records of the English Province*, by Br. Foley.   [2] Page 228.

relate, also, that 'the Society gave some property to Dr. Everard, with which he bought a house for £800.' Although there appears a slight confusion in the above accounts, it is quite evident that Dr. Everard had some transaction with the Jesuits in regard to the occupation of the school and mission of Ulverston. There is also some discrepancy as to the year in which Dr. Everard came to Ulverston. The *Collectanea* state that he 'was placed there [at Ulverston] by Father William Strickland as early as 1802.' If this means that Dr. Everard was certainly there at that date, it is true; but if it means to imply that he was not there before 1802, it seems incorrect, for the very reason why Mr. Burke obtained the appointment of Dr. Everard to Ulverston school was because he was thrown out of an occupation by the Revolution, in 1794 or '95. Besides, no mention of his being in Ireland, or in any other place than in Ulverston, between 1794 and 1802 can be found. On the contrary, all accounts seem to imply that he came straight to Ulverston after he left Bordeaux, with the exception of the short stay he then made in London. Had he been attached to some other mission in Ireland or England during those eight years, it would certainly have been known to Dr. Healy, who also would have mentioned the fact in his sketch of Dr. Everard's life before quoted. Very probably the word, 'placed,' meant that Father Strickland handed over the charge of the mission, as distinct from the school, to Dr. Everard in 1802. Nevertheless, the Jesuit Order seem to have reserved at least the right of investiture to themselves, because we find that as far back as 1678 until beyond the middle of this century in 1863, when this school had long since melted away into Stonyhurst, Ushaw, and Oscott, a long succession of Jesuits served the district of Ulverston.[1]

In the days of Dr. Everard the Catholics of Ulverston, exclusive of the students, were by no means numerous. Yet the few that were there were wealthy and aristocratic. Several titled families, such as the Belasyses and Mostyns,

---

[1] See *Records of the English Province*, by Br. Foley, vol. iii., addenda, p. 776. Also *State Papers*, P.R.O., Dom. Charles ii., b. n. 411, p. 45.

had fine houses here and resided as neighbours of the erudite
and polished Doctor.   Indeed, it is said that the school and
the Catholic gentry were the mainstay of the place at the
time.   The students had their own stables and horses and
dogs, and followed the hunt or rode out.   They dined and
danced with the neighbouring county families, who, in turn,
were entertained at the Catholic houses in the town.

Report has it that the great Doctor himself accompanied
his students on such occasions, and stayed as a spectator,
even for the dance.[1] Whether he was a *persona grata* during
the last-named portion of the entertainments, is not handed
down.   There is no reason, however, to suppose that he was
anything else, for the dances of the Catholic aristocracy
were then, and always have been, as decorous, nay, it might
be said, as ' sober, steadfast, and demure ' as a procession of
cloistered nuns.   A wise and paternal master, he had a
supervision over his pupils at all times.   He knew well how
to temper the useful with the pleasant, '*moresque viris et
præmia ponet.*'

But no one, who had the least knowledge of him, would
be scandalized in Dr. Everard.   On the contrary, all who
had the privilege of his acquaintance, and that was a great
privilege, were drawn to him by an irresistible attraction
quite his own.   Born and nurtured in a virtuous home,
inheriting the refinement of an ancient nobility, trained
for over twenty years in the conservatories of solid piety
and deep science, he was not only a priest, a scholar, and a
gentleman, but he was the model, the perfection, the very
pink and *beau ideal* of each.

In strange contrast with his whole character is the
following story, and quite authentic.   The good Professor
was one Sunday evening, above all other evenings, whiling
away the long, dreary candlelight, in a peaceful game of
whist with the parents of the lady who still relates the
event.   Suddenly the party were surprised red-handed, in
the very act of dealing, by the abrupt introduction into the
room of a very rigid and most correct old lady, yet not a

---

[1] See *Dublin Review*, October, 1892, p. 399, art. on ' Charles Langdale.'

Catholic. She was at first staggered, and could not believe her eyes, but when she had regained her scattered senses and her breath, and became calm enough to realize the awful situation she was in, she clasped her hands in an agony of scandal and horror, cast her eyes up to heaven, and screeched, ' My God ! has it come to this !' But Dr. Everard 'lived it down' and his reputation survived even this terrible *denouement*.

Judging from his portrait at Maynooth, and the one at the palace of his present successor in the see of Cashel, and from the fine bust set up to his memory in the chapel at Thurles College, Dr. Everard's personal appearance was as distinguished as were his mental accomplishments. He has the high forehead, the guileless eye, the aquiline nose, the well-formed mouth and chin of manly beauty. He was tall above the average, as most Tipperary men are, broad in the chest, and straight as a soldier.

For all that, his Catholicity and his nationality did not escape the profane ribaldry of the lower orders of the day, who shouted after him ' Irish Pat,' ' Yer Rivrince,' and ' Priest.' Cardinal Newman had not yet then whipped out of England that native insolence with his unmitigated castigation, remarking that *anything* can be a subject of ridicule with some people, even the bald head of a prophet. But none of those epithets were calculated to disturb the equanimity of Dr. Everard or caused him to blush. It was very ungrateful on their part, for many of them, if they did not owe to him their daily bread, were his debtors for the butter on it. To have his windows broken on the 5th November, was an affliction which he, in common with many other priests, could not cure, and so they endured. He used to close his inner shutters on the 5th, and send his glazier round on the 6th November, and his tradesmen on the 24th December with legs of mutton, pies, coals, sugar, and tea, for his persecutors.

The school itself was originally a fairly large gentleman's residence, and stands at the end of Fountain-street to this day. Long since it has been divided into four good-sized, respectable houses, in one of which the priests

of Ulverston have lived from Dr. Everard's day until the
year 1895, when a new church and presbytery were occupied,
and the old ones sold, exactly a century after Dr. Everard
came to the town. A large paved courtyard with stables
adjoining stands at the back of the old school premises
beneath the shade of a few ancient sycamores. Dr. Everard
also owned two fine gardens near the school and some fields
just outside the town, which are now called 'Gill Banks,'
and have become a public pleasure resort for the people.

The annual pension paid by Dr. Everard's pupils, according to Dr. Healy in his aforesaid work, ranged from '£200
to £400.' This seems a large sum for those days ; but when
it is borne in mind that the school was intended for the
sons of the nobility, and patronized by them alone, the
amount does not seem so very extravagant. Nevertheless,
if there were about twenty students under Dr. Everard, as
tradition says there were, and if we put the average pension
at £300, the income was one not at all to be despised. The
amount of money he realized as the proceeds of his school
may be estimated, to a certain extent, by the legacies he
left in his will. Among the items of his will are to be seen
£10,000 for the establishment of a college at Thurles for
the education of priests, and another of £5,000 to his old
friend Dr. Murray of Dublin, to be devoted entirely to
religious and educational purposes. It is known, on the
most trustworthy evidence, that not a penny of his earnings
went to a single member of his own family. Dr. Everard
did not acquire his comparatively large fortune from the
revenues of Cashel, as he was Archbishop of that see for only
three months, nor from his own family, for, as we have
already inferred, they were long ago denuded of most of the
ancestral property they once possessed.

Certainly the suggestion of selfishness, much less the
taint of avarice, cannot be laid at the door of his memory.
His was a cleanhandedness, a detachment from lucre,
worthy of St. Charles Borromeo. The nobility of England
would have gladly subscribed to the above-named objects the
amount Dr. Everard bequeathed to them, without ever
having heard of his name, or having had their sons educated

under his conscientious and indefatigable care. It is as pleasant to think of the success in England of the refugee from death in France as to recollect the triumphant affluence of Job. The emoluments he received at Ulverston were the natural outcome and fruits of his own prolific genius, peculiar skill, incessant toil. All his scorings, if we may use a modern schoolboy phrase, were 'off his own bat.' Only his equal could have attained an equal success. Yet, he did not go over to Ireland to buy back, which he was well able to do, the estates of his forefathers, and there build himself a house, wherein to rest, after the heats and burdens he had so long borne, and end his days in what would now be a boasted and laudable retirement. All his savings went to the building up of the spiritual edifice, the needy Church in Ireland, which, throughout the long periods of his exile, he had ever loved so well. With Bacon, he considered riches to be 'the baggage of virtue,' and his whole existence proclaimed with Fénelon, ' Secouez le joug du superflu, faites-vous riche sans argent.'

Beneath the handsome marble bust of Dr. Everard in Thurles College chapel there is a tablet which bears the following inscription : ' This Chapel has been Furnished and Decorated by the Archbishop and Priests of Cashel and Emly, in the Year of Grace 1889, in Memory of the Most Reverend Patrick Everard, Archbishop of Cashel and Emly, by whose Magnificent Bequest this College of St. Patrick was mainly Founded, A.D. 1837.'

Thus, the man who had sent over to Ireland from Bordeaux so many well-educated priests, conferred a perpetual boon upon England in furnishing us with lay gentlemen not less accomplished in their own spheres of influence and action; such men, for instance, as Charles Langdale, who achieved so much for the Catholics of his time. Nay, more, he utilized the very success of that boon to establish a great college in Ireland. To see that flourishing college with its grand broad corridors, its noble refectory and pretty chapel, its splendid libraries, its play-rooms and class-rooms, its superb suites of professorial apartments, its large imposing frontage dominating its beautiful gardens,

lawns, and avenues ; to see, above all, its learned and refined
staff of professors, with about a hundred earnest, merry,
busy, and healthy ecclesiastical students, is to form some
idea of the imperishable good Dr. Everard accomplished.

An intimate and unbroken friendship always existed
between Dr. Everard and Dr. Murray, Archbishop of Dublin.
The late Abbot Clifton, O.S.B., whose father was a pupil
under Dr. Everard at Ulverston, informed the writer of this
memoir that Dr. Murray himself, for some time at least,
assisted Dr. Everard in teaching at Ulverston—a fact which
in some measure accounts for the large bequest Dr. Everard
left to Dr. Murray.

A heroic and touching event, already alluded to, which
portrays in a halo of light the disinterestedness of
Dr. Everard, must not be forgotten. When he had passed
a year or two in prosperity at Ulverston, he chanced to hear
that his beloved former master, the Archbishop of Bordeaux,
poor old Monseigneur de Ceci, had escaped over to London,
and was living there in obscurity and poverty. The very
next ebb of the tide, the faithful disciple left Ulverston,
crossed over the dangerous sands of Morecambe Bay in the
stage-coach for Lancaster, and thence hastened on to London
with all possible speed, and with all the money he possessed,
to seek out and rescue his aged friend. And he found him.
The meeting of that Archbishop and his former Vicar-
General can be better imagined than described. They had
been driven asunder by a cruel storm and neither hoped to
see the other again. When the young priest was an exile
the Archbishop had raised him up to a high position, and
now it is in the power of the son to aid the father in his
homeless, sorrowful, and penurious exile. Needless to say
that opportunity was not let slip. Dr. Everard at once took
a respectable house for the foreign Archbishop, and maintained him there in a manner suitable to the dignity of so
great a prelate, until the storm abated and the shepherd
returned to his stricken flock in Bordeaux.

With the above exception, Dr. Everard's long sojourn of
over fifteen years in Ulverston was uneventful enough. It
was the calm, steady routine of a community life, day after

day, and year after year. As far as can be ascertained, he
did not publish any works except a certain pamphlet
addressed to the Duke of Wellington, which is said to have
caused a sensation at the time.

We now come to what may be called the last period in
the career of Dr. Everard, when we shall find him transferred
to new spheres of greater responsibility and higher dignity.
His fame was not confined to England and France; it was
known also in his own country. The Irish bishops not
unnaturally regarded with a jealous eye the employment of
their native Irish talent in the 'lay academy at Ulverstone.'
The gifted Tipperary priest had been ten years superior of
their own college in Bordeaux, and now, in 1810, he had
gained a long and varied experience in the training of young
gentlemen in England. They could submit to his being
raised to a high ecclesiastical position in France, where he
might still be useful to their cause ; but they would not
gladly allow his ability to be spent in England any longer
than they could help. The Irish bishops have more virtues
in their armoury than the simplicity of the dove. And, if
their charity had not in this case begun at home, they would
rightly endeavour to make it end there.

Accordingly, the Presidency of Maynooth College being
vacant in 1810, the bishops of Ireland elected Dr. Everard
President on the feast of SS. Peter and Paul in that year.
He was then in his own fifty-eighth year. This was a conspicuous honour conferred upon him by his own countrymen, and, of course, showed their high appreciation of his
rare virtues and capacity for training youth. To a great
extent, the spiritual fabric and welfare of all Ireland depends
upon the President of Maynooth College, where so vast a
number of priests are educated.

Unfortunately, the health of the new President was by
this time greatly impaired. In fact, his term of residence
at Maynooth seems never to have been very continuous.
The very year after his installation there we find him recruit-
ing his broken strength in the bracing sea and mountain air
of his English home at Ulverston. Dr. Maginnis, of Maynooth, in a letter to the Most Rev. Dr. Plunkett, of Meath,

dated St. Patrick's Day, 1811, says :—'Dr. Everard is still
in England.' Nevertheless, he still fought on, and returned
to his presidential duties as soon as he had regained sufficient strength.[1] But the climate of Maynooth did not suit
his shattered constitution. Ulverston, on the other hand,
lying, as we have said, in a basin surrounded by hills, which
shelter it from the cold north and east winds, is remarkable
for the mildness of its climate, and is even now a health
resort for invalids in winter time. Dr. Everard had become
acclimatized to this atmosphere, and so we find that he
again and again crossed over the Irish Sea from Dublin to
Ulverston, now struggling to fulfil his duties, now seeking to
restore his failing energies. The end of it all was that he
was obliged to retire from Maynooth altogether in 1812,
when, as Dr. Healy states, 'he returned to his school in
Ulverstone.' It was not, however, until the following year,
1813, that he wrote, sending in his final and formal resignation, which he did on the 25th of June of that year.
Dr. Murray, though he was then Archbishop of Dublin, held
the presidency himself as a *locum tenens* during Dr. Everard's
frequent relapses, hoping against hope that his friend would
be restored to health, and so retain the reins of office. But
it was not to be.

Although Dr. Everard returned again to Ulverston, after
his short and oft-interrupted rule as President of the great
college in Ireland, it is not known whether he then resumed
his teaching there or not. As he was in his sixty-first year,
and infirm, it is not likely that he did. In 1814, we find the
Rev. Nicholas Sewall, S.J., at Ulverston. Dr. Everard may,
therefore, have handed over the school to the Jesuit fathers,
from whom he is said to have originally bought it.

In that year, 1814, Dr. Everard was raised to the highest
rank and office to which a priest can attain, being elected
Coadjutor to the Most Rev. Dr. Bray, Archbishop of Cashel,
with the right of succession. According to the pontifical
brief of his election, dated 1st October, 1814, he received the

---

[1] It was probably through the instrumentality of Dr. Everard that
Dr. Lingard, the historian, was, in 1811, invited to assume the presidency of
Maynooth. They were clerical friends and neighbours at Ulverston and Hornby.

title of 'Archbishop of Malta, i.p.i., . . . and was consecrated at Cork on the 24th of April, 1815.'[1]   The elevation to the episcopate of an aged and feeble man may be regarded as rather *honoris* than *oneris causa* ; as an appropriate recognition of distinguished services rendered to the Church, rather than the road to future labours.   Yet, although his health prevented him from retaining the heavy responsibilities of Maynooth, there was no reason why he might not perform the less arduous duties of a coadjutor.   Maynooth is in as exposed a situation as Ushaw, while Tipperary is almost as undulating, and its valleys as sheltered, as Furness. His intellectual powers were not enfeebled.

Upon the death of Archbishop Bray, in the year 1820, Dr. Everard succeeded him, and became Archbishop of Cashel and Emly in December that year.   But he was not destined to wear the pallium for more than three months. He died in the following March, in 1821.   He was buried in the parish church of Cashel, where his remains still repose, unindicated as yet by any monument of stone, but remembered by the more lasting veneration of a hallowed tradition.

Thus the exile, after forty years of vicissitudes, of perils, labours, and successes, returned at last to the home and haunts of his childhood.   He returned, indeed, but not in the summer of his life, not to see those hoary ruins of Holy Cross and Cashel, those emerald hills and silvery . brooks and pleasant valleys, which team with the fascination of poetry and romance, lit up and engloried in the noon-day sun of his strength ; but he returned in the night of his life, when he was worn, and old, and feeble, when the friends of his youth were dead, to die himself, and'lay his bones, as was fitting, by the side of Erin's princes, and under the shadow of the sacred towers of Cashel.

The written records of the life of this great Archbishop are not at all copious, and these pages have been inscribed to his memory in an attempt to save the little that is known to a few from falling into undeserved oblivion.

T. B. ALLAN.

---

[1] M. l'Abbé Bertrand, op. cit. ib.

Notes and Queries

LITURGY

Rev. Dear Sir,—Will you be so kind as to relieve me of doubt on the two following points:—

1. As to whether the Annual Diocesan Solemn Mass for deceased diocesan prelates may be celebrated on a feast of a higher rite than semi-double; and (2) as to whether one prayer only, or three must be sung, in the event of (1) being answered in the affirmative.

M. C.

1. The rubrics of the Missal and the decrees of the Congregation of Rites recognise two kinds of anniversary requiem Masses. One kind may be called *foundation* Masses, as they should be founded by deed, donation, or last will for the repose of the founder's soul, or of the souls of others mentioned by the founder. The second kind of anniversary Mass is one which has not been founded or provided for by anyone, but is asked for annually by the relatives or friends of a deceased person. The privileges attaching to the first kind of anniversary Mass are more extensive than those attaching to the second. Both kinds may be celebrated on a feast of double, or even of double-major rite; but while the former kind can be transferred or anticipated as often as the anniversary day is impeded by a feast excluding an anniversary Mass, the latter kind cannot; in both cases, however, the Mass must be fixed for the actual anniversary of the day of death—*in die veri obitus*. And when a requiem Mass is celebrated for several deceased persons, whether it be a foundation Mass, or one asked for annually, it enjoys no privilege unless it be celebrated on the anniversary day of the death of one of those for whom it is offered.

Now, in the case about which our correspondent inquires the Mass is not, unless by accident, celebrated on the anniversary day of the death of any one of the prelates commemorated. Hence it possesses no privilege, and without a papal indult can be celebrated only on a day on which a private' Requiem Mass may be celebrated. This conclusion which we have deduced from general principles recognised by the rubrics has been made the subject of special legislation. Questions similar to the present one have been frequently addressed to the Congregation of Rites, and the invariable reply was one forbidding the annual Requiem Mass on any day of higher than semi-double rite. The latest question on this subject was addressed to the Congregation in the year 1850, and the reply was issued on September 7th of that year. We give the question and reply, and although there is no mention of deceased prelates, we think that this case is exactly similar to the one submitted by our correspondent, and consequently, that the same solution applies to both :—

Quando officium solemne, seu anniversarium pro animabus omnium defunctorum confratrum alicujus congregationis fit in festo duplici majori, poteritne cantari missa de Requie, praesertim ubi jam est antiqua praxis et consuetudo ?
Resp. In duplicibus non licere missam de Requie nec cum cantu celebrare absque Apostolico indulto hujus Sanctæ Sedis.

In the question, as may be seen, mention is made only of feasts of double-major rite, but the reply is quite general, and includes both doubles minor and doubles major.

2. Our correspondent's second question is based on the hypothesis that the first would be answered in the affirmative ; and as the first has not been answered in the affirmative we might leave the second unanswered. If, however, we left it unanswered we should create an erroneous impression by making it appear that the law regarding the number of prayers to be said in a Solemn Requiem Mass is the same now as it was always. And this is not so. Formerly in a Solemn Requiem Mass, whether it was celebrated on a privileged day or as *missa quotidiana*, only one prayer was said. But a change has been introduced by a decree of the Congregation

of Rites, dated June 30, 1896, according to which three prayers must be said even in a Solemn Requiem Mass, unless the Mass be celebrated on a privileged day or for an object to which some privilege attaches. This decree, to which attention has already been called in these pages, and which is published in the introduction to the *Ordo* for 1897, ordains :—

In missis quotidianis quibuscunque, sive lectis sive cum cantu plures esse dicendas orationes.

But an annual Mass, such as that about which our correspondent inquires, though not celebrated on a privileged day, is nevertheless not a mere *missa quotidiana*. For although the day is not privileged, the object is, according to the decree we have just quoted from. In the paragraph preceding that from which the above extract is taken it is laid down :—

Unam tantam esse dicendam orationem . . . quandocunque pro defunctis missa *solemniter* celebratur, nempe sub ritu qui duplici respondeat, uti in officio quod recitatur post acceptum nuntium de alicujus obitu, et *in anniversariis late sumptis*.

The last clause which we have italicized has special reference to anniversaries such as that to which our correspondent refers ; and hence only one prayer is to be said, although without a papal indult the Mass cannot be celebrated on a day of higher than semi-double rite.

D. O'LOAN.

CORRESPONDENCE

THE ANSWERS IN THE 'MAYNOOTH' CATECHISM:
A PRACTICAL QUESTION

ARCHBISHOP'S HOUSE,
DUBLIN, 24th *June*, 1897.

REV. AND DEAR SIR,—Kindly allow me to bring under the
notice of your readers a question of very great interest and
importance, upon which some of them, as the result of their
experience, may have formed a definite opinion, and may be
willing to state in the pages of the I. E. RECORD the conclusion at
which they have arrived.

It seemed a few years ago to be taken for granted that it
would be of great advantage in the religious instruction of the
young if the answers in the Catechism were recast, so that each
answer should form a complete sentence, stating, independently of any relation to the question, the religious truth intended
to be conveyed. Such a change was accordingly made in the
edition of the Catechism that was then brought out, and
that has come to be generally designated the 'Maynooth'
Catechism.[1]

Thus, instead of :—

'*Q.* Who made the world?
'*A.* God.'

We now have :—

'*Q.* Who made the world?
'*A.* God made the world.'

Again, instead of :—

'*Q.* What is faith?
'*A.* A divine virtue by which we firmly believe,' &c.

'*Q.* What is charity?
'*A.* A divine virtue by which we love God,' &c.

---

[1] As to this designation of the Catechism, see I. E. RECORD (Third Series),
vol. xiii., Jan. 1892, pages 3-5.

We have :—

' *Q*. What is faith ?
' *A*. Faith is a divine virtue by which we firmly believe,' &c.

' *Q*. What is charity ?
' *A*. Charity is a divine virtue by which we love God,' &c.

Also, to take some examples of a somewhat different class, instead of :—

' *Q*. Is it a great sin to neglect Confirmation ?
' *A*. Yes ; especially in those evil days, when faith and morals,' &c.

We have :—

' *Q*. Is it a great sin to neglect Confirmation?
' *A*. It is a great sin to neglect Confirmation, especially in those evil days when faith and morals,' &c.

Again, instead of :—

' *Q*. Are we to believe that the God of all glory is under the appearance of our corporal food?
' *A*. Yes; as we must also believe that the same God of all glory suffered death under the appearance of a criminal on the cross.'

We have :—.

' *Q*. Are we to believe that the God of all glory is under the appearance of our corporal food ?
' *A*. We believe that the God of all glory is under the appearance of our corporal food, just as we believe the same God of all glory,' &c.

And, instead of :—

' *Q*. What must persons do who did not carefully examine their consciences, or who had not sincere sorrow for their sins, or who wilfully concealed a mortal sin in confession ?
' *A*. They must truly repent of all such bad and sacrilegious confessions, and make them all over again.'

We have :—

' *Q*. What must persons do who did not carefully examine their consciences, or who had not sincere sorrow for their sins, or who wilfully concealed a mortal sin in confession ?
' *A*. Persons who did not examine their consciences, or who had not sorrow for their sins, or who wilfully concealed a mortal sin in confession, must truly repent of all such bad and sacrilegious confessions, and must make them over again.'

This extensive change in the form of the answers of the Catechism was made, it seems, for a two-fold purpose : first, to remove the opening, which undoubtedly was left in the older system, for the giving of irrelevant,—sometimes ludicrously irrelevant,—answers ; and, secondly, to secure that the children, by learning the answers of the Catechism, should get hold, in each case, of a definite statement of religious truth.

For my part, in so far as I formed, at the time, any definite view on the subject of the change, I regarded it as a decided improvement. I should think that this was the view then generally taken of it. At the same time I am aware that the opposite view was taken by not a few of the clergy. I understand too that it was taken by some of the Bishops. Indeed I have heard that, mainly on account of this change, there are parts of Ireland in which the so-called 'Maynooth' Catechism has never been admitted, and in which the unmodified 'Butler' has throughout continued to be the only recognised Catechism of the diocese.

Having recently had to consider some thoughtful criticisms in which this matter was discussed on the merits, I have found myself gradually brought round to recognise that there is at all events a good deal to be said in support of the view adverse to the change. For my own guidance, and believing that the point must be of interest to many of them, I have thought of thus bringing it under the notice of the readers of the I. E. RECORD, in the hope that some of them may contribute to its elucidation.

I. As to the supposed advantages of the change.

1. Has the change really excluded the giving of the wrong answers?

My own experience satisfies me that it has not, and that it is very far from having done so. Take, for instance, the questions, 'What is the Blessed Eucharist,' and 'What is the Mass.' In these two cases, is the wrong answer never substituted for the right one,—the first words, 'The Blessed Eucharist is,' or 'The Mass is,' being merely taken up as a sort of echo to the question, and the remainder being given from the wrong answer, which has happened to come to mind ? Is the same not true of the answers defining a sacrament and a sacrifice ; of the answers defining the several sacraments ; of the answers telling what is commanded, or what is forbidden, by the various commandments ;—in a word, is it not true in all those cases in which, under the form of answer in 'Butler,' such a substitution was in any way likely to occur ?

2. The second supposed advantage of the new system is that

it gives the children hold of intelligible doctrinal statements, not merely disconnected words or scraps of religious phraseology,— such as 'God;' 'to redeem and save us;' the devil, envying their happy state ; 'on Christmas Day, in a stable at Bethlehem;' and the like. Now, as to all this, it may be asked whether it is a fact that, in such cases as those illustrated by the answers just quoted, the children really got hold of nothing more than dis- connected scraps of phraseology,—whether, for instance, when they learned that, in reply to the question, 'Who made the world,' they were to answer, 'God,' they had not as firm a hold of the truth, 'God made the world,' as they have under the present cumbrous method ?

II. As to the considerations that may be urged against the change introduced in the 'Maynooth' Catechism, and in favour of a return to the older system.

1. It is very fairly urged that any arrangement which results in a substantial addition to the number of words that have to be learned by the children is, in so far, open to objection. Now. the examples which I have transcribed in the opening paragraphs of this letter,—examples, let me say, selected altogether at random, without any reference to the effect of the change as regards the length of the additions made to the passages quoted,—show the following results :—

Number of words in these six answers in ' Butler ' ...   78
     ,,   ,,   the 'Maynooth' Catechism ... 128

2. It is also a drawback that the answers as thus modified are, of necessity, rendered more complex in construction.

3. Moreover, the form of answer introduced by the change is undoubtedly a very unusual one ; probably it is altogether without parallel in any books of instruction that are drawn up as Catechisms, in the form of question and answer, in other subjects.

4. This method of answering questions is also constrained and unnatural, so that this method seems an undesirable one to put into the mouths of young children,—especially when so many answers, constructed upon the same artificial plan, have to be committed to memory and thus necessarily become familiar by frequent repetition.

5. A still more serious objection to the new form of answer is that it seems to have a tendency to check the exercise of in- telligence. In the old form of answer, a child, when asked, for instance, 'What is baptism,' had to attend carefully to the question, and to select the proper answer, out of the seven

answers in the Catechism that began with the words 'A sacrament.' In this, there was need for intelligent answering, as distinct from mere parrot-like repetition. But under the new system, in such cases, the last word of the question serves as a catchword to suggest the answer, and there is no evidence that we are getting anything more than a mere mechanical recitation when the child, echoing the last word of the question, continues the answer, ' Baptism is a sacrament,' &c.

I have already noticed the fact,—now fully established, I venture to say, by experience,—that whilst the present form of answer has the very grave defect to which I have just now directed attention, it has not, on the other hand, the advantage of really securing that the right answer shall be given.

A child, even slightly nervous, or answering at all inattentively, is by no means unlikely to give a wrong answer,—wrong, with the exception only of the first word, that one word being repeated, parrot-like, from the question. Thus, in answer to the question, ' What is Baptism,' I have heard, more than once, the absurd answer given, ' Baptism is a sacrament by which the sins are forgiven which are committed after baptism, —a result which those who object to the form in which the answers of the ' Maynooth ' Catechism are expressed would probably ascribe to the deadening effect of this form of answer upon the intelligence of the child.

A still better illustration of the same kind of defect is found in the case of the questions, ' What is Extreme Unction,' and ' What is Matrimony.' In this case, the beginning of each of the two answers contains the words, ' a sacrament which gives grace.' This, of course, adds to the confusion. And so it is not uncommon to hear,—in answer to the former question,—that ' Extreme Unction is *a sacrament which gives grace to* the husband and wife to live happy together, and to bring up their children in the fear and love of God,' and,—in answer to the latter,—that ' Matrimony is *a sacrament which gives grace to* die well, and is instituted chiefly for the spiritual strength and comfort of dying persons.'

This whole subject is plainly worthy of some careful consideration.

I remain, Rev. and Dear Sir,
Your faithful Servant,
✠ WILLIAM J. WALSH,
Archbishop of Dublin.
&c., &c

DOCUMENTS

IMPORTANT STATEMENT OF THE IRISH HIERARCHY ON
THE UNIVERSITY QUESTION.

AT a General Meeting of the Archbishops and Bishops of
Ireland, held in St. Patrick's College, Maynooth, on the
23rd ult., all the Irish Prelates being present, with the
exception of the Most Rev. Dr. Nulty, Bishop of Meath, who
was unavoidably absent, the following statement on the
Irish University question was unanimously adopted :—

Since our last meeting we have observed with great satisfaction the progress which the question of Catholic University
Education has made.

The striking Declaration in which the Catholic laity of
Ireland, renewing a similar Declaration made in the year 1870,
put forth their claim to educational equality with their Protestant
fellow-countrymen, has had a decided effect upon public opinion,
and has put beyond question the fact that the Catholic laity are
absolutely at one with the Bishops on this question, and feel as
keenly as we do the disabilities to which, on account of their
religious principles, Irish Catholics are still obliged to submit.

One of the first indications of the impression which that
Declaration made on the public mind was the very important
and hopeful debate which took place in the House of Commons
on the 22nd of January of this year, on an amendment to the
Address to the Throne, moved by Mr. Engeldew, M.P. for
Kildare. In that debate, one of the most remarkable features
was the unanimity with which, from every side of the House of
Commons, admissions were made of the existence of a grievance
on the part of Irish Catholics, and the hope was expressed that
the Government would proceed without delay to remove it.

We desire to mark in particular the fair and liberal attitude
taken up by Mr. Lecky. His own personal eminence, together
with the special authority attaching to his statements as the
representative of Dublin University, lend importance to his
speech, in which we very gladly observe a tone that does credit
to himself and to the distinguished constituency which he
represents. Naturally enough, viewing the question from a

different standpoint from ours, Mr. Lecky put forward, on the minor aspects of the question, some views from which we should dissent. But we note with very sincere pleasure the practical conclusion at which he arrived, and the expression of his hope ' that the Government would see their way to gratify the desire of the Irish Catholics.'

In some respects, the speech in which the late Chief Secretary for Ireland, Mr. Morley, went even farther in the same direction, is still more noteworthy and deserving of recognition at our hands.

With Mr. Morley's well-known views, we regard his hearty support of our claim to a Catholic University as an evidence of true liberality of mind ; and we are particularly grateful for the public spirit with which, refusing to make any party capital out of the question, he has raised it out of the arena of contentious politics, and has offered his support to the Government in their effort to deal with it.

There is then the remarkable speech of the First Lord of the Treasury, Mr. Arthur Balfour. From one occupying his position we could hardly expect a more favourable statement, and we will add that his speech, in its fairness, its friendliness of tone, and its appreciation of the views and wishes of Irish Catholics, is in keeping with the utterances of the right hon. gentleman on this question for many years ; and if the question is now ripe, as we think and trust that it is ripe, for settlement, that favourable condition of things is largely due to the statesmanship with which he has educated public opinion in the three kingdoms upon the fundamental issues that are involved.

In the course of his speech Mr. Balfour observed that upon this perplexing problem the Government have not had so much guidance from the leaders of Irish public opinion as they should like to have.

Perhaps he may have some reason for this complaint, but, for our part, we must say that we have always been ready to place any information which we possessed on the subject at the disposal of the Government, but we have never yet received an intimation that anyone in authority had any desire to receive it from us. Even now we should be glad if anyone on behalf of the Government were to formulate a series of questions on any points on which our views might be deemed of importance, so that we should know precisely the topics to which we might most usefully address ourselves. In this way we should effectually prevent the

contingency which, affecting the Government, Mr. Lecky and
Mr. Balfour seemed to apprehend, ' of proposing a scheme without being tolerably sure that it will be accepted.'

However, as we have not these definite points authoritatively
before us, we can only gather, as best we may, from the debate to
which we have referred, the issues of the case which seem to be
regarded as fundamental, and state our views upon them as clearly
and briefly as possible. They seem to be :—

1. What should be the proportion of laymen to ecclesiastics
on the governing body of the projected Catholic University ?

2. Do we ask an endowment for theological teaching ?

3. What security should be given to professors and others
against arbitrary dismissal ?

4. Are we prepared to accept the application of " The University of Dublin Tests Act " of 1873 ?

1. With regard to the constitution of the governing body we
have to remark that the question of the relative numbers of
laymen and ecclesiastics upon it is of very recent origin. For
forty years, during which Irish Catholics were engaged in
agitating for redress in University education, this question was
never once raised, nor was any opposition between these classes
even suggested ; and now we would impress upon the Government
that nothing, in our opinion, would be more fatal to the future of
the University than to approach its constitution in an anti-clerical
spirit, which is absolutely alien to the whole character and
disposition of our people.

If, however, such a spirit is excluded, and there is simply a
desire to give to the University the best and broadest constitution,
with a view to attaining the highest educational results, we have
to say that, whatever may be thought of the relative merits of
ecclesiastics and laymen as the directors of a University in the
abstract, we do not consider that in the particular circumstances
of this case it would be reasonable to propose that there should
be a preponderance of ecclesiastics on the Governing Body.

The new University will be called upon principally to provide
secular teaching. Our theological students are provided for at
Maynooth and other ecclesiastical colleges, and the need of a
Catholic University is mainly to teach secular knowledge to lay
students.

But, on the other hand, there are some considerations which it
is well not to overlook. One of the advantages which we expect

from the foundation of a Catholic University is the opportunity which it will afford of giving a higher education to the candidates for the priesthood in Ireland ; and these alone, it will be observed, will make, from the first, a large accession to the number of students in the University.

Then the whole system of secondary education, in which thousands of Catholic youths are now pursuing their studies, has come by the spontaneous action of the Catholics of Ireland to be almost entirely under ecclesiastical direction. For many of these students a University course is the natural completion of their studies, and we should hope that with our encouragement large numbers of them would pass on to the new University.

Finally, the Catholic University Colleges, notably those of St. Stephen's-green and Blackrock, and the Catholic University School of Medicine, would with our consent be merged in the contemplated University ; and hence it will be seen that we Bishops approach the settlement of this question, not empty-handed, but that, altogether independently of the rights which our Catholic people recognise as attaching to us as their religious teachers, we have claims to consideration which it would be neither just nor reasonable to ignore.

On this head, then, we have to say that if, in other respects, the Governing Body is properly constituted, we do not ask for a preponderance, or even an equality in number, of ecclesiastics upon it, but are prepared to accept a majority of laymen.

2. As to theological teaching, we accept unreservedly the solution suggested by Mr. Morley—a solution which was accepted in principle by all parties in Parliament in the year 1893 ; namely, that a theological faculty should not be excluded from the Catholic University, provided that the Chairs of the Faculty are not endowed out of public funds. We are prepared to assent to such a provision, and to any guarantees that may be necessary, that the moneys voted by Parliament shall be applied exclusively to the teaching of secular knowledge.

3. As to the appointment and removal of professors, Mr. Lecky raised an important point, and at the same time incidentally indicated at least the principle of its solution.

As reported in 'Hansard,' he said, referring to the appointment of professors :—' Of course they would be chosen not merely on the ground of competence, but also to a great extent on the ground of creed. This was inevitable, and, therefore, he did not wish to object to it; but he trusted that, having been chosen, something would be done to give them security of position.

Now it is perfectly obvious that reasons of religion which would prevent a man's appointment as professor, might in given circumstances tell against his continuance in office. But we think that both conditions—namely, absolute security for the interests of faith and morals in the University, and at the same time all reasonable protection for the position of the professor—may be met by submitting such questions to the decision of a strong and well-chosen Board of Visitors, in whose independence and judicial character all parties would have confidence.

4. There only remains the condition which Mr. Morley suggests, of the application of 'the University of Dublin Tests Act' of 1873. With reference to this we have to say that, with some modifications in the Act, in the sense of the English Acts of 1871, and the Oxford and Cambridge Act of 1877, we have no objection to the opening up of the degrees, honours, and emoluments of the University to all comers.

We have to add that in putting forward these views we assume that, if Government deals with the question, it will be by the foundation, not of a College, but of a University; and we venture to express our belief that by so doing they will best provide for all interests concerned, especially for those of higher education.

These are our views—and we trust they will be considered clear and frank enough—upon the fundamental principles which, as far as we can gather, the leading statesmen on all sides regard as the governing factors in the problem.

Should Her Majesty's Government desire any further statement from us, we shall at all times be quite ready to make it.

In conclusion, we may express the hope that, in the best interests of our country, material as well as intellectual, the question will not be again allowed to drop back from the position which it has reached, and that Government will remove this great grievance under which we labour, and, with it, one of the few remaining disabilities still attaching to the Catholic Church in Ireland.

✠ MICHAEL CARDINAL LOGUE, Archbishop of Armagh, Primate of All Ireland.
✠ WILLIAM, Archbishop of Dublin, Primate of Ireland.
✠ THOMAS WILLIAM, Archbishop of Cashel.
✠ JOHN, Archbishop of Tuam.

✠ Francis Joseph, Bishop of Galway and Kilmacduagh.
✠ Thomas Alphonsus, Bishop of Cork.
✠ John, Bishop of Clonfert.
✠ James, Bishop of Ferns.
✠ Abraham, Bishop of Ossory.
✠ Edward Thomas, Bishop of Limerick.
✠ Thomas, Bishop of Dromore.
✠ Patrick, Bishop of Raphoe.
✠ John, Bishop of Achonry.
✠ Edward, Bishop of Kilmore.
✠ John, Bishop of Kerry.
✠ Thomas, Bishop of Killaloe.
✠ John, Bishop of Derry.
✠ Richard Alphonsus, Bishop of Waterford and Lismore.
✠ John, Bishop of Killala.
✠ Robert, Bishop of Cloyne.
✠ Richard, Bishop of Clogher.
✠ Joseph, Bishop of Ardagh.
✠ John, Bishop of Elphin.
✠ Henry, Bishop of Down and Connor.
✠ Patrick, Bishop of Kildare and Leighlin.
✠ Denis, Bishop of Ross.
✠ Nicholas, Bishop of Canea.

IMPORTANT STATEMENT OF THE IRISH BISHOPS, ON THE AUTHORITY OF THE CHURCH IN POLITICAL QUESTIONS

At a General Meeting of the Archbishops and Bishops of Ireland, held in St. Patrick's College, Maynooth, on the 23rd ult., all the Irish Prelates being present, with the exception of the Most Rev. Dr. Nulty, Bishop of Meath, who was unavoidably absent, the following authoritative statement was unanimously adopted :—

Some dangerous errors, utterly subversive of Catholic truth, especially in relation to the teaching authority of the Church in what are called political matters, have recently been put forward by certain prominent Irish politicians. The Bishops of Ireland, as the divinely-appointed guardians of the faith and morals of their flocks, have read these utterances with deep regret, and all the more as most of them have emanated from persons who call themselves Catholics. Hence we feel it an urgent duty to point out these errors to our flocks, to warn them against the danger of being misled by such guides, and at the same time to set forth the true teaching of the Church, which all loyal Catholics are bound to believe and follow, in their public, no less than in their private conduct.

The errors to which we refer are the following :—That political acts are outside the sphere of morals, and that consequently they are not subject to the rules of morality, nor to any control on moral grounds, so that it is an invasion of civil rights if the pastors of the people, in the exercise of their pastoral office, pronounce upon the lawfulness of such acts in their moral aspect, or venture to condemn them, if necessary, as in conflict with the moral law. The public men now engaged in disseminating amongst our Catholic people these pernicious doctrines make formal claim to 'absolute freedom of thought and action in political matters in Ireland,' and assert that civil and religious liberty, as they phrase it, involves complete freedom from all moral control in their public action and political conduct.

They utterly repudiate all clerical interference in such matters, and deny that they are amenable in respect of their political action, either to the moral censure of their own pastors, or even of the Pope himself. As a natural consequence, their language, both in public and in private, regarding the clergy, is oftentimes highly offensive and unbecoming, so that there can be no reasonable doubt of their deliberate purpose to seduce our Catholic people from the loyalty and obedience which they certainly owe, and which hitherto they have always yielded, both to their local pastors and to the bishops of their respective dioceses.

Such teaching and such conduct cannot be any longer passed over in silence. These errors are in clear opposition to the teaching of the Catholic Church and to the observance of Christian morality. As our Holy Father Pope Leo XIII. has declared in his Encyclical *Immortale Dei*, ' the true mistress of virtue and guardian of morals is the Church of Christ ; ' ' to exclude her influence from the business of life, from legislation, from the teaching of youth, from domestic society, is a great and pernicious error.' Real freedom, he adds, is exercised in the pursuit of what is true and just : absolute freedom of thought and action, untrammelled by the laws of morality, is not liberty but licence.

There are, no doubt, many purely political matters about which the wisest and best men may disagree, and in which the pastors of the Church, as such, have no desire to intervene, nor to restrain freedom of thought and action, except when the means and methods employed are such as cannot be deemed conformable to the principles of Christian morality. Questions, for instance, about the best form of local or national government, the extension of the franchise, the operation of commercial and industrial laws, belong to this class. But there are many other questions—mixed questions as they are called in Canon Law—which have a moral and religious, as well as a political or temporal aspect, and in some of which the religious or moral question at issue is the predominant one. Such, in the past, were the Emancipation question, and the Disestablishment of the Protestant Church, and such, at the present time, are the Education question, Poor Law legislation, and many kindred subjects. To say that the clergy have no right to intervene in such questions, where oftentimes the highest interests of religion are at stake ; that they ought not to point out to their flocks the line of conscientious duty, and call upon them to follow it ; that they cannot and ought not to advise them in such political matters to choose as their leaders men of high character and sound principles, is, indeed, a great and pernicious error, involving a manifest denial of the teaching authority of the Church.

The commission which the Apostles received from Christ Himself, and which their successors inherit, was to teach the nations—politicians as well as private persons—all the truth of the Christian revelation—dogmatic truth and moral truth—and to condemn everything which, judged by that code, is untrue, immoral, or unjust. All this the Bishops are authorized to do, and this they mean to do, when the spiritual interests of their flocks require it, whether there be question of public or of private conduct, of the rulers, the politicians, or the people. The opposite principle is utterly subversive of Catholic truth, and would be fatal to Christian morality.

We venture to hope that by this word of warning, given in all charity, the politicians whose erroneous teaching has made the warning necessary may be moved to withdraw from their present reprehensible attitude. But if, unhappily, they should persist, by their speeches, newspapers, and manifestoes, in advocating the same erroneous principles, we shall feel it our duty to exercise to the

full our pastoral authority in order to protect our flocks, and
eradicate this great and growing evil.

We also most earnestly implore our faithful people to close
their ears against the hearing of such anti-Catholic teaching, and
to yield a willing and loyal obedience to the pastors, who are
responsible to God for their souls, and whose supreme concern is
to promote their spiritual and temporal welfare.

✠ MICHAEL CARDINAL LOGUE, Archbishop of Armagh,
    Primate of All Ireland.

✠ WILLIAM, Archbishop of Dublin, Primate of Ireland.

✠ THOMAS WILLIAM, Archbishop of Cashel.

✠ JOHN, Archbishop of Tuam.

✠ FRANCIS JOSEPH, Bishop of Galway and Kilmacduagh.

✠ THOMAS ALPHONSUS, Bishop of Cork.

✠ JOHN, Bishop of Clonfert.

✠ JAMES, Bishop of Ferns.

✠ ABRAHAM, Bishop of Ossory.

✠ EDWARD THOMAS, Bishop of Limerick.

✠ THOMAS, Bishop of Dromore.

✠ PATRICK, Bishop of Raphoe.

✠ JOHN, Bishop of Achonry.

✠ EDWARD, Bishop of Kilmore.

✠ JOHN, Bishop of Kerry.

✠ THOMAS, Bishop of Killaloe.

✠ JOHN, Bishop of Derry.

✠ RICHARD ALPHONSUS, Bishop of Waterford and Lismore.

✠ JOHN, Bishop of Killala.

✠ ROBERT, Bishop of Cloyne.

✠ RICHARD, Bishop of Clogher.

✠ JOSEPH, Bishop of Ardagh.

✠ JOHN, Bishop of Elphin.

✠ HENRY, Bishop of Down an Connor.

✠ PATRICK, Bishop of Kildare and Leighlin

✠ DENIS, Bishop of Ross.

✠ NICHOLAS, Bishop of Canea.

NOTICES OF BOOKS

THE IRISH UNIVERSITY QUESTION: THE CATHOLIC CASE.
By his Grace the Archbishop of Dublin. Dublin:
Browne & Nolan, Ltd.

WITH an energy that commands the admiration of friends
and foes, his Grace the Archbishop of Dublin has fought the
battle of Catholic education in Ireland during the past twenty
years. In season and out of season he has kept the grievances
of Irish Catholics in the matter of University education in the
very front of all actual and even burning questions. In speeches,
in articles, and in letters he has met every opponent, and has
practically made the denial of Ireland's claims for many years
longer an impossibility. It was only a few years ago that the
Archbishop published an exhaustive review of the whole situation
as regards University education in this country, in which he laid
bare before the eyes of the world the monstrous injustice from
which the vast majority of the people of this country suffer in
their own land.

In the present volume many new phases of the question are
discussed, and everything that the Archbishop himself has
recently said on the points of contention is embodied. Taken
in connection with the former work published by his Grace this
new volume will be found to contain a complete and exhaustive
treatment of the whole subject in all its phases. The Archbishop is so thoroughly versed in every aspect of the question
that he has been able to avoid, throughout, the faults of
the indiscreet and injudicious advocate on the one hand, and
of the timorous champion on the other. Indeed, it is very easy
for anyone not thoroughly equipped for the discussion of this
subject to do more injury than service to the claims for which he
pleads ; and one of the difficulties the Archbishop evidently had
to contend with was the energetic and audacious attempt that
was made by unauthorized and utterly unrepresentative writers
to set themselves up as exponents of the Catholic grievance and
the Catholic claim. His Grace is evidently determined that if
we are to have a Catholic university in Ireland it must be a
thoroughly national institution, and not the stronghold of any

section or party ; that the services of the best men must be
secured for its various faculties and chairs ; and that some other
proofs will have to be given of ability and capacity than flippant
speech and· superficial titles.   His Grace has in these pages
given vigorous expression to the views of the great majority
of Irishmen ; and in working out the realization of these views
he will have the whole country at his back.   J. F. H.

REPORT OF RELIGIOUS EXAMINATIONS OF SCHOOLS IN THE
    DIOCESE OF WATERFORD AND LISMORE FOR THE YEARS
    1895 AND 1896.   Waterford: N. Harvey & Co.

THE system of religious examination in primary schools which
for the past twenty years has been gradually spreading among
the dioceses of Ireland was introduced into the united dioceses of
Waterford and Lismore in the year 1895, and the Rev. Michael
P. Hickey was appointed first examiner.   The present interesting
and exhaustive report is from his pen.   The appearance so late
as the middle of 1897, of the report of examinations held in 1895
and 1896 is accounted for by the fact that Father Hickey was
called upon in October, 1896, to take up the arduous duties connected with the Chair of Celtic in Maynooth College, and, as a
consequence, had not leisure to compile the report for publication
at the proper time.   We learn that there were in 1896 as many
as 22,407 children on the rolls of· the various schools in the
diocese of Waterford and Lismore.   In the tabulated list of schools
are given the numbers on rolls in· each school, the average attendance, the attendance at the religious examinations, and the
proficiency of the children in the varied programme on which
they were examined.   But by far the most important section of
the report is the fourth appendix which deals with the religious
training of the teachers in the De la Salle Training College,
Waterford.   From this appendix we learn that the candidates for
the high office of instructing the youth of the country undergo a
searching half-yearly examination in Christian doctrine and Bible
history.   ' The Bishop,' says the report, ' holds the oral examinations in person, sets the papers for the written examinations, and
adjudges the certificates, which are also signed by his Lordship,
as well as by the brother director.'   The certificates are first,
second, and third class, to correspond with the certificates given
by the National Board.   It is obvious that these examinations,
conducted by the Bishop in person, must be a great stimulus to

the candidates to acquire a thorough knowledge of the subjects, and thus to fit them to efficiently instruct their pupils afterwards. The Most Rev. Dr. Sheehan, Bishop of Waterford, to whom is due the introduction of the religious examination in the schools of the diocese, as well as in the Training College, is to be congratulated on the good which must necessarily flow from both the one and the other. Father Hickey is also to be congratulated on the form, as well as on the fulness of his report.

MISSAE PRO DEFUNCTIS AD COMMODIOREM ECCLESIARUM USUM, EX MISSALI ROMANO DESUMPTAE. Accedit Ritus Absolutionis pro Defunctis ex Rituali et Pontificali Romano. Editio Quarta post Typicam. Ratisbonae, Neo Eboraci, et Cincinnati, Sumptibus, Chartis et Typis Friderici Pustet. 1897.

WE have received from the eminent publishing firm of Pustet two copies of the above. The larger copy measures fourteen inches by ten (14 × 10), the smaller twelve inches by nine (12¼ × 9¼). Both display to the fullest that beauty and excellence for which the liturgical books of this great Catholic firm have long been famous. The frontispiece—a crucifixion study—of the larger edition is a real work of art. The addition of the prayers, &c., used during the last absolution will be found extremely convenient.

THE OLD ENGLISH BIBLE AND OTHER ESSAYS. By F. A. Gasquet. London : John C. Nimmo.

WE are glad that these valuable Essays, published as they are without any preface or introduction, have been collected and produced in a volume well worthy, in every respect, of the title which it bears. It is quite unnecessary for us to say anything more than we have already said in various former reviews, in praise of Dr. Gasquet's great gifts as a writer of history. His labours have received the crowning acknowledgment of the Pope himself and all Catholics in these countries have rejoiced at the well-merited encomiums he has received.

The present volume deals mainly with a subject with which Don Gasquet is thoroughly familiar ; and it is greatly to be hoped that it may be widely read by the Bible-loving Protestants of England, as well as by Catholics everywhere. To many

Protestants we are sure the scholarly essay on the ' Pre-Reforma-
tion English Bible ' will come as a revelation ; whilst to Catholic
students of history the many new and interesting items of information regarding the early English versions of the Bible will afford
genuine pleasure. The Essays on ' Religious Instruction in
England during the fourteenth and fifteenth centuries ' on ' The
Canterbury Claustral School ' and on ' Hampshire Recusants '
are full of interest, and remind one very much both in style and
matter of Janssen's *History of the German People*. This volume,
though by no means the most important fruit of Dr. Gasquet's
labours, adds very considerably, nevertheless, to his already well-
established reputation.

J. F. H.

St. Nicholas de Tolentino. Par le Rev. P. Antonin
Tonna-Barthet, O.S.A. Societè de St. Augustin ;
Desclée, de Brouwer et Cie, 1896.

This last production of the Societé de St. Augustin which
we have received enhances the already well-established reputation
of the publishers for artistic printing and illustration. It is not,
however, to the cover and the letterpress that we desire to draw
attention, but to the contents of one of the most interesting
biographies that has appeared in recent times. As a priest, a
preacher, a wonder-worker, and an apostle, St. Nicholas of
Tolentino was one of the prodigies of his age. This new biography
cannot fail to make him better known and more revered than
he has ever been.

Popular History and Miracles of St. Anthony of
Padua. Translated from the French by the Rev.
Father Ignatius Beale, T.O.S.F. Dublin : M. H. Gill
and Son.

The devotion to St. Anthony of Padua is now so wide-spread
that this popular account of his life, and of the wonderful miracles
attributed to him, should have a very large circulation.

Ut Christiani sis et Romani sitis.   "As you are children of Christ, so be you children of Rome."
Ex Dictis S. Patricii, In Libro Armacano, fol. 9.

The Irish
Ecclesiastical Record

A Monthly Journal, under Episcopal Sanction.

Thirtieth Year]   **AUGUST, 1897.**   [Fourth Series
No. 356.]   Vol. II.

Nihil Obstat.
GERALDUS MOLLOY, S.T.D.,
Censor Dep.

Imprimatur.
✠ GULIELMUS,
Archiep. Dublin.,
Hiberniae Primas.

BROWNE & NOLAN, Limited

Publishers and Printers, 24 & 25

NASSAU STREET, DUBLIN.

A New and Cheaper Edition, in Six Volumes, large crown 8vo, cloth, gilt top, price 42s. net, with an Introductory Essay on "Monastic Constitutional History," by the Rev. F. A. GASQUET, D.D., O.S.B., *Author of "Henry VIII. and the English Monasteries."*

THE MONKS OF THE WEST

From St. Benedict to St. Bernard.

BY THE COUNT DE MONTALEMBERT,

Member of the French Academy.

With an Introduction by the Rev. F. A. GASQUET, D.D., O.S.B., Author of "Henry VIII. and the English Monasteries."

Extract from Dr. GASQUET's *Introductory Essay on Monastic Constitutional History :—*

"Writing, to Montalembert, with the design of presenting to the world a popular account of the workings of the monastic system in Europe, as exemplified in the lives of those monks whose names are chiefly known to us in the history of nations, it did not enter into the scope of his work to give any account of this side of monastic history. It is obvious that during a past which covers fourteen hundred years, the principles of monastic organization will have varied to meet various and varying conditions of time and place. It would seem desirable that those who may wish to understand the full bearing of Western monachism should have at hand some consecutive account of the purely constitutional side of monastic government. In this belief, the chief part of the present Introduction is devoted to a sketch of the changes of policy and government inaugurated at various stages in the history of the Order."

A BATCH OF LETTERS

I HAVE reason to believe that in many Irish presbyteries, and also in the hands of laymen, there are lying old letters by deceased prelates, and other documents of some ecclesiastical interest and value. Sometimes a priest of antiquarian tastes will make a collection of such materials, which at his death will probably be scattered and lost. I have known some cases of the sort. It would be very desirable to confer upon as many of these papers as possible the immortality of print, for which numerous facilities are afforded nowadays. If the Editor of the I. E. RECORD should now kindly allow me to make an attempt in this direction the example might have a good effect on priests who have more precious papers in their keeping.

As I have already urged that the chief object to be aimed at is, in the first instance, to transmute frail and illegible manuscript into immutable print, I will neglect chronological order, and abstain rigidly from comment and illustration.

Though some of the materials lying beside me belong to early years of the century, let us begin with an unpublished letter of Cardinal Newman. The Cardinal's literary executor, Father W. P. Neville, kindly gave me leave on a previous occasion to print letters addressed by the great Oratorian to Dr. Russell of Maynooth ; but the letter which follows was written to an English lady who, after her conversion, joined Mother Macaulay at an early stage of the wonderful development of the Irish Sisterhood of Mercy, and who, nevertheless, is still at this present moment the Mother Superior of the Convent of Mercy at Birr. At the date of the following letter, more than thirty years ago, Mother Anastatia Beckot already occupied this position :—

THE ORATORY, BIRMINGHAM,
January 18*th*, 1865.

DEAR REV. MOTHER,—I return the letter which you have allowed me to read ; but I am puzzled by it, as you have been. By which I do not mean that the writer differs from many others whom one meets with, in her views of religion, but because all those cases—that especially *Anglican* view of doctrine is difficult to deal with. Anglicanism is a theory which is tolerably consistent with itself, and comes home to sensible minds as being very likely and sensible. Its fault is—its fatal fault—that it is not borne out by historical facts. But what can the bulk of people know about historical facts ? One man says one thing, another another. And of those who know them, some will look at some facts, others at others. Some make these the rule, and that the exception ; others make those the rule, and this the exception. The two parties are like the knight who fought about the shield, which on one side was gold and on the other silver.

I am not for an instant supposing that the Catholic side is not right in point of historical facts, and the Anglican wrong ; but the question is how is this to be brought home to any except the few who have the means of historical research ? The best proof that Catholics are right is that unbelievers like Gibbon, who are on neither side, but are profound students, give the decision in favour of Catholics. When these people defend themselves by reference to 'rubrics,' the 'fathers,' and 'the mode' of the Real Presence, and have not the means of learning, except from Anglican clergymen, the facts of the case, as history discloses them, I do not see the good of pursuing the argument.

I should be rather inclined to attempt another way. If men have lived in the world, and lived as other men, then they are often most powerfully affected by the question, 'What shall I do to be saved ?' Their sins stare them in the face, and thus they recognise the superiority of a religion which so strikingly carries out our Lord's words, 'Whose sins ye remit,' &c., over others which either do not profess, or do not practise, the ordinance of absolution.

Again, supposing a person once can be brought to see that the Bible does not answer some of the most important questions of religion, then he will necessarily be led to look for a teacher elsewhere.

This last seems to me the best ground to take against this

lady's defence of herself. *Who* taught her her creed? Did she gather it from the Bible? Impossible! Did she gather it from the Anglican prayer book? If so, why should the prayer book be infallible? Who taught her that there were two Sacraments and two only, &c., &c.?

Till she is *in doubt* whether she is in possession of the very truth as our Lord gave it, of course a Catholic can do nothing with her. She ought to be put on her defence, how she knows — since our Lord *must* have given us a teacher — how she knows that the Bible is that teacher? How she knows, even though the Bible be the teacher, that she has really mastered all that, and nothing but what the Bible teaches.

My ordinary judgment is that a person at a distance who attempts to convert, does more harm than good. He is sure to use the wrong arguments. Persons often write to me and say, 'Do say a few words to so and so,' whom I do not know; and I have so constantly found, when I have attempted it, that I have been worse than unsuccessful, that now my rule is to refuse to do so.

In writing thus to you now, I am (I grieve to say) induced by no hope that anything I say will be useful, but because you ask me. I pray God you may have every success; but you must watch the times and the moments, which are in His hand.

I shall be much pleased at anything which you are kind enough to tell me about Father Spencer.

Begging your good prayers,

I am, dear Rev. Mother,

Sincerely yours in Christ,

JOHN H. NEWMAN.

The following letter may be preserved as one of the few references that are likely to be made to an Irish ecclesiastic of great ability, whom circumstances did not allow to acquire as wide a reputation as his friends desired for him. Dr. Michael Kieran was considered by many excellent judges to be the most effective preacher of his time in Ireland, full of massive thought, and very earnest in his delivery. He became Archbishop of Armagh on the death of Dr. Joseph Dixon, in 1866; but his health was so unsatisfactory that his medical adviser, Dr. John Gartlan of Dundalk, strongly urged him not to accept the new responsibility, and in fact he died in less than three years, September 16th, 1869. He obtained leave to retain as his mensal parish Dundalk, where he had laboured so long, and was so much loved and

reverenced.   From his residence about a mile distant from
that flourishing town this letter was written to the President
of Maynooth, in the last year of the Primate's life :—

FORTHILL,
February 17*th*, 1869.

MY DEAR DR. RUSSELL,—I feel great pleasure in approving of
anything you may think it necessary to do in order that you may
be able to attend to the important business to which you refer in
your last letter.

The favourable opinion you have been pleased to express of my
Lenten Pastoral for 1869 is extremely gratifying to me, as there
is no ecclesiastic in these Kingdoms on whose opinion in matters
of the kind I would place a higher value than yours.

I think I am able to say that I am on the whole better, notwithstanding the severity of the season since the beginning of the
winter ; and, when the weather becomes milder, my health will,
please God, undergo a corresponding improvement.

I remain yours truly,

✠ M. KIERAN.

The following letter will have no interest for those who
are unacquainted with the great reputation that Father
Peter Kenney, S.J., enjoyed amongst the priests and people
of Ireland in the first half of this century, which is now
hastening to its close.   An emphatic testimony to that
reputation has just come under my notice in another manuscript, which I hope to be allowed to print in these pages
—namely, the lettter which the priests of the diocese of
Dromore addressed to Cardinal Somaglia, Prefect of the
Propaganda, in January, 1826, proposing three names out of
which a successor might be appointed to Dr. Hugh O'Kelly,
who had died after a short episcopate of five years.   They
named in the first place Dr. Thomas Kelly, a dean and
professor of Maynooth, who was actually appointed, but
promoted six years later to his native diocese of Armagh,
which he governed only two years.   The second was
Dr. Arthur McArdle, Vicar-General of Dromore; and the third
was Father Peter Kenney, S.J., ' de quo loqui ut meretur
perdifficile est, quia res ab eo gestae religionis ergo tam multae
tamque praeclarae sunt ut laudem nostram superent.'

This may seem a little unfair to give as a relic of this

'sacerdos magnus' a trivial letter which has chanced to survive; but the judicious reader will be edified as well as amused by the Johnsonian dignity of style with which the Rector of Clongowes College, then recently founded—for this undated letter is now some eighty years old—refused the request of a lady who had craved permission for her son, a Clongowes pupil, to attend his sister's wedding.

MY DEAR MADAM,—It is impossible for me to consent to a measure which I cannot think judicious in itself, or advantageous to the child in present circumstances. To-morrow is one of the days on which the scholars compose themes in their respective schools, and contend with each other for priority of place. Were he allowed to be absent, he would be deprived of all his chance of the past compositions, made on Monday and Wednesday last. and be obliged to remain in the last place in his school, without any chance of rising to a higher one before next Easter. I am sure that his sister would not allow him to purchase the honour of being present at the marriage by such a degradation. The examination soon follows this exercise, and a day's absence would materially retard his efforts.

So much for his particular case. May I beg to remind you that it is expressly required in the prospectus that the children be not taken from the College during the academical year? The vacation is the only time at which it is optional with the parent to take the pupil home; at other times of the year it is not allowable.

I hope that these reasons will plead my apology for begging that you will not urge the request contained in your letter.

Yours truly,

P. KENNEY.

If a similar application were made to-day to the Rev. Matthew Devitt, S.J., *nunc feliciter regnans*, as Father Kenney's successor, I wonder would his reply be much the same. Whatever the substance of it might be, the form would probably be different; it would be condensed into three sentences on the first page of a sheet of notepaper. The age of letter-writing is gone, and Johnsonese is out of fashion.

Here are the terms in which Dr. Robert Ffrench Whitehead, the well-remembered Vice-President of Maynooth College, submitted to some bishop, probably to his devoted friend Dr. George Butler of Limerick, his Latin ode on the laying of the foundation-stone of the beautiful College Church, which the President, Dr. Russell, issued in the form of a handsome brochure, along with the sermon of Dr. Moriarty, Bishop of Kerry, Mr. Aubrey de Vere's trio of sonnets on the same subject, and the stately blank verse of the Rev. Joseph Farrell, C.C., the gifted author of "The Lectures of a Certain Professor." We print this letter from Dr. Whitehead's most legible and careful manuscript. He ought to have dated it "St. Patrick's Day."

St. Patrick's College, Maynooth,
March 17th, 1875.

My Dearest Lord,—Yesterday, after dinner, I had the impudence to read the accompanying ode for the superiors and professors at table. They found no fault with it, except the rather complimentary one that it is too short. It goes on the supposition that the College has hitherto been lamenting the want of a suitable place of worship, and it is to be intoned the moment the first stone is laid. I intend to get copies of it printed for all the students, so that they may know it, and be accustomed to sing it when the occasion arrives. Before doing so, I submit it to your judgment, that you may tell me of any change it may require. It is so long since I heard from you that I am glad of an opportunity of inducing you to write to me.

Ever most respectfully and affectionately yours,

Robert Ffrench Whitehead.

Nothing certainly of great importance is contained in these letters; but I hope they will be considered to possess some interest as reminding us of two or three notable Irish priests. Of Cardinal Newman no one needs to be reminded.

Matthew Russell.

ST. AUGUSTINE AND THE PELAGIANS[1]

IT is not intended in this paper to discuss Pelagian doctrines, but merely to vindicate, against Anglican misrepresentation, St. Augustine's Church principles in dealing with it. Readers of the I. E. RECORD who have not had their attention specially directed to the subject, could not imagine that respectable public writers would be guilty of the barefaced falsifications of history which have been resorted to in this matter. Although some of the writers to whom we allude are not very recent, and have been again and again refuted, their works are still the great authority on this subject among Anglicans.

St. Augustine gives a summary of Pelagian doctrine in his work, *De Hæresibus;* and Peronne briefly describes it in the following words :—

As in the Pelagian system the first man was neither elevated by sanctifying grace above his natural condition, nor endowed with the gift of integrity, Adam neither fell by sin from such a state, nor contracted any infirmity ; that is, he was neither deprived of supernatural, nor wounded in his natural endowments. Hence his children are born without sin, and in the same state in which the first man was made by God, with that native imbecility which belongs to human nature, subject to ignorance, concupiscence, and death. From this it was easy to infer, that neither Adam after his sin, nor his posterity, need any supernatural help to be restored to a supernatural state, nor anything by which their understanding might be illuminated or their will strengthened to do any good or to overcome the force of temptation. But if God should grant such aids, it could only be to lessen man's labour in his efforts to arrive at truth or do good.[2]

Pelagianism was therefore the very opposite of Calvinism, and was almost identical with our modern Naturalism.

A word now about Pelagius himself. He was a British monk named Morgan, who towards the end of the fourth century, travelled into the East in quest of knowledge, little

---

[1] *Opera S. Augustini*, t. x , Ed. Migne.
[2] *De Gratia*, Art. i.

thinking what a seed plot of error all that region had become, owing to the long Arian troubles of the preceding half-century. We find him at Constantinople in the time of St. John Chrysostom—398-405—with his name changed to Pelagius, the Greek synonym for Morgan (of the Sea). So great was his reputation at this time for study and austerity of life, that he attracted the attention of St. John himself, always a great patron of monks. We must bear in mind, that in those days it was no unusual thing to see learned and holy men wearing the monastic habit, without being attached to any particular community ; just as philosophers wore the *pallium*. Although we have no reason to question the sincerity of Pelagius, at this time, an incident which took place reveals to us a serious flaw in his character : he deserted his patron and friend St. John, in the celebrated court persecution raised against him.

We next find him at Rome, where he spends five years— 405-410—with the same reputation for study and austerity of life ; making converts to his monastic profession, among whom was a rich and learned young man named Celestius, whom St. Augustine calls long after *homo acerrimi ingenii*.[1] There was then at Rome a Syrian priest named Rufinus who made the acquaintance of Pelagius ; he was deeply imbued with strange errors, but dared not endeavour to propagate them himself, probably on account of his position in the family of Pammachius, a Roman senator, very dear to St. Augustine.[2] He soon found in Pelagius a soil already prepared, and having deeply imbued him with his novel doctrines, committed the cause entirely to his keeping. Pelagius soon began to indoctrinate his disciples, probably with no worse intention than that of urging them to greater energy in their efforts to attain greater perfection in their monastic state ; for, at first he seems quite unconscious that he is broaching a heresy. His character is still so high that he can count among his admirers such men as St. Paulinus of Nola, and St. Augustine. But the narrow circle of his disciples was too restricted for his zeal; he began

---

[1] *Ad. Bonif.*, ii. 5.   [2] *Ep.* 58.

to teach the new doctrine more openly, and even to write
books, which, although primarily on subjects of piety,
contained new ideas on almost every page. All this reached
the ears of St. Augustine, but such was his esteem for
Pelagius that he resolved to abstain from all criticism
until he could procure more ample information.[1] For some
time before the sack of Rome, by Alaric, in 410, there was
great alarm in the city, and many fled for safety to Africa.
Pelagius landed at Hippo ; but, as St. Augustine was absent,
he went on to Carthage.

Being obliged to go to Carthage in 411 for the great
conference with the Donatists, St. Augustine had a friendly
but very brief interview with him, and seems to have invited
him to Hippo, to talk matters over at leisure, the great
conference not leaving a moment to spare for anything else.
Pelagius never came to Hippo, but went on immediately to
the East, leaving Celestius at Carthage to evangelize the
Africans.

We next hear of Pelagius in 412, earnestly engaged in
spreading his ideas in Palestine. Celestius laboured quite
as earnestly at Carthage, but not as cautiously, for,
endeavouring to get ordained to the priesthood, he only
succeeded in attracting the attention of the Primate
Aurelius, who in 412 called a synod to examine his teaching
and ended by excommunicating him. To evade the force
of the excommunication Celestius appealed at once to Rome,
and then went on to Ephesus, where he must have succeeded
in getting ordained, as we find him ever after called a
priest. Pelagius was never ordained. After a few years
Celestius quitted Ephesus, and settled down at Constantinople ; but the patriarch, Atticus, although by no means
blameless himself in other respects, soon put a stop to his
propagandism, and even had him expelled from the city.
Constantinople had harboured many a heresy, but it refused
to tolerate Pelagianism ; in all the East it never had but
one open defender of any note, the notorious Theodore of
Mopsuesta.

---

[1] *De Gestis Pelag.*, 46-53.

At this time Pelagius wrote a letter to St. Augustine,
which we know only from the following brief answer written
in 413.

Domino dilectissimo, et desideratissimo fratri Pelagio,
Augustinus, in domino salutem.

Many thanks for your condescension in sending me your
refreshing letter, and informing me that you are well.   May God
reward you, and may this reward be always with you; may you
live with Him for ever, most beloved sir and brother.   Although
I can see in myself no ground for the praise contained in your
letter, I cannot be ungrateful for your very kind sentiments
towards one so insignificant as myself.   Pray rather to the Lord
to make me such as you imagine me to be already.   Remember
me; may the Lord keep you, and may you be pleasing to Him,
sir and most beloved brother.[1]

Speaking of this letter in 417, he says[2] that when writing
it he was quite aware of Pelagius' teaching, and therefore
abstained from praising him; while showing him all the
ordinary civilities in order to induce him to discuss matters
in a personal interview.   He also says, that without
explicitly raising the question, he endeavoured to instil
proper ideas about grace indirectly.   All this time he was
actively engaged in refuting the Pelagian doctrines, by
letters, sermons, conferences, and even by two important
works, *De Peccatorum Meritis, De Spiritu et Littera*, and
yet he never mentioned the innovators' names, hoping
against hope to soften their obduracy, and save them from
the fate that awaited them.

Things went on in this way until 415, when Augustine
received a letter from two gentlemen, named Timasius and
Jacobus, former disciples of Pelagius at Rome, who had
been greatly scandalized at his doctrine; with their letter
they sent a work of his which Augustine, without naming
him still, refuted in his work, *De Natura et Gratia*.   About
the same time he received from two bishops some writings
of Celestius, which he refuted in his work *De Perfectione
Justitiæ Hominis;* in this work he names Celestius for the
first time.   In this same year he sent Orosius to Bethlehem

---

[1] Ep. 146.   [2] *De Gestis Pelag.*, 61.

to consult St. Jerome on quite another subject; but
Orosius found all Palestine in commotion about the new
heresy, and St. Jerome up in arms against it.   Urged by his
clergy, John, Bishop of Jerusalem, had to call a synod to
discuss the subject ; Orosius was specially invited by the
clergy ; Pelagius was summoned to answer the charges
made against him, and when Orosius produced a letter of
St. Augustine's on the subject, he simply answered, ' What is
Augustine to me ?'   This insolence towards so great a man
raised a storm of indignation in the assembly, and Orosius
seeing the bias of John in favour of Pelagius, proposed that
as the accused was a Latin the whole matter should be
referred to Pope Innocent.   John gladly acceded to this,
imposing silence in the meantime on both parties, and
saying, ' that whatever Pope Innocent might decide should
be final for all.'

This diocesan synod had no appreciable effect on the
course of events, and a few months later the bishops of
Palestine met in Provincial Synod at Diospolis (Lydda).
There were fourteen bishops present, under the presidency
of the Metropolitan Eulogius of Cesarea.   Pelagius pleaded
his own cause in fluent Greek ; his judges were Greeks; his
writings were in Latin, the extracts selected from them
were in Latin; the interpreter was incompetent or worse.
No wonder the accused had an easy victory ; the heretical
propositions attributed to him were indeed condemned, but
he left the assembly with a certificate of personal orthodoxy.
St. Jerome calls this Synod 'the miserable Synod of Diospolis,'
but St. Augustine always quotes it against Pelagius,
constantly reminding him of all the retractations and
professions by which he extorted his fraudulent certificate.

. But it was this victory that contributed to wreck his
fortunes at last ; it simply turned his head, and drove him
to such extremes, that no moderate or respectable man could
stand by him.   He defied all his enemies, laid aside his
austerities, lived an easy and luxurious life, roused the
passions of the mob, and stopped at no calumny or untruth.
His fanatical followers sacked and burned the monasteries
of St. Jerome and St. Paula of Bethlehem.   When all this

reached Hippo there was an end to St. Augustine's reserve ; although Pelagius, anticipating the publication of the *Acts*, had sent him a *chartula*[1] containing a distorted account of what had taken place at the Synod ; this *card* had been also sent to the ends of the earth already.

Short as was their stay at Carthage, the two innovators succeeded in forming a party, active, insolent, and intolerant, as such parties always are. In 413 the Primate invited Augustine to preach against them ; in concluding this sermon, he says :—

Let us therefore try to induce our brethren no longer to call us heretics, an appellation which we could perhaps bestow on them, if we liked, for these disputes ; but we do not inflict it on them. May their Mother still bear with them in her maternal tenderness, to be healed and taught, lest she should have to deplore their death. We know to what excesses they go; very great, almost unendurable, and demanding the greatest patience. Let them not abuse this patience of the Church ; let them correct themselves; it is their own interest. We do not dispute with them as enemies ; we exhort them as friends. They calumniate us, and we bear with it ; but let them not calumniate the rule ; let them not calumniate the truth ; let them not calumniate the Holy Church which labours daily for the remission of original sin in children. This is a settled question. Should anyone dispute about other points not yet fully discussed, not yet settled by the full authority of the Church, his error may be endured, but he must not go so far as to try to shake the very foundation of the Church.[2]

Writing about them a year later, he says :—

Nor do I think we are entirely free from them as yet, especially at Carthage ; but they now whisper in secret, dreading the immovable faith of the Church. . . . However, we prefer to see them healed in the Church, rather than cut off from her body as incurable members ; unless the necessity of preserving others should require it.[3]

Nothing in Pelagianism alarmed him so much as its tendency to introduce laxity regarding infant baptism ; again and again he returns to this subject, entreating the faithful ' to have pity on these helpless little ones.'[4]

<hr>

[1] *De Gest. Pelag.*, 57.
[2] Serm. 294.
[3] Ep. clvii. 22.
[4] Serm. 174, 176, 293, 294.

But there was as yet no manifest *contumacy;* the innovators explained, denied, retracted, like Pelagius at Diospolis; they were inconsistently zealous for the baptism of their children,[1] and above all they protested that they were ready *to hear the Church.* Even Donatists he did not regard as formal heretics without *contumacy;* thus writing in 398 to some well-disposed Donatist gentlemen who were . seeking for light, he says :—

The Apostle tells us *to avoid a man who is a heretic,* &c.[2] But those, who, without any *pertinacious* spirit, defend their opinion, though false and perverse, are by no means to be accounted heretics, especially when this opinion is derived not from their own audacity or presumption, but from the teaching of parents who had been seduced themselves ; and when they anxiously seek the truth, intending to be corrected when they find it. Did I not think you to be such, I should perhaps not have written to you at all.[3]

But we are now about to witness a great change in his attitude towards the Pelagians. In 416 two African synods took up the question; the Provincial Council of Proconsularis, at Carthage, with sixty-eight bishops ; and the Provincial Council of Numidia, at Milevis, with sixty-one bishops including St. Augustine. Both sent synodical letters to Pope Innocent. The Council of Carthage asks him, ' to confirm by the authority of the Apostolic See the decrees, *statuta,* of their mediocrity.' Yet the synodical letter contains no formal decrees, but merely states, discusses, and condemns in an informal way the Pelagian errors against grace and original sin. It recites the sentence pronounced against Celestius, at Carthage, in 412, the certificate of orthodoxy granted to Pelagius by the Synod of Diospolis, and prays that even though both should be found personally worthy of absolution, their errors might be condemned under *anathema.* The Numidian synodical letter goes over the same ground, urges immediate action, hopes the mere weight of the Pope's authority will prevent the necessity for severe measures, and says ' they would consider themselves guilty of great negligence had they omitted to suggest what

---

[1] Serm. 174-176.   [2] Ep. 43   [3] Tit. iii.

the needs of the Church demanded.' It mentions also another question, but without pressing for an answer; both letters teem with expressions of filial reverence. These letters were accompanied by a third, signed by Aurelius, Alypius, Augustine, Evodius, and Possidius; much longer on all the points, but unofficial and purely confidential, These four bishops were Augustine's bosom friends, and among the most distinguished in the African Church. This letter, like the others, abounds in expressions of filial reverence, and concludes thus:

> The rest your Beatitude will find in the *Acts*, and will no doubt judge. Your kind and gentle heart will surely excuse this letter, which is perhaps longer than your Holiness would desire. Our intention is not to replenish your great fountain from our own rivulet, but to see in those troubled times whether our little stream comes from the same source as your own abundance; hoping to be consoled by your rescripts in the participation of the same grace.

While awaiting these rescripts, Augustine had to give a letter of introduction to a gentleman named Palladius who was going to Narbonne; he takes advantage of the occasion to inform the Bishop Hilary of what had been done in the two councils, saying that 'Pelagianism is a new heresy which is striving to arise against the Church of Christ, and opposed to the grace of Christ; but not as yet evidently separated from the Church; *sed nondum evidenter ab Ecclesia separata est.*'[1] This was after its condemnation by four Provincial Synods, to say nothing of all the bishops and theologians, including St. Jerome and St. Augustine himself.[2]

---

[1] Ep. 178.

[2] This letter, so explicitly worded, puts an end to the old Gallican pretence that St. Augustine thought local councils capable of *finally* deciding such controversies. In his work *De Gestis Pelagii*, No. 30, he calls Pelagianism a *damnata haeresis* after the sentence of the Council of Diospolis, which St. Jerome called 'the miserable Synod of Diospolis;' it is manifest that *damnata* is taken here in an informal sense, and *quantum valeat.* The same explanation applies to other instances noted by the Benedictine editors (Ep. ccxv. 2, *note*), who wrote in a very Gallican atmosphere. The other instances noted by them, were actually posterior, not only to the rescripts of Innocent, but to the more comprehensive Encyclical of Zosimus.

At last, after a delay of about six months, the rescripts arrive in the spring of 417. The answer to the five bishops is merely a letter of confidence and friendship like their own; the two other rescripts contain the official answer, and are manifestly intended to supplement each other. The Pope's decision had been asked on two points—grace and original sin; and on these he pronounces a *doctrinal* decision, condemning the errors of Pelagius regarding them. To this was added a *judicial* sentence of excommunication against Pelagius and Celestius and all others who might endeavour *pertinaciously* to defend the same errors. He gives the bishops *power* to absolve the delinquents whenever they should be found to have sincerely repented; but in the Numidian document he adds an *express command* to this effect. These official rescripts are more in the tone of one having supreme authority, than of a theologian obliged to give his reasons; indeed he says that the bishops themselves had so exhaustively furnished the reasons, that it would be superfluous for him to spend much time in directing their attention to them. He also praises their great zeal and vigilance; as well as their fidelity to sacerdotal duty in conforming to the decrees of the fathers, ' who had decided, not by human, but by divine authority, that nothing should be concluded even in the most distant provinces without the knowledge of this see.' All these documents can be seen among the letters of St. Augustine.[1]

The tone of the controversy is now completely changed. Preaching at Carthage in the autumn of this year, St. Augustine says :—

My brethren, share in my compassion for them [the Pelagians]. When you meet with any, do not conceal them through a pernicious kindness ; no, absolutely no, do not conceal them. Reprove them, and if they resist bring them to us. For, already the deliberations of two councils on this matter were sent to the Apostolic See ; rescripts have thence arrived ; the cause is ended ; would that the error were ended at last. We, therefore, advise them to reflect ; we make known to them the truth ; let us pray for their conversion. [2]

---

[1] Ep. 175, 176, 177, 181, 182, 183.　　　　[2] Serm. cxxxi. 10.

Writing at this time to his friend St. Paulinus, of Nola,
and sending a copy of the rescripts, he says : ' They are
just such as become a bishop of the Apostolic See . . . This
new and pernicious error is now so crushed by ecclesiastical
authority, that it is astonishing how anyone can still hold
erroneous opinions about the grace of God.'[1] Henceforth,
Pelagianism is to him a condemned heresy, and its teachers
contumacious heretics.

Pelagius and Celestius, dreading the effect of the excommunication, at least on their fortunes, appealed at once to
Rome for the absolution promised by Pope Innocent to all
who should be found to deserve it. Having already[2]
given the details of this appeal, I shall now only ask my
readers to recall the following points about which no
doubt can be raised. (1) There never was any question
of revising the *doctrinal* decision of Pope Innocent.
(2) On the contrary, Pope Zosimus, from first to last,
sternly enforced that decision on the innovators. (3) The
only question at issue was whether they had given
sufficient satisfaction to be absolved from the personal
censure. (4) There was not a shadow of *doctrinal* difference
between Carthage and Rome; the whole difference was
about the *sufficiency* of the satisfaction, for the security of
the faithful against the wiles of the innovators. (5) As a
matter of fact, they never were absolved. (6) Pope Zosimus
solemnly republished the decisions of Innocent, both doctrinal and judicial, in an Encyclical directed to all the
bishops in the world. (7) This Encyclical had been already
published when the great African Council of 418 met.

Let us now hear the most authoritative Anglican
versions of the matter. Dean Milman's version, in 1854,
runs thus :—

Once at this period, and but for a short time, the Bishop of
Rome threw himself across the stream of religious opinion.
Zosimus, the successor of Innocent, was by birth a Greek, and
seemed to treat the momentous questions agitated by the
Pelagian controversy with the contemptuous indifference of a
Greek. Whether from the uncongeniality of the Eastern mind

---

[1] Ep. 186.   [2] *The Dublin Review*, July, 1890.

with these debates ; whether from the pride of the man, which
was flattered by the submission of both these dangerous
heresiarchs to his authority ; whether from the earnest and well-
intentioned, but mistaken hope of suppressing what appeared to
him a needless dispute, Zosimus annulled at one blow all the
judgment of his predecessor, Innocent, and absolved the men
whom Innocent, if he had not branded with direct anathema,
had declared deserving to be cut off from the communion of the
faithful.[1]

Archdeacon Farrar's version, in 1889, runs thus :—

Celestius hastened to Rome where Innocent had been succeeded by Zosimus, who, being a Greek, had little taste for these
questions, accepted the favourable view of their opinions, and
held with them that original sin was not a recognised doctrine of
the Church, and that other points at issue were mere school
problems. . . . Another African Council of two hundred bishops,
in 418, anathematized the views of Pelagius. Thereupon, Zosimus,
in sudden alarm, turned completely round, and declared strongly
against Pelagius in an *Epistcla Tractatoria* [the Encyclical].[2]

This is the way history is *cooked* for Anglican palates
whenever Rome is in question. But, we must say a word
about this African Council of 418, which plays so important
a part in Anglican versions of this appeal. Unfortunately,
all that remains to us of its *Acts*, is the date, the final
signatures, and its eighteen or nineteen canons ; nor have
we any outside account of its proceedings. We are, therefore, in complete ignorance about its debates ; we do not
know who spoke, what was said ; much less how it was
said. The canons are so evenly divided between the
Donatists and the Pelagians, that it is impossible to say for
which of these questions it was assembled. Anglicans take
care to remind us that it was a *plenary* council ; but such
councils were not at all unusual in Africa, even for general
business ; and some of the canons of this very council, which
we must remember met at the usual season, have reference
only to general discipline.[3]

[1] *Hist. Lat. Christ.*, vol. i., p. 121,
[2] *Lives of the Fathers*, vol. ii., p. 554.
[3] In Africa there were two classes of National Councils, the *Plenary* and
the *General* or Universal. The former consisted *de jure* of all the bishops ; the
latter, of deputies from each of the six provinces, as arranged by the Council
of Hippo in 393, which enacted that the National Council should meet annually :

There is no evidence to show in what spirit this Synod was called, in what spirit the bishops assembled, or in what spirit they conducted their debates; nor do we know what Augustine said, or how he said it, although we may assume that he spoke. But we have ample evidence, that anything like an anti-Roman spirit would be thoroughly un-African.

Let us now listen to 'another Anglican writer, Julius Lloyd, M.A., the mouthpiece of the Christian Knowledge Society :—

Numerous as was this Council [of 417,] it was not sufficiently representative of the whole African Church, to carry the united weight of the entire body, and another Council was summoned in the following year. At this Plenary Council, as it was called, the numbers were not greater than before, but the members, drawn from the most remote districts, gave an extraordinary importance to their assembly which met on May 1, A.D. 418. Along the whole southern coast of the Mediterranean for more than a thousand miles, from the sultry land of Tripolis, the home of the lotos-eaters, to the slopes of the western Atlas, which faced the open Atlantic, beyond the Pillars of Hercules, the prelates of all the African provinces left their homes to meet together for deliberation at Carthage . . . Every cause which could tend to excite deep and strong emotion in human hearts, was abundantly supplied by the circumstances under which the Council was assembled. The question to be debated was one which had arisen on their own African soil, and had since filled the world with controversy. It had assumed the form of a dispute between the ancient rivals, Rome and Carthage. The Bishop of Rome had unexpectedly shown a disposition to stand by men whom the Synods of Africa had repeatedly condemned as heretics. Nor were more private grievances wanting; for, the tone of Zosimus

---

of course every *plenary* council was *general*, but not *vice versa*. All the *plenary* councils, as far as we can judge at present, ended by being merely *general*, deputies being elected to dispose of the ordinary business. Of the *Acts* of most of these councils, known in Ecclesiastical History as *The Councils of Carthage*, we have only a few fragments; but, we have nearly all their canons, and some of their synodical letters to the Popes. As far as can be made out now, the lowest legal number of deputies was sixteen, which, with the six metropolitans, who were members *de jure*, makes twenty-two. The distinction between *plenary* and *general* Synods is not observed in our great *collections*, but it was well understood among the Africans themselves; thus, St. Augustine always calls the great Donatist Synod of Bagaia, consisting of 310 bishops, *plenarium concilium vestrum* (Ep. li. 2; *In Baptis*, iii. 3); just as he does similar Catholic Synods (Ep. ccxv. 2; *Retrac.*, i. 17). During all St. Augustine's time, he and Alypius and Possidius were almost invariably the deputies for Numidia; and, as a general rule, only the most distinguished bishops of each province were elected deputies.

and his predecessor Innocent in writing to the Bishop of Carthage, had betrayed an arrogance which the Africans hotly resented. Zosimus had told them they were hasty ; Innocent had addressed to Aurelius, a few years before, a letter of reproof for ordaining illiterate men. Bishops, he said, were elected so carelessly, that complaints were in everyone's mouth. With such words fresh in their memory, the Bishops at Carthage were in no mood to bear Roman dictation on a question of a doctrine on which they felt, with legitimate pride, that the ablest living defender of the faith was their own Bishop of Hippo . . . Two bishops presided over the Council, Aurelius of Carthage and Donatian of Telepte, the Primate of Byzacena. The object of this arrangement was, no doubt, to allay the ancient jealousy which was felt in the rural districts, where the clergy were always in fear that Carthage might become what Rome actually became. It was not, however, to either of the two presidents that the Council looked for guidance, so much as to Augustine. Most of those present had seen him before, and had heard him argue, point by point, against the Donatists with admirable temper and skill in the conference of A.D. 411. He stood before them now with the augmented dignity of a reputation which the Universal Church had learned to confirm. His voice, his language, his gestures were trained by long practice to convey effectively to his hearers the emotions of his own fervid soul ; and the theme on which he had to speak was one on which he had more cause than most men to feel intensely . . . His hearers were men of the most various degrees of culture. Some were highly educated and had a large share of the artificial refinement of the declining empire. Others were uncivilized bishops from the hill country, who could neither read nor write, mitred savages. Educated and uneducated alike were carried along by Augustine's eloquence ; and the articles of the Council [nine in number], relating to Pelagianism bear the impress of his mind in almost every word . . . The Acts of the Council of Carthage arrested the advance of Pelagianism at a moment when both the eastern and western Churches of Europe were inclining to approve, or at least to absolve, Pelagius and those who held with him. From that moment a new turn was given to the controversy : and the main definitions of the African Church were recognised before long as part of the doctrine of the Church Universal. Zosimus did not wait for the official report of the proceedings of the Council . . . He pronounced sentence without delay, confirming the judgment of his predecessor Innocent, against Pelagius and Celestius.

The only authority quoted for all this is Fleury. We turned at once to the pages of the celebrated Gallican,[2] fully

---

[1] *The North African Church*, 1880, p. 250.   [2] 4th Ed. Caen., 1781.

prepared to find him guilty and give him his deserts, but what was our astonishment at finding that he does not say a single word about ' uncivilized bishops who could neither read nor write,' nor about 'mitred savages,' nor about 'the hill country,' nor about 'the Conference of Carthage,' nor about ' Roman dictation,' nor about any ' speech of St. Augustine's,' nor about 'hot resentment,' nor about ' private grievances,' nor about ' the jealousy of the rural clergy,' nor about the Council having been called for the Pelagian question, or in any anti-Roman spirit, nor about any anti-Roman spirit in the debates, nor about its canons having finally settled the Pelagian controversy. No, some one else has invented all this. Fleury seldom makes such easily detected assertions ; he deals more in sly hints and *suppressio veri ;* thus, in his account of this transaction he entirely suppresses the letter of Zosimus to the African bishops, dated March 12, 418, and received at Carthage, April 29, just on the eve of this very Council, which was opened May 1, 418, and continued for a month in its second or *general* form, as we learn from St. Augustine in his work *De Peccato originali,*[1] written during the month. He also suppresses what remains to us in Prosper's *contra collatorem,*[2] of the answer sent to the Pope, most probably at the close of this Council.[3] In his letter, the Pope says :—

The tradition of the fathers has attributed to the Apostolic See an authority so great that no one would dare to question its judgments, and has always observed the same in its canons and rules. . . . Such then being the authority derived from Peter and confirmed by the respect of all antiquity, and the Roman Church being sustained in it by all laws, human and divine, over which Church, beloved brethren, you know we are placed with all the powers and authority attached to the name. Nevertheless, although our authority is such that no one can reform our sentence, we have done nothing which we have not communicated to you of our own accord, in order that we might consult together in the spirit of fraternal charity. . . . A sovereign sentence is not to be pronounced without great deliberation. Know then, my brethren, that since the date of your letters and ours, in accordance with your request, nothing has been changed.

---

[1] N. 24.   [2] N. 15.   [3] *Pagi. Gest., Rom. Pont.,* ad An. 41"

To one sentiment expressed in this letter, and repeated in the Encyclical, which they must have received before the close of the Council, they respond in these words :—' What act of yours was ever more free than that by which you communicated all this to our littleness.' All this can be seen at the end of vol. 10. of St. Augustine's works.

Another of Fleury's convenient omissions is, that with this letter Pope Zosimus sent another which appointed a commission of bishops to try some important case—an appeal, of course—in Mauritania, and that at the end of the Council St. Augustine, as a member of the commission, set out on his long journey in presence of the Primate, and absented himself for five months from his dear flock at Hippo, ' because of an ecclesiastical necessity laid upon us by the venerable Pope Zosimus, Bishop of the Apostolic See.'[1]

From all this the reader can see that Fleury had a very convenient Gallican memory.   But this is not all; he is also a master in the art of sly insinuations.   Thus, not daring on this subject to swear like his Anglican followers, he contents himself with the sly hint, *on croit que ces canons furent dressés par S. Augustin qui etoit l'ame de ce concile*.   Anglicans have taken the hint, and invented the fiction so graphically set forth by Mr. Lloyd.   In this fiction St. Augustine and the African bishops are made to march, as we have seen, under the No-Popery flag; the other false assertions are but props for this.   Now, as to the main error, we cannot imagine how any honest writer, acquainted with the events of the three years—416-419—within which this Council took place, could possibly have fallen into it. In 416 we find the Councils of Carthage and Milevis--one hundred and twenty-nine of these very bishops—sending to Pope Innocent the synodical letters already mentioned. In 419 a Plenary Council of two hundred and seventeen bishops met at Carthage; its *Acts* were signed by the two presidents, then by the Papal Legate, Faustinus, then by the other bishops, and finally by the two Roman priests who

---

[1] Ep. 190.

accompanied the Legate; they were then handed over to the Legates to be brought off to Rome. They contained the celebrated *Codex Canonum Ecclesiæ Africanæ*, compiled at this synod from all previous collections, so that the whole Canon Law of the African Church is now submitted to Rome. They concluded by a synodical letter which begins thus :— ‘ Domino beatissimo et honorabili fratri Bonifacio, Aurelius, Valentinus, primæ sedis provinciae Numidiae et coteri qui presentes adfuimus numero. ccxvii. ex omni concilio Africae.'

Since it has pleased the Lord that all that has been done between us and our holy brethren, our fellow-bishop Faustinus, and our fellow-priests Philip and Asellus, should be reported by our humility, not to Bishop Zosimus of holy memory, whose commands and holy letters they brought us, but to your venerability divinely substituted for him; we feel bound to state briefly what has been amicably arranged between us, not what is contained in the voluminous *Acts*. . . . How all this would have gladdened the heart of Zosimus were he still alive. . . . But, we had already intimated to him this past year *that to avoid all want of respect for him* we should permit these canons to be observed pending the inquiry, &c.[1]

---

[1] Not a word of this preamble does Fleury give, although he quotes the document. For the words out of respect *for him*, he has *pour le respect direc concile* (Nicea), How are honest Anglicans to guard themselves against the wiles of such a man ? The synod of 418 is known to us only from this synodical of 419 ; of this Fleury was well aware when giving his account of it under its proper date, but he does not indicate the source of his information.

As this Synod is almost the only African Synod of which we have the complete *Acts*, we take a few additional extracts from its synodical letter, to enable our readers to compare a genuine African document of this kind with the spurious one of the Synod of 424. Its conclusion runs thus :—‘ Quod donec fiat, haec quae in commonitorio supradicto nobis allegatar sunt. . . . Nos usque ad probationem servaturos esse profitemur, et beatitudinem tuam ad hoc nos adjuturam in Dei voluntate confidimus. Cetera vero quae in nostra synodo gesta vel confirmata sunt, quoniam supradicti fratres nostri, Faustinus Coepiscopus, Philippus et Asellus presbyteri, secum ferunt si dignatus fueris, tuae nota facient sanctitati.

The signatures are often repeated in the *Acts ;* here is a specimen :—

Aurelius Epus, his gestis subscripsi. Valentinus primae sedis epus provinciae Numidiae his gestis subscripsi.

Faustinus Epus ecclesiae Potentinae provinciae Piceni, legatus ecclesiae Romanae, his gestis subscripsi.

Alypius Epus Thagastensis, legatus provinciae Numidiae; his gestis subscripsi.

Augustinus Epus Hipponensis, legatus provinciae Numidiae, his gestis subscripsi.

Possidius Epus calamansis legatus provinciae numidae his gestis subscripsi.

The *deputies* of 419 are nearly the same as those of 418, and are as usual the first men in the country. The date is also most precisely given.

And these ultra-Papists of 416 and 419 are the No-Popery fanatics of 418.

There is no excuse for the offensive words 'mitred savages,' for Roman Africa was one of the most civilized provinces in the empire, and the uncivilized Moors and Getulians had no bishops, being still Pagans, as St. Augustine tells us,[1] about the year 420. Fleury does not even speak of illiterate bishops or priests, he does speak of illiterate deacons, and on very slight grounds. The Bishop of Carthage in 401, asked Pope Anastasius to permit the ordination of Donatist converts, as there were churches without 'even an illiterate deacon.' Fleury does speak of ' the careless election of bishops;' but he is quite mistaken ; for the complaint sent to Rome was, that some bishops ordained to the priesthood, *worldly men*, in preference to deserving clerics ; and the letter sent by Pope Innocent to the Bishop of Carthage, to be communicated to the other bishops, had reference only to this abuse.[2] There is no trace in African history of any friction caused by this letter.

The only excuse I can see for these fictions is, that Anglicans lose their senses when Rome is in question. Thus, Dr. Salmon, in his *Introduction to the New Testament*,[3] denies that Peter was Bishop of Rome ; while admitting[4] that he lived and died at Rome. Now, his chief witnesses for the authenticity of the Gospels, &c.,[5] are just as strong for Peter's Roman episcopacy ; and Christian tradition, on which he has to rely so much,[6] is just as strong, if not stronger, for the episcopacy. He, therefore, blindly gives away his case against his adversaries, ' the destructive critics,' for the poor consolation of having a fling at Rome.

Why are Anglicans so anxious to prove that the popes were aided by the African bishops in this matter ? St. Augustine thus expresses the relative positions of popes and councils. Thus speaking of himself he says :—

After the Pelagian heresy with its authors was refuted and condemned by the Bishops of the Roman Church, Innocent first,

---

[1] Ep. 199, n. 46.
[2] Baron ad.. An 416.
[3] 4 Ed., p. 15.

[4] Page 48.
[5] Pages 35, 41, 51, 89, &c
[6] Pages 129, 190, 398, 443, 454.

and then Zosimus, the letters of African councils co-operating, I wrote two books against them, one *On the Grace of Christ*, the other *On Original Sin*.' [1]

Again, writing to Optatus, a Mauritanian Bishop, in 418, and sending him copies of the rescripts and the Encyclical, he says :—

Through the vigilance of episcopal councils, aided by the Saviour who protects His Church, Pelagius and Celestius have been condemned over the whole Christian world by the two venerable bishops of the Apostolic See, Pope Innocent and Pope Zosimus . . . In these words of the Apostolic See, the Catholic faith is so ancient and firm, so clear and certain, that it would be criminal (nefas) for any Christian to question it.' [2]

Writing about the same time to a bishop named Asellicus, he says :—

These men had for leaders Pelagius and Celestius, the most strenuous propagators of this impiety ; who, by the recent judgment of God through His diligent and faithful servants, have been deprived of Catholic Communion.[3]

Thanking the Roman priest Sixtus for his early news of the Encyclical, he says : 'This pestilence is now condemned by a most manifest judgment of the Apostolic See.' [4]

This was his formula in speaking to Catholics, and therefore in expressing the pure Catholic doctrine; the councils *co-operating*, the Pope's *pronouncing final judgment*. Of course, this formula will not do for *contumacious* Pelagians who have to be fought upon their own ground, with his familiar weapon, the *argumentum ad hominem*.

In St. Augustine's estimation, the Encyclical added nothing to the rescripts as far as they went; but they had only decided two points, and others had been since raised in the course of the controversy. These the Encyclical now embraced, while reaffirming the decisions of the rescripts. It was also more effective, by its greater publicity, and its more solemn promulgation. Of this Encyclical we have only some fragments preserved by St. Augustine and others ;

---

[1] *Retrac.*, ii. 50.
[2] Ep. cxc. vi. 22, 23.
[3] Ep. cxcvi. 7.
[4] Ep. cxci. 2.

but we know that it was a very long and complete document, and that it was directed to all the bishops of the world, and demanded their unqualified acceptance attested by their signatures. These signatures were given by all, except by eighteen Italians headed by Julian of Eclanum (Avellino); these were deposed by the Pope and banished by the Emperor. They complained ' that the signatures of simple bishops had been extorted in their own homes without assembling a synod ;' and Augustine answers :—

> Was a Synod required for the condemnation of an open pestilence? Was no heresy ever condemned without assembling a Synod? Is it not rather the fact that heresies requiring such a remedy have been very rare? By far the greater number have been condemned where they arose, and have thus become known to the other lands that had to avoid them. But, the pride of these men [Pelagians] must have the glory of a Synod of the East and the West, specially summoned for themselves. As they cannot pervert the Catholic world, they must try at least to disturb it. But a competent judgment having been pronounced, pastoral vigilance and zeal must now drive away these wolves, wherever they may appear ; thus providing for their conversion and salvation ; as well as for the security of others ; the pastor of pastors aiding, who seeks the lost sheep even among the lowly.[1]

These are the concluding words of his *Books to Boniface*, written in 420, at the special request of the Pope himself. In sending him the work, he says : ' They are sent to your Holiness, not to teach, but to be examined, and corrected if necessary.'[2] It is manifest that in speaking of heresies being ' condemned where they arose,' he supposes the concurrence of Rome, as in the case of the rescripts.

Having failed with pope and bishops, the Pelagians turned to the Emperor Honorius for the Council; but he gave them no encouragement. They then demanded such a conference as he had granted to the Donatists in 411. To this Augustine replied :—

> Your cause is ended, having been already treated by a competent assembly of bishops. There can be no further question of treating with you about the right of discussion.

---

[1] Ad. Bonf. iv. 34,   [2] i. 3.

What you have to do, is to accept peacefully the decision already given. If you refuse this, your turbulent and insidious movements shall be restrained. You are just like the Maximianists, who, wishing to console themselves for their insignificance, and to make some show before those who despised them, endeavoured to enter into a contest with us ; but we contemptuously rejected all their proposals. . . . If then you now boast of being the victors, merely because further discussion is denied to you, remember the Maximianists made the very same boast before you. The Catholic Church gave you a full and proper hearing, and your cause was ended ; but to them she gave none, because their separation was from the Donatists, not from us . . . It should be enough for you, that the Catholic Church having long borne with you in her maternal tenderness, has at last condemned you, more from medicinal necessity than from judicial severity.'[1]

We here enter upon his *argumentum ad hominem*. They clamoured for an assembly of bishops, and he answers, that even if the decision were to rest with synods and assemblies of bishops, the cause is already ended. They kept up this demand for a synod to the end ; thus, in his very last work against Julian, he says: 'Why do you still look for an examination which has been already completed at the Apostolic See ? completed even in the Episcopal Council of Palestine.'[2]

Here we have a perfect specimen of his *argumentum ad hominem ;* which he never scruples to use when there is no danger of being misunderstood. Julian knew well that he had no idea of placing the Apostolic See on a level with ' the miserable Synod of Diospolis ;' he also knew that with Augustine *factum apud sedem Apostolicam* meant *causa finita est.* Modern writers often mistake his meaning, by not adverting to his habit of taking the adversary on his

---

[1] Cont. Jul., iii. 5. To understand some of the allusions in this passage, we must remember that in '391 the main body of the Donatists split up into two factions, called after their respective Primates, Maximianists and Primianists. The Maximianists held a Council of one hundred, the Primianists, one of three hundred and ten bishops. By the aid of the Civil power, the Primianists had so weakened their rivals, that in the Conference of Carthage in 411, their claim to be recognised as a distinct party was rejected. We do not know how many bishops they had at this time ; but we know that the Rogatists, Claudianists, and Urbanists, were treated in the same way, and that the Rogatists had at least ten bishops. (Ep. xciii. 21.)

[2] *Opus Imperf.*, ii. 103.

own ground ; but his contemporaries do not seem to have ever misunderstood him, probably because all the circumstances were present to their minds, especially his avowed principles and teaching.   The Pelagians complained, that he relied on Rome, not on Synods ; and he answers by quoting against them, as quite sufficient, the very least of the Synods that had examined their cause.

Having completely failed in the West, Julian and his party beset the Court of Constantinople about the Council ; but they failed there too, until Nestorius became Patriarch ; he went so far as to write to Pope Celestine in their favour. Nestorius was anxious for a Council, because he hoped to be able to use it in favour of his own heresy ; Julian longed for a Council in which the whole Pelagian question could be re-opened.   Well, the General Council met at Ephesus in the Summer of 431 ; everyone knows how it dealt with Nestorius ; but it is not so generally known that the Pelagians too got a hearing.   It was, however, a terrible disappointment for them ; the Council refused all *re-examination* of doctrine, and simply promulgated the Roman decrees passed against them.   And this, be it remembered, was an almost exclusively Greek Council.   So much for the Anglican assertions that Pelagianism had a special attraction for the Greek mind ; it certainly had, but only for Arian and Nestorian minds.

How all this would have gladdened the heart of Augustine were he still alive ; he had been specially invited to the Council, but died before it met.   Had he lived a few months longer, he and Julian might have met on one of the most solemn occasions in the history of the Church ; met, after twelve years of incessant controversy ; met, perhaps with some good result for Julian himself, who died as he had lived, nearly twenty years later.

Julian and his party were never able to organize their schism ; they scattered themselves as Propagandists over the East and West.   So opposed and detested were they in the East, that even Theodore of Mopsuesta deserted them. In the West, their chief success was in Britain, whither Pope Celestine sent St. Germanus of Auxerre against them in 429, as we see in his *Life*, July 26, and in Lingard's *Anglo-Saxon Church*, chap. i.

After their final condemnation by Pope Zosimus, Pelagius and Celestius gradually disappear, but not without a struggle. We last hear of Pelagius in 420, when he was banished from Palestine. Celestius being a much younger man was able to hold out longer, and to traverse the East and the West. He was banished from Rome by the Emperor Constantius, in 421; and yet we find him about 425 asking an audience of Pope Celestine. When or where he ended his career is unknown.

In this contest the following points of St. Augustine's teaching stand out clearly : (1) In a doctrinal controversy, no Synod, or number of Synods, would be final with him, without the confirmation of Rome. (2) Once Rome had spoken, the cause was ended. (3) What was endurable before, was rank heresy after Rome had spoken. (4) The decision of Rome was binding on all Christians. (5) From the decision of Rome there was no appeal.[1]

But did St. Augustine regard all this as *de jure divino?* Most certainly; for by what other right could the Roman Pontiff bind the consciences of all Christians in the Pelagian question? By what other right could union with Rome be obligatory on Donatists on pain of salvation? That these were his doctrines I have already shown in the *Historical Study* and elsewhere. This was the doctrine preached to the Africans by his favourite Popes, Innocent and Zosimus.

---

[1] The only passage in all his works that could at all be urged against this is where he says (Ep. xliii., n. 19), in discussing the origin of their schism with some Donatists, that after their condemnation in 313 by the Council of Rome under Pope Melchiades, there remained to them an appeal *ad plenarium Ecclesiae Universalis Concilium*. And in the same letter he reminds them of all the irregular appeals they had made, and that this was the only one which they took care to omit. Now, this Roman Council refused to discuss at all the doctrinal question they had raised as an excuse for their rebellion, and simply decided the *judicial* question regarding the validity of Cecilian's ordination. And even as regards this, they acted only as a Court of Appeal on the appointment of Constantine. As to the way being still open for an appeal from this Court, it is not clear that he regarded it as anything more than one of the concessions of the Pope and the Emperor to cure their madness, and leave them no excuse. This letter mentions (n. 16) an *ultima sententia* of the Pope himself; but it consists entirely of extraordinary concessions to enable them to recede from the schism, and has nothing to say to this appeal.

So well was all this understood by his contemporaries, friend and foe, that no question was ever raised about it. That the Bishop of Hippo regarded the Roman Pontiff as the heir of Peter, was as well known as that his name was Augustine.

PHILIP BURTON, C.M.

IRISH EXILES IN BRITTANY
III.

TOWARDS the opening of the second half of the seventeenth century two Irish exiles of particular note took refuge in Brittany, and became figures of mark in its annals. They were splendid types of the Irish ecclesiastic, and by their virtues and nobility of character won the respect and esteem of both clergy and people. The high opinion even still prevalent here in regard to our countrymen may be, perhaps, largely attributed to the influence of these confessors of the faith, who were so severely tried in the crucible of persecution, and who so triumphantly proved the sterling gold of their piety and faith. The honour and respect shown to them during their stay reflects eternal credit on the Breton character, and should not be forgotten by us in making our estimates of this noble people. The kindness and hospitality shown these pilgrim bishops bind with links of gold two sections of the Celtic race, and indicate their never-failing kinship in blood as in the supernatural brotherhood of faith.

Monsignor Patrick Comerford, Bishop of Waterford, arrived in Nantes towards the opening months of 1652. His city had been captured by Ireton on August 6, 1650, and the Bishop received orders to quit the country within three months.[1] He had but to obey, as there was no hope of successful resistance to this decree which divorced him from his diocese ; and he turned his footsteps towards Brittany,

---

[1] Cardinal Moran, *Persecution of Irish Catholics*, pp. 163, 169.

where he arrived at San Malo at the close of August. Dr. Comerford was not a stranger to continental life, as he had had long-sustained relations with many parts of Europe, in whose schools and monasteries he had been educated, and whose influences had largely shaped his character, and given a fixed determination to his life. He was born in Waterford, in the year 1586, and within the walls of the *Urbs Intacta* passed his early years. He went abroad for his studies, and finished his classical course at Bordeaux. On their conclusion he proceeded to Lisbon, where he became a member of the Order of Hermits of St. Augustine. The outline of his life is well preserved in the annals of his order, which really give us all the evidence now to be had concerning his character, studies, and the various duties which marked his very active career. We read of him, in this authentic collection, enough to give us a high opinion of his disposition and ability. His talents would seem to have been very extensive ; he was Professor of Eloquence, poet and preacher of note, while attaining the highest honours in the dryer studies of sacred science. His service to his institute was mainly given abroad, and in this he followed the fortunes of so many others of his countrymen of that age who found on the Continent a use for their talents or their swords which was denied them at home. It will serve good purpose if we transcribe here the section of the annals of his order which treat of this gifted and remarkable Irishman. The Latinity is indeed very plain, but the careful preservation of facts and dates indicates with what security the religious institutes preserve the *res gesta* of their more distinguished sons. In their present form they were published at Rome in 1875, by Father Joseph Lanteri, O.S.A., who was a born chronicler, and who devoted himself to the preservation of the history of the order of which he was himself a distinguished member. He devoted one volume to the lives of the brethren who from the year of the union of the Hermits of St. Augustine, 1256, had been elevated to the episcopal office, and in this work, page 19, we read the following :—

Fr. Patritius Quemerfort, alias ab Angelis cognominatus, nobilis Hibernus, Waterfordiae, honestis Catholicisque parentibus

natus, ex parte patris ex familia Quemerfordorum et Wascheorum,
ex parte vero matris ex progenie Whiteorum, et Butleorum
affinitate S. Thomam Cantuariensem attigentium, vir fuit magnae et
insignis staturae, eloquens et suavis, qui amoenas litteras didicit
Burdigalae in Gallia, et philosophiam Ulyssipone in Lusitania
ubi Augustiniano Ordine nomen dedit. Coimbriae S. Theologiae
operam navavit, ac postea in Tertiarias insulas missus fuit
eloquentiae publicam cathedram moderaturus. Fuit etiam poeta
atque orator praecellens necnon S. Theologiae doctor Florentinus.
In Lusitania P. Provincialis secretarium egit, atque pro insulis
Tertiariis consiliarum. An. 1618 Bruxellis in Belgio nostrates
alumnos philosophiam docebat. Romae postea fuit suae provinciae definitor ac procurator. A Paulo V. pro fide propa-
paganda missionarius et Coenobii Kellensis Prior perpetuus in
Hiberniam remittitur. Tandem ab Urbano VIII. an. 1629, die
12 Feb. creatur episcopus Lismoriensis et Waterfordiensis in
provincia Casheliensis, et par manus Cardinalis Bentivoglio,
eodem anno die 18. Martii Romae in ecclesiae S. Sylvestri ad
montem Quirinalem Consecrationem accepit. Interfuit an. 1648
celebri synodo Waterfordiensi cui praefuit Nuncius Apostolicus.
Io Baptista Rinuccini et in qua damnatae fuerunt *conditiones
pacis* ab Ormondae Anglo duce tempore belli civilis propositae,
quippe quae injustae videbantur atque pernicivae cum religioni
tum patriae Hibernorum. [1]

In this passage we have a sufficiently graphic story of
this scholar and priest, who was a type of his times in many
ways. He was one of many whose love of letters made them
eat the bread of exile in order to accomplish their task
which was become impossible at home, and whose love of
religious life burned with heroic flame during that dark
period when the monk's habit was in Ireland a mark for
the worst fury of the enemies of our race. If one had the
gift of word-painting it would be a pleasant task to follow
this gigantic Celt in his search for knowledge through the
cities of the Continent. How he must have towered above
the diminutive Gascons at Bordeaux, and the sound of his
rich Irish voice must have been sweet to hear as he spoke
the sweet languages of the South! Whether any of his
poems remain to attest his genius for song, we cannot say;
but it is safe to assert that he must have accomplished

---

[1] Lanteri : *Eremi Sacrae Augustinianae*, pars altera, p. 19.

something above the ordinary level of amateur verse to have merited any mention of this gift being linked with his name. It is a curious fact that his theological studies were made in the same University, where, nearly two hundred years after him, another Irish Augustinian, who in his turn became a great Irish bishop, also made his course of the sacred sciences. Our country owes a great deal to the educational institutes of Southern Europe; they gave our students asylum during the passion-tide of our history; but to none are we more conspicuously indebted than to Coimbra, in Portugal, which moulded the minds and hearts of Bishops Comerford and Doyle.

It would be an agreeable work to sketch even a short period of Dr. Comerford's life in immediate connection with Brittany; the opportunity would then be given us to make a critical estimate of him in regard to some one side of his character at least; but, alas! we have only to tell that he came, not for life and signal deeds, but simply to die and find a grave worthy of his genius and his virtues. Arriving at St. Malo, as we above noted, about the close of August, 1650, he came to Nantes in the early part of 1652, and died in this city on March 10 of that year.[1] His death so soon after his arrival hindered any honours being paid to this most distinguished prelate; but we may assume that, had he lived, he would have been the object of the most marked solicitude on the part of the clergy and citizens, who at his death showed him extraordinary marks of their pious consideration. We read in the archives of the Cathedral Chapter that the canons felt themselves honoured by celebrating his obsequies in the Cathedral, where every rubrical resource was exhausted in manifesting their appreciation of the dignity and worth of the deceased prelate. The minutes of the Chapter remain to attest the solemnity of the burial functions, and a few extracts will not be without interest to our readers. The first mention of the bishop's death and burial occurs on March 11, 1652, under the title :—'Le XI

---

[1] I. E. RECORD, December, 1887, p. 1062, et seq.

Mars. Enterrement de l'evesque Comerford, Irlandois ;'
and proceeds to say :—

Le chapitre à arresté de faire demain solennellement l'enterrement du Révérend Pere Patrice Comerford, de l'ordre de
S. Augustin, evesque de Waterford et Lismore d'Irlande exillé
de son pays pour la foi, decedé dimanche dernier, à la Fosse.
Et pour ce, on sonnera à Midy touttes les cloches, comme est de
constume des enterrements solennels. Et au soir, et demain, on
dira tout le service avant le sermon. Immédiatement à l'issue
du dict sermon aller processionellement à la Fosse quèrir le corps
qui sera conduit en cette eglise où sera chantee la Messe des
deffuncts. Et après les cérémonies faictes le corps sera inhumé
dans l'enfen desoubz les marches devant l'autel S. Charles : et le
sacristie sera advorti de faire sonner à cinq heures, le Mercredi
13 Mars. 1652.[1]

If the exiled Bishop had died in his own palace on the
banks of the Suir he could hardly have received more
honours from his own people than came to him from those
stranger hands. His friends who had accompanied him
abroad, and whose loving care had sweetened his last hours,
were not untouched by the pious generosity of the Canons,
and we find in the same collection cited above, and on the
following page, this notice of their gratitude :—

Les parentz du feu Révérend Evesque Patrice Comerford,
enterré hier, en cette Eglise, sont entrés au chapitre, qui ont
remercié Messieurs d'avoir honoré le defunct, d'avoir fait ses
obsèques et funorailles (et) qui en ont promis le faire en son
service d'octave.

This promise was honoured by the observance, as is
proved by the following page of the chapter record. From
this we gather that the Canons again met to consider what
further measures should be taken with respect to Monsignor
Comerford, and the result of this meeting is recorded in the
following entry :—

Le chapitre a arresté de faire le service d'octave du defunct
Révérend Évesque Patrice Comerford et Lismore, et pour ce, on
sonnera un appeau d'une grosse cloche pendant Vespres ; et a
l'issue, ou dira la messe solennelle, au Grand-Autel, qui sera
chantée en musique et pendant ladite messe ou sonnera un glas
de toutes les cloches. Le Mercredy, 20 Mars. 1652.

---

[1] *Archiv. du Chapitre.* Nantes: 1652, p. 76.

These extracts leave nothing to be desired in determining
the facts they concern; they are plain and direct, as such
records ought always be. Some of the particulars given are
worthy of note. We see what a conspicuous place the bells
play in these funeral functions; the number to be rung and
the various forms to be followed are carefully determined by
the authorities. Another point in the last entry may need
explanation. It is ordered that a mass be solemnly sung
after Vespers, and this may seem to many an extraordinary
proceeding. But the wonder will cease when it is remembered that these ceremonies took place in Lent, when the
chapter was *bound* to recite Vespers *before noon*, and consequently the mass would commence before or at 12 o'clock,
which is not at all an unusual custom in France even in
our own time. Having laid the bishop in his tomb these
generous strangers were unwilling that his grave should be
forgotten. They placed above it a slab on which was written
the following inscription :—

Ici repose révérend père en Dieu, Patrice de Comerford,
evesque de Waterford et de Lismore en Irlande. Persécuté dans
son pays par les factieux d'Angleterre, il se retira en France où
il trouva sureté et protection. Plein de confiance dans les bontés
de l'Eternel, il vécut avec patience et supporta les malheurs de
cette vie avec resignation. Il mourut l'an du Seigneur 1652.[1]

It is a remarkable fact, and worthy of special mention
here, that when his grave was opened ten years after, in
order to place beside this confessor of the faith the bones
of another exiled Irish bishop, the body of Dr. Comerford
was found intact, and without the slightest trace of corruption.[2] In this we may see a testimony to the sanctity
of a life whose holiness may yet receive a still higher
sanction from the Church he served so well.

At this period Nantes gave a home to another Irish
bishop who had been constrained to abandon the administration of his diocese by circumstances precisely similar
to those which drove the Bishop of Waterford into exile.

---

[1] This slab was removed to a more conspicuous place in 1779, 'pour
perpetuer la mémoire du dit Seigneur evêque.' During the reign of terror,
however, it was destroyed together with many other monuments in the Cathedral,
and of it there is now no trace. (*Archives du Chapitre*, 29 October, 1779.)
[2] Cardinal Moran, *Persecutions of Irish Catholics*, vol. i., p. 279.

Monsignor Robert Barry, Bishop of the united dioceses of Cork and Cloyne, was born in the parish of Brittway, in Cloyne, in the year 1588. His early studies were made with the Jesuit fathers, in their College at Bordeaux, but we have no evidence that might enable us to fix the place of his theological training. He would seem to have returned immediately after his ordination to Ireland, where he became chaplain to the Countess of Ormond, and in this position did some good service to the cause of religion. Dr. Brady, in his work on *Episcopal Succession in Ireland*, attests to the active ministry of this young priest, who laboured in the cause of the faith in England, Dublin, and other places. This would seem to have been the testimony of no less authority than Rinuccini, through whose favour, no doubt, at the age of thirty-two Dr. Barry was appointed by Paul V. Vicar Apostolic of Cork and Ross. His career was singularly active, and he would seem to have played a leading part in the political events of which that period was so notably fertile. He was appointed delegate to the Supreme Council of the Confederate Catholics, and as such undertook journeys to England and France. From these political associations he was obliged to take sides in the urgent controversies of his times, and as a natural consequence was compelled to oppose the opinions of many others who differed from his views and policy. This explains the determined opposition made to his nomination as bishop of Cork and Cloyne, to which see he was, however, preconized in 1648, and received consecration at the hands of his staunch friend the Apostolic Nuncio. His zeal in his new office justified the choice of the Holy See; his labours were multiplied, and at the constant risk of his life he discharged the duties of the pastoral office. The vigilance of the enemies of the faith was at that time almost impossible to evade; but, disguised, the Bishop lived with his people, held his pastoral visits, confirmed the persecuted flock by his example, and consoled them by the ministry of the sacraments. This successful defiance of the law made him a marked man among the many who fought the good fight at that time, and he was signalled out for especially hard treatment. The faculty given to others to leave the country was withdrawn from him, and he was compelled to hide in fens and marshes in order to escape the fury of the Cromwellian officials. At length he found means to leave Ireland, and turned for his place of refuge to the shores of Brittany. He arrived in San Malo, during the residence there of Monsignor Comerford ; and having in vain waited for signs of better times at home, he came to Nantes, in 1652.

His life here was a fitting sequel to his record at home. Of him it may be truly said that, having crossed the seas, he changed only his climate, and amid the peaceful surroundings of a Breton city, preserved all the ardour and zeal of his youthful ministry spent in the service of Ireland.

It is really pleasant to read of his life in Nantes ; on his side and on that of his new friends the record is of the most honourable description. He was received by bishop and people with hospitality similar to that which greeted the Bishop of Waterford ; but he was happier in that God gave him some years of further life which were consecrated to the paying off the debt he owed to Catholic Brittany. The Bishop of Nantes at this time was Monsignor Gabriel de Beauveau, who exhausted every means within his power to honour his persecuted brother, and sweeten the bitterness of his exile. Dr. Barry became practically coadjutor of the diocese. Cardinal Moran tells us[1] that he discharged various functions of the pastoral office, and the archives of the see testify to numerous ordinations held by the Bishop of Cork and Cloyne.[2] This fact is also attested by the historian Lynch, who calls him choreveque de Nantes ; and in the Carte papers this mention of him occurs :—' Muneribus episcopalibus, praesulis Nanetensis vice, saepius fungens Chorepiscopus Nanetensis, prisco more, dici poterit.'[3]

In the midst of these new duties Dr. Barry never forgot his own people, and administered his diocese through his vicars. His correspondence with them is said to have been

[1] *Persecutions of Irish Catholics*, p. 159.
[2] *Insinuations, archives de l'evêche de Nantes*, années 1656, and *seqq.*
[3] 172 (p. 510), Bodleian Lib., Oxford.

frequent, and while we have not at hand any extracts from his letters, his active and apostolic character makes it easy to believe with what zeal and pastoral charity he provided for the spiritual good of the flock from which the enemies of his country and faith divided him. But the end came very soon to this double ministry. Consumed by the labours of his early career, and worn out by the fatigues and hardships of his life as a bishop, the constitution which had stood so many trials at length gave way, and he died at Nantes on Friday, July 7, 1662. For ten years he had borne the lengthening chain of exile, and in that interval had won the love and reverence of all who had known him. He was buried in the Cathedral, and lies beside his friend and brother exile, Dr. Comerford; so that they whom a similar dignity and common sorrows had united during life, in their death and long rest were not divided.

The municipal archives of Nantes contain the following notice of Dr. Barry's death :—

Le sept de Juillet mil six cent soixante et deux, le corps de Révérend Père en Dieu, Robert evêque de Corq (Irlande) refugié à Nantes pour la persecution des hérétiques d'Angleterre, depuis huit on dix ans, fut sépulturé en l'eglise Cathédrale devant l'autel S. Charles. Décedé près la chapelle de Toussaint de Nantes.

The last wish of this great confessor of the faith was that he be buried in the Cathedral of the city that had become so dear to him. With what willingness this wish was acceded to by the Chapter may be gathered from the following extract from their archives. Under the date Juillet, 1662, we read :—

Enterrement de Monsigneur l'evesque de Cork, Hibernie. Robert Barry evesque de Cork et de Cloyne en Hibernie, exilé pour la foy catholique.

Estant entré en chapitre a representé que ledit seigneur evesque estoit décedé aujourd'hui sur les trois heures du matin et que durant sa vie il avoit temoigné grand desir d'estre inhumé dans cette église pourveu que Messieurs du Chapitre leussent agréable. Et cela estant, supplié mes dits sieurs d'ordonner l'heure et la solemnité de l'enterrement comme il leur plairoit. Sur quoy le chapitre aprés avoir deliberé a arresté de faire demain le dit enterrement a l'issue de la grande messe avec toute la solemnité accontumée des enterrements solennels. Et pour ce, on sonnera aujourd'hui trente gobets de la plus grosse cloche depuis Midy jusqu'a[1] Midy et demy, et ensuite un glas de toutes les cloches jusqu'a une heure et demie: et autre semblable glas ce soir a huit heures et demain a six heures du matin suivant le coustume. Plus demain aprés la grande messe l'on ira processionellement en la maison oú est décédé ledit Seigneur Evesque, près de Sainte Radegonde pour lever le corps lequel sera conduit par la rue de chasteau et par la grande rue en cette eglise où sera chantée solennellement la messe des defuncts. Et aprés les cérémonies faictes le corps sera inhumé dans l'enfeu qui est sous les maiches devant l'autel de S. Charles. Et pour faire l'office audit enterrement, est deputé Monsieur Robin chanoine.

Le Vendredi, septiém jour de Juillet, 1662.[1]

With such fitting pomp, and in the midst of general sorrow throughout the city, the Bishop was laid to rest beside the Bishop of Waterford, and a second slab above the tomb bore the following inscription :—

Messire Robert (Barry) par la gráce de Dieu et du Saint Siege apostolique evêque de Cork (et de Cloyne) on Hybernie, refugié à Nantes par la persecution des heritiques en Angleterre, lequel mourut le 7 Juillet, 1662.[2]

The fact that it holds such precious relics of these remarkable exiles, adds for us a new solemnity to the magnificent Cathedral of Nantes. It should be a place of pilgrimage to every Irishman whose fortunes bring him towards this ancient and most Catholic city. It has other titles to our admiration in the beauty of its architecture and the many monuments that bind it with the past, and make it 'familiar with forgotten years ;' but to the eyes of the Irish pilgrim it is above all sacred, because these two glorious exile bishops rest beneath its vaulted roof, and mingle their ashes with its consecrated soil.

A lasting monument to the piety and zeal of Monsignor Barry remains to this day in the devotion to the Mother of Mercy, which is one of the most popular religious exercises of the City of Nantes. Its origin goes back over six hundred years to a time when the people were delivered from a great public calamity through the intercession of the Blessed Virgin. In recognition of her goodness to them a chapel was built in her honour, and for a long period a special

---

[1] *Archides Chapitre*, vol. 1659-1666, p. 67.
[2] *Mallinat Commune do Nantes*, tome i., p. 282.

cultus was given her under the title of the Mother of Mercy. While this act of gratitude was a great religious feature of the city, yet there was long wanting to it the peculiar strength which comes to every pious practice when the Church officially recognises its worth and accepts respon· sibility for its administration. In point of fact, it was not until the middle of the seventeenth century that the diocesan authorities formally accepted their devotion, and undertook its direction; and this was done, according to all authorities, at the instance of an Irish bishop, who can, according to the historical evidence of the case,. be none other than the Bishop of Cork and Cloyne.

The foundation of the Novena in honour of the Mother of Mercy dates more probably from the year 1654, when Dr. Barry had already begun his Apostolic labours in the diocese. Through his initiative the Chapel of the Madonna in the parish of St. Similien was renovated and restored to more than its ancient splendour, and it soon became the centre of a magnificent movement which affected every section of the people. The Novena takes place during the interval between the Ascension and Pentecost, and commemorates, according to an ancient writer, ' the eleven days spent by the Blessed Virgin in the desert after the Ascension of our Lord.'[1] The devotion is as active now as at any time in the past, and from eight to ten thousand people make the Novena every year. I have before me as I write the elenchus of the feast for a recent year, and it would seem that the whole city took part in it. The students of the Petit Seminaire came on the first day; later on those of the Grand Seminaire, and in their turn all the schools and colleges of the city. To the programme the following touching words are added :—

Au milieu des difficultés de l'heure actuelle, le secours certain, efficace, est aux pieds de Notre Dame de Misericorde. Venons tous frapper à la porte de son coeur maternel faire appel à sa puissante protection.[2]

---

[1] En mémoire deceque la Sainte Vierge resta onze jours dans le desert, apres l'Ascension de Jésus Christ.   Ogée, edition *Marteville*, vol. xii., p. 196.
[2] The Novena now takes place in the magnificent new Church of St. Similien. The arms of the Bishop of Cork are worked into the stain-glass windows above the Altar of the Mother of Mercy.

That Monsignor Barry was the first promoter of this great religious work cannot be doubted. The following testimony taken from the *Manual* speaks only of an Irish bishop, and does not determine which of the exiled prelates had the honour of this work. But the question is narrowed to Bishops Comerford and Barry, and as the first of these could have done no missionary labour at Nantes, owing to his illness and early death so soon after his arrival, it remains to accept Dr. Barry as the founder of a devotion which, while it sanctifies souls by its blessed influence unites by another tie Catholic Brittany with Catholic and suffering Ireland.

The historical proof of Dr. Barry's action with respect to this devotion is stated in the following extract; the Irish bishop in question can be none other than the zealous and active Bishop of Cork and Cloyne :—

Un Evêque d'Hybernie, exilé de son pays, persecuté pour la foi catholique, et refugié dans cette ville de Nantes qu'il édifia par les exercices d'une piété exemplaire, établit cette station dans la chapelle dédiée à l'honneur de la Sainte Vierge sous le titre de Misericorde, Mater Misericordiae, dans la paroisse de Sainte Similien, rebatie dans l'aée 1544 (1554 ?) sur un plan plus orné que l'ancienne, alors en partie tombée de vetusté. Cet evêque ayant communiqué ses intentions à Gabriel de Beauveau, Evêque de Nantes, célébra la Sainte Messe dans cette chapelle, et s'y rendit tous les jours, depuis l'Ascension jusqu'a la fête de la Pentecôte, accompagné de quelques ecclesiastiques et de plusieurs personnes de piété avec qui il recita les priéres analogues aux pieux motifs qui les assemblaint. Plusieurs villes du Royaume et un très-grand nombre dans l'univers chretien avaient déjà les unes des confrairies, les autres des devotions semblables à celle-ci ; d'autres des exercices particuliers de piété pour preparer les fidéles à la venue du Saint Esprit, lorsque ce digne confesseur de la foi entreprit à Nantes cet establissement. La parvoisse de Saint Similien fut honorée par la choix qu'il fit de la chapelle de Misèricorde.[1]

This closes our record of the Bishop of Cork in Brittany. It is one of which his countrymen may be well proud. It shows him in exile and comparative old age, still active and zealous in the cause of his Master. The energy which

---

[1] Sele de Gaubert, *Manual*, pp. 37-38.

characterized him in the evil days he spent with his own people followed him abroad, and assures him undying remembrances among the people who honoured him while living, and who treasure still the tomb where his ashes lie awaiting the resurrection of the just.

This chapter would not be complete without a passing mention of some other Irish prelates who sojourned for some little time in Nantes during the troubles of the seventeenth century.

Monsignor Nicholas French, named Bishop of Ferns in 1646, after three troubled years spent in the work of his diocese, at length was compelled to leave Ireland and take refuge in France. He came to Nantes, where he delayed only a short time, proceeding thence to Compostella, in Spain. During his stay in Brittany he wrote a letter to the Archbishop of Tuam, then a prisoner in Galway Jail, and this remains as a testimony to his sojourn in this city. It was written on January 30th, 1654, and exhorts the venerable prelate to bear his persecutions in the spirit of martyrdom. The letter is a magnificent composition, and shows the splendid spirit that animated our prelates in these days of trial, when the faith of our people was so severely tested. Dr. French died in Ghent, on August 23rd, 1678 ; he was then coadjutor to the Archbishop of that city.[1]

The Archbishop of Tuam, John de Burgh, who had succeeded in escaping from prison, in his turn sought refuge in this city. He came here in 1654, and remained until 1659. His name is associated in Ireland with a political inconstancy unusual at that period ; and in Nantes he has left no trace of his years that were passed in Brittany. The only memory left of him is that he was reduced to the most extreme poverty. He eventually succeeded in returning homewards, and died an edifying death in 1667.[2]

The last Irish prelate who, at this epoch, came to Nantes, was the Bishop of Killala, Monsignor Francis Kirwan, towards 1655. He had been imprisoned in Ireland, but after a few days of captivity made good his escape through

---

[1] Brady, *Episcopal Succession*, p. 378.
[2] Meehan, *Franciscan Monasteries*, p. 134.

the help of his friends, and came to Brittany. He arrived
in a state of pitiable destitution, and received from the
Breton Parliament the sum of fifty pieces of gold. Of this
slender pittance he gave a third part to the poor, and spent
the rest in procuring food and clothing. It is said of him
that he refused to dress in episcopal purple, and always wore
the cassock of a simple priest. He was appealed to by the
parliament for his opinion concerning the subsidies to
be divided among the Irish exiles, of whom many were
of noble birth, and had petitioned for succour from the
authorities. His reply reflects the best light upon his
character. He said the first aid should be extended to the
nobles as they had suffered in the same good cause as the
clergy, and, further, while in the possession of their fortunes
had befriended the priests who were in need. He added
that the latter had always the *honorarium* of the Mass to
support them, while the nobles were without any resource.
This reply, while it did honour to him, was not well received
by his brethren of the clergy, who criticized him very severely
on this occasion. Monsignor Kirwan remained two years
in Nantes, and died at Rennes, on August 27th, 1661.[3]

We can find no record of other Irish bishops who made
any stay in Nantes at this period. The Primate of all
Ireland, Edmund O'Reilly, had made some efforts to reach
this hospitable and friendly city, but died on the voyage to
Brittany. Enough, however, has been said to show how
close were the relations between this province and Ireland,
during one of the darkest and stormiest portions of our
history; and I think anyone who has followed the narrative
will agree with me in holding that it honours the country
for whose faith and nationality so many of her sons were
ready to sacrifice all that is best and dearest in life, and
certainly does not discredit Brittany, who so nobly opened
her hand and her heart to these helpless and harmless exiles
of Erin.

A. WALSH, O.S.A.

[1] *Pii Antistites Icon.* Auctore Joanne Lynch.

PARIS UNIVERSITY AND THE SCHOOLMEN

I.

THE history of the Paris University and the great theologians connected with it will ever be a subject of the greatest interest to the theological student. It has somewhere been said, that ' to thoroughly understand any scientific system one must study its origin and development.' Such, we think, is also true of theology. To understand its connections, one part with another, and its relations to the different errors it was employed to combat, one must go to its first beginning, and advance with it through its gradual development; one must study the ends the great theologians had in view when they wrote their huge tomes, and enter with them into the spirit of their subject. No one has ever yet been an expert in theology who has not closely studied its history and the history of the great theologians. Paris was the great centre where such men flourished, and the University of Paris is too closely connected with their works to be separated from their history. It is with the view to interest those who devote most of their time to the study of theology in the labours of the great founders of theological science that the following pages have been written.

From the time that Christianity began to take a firm footing in the West under the patronage of the Frankish Emperors the work of education was carried on almost exclusively by the great monastic institutions. The monasteries were the recognised homes of intellectual labour, and outside their stately halls education was little known. Charlemagne endeavoured to establish a school in his court, and with the aid of the famous Alcuin, was to a great extent successful in doing so, but the Court School of Charlemagne was principally intended for the education of the future dignitaries of the Church and State. Yet the Emperor's zeal extended beyond the court. Monasteries that till then

were not devoted to intellectual training were obliged to
open schools, and a like obligation was extended to all
cathedrals. Bishops, it is true, had always endeavoured to
gather round them young subjects, whom they trained in
ecclesiastical sciences and liturgical observances, that they
might afterwards supply the wants of the dioceses; but such
an education was strictly ecclesiastical. The cathedral
school, where it did exist, was a school for clerics, and the
laity, as a rule, were denied entrance to it. The monastic
schools were more liberal, and the monks devoted their
time to the education of lay students, as well as of those
who intended to afterwards embrace the monastic life.

Charlemagne thus brought about by his influence that all
monasteries and cathedrals in his kingdom should have
schools attached to them. If teachers could not be had in
the cathedrals they were supplied by the monasteries, and
thus a great stimulus was given to education throughout.
the West. Yet the spirit of these schools was necessarily
ecclesiastical. Lay students were admitted, but they had
to join in the same studies with those who were being
prepared for the ecclesiastical state. Holy Scripture and
the fathers were the principal subjects taught; other subjects were studied only inasmuch as they were necessary
for the well understanding of the former. The division
of the Seven Arts, which properly formed the secular
course, into two classes called the *Trivium* and the
Quadrivium was an established rule in all the colleges of
the ninth and tenth century. The Trivium, which included
grammar, rhetoric, and dialectics, was more insisted on than
the advanced course of the Quadrivium, which comprised
music, arithmetic, geometry, and astronomy. These latter
subjects were merely dealt with in a cursory way, though
they remained on the curriculum until the renaissance of the
twelfth century; the subjects of the Trivium were what we
might call the only secular subjects then taught in the
schools. Grammar included not merely a knowledge of the
fixed grammatical rules, but it extended to a systematic
study and interpretation of the classical authors of ancient
Rome; rhetoric chiefly consisted in a close study of Cicero's

De Oratore, and some other works of the Roman orator; but it was logic that specially attracted the minds of the youths of these ages.

The art of logic was studied ardently and practised unsparingly by the students of the Middle Ages. Dialectics could be no hindrance to the welfare of religion; on the contrary, its practice would sharpen the mind to proceed with ease through the often subtle distinctions of the fathers; and for these reasons dialectics was above all others the one subject to which the monastic and cathedral schools then devoted most of their labour and time. The translations of Aristotle's *Categoriae* and *De Interpretatione*, and Porphyry's *Isagoge*, by Boethius, were the principal text books of logic then in use. It was the logic of Aristotle that most attracted attention, and though Plato's contemplative mind had exercised much influence over the monastic intellects, still he was little known in the schools, except on account of his controversy on the origin of ideas. Yet, this one question was ever fresh in the minds of the young students, and it was again and again as warmly debated among them as it ever had been in the walks of Athens. The question of Universals which had a close connection with the question of ideas was another leading point of dispute. Porphyry's exposition of the question on the reality of genera and species, which ended in his *dicere recusabo*, was placed as an introduction to Aristotle's logic, and both supplied matter for many intellectual combats. Such was the spirit of the schools from the Carolingian era on to the end of the twelfth century.

A new epoch of intellectual fervour then began. The question of the Universals still continued to be the great subject of dispute, and though unsettled the question led to far-reaching consequences. While kept within the domain of logic no great evil could arise, but when carried on to physics, metaphysics, and theology, grave results were soon found to follow. Roscelin, a canon of the diocese of Compiègne in Brittany, insisting on the non-reality of the Universal, openly taught that nothing was real except the individual, that genera and species were but mere figments

of the mind, *merae voces*, with no external reality whatever :
the individual alone was the sole objective reality. This
nominalism, as it was called, when carried into the domain
of theology was found to clash with the chief doctrines of
Christianity. By admitting such a theory the mystery of
the Blessed Trinity fell to the ground. If no reality could
be common to many, therefore the Three Persons of the
Holy Trinity were three separate individuals with nothing
common to all. Many intellectual champions appeared in
the field to combat the new false theory, foremost amongst
whom was William of Champeaux, the Chancellor of the
Cathedral School of Paris. Possessed of a keen well-
trained intellect, and a comprehensive knowledge of the
fathers, William boldly attacked Roscelin's theory, and
showed how the Universal could exist in many ; how though
inseparable from the individual it pervaded several. Such
were the opinions that formed the intellectual atmosphere
of the schools, and divided professors and students into
separate parties when the brightest genius of the age made
his appearance. This was the famous Peter Abelard.

Abelard, who was born in Brittany in the year 1079,
became at an early age the disciple of Roscelin. He
wandered from school to school eagerly seeking everywhere
for knowledge. Dialectics had special attraction for him,
and his subtle mind was soon drilled in the art of fine
distinctions. Of all the masters he had listened to Roscelin
pleased him best, and from him he quickly imbibed the
spirit of critical examination, and the practice of applying
logic to questions of religion. At the age of twenty he
came to Paris to attend the lectures of the famous Chancellor. But he was not long satisfied to hold the humble
place of one seeking for knowledge ; he wished to become a
master. Hearing William of Champeaux one day exposing
his doctrine on Universals, and their essential existence in
each individual, Abelard quickly asked : ' If the Universal
essentially exists in one individual how is any of it left to
exist in another ? ' William, we are told, hesitated before
replying, and then offered an explanation. But from that
moment his fame was gone. Students who till then had

given full credence to his words now turned their eyes on
Abelard, and volunteered to become his disciples. But to
become a teacher at Paris was not then a matter of personal
choice. Permission to teach should be obtained from the
Chancellor of the Cathedral School, and such permission
William refused to Abelard. But though hindered from
establishing a school at Paris Abelard retired with his
students to Melun, where he began to teach. William,
seeing many of his students leaving him, and wishing for a
quiet and peaceful life, retired to a lonely wilderness not
far from Paris where he founded the afterwards famous
monastery of St. Victor's. He entrusted his chair to the
ablest of his pupils, but the greater number of his students
had departed for Melun.

Abelard soon grew tired of his retreat, and returned to
Paris in search of greater honours. He attended the
lectures of the new teacher in the Cathedral School, and
after some questions and distinctions the master offered to
change places with Abelard, declaring that he would consider
it a privilege to sit at the feet of such a brilliant philosopher.
William returned to oppose such a measure, and appointing
a man of more determined mind to the office of teacher,
Abelard, had to return again to Melun. But he did not long
remain at rest. He returned to Paris, and crossing the
Seine he established a school at Mount St. Geneviève, a
place which was then outside the Chancellor's jurisdiction.

So far, dialectics had been Abelard's principal study ; he
now resolved to become a theologian. Leaving his school
at St. Geneviève he went to attend lectures in theology at the
School of Anselm of Laon. There his spirit of criticism
soon became apparent. Anselm who had devoted all his
lifetime to teaching could bring forward the testimony of
the Holy Scriptures and the fathers for every point of
doctrine ; his method, like the universal method of the time,
was strictly positive; reason was then a stranger in the field
of theology ; authority was the one great basis of doctrine.
Abelard listened to his master's lectures, but soon began to
make little of them before his fellow-students. He boasted
that with a copy of the fathers he could, after one night's

study, explain the Holy Scriptures better than had hitherto been done for them. His companions took him at his word, and next morning Abelard came forth to explain a difficult chapter of Ezechiel. His rich voice, his easy rhetorical flow of words, and his ingenious distinctions captivated the minds of the students. He more than kept his promise, and those who listened to him begged him to become their master. This he refused, and departing from Laon he came again to Paris. The chair in the Cathedral School was now vacant, and William had been appointed Bishop of Châlons-sur-Marne. Abelard volunteered to become master, and his friends succeeded in soon placing him in the vacant chair.

While Abelard was thus advancing to the height of intellectual renown, his downfall was fast approaching. His works were being examined by many theologians, and everywhere met with disapproval. William of St. Thierry, a monk of an abbey near Rheims, sent a list of the most manifest errors in Abelard's works to St. Bernard, and besought the saint to come forth from his retreat and impose silence on one so dangerous to orthodoxy. It is not for us to trace here the active part the great saint took in maintaining the doctrine of the Church against the dangerous systems of Abelard. Abelard's appearance at the Council of Sens, in 1141, his appeal from the Council to the Pope, his after reconciliation with St. Bernard and the Pope, his humble edifying life in the monastery, and his pious holy death in 1142, are too well known to be here dwelt upon. Our object is to show the great part he took in the intellectual movement of the beginning of the twelfth century.

Abelard was undoubtedly a man of wonderful intellectual power, but he directed it in a dangerous course. His test of truth was the light of reason: what could not be seen by that light, and subjected to the distinctions of dialectical art, was to be discarded. This was his mistake, and against this the theological teachers of his time loudly protested. His system, too, at the time was a new movement, and sounded strange to ears that till then were accustomed to the voice of authority alone in questions of doctrine; and to some extent that accounts for the perhaps exaggerated feeling that was raised against him. Much of his system was afterwards adopted by the great lights of the theological schools, notably by St. Anselm, the Lombard, Albert the Great, and St. Thomas; but the difference was that they gave reason but a secondary place, and made it harmonize with the old spirit of authority. Abelard relied too much on reason to the detriment of authority; they made reason go hand in hand with authority, and thus built up the noble fabric of theological science.

When Roscelin's nominalism aided by Abelard's rationalistic spirit began like a burning cancer to extend its poisonous roots into the life-giving principles of theology, it was soon seized and cut out by the famous Abbot of Bec. What William of Champeaux had done to maintain true philosophy, St. Anselm came forth to do in support of theology. After having spent many years in the silence of his monastery in prayer and contemplation, and with a mind well trained to the subtle wanderings of dialectical skill, he faced the poisonous stream of error and stopped its advance. Like a practised specialist who subjects a new disease to a careful analysis, and points out where the danger to health dwells, St. Anselm seized nominalism, cut it in pieces, and showed to the schoolmen the venemous dregs that it concealed under the deceptive name of Reason. He laid bare its component parts, and with his keen intellect pointed out where the poison lay. Yet his method was not wholly destructive. Whatever sound parts he could find in nominalism he carefully retained to be afterwards utilized in the domain of theology; the unhealthy poisonous parts he condemned to the flames.

After giving the death-blow to nominalism St. Anselm laid the foundation of the great work of the theological schools of the Middle Ages, the harmonizing of reason with authority. In his lonely monastery of Bec he had spent years in the close study of Holy Scripture and the fathers, and had learned to subordinate all human authority to the unerring Word of God. His well-known maxim *credo ut intelligam* had been the rule by which he disciplined his mind in the investigation of truth, by which

he made reason submissive to faith. Yet he did not reject
reason; he knew too well its importance to eliminate it
from the investigation of truth, and it was his appreciation
of reason, and his constant application of its principles,
that so well equipped him for the bold stand he was able to
take against the errors of nominalism. With his mind
thus alive to the value of reason he knew how far it ought
to go, and where it ought to stop, in the investigation of
truth; he saw with one glance that it had exceeded its
bounds in the nominalistic and rationalistic theories; then
recalling reason to its due limits, he allowed it to enter the
domain of theology, and clearly assigned it its place therein.
He was the first of the schoolmen that made use of logic
in the cause of religion. This system suited the minds of
the leaders of the schools, and towards the end of the
twelfth century a new theological spirit had sprung up;
pious, learned doctors, who had always echoed the voice
of authority from their lecture chairs, were now wont to
add the *favetur ratione* to show the reasonableness or non-
reasonableness of the doctrine they were expounding.

Since the time of Abelard's teaching in the cathedral
school of Notre Dame a new movement developed among
the Paris students. The intellectual celebrity of William
of Champeaux, and his logical rival Abelard gave Paris a
world-wide renown. Students came from all countries of
Europe, from England, Ireland, and Germany, from Spain,
Normandy, and far-distant Constantinople, to attend the
lectures of the Paris teachers. This great gathering of
students led to one of the most important events of the
then intellectual world, the growth of the Paris University.

In the cathedral schools the Chancellor alone had
authority to teach, and without his permission or the
licentia docendi, as it was called, no new master could
begin to lecture. If a student wanted to become a teacher
in any of the arts, he should first assist for a given time
at the lectures of some master, and then with his master's
approval present himself to the Chancellor for permission
to teach. Without this qualification no one was considered
a competent teacher, and it was because Abelard undertook

to lecture to the students at Laon without the sanction
of the Chancellor, and without having spent the required
time in attending the lectures of his master, that a general
cry of the masters was raised against him.

During the second quarter of the twelfth century the
number of students in Paris had become so great that it was
impossible for all to attend the cathedral school; accordingly many of the most brilliant students received permission
to open separate schools, and there give lectures. This gave
rise to a number of masters, and all being engaged in the
same work of teaching, they soon formed themselves into
an organized body. But before any new master received
the *licentia docendi* from the Chancellor he had to give
an 'Inception' or 'Determination,' by which he showed
himself to be fit for the office of teacher; he was then, if.
successful, enrolled by the Chancellor into the guild of
masters, and became thereby partaker of all their privileges.
At what exact date the masters came to be formed into a
separate body is not known, but from a reference in the life
of a monk named John of the Cell, who, it is said, was
enrolled into 'the fellowship of the masters' about the
year 1170, it has been inferred that the body of masters
must have been formed into a united guild between the
years 1150-70. This also seems to be the nearest date
of the foundation of the Paris University. It was never
formally established ; it gradually developed into a separate
body which by degrees succeeded in securing for itself
certain rights and privileges. It was the gradual growth
of the acknowledged rights of the masters, and the
formalities gone through before one became a member of
their guild, that made them appear in the eyes of the
students and citizens as the lawful possessors of certain
privileges and dignities.   Louis VII., towards the end of
the twelfth century, is said to have authorized the masters
as a body to suspend lectures if any of their rights were
interfered with ; thus were they, at least, recognised by the
crown as a separate body with their own rights.

It was not till the beginning of the thirteenth century
that the privileges of the Paris students began to be

acknowledged. They had then none of those large buildings
and spacious halls that we now attach to the idea of a
University; even outside the lecture hall they had no
recognised superior. They generally lived together in
tenanted rooms, often whole streets such as the Rue du
Fouarre being in their possession. This liberty of the
students often led to much disturbance with the citizens
open riots were of frequent occurrence, and the repeated
'town and gown fights' were, as later on at Oxford, often
the scenes of bloodshed and murder. To prevent such
riots Philip Augustus, in the year 1200, granted the privilege
of exemption from civil authority to the students of the
University. The famous riot that led to granting of this
privilege began in a tavern. A German student was insulted
by the proprietor, whereupon his fellow-countrymen came in
a band to the tavern, and dragging forth the host, so severely
beat him that, in the words of a chronicler, he was 'left
half dead.' The citizens headed by the chief magistrate
rose up to seek revenge ; they attacked the hall of the
students, and an open fight followed in which several of the
students were killed. The masters appealed to the King,
and threatened, if redress was not granted they would
leave the city. Fearing lest they should depart the King
sentenced the magistrate to banishment from the city, and
threatened the offending citizens with a like punishment
except they got the injured students to intercede for them.
This the students did, but with the curious condition, so
worthy of students, that they would be allowed to flog the
offenders 'after the manner of scholars' in their schools; a
condition which the King humanely refused to have fulfilled.
When the masters and scholars were thus pacified the King
drew up a royal charter in favour of the students. Any of
them who should afterwards be arrested for an offence were
to be handed over for trial to an ecclesiastical judge, and
the magistrate on admission to his office was to take an
oath that he would respect the privileges of the masters and
scholars. At about the same period the University was
formed into a legal corporation by a Bull of Innocent III.
(himself a former master of the University), with power to

elect a representative who should maintain its rights. Thus did the Paris University gradually grow into a legal independent body governed by the society of masters, and endowed alike by Papal and Royal privileges, and from its beginning it maintained the reputation of being the chief centre of education in all Europe.   In another paper we shall speak of its material and intellectual development, of its colleges and educational course.

Contemporary with the growth of the University was the great Monastery of St. Victor, that institution which helped so much to direct the intellectual course of the Middle Ages, and it is so connected with the history of the University that an account of its foundation and spirit may not be irrelevant.   When William of Champeaux ceased to lecture' in the cathedral school of Notre Dame he withdrew from the noisy tumult of Paris, and buried himself with God in the silence of a remote wilderness.   He found hidden away among rocks and trees a little grotto which was dedicated to St. Victor, martyr, and there he resolved to pass the remainder of his life in prayer and contemplation. Some of his old pupils followed him into his retreat, and joining him in his quiet holy life, they laid the foundation of the congregation of St. Victor.   They lived a most austere life, practised long fasts, never ate meat, rarely even fish, and divided their time between prayer, study, and manual labour.   The congregation which was called Canons Regular of St. Victor was approved of by Paschal II., and richly endowed by Louis VI.   In 1113 St. Victor's was raised to an abbey, and was henceforth governed by an abbot ; in the same year William of Champeaux, its first Prior, was appointed to the see of Châlons-sur-Marne.   The Congregation which from its beginning was remarkable for men of great sanctity and learning spread with great rapidity; before the death of its second abbot, about thirty years after its foundation, it possessed over forty houses, and had given many abbots, bishops, and cardinals to the Church.

The spirit of the religious of St. Victor's was essentially comtemplative.   St. Bernard was the intimate friend of William, its founder, and it was the spirit of St. Bernard

that William determined to develop in his new retreat.   He
had grown weary of the logical displays of the Paris School;
he was much averse to the rationalistic spirit introduced by
Abelard; he loved the fathers and the Holy Scriptures,
and in the quiet study of these he resolved to spend the
remainder of his life.   Those who came to join him were
animated with a like spirit, and soon St. Victor's became
renowned for its theological learning.   But it was not
theology as treated by the new dialecticians that was taught
therein, it was more the theology of the fathers, the
theology that nourishes the soul rather than puffs up the
intellect.   St. Victor's was intended as the counter-agent
to the intellectual fever of the Paris schools, and while
reason and logic were battling for the day in Paris, contemplation and love found a home in St. Victor's.   Paris
was intellectual, active, and fond of display; St. Victor's
was likewise intellectual, but calm, recollected, and jealous
of retirement; Paris gave little to theology, or to the
Church; St. Victor's gave many great men to the Church,
and sheltered within its walls the founders and leaders of
theology in its most attractive form—mystical theology.
Hugh from Saxony, and Richard from Scotland, were
its brightest lights; they were both endowed with extraordinary intellectual power, and they both used that
power to build up a systematic course of mystical
theology.

To the modern mind mystical theology seems something
unreal, something far-fetched, and unpractical; yet of all
the sciences worthy of man's consideration there is none
that so ennobles man and raises him up from the gross
material things of this world as the science of mysticism.
The human mind never rests satisfied except in the possession of the Supreme Good; it may interest and worry itself
with the things of this world, but it will never rest fully
satisfied in their possession: God alone can satisfy man's
heart; and to lead man to possess God, as far as He can
be possessed in this life, is the primary end of mystical
theology.   By reason the human mind investigates, divides,
and concludes; it, in a way, masters and domineers over the

question put before it for consideration; but in that work it does not find peace and rest: by contemplation, which is the chief act of mysticism, the soul believes, adores, loves, and is happy. In contemplation the soul forgets the world and the senses, it rises high above reason, and with an intuitive glance it sees and possesses God, and in that vision and possession it finds true happiness.

And yet mysticism is practical. Who has such power of doing good, of influencing others, and of leading them safe through the continual struggle of daily life, as he who has his soul fixed firmly on God. Anyone who studies the history of the Catholic Church will easily see that any great work that was ever done for God was not the work of men who relied on reason alone, or on any other human agency, but that it was the work of souls of love, and prayer, of contemplation and reverence; of souls that saw God in all things, that worked for and with God in all things. A soul that is truly anxious to do good will get more strength to do it from one-half hour spent in silent prayer at the foot of the crucifix, or in holy love before the tabernacle, or in devout meditation on the pages of Holy Scripture, than from any means that human agency can supply. If there is anything wanted at the present day to help in promoting God's work it would seem to be the development of the contemplative spirit—the fixing of the soul on God alone—and then aided by His all-powerful grace, boldly and perseveringly setting to work. The rationalistic spirit is not now more powerful than it was in the Paris schools of the twelfth and thirteenth centuries, yet it was by prayer and contemplation supplemented by long patient study that it was then combatted and subdued. It was prayer and contemplation that prepared the minds of St. Bernard, St. Anselm, William of Champeaux, and the Lombard, for that deep broad grasp of truth which made them the brave upholders of the doctrines of Christianity; it was a like spirit that afterwards prepared Albert the Great, St. Thomas, and St. Bonaventure, to enter the arena with the rationalistic schoolmen, and do battle for the

Church ; and it is a like spirit that must animate those brave champions who will crush and break in pieces the many erroneous systems of modern times, and show to scientific men the harmony, beauty, and sublimity of the doctrines of our holy faith.

P. T. Burke, o.d.c.

A POSTSCRIPT TO REMARKS ON ST. CUMMAIN FOTA'S HYMN

I DESIRE to give here a few words of reply to queries touching some remarks in the article on St. Cummain Fota's hymn in honour of the Apostles, which I contributed to the May number of the I. E. Record. First, I am asked, beyond the statements of modern Irish Catholic hagiologists, what was my authority for assuming that the Cummain who composed the hymn in question was the one who, according to all accounts, was in his time educated at St. Finbarr's Seminary, Cork ? I am reminded that not only were there many forms for the name, both in Latin and Irish, but there were different persons known by it, and each indifferently under its various forms, such as Cummain, Cummian, Cumin, &c. In my article I noticed one other than Cummain Fota, namely, Cummain [Cummian or Comin] Finn, or the Fair. Some count many more, but most likely counted the different forms of the name as representing different persons.[1] Be that as it may, I have never seen it asserted or suggested, nor do I see any reason for supposing that there was any other known by the distinguishing term *Fota* [*Foda* or *Fada*], the Tall. But whether there was or not, I had sufficient

---

[1] For remarks on the different ways of writing the name, see article in May number, p. 441. Colgan (*Acta SS.*, 59, No. 6) gives a list of twenty-one named *Cumminus*, *Cumineus*, or *Cumianus* (Latin forms), and Mart. Doneg gives one of eighteen named *Cuimin*, *Cummein*, *Cuimmin* (Irish forms). All these, it will be observed, phonetically give the same word, and, as a matter of fact, several are admittedly employed to designate the same person.

authority for what I assumed, and in the way required. Passing by the statements of modern, or even comparatively modern writers, non-Catholic as well as Catholic, who refer to the subject, and who, as far as I have seen, are unanimous on the point, my immediate authority for what I assumed was the short biographical notice [mixed Latin and Irish] prefixed to the hymn itself, and by the same hand that copied it, in the Trinity College MS. '*Liber Hymnorum.*' There, having distinctly declared that it was composed by 'Cummain Fota MacFiachna' and then said something of his early life, the ancient scholiast adds that he 'afterwards studied in Cork until he became *Sai*' (or *Saoi*), that is, Doctor.[1] Now there can be no doubt that the only school 'at Cork' in which that then highest of academic degrees could have been taken, indeed the only school ever spoken of as 'at Cork,' at the time, was St. Finbarr's. And not Irish Catholic hagiologists alone take that for granted; in Smith and Ware's *Dictionary of Christian Biography* (a work mainly composed of articles contributed by English, Scotch, and Irish Protestant clergymen), in the notice of Colman Ua Clusaigh, we read: 'He was Fer-legind or Lecturer in the Theological School at Cork, and is best known as the tutor or master of St. Cumin Foda of Clonfert.'

But, again, I am asked, why assume that the latter was the Cumin (Cummain or Cummian) who wrote the famous epistle on the Paschal controversy. This having been but a

---

[1] *Sái*, sometimes written *Sai*, most commonly *Saoi*, seems to be radically the same word as *Sápiens*, our own word *Ságe*, and similar terms in many modern languages, all apparently from the old root *Sa* to *see*, or know thoroughly. It is of frequent occurrence in our oldest annals, and is often translated 'Professor,' but more generally 'Doctor.' In the library of Trinity College, Dublin, there is a MS. (classed H. 5. 30) said to be a Law Glossary compiled by the celebrated Duald MacFirbis (*circa* 650), which purports to explain 'the *seven* orders of wisdom' (or *science*). These seem to be the received 'classes' or grades in the academic course of ancient Erinn. As one passed in each of them he was known by an appropriate name; thus in order—1. *Caoydach* (one of degree —matriculated ?) 2. *Foglaintidh* (a Student). 3. *Deagibal* (Disciple—Scholar). 4. *Starridhe* (Narrator or Expounder. 5. *Foirreadlaidhe* (Lecturer or Reader in grammar, enumeration, and the courses of the year, of the sun and moon), 6. *Saoi Canoiné* (Doctor of the Canons). 7. *Druimcli* (one who has complete knowledge). *Druimcli* would thus seem to mean one who finished the academic course, was fully taught, was the *Doctus*; while *Saoi* (simply so called) would mean *Doctus satis ad esse* 'Doctor,' as such taken from the final grade, but not necessarily one engaged in teaching.

passing remark, and of little consequence to the immediate
object of my article, I might well content myself with
answering : I assumed he was so, because, having looked
the matter up, I believed he was, and I believe so still.
There is certainly not the same sort of evidence for this that
there is for the previous point, and some modern English
Protestant writers refuse to admit it.   For instance, take
the *Dictionary* I have just quoted. In the notice of Cummain
Fota (there written *Cumin Foda*), who, the writer says,
'appears to have been a man of great learning,' and was
'author of a hymn in praise of the Apostles and Evangelist,'
we read, 'Lanigan and Butler identify him with St. Cummain
who took such a prominent part in the Paschal controversy,[1]
but their supposition appears groundless.'   The animus
of the writer was previously shown by his referring to the
latter as 'the Romanizing Cummain.'   But in the following
article on this 'Romanizing Cummain' it is admitted that,
assuming him not to be the same as the author of the hymn
on the Apostles, 'there is no account of his parentage or
race;' and further on, that 'there is no account of his death.'
Moreover, no reason is given either there or elsewhere for
the assertion that the 'supposition' of Lanigan and Butler
'appears groundless.'   A reason, however, appears to be
suggested ; it is that the 'Cummain who composed the
hymn on the Apostles, and who was previously represented
as a man of great learning, as well as other ways praised,'
could not be the same as 'that Romanizing Cummain,' who
'took such a prominent part in the Paschal controversy,' and
who, it is added,[2] 'espoused the Roman as against the
national or Scotic side.'   The writer of those words forgot, if
he ever read, the verse of Cummain's hymn in praise of the
Apostles, which I quoted, commencing, '*Claviculari Petri
primi pastoris.*' No line in the Paschal letter is more
'Romanizing' than that.   Furthermore it may be observed
that the very unusual and particularly Romanizing title of

---

[1] So do many other naturally most reliable authorities on such a subject.
See Dr. Healy's *Insula Sanctorum et Doctorum*, art. on 'School of Clonfert,'
where the supposition of Lanigan and Butler is maintained throughout.
[2] Page 723.

clavicularis is given to St. Peter in this same Paschal letter. Then, surely it might be said there is no *a priori* reason for assuming, rather every such reason for denying, that throughout this crisis of our national Church's life any ecclesiastic in the land would have proved more 'Romanizing' than one trained in the school of St. Finbarr, whose own teacher, MacCuirp, was a Roman student, taught by St. Gregory the Great;[1] who moreover, when founding his school at Cork, if ancient accounts of him be true, went to thoroughly Romanize his spirit in the City of Rome, most difficult of access, for various reasons, as that city was for a traveller from Ireland in those days.[2]

For a well-edited text of this Paschal letter, having quoted Migne's Collection of the fathers, I may add, it is there ascribed to Cominus Longus (that is Cummian Foda or the Tall), as distinguished from Cominus Albus (Finn or the Fair). As to the Paschal letter itself, undoubtedly the text as we have it exhibits faults, both of matter and form. With regard to these, I would only remark that a Latin text, written in the seventh century, and in a country situated as Ireland then was in regard to the Continent of Europe, for a document moreover on such a complex subject, at once theological, liturgical, historical, linguistic, and semi-scientific, neither matter or form could fairly be criticized from the standpoint of a savant living at the latter end of the nineteenth century; even supposing its

---

[1] In one of the ancient MS. lives of St. Finbarr (Codex Marsh), this 'Sanctus Maccuirp' is spoken of as 'sanctissimus vir et sapiens multum discipulusque Sancti Gregorii Romae, et magister Sancti Barri.' Referring to the same in a previous part of the life we read : 'Cum autem (S. Barrus) pervenisset ad ætatem maturam venit ex Roma sapiens vir et sanctus qui fuit alumpnus Sancti Gregorii papae et peritus in regulis ecclesiasticis.   Illi sancti seniores magistri Sancti Barri miserunt eum ad illum ut disceret et legeret apud ipsum.''   Another apparently more recently written MS. life (Codex Bodl.) in much better Latin, thus, gives the fact : ' Eo tempore venit quidem sanctus de urbe Roma, discipulus Sancti Gregorii papae ad Hiberniam, qui in divinus scripturis sufficienter erat instructus, cujus formam ut audirent, nutriores Sancti Finbarri dixerunt ei, ut ad illum virum in Sacra scriptura expertum propararet qui aitem ardentis sui ingenii, tamquam in fonte de novo scaturiente, plenius ipse refrigeraret.'
[2] ' Alio tempore posteasquam limina visitavit apostolica, redeundo ad propria declinavit ad Sanctum David.'   (*Id. Codex Bodl.*)

existing text to be pure, which in several places that of this
epistle clearly is not.

One other observation regarding it I wish to notice as
being one which is often made by way of comment on the
character of its author as a man and a priest. This is that
certain passages seem strangely rude to the eminent ecclesiastic to whom it was addressed, as well as to the many
learned and holy men throughout the country, who still
maintained what has been since honoured with the qualification of 'the national side of the Paschal controversy.'
Certainly, some passages, and these the ones generally quoted,
if read apart from the rest, and according to our modern
notions of propriety, would at first sight seem 'strangely
rude' in the sense objected. Reading these, however, in the
light of the whole and of the known character of the writer
as of his place and time, their apparent rudeness will be seen
to be only that of strength of expression ; that natural to the
writing of a strong man, strong in faith and mind-power
and conscious fulness of knowledge touching the subject he
was treating; strong, above all, in consciousness of the
momentous character of its final issue for Church and country,
and the right of the side he had taken. In effect, that
meant whole-hearted adhesion to the centre of Christian
unity, in spite of all manner of adverse natural tendencies,
racial sympathies, national prejudices, strong party-feeling
as well as family interests, and, consequently, many forms
of persevering local opposition. It meant taking a stand
before the country and its people elsewhere that some
of the best men of the day could not get themselves to take,
and from which those who had been reasoned into taking it
had been afterwards induced to recede, but which every
ecclesiastic in Ireland and every Irish ecclesiastic abroad felt
bound to take up later on. In short, for Church and country,
at the time, St. Cummain felt called to take an unpopular
stand, and he took it ; to speak unpopular truths, and he
spoke them. Ever since his day Christendom has felt the
force of those outspoken truths, of that in particular which
is the term-thought of his Paschal Epistle—*Quid pravius
sentiri potest de Ecclesia Matre quam si dicamus; Roma errat,*

Hierosolyma errat, Antiochia errat, totus mundus errat, soli tantum Scoti et Britones rectum sapiunt[1]*?* In that question (Irish fashion) is the one all-satisfying answer to sectaries be their sectarianism political, social, or religious. Thus, assuming the author of *Celebra Juda*, that is St. Cummain Fota to have been the writer of this famous epistle, it seems to me that, not merely though he was, but because he was so, Cork has reason to be proud of the 'Romanizing' graduate St. Finbarr's Seminary gave to Ireland nearly thirteen hundred years ago.

Still, as I have said, whether the Cummain who wrote this epistle, and throughout figured so prominently in the Paschal controversy, was or was not the Cummain who wrote the hymn I noticed, but indirectly affects my main assumption as to the latter's character. This was simply that being Cummain *Fota* he was the 'Cummain' educated at St. Finbarr's Seminary, Cork, under St. Colman O'Clusaigh, and so was the learned and holy prelate likened to St. Gregory the Great, by that same St. Colman, in the Rann or commemorative poem which is given as by him in the Annals of the Four Masters. Nor should such a comparison be deemed but the passing compliment of an old poet to the memory of a distinguished pupil. It was acknowledged at the time as his country's verdict, and as such remained. In a popular list of parallelisms or ideal associations of characteristics between the saints of Ireland and those o the Universa Church, a list drawn up about a century after St. Cummain's death, his name appears facing that of St. Gregory the Great as being the name of one wholly like him in life and manner— *unius vitæ et moris.*

Touching my textual treatment of his Alleluiatic Hymn, a learned correspondent while agreeing with my 'conclusions' in regard to it, maintained it was a mistake not to have

---

[1] In his, on the whole, excellent work, entitled *The Liturgy and Ritual of the Celtic Church* (Oxford, 1881), Warren sneers at those famous words from St. Cummain's Paschal Epistle as a parody on 'the Irish position.' Other modern English writers treat them more contemptuously still. Heretical hisses of the sort from Oxford and Cambridge houses, and like places, at the end of the nineteenth century, serve well to accentuate the applause of the Christian schools of the world for over a thousand years.

given the whole of the text, ' so few I. E. RECORD readers,' he observed, ' know it save in name.' It would have been very easy to have given the whole, but, besides that I considered this would be claiming a great deal too much space for my part in the month's number, the immediate object of my article was to stimulate rather than satisfy the reader's interest in its subject. I took care, however, to note that the full text of the hymn is printed in Dr. Todd's annotated issue, or rather part-issue of the Trinity College *Liber Hymnorum.* I here note, in addition, I understand that a complete issue of it, most carefully edited and collated with the Franciscan Codex is in active preparation and will soon be published.

At the end of my article, when comparing St. Cummain's with the other oldest alleluiatic hymns at present known to hymnologists, I observed, '*Celebra Juda* is at present to be seen in Dublin MSS. of the ninth or tenth, or, at latest, eleventh century, and is there given, not as an anonymous production or one of uncertain age, but is distinctly ascribed to an author known to have been born towards the end of the sixth century, an inscription that independent data of traditional and documentary evidence fully confirm.' Now, setting aside what may be called data of tradition, I am asked, is there any documentary evidence of the kind in question, previous to or about the *ninth century* among generally accessible MSS. at present existing in Ireland? There is. It is found in the hitherto unprinted MS. known as the *Book of Mulling*, in part a liturgical Codex like the *Book of Dimma*, and with it, preserved in the Library of Trinity College, Dublin. Both these codices are highly interesting from many points of view, theological as well as archæo-logical. Yet they have been little studied; from the Irish Catholic standpoint, scarcely at all. In Gilbert's list of our national MSS., the one I have here to do with is given as ' ascribed to Mulling, Bishop of Ferns, who died A.D. 697 :' thus within the seventh century and about forty years after the death of St. Cummain Fota. This *Book of Mulling*, Gilbert notes, ' is a copy of the four Gospels in Latin with formulary for visitation of the sick.' It has something

more, something which Irish Catholic archæologists will,
I think, yet find the most interesting page in the book.
This comes immediately after the Gospel of St. John and,
it should be particularly noted, unlike the 'formulary for
visitation of the sick,' is evidently written by the same hand
that wrote the four Gospels. If there be an older part,
therefore, it belongs to that.   Upon the page, over a very
curious liturgical synopsis, there is what appears to be the
Ordo of a daily office or form of night and morning prayer.
On the first line we now find only the letters *Al* : which we
should naturally say stand for *Alleluia* as opening of the
Office or 'Invitatory.' Then, among the items prescribed
after the *Magnificat* and *Benedictus*, we find a portion of
the Hymn of Secundinus to St. Patrick, and, after that,
the last part of the Alleluiatic form of St. Cummain Fota.
I should like to say something more about this interesting
most ancient *Officium laudis* of our fathers in the faith.
But here I must stop, content with having at least indicated
original sources of information for that and the other points
I touched on.

T. J. O'MAHONY, D.D.

Notes and Queries

THEOLOGY

APPLICATION OF A MASS FOR WHICH A 'HONORARIUM' HAS BEEN RECEIVED

REV. DEAR SIR,—Having received a *honorarium* to say Mass for A. B. deceased, I offered a Mass for A. B. and all the souls in purgatory. Have I satisfied my obligation ? . . .

C. C.

Viewed in the abstract, the solution of the question depends on the issue of the well-known controversy, regarding the infinite or indefinite efficacy of the fruits of the Mass. Our correspondent, as he gives us to understand, believes that the fruits of the Mass are infinite, and that, therefore, a Mass offered, say, for a thousand persons avails as much for each, as if it had been offered for him alone. No doubt, our correspondent has a right to his speculative opinion. We cannot, however, share his view. To our mind, the practice of the Church has always seemed a conclusive argument against the opinion which he adopts. For, in consistency, he should hold that *every* Mass *ought* to be offered for *all* to whom it may be validly and lawfully applied. And yet, the Church not merely tolerates, but recommends that Masses should be offered for individuals. Surely, this would be senseless and reprehensible, if the opinion of our correspondent were true. The individual for whom the Mass is specially offered would gain nothing additional, while all the world beside would be the poorer, owing to the restricted application: and the bounty of Christ, which might be extended to all, though the celebration of each Mass, would be narrowed down to relieving the wants of a single individual. And, we may ask, in passing, why our correspondent restricts the application of the Mass to 'the souls in purgatory.' Why are the living excluded, if they may be included without detracting from the benefits accruing to the dead ?

But even though the speculative probability of our correspondent's opinion were admitted, he would not be justified in attempting to satisfy his obligation towards A. B. by offering Mass for A. B. and all the souls in purgatory. His obligation *ex stipendio* is a certain obligation binding in justice, and it is not to be satisfied by what, at best, is a return of *doubtful* value.

In practice, our correspondent can satisfy at once his obligations and his commendable zeal and charity by means of a secondary intention.

In the case proposed, he should offer the Mass, in the first instance, for A.B. But, by a secondary intention, he might offer the Mass for all the faithful departed, in so far as this secondary intention would not interfere with the rights of A. B. or the intention of the person who gave the honorarium. In this way he can, at the same time, avail himself, to the full, of the advantages of his own opinion, without incurring the censure of those who think differently, or endangering the fulfilment of his obligations.

ABSOLUTION FROM HERESY

Rev. Dear Sir,—A penitent accuses himself of formal heresy. Can I absolve without special faculties? The sin of heresy was purely internal. Some to whom I have referred the matter are doubtful. An answer in the I. E. Record will oblige.

CHAPLAIN.

If the sin was internal, *i.e.*, externated neither by word or act, you can certainly absolve. No censure or reservation attaches to a sin purely internal. Hence internal heresy can be absolved by any confessor.

If the heresy were externally manifested by any grievously sinful word or act, your penitent would, of course, be subject to an excommunication specially reserved to the Holy See.

D. MANNIX.

LITURGY

REV. DEAR SIR,—Will you kindly answer the following in the
next issue of the I. E. RECORD. (1) What promulgation is necessary that the decrees of Sacred Congregation be binding on all the
faithful? (2) Some months ago I saw by the I. E. RECORD it
was decreed at Rome that the prayers of a private Requiem
Mass be said in a different order to that in which they occur in
the Missal, *i.e.*, that first prayer be for the deceased for whom
Mass is said, the second prayer *ad libitum*, and the third
Fidelium Deus omnium Conditor. (a) Are all priests bound to
this order? (b) Is a priest justified in adhering to the old method,
disregarding the decree till it is formally promulgated by *his*
bishop? (c) What of those priests who do not get I. E. RECORD,
and are in ignorance of the existence of such a decree?

SACERDOS.

Decrees of the Congregation of Rites are either *general*
or *particular.* The former are addressed to the Universal
Church, and bind everywhere; the latter are addressed only
to particular churches or countries, and are usually founded
on a petition sent to the Congregation in the name of the
bishop of a particular diocese, or of the hierarchy of a particular
country. Decrees of the latter kind doubtless require some
kind of promulgation, but as the decree about which our
correspondent inquires does not belong to this class, it is
unnecessary to discuss here what special form of publication
or promulgation particular decrees require. The decree
regarding the order of the prayers in a Requiem Mass is a
general decree. *Decretum Generale* is its heading, as a
reference to the *Ordo* for this year will show,[1] and consequently the rules applying to the promulgation of general
decrees apply to this one.

Now general decrees of the Congregation of Rites require
no special promulgation. They bind *in actu primo* from the

[1] Introduction, p. xxxii.

moment that the authentic copy has been signed by the Prefect and Secretary of the Congregation ; and *in actu secundo* in the case of each individual, as soon as he becomes aware, through an authentic source, of the purport of the decree. This is the general teaching of theologians, and is thus expressed by De Herdt :— [1]

' Ut autem decreta et responsiones quae a S. R. C. datae sunt, tamquam formaliter editae habendae sint, ac si ab ipso Summo Pontifice immediate promanarent, non requiritur ut sint vel Romae, vel ab Episcopis in suis dioecesibus promulgatae, sed sufficit quod sint subscriptae a S. R. C. Praefecto et Secretario, ac ejusdem sigillo munita.

This passage, which is merely a transcript of a decree issued by the Congregation of Rites, on April 8th, 1854,[2] shows clearly that no formal promulgation is required, in order that general decrees of the Congregation of Rites should have the force of papal laws.

2. (*a*) All priests following the Roman rite are bound to say the prayers in a Requiem Mass in the order prescribed by the decree of June 30th, 1896. Ignorance, of course, excuses from this obligation on the same conditions on which it excuses from other obligations ; but the only ignorance that avails is ignorance of the existence of this decree. Ignorance regarding its promulgation cannot excuse him who knows of its existence.

(*b*) From what has been already said it follows that a priest who is aware of the publication of this decree is no longer justified in saying the prayers in a Requiem Mass according to the old order. No formal promulgation by the bishop is required, as we have seen, and consequently the decree binds *in actu secundo* from the moment its terms are learned from any authentic source.

(*c*) We pity the priests who do not get the I. E. RECORD, and we feel sure they are ignorant of a great many other things besides the present order of reciting the prayers in a

---

[1] *Praxis Liturg.*, tom. i., n. 8.
[2] See Gardellini, in 5066-5202.

Requiem Mass. Ignorance in matters of this kind in a priest who does not subscribe for the I. E. RECORD, might almost be described as *ignorantia affectata*, and consequently not an excusing cause ; but there is another publication for which all Irish secular priests are supposed to subscribe, and in which all decrees bearing on the recital of the Divine Office and the celebration of Holy Mass are published. This is the *Ordo*, in the copy of which for last year our correspondent and all else concerned will find at a place already indicated the decree in question. The *Ordo* has the formal sanction of the archbishops and bishops of Ireland, and even though certain decrees did require episcopal promulgation, it would, we think, be sufficient to have them published in its pages.

D. O'LOAN.

CORRESPONDENCE

THE ANNUAL DIOCESAN MASS FOR DECEASED PRELATES

REV. DEAR SIR,—According to a decision given in the last number of the I. E. RECORD, by a very accurate rubricist, the above Mass cannot be said on a festival of a double rite. This decision does not seem consistent with a liberal and fair interpretation of the late legislation in favour of Masses for the dead. The offices of a double rite had so multiplied latterly, and thus shut out semi-doubles that the Holy Father, in June, 1896, gave increased facilities for saying private Requiem Masses on festivals of a double rite; and in the course of the year the Sacred Congregation of Rites issued a decree in regard to the prayers and the use of the Sequence to be employed in the four different Requiem Masses in the Missal. While the three first are privileged—those (1) for All Souls' day—(2) for the death, burial, the third and seventh day—(3) for the anniversary—the fourth Mass or "daily" had and has not as such the privilege of superseding a double rite.

The general decree, S. C. R., issued last year, is given under five sections, as may be seen in the introductory matter in the Latin *Ordo.* (i) The first section decreed that only one prayer was to be said in Masses private and solemn on the following days:—' Commemoratione omnium Fidelium Defunctorum, die et pro die obitus seu depositionis, atque etiam in Missis Cantatis et lectis, permittente ritu, diebus iii., vii., xxx., et die anniversaria, necnon quandocunque pro defunctis Missa solemniter celebratur, nempe sub ritu qui duplici respondeat in officio quod recitatur post acceptum nuntium de alicujus obitu, et in *anniversariis late sumptis.*'

(ii) The second section dealing with the *Missis quotidianis quibuscunque* requires that three prayers should be said, which are described in this and the following sections according to the person or persons to be commemorated.

The concluding section in reference to the *Dies Iræ* runs thus:—

' V. Quod denique ad sequentiam attinet, semper illam esse dicendam in quibusvis Cantatis Missis uti etiam in lectis quæ diebus *ut supra* privilegiatis fiunt, &c.'

Now the *anniversariis late sumptis* as distinguished from the real, strict *anniversaria die*, mentioned in the (1) section, comprehend our diocesan anniversaries, and, as the I. E. RECORD rubricist states, ' have special reference' to them ; and these are privileged according to the decree in Section V. : therefore Mass can be said on them on a day of a double rite.

The position taken by the writer in the I. E. RECORD has led him to say that the Mass said on the *anniversariis late sumptis* is not on a privileged day, though the decree says otherwise— *diebus ut supra* (sec. i) *privilegiatis.*

I may mention that the privileged days mentioned in sec. i. are such as found in the Rubrics of Missal, Sec. V., No. 3, except the *anniversaria late sumpta;* and I am not at all surprised at this addition. For scores of pages are devoted by Gardellini to the petitions presented to the Sacred Congregation during hundreds of years by private individuals and religious bodies to be allowed to treat the *anniversaria late sumpta* as privileged. The favour was granted almost always as a grace, and not as a right. During some time there was an annual commemoration of the deceased of the three Franciscan Orders on a double, but on a fixed day ; and it was allowed on the supposition that it was equivalent to a commemoration of all the faithful departed.

SYLVESTER MALONE.

THE ANCIENT IRISH CHURCH

REV. DEAR SIR,—In view of the ' larger volume intended (p. 163), it becomes incumbent to set forth some of the defects which materially mar *The Ancient Irish Church as a Witness to Catholic Doctrine.* That a compilation demands something more than mere industry,—some such acquaintance with the subject as shall ensure due discrimination of the material, is a proposition which needs no proof. This minimum is all the more necessary when one deals controversially with disputed topics ; defective treatment must needs damage the most excellent cause.

Chief among the sources of the work is the Bobbio Missal, to which an appendix (p. 225-8) is devoted. The Missal, it is admitted, ' is most likely Gallican ;' but, ' it would not be extraordinary if some of the native clergy transcribed and used a Gallican Missal, especially having regard to the connection anciently existing between Gaul and this country' (p. 227). Reasoning of this kind is of ominous import respecting the state of Sacred Archæology amongst us. Having regard to the number of Irish missionaries and pilgrims who went over sea, and the recognition there accorded to the superiority of their caligraphy, the question whether any of the numerous works in Scottic hand preserved abroad was executed for native or foreign use has to be decided without reference to the script. To assume offhand that every such document was employed in Ireland, or represents an Irish state of things, would lead to some startling conclusions. Now, to all who have studied the monuments of early Western Liturgy, the omissions and insertions of the Bobbio Missal, taken in connection with the omissions and insertions of the Stowe and St. Gall Missals, are evidence conclusive that the first-named was drawn up for a church in France, most probably in Burgundy. All the citations therefrom (and they total pretty large) must accordingly be omitted as irrelevant.

Similarly, as regards the Penitential 'attached to the Missal' (p. 128). No doubt, the compiler can plead that, according to one of his 'works quoted,' 'of its forty-seven canons there is not one that is not purely Irish' (Moran: *Essays*, &c., p. 285). But he could have learned from another work on his list (*On the Stowe Missal*, Trans. R.I.A., xxvii., p. 152) that the sole proof of this sweeping assertion was drawn from transforming an *old woman* into a *village !*

Equal importance is assigned to the Penitential of Cummian, amongst the quotations from which are fifteen consecutive items, translation and text (pp. 20-22 ; 228-30), to prove, 'that in the system of early Irish Christianity there was no latitude for any exhibition of the private spirit' (p. 22). But the fact has been overlooked that, according to Wasserschleben, whose edition is used, every indication denotes decisively that Cummian wrote his work not in his native but in another land, and drew from Irish, Anglo-Saxon, and Frankish Penitentials (*Bussordnungen*, &c., pp. 53, 65). This being so, ordinary prudence would suggest what has, unfortunately, not been done here,—to verify the origin before adopting the citation. Nor, in the case of the fifteen enactments in question, would that have postulated any special critical acumen. For, not to mention that every item is traced by Wasserschleben to the source, in the well-known passage which the compiler could scarce fail to quote, St. Columbanus boasts that Ireland produced no heretic. That brings us to the close of the sixth century. Assuredly then it strains credulity (seeing that Penitentials deal with actual, not supposed, cases) that in the century next ensuing Ireland produced heretical congregations, heretical priests; abbots and bishops favouring heresy ; heretics whose relics were venerated as those of saints, and finally Quartodecimans.

To the same lack of discrimination is due a still more aggravated libel on the morality of the Ancient Irish Church. ' Among the St. Gall MSS. there is an ancient Irish Order for the Administration of Penance (*Ordo ad Poenitentiam dandam*),' in which, after questioning the penitent as to belief in the Trinity, Unity, Resurrection, future reward and punishment, and forgiveness of injuries, the priest is directed to inquire diligently whether he is incestuous, and if he is, not to give him penance, unless he be willing to put away the incests; if willing, to hear his confession (p. 107). The ' Ancient Irish Order ' is, however, purely Anglo-Saxon ! In two Penitentials of that nationality which the compiler had under his hand (*Bussordnungen*, &c., pp. 252, 319-50), two *Ordines* are given : both containing the title, queries, and rubrics ; the latter, the title, queries, rubrics, and prayers, of the ' Irish ' *Ordo*. And, to anticipate the objection that the last-mentioned was the source of the two first, the proof can be completed from a classic familiar to the world of workers for more than two centuries, but not found amongst the works here 'quoted,' namely, the *Commentarius Historicus de disciplina* . . *Poenitentiae* of Morinus (Brussels, 1685).

Ordo of St. Gall (*The Ancient Irish Church*, &c., p. 108).

Et si homo ingeniosus est, da ei consilium ut veniat tempore statuto ad te aut ad alium sacerdotem in Coena Domini, et reconciliaretur [-lietur] sic[ut] in Sacramentario continetur. Quicquid manens in corpore consecutus non fuerit (h.e. reconciliatio), exutus carne consequi non poterit.

Si vero minus intelligens [fuerit], quod ipse non intelligit, in uno statu reconciliare eum potes, dicendo.

Oremus.

Presta, quaesumus [etc.]   Si infirmus est homo, statim reconciliare eum debes.

Ordo of Penitential of Egbert (abp. of York, 734-766 : Morinus, Ap. p. 19A).

Tunc expleta poenitentia, si homo intelligibilis est, veniat ad sacerdotem et reconciliet eum. Si vero simplicem vel brutum eum intellexeris, statim reconcilia eum, ita dicendo.

Oratio.

Praesta, quaesumus [etc.]

Alia.

Omnipotens [etc.]

Si tempus ut [? tibi] vacet, dic illas alias : si non, istae duae sufficiant, et omni tempore quando ad aegrotum venerit [-is], statim reconcilia eum dicendo.

[Four Prayers.]

It only remains to add that the ' Sacramentary ' ceremonial for Holy Thursday is given in Egbert's Penitential, and contains the Praesta quaesumus (*ib.*, p. 19, 20).

The Latin excerpts do not afford much latitude for misunderstanding. Withal, one page (89) contains the following :—(1) The Memento of the living in the Stowe Missal has pro . . . actuum emendatione eorum. This is amended by [? nostrorum], ' for . . . the amendment of our actions.' A single letter, however, supplies the correction : [r]eorum, culpable (actions). (2) The same Memento has uti eos in aeterna summae lucis quietae pietas divina suscipiat, ' that the divine piety may receive them into the eternal regions of sovereign light and peace.' Here, notwithstanding ' classified examples ' of, and references to authorities on, Irish-Latin orthography (p. 226), we have failure to perceive a commonplace peculiarity,—the *e* sound denoted by *ac*. Read *in eterna quiete*, into eternal rest. (3) The Stowe Offertory has Sacrificium tibi celebrandum placatus intende, ' graciously dispose the Sacrifice to be celebrated to Thee.' But, if one must play the pedagogue, the regimen is the same as in the Vesper hymn of Christmas :—

> Intende quas fundunt preces
> Tui per orbem servuli.

The meaning is, graciously regard the Sacrifice to be celebrated to Thee.

The Tripartite Life of St. Patrick reads (with reference to bishop Cairell of Taunagh, Co. Sligo) quem ordinaverunt episcop Patricii .i. Bronus et Biteus (Rolls' ed., p. 98). This, it is suggested, could be made to give three bishops at the consecration, ' by a very slight and apparently necessary emendation, thus :—quem ordinaverunt episcopi l'atricius Bronus et Biteus ' (p. 118). But the corresponding passage in the Book of Armagh has ordinaverunt episcopi Patricii, id est, Bronus et Bietheus (Rolls' ed., p. 314).

The testimonies given in Irish, owing to the retention of the arbitrary scribal joining and disjoining of words and the comparatively numerous errors of the press (one page, 231, has as many as thirty), will scarcely afford ' special satisfaction ' (p. xiii.) to scholars.

The ' ancient treatise, in Irish, preserved in the *Leabhar Breac* ' (p. 18), it is well known, is a Latin original, the sentences of which are respectively followed by versions, sometimes literal, sometimes paraphrastic, in the native tongue. In the treatise, the Scriptures, we learn ' are compared to food . . . But, as food, this simile continues, is innutritious for the body when not prepared for digestion by the teeth, so the Scriptures are unwholesome for the soul, dissociated from the expositions of the Doctors ' (ib.).

The original (not given by the compiler) is : Sicut enim sine dentibus caput egrotat, ita [hita, MS.] sine doctoribus ecclesia [ecclesiae, MS.] non valet. This is expanded thus in the Irish. Since the head is useless without its teeth, by which the foods are minced for the members, similarly, the Church is useless without her learned, who mince the pure mysteries of the Holy Scripture for the faithful (L. B. 196 b, ll. 15-19.)[1]

Yet, so confident is the compiler (p. 135), that he does not hesitate to impute folly to O'Donovan for not taking ' in the metaphorical sense' a word which the most elementary knowledge of Irish shows was employed with the primary meaning.

Finally, the statements regarding the Paschal question may, perhaps, lay claim to the doubtful merit of originality. The Quartodecimans ' kept Easter on the 14th day of March, no matter what day of the week it fell upon' (p. 22.) ! That this is no mere lapse, is shown by the following. ' In strictness, the Irish were not Quartodecimans. They did not celebrate Easter on the 14th March, unless that day fell on a Sunday" (p. 230) ! Now, with respect to the Quartodecimans, 14th day signifies the *14th day of the Jewish lunar month, Nisan,*—a date which, it is well known, did not fall on March 14,[2] but fell either in the second half of March, or in April. The Irish, on the other hand, kept Easter (not on March 14, but) on the 14th of the Paschal moon, provided the Sunday on which it fell was not earlier than March 25, inclusive, their earliest Paschal date.

The foregoing, *though not exhaustive,* are, it is submitted, amply sufficient to justify the Horatian counsel relative to the proposed enlarged edition,—nonum prematur in annum.

B. MAC CARTHY.

---

[1] Uair nach tarba in ccnd con n dcnta, ho minigther na biada do na ballaib, is amal sin nach tarba in cclais ccn a hccnaido[-iu] minigit glanrúin na Screptra noibe do na hiresechu[-hib].

[2] One of the ' works quoted' (Leabhar Breac, p. 85) states that Nisan began with the April moon. (The lunar month is named from the solar in which it ends.) Allowing for the present purpose that the April moon had 30 (not 29) days, the earliest Nisan would thus begin on March 3 ; Nisan 14 would fall on March 16.

DOCUMENTS

ENCYCLICAL OF HIS HOLINESS LEO XIII.

EX ACTIS LEONIS XIII. ET E SECRETAR. BREVIUM
SANCTISSIMI DOMINI NOSTRI LEONIS DIVINA PROVIDENTIA PAPAE XIII.
EPISTOLA ENCYCLICA AD PATRIARCHAS, PRIMATES, ARCHI-
EPISCOPOS, EPISCOPOS, ALIOSQUE LOCORUM ORDINARIOS PACEM
ET COMMUNIONEM CUM APOSTOLICA SEDE HABENTES.

VENERABILIBUS FRATRIBUS PATRIARCHIS, PRIMATIBUS, ARCHIEPIS-
COPIS, EPISCOPIS, ALIISQUE LOCORUM ORDINARIIS PACEM ET
COMMUNIONEM CUM APOSTOLICA SEDE HABENTIBUS

LEO PP. XIII.

VENERABILES FRATRES SALUTEM ET APOSTOLICAM BENEDICTIONEM

Divinum illud munus 'quod humani generis causa a Patre
acceptum Iesus Christus sanctissime obiit, sicut eo tamquam ad
ultimum spectat, ut homines vitae compotes fiant in sempiterna
gloria beatae, ita huc proxime attinet per saeculi cursum, ut
divinae gratiae habeant colantque vitam, quae tandem in vitam
floreat coelestem. Quamobrem omnes ad unum homines cuiusvis
nationis et linguae Redemptor ipse invitare ad sinum Ecclesiae
suae summa benignitate non cessat : ' Venite ad me omnes ;
Ego sum vita ; Ego sum pastor bonus.' Hic tamen, secundum
altissima quaedam consilia, eiusmodi munus noluit quidem per
se in terris usquequaque conficere et explere ; verum quod ipse
traditum a Patre habuerat, idem Spiritui Sancto tradidit per-
ficiendum. Atque iucunda memoratu ea sunt quae Christus,
paulo ante quam terras relinqueret, in discipulorum coetu affirmavit : ' Expedit vobis ut ego vadam : si enim non abiero, Paraclitus non veniet ad vos ; si autem abiero, mittam eum ad vos.' [1]
Haec enim affirmans, causam discessus sui reditusque ad Patrem
eam potissimum attulit, utilitatem ipsis alumnis suis profecto
accessuram ab adventu Spiritus Sancti : quem quidem una mons-
travit, a se aeque mitti atque adeo procedere sicut a Patre,
eumdemque fore qui opus a semetipso in mortali vita exactum,
deprecator, consolator, praeceptor, absolveret. Multiplici nempe
virtuti huiusce Spiritus, qui in procreatione mundi ' ornavit

---

[1] Ioann. xvi. 7.

coelos '' et ' replevit orbem terrarum,'[2] in eiusdem redemptione-
perfectio operis erat providentissime reservata.   Iamvero Christi
Servatoris, qui princeps pastorum est et episcopus animarum nostra-
rum, exempla Nos imitari, ipso opitulante, continenter studuimus;
religiose insistentes idem ipsius munus, Apostolis creditum in
primisque Petro, ' cuius etiam dignitas in indigno herede non
deficit.'[3]   Hoc adducti consilio, quaecumque in perfunctione iam
diuturna summi pontificatus aggressi sumus instandoque perse-
quimur, ea conspirare voluimus ad duo praecipue.   Primum, ad
rationem vitae christianae in societate civili et domestica, in
principibus et in populis instaurandam ; propterea quod nequaquam nisi a Christo vera in omnes profluat vita.   Tum ad eorum
fovendam reconciliationem qui ab Ecclesia catholica vel fide vel
obsequio dissident ; quum haec eiusdem Christi certissima sit
voluntas, ut ii omnes in unico Ovili suo sub Pastore uno censean-
tur.   Nunc autem, quum humani exitus adventantem diem
conspicimus, omnino permovemur animo ut Apostolatus Nostri
operam, qualemcumque adhuc deduximus, Spiritui Sancto, qui
Amor vivificans est, ad maturitatem fecunditatemque commen-
demus.   Propositum Nostrum quo melius uberiusque eveniat,
deliberatum habemus alloqui vos per sollemnia proxima sacrae
Pentecostes de praesentia et virtute mirifica eiusdem Spiritus :
quantopere nimirum et in tota Ecclesia et in singulorum animis
ipse agat efficiatque praeclara copia charismatum supernorum.
Inde fiat, quod vehementer optamus, ut fides excitetur vigeatque
in animis de mysterio Trinitatis augustae, ac praesertim pietas
augeatur et caleat erga divinum Spiritum, cui plurimum omnes
acceptum referre debent quotquot vias veritatis et iustitiae sec-
tantur: nam, quemadmodum Basilius praedicavit, ' Dispensationes
circa hominem, quae factae sunt a magno Deo et Servatore
nostro Iesu Christo iuxta bonitatem Dei, quis neget per Spiritus
gratiam esse adimpletas ? '[4]

Antequam rem aggredimur institutam, nonnulla de Triadis
sacrosanctae mysterio placet atque utile erit attingere.   Hoc
namque ' substantia novi testamenti ' a sacris doctoribus apel-
latur, mysterium videlicet unum omnium maximum, quippe
omnium veluti fons et caput; cuius cognoscendi contemplandique
causa, in coelo angeli, in terris homines procreati sunt, quod, in
testamento veteri adumbratum, ut manifestius doceret, ab angelis

---

[1] Iob xxvi. 13.   [3] S. Leo M., *ser. II. in annit. ass. suae.*
[2] Sap. i. 7.   [4] *De Spiritu Sancto,* c. xvi., n. 39.

ad homines Deus ipse descendit : ' Deum nemo vidit unquam :
Unigenitus Filius qui est in sinu Patris, ipse enarravit.'[1] Quis-
quis igitur de Trinitate scribit aut dicit, illud ob oculos teneat
oportet quod prudenter monet Angelicus : ' Quum de Trinitate
loquimur cum cautela et modestia est agendum, quia, ut Augustinus
dicit, nec periculosius alicubi erratur, nec laboriosius aliquid
quaeritur, nec fructuosius aliquid invenitur.'[2] Periculum autem
ex eo fit, ne in fide aut in cultu vel divinae inter se Personae
confundantur, vel unica in ipsis natura separetur ; nam, ' fides
catholica haec est, ut unum Deum in Trinitate et Trinitatem in
unitate veneremur.' Quare Innocentius XII. decessor Noster,
sollemnia quaedam honori Patris propria postulantibus omnino
negavit. Quod si singula Incarnati Verbi mysteria certis diebus
festis celebrantur, non tamen proprio ullo festo celebratur Verbum,
secundum divinam tantum naturam : atque ipsa etiam Pentecostes
sollemnia non ideo inducta antiquitus sunt, ut Spiritus Sanctus
per se simpliciter honoraretur, sed ut eiusdem recoleretur adventus
sive externa missio. Quae quidem omnia sapienti consilio sancita
sunt, ne quis forte a distinguendis Personis ad divinam essentiam
distinguendam prolaberetur. Quin etiam Ecclesia ut in fidei
integritate filios contineret, sanctissimae Trinitatis festum insti-
tuit, quod Ioannes XXII. deinde iussit ubique agendum ; tum
altaria et templa eidem dicari permisit ; atque Ordinem religiosorum captivis redimendis, qui Trinitati devotus omnino est
ciusque titulo gaudet, non sine coelesti nutu rite comprobavit.
Multaque rem confirmant. Cultus enim qui sanctis Coelitibus
atque Angelis, qui Virgini Deiparae, qui Christo tribuitur, is
demum in Trinitatem ipsam redundat et desinit. In precationibus
quae uni Personae adhibentur, item de ceteris mentio est ; in
forma supplicationum, singulis quidem Personis seorsum invocatis,
communis earum invocatio subiicitur ; psalmis hymnisque idem
omnibus praeconium accedit in Patrem et Filium et Spiritum
Sanctum ; benedictiones, ritus, sacramenta comitatur aut con-
ficit sanctae imploratio Trinitatis. Atque haec ipsa iampridem
Apostolus praemonuerat in ea sententia ; ' Quoniam ex ipso et
per ipsum et in ipso sunt omnia ; ipsi gloria in saecula ;'[3] inde
significans Personarum trinitatem, hinc unitatem affirmans naturae quae quum una eademque singulis sit Personis, ideo singulis,
tamquam uni eidemque Deo, aeterna aeque maiestatis gloria

---

[1] Ioann. i. 18.
[2] *Summa. th.* 1ª, q. xxxi. a. 2. *De Trin.*, l. i., c. 3.
[3] Rom. xi. 36.

debetur.   Quod testimonium edisserens Augustinus : ' Non con-
fuse,' inquit, ' accipiendum est quod ait Apostolus, ex ipso et per
ipsum et in ipso; ex ipso dicens propter Patrem, per ipsum
propter Filium, in ipso propter Spiritum Sanctum.'[1] Aptissi-
meque Ecclesia, ea Divinitatis opera in quibus potentia excellit,
tribuere Patri, ea in quibus excellit sapientia, tribuere Filio,
ea in quibus excellit amor, Spiritu Sancto tribueri consuevit.
Non quod perfectiones cunctae atque opera extrinsecus edita
Personis divinis communia non sint; sunt enim ' indivisa
opera Trinitatis, sicut et indivisa est Trinitatis essentia,'[2] quia,
uti tres Personae divinae ' inseparabiles sunt, ita inseparabiliter
operantur :'[3] verum quod ex comparatione quadam et prope-
modum affinitate quae inter opera ipsa et Personarum proprietates intercedit, ea alteri potius quam alteris addicuntur sive,
ut aiunt, appropriantur : ' Sicut similitudine vestigii vel imaginis
in creaturis inventa, utimur ad manifestationem divinarum Personarum, ita et essentialibus attributis; et haec manifestatio
Personarum per essentialia attributa appropriatio dicitur.'[4] Hoc
modo Pater qui est ' principium totius Deitatis,'[5] idem causa est
effectrix universitatis rerum et Incarnationis Verbi et sanctifica-
tionis animorum, ' ex ipso sunt omnia ;' ex ipso, propter Patrem.
Filius autem, ' Verbum, Imago Dei,' idem est causa exemplaris
unde res omnes formam et pulchritudinem, ordinem et concentum
imitantur ; qui extitit nobis via, veritas, vita, hominis cum Deo
reconciliator, ' per ipsum sunt omnia ;' per ipsum, propter Filium.
Spiritus vero Sanctus idem est omnium rerum causa ultima, eo
quia sicut in fine suo voluntas lateque omnia conquiescunt, non
aliter ille, qui divina bonitas est ac Patris ipsa Filiique inter se
caritas, arcana ea opera de salute hominum sempiterna, impul-
sione quadam valida suavique complet et perficit, ' in ipso sunt
omnia ;' in ipso, propter Spiritum Sanctum.

    Rite igitur inviolateque custodito religionis studio, toti debito
Trinitati beatissimae, quod magis magisque in christiano populo
aequum est inculcari, ad virtutem Spiritus Sancti exponendam
oratio Nostra convertitur.   Ac principio respici oportet ad
Christum, conditorem Ecclesiae et nostri generis Redemptorem.
Sane in operibus Dei externis illud eximie praestat Incarnati
Verbi mysterium, in quo divinarum perfectionum sic enitet lux

[1] De Trin., l. vi., o. 10; l. i., c. 6.
[2] S. Aug., de Trin., l. i., c. 4 et 5.
[3] S. Aug., ib.
[4] S. Th. 1ª, q. xxxix., a. 7.
[5] S. Aug., de Trin., l. iv., c. 20.

ut quidquam supra ne cogitari quidem possit, et quo aliud nullum humanae naturae esse poterat salutarius. Hoc igitur tantum opus, etsi totius Trinitatis fuit, attamen Spiritui Sancto tamquam proprium adscribitur : ita ut de Virgine sic Evangelia commemorent : ' Inventa est in utero habens de Spiritu Sancto ; ' et : ' Quod in ea natum est, de Spiritu Sancto est.'[1] Idque merito adscribitur ei qui Patris et Filii est caritas ; quum hoc ' magnum pietatis Sacramentum '[2] sit a summa Dei erga homines caritate profectum, prout Ioannes commonet : ' Sic Deus dilexit mundum ut Filium suum unigenitum daret.'[3] Accedit quod natura humana evecta inde sit ad coniunctionem ' personalem ' cum Verbo : quae dignitas non ullis quidem data est eius promeritis, sed ex integra plane gratia, proptereaque ex munere veluti proprio Spiritus Sancti. Ad rem apposite Augustinus : ' Iste modus,' inquit, ' quo est natus Christus de Spiritu Sancto, insinuat nobis gratiam Dei, qua homo nullis praecedentibus meritis, in ipso primo exordio naturae suae quo esse coepit, Verbo Dei copularetur in tantam personae unitatem, ut idem ipse esset Filius Dei qui Filius hominis, et Filius hominis qui Filius Dei.'[4] Divini autem Spiritus opera non solum conceptio Christi effecta est, sed eius quoque sanctificatio animae, quae ' unctio ' in sacris libris nominatur :[5] atque adeo omnis eius actio ' praesente Spiritu peragebatur.'[6] praecipueque sacrificium sui : ' Per Spiritum Sanctum semetipsum obtulit immaculatum Deo.'[7] Ista qui perpenderit, nihil erit ei mirum quod charismata omnia almi Spiritus in animam Christi affluxerint. Namque in ipso copia insedit gratiae singulariter plena, quanto maximo videlicet modo atque efficacitate haberi possit ; in ipso omnes sapientiae scientiaeque thesauri, gratiae gratis datae, virtutes, donaque omnino omnia quae tum Isaiae oraculis nunciata,[8] tum significata sunt admirabili ea columba ad Iordanem, quum eas aquas suo Christus baptismate ad sacramentum novum consecravit. Quo loco illa eiusdem Augustini recte conveniunt : ' Absurdissimum est dicere quod Christus, quum iam triginta esset annorum, accepit Spiritum Sanctum, sed venit ad baptismum sicut sine peccato, ita non sine Spiritu Sancto. Tunc ergo,' scilicet in baptismate, ' corpus suum, idest Ecclesiam, praefigurari dignatus est, in qua praecipue

---

1 Matth. i , 18, 20.
2 1 Tim. iii. 16.
3 iii. 16.
4 *Enchir.*, c. xl.   S. Th. 3ª., q. xxxii., a 1.

5 Actor. x. 38.
6 S. Basil. *de Sp. S.*, c. xvi.
7 Hebr. ix. 14.
8 iv. 1 ; xi. 2, 3.

baptizati accipiunt Spiritum Sanctum.'¹ Itaque Spiritus Sancte et praesentia conspicua super Christam et virtute intima in anima eius, duplex eiusdem Spiritus praesignificatur missio, ea nimirum quae in Ecclesia manifesto patet, et ea quae in animis iustorum secreto illapsu exercetur.

Ecclesia, quae iam concepta, ex latere ipso secundi Adami, velut in cruce dormientis, orta erat, sese in lucem hominum insigni modo primitus dedit die celeberrima Pentecostes, Ipsaque die beneficia sua Spiritus Sanctus in mystico Christi corpore prodere coepit, ea mira effusione quam Ioël propheta iampridem viderat : ² nam Paraclitus ' sedit super Apostolos ut novae coronae spirituales per linguas igneas imponerentur capiti illorum.' ³ Tum vero Apostoli ' de monte descenderunt,' ut Chrysostomus scribit, 'non tabulas lapideas in manibus portantes, sicut Moyses, sed Spiritum in mente circumferentes, et thesaurum quemdam ac fontem dogmatum et charismatum effundentes.' ⁴ Ita plane eveniebat illud extremum Christi ad Apostolos suos promissum de Spiritu Sancto mittendo, qui doctrinae, ipso afflante, traditae completurus ipse esset et quodammodo obsignaturus depositum : 'Adhuc multa habeo vobis dicere, sed non potestis portare modo ; quum autem venerit ille Spiritus veritatis, docebit vos omnem veritatem.' ⁵ Hic enim qui Spiritus est veritatis, utpote simul a Patre, qui verum aeternum est, simul a Filio, qui veritas est substantialis, procedens, haurit ab utroque una cum essentia omnem veritatis quanta est amplitudinem : quam quidem veritatem impertit ac largitur Ecclesiae, auxilio praesentissimo providens ut ipsa ne ulli unquam errori obnoxia sit, utque divinae doctrinae germina alere copiosius in dies possit et frugifera praestare ad populorum salutem.   Et quoniam populorum salus, ad quam nata est Ecclesia, plane postulat ut haec munus idem in perpetuitatem temporum persequatur, perennis idcirco vita atque virtus a Spiritu Sancto suppetit, quae Ecclesiam conservat augetque : ' Ego rogabo Patrem, et alium Paraclitum dabit vobis, ut maneat vobiscum in aeternum, Spiritum veritatis.' ⁶ Ab ipso namque episcopi constituuntur, quorum ministerio non modo filii generantur, sed etiam patres, sacerdotes videlicet, ad eam regendam

---

¹ *De Trin.*, l. xv., c. 26.
² ii. 28, 29.
³ Cyr. hierosol. *catech*, 17.

⁴ *In Matth. hom.* i., 2 Cor. iii. 3.
⁵ Ioan. xvi. 12, 13.
⁶ *Ib.*, xiv. 16, 17.

enutriendamque eodem sanguine quo est a Christo redempta : ' Spiritus Sanctus posuit episcopos regere Ecclesiam Dei, quam acquisivit sanguine suo.'[1] Utrique autem, episcopi et sacerdotes, insigni Spiritu munere id habent ut peccata pro potestate deleant, secundum illud Christi ad Apostolos : ' Accipite Spiritum Sanctum ; quorum remiseritis peccata, remittuntur eis, et quorum retinueritis, retenta sunt.'[2]   Porro Ecclesiam opus esse plane divinum, alio nullo argumento praeclarius constat quam charismatum quibus undique illa ornatur splendore et gloria ; auctore nimirum et datore Spiritu Sancto.   Atque hoc affirmare sufficiat, quod quum Christus caput sit Ecclesiae, Spiritus Sanctus sit eius anima : ' Quod est in corpore nostro anima, id est Spiritus Sanctus in corpore Christi, quod est Ecclesia.'[3]   Quae ita quum sint, nequaquam comminisci et expectare licet aliam ullam ampliorem uberioremque ' divini Spiritus manifestationem et ostensionem' : quae enim nunc in Ecclesia habetur, maxima sane est, eaque tamdiu manebit quoad Ecclesiae contingat ut, militiae emensa stadium, ad triumphantium in coelesti societate laetitiam educatur.

Quantum vero et quo modo Spiritus Sanctus in animis singulorum (agat, id non minus admirabile est, quamquam intellectu paulo est difficilius, eo etiam quia omnem intuitum fugiat oculorum.   Haec pariter Spiritus effusio tantae est copiae, ut Christus ipse, cuius de munere proficiscitur, abundantissimo amni similem dixerit, prout est apud Ioannum : ' Qui credit in me, sicut dicit Scriptura, flumina de ventre eius fluent aquae viuae ' : cui testimonio idem Evangelista explanationem subiicit : ' Hoc autem dixit de Spiritu, quem accepturi erant credentes in eum.'[4] Certum quidem est, in ipsis etiam hominibus iustis qui ante Christum fuerunt, insedisse per gratiam Spiritum Sanctum, quemadmodum de prophetis, de Zacharia, de Ioanne Baptista, de Simeone et Anna scriptum accepimus ; quippe in Pentecoste non ita se Spiritus Sanctus tribuit, ' ut tunc primum esse sanctorum inhabitator inciperet, sed ut copiosius inundaret, cumulans sua dona, non inchoans, nec ideo novus opere, quia ditior largitate.'[5]   Verum, si et illi in filiis Dei numerabantur, conditione tamen perinde erant ac servi, quia etiam filius ' nihil differt a servo,' quousque est ' sub tutoribus et actoribus :'[6] ac,

---

[1] Act. xx. 28.
[2] Ioann. xx. 22, 23.
[3] S. Aug., *serm.* clxxxvii., *de temp.*
[4] vii. 38, 39.
[5] S. Leo M. *hom.* iii. *de Pentec.*
[6] Gal. iv. 1, 2.

praeter quam quod iustitia in illis non erat nisi ex Christi meritis adventuri, communicatio Spiritus Sancti post Christum facta multo est copiosior, propemodum ut arram pretio vincit res pacta, atque ut imagini longe praestat veritas. Hoc propterea affirmavit Ioannes : ' Nondum erat Spiritus datus, quia Iesus nondum erat glorificatus.',[1] Statim igitur ut Christus, ' ascendens in altum,' regni sui gloria tam laboriose parta potitus est, divitias Spiritus Sancti munifice reclusit, ' dedit dona hominibus.'[2] Nam ' certa illa Spiritus Sancti datio vel missio post clarificationem Christi futura erat qualis nunquam antea fuerat, neque enim antea nulla fuerat, sed talis non fuerat.'[3] Siquidem natura humana necessario serva est Dei : ' Creatura serva est, servi nos Dei sumus secundum naturam : '[4] quin etiam ob communem noxam natura nostra omnis in id vitium dedecusque prolapsa est, ut praeterea infensi Deo extiterimus : ' Eramus natura filii irae.'[5] Tali nos a ruina exitioque sempiterno nulla usquam vis tanta erat quae posset erigere et vindicare. Id vero Deus, humanae naturae conditor, summe misericors praestitit per Unigenam suum : cuius beneficio factum, ut homo in gradum nobilitatemque, unde exciderat, cum donorum locupletiore ornatu sit restitutus. Eloqui nemo potest quale sit opus istud divinae gratiae in animis hominum ; qui propterea loculenter tum in sacris litteris tum apud Ecclesiae patres, et regenerati et creaturae novae et consortes divinae naturae et filii Dei et deifici similibusque laudibus appellantur. Iamvero tam ampla bona non sine causa debentur quasi propria Spiritui Sancto. Ipse enim est ' Spiritus adoptionis filiorum, in quo clamamus : Abba, Pater ; ' idemque paterni amoris suavitate corda perfundit : ' Ipse Spiritus testimonium reddit spiritui nostro quod sumus filii Dei.'[6] Cui rei declarandae opportune cadit ea, quam Angelicus perspexit, similitudo inter utramque Spiritus Sancti operam ; quippe per eum ipsum et ' Christus est in sanctitate conceptus ut esset Filius Dei naturalis,' et 'alii sanctificantur ut sint filii Dei adoptivi.'[7] Ita, multo quidem nobilius quam in rerum natura fiat, ab amore oritur spiritualis regeneratio, ab Amore scilicet increato.

Huius regenerationis et renovationis initia sunt homini per

---

[1] vii. 39.
[2] Eph. iv. 8.
[3] S. Aug., *de Trin.*, 1, iv., c. 20.
[4] S. Cyr. Alex., *Thesaur.* l. v., c. 5.
[5] Eph. ii. 3
[6] Rom. viii. 15, 16.
[7] S. Th. 3, q. xxxii., a. 1.

baptisma : in quo sacramento, spiritu immundo ab anima depulso,
illabitur primum Spiritus Sanctus, eamque similem sibi facit :
' Quod natum est ex Spiritu, spiritus est.' [1] Uberiusque per
sacram confirmationem, ad constantiam et robur christianae
vitae, sese dono dat idem Spiritus ; a quo nimirum fuit victoria
martyrum et virginum de illecebris corruptelarum triumphus.
Sese, inquimus, dono dat Spiritus Sanctus : ' Caritas Dei
diffusa est in cordibus nostris per Spiritum Sanctum qui datus
est nobis.' [2] Ipse enimvero non modo affert nobis divina munera,
sed eorumdem est auctor, atque etiam munus ipse est supremum ;
qui a mutuo Patris Filiique amore procedens iure habetur, et
nuncupatur ' altissimi donum Dei.' Cuius doni natura et vis
quo illustrius pateat, revocare oportet ea quae in divinis litteris
tradita sacri doctores explicaverunt, Deum videlicet adesse rebus
omnibus in eisque esse, ' per potentiam, in quantum omnia eius
potestati subduntur ; per praesentiam, in quantum omnia nuda
sunt et aperta oculis eius ; per essentiam, in quantum adest
omnibus ut causa essendi.' [3] At vero in homine est Deus non
tantummodo ut in rebus, sed eo amplius cognoscitur ab ipso et
diligitur ; quum vel duce natura bonum sponte amemus, cupiamus,
conquiramus. Praeterea Deus ex gratia insidet animae iustae
tamquam in templo, modo penitus intimo et singulari ; ex quo
etiam sequitur ea necessitudo caritatis, qua Deo adhaeret anima
coniunctissime, plus quam amico amicus possit benevolenti
maxime et dilecto, eoque plene suaviterque fruitur. Haec autem
mira coniunctio, quae suo nomine ' inhabitatio ' dicitur, conditione
tantum seu statu ab ea discrepans qua coelites Deus beando
complectitur, tametsi verissime efficitur praesenti totius Trinitatis numine, ' ad eum veniemus et mansionem apud eum
faciemus,' [4] attamen de Spiritu Sancto tamquam peculiaris prae-
dicatur. Siquidem divinae et potentiae et sapientiae vel in
homine improbo apparent vestigia ; caritatis, quae propria
Spiritus veluti nota est, alius nemo nisi iustus est particeps.
Atque illud cum re cohaeret, eumdem Spiritum nominari
Sanctum, ideo etiam quod ipse, primus summusque Amor, animos
moveat agatque ad sanctitatem, quae demum amore in Deum
continetur. Quapropter Apostolus quum iustos appellat templum
Dei, tales non expresse Patris aut Filii appellat, sed Spiritus

---

[1] Ioann. iii. 7.
[2] Rom. v. 5.
[3] S. Th. 1ª, q. viii., a. 3.
[4] Ioann. xiv. 23.

Sancti : ' An nescitis quoniam membra vestra templum sunt
Spiritus Sancti, qui in vobis est, quem habetis a Deo ? ' [1] Inhabi-
tantem in animis piis Spiritum Sanctum ubertas munerum
coelestium multis modis consequitur. Nam, quae est Aquinatis
doctrina : ' Quum Spiritus Sanctus procedat ut amor, procedit in
ratione doni primi ; unde dicit Augustinus, quod per donum quod
est Spiritus Sanctus, multa propria dona dividuntur membris
Christi.' [2] In his autem muneribus sunt arcanae illae admoni-
tiones invitationesque, quae instinctu Sancti Spiritus identidem
in mentibus animisque excitantur ; quae si desint, neque initium
viae bonae habetur, neque progressiones, neque exitus salutis
aeternae. Et quoniam huiusmodi voces et motiones occulte admodum in animis fiunt, apte in sacris paginis similes nonnunquam
habentur venientis aurae sibilo ; easque Doctor Angelicus scite
confert motibus cordis, cuius tota vis est in animante perabdita :
' Cor habet quamdam influentiam occultam, et ideo cordi com-
paratur Spiritus Sanctus, qui invisibiliter Ecclesiam vivificat et
unit.' [3] Hoc amplius, homini iusto, vitam scilicet viventi divinae
gratiae et per congruas virtutes tamquam facultates agenti, opus
plane est septenis illis quae proprie dicuntur Spiritus Sancti donis.
Porum enim beneficio instruitur animus et munitur ut eius vocibus
atque impulsioni facilius promptiusque obsequatur ; haec
propterea dona tantae sunt efficacitatis ut eum ad fastigium
sanctimoniae adducant, tantaque excellentiae ut in coelesti regno
eadem quamquam perfectius, perseverent. Ipsorumque ope
charismatum provocatur animus et effertur ad appetendas
adipiscendasque beatitudines evangelicas quae, perinde ac
flores verno tempore erumpentes, indices ac nunciae sunt
beatitatis perpetuo mansurae. Felices denique sunt fructus
ii, ab Apostolo enumerati, [4] quos hominibus iustis in hac
etiam caduca vita Spiritus parit et exhibet, omni refertos
dulcedine et gaudio ; cuiusmodi esse debent a Spiritu, ' qui est
in Trinitate genitoris genitique suavitas, ingenti largitate atque
ubertate perfundens omnes creaturas.' [5] Itaque divinus Spiritus
in aeterno sanctitatis lumine a Patre et a Verbo procedens, amor
idem et donum, postquam se per velamen imaginum in testamento veteri exhibuit, plenam sui copiam effudit in Christum in

---

[1] 1 Cor. vi. 19.
[2] *Summ. th.* 1ª q. xxxvii., a. 2. S. Aug., *de Trin.*, l. xv., c. 19.
[3] *Summ. th.* 3ⁿ, q. viii., a. 1, ad 3.
[4] Gal. v. 22.
[5] S. Aug., *de Trin.*, 1, vi., c. 9.

eiusque corpus mysticum, quae est Ecclesia ; atque homines in
pravitatem et corruptelam abeuntes praesentia et gratia sua tam
salutariter revocavit, ut iam non de terra terreni, longe alia
saperent et vellent, quasi de coelo coelestes.

Haec omnia quum tanta sint, quumque Spiritus Sancti bonitatem in nos immensam luculenter declarent, omnino postulant
a nobis, ut obsequii pietatisque studium in eum quam maximo
intendamus. Id autem christiani homines recte optimeque
efficient, si eumdem certaverint maiore quotidie cura et noscere
et amare et exorare : cuius rei gratia sit haec ad ipsos, prout
sponte fluit paterno ex animo, cohortatio.—Fortasse ne hodie
quidem in eis desunt, qui similiter rogati ut quidam olim a Paulo
apostolo, acceperintne Spiritum Sanctum, respondeant similiter :
'Sed neque si Spiritus Sanctus est, audivimus.'[1] Sin minus,
multi certe in eius cognitione valde deficiunt ; cuius quidem
crebro usurpant nomen in religiosis actibus exercendis, sed ea
fide quae crassis tenebris circumfusa est. Quapropter quotquot
sunt sacri concionatores curatoresque animarum hoc meminerint
esse suum, ut quae ad Spiritum Sanctum pertinent diligentius
atque uberius populo tradant ; sic tamen ut difficiles subtilesque
absint controversiae, et prava eorum stultitia devitetur qui omnia
etiam arcana divina temere conantur perscrutari. Illud potius
commemorandum enucleateque explanandum est, quam multa et
magna beneficia ab hoc largitore divino et manaverint ad nos
et manare non desinant ; ut vel error vel ignoratio tantarum rerum,
'lucis filiis' indigna, prorsus depellatur. Hoc autem propterea
urgemus, non modo quia id attingit mysterium quo ad vitam
aeternam proxime dirigimur, ob eamque rem firme credendum ;
verum etiam quia bonum quo clarius pleniusque habetur cognitum,
eo impensius diligitur et amatur.—Nempe Spiritui Sancto, quod
alterum praestandum esse monuimus, debetur amor, quia Deus
est : 'Diliges Dominum Deum tuum ex toto corde tuo, ex tota
anima tua et ex tota fortitudine tua.'[2] Amandusque idem est,
quippe substantialis, aeternus, primus amor ; amore autem nihil
est amabilius : multoque id magis quia summis ipse nos cumula-
vit beneficiis, quae ut largientis benevolentiam testantur, ita
gratum animum accipientis reposcunt. Qui amor duplicem habet
utilitatem neque eam exiguam. Nam tum ad illustriorem in
dies notitiam de Spiritu Sancto capiendam nos exacuet ; 'Amans'

---

[1] Act. xix. 2.   [2] Deut. vi. 5.

enim, ut Angelicus ait, ' non est contentus superficiali apprehen-
sione amati, sed nititur singula quae ad amatum pertinent intrinsecus disquirere, et sic ad interiora eius ingreditur, sicut de
Spiritu Sancto, qui est amor Dei, dicitur quod scrutatur etiam
profunda Dei ;'[1] tum coelestium donorum copiam nobis concilia-
bit largiorem, eo quod donantis manum ut angustus animus contrahit, ita gratus et memor dilitat.   Curandum tamen magnopere
ut iste amor eiusmodi sit qui non in cogitatione arida externoque
obsequio subsistat, sed ad agendum prosiliat, refugiat maxime a
culpa; quum haec Spiritui Sancto, peculiari quodam nomine,
accidat iniuriosior.   Quanticumque enim sumus, tanti sumus ex
bonitati divina ; quae eidem Spiritui praesertim adscribitur ; hunc
benigne sibi facientem is offendit qui peccat, quique ipsis eius
abusus muneribus et bonitati confisus, quotidie magis insolescit.
—Ad haec, quum veritatis ille sit Spiritus, si quis ex infirmitate
aut inscitia deliquerit, forsitan excusationis aliquid apud Deum
habeat; at qui per malitiam veritati repugnet ab eaque se avertat,
in Spiritum Sanctum peccat gravissime.   Quod quidem aetate
nostra increbruit adeo, ut deterrima ea tempora advenisse videantur a Paulo praenunciata, quibus homines iustissimo Dei
iudicio obcaecati, falsa pro veris habituri sint, et ' huius mundi
principi,' qui mendax est et mendacii pater, tamquam veritatis
magistro credituri : ' Mittet illis Deus operationem erroris ut cre-
dant mendacio ;'[2] ' in novissimis temporibus discedent quidam a
fide, attendentes spiritibus erroris et doctrinis daemoniorum,'[3]—
Quoniam vero Spiritus Sanctus in nobis, ut supra monuimus,
quasi suo quodam in templo habitat, suadendum est illud Apostoli : ' Nolite contristare Spiritum Sanctum Dei, in quo signati,
estis.'[4]   Idque ipsum non satis est, indigna omnia defugere, sed
omni virtutum laude christianus homo nitere debet ut hospiti tam
magno tamque benigno placeat, castimonia in primis et sancti-
tudine ; casta enim et sancta addecent templum.   Hinc idem
Apostolus : ' Nescitis quia templum Dei estis, et Spiritus Dei
habitat in vobis ?   Si quis autem templum Dei violaverit, disperdet
illum Deus ; templum enim Dei sanctum est, quod estis vos :'[5]
formidolosae eae quidem, sed perquam iustae minae.—Postremo,
Spiritum Sanctum exorari et obsecrari oportet, quippe cuius prae-
sidio adiumentisque nemo unus non egeat maxime.   Ut enim
quisque est inops consilii, viribus infirmus, aerumnis pressus,

---

[1] 1 Cor. ii. 10.—*Summ. th.* 1ª 2ᵃᵉ, q. xxviii, s. 2.   [4] Eph. iv. 30.
[2] 2 Thess. ii. 10.   [5] 1 Cor iii. 16, 17.
[3] 1 Tim. iv, 1.

pronus iu vetitum, ita ad eum confugere debet qui luminis, fortitudinis, consolationis, sanctitatis fons patet perennis. Atque illa homini in primis necessaria, admissorum venia ab eo potissimum expetenda est : 'Spiritus Sancti proprium est quod sit donum Patris et Filii ; remissio autem peccatorum fit per Spiritum Sanctum, tamquam per donum Dei:'[1] de quo Spiritu apertius habetur in ordine rituali : 'Ipse est remissio omnium peccatorum.'[2] — Quanam vero ratione sit exorandus, perapte docet Ecclesia, quae supplex eum compellat et obtestatur suavissimis quibusque, nominibus : 'Veni pater pauperum, veni dator munerum, veni lumen cordium : consolator optime, dulcis hospes animae, dulce refrigerium :' eumdemque enixe implorat ut eluat, ut sanet, ut irriget mentes atque corda, detque confidentibus et 'virtutis meritum' et 'salutis exitum' et 'perenne gaudium.' Nec dubitare ullo pacto licet an huiusmodi preces auditurus ille sit, quo auctore scriptum legimus : 'Ipse Spiritus postulat pro nobis gemitibus inenarrabilibus.'[3] Demum hoc est fidenter assidueque supplicandum, ut nos quotidie magis et luce sua illustret et caritatis suae quasi facibus incendat ; sic enim fide et amore freti acriter enitamur adpraemia sempiterna, quoniam ipse 'est pignus hereditatis nostra.'[4]

Habetis, Venerabiles Frates, quae ad fovendum Spiritus Sancti cultum monendo hortandoque placuit edicere : minimeque dubitamus, quin ope praesertim navitatis sollertiaeque vestrae praeclaros in christiano populo sint fructus latura. Nostra quidem tantae huic rei persequendae nulla unquam defutura est opera, atque etiam consilium est ut, quibus subinde modis videbitur opportunius, idem pietatis studium tam praestabile alamus et provehamus. Interea, quoniam biennio ante, datis litteris 'Provida matris,'[5] peculiares preces, easque ad maturandum christianae unitatis bonum, in sollemnibus Pentecostes catholicis commendavimus, libet de hoc ipso capite ampliora quaedam decernere. Decernimus igitur et mandamus ut per orbem catholicum universum, hoc anno itemque annis in perpetuum consequentibus, supplicatio novendialis ante Pentecosten, in omnibus curialibus templis et, si Ordinarii locorum utile iudicarint, in aliis etiam templis sacrariisve fiat. Omnibus autem qui eidem novendiali supplicationi interfuerent, et ad mentem Nostram rite

---

[1] *Summ. th.* 3ª q. iii. a. 8, ad 3ᵐ.
[2] *In Miss. rom. fer.* iii. *post Pent.*
[3] Rom. viii. 26.
[4] Eph. i. 14.
[5] Cf. *Anal. Eccl.*, vol. iii., p. 193.

oraverint, eis annorum septem septemque quadragenarum apud Deum indulgentiam in singulos dies concedimus; tum plenariam in uno quolibet eorumdem dierum vel festo ipso die Pentecostes, vel etiam quolibet ex octo subsequentibus, modo rite confessione abluti sacraque communione refecti ad eamdem mentem Nostram pie supplicaverint. Quibus beneficiis frui pariter eos posse volumus quos publicis illis precibus legitima causa prohibeat, vel ubi non ita commode, secundum Ordinarii prudentiam, in templo res fieri possit; dum tamen supplicationi novendiali privatim detur opera ceteraeque conditiones expleantur. Hoc praeterea placet de thesauro Ecclesiae in perpetuum tribuere, ut si qui vel publice vel privatim preces aliquas ad Spiritum Sanctum pro pietate sue iterum praestent quotidie per octavam Pentecostes ad festum inclusive sanctae Trinitatis, ceterisque ut supra conditionibus rite satisfecerint, ipsis liceat utramque iterum consequi indulgentiam. Quae omnia indulgentiae munera etiam animabus piis igni purgatorio addictis converti in suffragium posse, misericorditer in Domino concedimus.

Iam Nobis mens animusque ad ea revolat vota quae initio aperuimus; quorum eventum summis precibus a divino Spiritu flagitamus, flagitabimus. Agite, Venerabiles Fratres, Nostris cum precibus vestras consocietis, vobisque hortatoribus universae christianae gentes coniungant suas, adhibita conciliatrice potenti et peraccepta Virgine Beatissma. Quae ipsi rationes cum Spiritu Sancto intercedant intimae admirabilesque, probe nostis; ut Sponsa eius immaculata merito nominetur. Ipsius deprecatio Viginis multum profecto valuit et ad mysterium Incarnationis et ad eiusdem Paracliti in Apostolorum coronam adventum. Communes igitur preces pergat ipsa suffragio suo benignissima roborare, ut in universitate nationum tam misere laborantium divina rerum prodigia per almum Spiritum feliciter instaurentur, quae vaticinatione Davidica sunt celebrata: 'Emittes Spiritum tuum et creabuntur et renovabis faciem terrae.'[1]—Coelestium vero donorum auspicem et benevolentiae Nostrae testem vobis, Venerabiles Fratres, Clero populoque vestro Apostolicam benedictionem peramanter in Domino impertimus.

Datum Romae apud Sanctum Petrum die ix Maii anno MDCCCLXXXXVII, Pontificatus Nostri vigesimo.

LEO PP. XIII.

---

[1] Ps. ciii. 30.

IN PRAISE OF FRUGAL LIVING

A NEW POEM BY HIS HOLINESS LEO XIII.

PARCO AC TENUI VICTU CONTENTUS INGLUVIEM FUGE.

AD FABRICIUM RUFUM EPISTOLA

Quo victu immunem morbis, et robore vitam
  Ducere florentem possis, sermone diserto
  Sedulus Hippocratis cultor rigidusque satelles
  Haec nuper praecepta bonus tradebat Ofellus ;
  Multa et de tristi ingluvie gravis ore locutus.

Munditiae imprimis studeas ; sine divite cultu
  Mensa tibi, nitidae lances et candida mappa.—
  Albana e cella iubeas purissima vina
  Apponi ; exhilarant animos curasque resolvunt ;
  Sobrius at caveas, nimium ne crede lyaeo,
  Neu crebra pigeat calices perfundere lympha.—
  E munda cerere atque excoctos delige panes.—
  Quas Gallina dapes et bos agnusve pararint,
  Sume libens ; firmandis viribus utilis esca :
  Sint tenerae carnes ; instructaque fercula spissum
  Non ius vel siser inficiat, non faecula coa.—
  Tum laudata tibi sint ova recentia, succum
  Lento igne aut libeat modicis siccare patellis,
  Sugere seu mollem pleno sit gratius ore ;
  Atque alios sunt ova tibi percommoda in usus.—
  Neve accepta minus spumantis copia lactis :
  Nutriit infantem ; senior bene lacte valebis.—
  Nunc age, et aerei mellis caelestia dona
  Profer, et hyblaeo parcus de nectare liba.—
  Adde suburbano tibi quod succrescit in horto
  Dulce olus, et pubens decusso flore legumen ;
  Adde et maturos, quos fertilis educat annus,
  Delectos fructus, imprimis mitia poma,
  Quae pulcre in cistis mensam rubicunda coronent.—
  Postremo e tostis succedat potio baccis,
  Quas tibi Moka ferax, mittunt et littora eoa :
  Nigrantem laticem sensim summisque labellis
  Sorbilla ; dulcis stomachum bene molliet haustus.
  De tenui victu haec teneas, his utere tutus ;
  Ad seram ut vivas sanus vegetusque senectam.

At contra (haec sapiens argute addebat Ofellus)
    Nectere nata dolos, homines et perdere nata
    Vitanda ingluvies, crudelis et improba siren.

Principio hoc illi studium ; componere mensas
    Ornatu vario, aulaeis ostroque nitentes.
    Explicat ipsa viden' tonsis mantelia villis ;
    Grandia stant circum longo ordine pocula, aheni
    Crateres, paterae, lances, argentea vasa :
    Mensa thymo atque apio redolet florumque corollis.—
    His laute instructis, simulata voce locuta
    Convivas trahit incautos ; succedere tecto,
    Mollibus et blanda invitat discumbere lectis ;
    Continuoque reposta cadis lectissima vina
    Caecuba depromit, coumque vetusque falernum ;
    Quin exquisitas tillatos arte liquores
    E musto et pomis, ultro potantibus offert.
    Convivae humectant certatim guttura, et una
    Succosas avido degustant ore placentas.
    Ecce autem lucanus aper perfusus abunde
    Mordaci pipere atque oleo, profertur edendus,
    Et leporum pingues armi, et iecur anseris albi,
    Assique in verubus turdi, niveique columbi.
    Carnibus admixti pisces ; conchylia rhombi,
    Mollia pectinibus patulis iuncta ostrea, et ampla
    In patera squillas inter muraena natantes.—
    Attonitis inhiant oculis ; saturantur opime ;
    Cuncta vorant usque ad fastidia ; iamque lyaeo
    Inflati venas nimio, dapibusque gravati
    Surgunt convivae, temere bacchantur in aula,
    Insana et pugiles inter se iurgia miscent,
    Defessi donec lymphata mente quiescunt.
    Laeta dolum Ingluvies ridet, jam facta suorum
    Compos votorum, et gaudet, memor artis iniquae,
    Ceu nautas tumida pereuntes aequoris unda,
    Mergere convivas miseros sub gurgite tanto.·
    Nam subito exsudant praecordia, et excita bilis
    E iecore in stomachum larga affluit, ilia torquet,
    Immanemque ciet commoto ventre tumultum ;
    Membra labant incerta, stupent pallentia et ora.
    Corpore sic misere exhausto fractoque, quid ultra
    Audeat ingluvies ? Ipsum, proh dedecus ! ipsum
    Figere humo, ac (tantum si fas) extinguere malit
    Immortalem animum, divinae particulam aurae.

PRELATES HAVING A RIGHT TO A PRIVATE ORATORY CAN HAVE PERMISSION TO CELEBRATE ONE REQUIEM MASS EACH WEEK

FACULTAS APPLICANDI LITANDI UNAM MISSAM 'DE REQUIE' IN HEBDOMADA

Sanctissimus Dominus Noster Leo Papa XIII., ad levamen animarum quae in Purgatorio detinentur, Sacrae Rituum Congregationi facultatem indulgere dignatus est, qua singulis petentibus S. R. E. Cardinalibus, Episcopis, aliisque Praelatis, quibus Oratorii privati privilegium de iure competit, permitti possit in eodem Oratorio unica Missa privata de Requie, defunctis applicanda, infra hebdomadam diebus non impeditis a Festo ritus duplicis, quod iure translationis pollet, a Dominicis aliisque Festis de praecepto servandis, nec non a Vigiliis, Feriis Octavisque privilegiatis; et servatis Rubricis. Contrariis non obstantibus quibuscumque.

Die, 8 Iunii, 1896.

NON-LITURGICAL LITANIES MAY NOT BE RECITED OR SUNG IN A CHURCH OR PUBLIC ORATORY

MONTIS ALBANI, DUBIUM QUOAD LITANIAS SANCTORUM

Rmus Dominus Adulphus Fiard Episcopus Montis Albani a S. Congreg. sequentis dubii solutionem humillime flagitavit, nimirum: Utrum prohibitio recitandi aut cantandi in Ecclesiis seu Oratoriis publicis Litanias, de quibus agitur in Decretis S. Rit. Congregationis 6 Martii 1894 et 28 Nov. 1895,[1] complectatur etiam quamlibet earum recitationem, a pluribus coniunctim in Ecclesiis vel Oratoriis publicis, absque ministri Ecclesiae, qua talis, interventu factam?

Et S. eadem Congr. referente subscripto Secretario, exquisito voto Commissionis Liturgicae, omnibus mature perpensis, ad propositum dubium respondendum censuit. *Affirmative.*

Atque ita rescripsit.

Die 20 Iunii 1896.

G. Card. ALOISI-MASELLA, S.R.C., *Praefectus.*

L. ✠ S.

ALOISIUS TRIPEPI, *Secretarius.*

INDULGENCES FOR CERTAIN PRAYERS

URBIS ET CRBIS.   DECRETUM EX AUDIENTIA SANCTISSIMI DIE
2 FEBRUARII 1897 QUOAD LAUDEM, CUIUS INITIUM EST 'DIO SIA
BENEDETTO '

Iam diu apud Christifideles, praesertim Italos, ea in more est piarum laudum formula, cuius initium, ' Dio sia benedetto ' : qui religionis actus, praeter quam per se optimus, etiam opportune valet, quemadmodum initio institutus fuit, ad honorem compensandum divini Nominis rerumque sanctissimarum, tam multis quotidie impiis vocibus passim violatum.   Proximis autem temporibus inductum est multis locis, Episcoporum concessu vel iussu, ut ea ipsa formula recitetur publice in ecclesia, sive ad benedictionem cum Venerabili Sacramento impertitam, sive post divini sacrificii celebrationem.   Huiusmodi increbrescentem consuetudinem SSmus Dominus Noster Leo PP. XIII. non semel, data occasione, probavit et commendavit.   Nuper vero, quo illam vehementius commendaret eoque amplius foveret, constituit, tum eidem formulae laudem interserere in sacratissimum Cor Iesu, tum augere munera sacrae Indulgentiae, quibus ea donata est a Decessoribus suis sa. me. Pio VII. et Pio IX.   Alter enim die 23 Iulii 1801 concessit ' indulgentiam unius anni pro qualibet vice laudes eas corde saltem contrito ac devote recitantibus.'   Alter vero, die 22 Martii 1847, ' eam ipsam indulgentiam animabus quoque in Purgatorio detentis applicabilem esse declaravit ' ; tum etiam eodem anno, die 8 Augusti, indulsit ' ut omnes utriusque sexus Christifideles semel saltem in die dictas laudes per integrum mensem recitantes, indulgentiam plenariam, una tantum cuiuslibet mensis die, uniuscuiusque arbitrio eligenda, dummodo vere poenitentes confessi ac sacra Communione refecti fuerint, et aliquam ecclesiam seu publicum oratorium visitaverint, ibique per aliquod temporis spatium iuxta mentem Sanctitatis Suae pias ad Deum preces effuderint, lucrari possint et valeant ; facta insuper potestate ipsam etiam plenariam indulgentiam fidelibus pariter defunctus applicandi.'

Itaque SSmus Dominus Noster, quod spectat ad contextum formulae earumdem laudum, statuit ut laudi quarto loco positae, scilicet ' Benedetto il Nome di Gesù,' haec subiungatur, ' Benedetto il suo sacratissimo Cuore.'   Quod vero ad indulgentiam attinet, benigne tribuit ut, confirmatis indulgentiis partiali et plenaria supra commemoratis, duplicetur ipsa indulgentia partialis, quoties eaedem laudes publice devoteque (quocumque idiomate expressae sint) recitentur vel post divini sacrificii celebrationem vel ad benedictionem cum Venerabili Sacramento ; quae item indulgentia cedere in suffragium possit animabus piis Purgantibus —Praesenti perpetuis futuris temporibus valituro, absque ulla Brevis expeditione.

Datum Romae ex Secretaria S. Congregationis Indulgentiis et SS. Reliquis praepositae die 2 Februarii, 1897.

Fr. HIERONYMUS M. Card. GOTTI, *Praefectus.*
A. ARCHIEP. NICOP., *Secretarius.*

Hic subiicitur integra laudum formula, de qua supra, in commodum eorum quibus non satis ea sit cognita :

Dio sia benedetto :
Benedetto il suo santo Nome :
Benedetto Gesù Cristo, vero Dio e vero Uomo :
Benedetto il Nome di Gesù :
Benedetto il suo sacratissimo Cuore :
Benedetto Gesù nel Santissimo Sacramento dell'Altare :
Benedetta la gran Madre di Dio Maria Santissima :
Benedetta la sua santa e immacolata Concezione :
Benedetto il nome di Maria Vergine e Madre :
Benedetto Iddio ne'suoi Angeli e ne'suoi Santi.

NOTICES OF BOOKS

THE PAROCHIAL HYMN BOOK. Complete Edition, with Words and Accompaniments. Edited by Rev. A. Police, S.M. Boston, Mass.

THIS is more than a hymn book. It is a prayer book, a treatise set to music on the three theological virtues, the end of man and the last things, as well as a complete vesperal. As a hymn book it is intended for congregational singing; and, to obviate the necessity of carrying another book to and from church, the editor, as he modestly styles himself, has added the various prayers and devotions to be found in our best and most modern prayer books. The hymns, with music, occupy upwards of 370 pages, and though the subjects are as varied as could be desired, yet the hymns are classified, and connected together in a manner which displays both originality and ingenuity on the part of the compiler. The collection of hymns consists of three parts, with an appendix. Each part is intended to inculcate and illustrate one of the theological virtues, while the appendix brings before the mind the four last things. It might seem that this apparently restricted scope would have restricted the selection of hymns, and would have made it necessary to omit many that should be found in every collection of Catholic hymns. This, however, is not the case, The compiler views the three virtues of Faith, Hope, and Charity, from the lofty standpoint of a great theologian, and makes them to include within their ample limits the entire course of doctrinal and devotional teaching.

This book should be in every Catholic school, and, as far as possible, in the hands of every Catholic child in English-speaking countries. We believe if the half hour which is daily devoted to Catechism were, in whole, or in part devoted to singing hymns from this collection, prefaced or followed by a short doctrinal exposition from the teacher, that it would be an improvement on the present system. If it be the ballads of a people that keep alive their love for native land, why should not Catholic hymns make the spirit of Catholicity burn more brightly? Luther, keen-minded student of human nature that he was, well knew the power of hymns in moulding the religious belief of a people, and relied more on the hymns which he himself composed and set to music than on his sermons, for the propagation of his errors.

The hymns are collected from every source ; some are translations, some are written originally in English, and some have been written specially for the present collection. The music, too, is old, where old, and at the same time suitable music could be found ; otherwise, but only in comparatively few cases, it is the work of Father Police. But in all cases it is a true, simple, and devotional interpretation of the words. The book, we understand, can be had from Messrs. M. II. Gill & Son, Dublin, direct, or through any bookseller.

D. O'L.

BEATI PETRI CANISII SOCIETATIS JESU EPISTOLAE ET ACTA. Collegit et adnotationibus illustravit Otto Braunsberyer, ejusdem Societatis Sacerdos. Volumen Primum, 1541-1556. Friburgi Brisgoviae, Sumptibus : Herder.

PETER CANISIUS, who was beatified by Pius IX. on November 20th, 1864, was one of the first followers of St. Ignatius. In company with Lejay, he went into Germany, in 1551, on the invitation of Ferdinand I., and by his zeal in catechizing the people, and the example of his saintly life, he succeeded not only in stemming the tide of Protestant successes amongst the peasantry, but won back many to the true faith. This collection of letters, written to him and by him, when completed, will prove a valuable contribution to the documentary history of the sixteenth century. The publishers promise a yearly volume for six or eight years. When the collection has been completed we shall give it a notice worthy of its importance.

THE INVENTION OF GOD'S LOVE FOR MAN. By Very Rev. T. Brady, P.P., V.F., Cootehill. Dublin : M. H. Gill and Son.

THIS is an edifying and instructive little book on the Sacrifice of the Mass, by one whose erudition and piety have already added considerably to sound ascetic literature. His asceticism, unlike that of some of the mediaeval mystics, is founded on dogma, as the opening chapters of the present booklet amply testify. Everything the laity need to know about this sublime Sacrifice will be found clearly and pleasingly told in these pages.

A SUMMER AT WOODVILLE. By Anna T. Sadlier. Benziger
 Brothers. New York, &c.

MRS. SADLIER has done so much for Catholic literature that
no one will be surprised to hear a word of praise in favour of this
latest of her productions. Religious novels and stories are
certainly not popular now-a-days. We doubt if they have ever
been ; and yet they are welcomed and read by a large circle of
readers, who would probably devote their time to more worldly
productions if these were not to be had. A " Summer at
Woodville " is indeed, professedly a Catholic novel; but it has
none the less on that account a considerable flavour of the world,
and may well be read not alone by young people but even by
more seasoned lovers of fiction.

MANUAL OF THE HOLY EUCHARIST, CONFERENCES ON THE
 BLESSED SACRAMENT AND EUCHARISTIC DEVOTION.
 Rev. F. X. Lasance. Benziger Brothers. 1897.

IN the midst of the evils that abound on all sides in modern
society the Church unceasingly directs the attention of the
faithful to the adorable Sacrament of the Eucharist, that they
may derive from it those graces which enlighten the mind and
strengthen the heart, and enable men to steer their course in
safety and avoid the dangers that lie in their way. Of the many
useful manuals compiled for this purpose one of the most useful
is undoubtedly that which we have now before us, and which has
just been published by Messrs. Benziger Brothers of New York.
We recommend it most heartily to all who are interested in
sodalities and confraternities.

The Irish Ecclesiastical Record

A Monthly Journal, under Episcopal Sanction.

Thirtieth Year] No. 357.   **SEPTEMBER, 1897.**   [Fourth Series Vol. II.

Nihil Obstat.
GIRALDUS MOLLOY, S.T.D.
Censor Dep.

Imprimatur.
✠ GULIELMUS,
Archiep. Dublin.,
Hiberniae Primas.

BROWNE & NOLAN, Limited

Publishers and Printers, 24 & 25

NASSAU STREET, DUBLIN.

. . PRICE ONE SHILLING . .

THE SPIRIT OF THE PRIESTHOOD

AMONG the writings of the late Cardinal Manning, there are two works which stand out conspicuous above the rest—*The Temporal Mission of the Holy Ghost*, and *The Eternal Priesthood*. Both of these works have a real worth of their own; for in well-chosen words they tell great spiritual truths of which the world needs to be reminded. But to those who are acquainted with the writer's life and labours, they have a further importance, and bear a meaning which does not meet the eyes of the casual reader. Rightly understood, they throw back a flood of light on the story of that life, and show the spirit working in his years of active labour. In that long, eventful course he had, no doubt, many and varied ends in view at different times; yet it needs no very keen sight, and certainly no far-fetched fancy, to recognise two leading ideas, by which all else was swayed, and ruled and moulded. With whatever change of circumstance, and with whatever measure of failure or success, he was still seeking to accomplish a two-fold task :—to kindle a deep devotion to the Holy Ghost, founded on a right understanding of his office and mission, both in the guidance of the visible Church, and in the hidden hallowing of the individual soul ; and to fill the clergy with a keener sense of their high calling, and a fuller knowledge of the dignity and of the duties of the eternal priesthood.

Not that in either case he was standing apart, and advocating anything new or strange. In truth, he was by no means the only worker in this field, and has no claim to the somewhat dubious merit of originality. In his *Temporal Mission of the Holy Ghost*, as well as its sequel, *The Internal Mission*, and other minor writings on the same subject, he does but set forth in his own words and in his own way, the teaching of the early fathers and the great mediæval schoolmen. But if the doctrine, and the practical devotion flowing from it, are indeed as old as the Church herself; there is yet a new and special reason for preaching them prominently at the present day. As the heresies and divisions of the fifth century arose from a denial or distortion of the dogma of the Incarnation ; the troubles of the Church in the last three hundred years may be said to have their origin in a like denial or misconception of the doctrine set forth in the third main division of the baptismal creed :—

It would seem to me [says Cardinal Manning] that the development of error has constrained the Church in these times to treat especially of the third and last clause of the Apostles' Creed: 'I believe in the Holy Ghost, the Holy Catholic Church, the Communion of Saints.' The definitions of the Immaculate Conception of the Mother of God, of the Infallibility of the Vicar of Christ, bring out into distinct relief the two-fold office of the Holy Ghost, of which one part is His perpetual assistance in the Church, the other His sanctification of the soul, of which the Immaculate Conception is the first fruits and the perfect exemplar.[1]

And it is surely significant that these two questions of the Church's authority and justification, were, after all, the two main issues at the outset of the Reformation movement.

It is only in keeping with this trend of theological controversy, that we find spiritual writers, such as the blessed Louis Grignon de Montfort, in the last century, preaching a special devotion to the Holy Ghost, and dwelling on the mysteries of His working in the whole Church, and in the souls of her children. And in the present century another

---

[1] *The Internal Mission of the Holy Ghost*, p. x.

French writer, the late Abbé Gaume, has written largely on the same theme. Elsewhere, we find the subject treated, in our own days, by Mgr. Otto Zardetti, who has lately resigned the archiepiscopal see of Bucharest. Before his promotion to the episcopate he had helped to spread the devotion in America by means of the Archconfraternity of the Servants of the Holy Ghost, an institution founded by the late Father H. A. Rawes, of the English Congregation of Oblates of St. Charles. How heartily Mgr. Zardetti entered into Cardinal Manning's feelings on this matter, may be seen in some little spiritual works which he published when he was Professor of Theology at the Provincial Seminary of the Archdiocese of Milwaukee.[1]

In the very same way, Cardinal Manning's labours in seeking to raise the standard of priestly perfection, have the support of high authorities and weighty reasons. If the errors of modern sectaries are largely concerned with the office of the Holy Ghost, in His guidance of the Church, and in the hidden work of justification, the widespread triumph of these errors in so many nations of Europe was due in great measure to the corruption and worldliness of too many of the clergy. Hence, the council called together to check the spread of the new heresies had to deal *pari passu* with definition of doctrine, and with moral reformation. This same need of the times may be plainly read in the lives or writings of such real reformers as St. Philip Neri, St. Vincent de Paul, and St. Charles Borromeo.

Cardinal Manning was thus by no means striking out a new line of his own in his writings on these two important topics, or in the practical effect which he gave to his

---

[1] *De Relatione Triplici Sancti Spiritu ad SS. Eucharistiam. De Relatione Triplici Sancti Spiritus ad B. Virginem. De Relatione Triplici Sancti Spiritus ad Verbum Incarnatum. Die Bedeutung besonderer Andacht zu Gott dem H. Geiste für Studirende und für Candidaten des Heiligthumes.* In the last-named work, the author pays the following tribute to Cardinal Manning: ' In ihm haben wir den Basilius redivivus, nur gekleidet in den Purpur. Des Geistes Wünderkraft schildern seine Werke, aber verherrlichen noch mehr als in *humanae sapientiae persuasibilibus verbis* die Werke und |Resultate seines Wirkens, in der That einer Wirksamkeit *in spiritu et virtute.* Seine ganze Erscheinung ist das Abbild eines Basilius und die fleischgewordene Bestätigung des Wortes Spiritus vivificat.' s. 9.

convictions. In both cases he did but seize and set forth the teaching and belief of the chief champions raised up to grapple with the evils of the Reformation period.

It is not our present purpose to give a *resumé* of that teaching as it is set forth by Cardinal Manning. Still less shall we presume to criticize it, or attempt the needless task of defending it from the criticism of others. Our readers will, doubtless, prefer to betake themselves to the original works of the Cardinal, which are still easily accessible. It may, however, be worth our while to consider these two important questions in a somewhat different way, and see if there is not some simple means of bringing them together in one. In insisting on the importance of sanctity, and perfection of life in the Christian priesthood, Cardinal Manning was wont to dwell especially on the Pastoral Office, a phrase which forms the title of a privately printed work in some sense supplementing *The Eternal Priesthood*. To put the matter briefly, in our own words, the argument would seem to be that the parochial clergy and priests engaged on the mission, as sharing in the bishop's pastoral duties, must needs have some share also in the perfection which belongs to the order of bishops. Now, we are in no wise disposed to question the validity of this line of reasoning. Their duties to the flock, on the one hand, and their associations with the pastor, on the other, are doubtless among the strongest motives to lead the clergy to aim at holiness and perfection of life—as even those who cannot agree with all that Cardinal Manning has written on this topic will readily allow. At the same time it may be admitted that the argument lends itself very easily to misconceptions and exaggeration in the hands of indiscreet advocates or captious critics. By some it may be understood as claiming for the priest the fulness of episcopal perfection, or as tending in some degree to lower or disparage the position which belongs to the Religious Orders. While, if it may thus be pressed too far in one way, to some of us it may seem to fall short in apparently limiting the perfection claimed for the priesthood to those who are actually associated in the labours of the pastoral office.

Yet, after all, that office, sublime though it be, is neither the first nor the most fundamental duty of the priesthood. There is another office yet more exalted—and it is common to all who bear the name of priest—the offering of sacrifice. Among the various words by which this title is denoted in the different languages of Europe, that which most happily expresses the true meaning of the priestly office, is the Welsh *offeiriad* or *offerenwr*—one who offers up the Mass.[1]

And it is in this same office of sacrificing that we must look for the real source and standard of priestly perfection, and the true spirit which should animate the priesthood.

Much has been written on the subject of sacrifice, and its symbolical character. But the true meaning of this great central act of divine worship has been nowhere more fully and forcibly expressed than in the well-known words of St. Augustine.[2] 'The visible sacrifice, therefore, is the sacrament; that is, the sacred sign, of the invisible sacrifice.' And again, 'Hence man himself consecrated in the name of God, and vowed to God, inasmuch as he dies to the world that he may live to God, is a sacrifice.' The outward destruction, the slaying of the victim, or the pouring out of the libation, or the burning of the holocaust, was thus a real or visible word, speaking and declaring the inward sacrifice of heart by which the offerer gave himself to God. Hence

---

[1] So, the verb *offerena* means to celebrate Mass. In most other European languages, the word used for priest is only some modified form of *presbyter* and *sacerdos*, e.g., *priester, prêtre, priest, prest ; sacerdote, soggarth*. There are, however, some notable exceptions, such as the Finnish *pappi*, the Hungarian *pap*, and the Polish *ksiandz*.

[2] 'Sacrificium ergo visibile invisibilis sacrificii sacramentum, id est, sacrum signum est. Unde ille penitens apud prophetam, vel ipse propheta quaerens Deum peccatis suis habere propitium : Si voluisses, inquit, sacrificium, dedissem utique, holocaustis non delectaberis. Sacrificium Deo spiritus contribulatus, cor contritum et humiliatum Deus non spernet. Intuemur quemadmodum ubi Deum dixit nolle sacrificium, ibi Deum ostendit velle sacrificium. Non vult ergo sacrificium trucidati pecoris, sed vult sacrificium contriti cordis. Illo igitur quod eum nolle dixit, hoc significatur quod eum velle subjecit. . . . . Ac per hoc ubi scriptum est : Misericordiam volo quam sacrificium ; nihil aliud quam sacrificio sacrificium praelatum oportet intelligi; quoniam illud quod ab omnibus appellatur sacrificium, signum est veri sacrificii.' (*De Civitate Dei*, lib. x., c. 5.) And a little later on : 'Unde ipse homo Dei nomine consecratus, et Deo votus, in quantum mundo moritur ut Deo vivat sacrificium est.' (*Ib.*, c. 6.)

St. Augustine says, again, that those who think that visible
sacrifices belong to other gods,

Surely know not that these are the signs of those [invisible
sacrifices] even as sounding words are the signs of realities.
Wherefore, as when we pray and praise, we send up words with
meaning to Him to whom we offer in the heart those same
realities which we mean thereby ; so when we sacrifice, we must
know that visible sacrifice is to be offered to no other than to
Him whose invisible sacrifice we ourselves must be in our
hearts.[1]

Such is the inward meaning of the sacramental rite of
sacrifice. And for this reason the most perfect sacrifice is
that in which the priest is himself the victim, not offering
some lower being in his stead, but sacrificing himself in deed
and in truth. The olden sacrifices were doubly imperfect,
in the little worth of the victims, which were as nothing in
the sight of God ; and, again, by the very fact that they were
but vicarious symbols, and the sacrifice of heart which they
betokened was too often wanting. But in the one great
sacrifice which these olden rites faintly foreshadowed, there
is a victim worthy of God, and the great High Priest who
offers is Himself the victim. ' Per hoc,' says St. Augustine,
' et sacerdos est, ipse offerens, ipse et oblatio.'[2] Or as the
Church sings in her Easter hymn :—

> Almique membra corporis
> Amor sacerdos immolat.

By that one perfect sacrifice on Calvary the debt of
mankind was paid ; and by its bloodless renewal on the
altar, day by day, its fruits are ceaselessly applied to those
for whom it was offered. And, at the same time, men are
enabled to give a worthy worship to God by joining in its
offering. As of old the priest and people offered themselves
in and through the beasts which were their substitutes and
symbols, so here do they offer themselves in and through
the oblation of the divine Priest who has deigned to give
Himself as their Victim. As St. Augustine says once more :
' This is the sacrifice of Christians : many one body in

[1] *Ib.*, c. 19.   [2] *Ib.*, c. 20.

Christ : which the Church also frequenteth in the sacrament of the altar which is known to the faithful, wherein it is shown to her, that in that which she offereth she herself is offered.'² In like manner, the Church herself says in the *Secreta* on Whit Monday, *et hostiae spiritalis oblatione suscepta, nosmetipsos tibi perfice munus aeternum.*

Now, if this self-offering, this inward sacrifice of heart and consecration of life, is the spirit in which all the children of the Church should join in the Eucharistic Sacrifice, it needs no laboured argument to show that a double portion of that spirit should fall on those who are called to a closer share in this supreme act of divine worship. The priest by whose hands and lips the great Victim offers Himself in sacrifice, is therefore rightly set apart by his ordination, and consecrated to the sacred service, like the vessels of the altar at which he ministers. And in his case there is surely a special fulfilment of the words : 'ipse homo Dei nomine consecratus, et Deo votus, in quantum mundo moritur ut Deo vivat sacrificium est.' The spirit of the priestly life is thus found in its true source in the Eucharistic Sacrifice.

We may see an instance of this looking to the pattern shown us on the altar, in the words of the Apostle St. Andrew, when he was bidden to offer sacrifice to heathen idols : ' I sacrifice, every day, to the Almighty God, who is one and true, not the flesh of bulls nor the blood of goats, but the immaculate Lamb on the altar.'¹ And every priest may well find in this same thought a constraining motive for shunning any homage in the temple of Remmon, or any burning of incense at rival shrines. For the idolatrous worship asked of the Apostle is not the only thing that is incompatible with the service of the altar. As St. Augustine says elsewhere, ' non uno modo sacrificatur traditoribus angelis.'

> In heart the world is pagan, it is still in evil set,
> And offers many a sacrifice at Mammon's altar yet

---

¹ *Ib.*, c. 6 : cf. c. 20 : ' Cujus rei sacramentum quotidianum esse voluit Ecclesiae sacrificium : quae cum ipsius capitis corpus sit, se ipsam per ipsum dicit offerre.'

⁹ See the Breviary Lessons, and the original Acts of the Martyrdom in Gallandius

But the thought which is thus powerful to restrain from evil, should surely prove an equally urgent motive for doing good deeds, and for striving after greater perfection.

The spirit of the priesthood may thus be regarded as neither more nor less than the spirit of sacrifice, by which the priest daily, nay hourly, gives himself in union with the sacred Victim offered by his ministry. And this offering must surely be kindled by the selfsame fire which consumes the Eucharistic holocaust, the flames of divine love and the living fire of the Holy Spirit. Here we are brought to the bond of union which links the teaching of the *Internal Mission* with that of the *Eternal Priesthood.*

Among the works specially ascribed by appropriation to the Holy Ghost, the consecration of the Eucharistic Sacrifice is conspicuous. We may find some trace of this in the Scriptures, for the Apostle contrasts the olden sacrificial rites with the sacrifice of the 'blood of Christ who by the Holy Ghost offered Himself unspotted unto God' (Hebrews ix. 14). And what is here said of the sacrifice of Calvary is repeated by the fathers when they are speaking of the bloodless offering on the altar. 'The priest stands,' says St. John Chrysostom, ' bearing not fire, but the Holy Spirit.'[1] And it is this same Spirit who ' accomplishes this tremendous sacrifice. Comparing this work with the original creation, St. John Damascene says :—

He said in the beginning : 'Let the earth bring forth the green herb': and until now, when the rain cometh, it bringeth forth its own blossoms, impelled and empowered by the divine command. God said:' This is My Body;' and : ' This is My Blood ': and: 'Do this in commemoration of Me.' And by His almighty ordinance, until His coming ; for thus the Apostle saith : ' until He come: ' and by the invocation, there cometh a rain upon this new husbandry, the overshadowing might of the Holy Spirit. For as all whatsoever God made, He made by the operation of the Holy Ghost, so now also the operation of the Holy Ghost worketh the things above nature which faith alone can receive. ' How shall this come to me,' saith the holy Virgin, ' for I know

---

[1] *De Sacerdotio,* lib. iii., c. 4., and lib. vi., c. 4. Compare with this, the language of our own St. Bede : ' Lavat itaque nos a peccatis nostris quotidie in sanguine suo, cum ejusdem beatae passionis ad altare memoria replicatur, cum panis et vini creatura in sacramentum carnis et sanguinis ejus ineffabili Spiritus sanctificatione transfertur.' (*Hom. in Epiphan. Domini, in Joan,* 1.')

not man ? '   The Archangel Gabriel answereth : ' The Holy Ghost shall come upon thee, and the might of the Most High shall overshadow thee.'   And now thou askest : How doth the bread become the body of Christ, and the wine and the water the blood of Christ?   And I say to thee, the Holy Ghost cometh upon them, and worketh those things which are above nature, reason, and understanding.[1]

Yet more significant than these utterances of the fathers, is the prayer of invocation to the Holy Ghost, which holds such a prominent place in all the ancient liturgies.   Its venerable antiquity, and the importance attached to it in the earliest ages, may be gathered from the fact that St. Basil cites it as one of the things handed down by unwritten tradition.[2]   So great, indeed, was the stress laid on this invocation by some early writers, that their language has unfortunately seemed to countenance the opinion that the Consecration is wrought by this Epiclesis, and not by the words of institution.   Theologians and apologists are naturally at pains to show that the words of the liturgies, and the Greek fathers, do not really bear this meaning.[3]   And possibly, in some quarters, the little attention bestowed on this matter is mainly spent on this barren controversy. By a very common reaction, the view which exaggerates the importance of the Epiclesis, is followed by one which unduly disparages it ; and satisfied that the words do not imply what some Eastern schismatics and Western antiquarians have asserted, we pay too little heed to their real meaning.

That there is some deep significance in this invocation of the Holy Ghost, can hardly be questioned by those who know anything of the teaching of the fathers on this matter.   And, it is well to add, this special association of the Holy Spirit with the Holy Eucharist is by no means confined to the Greek, or other Eastern liturgies.   Some counterpart of the Epiclesis, if not so prominent, or in the same position or the same form of words, may yet be found in our Roman Missal.   It is true that the chief Latin

---

[1] *De Fide Orthodoxa*, lib. iv., c. 13.
[2] *De Spiritu Sancto*, c. 27.
[3] Cf. Franzelin, *De Eucharistia*, thes. vii. The subject has been treated at length by Orsi in his valuable *Dissertatio de Spiritus Sancti Invocatione Liturgica*.

equivalent of the Greek invocation, the *Quam oblationem*, which comes immediately before the Consecration, is addressed to the Father, and not to the Holy Spirit. But there is another prayer, in an earlier part of the service, in which a special and direct invocation of the Holy Ghost is plainly discernible. After offering the elements, and saying the prayer *In spiritu humilitatis*, the priest calls down a blessing on the bread and wine, saying: ' Veni, Sanctificator, Omnipotens aeterne Deus, et benedic hoc sacrificium Tuo sancto nomini praeparatum.' That this is addressed to the Holy Ghost, may be gathered from the title *Sanctificator*, which describes the office generally appropriated to the Third Person. But, as Le Brun has shown, we are not left to conjecture, as there is plain evidence, in other Latin liturgies, as to the original purport of this prayer. The invocation, it would seem, was taken from the Missals of the early Gallican Church. Many of these have the words: ' Veni Sancte Spiritus', or, ' Veni, Creator Spiritus'; while the Mozarabic liturgy has the fuller form: ' Veni Sancte Spiritus Sanctificator.' [1]

In these words of the liturgy the Church shows us how the great sacrifice is accomplished by the operation of the divine power, and as a work of love and sanctification it is appropriated to Him who is the Spirit of love and of holiness. [2] And this, and no other, is the source of that sacrificial fire which should burn in the hearts of those who are called to offer the Eucharistic Victim.

In the admonition addressed to the *Ordinandi* the bishop tells how Moses was bidden to choose the seventy elders to whom he was to impart the gifts of the Holy Ghost; and in these, he adds, the priests were signified, if they live worthily, ' by the sevenfold Spirit.' And again after the laying on of hands, in the prayer of consecration, he calls down upon them ' the blessing of the Holy Ghost and the power of priestly grace.' And in a later prayer he prays that the new priests may live worthily of their calling, and may rise up in

---

[1] *Explicatio Missae*, tom. i., pp. 159-60.
[2] Cf. the Secreta for the Friday in Whitsun week : ' Sacrificia, Domine, tuis oblata conspectibus, ignis ille divinus absumat, qui discipulorum Christi Filii tui per Spiritum sanctum corda succendit '

the day of judgment 'Spiritu Sancto pleni.'   So also, during the anointing of their hands, the strains of the Veni Creator call down the Holy Spirit, whose grace it symbolizes.   The versicle, 'Accipite Spiritum Sanctum in vobis Paracletum' is sung in the Responsory after the Communion, and the last imposition of hands is accompanied by the words, 'Accipe Spiritum Sanctum;' while the first of the three Votive Masses which the new priest is bidden to say is the Mass of the Holy Ghost.   Thus the rite of Ordination agrees with the language of the Missal in associating the Holy Spirit in a special manner with the sacrifice, and with the Priesthood.

Monsignor Zardetti has drawn attention to another place in the Missal which enforces the same lesson.   The beautiful prayers of preparation for Mass, ascribed to St. Ambrose, lay great stress on the office of the Holy Ghost in accomplishing the Eucharistic Sacrifice, and pray that His grace may fill the heart of its earthly minister.   Thus the prayer for Sunday says: 'Thou didst set this mystery in the might of Thy Holy Spirit;' and, further on, 'Teach me, I beseech Thee, by Thy Holy Spirit.'   In the prayer for Thursday, again, we read, 'Kindle in us the fire of Thy Holy Spirit;' and on Friday: 'Descendat etiam, Domine illa Sancti Spiritus tui invisibilis incomprehensibilisque majestas, sicut quondam in hostias patrum descendebat, qui et oblationes nostras Corpus et Sanguinem tuum efficiat, et me indignum sacerdotem doceat tantum tractare mysterium cum cordis puritate et lachrymarum devotione.'   These prayers of preparation speak of a special working of the Holy Spirit both in the accomplishment of the sacrifice and the heart of the priest, by whose ministry it is offered.   And assuredly no other form of devotion could be more in harmony with the language of the ancient liturgies and with the true ideal of the priestly office.   For the priest who offers worthily must have the same mind which is in the great High Priest who is Himself the Victim, and the inward holocaust of the heart must be kindled by Him who lights the flames of the altar—and the Spirit of the Sacrifice is the Spirit of the Priesthood.

W. H. KENT, o.s.c.

MODERN SCIENTIFIC MATERIALISM

PART II.—LIFE

BEFORE entering on this part of the subject, where wild assertion and sly assumption do most prevail, let us quote a few sentences from a remarkable address delivered at Munich in 1877 by Professor Virchow. The whole address is virtually a condemnation pronounced by the most learned German materialist on the rash and unwarrantable methods of his fellows. The license of assertion and assumption must have appeared to him to pass all reasonable bounds when, to use his own words, ' it seemed to him high time to enter an energetic protest against the attempts that are made to proclaim the problems of research as actual facts, and the opinions of scientists as established science':—

> We ought not to represent our conjecture as a certainty, nor our hypothesis as a doctrine. . . . The objects of our research are expressed as problems or hypotheses ; but the problem or hypothesis is not, without further debate, to be made *a doctrine.* . . . ' *Scientia est potentia* '—not speculative knowledge, not the knowledge of hypotheses, but objective and actual knowledge. Gentlemen, I think we should be abusing our power, we should be imperilling our power, unless in our teaching we restrict ourselves to this perfectly safe and unassailable domain.

A counsel surely more honoured in the breach than the observance! How necessary—and how futile—it was, will more and more appear as we proceed. We start with a typical instance from a typical transgressor :—

> To account for the origin, growth, and energies of living things it was usual to assume a special agent, free to a great extent from the limitations observed among the powers of inorganic nature. This agent was called *vital force ;* and under its influence plants and animals were supposed to collect their materials and to assume determinate forms. Within the last few years, however, our ideas of vital processes have undergone profound modifications. . . . In tracing the phenomena of vitality through all their modifications the most advanced philosophers of the present day declare that they ultimately arrive at a single source

of power, from which all vital energy is derived : and this source is not the direct fiat of a supernatural agent, but a reservoir of what must be regarded as *inorganic* force.   In short it is considered as proved that all the energy which we derive from plants and animals is drawn from the sun.[1]

The first thing we notice about this passage is the studied use of the past tense when referring to *vital force*, as if it was now quite out of date and possessed of only a historical interest.   In the opening words the foundations of a favourite fallacy are neatly laid.   The ' origin, growth, and energies of living things ' are classed together as if in all respects on exactly the same level and accountable for in the same way. Now it seems almost superfluous to point out that the ' origin ' of a living thing is quite a different process from its ' growth,' and that what may be necessary or sufficient for the one cannot be assumed to be so for the other.   Tyndall, in the course of the essay, shows how sunlight is *necessary* for the ' growth and energies ' of plants and animals, and then concludes that it is *sufficient for all three processes.*   Because plants wither away and die in the dark, therefore sunlight is *sufficient*, not only for the ' growth,' but for the ' origin ' of plants !   We might just as well say that because moisture is *necessary* for the ' growth ' of plants, it is also *sufficient*, not only for their ' growth,' but for their ' origin.'   Fresh air too is *necessary* for plants and animals, but it is hardly *sufficient* for either.   All this looks like trifling ; yet it is by such shallow dodges that ' the most advanced philosophers of the present day ' give their fallacies an appearance of truth.

The last sentence of the extract affords an excellent example of the ' scientific method ' of cooking facts to suit ' advanced philosophy.'   Here we have a collossal assertion —nothing less than that the materialistic theory of life ' is considered as proved '—resting on a misrepresentation of an elementary fact of biology.   This is how the trick is done. It is well known that plants derive the material of their solid structures chiefly from the air.   The leaves absorb the carbonic acid of the air into their pores.   By the combined

---

[1] Tyndall, *Vitality.*

action of the sun and the protoplasm of the leaves this carbonic acid is decomposed, the carbon being assimilated and built up into the solid framework of the plant. To make this process serve his purpose Tyndall represents it as entirely the work of the sun :—' The building up of the vegetable is effected by the sun through the reduction of chemical compounds.' After this the rest is easy. The animals eat the plants ; we eat the animals ; and so ' all the energy we derive from plants and animals is drawn from the sun.' In the process described the protoplasm of the leaf does not, of course, count for much, and may be neglected. On the same principle it might be ' considered as proved' that the chicken is due to the warmth of the sitting hen, the egg not contributing anything worth mentioning ! And this is the Philosophy of Science with capital letters ! A little further on we shall see that nature's *only* builder of her organic structures, whether vegetable or animal, is *living protoplasm.* Without that mysterious worker in the living leaf as in the fruitful egg, the sun might shine on seas of carbonic acid for all time and never raise a twig. Other influences may favour its work, may be necessary for its work; but no known influence can *do* its work.

WHAT IS LIFE ?

What then is *life* according to the materialists ? What is their substitute for that antiquated and unscientific *vital force* with which less ' advanced ' thinkers were and are satisfied ? Life, they tell us, is a purely mechanical phenomenon due to the affinities of ordinary matter. But their own words lend their theory a picturesqueness of which it ought not to be shorn.

Says Tyndall : ' It is the compounding, in the organic world, of forces belonging equally to the inorganic, that constitutes the mystery and miracle of vitality.' [1]

In an important article on Biology in the latest edition (1875) of the *Encyclopædia Britannica* Huxley says :—' To speak of vitality as anything but the name of a series of

---

[1] *Vitality.*

operations is as if one should talk of the horology of a clock.'

Herbert Spencer is sufficiently positive if a trifle inaccurate:—

That the forces exhibited in vital actions, vegetable and animal, are similarly derived [as in inorganic actions], is so obvious a deduction from the facts of organic chemistry that it will meet with ready acceptance from readers acquainted with those facts. [1]

And then, wonderful to relate, he goes on to show his own ' acquaintance with those facts ' by giving a wholly inaccurate account of the process of plant life above described. Like Tyndall he attributes the decomposition of the carbonic acid *altogether* to the sunlight, taking no account of the protoplasm of the leaf, which is the real agent, the sunlight only favouring its action. Huxley indeed shows that certain vegetable growths get on splendidly *in the dark*.[2]

Here then are what, in the case of most men, we should be bound to accept as statements of *fact*. Their words leave no room for a second opinion. It is not a question of hypothesis. We are told in so many words that vitality is as mechanical as the force by which a magnet draws iron or a stone falls to the ground.

When we ask for some proof of all this we get misrepresentations of facts of chemistry or biology such as we have just seen in regard to plant growth. From that typical specimen of ' advanced philosophy ' Tyndall has no hesitation in drawing the required conclusion. He puts it, no doubt, with an *If*; but the hypothetical character of that *If* is carefully eliminated by its surroundings. ' If then from solar light and heat we can derive the energies which we have been accustomed to call *vital*, it indubitably follows that vital energy may have a proximately mechanical origin.'[3] Or we get wholly unwarrantable analogies, as when Tyndall makes out vital force to be little more than a rather complex development of crystalline force, or when Sir R. Ball traces a relationship between animal motion and the supposed

---

[1] *First Principles.*   [2] *Yeast.*   [3] *Vitality.*

vibratory motion of the ultimate atoms of matter.[1] Or we are treated to a disquisition on the correlation of the inorganic forces, and assured that either vital force is an 'undiscovered correlative' of some of these forces, or else that having no correlation with them it can have no existence at all—which is something like saying that because Tom is not sometimes Jack or Bill, there is no Tom! Or again, we get assumptions and assertions piled up until the reader loses sight of the fact that the first of them has as little to stand on as the tortoise of ancient cosmology. Or finally, we are led away into the region of prophecy, and bidden to put faith in the power of science to produce in the future evidence which unfortunately, owing to the difficulty of the subject, is not forthcoming in the present.[2] After a due amount of this sort of 'advanced philosophy' the proposition is 'considered as proved, all reasons to the contrary being classified as ignorance or narrow theological prejudice.

So long as the human mind continues to be constituted as it is it must reject this so-called 'mechanical' theory of life as utterly irrational. It is, in fact, repugnant to one of those intuitions that lie at the root of all certainty. To accept it we must give up our belief in the necessity of adequate causes to produce effects. Natural phenomena of all kinds are simply *effects* which it is the proper business of science to trace to adequate causes. We note that certain of these phenomena are peculiar to living things, vegetable or animal ; that no trace of them, or of anything in the least like them, can be discovered in inanimate nature. Experts on both sides confirm this view. 'The phenomena which living things present,' says Professor Huxley, 'have no parallel in the mineral world.'[3] Mivart says : 'Scientific

---

[1] *Vide* I. E. RECORD, Fourth Series, vol. i., p. 253.

[2] Professor Marsh in a presidential address thus preaches a sort of scientific 'salvation by faith' to the American Association—' Possibly the great mystery of life may thus be solved (*i.e.*, by the mechanical theory) ; but whether it be or not, a true faith in science knows no limits to its search for truth.' We do not pretend to know what the latter portion of the sentence means, except that it calls for an unlimited and apparently an unreasoning faith in science whether it solves difficulties or not.

[3] *Ency. Brit. Biology.*

men are agreed that there is an absolute break between the living world and the world devoid of life.'[1] Dr. Lionel Beale, a veteran authority on this subject, says: ' Surely it is very significant that every particle of living matter of every sort known should manifest phenomena of a particular kind, while no form of non-living matter has been discovered which exhibits any like phenomena.'[2] And again :—

I have never been able to discover in any non-living bodie whatever any phenomena which can be fairly said to correspond to, or be comparable with [the phenomena of living bodies]. Nor can I discern the faintest analogy between the marvellous changes which affect every kind of living matter in nature, and any changes which have been proved to occur under any circumstances in matter which does not live.[3]

The characteristic features that thus clearly mark off the living from the not-living are chiefly these :—(1) organized structure, which is quite unlike anything found in lifeless matter ; (2) extraordinary chemical complexity ; (3) mode of origin, which is invariably from pre-existing life, and in no other way; (4) growth and conservation by the absorption of nutritive material and its conversion into their own substance ; (5) reproduction of their own like ; (6) healing power in case of wounds ; (7) decay and death, followed by the speedy break up of the whole complex organism. These phenomena in one shape or another are common to all kinds of living things; while, as Huxley says, they are absolutely without parallel in the mineral world. We naturally conclude that the same is true of the *cause* which lies behind these *effects*—it must also be something which ' has no parallel in the mineral world.' The effects show this cause to be of the nature of what we call a force or power ; and so we name it *vital force*, or *life* in its widest sense.

The point is of such importance that we may be allowed to quote another statement of the argument from a recent work :—

These various features mark off by an impassable barrier the living organism from dead matter. . . . The several processes of

[1] *Origin of Human Reason.*   [3] *Lumleian Lectures*, p. 51.
[2] *Mystery of Life*, p. 26.

evolution, conservation, and reproduction constitute a group of operations completely transcending the chemical and mechanical powers of matter. The innate tendency to build itself up according to a specific type, to restore injured or diseased parts, to conserve itself against the agencies perpetually working for its dissolution, and to reproduce its kind, manifest an internal principle which dominates and governs the entire existence of the being. On the strength of the axiom that every effect must have an adequate cause, we claim a special ground for vital phenomena in those material substances which possess life. It is true, of course, that life is subject to the conditions imposed on its existence by the chemical and mechanical properties of matter, but this is quite a different thing from saying that life is only the *result* of these properties. Mere aggregation or combination of chemical elements could never be the sufficient reason for the evolution of a plant or animal according to its specific type. Reproduction and uniformity within the same species, and the persistent differences which keep separate species apart, would never proceed from such a cause. We are justified, then, in assuming a new internal energy, a directing force which determines and governs the stream of activities described as the phenomena of life. This force is what is meant by the so-called ' *vegetative scul* ' or ' *vital principle*.' [1]

Of course this conception of a special vital force to account for vital phenomena is not of to-day or yesterday. It did not need to wait for modern science to establish it. The broad face of nature lay open to view in the past as in the present, and thinking men long ago noted the chief characteristics which distinguish living from lifeless things, and drew from them the conclusion which we now draw. These observers doubtless had very crude notions of organic structure. They knew nothing of the chemical complexity of organic substances. They were not at all sure of the invariable necessity of antecedent life for the production of life. But they saw quite enough on the surface of things to convince them of the existence of that 'impassable barrier' whose deep foundations science has since partly laid bare. They saw living things grow by the assimilation of other

---

[1] *Psychology*, by M. Maher, S J. (1893). For an elegant illustration of the nature of the argument for the existence of a special vital force, see Dr. Elam's *Winds of Doctrine*, p. 100 to end of chapter.

substances into their own. They saw them reproduce and perpetuate their own kind. They saw the gashed tree or the wounded animal put forth a wonderful self-healing power. They saw all these vital processes fail, and the living thing die and speedily decompose. They saw that this cycle of phenomena was common to all living things of whatever kind, vegetable or animal, that came under their observation. They saw as clearly as Professor Huxley that it 'had no parallel in the mineral world.' They saw with greater clearness, because with less prejudice than the Professor, that effects so utterly contrasted as were those observable in living and not-living things could not be traceable to the same cause or causes. Not having a pre-conceived 'mechanical' theory to sustain they therefore concluded that there must be some activity, power, principle—call it what you will—at work in the one, of which there was no trace in the other. Further, they concluded that this vital power or principle must, from the peculiar and quite exceptional nature of its effects, be something entirely different from the forces of inanimate matter—something 'apart from the domain of physics, and beyond the empire of physical law.'[1]

That is how the argument stood long before the great-grandfathers of 'the most advanced philosophers of the present day' appeared on the scene. That is how it stands now, only still further confirmed by the results of modern research. The microscopist, peering into the living cell, beholds there phenomena as peculiar to, and distinctive of life as those more evident ones already referred to—absorption of nutriment, growth, ceaseless movement—all of which 'differ absolutely from any actions known to occur in any kind of non-living matter whatever.'[2]

It may be well to notice a sort of pantheistic theory of vitality maintained or approved by some of our 'advanced

---

[1] Beale, *Lumleian Lectures*, p. 50.   [2] *Ibid.*, p. 21.

philosophers.'   We borrow a statement of it from *The Dublin Review* :—[1]

Life in this or that living being may be imagined to be a portion of a universal life, which concentrates itself in living organisms, but is yet diffused throughout the universe—which sleeps in the mineral, dreams in the animal, and first wakes to consciousness of itself in man.   The starting-point of speculation may be made neither matter alone nor a Divine mind alone, but an obscure synthesis of mind and matter, . . . so that wherever we have matter we have mind in a more or less rudimentary or developed state ; and where in man we have the highest material organisation and complexity, we have also the fullest development of mind.   On this opinion the phenomena of life and mind . . . would belong to the same order [as the phenomena of the non-living world].   The difference between the living and what we call the non-living would be one not of kind but of degree. . . . The first appearance and subsequent activity of *recognised* life in the world would be—not an interference with the previous course of nature, not the introduction from without of a new agency, . . . but the self-revelation of the agency which had been at work all along, and had now attained in particular organisms such development that its true character could no longer be mistaken.

We have already seen the way prepared for this view by Bain's ' double-faced ' definition of matter.[2]   That definition supplied the requisite synthesis of mind and matter, so that wherever we have matter we have the elements of mind.   Development in the direction of life, sensation, and finally consciousness, could then be described as simply keeping pace with chemical complication.   Later on we shall see this theory advanced by Häckel, Tyndall, and others, as one way of accounting for the origin of life.   It has, of course, no more solid support than the ' scientific imagination.'

The adoption of this theory of vitality *ought* to mean the abandonment of the purely physical or mechanical theory, which ascribes life to the forces of ordinary matter as commonly defined, without assuming the existence of any extraordinary *mind-matter*.   However, our ' advanced philo-

---

[1] July, 1873, pp. 258-9.
[2] I. E. RECORD, fourth series, vol. i., p. 345-6.

sophers' show a wonderful aptitude for holding quite
contradictory theories; and so we must not be surprised
to find them maintaining that life is due to the forces of
ordinary matter as we all know it, and also to the properties
of extraordinary matter as known only to Professors Bain
and Tyndall and a few other 'privileged spirits.'

About the *nature* of vital force science—with whose
teachings alone we are here concerned—can tell us nothing.
Biology can inform us of the inadequacy of the chemical or
physical forces to account for vital phenomena, and so
authorize us to affirm the existence of some other force that
can account for them; but that is all. What further
knowledge we may acquire about it—as that in the case of
man the vital principle is an immaterial and immortal
spirit—we get from quite other sources.

PROTOPLASM

The manifestations of vital force are always found to be
associated with a particular substance which has received
various names, but which will probably be best known to
the general reader under that of *protoplasm*. As this protoplasm is, so to speak, the physical machinery through
which life force does it work, it demands somewhat detailed
notice. We shall arrange what we have to say under the
following heads:—(1) general description of protoplasm;
(2) function or work; (3) differentiation; (4) materialistic
difficulties. In such a highly technical matter we shall be
careful to confine ourselves to statements for which we can
produce unexceptionable authority. No one, we think, will
gainsay Dr. Lionel Beale's claim to a foremost place amongst
British specialists on protoplasm. For continental opinion
we shall refer to a splendid French work published last year,
La Cellule, by Professor L. F. Henneguy, Lecturer on
Embryology at the College of France, &c.

GENERAL DESCRIPTION

In every living thing [says Dr. Beale], at every period of
life there exist in every part of it portions of *bioplasm* upon which

the life of the being or part thereof absolutely depends.[1] . . .
As far as can be ascertained by examination under an amplifying
power of 5,000 diameters, living matter throughout nature is
colourless and structureless.[2] . . . If motionless, its presence
[under the microscope] can only be recognised by the fact of
its being a very little less perfectly transparent than the fluid
which surrounds it, and by its refracting property being
slightly different from that of the medium in which it lives.[3]

Writing on the subject as late as last year he still
describes protoplasm as 'colourless, structureless matter,
consisting largely of water.'[4] In fact, twenty years of active
research by the most eminent histologists of all nations have
but confirmed Dr. Beale's description in every particular.
Though protoplasm has from time to time during these
years been described by different investigators as *striated*,
fibrous, reticulated, granulated, &c., yet in the end we find
the ablest of all the continental histologists, Kölliker,
describing the pure protoplasm found in young cells as
'absolutely homogeneous, without any structure, made
up of a mixture of semi-fluid substances.'[5] With the
results of all these investigations before him, Kölliker's
description is fully endorsed and adopted by Henneguy,[6]
who also elsewhere describes pure protoplasm in almost the
exact words used by Dr. Beale—'a viscous, semi-fluid,
colourless substance, insoluble in water, and of higher
refracting power than the liquid.'[7] According to Kölliker
the various formations above referred to—*granules, fibres,
net-work processes*, &c.—appear later on,[8] and hence must be
regarded rather as products of the activity of protoplasm
than as essential constituents. Some of them are regarded
as results of the action of the chemical tests employed,

[1] From a letter of March 21st, 1897. Dr. Beale generally prefers the term
bioplasm to protoplasm.
[2] *Lumleian Lectures* (1875), p. 26.
[3] *Ibid.*, p. 27.
[4] *Lancet*, June 13th, 1896.
[5] *La Cellule* (1896), p. 59.
[6] *Ibid.*, p. 60.
[7] *Ibid.*, p. 19.
[8] *Ibid.*, p. 59. See this confirmed by Nicholas (1892), Saint Remy (1892),
and others, *ibid.*, p. 235-6.

or of the coagulation of the protoplasm after death,[1] or as secretions to be afterwards cast out.[2]

Protoplasm is never found in large quantities together. ' In man and the higher animals it is the exception to find a single mass of protoplasm which measures as much as the one-thousandth of an inch in any direction.'[3] These minute specks are nearly always enclosed in a transparent membrane, forming a *cell*. A portion of the protoplasm of every living cell is found to be thickened and altered in some unexplained way, forming what is called the *nucleus* of the cell. Such a nucleus, it is found, is essential to the life and activity of the cell. Hence a living cell may be described as a minute mass of protoplasm containing a nucleus and surrounded by a transparent membrane.

A notable characteristic of living protoplasm is its state of ceaseless movement. The movements are various and peculiar, and include a species of *circulation* within each cell. This state of ceaseless movement is believed to be essential to its life.[4]

As regards the chemical nature of protoplasm it is found to be, not a single, definite chemical compound, but a mixture of several complex bodies, together with traces of simpler ones.[5] However, the chemical analysis of protoplasm cannot be relied on as deciding the constitution of *living* protoplasm, inasmuch as protoplasm submitted to chemical analysis is necessarily deprived of life; and loss of life means loss of those very characters that distinguish protoplasm from all other substances.[6] ' The essential character of protoplasm is that it is *living*, and that it loses its properties with its life. Protoplasm that is no longer alive is no longer protoplasm.'[7] Henneguy entirely agrees with those biologists who maintain that ' living, active protoplasm has a different molecular constitution from dead protoplasm.'[8] The change,

---

[1] *La Cellule*, p. 60.
[2] *Ibid.*, pp. 57-58.
[3] *Lumleian Lectures*, p. 18.
[4] *Ibid.*, pp. 28-36. *La Cellule*, pp. 29-30.
[5] *La Cellule*, p. 25, *et seq.*
[6] *Ibid.*, p. 20.
[7] *Ibid.*, p. 18.
[8] *Ibid.*, p. 23.

be admits, may be 'merely an alteration in the grouping of the molecules. We do not know. We know no more of the cause of death than of the origin of life.'[1]

FUNCTION

The function or work or protoplasm is the conversion of nutriment into organic tissue. Nutriment when presented in a proper form is absorbed into the protoplasm, converted instantaneously into living matter (*i.e.*, more protoplasm) *by some utterly unknown process*, and finally into *formed material* or *tissue* of one kind or another—bone, muscle, nerve, flesh, skin, &c.—bark, wood-fibre, pith, &c.

These two processes—the formation of tissue by bioplasm, and the production of new bioplasm by the appropriation of nutritive matters—proceed at the same time.[2] . . . Nutrient pabulum dissolved in water permeates the capsule of formed material (*i.e.*, the membrane), and comes into contact with the bioplasm within. The non-living matter then undergoes changes most wonderful, in the course of which it acquires the same properties and powers as the bioplasm already existent possesses?[3] . . . In the formation of every tissue, in the construction of every organ and of every form of mechanism existing in a living being, bioplasm is the sole essential and active agent.[4]

Its mode of operation constitutes the unsolved 'mystery of life.'—'The field is open for research regarding the internal phenomena of which living matter is the seat—phenomena of which, for the most part, we still know nothing.'[5] Dr. Beale tells us that 'there is not the slighest reason to think that the nature of the changes which proceed in living centres will ever be ascertained by physical investigation, inasmuch as they are certainly of an order or nature totally distinct from that to which any other phenomena known to us can be referred.'[6] In fact he tells us that the proper means for investigating them have yet to be discovered.[7]

Note that the function of protoplasm does not stop with the formation of organic *substances* from inorganic or other materials; the chemist can do that to a limited extent. It

---

[1] *La Cellule*, p. 467.
[2] Beale, *Mystery of Life*, p. 39.
[3] *Lumleian Lectures*, p. 20.
[4] *Ibid.*, p. 60, *et seq.*
[5] *La Cellule*, p. 465.
[6] *Mystery of Life*, p. 55.
[7] *Lancet*, June 13th, 1896.

goes on to build up the converted substances into organic *structures*—a process entirely transcending the powers of chemistry.

No forces known except those operating in living matter have been found competent to effect special structural arrangements[1] —(*i.e.*, such as are found in living things). . . . The idea of a particle of muscular or nerve tissue being formed by a process akin to crystallization appears ridiculous to anyone who has studied the phenomena, or who is acquainted with the structure of these tissues.[2]

We must bear in mind that the *living matter* or protoplasm is very different from the *formed matter* or tissue which is its work.

In all parts of all organisms, and at every period of life, we find the greatest contrast between living and formed matter— between the active living matter that selects, grows, forms, and possesses vital movements, and the formed material which, though it performs very important offices, does not grow or reproduce itself, and has no power of selection or construction.[3]

In fact the difference amounts to this that formed tissue is no longer *alive.* ' The production of the formed material is coincident with the death of the bioplasm. As the formed material is produced, the bioplasm ceases to live.'[4]

Part of the function of protoplasm is to be the vehicle of hereditary traits, and this not merely in the broad sense of reproducing the general characteristics of the species, but the special peculiarities of the individual. ' Hereditary characters can be transmitted by the bioplasm only. . . . Bioplasm is the agent concerned in the transmission of all hereditary structural peculiarities; nay, this living matter alone can inherit.'[5] Family resemblances extending even to the most trivial details are matter of common observation. No one is surprised to see a particular tilt of an ancestor's nose or the curl of a lock of hair reappear in some or all of the descendants. Yet what a wonder such a trifling thing is when we consider the mode of transmission. The

---

[1] *Lumleian Lectures*, p. 61.   [4] *Lumleian Lectures*, p. 21.
[2] *Mystery of Life*, p. 39.   [5] *Ibid.*, pp. 66-7.
[3] *Lancet*, Aug. 29, 1896.

architectural power that was to produce not only the specific
feature but the special family peculiarity must have been
present in the protoplasm of the germ speck, must have
lain dormant until the proper time for its operations arrived,
must then have woke up to activity, and guided the formative protoplasm to reproduce the plan traced by ancestral
protoplasm perhaps centuries before. Needless to say, all
this is an impenetrable mystery. The facts are evident,
but the cause baffles scientific skill to discover. Even the
omniscient ' scientific imagination ' has failed to supply a
reasonable theory on the subject. ' Certain biologists have
attempted to explain the properties of organized matter by
its peculiar molecular constitution.[1] . . . But such a
hypothesis is powerless to give us any idea of the development or reproduction of living matter, or the manner in
which the hereditary peculiarities of parents are transmitted
to their descendants.'[2] All the theories of heredity hitherto
put forward, from Darwin to Weismann, are characterized
by Henneguy as ' pure conceptions of the mind, . . . fated
to disappear.'[3] They remind him of Molière's explanation
of the effects of opium—' *Opium facit dormire quia est in
eo virtus dormitiva !* '[4]

The phenomena of heredity still further emphasize the
absolute distinction that exists between living and not-
living matter. ' There is nothing in the non-living world,
it need scarcely be remarked, that presents any analogy
with this marvellous power of inheriting from predecessors
definite characters, and transmitting them to those that
succeed.'[5]

---

[1] This, of course, refers to the ' mechanical theory ' of life.
[2] *La Cellule*, p. 480.
[3] *Ibid.*, p. 484. It must be admitted that the theorists themselves
help vigorously towards the accomplishment of this ' disappearance.' Darwin's
theory of heredity is declared by Weismann to be ' inconceivable,' and
Weismann's is, in turn, pronounced by Professor Romanes to be if anything still
more inconceivable—' a work of artistic imagination rather than of scientific
generalization.' Indeed Dr. Romanes impartially declares ' all theories of the
ultimate mechanism of heredity hitherto published,' owing to ' the necessary
absence of verification,' to be purely imaginary. *Examination of Weismannism*
(1893), pp. 119, 120.
[4] *Ibid.*, 488.
[5] *Lumleian Lectures*, p. 67.

DIFFERENTIATION

It was long believed that protoplasm from all sources was in every respect identical. Between protoplasm and protoplasm when pure, the most powerful microscope shows absolutely no difference. 'The highest known form of living matter cannot be distinguished from the lowest.[1] For neither in dimensions, nor in form, nor in composition, nor in any other essential character, property, or quality, to be demonstrated by physics, chemistry, or observation, does the one particle differ from the other.'[2] Moreover, when submitted to chemical decomposition, pure protoplasm always yields the same products. These facts were regarded as establishing the complete identity of all protoplasm. Huxley strongly insisted on this complete identity—the protoplasm of all living things was ' substantially the same,' identical in matter, form, and function. In his skilful hands this universal identity of life stuff was made to serve as proof of the common origin and all-round relationship of living things, animal and vegetable. All are made of the same stuff in the same mill. There is no more in any of the products than what the mill has put into them. It is as vain to look for specific differences among the products of protoplasm as among those of a cotton mill.

But there were other facts equally well known that tended to establish the very opposite of all this—to substitute for Huxley's universal identity a universal difference. The varied functional activities of protoplasm indicated the existence of differences too subtle for microscope or chemical test. There was machinery in the mill that could not be detected. Day by day it became more clear that while the identity was only superficial, the differences were fundamental. Thus vegetable and animal protoplasm afford an example of that physical and chemical identity just described; yet that there is some fundamental difference is shown by the fact that while the former will assimilate and work up *inorganic* material, the latter will not—its nutriment

---

[1] *Lumleian Lectures*, p. 26.   [2] *Mystery of Life*, p. 29.

must be supplied in an organized form.[1] Then the protoplasm of each kind of living thing shows itself by its work
to be in some mysterious way different from the protoplasms
of all other kinds. Thus the protoplasm of a fish and that
of a man convert the same nutriment into quite different
formations. Further, the protoplasm of each particular organ
of each living thing is in like manner different from the
protoplasms of all the other organs, and is not interchangeable
with them. 'Of no one living thing, and of the organs
of no one living thing, is the protoplasm interchangeable
with that of another.[2] . . . There is nerve-protoplasm,
brain-protoplasm, bone-protoplasm, muscle-protoplasm, and
protoplasm of all the other tissues, no one of which but
produces only its own kind, and is uninterchangeable with
the rest.'[3]

Cells which to us, with our present means of investigation,
appear to be composed of identical protoplasm have, nevertheless,
very different functional properties. Cells from the different
salivary glands and from the pancreas of a dog, for instance, are
to all outward appearance so much alike that it is impossible to
distinguish them, and yet each has its own peculiar function.
The most skilful embryologist could not distinguish the ovule of
a cow from that of a dog, yet these ovules will produce very
different animals.[4]

So also Dr. Beale:—

Here are two minute masses of perfectly structureless,
colourless living matter. No difference between them can be
demonstrated by physics or chemistry. One placed under certain
conditions will become a dog, the other a man ; but from the dog-
germ you cannot by any alteration of conditions obtain a man,
any more than from the man-germ anything but a man can be
evolved. Now what is the difference [between the germs] which
cannot be distinguished by physical or chemical investigation ? I
would answer—a transcendent difference, but *in power*.[5]

[1] Reference has already been made to the process of plant growth. The
protoplasm of the leaves, aided by sunlight, has the power of forming protoplasm
from what we may call its raw materials, viz., carbonic acid, water, and
ammonia. Animal protoplasm has no such power. It is a common saying
that ' we cannot live on air.'
[2] *As Regards Protoplasm*, by Dr.J. H. Stirling, p. 4. This pamphlet, though
somewhat tough in style, is excellent in matter.
[3] *Ibid.*, p. 31.
[4] *La Cellule*, p. 18.
[5] *Mystery of Life*, p. 13.

Yielding to the force of such facts as these, expert opinion has veered round to the opposite pole, and is now expressed by the sweeping statement that ' there are in reality as many protoplasms as there are different beings, and organs in each of these beings fulfilling different functions.'[1]   In fact protoplasm has come to be regarded as a sort of generic term like *bird* or *mammal*, an expression covering a whole category of more or less different things united by certain common characteristics.[2]

The only explanation offered of this endless diversity of power in connection with apparent identity of substance is a purely hypothetical one.

Organic chemistry teaches us that certain bodies of absolutely identical chemical composition may have very different properties. Such bodies are called *isomeric ;* and the idea is that difference in properties is due to corresponding differences in the grouping of the component atoms, whose number and relative proportions are the same. It may possibly be the same with regard to different protoplasms, their diversity of properties being due to the phenomenon known in organic chemistry as *isomerism.*[3]

No doubt protoplasm, with its wonderfully complex structure, affords exceptional opportunities for the working of the principle here described ; but it must be borne in mind that there is not the smallest experimental foundation either for principle or application. They are as purely imaginary as theories of heredity, and suffer from the same ' necessary absence of verification.'

We are now prepared to realize to some extent the difficulty biologists find in framing a definition of protoplasm. As a picturesque and suggestive synonym Huxley's ' physical basis of life ' is excellent. Few could name or, when it suited him, misname a thing more aptly than the versatile Professor. However, in accepting his expression we must be careful not to accept the theories he founded on it. Many of Dr. Beale's references to protoplasm are almost definitions, as, for instance, when he speaks of it as

---

[1] *La Cellule.* p. 18.   [2] *Ibid.*, p. 18.   [3] *Ibid.*

'living matter which throughout nature is devoid of structure, exhibits spontaneous movement, and consists of comparatively few elements.'[1] This serves very well to recall some of its leading physical and chemical characteristics. But, as we have seen, all such characteristics are of secondary importance, and 'its essential character is that it is *living*, and that it loses its properties with its life'—to which may also be added 'that it can only come from preexisting protoplasm.'[2] These are the only characteristics that are entirely peculiar to protoplasm, and in comparison with them its physical and chemical properties must be regarded as of only secondary importance.[3] Hence little of any moment can be added to the bare statement that 'protoplasm is organic living matter.'[4]

Protoplasm once dead, whatever be the nature of the change that takes place in it, can no longer be called 'life-matter.' There is a fallacy hidden in such a use of words. It suggests a capacity in dead protoplasm to be revitalized. But there is no such capacity. Protoplasm once dead can never again by any process known to science be revitalized 'Under no circumstances can the living thing once dead be made to live again.'[5] Dead protoplasm simply decays and decomposes like any other organic substance. *Living* protoplasm alone is 'life-matter.'

MATERIALISTIC DIFFICULTIES

The scientific philosophers, as we know, deny that there has been 'any intrusion of purely creative power' anywhere in nature. Tyndall has assured us that that sleepless Cerberus, 'the eye of science,' has hitherto sought in vain for the faintest trace of such a thing. Therefore protoplasm with all its wonderful properties must be a product of the action of the natural forces ; and some reasonable account of its development out of

---

[1] *Lancet*, June 13, 1896.
[2] *La Cellule*, p. 19.
[3] *Ibid.*
[4] *Ibid.*, p. 18.
[5] *Mystery of Life*, p. 81. We do not, of course, contemplate *miraculous* restoration to life.

elementary matter has to be given.   The difficulty is three-fold.   (1) Looking at it from a chemical point of view, how did such an extraordinarily complex chemical substance as protoplasm ever come to be formed from inert matter by any known or conceivable action of the ordinary forces of nature?   (2) Supposing the chemical substance to be formed by some inconceivable combination of circumstances, how did it grow alive?   (3) How did it acquire that marvellous diversity of architectural powers which it displays throughout nature?

Most of the leading materialistic philosophers have tried their hands at this three-fold puzzle.   The most eloquent of 'lay sermons' has been preached upon it; the 'scientific imagination' has run riot in discoursing of it; chemists have left their crucibles, and geologists their rocks, to talk about it; and at least one astronomer has abandoned 'the high heavens' to favour earth with a solution which had better have been confided in passing to the man in the moon. All the solutions will be covered by one description—the throwing of unlimited verbal dust in the public eye.   Of all the scientific jugglers who have attempted this dust trick Professor Huxley may be fairly regarded as the most expert, and his method of disposing of the three difficulties above enumerated supplies a high class specimen of his powers.

1. The first difficulty, viz., the formation of protoplasm from its elements, seems to vanish away before his mere statement, ceasing to be a difficulty at all, and shrivelling up to the dimensions of a beggarly chemical experiment. In his famous essay on *The Physical Basis of Life* he teaches the public the chemistry of protoplasm in this wise : [1]—

Carbon, hydrogen, oxygen, and nitrogen, are all lifeless bodies. Of these carbon and oxygen unite in certain proportions and under certain conditions to give rise to carbonic acid; hydrogen and oxygen produce water; nitrogen and hydrogen

[1] *Lay Sermons* (1893), pp. 117-8.

give rise to ammonia. These new compounds, like the elementary bodies of which they are composed, are lifeless. But when
they are brought together under certain conditions, they give
rise to a still more complex body, *protoplasm;* and this protoplasm exhibits the phenomena of life.

Nothing simpler, you will say. The non-chemical reader ·
must feel perfectly helpless in face of such a statement
from such an authority. In fact, be must feel prepared to
admit the probability of protoplasm becoming an article
of commerce, opening up new and delightful possibilities
for the pictorial advertiser! The vague little phrase 'under
certain conditions' would not attract attention, and might
mean anything—boiling, or pressure, or ignition, as in the
production of carbonic acid or water. A little farther
on we are told in a passing way, as if it was of no great
consequence, that the *condition* is '*the influence of pre-
existing protoplasm*'—surely a most unexpected condition
for the production of this very substance from its constituents! If 'pre-existing protoplasm' is a 'condition' of
the production of protoplasm, how was the *first* protoplasm
produced?

Professor Huxley sees 'no break in the series of steps
in molecular complication,' and is unable to understand
why the language which is applicable to any one term
of the series may not be used to any of the others.
Does carbonic acid, or water, or ammonia require 'the
influence of pre-existing' carbonic acid, water, or ammonia
for its production? If not, what an enormous change
must be made in the 'language applicable' in the two
cases!

Nor does Professor Huxley think it necessary to tell the
non-chemical reader that, while the making of carbonic
acid, water, and ammonia are mere elementary experiments,
*no known chemical process can produce from these under any
conditions any substance ever so remotely resembling protoplasm!* What is to be thought of the man who, with full
knowledge of all this, could still tell the unsuspecting
public that there was 'no break in the series of steps' from
lifeless elements to living protoplasm?

Professor Huxley goes on to take advantage of whatever slight knowledge of chemistry his readers may have, to make his reasoning still more crushing :—

When hydrogen and oxygen are mixed in a certain proportion, and an electric spark is passed through them, they disappear, and a quantity of water equal in weight to the sum of their weights appears in their place. Is the case in any way changed when carbonic acid, water, and ammonia disappear, and in their place, under the influence of pre-existing living protoplasm, an equivalent weight of the matter of life makes its appearance ?

Here we have 'the language applicable to one term of the series' applied to another with a completeness that leaves nothing to be desired. The two processes, viz., the chemical production of water and the chemical production of protoplasm, are, as far as words can do it, placed on exactly the same level. Now the merest tyro in chemistry has seen the first experiment performed, and knows that it is quite easy. With his limited knowledge he can only suppose, from the language used, that to a man of Professor Huxley's scientific eminence the second is equally easy. He is quite unaware of the fact that neither electric sparks nor any other known agency would be of the smallest use in the case ; but he naturally supposes Professor Huxley an honest reasoner, and remains confounded if not convinced.

Here is what the leading English chemist of our day, Sir H. Roscoe, has to say of Professor Huxley's chemistry of protoplasm :—

It is true that there are those who profess to foresee that the day will arrive when the chemist, by a succession of constructive efforts, may pass beyond albumen, and gather the elements of lifeless matter into a living structure. Whatever may be said of this from other standpoints, the chemist can only say that at present no such problem lies within his province. Protoplasm, with which the simplest manifestations of life are associated, is not a compound, but a structure built up of compounds. The chemist may successfully synthesize any of its component compounds, but he has no more reason to look forward to the synthetic production of the structure than to imagine that the synthesis of gallic acid leads to the artificial production of gall-nuts.[1]

---

[1] *Presidential Address to the British Association*, 1887.

Professor Henneguy is equally decided :—

In the present condition of our knowledge we must speak of protoplasm as a body *whose synthesis we cannot effect*, and whose origin we do not know. This much we do know since spontaneous generation was finally disposed of by Pasteur and Tyndall— *that protoplasm can only come from pre-existing protoplasm.*[1]

Dr. Stirling takes us even a step farther : —

Protoplasm can only be produced by protoplasm, and each of all the innumerable varieties of protoplasm only by its own kind.[2]

All honest men will endorse Dr. Beale's demand for open and straightforward dealing in this matter :—

If the method by which non-living matter is converted into living matter is understood, by all means let it be explained. If conversion like that effected by living matter can be carried out in the laboratory, let it be done ; but if the change can be effected by living matter alone, let this be openly admitted ; and let it be clearly stated, and in the most public manner possible, that the phenomena in question are peculiar to living matter, and cannot be shown to be due to physical and chemical changes apart from life.

One of Professor Huxley's smart sayings is that 'the man of science has learned to believe in justification, not by faith, but by verification.'[4] He seems to have conveniently forgotten this maxim when writing *The Physical Basis of Life.*

2. It is always quietly assumed that protoplasm, if once formed, would necessarily be *alive*. It always is so when formed by nature's mysterious chemistry under the influence of pre-existing living protoplasm. But there is such a thing as *dead* protoplasm, differing no doubt, as we have seen, in some unknown way from living protoplasm, but still at least the corpse, so to speak, of protoplasm, and still called protoplasm by materialists themselves. They are bound to show that their protoplasm, even if they could make it, would ever get beyond this stage—would ever 'exhibit the phenomena of life.' In the whole range of scientific achievement

---

[1] *La Cellule*, p. 19.
[2] *As Regards Protoplasm*, p. 48.
[3] *Lumleian Lectures*, p. 41.
[4] *Lay Sermons*, p. 16.

is there anything to teach them how to make a thing *alive*? Can they learn nature's secret by watching her work under the microscope? Alas! Professor Huxley's despairing answer is that 'the influence of pre-existing living matter is something quite unintelligible,'[1] and therefore not likely to serve as a guide in practical chemistry!

> In living centres [says Dr. Beale] proceed changes of the nature of which the most advanced physicists and chemists fail to afford us the faintest conception. Nor is there the slightest reason to think that the nature of these changes will ever be ascertained by physical investigation.

The nearest approach to a solution of this second difficulty which we get from Professor Huxley is a reference to 'subtle influences' which 'will convert dead protoplasm into living protoplasm.' What these 'subtle influences' are, or whence they are derived, or how they effect this important conversion, is not stated. What, by the way, is the difference between these subtle influences and *vital force*? And how comes it that the theory of 'subtle influences' is quite scientific, while that of vital force is not?

3. The third difficulty is the specialization of protoplasm in different organisms and in different parts of the same organism. If all protoplasm is 'substantially the same,' how has it learned so to specialize its powers as to weave out of the same material tough muscle here, delicate nerve tissue there—here build an oak, there colour a rose leaf? If it be answered that its position determines its work—in the bone it builds bone, in the muscle it weaves muscle—how, we ask, did it *begin* to form bone or muscle in the course of development from the germ where there was neither? If living protoplasm is merely a peculiar chemical substance and nothing more, how in the name of chemistry can we account for the infinite subdivision and specialization of its powers in the process of development of the germ into the plant or animal? Take the speck of protoplasm in a fertile egg, and try to imagine the subdivision and specialization

---

[1] *Lay Sermons* (1893), p. 118.   [2] *Mystery of Life*, p. 54-5.

of its powers as the chicken is developed. Skeleton and skin and feathers—digestive, blood, and nervous systems— bright eye and keen ear—nay, the very cock-a-doodle-doo that will in due time salute the dawn—all must come out of that speck. And they will, and without the slightest confusion or the smallest mistake. Is there any conceivable explanation of this on the supposition that living protoplasm is merely a very intricate chemical structure, and no more? Surely there was every need for Huxley to summon 'subtle influences' to his aid—and very subtle indeed they must be? But then, when we get to 'subtle influences,' we are entitled to ask—Where are we now? Is this *chemistry* of any kind or sort that ever was heard of? Chemical elements we know, and chemical compounds we know, but what are 'subtle influences'?

But we have pursued this argument far enough, perhaps too far for the patience of the reader. However, it exemplifies the straits into which the 'advanced philosophers' are led by their theory, and the miserable shuffles to which they must have recourse to try to get out of them. It will be worth while to remember that one of the keenest intellects of them all had no more definite theory of life than that it is due to complexity of chemical structure *plus* 'subtle influences.'

E. GAYNOR, C.M.

PARIS UNIVERSITY AND THE SCHOOLMEN
II.

THE future history of the Paris University[1] is marked by three distinct events—the struggle with the Chancellor, the great dispersion of 1229, and the coming of the Mendicant Orders. All these contributed much to the establishing of the great institution into an organized body. From the beginning the Chancellor of Notre Dame exercised almost absolute control over the masters and scholars of the University; no new master could begin to teach without his sanction, and being at liberty to grant or refuse his sanction as he wished, he often rejected scholars who were judged fit for the teacher's chair by a majority of the masters. He also had the power to suspend masters for any offence, and to inflict punishment on refractory scholars. Such unlimited power in the hands of one not always favourably disposed towards the rising University much displeased the masters, and they determined to use every effort to restrict it. They refused to recognise any teacher appointed by the Chancellor who had not been presented by them for approval; they denied such teachers admission to the Masters' Guild, and persuaded students not to attend their lectures. Thus a system of " boycotting" was continually carried on by the masters; but even that proved ineffectual in limiting the Chancellor's power, and the masters finally appealed to the Pope against him. Their appeal was duly considered in Rome, and in 1212 a Papal Bull was issued by which the jurisdiction of the Chancellor over the masters and scholars was greatly restricted. Henceforth he was not to refuse permission to teach to any scholar whom a majority of the masters judged fit for such an office, and he was not to suspend a master or inflict punishment on any student till after a formal trial. With this Papal recognition and exemption from the unbounded control of the Chancellor,

---

[1] Vide I. E. RECORD, August, 1897, page 139, et seq.

the masters began to gradually make statutes for their own government; they also elected one who should represent them in cases of litigation and in any future appeal to Rome. This was the origin of the Rectorship of the University, a step which helped much to make the institution an independent body with its own governing head.

The great dispersion of the masters by which the University had for a time ceased to exist took place in 1229-30. We saw before[1] how the 'town and gown" disturbance of 1200 ended by the obtaining of a Royal Charter granting many new privileges to the University; the dispersion we are now considering arose from a like disturbance, and also ended by obtaining new privileges. Thus the University may be said to have advanced by its misfortunes.

During the Carnival of 1228-29 some of the students who had been enjoying the country air for the day entered a tavern on their way home, and, in the words of the chronicler, found 'good and sweet wine.' They all drank in plenty, but when about to leave a dispute arose with the landlord regarding the payment. From words the disputants came to blows, ' to pulling of ears and tearing of hair,' and the neighbours gathering to help the injured proprietor, severely beat the riotous students. Next day a strong reinforcement of gownsmen returned to seek revenge, and breaking into the tavern, they set the wine taps running, drank in abundance, and then going forth into the streets attacked every citizen they could find. News of the riot soon spread throughout the city, and the magistrate, authorized, it is said, by the queen, marched a number of police to suppress the riot. Filled with rage, the half savage police attacked a party of unoffending students who were occupied in their holiday games, and left many of them dead on the playground. The masters loudly complained of such brutal treatment, and using their privilege of ' cessation,' they appealed to the King, threatening if the offending citizens were not punished within fifteen days they would stop their lectures. The fifteen days passed, and no redress was

---

[1] *Ibid.*, 148.

granted ; the masters then appealed anew to the King, and announced that if justice was not done them in a month they would all quit the city for a period of six years. Even this did not obtain redress, and after the month had expired, the masters dissolved the University and departed in a body for the other great centres of education, many of them coming to the then rising Universities of Oxford and Cambridge, while others went to Toulouse, Orleans, Rheims, and Angers.

Things remained in this unsatisfactory state for over a year, when the Pope interceded for the injured masters, and the court, seeing the prosperity and prestige of Paris rapidly decreasing, easily granted redress. Ample satisfaction was promised by the King; the Pope, Gregory IX., issued a new Bull securing the masters and scholars from any future interference, and in 1231 they returned again to their work. The exemption from civil authority granted by Philip Augustus was henceforth to be strictly observed; the masters were authorized to have their own rector and the power of making their own statutes ; in short, the University may be said to have then become fully autonomous.

Yet there was another great crisis through which it had to pass—the coming of the Mendicant Orders. From their first establishment the Mendicants, especially the Dominicans, sought learning as the one great means of carrying on the work to which they devoted their lives. They came as champions of the Church, ready to meet the enemy in open battle-ground, and armed with prayer and learning, they boldly carried on the fight against the Church's opponents. Some of the most brilliant masters of the schools enrolled themselves among them, and every effort was made to perfect their young members in the different sciences. It was with this end in view that they came to establish themselves in Paris at an early stage of the University's existence. At the date of the great dispersion we find the Dominicans and Franciscans having schools in the University ; the Carmelites and Augustinians came soon after the masters' return. Other religious orders—the Trinitarians, the old Benedictines, and the Cistercians—

established schools in the city, that their young members might assist at the University lectures.

When the Mendicants first came to Paris they were received with every show of respect by the University authorities; even the Convent of St. James was freely given to the Dominicans, on condition, however, that they would perform some spiritual offices for the members of the University. It was only on the return of the masters after the great dispersion that the Seculars first began to manifest displeasure with the Mendicants. During the masters' absence the Friars had continued to open their schools and give public lectures; to this the masters objected, because the loss caused by their departure was thereby greatly lessened, and when they again began to teach they refused to recognise the Mendicant Doctors as forming part of the University. Not having observed the 'cessation,' prevented them, the masters declared, from any longer partaking in any privileges of the University. The masters then used every effort to prevent students from attending the lectures of the Mendicants, and they ignored any master who had not attended their own course of lectures, and 'incepted' according to their rules. This state of things lasted on till 1250, when an event took place that led to open opposition between the Seculars and the Friars.

The occasion was brought about by another tavern brawl in which one of the students was killed. The masters consequently proclaimed a 'cessation' till satisfaction was made, but the Friars refused to comply with the masters' decision; they even appealed to Rome to be freed from any obligation they might be under to observe a 'cessation.' Reparation not being made, the masters determined to bind themselves by oath to insist on obtaining justice. The Mendicants were again unwilling to bind themselves by such an oath, and though redress was soon obtained by the hanging of two of the offenders, the question between the masters and the Friars still remained unsettled. The masters now drew up a statute according to which no new master should be admitted into the 'College of Masters or Fellowship of the University,' unless he would first bind

himself by oath to obey all the statutes of the University, and
to observe a 'cessation' whenever ordered by a majority of
the masters. This regulation was primarily intended for
the Friars, since their doctors had been always unwilling to
be bound by the arbitrary rules of the Seculars. The Friars
claimed the right of being free to lecture in their schools
and open their halls to all who should come to them for
knowledge, and they refused to be hampered in their work
by the often whimsical regulations of frivolous masters ; but
the masters as persistently refused to acknowledge the Friars
or to allow them any share in the privileges of the University
unless they promised submission to whatever statutes had
been or should be made ; the great success of the
Mendicants, owing to such teachers as Alexander of Hales,
Albert the Great, and St. Thomas, and the immense number
of students who frequented their schools, also helped to
rouse the Seculars to limit the liberty of the Mendicants.

The struggle lasted on till 1254, when Innocent IV.
endeavoured to bring about a compromise by restricting the
privileges of the Friars.   But that same year the Sovereign
Pontiff died, and his successor Alexander IV. turned the tide
in favour of the Mendicants.   The Bull of Innocent was
immediately revoked, and in April, 1255, a new Bull was
issued by which the Friars were secured against the attacks
of the Seculars.   The Chancellor was in future to grant the
licence to teach to as many of the Mendicant students as he
in conscience should judge fit; they were exempted from the
necessity of requiring a majority of the secular masters in
order to be presented to the Chancellor for the *licentia
docendi*, and they were at liberty to observe a 'cessation,'
except when declared by two-thirds of the masters of each
faculty, and even in this they were secure, for the Mendicant
masters in theology numbered more than one-third.

The masters now had recourse to another alternative.
Though they were recognised as a legal society, and were
granted many privileges both by the Pope and the King,
they were still, they maintained, a free society, and being
such they declared that they could dissolve the University in
the same way as they had formed it.   By doing so they

would evade the Papal restrictions, and succeed in depriving the Friars of the University privileges they enjoyed. The masters, accordingly, drew up a formal declaration dissolving the University which they forwarded to the Pope. The answer to this declaration, if any answer was ever given, has nowhere been preserved. The Friars, though still unrecognised by the masters, continued to hold lectures and 'inceptions' in their own schools, and so great was the envy raised against them, that they had often to call in an armed force to prevent the mob from entering their halls. It was during this troublesome time that St. Thomas 'incepted' for his degree in theology, and it is said, that while doing so men in arms had to be present to preserve peace. The appearance of a Friar in the streets was the signal of a general uproar equalled only by the after degrading scenes of the Paris Commune of later days. But such persecution of the Friars was only weakening the cause of the Seculars. Reports of their mode of acting soon reached Rome, and Bulls were issued commanding them under threat of excommunication not to molest the Mendicants, and to admit them to the enjoyment of all the University privileges. By degrees the opposition of the Seculars calmed down : the Mendicant Doctors were again received into the meetings of the University on formal occasions, though many of the rebellious masters still refused association with the Friars. It was not till 1258 that peace was finally restored, and the long-wished-for harmony reigned between the Regular and Secular Masters of the University. The Friars had apparently triumphed, though the Seculars by their stern opposition had succeeded in securing for themselves many of the favours they had so ardently sought for. Nor were they still wholly satisfied ; they were ever ready when any occasion offered to endeavour to curtail the Mendicants' favours, and sooner than again begin a new warfare, the Friars consented, in 1318, to submit to the statutes of the University, but with the provision that their own privileges would not be interfered with. The University then got into organized working form ; each of the Mendicant Orders had a separate school attached to its convent, and their distinguished doctors attracted numbers of students to their lectures : the Seculars had their own schools, and secured the attendance of students by the fact that in their schools alone could secular students take out their degrees. The Friars could have 'inceptions' in their own schools, but only for their own students, and no secular student could 'incept' for degrees unless he had attended the course of lectures in the schools of the Seculars.

So far we have been considering but the material growth of the Paris University, yet it is its intellectual growth that principally deserves our consideration. Like every new intellectual movement the new system introduced by St. Anselm into the theological schools remained for a time devoid of systematic order. The system was developed by professors, and eagerly grasped by students who rejoiced at being able to display their logical skill in theological disputes, but it wanted order and method. To establish order in the whole teaching of theology was the next great work to be done, and it was the monastery again that supplied the man—the famous Lombard—who accomplished the task. Peter Lombard (1164), a native of Lombardy, had laboured and studied with the great mystics of St. Victor's. He saw the great hold the system of St. Anselm was taking on the schools; he saw also the defect of the system—its lack of unity, and this he determined to remedy. He ardently set to work on the foundations supplied him by Holy Scripture, the fathers and reason, and worked out a systematic plan of all theological truth. The result of his labours was the famous ' Book of the Sentences,' a work which merited for him the title of Master of the Sentences. He divided all theology into four parts. He first considered God in Himself as the primary object of theological science; and accordingly, he treated in the first part of his work of God and the Blessed Trinity. All things outside of God he considered as effects of God's creative power, and as so many means of tending to Him, and of promoting His glory ; and viewed, in that light he treated in the second part of the angels and their fall, of man before and after the fall, of nature and grace : in the third part he treated of the Incarnation and the means

God has given man to attain his ultimate end; and in the fourth part the four last things were dealt with. Such a division brought clearness and precision into the theological course. Masters took up each 'Book of the Sentences,' and commented on it, and students were overjoyed that they could now advance in clear logical order.

It was the systematic unity which the Lombard showed to exist in theology that gained for the Sentences such great popularity, and made them for years the text book of the schools. The method of the Sentences also helped to secure their stay with masters and students. The author first divided each part into a certain number of Distinctions, then each Distinction into several theological propositions in support of which he adduced arguments from the Scriptures, the fathers, and reason. Where the fathers seemed to clash in their opinions he brought about a reconciliation by distinctions and explanations. These collated Sentences of the Scriptures and the fathers with the arguments and distinctions of reason met exactly the intellectual want of the time: those who wished to maintain authority could not but feel fully satisfied by the many authorities adduced in confirmation of the doctrine in question; while the new spirit of allowing reason to enter the domain of theology found full scope for exercise in the arguments, distinctions, and explanations that followed the list of authorities. The Sentences thus became the book of the schools, and were commented on by all the distinguished schoolmen.

But there was another intellectual movement that must not be passed over in an account of the intellectual advancement of the University. The great intellectual contest that lasted on till close on the end of the twelfth century was the growth of the intellectual movement that sprung up among the Churchmen themselves. Roscelin and Abelard, with William of Champeaux, St. Bernard, and St. Anselm, were the chief leaders in the contest, and none of these once thought of rejecting the authority of the Church or the fathers, or of misinterpreting the Word of God. The contest was never intended to in any way belittle the truths of Christianity, though unintentionally the system of the former had done so ; on the contrary, it was pushed on with the hope of bringing these truths more within the reach of men's minds. But where danger lay it was soon pointed out by the defenders of orthodoxy, and the sound part of the movement was permitted to live, so that the great alarm the use of dialectics in theology had caused in the beginning had almost entirely subsided towards the end of the twelfth century. The scholastic method which may be said to have been the result of the contest suited the logical-trained minds of the age, and it easily found entrance into the schools of theology.

Yet scarcely had the great contest calmed down when a new intellectual movement was set on foot. This time it was caused by the introduction of the unknown works of Aristotle into the schools. The schoolmen were never so happy as when able to find some new doctrines in the examination of which they could display their intellectual skill ; hundreds of students would crowd to hear any doctor who propounded any new system, or undertook to destroy some received one. With ears intent on every word that fell from his lips they would carefully take in the new opinions and go away to fight out among themselves the strong and weak points of the teacher's novelties. Great then was their delight when the hitherto unknown works of Aristotle were presented to them. But few of Aristotle's works, such as the *Catagories* and *De Interpretatione,* were known in the schools up to the end of the twelfth century ; it was only then that his other works became known in the West ; and what added principally to their novelty and their after evil influence was, that they were presented in Oriental dress.

The Nestorian doctors after their condemnation brought with them into their exile in the East many works of the Grecian philosophers. They translated Aristotle into Arabic, and the subtle mind of the Eastern philosophers eagerly took in the systems of the Stagyrite and taught them in their crowded schools of Edessa and Bagdad. Avicenna (980-1037), the greatest of Arabic philosophers, took each of Aristotle's treatises, and giving equal credence to all his words, he added paraphrases and adaptations in which the true

and false principles and systems of the philosopher were
equally set forth, interspersed with many Eastern false ideas.
This great love of Grecian philosophy was carried into Spain
by the Arabs and Jews. Averroës (1105), of Cordova, studied
Aristotle himself in the Arabic translations, and as expounded
in the paraphrases of Avicenna. He then took the text
itself, added new commentaries on each assertion, and his
unbounded belief in the philosopher, who, he said, had never
erred, and whose works were perfect, led him into some of
the greatest philosophic errors, such as the pantheistic idea
of the unity of the human intellect, the denial of God's
providence with regard to individual beings, and the negation
of individual immortality.

In the beginning of the thirteenth century Aristotle and
the paraphrases of Avicenna were translated from the Arabic
into Latin, and introduced into the Paris schools ; soon after,
the Commentaries of Averroës passed through a like process
and one can well imagine the intellectual uproar that met
their coming. Aristotle alone would have caused excitement,
and would perhaps have been dangerous material in such
unsafe hands, but when accompanied by the speculations of
Oriental minds, a terrible explosion was destined to follow.
Students wished to hear nothing but Aristotle, and proud
masters daily appeared to interpret to them the new systems.
One master, after endeavouring to use Aristotle in proving
the doctrine of the Blessed Trinity, proudly boasted that he
could as easily overthrow the doctrine on the morrow by
equally plausible arguments. The morrow came, but the
master when about to begin his discourse was seized by a
stroke of paralysis by which he instantly lost his speech and
memory. Such like daring attempts to test all doctrine by
the new system soon led to the overthrow of Christian truths.
Almaric of Bena, and David of Dinanto, two Paris doctors,
became the leaders of free-thought and the rejection of
authority ; reverence for Holy Scripture and the fathers
daily disappeared, and the system of judging by reason alone,
fanned by Oriental ideas about the eternity of matter and the
universal unity of the human soul, spread like a rapid conflagration among masters and scholars.

This wide-spreading evil soon roused the authorities of the Church, and determined steps were taken to stop the onflow of error.   Almaric had died before his erroneous teaching had become known, and now his body was disinterred, and· cast with an excommunication into unconsecrated ground.   David of Dinanto and many of his followers were delivered over to the secular power for punishment, and the books of Aristotle and his commentators were forbidden to be read either publicly or in private.   A new statute was drawn up by the Papal Legate, in 1215, by which masters on ' incepting' were to take an oath that they would not read the works of David or Almaric or the Commentaries of Averroës.   To this oath of the masters, Gregory IX., in 1231, added the restriction, ' until these works shall have been examined and purged from all heresy.'

While Aristotle, thus presented in Oriental dress, fared so badly in the schools of Paris, his works found'another safer and more lasting introduction to the schoolmen.   The conquest of Constantinople by the Crusaders, in 1204, opened the way to new literary discoveries.   Latin scholars accompanied the Crusades, and after spending some time in the East they were able to collect most of the works of Grecian philosophers in the original form.   They eagerly sought for every remaining fragment of Aristotle's works, and soon succeeded in being able to present him to the West without the interpolations of Arabic translators and commentators.   Translations of his most important works, such as the *Metaphysics*, some books of the *Ethics*, the *Politics*, and the *Magna Moralia*, were made by able Greek scholars, and circulated in the schools.   This version supplanted the Arabic translation, though both remained for a time current among masters and scholars.

With the introduction of the Greek version of Aristotle a distinction was soon pointed out between Aristotle himself and his Arabic commentators, and the great object of teachers was henceforth to christianize the Philosopher, as Aristotle was called ; to eviscerate his false systems, and make his sound principles become the handmaid of Christian theology.   The first who set himself to carry out this idea

was the renowned Franciscan Doctor, Alexander of Hales.
He made free use of the Aristotelian treatises in support of
the Catholic truths, and his example was followed by other
schools of the University. But Alexander was principally
a theologian, and as such could not deal with Aristotle to
advantage ; it was in philosophy that the Philosopher had
first to be christianized, and such a work was fully accomplished by the two great Dominican doctors, Albert the Great,
and his yet more celebrated disciple, St. Thomas Aquinas.
Albert took Aristotle, and, proceeding in a method similar
to that of Avicenna, paraphrazed each treatise according to
Christian ideas ; where Aristotle was found to teach any
unchristian system he was rejected, and students were
warned against him ; but where his principles and systems
were sound, he was retained and turned to advantage. Such
a method of treatment resulted in the production of a vast
encyclopædia of development of principles that served as
a valuable safeguard against all future encroachment on
truth.

St. Thomas, who had studied under Albert the Great,
excelled his master in method and precision. He handled
Aristotle more after the method of Averroës, commenting on
the words of the text itself, and then adding new *opuscula*
where required. With clear and accurate distinctions he
met the arguments of the Arabic commentator, and showed
where the truth and the error lay. His keen intellect was
also well sharpened against the dangers of exaggerated
Realism and Nominalism, and with a deep, broad grasp of
far-reaching principles he succeeded in producing harmony
between the divergent systems.

The great success of St. Thomas must be attributed to
his clear insight into every system that came before him for
consideration. As a rule, every erroneous system contains
at bottom some element of truth, and the chief work of the
assailant is to clearly grasp how far that remnant of truth
reaches, and to point out where it comes in contact with
error. This insight into the errors hinging on some mis-
applied principles, and into the difficulties surrounding each
point of true doctrine, was never so clearly or so fully seen

by any human intellect as by the great Aquinas.   His
method was to meet the opponents of truth on their own
prepared ground, to bring with them as many difficulties as
possible against a point of doctrine ; then by a short quotation
to show the sense of Scripture, the mind of the fathers or
the philosopher regarding the doctrine in question ; next
followed a short pointed argument in defence of the reasonableness of the doctrine ; and finally, an ingenious answer to
each of the difficulties adduced.   St. Bernard, perhaps, would
have been shocked at any doctor of the orthodox faith
bringing objections against any Catholic doctrine; but in
the time of St. Thomas such a system was the only means
of satisfying the minds of the schoolmen and refuting
erroneous opinions.   And such a system could not but
succeed.   Let an upholder of error first bring forth all the
grounds of his belief, and his difficulties regarding any truth;
then briefly set forth for him the true doctrine, and lay bare
the hollowness of the objections and difficulties brought
forth, and he must be very obstinate in his belief who will
not be convinced of the truth.   By this invariable method
of proceeding, the Angelical met the wants of his time.   The
dialecticians had ample scope for exercising their skill by
raising difficulties, and by ingeniously answering them with
logical distinctions ; the rationalist could delight in the free
exercise of reason ; and the upholder of authority could feel
confident that his position was secure and well provided for.
The Angelical drew a clear distinction between natural and
revealed religion, and where reason could not demonstrate,
she was allowed to freely enter and show the reasonableness
or non-unreasonableness of revealed truth.   This method of
St. Thomas and the works that he produced formed the
groundwork on which theological science then caught a firm
footing, and from which she has not yet been, nor ever
shall be moved so long as the method and works of the
Angelical are kept alive in the theological schools.

    With St. Thomas the Paris University may be said to
have reached its intellectual perfection.   Other great doctors
such as St. Bonaventure, Roger Bacon, and Duns Scotus
were bright luminaries of its schools ; yet, it is to St. Thomas

is principally due the great renown the University gained as
being the first great mediæval centre of theological learning,
and it was his fame that made its colleges become an
attraction to students from all parts of Europe.

It was not till long after the establishment of the
University that any attempt was made to found colleges for
its students.   University colleges, as we understand them,
were unknown when the University began, and students
who came to the University had to fare for themselves
among the citizens as best they could.   They assembled to
hear their masters' lecture in large halls in which they were
seated on planks, stones, many even on the straw on the
floor; heated halls with cushioned seats and carpeted floors
were then unknown to students.   Outside these lecture
halls the only classification recognised among them was
their division into nations.   Four nations were represented—
the French, which included all the Latin races; the English
with whom were classed the Germans, Hungarians, and all
students from the north and east of Europe; the Picards
which embraced all the low countries: and the Normans.
With this nominal classification the students were at liberty
to live in whatever manner they chose, and when we consider that the number of students thus free to live and act
as they pleased was often considerably over twenty thousand, we may well make allowance for the repeated riots
and disturbances that occurred.   The rich students lived
sumptuously with their friends or wealthy acquaintances,
and studied little; the middle class lived together in rented
houses in which they appointed one of themselves to preside ;
the poor students, many of whom had travelled on foot from
far-distant countries to seek learning in Paris, lived in
miserable hovels or garrets with scarcely enough food or
clothing to enable them to study and attend the lectures.
Many incidents are related of the sacrifices students then
made in order to acquire learning.   In one room three
students lived together and possessed between them but one
suit of clothes.   While two studied in bed the other went
to attend the lecture ; the other two succeeded in turn, and
each brought home to his indigent prisoners the knowledge

he had acquired from the latest lecture. Another student when dying had nothing but some torn clothes and an old black parchment book, all which he left to his fellow-student, but with the condition that he would get Mass said for the repose of his soul.   It was to remedy the sad state of these poor scholars that attempts were first made to establish a college or house where they could live together in common.

The only colleges then in Paris were those of Notre Dame, St. Genevieve, St. Victor's, and the colleges of the Mendicant orders, but these latter were for their own respective students.   Only a small number of ecclesiastical students were allowed to remain within the cloisters of Notre Dame ; St. Victor's was the home of its monks, though its doors were ever open to poor students who came for help. St. Genevieve, which was then considered outside the Paris boundaries, and which is said to have been founded by Clovis and Clotilda at the solicitation of the saint, was inhabited by canons who were exempt from episcopal jurisdiction ; the Mendicants and the other Religious Orders had their own colleges where their masters lectured and their students studied ; but beyond these centres there were no other fixed and authorized homes for the students.

The first secular college mentioned in the history of the University is the college for poor clerks, founded in 1180, close to the Cathedral of Notre Dame ; it was established by Jocius, of London, who had recently returned from the Crusades. He was so touched by the pitiful state of the poor scholars that he founded and endowed a house in which many of them were to be received and cared for. Two similar institutions were founded in 1186 and 1208, both of which were governed by ecclesiastical authorities. Another early foundation was the College of Constantinople, founded soon after the taking of Constantinople, in 1204, for the education of young Greeks in the orthodox faith. After these foundations and the stimulus given to like institutions by the coming of the Religious Orders, colleges began to rapidly multiply, so much so, that in less than two centuries after, more than fifty colleges, besides those of the Friars, were established and flourishing in Paris.

But among all these colleges there is one that especially claims attention, the College of Sorbonne. It was founded in 1257 by Robert de Sorbonne, St. Louis's private chaplain. Moved by the inorderly life of the University students, and the many temptations to which they were exposed, Robert conceived the idea of bringing masters and students together, and establishing a house where they would be free to devote all their time to lectures and study, and be secure from the many temptations of city life. Some attribute its foundation as an intended check on the Friars, who on account of their regular conventual life and their large, valuable libraries easily gained the day over the seculars. Robert used every effort to have it a success, to have it for secular doctors and students what the convents were for the Mendicants. He selected the best men he could find to become members of it, and at his request the King favoured it from its beginning, granting a suitable site for its erection, and afterwards contributing richly to its endowment. It was under the control of the secular ecclesiastical authority. Robert, after being its superior for twenty years, died in 1274.

The Sorbonne was intended for secular students who had already taken their Degree in Arts, and who intended to enter on the long course necessary for the doctorship in theology. Sixteen students, four from each nation, were all that were first admitted to residence, but the number was soon raised to thirty-six. Besides this established number of residences new bachelors of theology sought admittance to it, and in the sixteenth and seventeenth centuries the Sorbonne came to be understood for the whole theological faculty of the Paris University. In its halls or schools were held all the public disputations of the theologians, and from its doctors pronouncements on heresies and decisions of cases were sought from all parts of Europe. Even in modern days the Sorbonne has made itself remarkable for its independent position in questions of theology, and its conniving at Jansenism and Gallicanism often brought itself and its doctors under the censures of ecclesiastical authorities. It is still the theological faculty of Paris.

The college system thus introduced into the Paris University brought about a period of peace and calm in the city, and the riotous 'martinets' were looked on as a thing of the past. Each faculty had its own masters who lectured and held 'inceptions' in their different schools, and the carrying out of the fixed curriculum was much insisted on by the authorities of the University.

By a Bull of Innocent III., given in the beginning of the thirteenth century, a curriculum or university course, and the time required for attending lectures before taking degrees in any faculty had been determined. The faculties then recognised were—Arts, Law, and Theology; the Faculty of Medicine was not introduced till about half a century later. The young student had to spend a certain number of years as a simple auditor attending his master's lectures, then he had to hold a 'determination,' and if successful was admitted to the Baccalaureate, and commissioned to lecture under his master's guidance for some years more, after which he had to hold his final 'determination' before the body of masters. He was then presented to the Chancellor from whom he received the *licentia docendi*, a necessary requirement before he could begin to teach in any public school.

In the Art Faculty the term required before 'determining,' was six years—four as an auditor, and two as a bachelor. The course included grammar, logic, psychology, natural and moral philosophy, and no student could become a Master of Arts till he had attained his twenty-first year. To obtain mastership in theology the course was much longer. A student should first spend six years attending lectures on Holy Scripture and the Lombard; then, provided he had attained the age of twenty-five, he should present himself for examination before four masters, and if successful, he was made bachelor, and admitted to his 'first course.' He then delivered lectures for two years on different books of the Bible, at the end of which term he held his 'principium,' by defending a thesis against a number of young students who were waiting for their bachelorship. After this he began a two years' course of lectures on the

Sentences, and at the end of the course held a theological disputation in the bishop's hall. The Chancellor, the presiding master, and the other masters present tested his knowledge of different theological questions, and if his answers proved satisfactory, the Chancellor placed the *Birretum Doctorale* on his head, and assigned him a place among the doctors. The prescribed age for doctorship was thirty-five, though in this, and in the time required for attending the master's lectures, the University had the power to dispense. St. Thomas, owing to his great ability, was made doctor at thirty-one. The Faculties of Law and Medicine required six years' attendance at lectures, and degrees were conferred in much the same way as in the Faculties of Art and Theology.

Such was the curriculum according to which the intellectual training of the great schoolmen was perfected, and with it we conclude our already too extended, yet incomplete account, of the intellectual life of Paris. It may not be too much to hope that what we have said may lead others interested in scholastic theology to study for themselves the fascinating history of the Paris University and the Schoolmen.

P. T. BURKE, O.D.C.

THE LATIN LANGUAGE IN CONVENTS

THE following lines are the immediate consequence of a
visit to a convent where my daughter was to make her
final vows. Many and deep were the feelings aroused on
that solemn occasion ; yet they did not prevent a lively
recollection of an occurrence in my early boyhood taking a
particular hold of me. My daughter mentioned, among
other things concerning her profession, how she and her
two companions had of late, during Lent, had to say
numerous and hard prayers in Latin ; how she often would
have willingly given up her knowledge of German for an
equal amount of Latin. This observation exactly corresponded with ideas and feelings long ago impressed on my
mind, and brought them, as it were, to a point.

When I was still at school, now more than half a century
ago, I used to spend my Sundays and part of my vacations
at the quiet home of an old aunt who had been in a convent
in Germany. On the arrival of the French republican armies
she had been driven away, and lived ever since with three of
her fellow-sufferers in a retired place, keeping up as much as
possible the rules of their order. Often I handled their
Latin breviary, and once or twice I was bold enough to ask
the pert question : How is it you say prayers in Latin when
you do not understand the words ? One of the good nuns
seemed prepared for such a taunt ; she must have heard it
before, for she replied quite readily : Have you not a canary
at home that sings a nice tune ? Does the bird understand
what it sings ? and yet you are pleased to hear it. So it is
with us. Almighty God is pleased with our prayers although
we do not understand the words. This reply, uttered with
great confidence and self-satisfaction, settled, for the time,
the discussion ; yet a feeling remained behind within me
that also something else, even something better, might be
said on the subject.

Since then the importance of the Latin language for

our Catholic Church has become a favourite theme of my thoughts. I have learned to consider it as a dowry, an absolutely necessary dowry, prepared by Providence, for the spouse of Christ, and thus a powerful evidence in favour of the Catholic against all national Churches. We Catholics cannot esteem and cultivate that language too much. Now, if this is true, the simple conclusion from such a view with regard to the object now under consideration, is the question : Why should not young nuns learn Latin ?

The advantages of such a course of study are obvious ; the difficulties that may appear at first sight are not serious, and are easily overcome. In former ages, when modern languages, with their noble literatures were not yet developed. Latin and Greek were learned by ladies who pretended to a higher education; everyone knows how Lady Jane Grey, not to mention other historical persons of the same period, was even at her young age an excellent classical scholar. And even now-a-days, ladies here, and more yet in America, have again turned their attention to those ancient languages and literatures. There is scarcely any young person among those classes that enter into convents who has not learned something of German, French, or Italian. Why should not the same persons study a little Latin, just enough to understand such books as in a convent come into their hands ? We do not want them to dive, like our students of philology, into all the difficulties of syntax and composition, to study Roman law, constitution, philosophy ; to master the obscure passages of historians, orators, or poets; but to read in Latin what they mostly have read already in their mother tongue. The first, and almost only thing required, would be a book specially intended for our purpose, quite different from the manuals used in grammar schools, containing the simplest rules of grammar and syntax, with copious vocabulary, exercises, and suitable extracts. There might be, in the beginning, here and there some difficulty in procuring masters to teach ; but when the system has been once generally introduced, there will be in every convent Latin scholars able to impart their own knowledge, and who going thus over the same ground again, will themselves become more perfect, according to the saying, *docendo discimus*. The cost of such a publication would soon be covered; there will be plenty of copies required every year, especially also when young ladies intending to enter a convent take to these studies as a kind of preparation.

General success for an undertaking like the one here proposed, depends, in our Catholic Church, on action emanating from the centre. What we therefore wish, and the ultimate intention of these lines is, to draw the attention of some one of high position to the subject with a view of getting the approval and encouragement of the highest authorities. Very few words would be sufficient.

PREFACE TO A LATIN GRAMMAR FOR NOVICES

The Latin language is for the Catholic Church, and consequently for each individual member of it, of the utmost importance, more so than is generally thought. People that look on the subject only superficially are rather struck with the opposite view that public worship in an unknown tongue has only inconvenience. But we need not shrink from the controversy: we have a good cause to plead, and can enter boldly on the question. A Church established and intended for one nation only could eventually do without the use of any foreign tongue, without Latin; not so that one Church which is destined equally for all races, tribes, and nations, as well as for all ages. The introduction and general adoption of that language by our holy Church was evidently something more than the result of human calculation and wisdom; we can clearly see how Providence itself prepared, in many ways, centuries before the coming of the Messiah, the spread of His kingdom in many ways; especially also, by getting ready a kind of dowry, a dowry absolutely necessary for His bride the Church, in the shape of a grand, rich unchanging language, fit to express and preserve intact the doctrine and precepts of the Messiah; able to render the loftiest ideas and the deepest feelings inspired by the spirit of religion. It is, therefore, suitable and useful before we begin the study of that language to pursue a little further and deeper these reflections, to examine the importance and necessity of Latin for our Church, and humbly, adoringly follow the ways of Providence with regard to this subject.

At the time when our Saviour was born, although Rome formed a strong tyrannical political centre, the whole human race was split up into numberless nations, tribes, and classes, each having its own religious belief, moral code and practices; many went to extremes of folly and horror; the most respectable amongst those religious societies were confined to a few select disciples or classes who often guarded timidly and zealously their dogmas from the knowledge of the crowd. The consequence of all this was universal division, contempt, hatred, open enmity; an almost insuperable barrier to general civilization, progress, and happiness. If that state of things had continued, we all would probably be nothing but vile slaves under a few insolent tyrannical masters. God had mercy on poor man.

Christ appeared, and brought from on high a doctrine as different from all existing ones as heaven is from earth : 'Only one God, an infinitely perfect, eternal Being, ye men are His creatures, made to His image, nay, His children, all but one family, brethren bound to esteem and love one another, all alike destined for eternal happiness. Unite therfore to adore and serve Him, in that one Church which I came to establish, and of which I shall always be the head.' And behold, His apostles, contrary to the doings of all other teachers of religion, go out, immediately after the establishment of that Church, in all directions to preach the Gospel, not even knowing how far their mission would carry them, for they had no idea of the extent of our globe. But what would have become of those twelve single men amongst the barbarians if every tribe had been constantly at war with their neighbours ? What connection would have been possible between the Apostles or their successors among themselves and with their centre? They would all have miserably perished in an unknown spot and been forgotten. Providence had provided against that.

There was a vigorous race of men in Italy called the Romans. They first conquered their immediate neighbours, then the whole of Italy, and now the idea came into their heads, that they were destined to subdue all other nations of the earth. By valour and prudent policy they actually succeeded in this. By the time Christ was born the Romans had extended their sway over the whole known globe. There was, for some time, no great war, the so-called Magnificent Roman Peace prevailed; and this, of course, favoured the spread of the Catholic religion; communications between the different parts of the empire and with the capital were kept up; and St. Peter, no doubt guided by Providence, had, in the meantime, made Rome the city of his final abode, the centre of the Church.

But something else was even more necessary than the universal empire, namely, a language. Let us imagine the Apostles going out among the barbarians whose rude language might not be able even to express fully all doctrines, those idioms besides changing every generation. The Apostles themselves had indeed all the same language, that used by our Lord Himself, but their immediate successors had only that imperfect idiom belonging to the spot where they were engaged. Humanly speaking it would have been impossible, under such circumstances, to preserve the Christian doctrine complete and pure. If after a few generations two Christians had met, the one coming from the far East, the other from Ireland, they would not have recognised each other's teaching as being one and the same. But there was one language provided by Providence for the East and West, and this prevented all confusion.

The same Romans who had so firmly persuaded themselves they were destined to extend their empire over the whole globe, and had carried out this idea with admirable firmness and wisdom, insisted also, as one of the means for preserving their universal sway, that no language but their own should be used in dealing with kings or chiefs of foreign nations, or in the courts of justice among them. And that language had, just before the beginning of the Christian era, been brought to its perfection; historians, philosophers, lawyers, politicians, and poets, endowed from on high with eminent talents for their task, had

done their best to render Latin fit for expressing all the
loftiest thoughts, and all impulses of the human mind and
soul. And the barbarians, especially their leaders, adopted,
readily enough, this language; they could not help feeling
its superiority, they were partly forced, partly proud, to learn
it, to be able to go to Rome on private or on public business.
Thus the Latin language spread amongst all nations; it was
a means of communication among them, and with the centre
of the empire. And this same language was naturally, with
more or less consciousness of its utility and necessity,
adopted by the Church for the same purpose of communication and union amongst all, and with the common
centre.

Yet there was a new danger ahead for that very language,
a danger of which the early Christians themselves certainly
never thought, but which Providence again foresaw and
prevented. All languages change in the course of time.
Our modern languages, in spite of the standard works of
literature, in spite of schools, and all efforts to the contrary,
are subject to that law of change; words and expressions are
now used in a different meaning from what they had a
hundred years ago: compare the works of Chaucer, with
those of modern authors. But among uncivilized people
these changes are much more striking. To mention only
one example. Some missionaries went to the west of Africa,
and established a small colony; they were, however, obliged
to leave; and when they returned, after many years, they
found the idiom of the natives quite altered. The pure
Latin of Rome was exposed even to special danger in this
respect. Being taken up by many half-civilized people it
got mixed up with the local idioms, and thus spoiled. This
corruption went actually so far, the Latin in distant countries
became so bad, that serious doubts were raised whether
sacraments administered in this way were really efficient.
What would have been the end of this? But what does
history tell us?

Innumerable hords of savages came from the north, from
the east; learned men cannot yet account for this immense
inroad; they overran and destroyed the great Roman empire,

and divided it into many independent parts. Terrible
ravages occurred; but even in a worldly sense the change
proved ultimately a benefit to mankind at large. The
Romans had lost their former high national character, riches
and power had rendered them voluptuous, tyrannical, a
scourge to all nations; the Roman empire had fulfilled its
destiny, and went down.

With regard to language, the invaders followed the
example of the other nations, and adopted the Latin tongue;
but they did so not as docile pupils, but as conquerors and
masters; they mixed with it so much of their own, that
Latin lost entirely its character, and turned into quite new
idioms, Italian, Spanish, French. Latin thus vanished as
a spoken language, but its most perfect form of the classical
period remained intact in a rich literature, and that is now
the Catholic language in which the purity of Christian
doctrine is preserved for ever.

Who does not perceive the importance of such a treasure ?
Who does not distinctly see the hand of Providence, which
for ages had been preparing that gift ? And not only that.
The early fathers of the Church who carefully studied the
great Roman authors, and made themselves complete
masters of this language, adopted it as a new mother tongue,
then used it for higher purposes, and composed prayers
and liturgies which no translation can adequately render, and
in some of which, as in the preface before the *Sanctus*, the
most magnificent language is found that ever issued from
human lips.

You who are about to enter on these studies will be
rewarded in many ways for the trouble that is always
attached to a new beginning. And when you afterwards
say, or join in the singing of the *Pange Lingua*, or other
hymns, you will be stirred by some of the most sublime and
lovely poetry that ever came from and moved a human
heart. And then remember that exactly these same words
resound all over the globe wherever an altar is raised
round which assemble, in union with their brethren all
over this earth, the members of the one Holy Catholic
Church.

The publication of a Preface to a Latin Grammar for
Novices, implies, of course, that the writer has completed, or
at least has on hand, a sketch for such a work. This is,
indeed, a fact; the general plan and a few chapters are
ready, and afford to a competent judge an opportunity to
give his opinion about the whole. But it would be useless
to finish the sketch unless first some chances of success
appear. As a mercantile undertaking it is, however, not
intended. The views of the writer go a little higher; he
thinks that, in matters of this kind, personal interests must
be, as much as possible, set aside, and only the advantage of
the Church at large be considered. Thinking of this, a late
communication from Rome in the newspapers came just in
time to confirm him in his ideas, and, at the same time,
suggests the following proposal :—

· The Holy Father, in an Encyclical letter, speaks of his
sincere wish and intention to promote more vigorously
missionary work, especially also in the East. For assistance
he refers to the well-known Catholic Association for the
Propagation of Faith, and applies to all Catholics to
contribute, now even more liberally, to the funds of that
Society, as pecuniary help will be one of the first requirements.

Now, here is a plan for connecting our proposal to
introduce the study of Latin in convents with that wish
expressed by the Holy Father.

1. It may be taken for granted that all admit how
desirable it is that novices should learn enough Latin to
understand what they read.

2. To get this opinion generally acknowledged, and
eventually carried into effect, some encouragement from
headquarters, from Rome, would be required.

3. The book in question, the Latin class-book, will then
be completed by competent, experienced men, and approved
of by competent authorities.

4. A subscription (rather moderate) is raised to defray
the expenses of a first edition.

5. These books are placed at the disposition of the above-
mentioned Association, who have agents everywhere. They

apply to all convents, referring to the decision from Rome, and supply the required number of copies.

6. The money received goes, with scarcely any deduction, to the said Association, who apply it according to the intentions of the Holy Father.

7. An extension of the work and of the respective income is produced by getting the Grammar translated into different languages, and then following the same plan for distributing it.

8. In convent schools, classes could be formed where pupils learn enough Latin to understand the Offices of the Church.

HERMANN DACUS.

WAS ST. AUGUSTINE UNCRITICAL?

ANGLICANS, even when great admirers of St. Augustine, take it for granted that, on Biblical questions, he was uncritical; and for this they have the very highest authority in their Church, that of Dr. Westcott. In *Smith's Dictionary of the Bible*, 1863,[1] he gladly avails of St. Augustine's help to prove our present New Testament Canon, which is also the Anglican Canon; but, on our Old Testament Canon, which was also the Canon of St. Augustine, but is not the Canon of the Anglican Church, he completely rejects his testimony. To account for this inconsistency he falls into a number of inconsistencies and errors which are best given in his own words:—

The real divergence as to the contents of the Old Testament Canon is to be traced to Augustine, whose wavering and uncertain language on the point furnishes abundant materials for controversy. By education and character he occupied a position more than usually unfavourable to historical criticism, and yet his overpowering influence, when it fell in with ordinary usage, gave consistency and strength to the opinion which he appeared to

---

[1] Art. ' Canon.'

advocate, for it may be reasonably doubted whether he differed intentionally from Jerome except in language . . . . And the original catalogue [of Augustine] is equally qualified by an introduction which distinguishes between the authority of books which are received by all, and by some of the Churches; and again between those which are received by Churches of great or of small weight,[1] so that the list which immediately follows must be interpreted by this rule . . . . But, on the other hand, Augustine frequently uses passages from the apocryphal books as co-ordinate with Scripture, and practically disregards the rules of distinction between the various classes of sacred writings which he had himself laid down. He stood on the extreme verge of the age of independent learning, and follows at one time the conclusions of criticism, at another the prescriptions of habit, which from his date grew more and more powerful. The enlarged Canon of Augustine, which was, as it will be seen, wholly unsupported by any Greek authority, was adopted at the Council of Carthage (A.D. 397), though with a reservation (Can. 47) : *De confirmando isto canone transmarina ecclesia consulatur.*

All this might have been said in this one sentence, ' Augustine differs from the Church of England ; but it makes no matter, for he was a bad critic, he was incapable of testing historical evidence, and did not even know his own mind.'

Passing over for the present the errors of fact and date contained in this long extract, I will call St. Augustine himself to answer this charge of incompetence. Having occasion recently[2] to analyze St. Augustine's *contra Faustum*, I lighted on a passage which was too long for my space, but which seems almost intended as an answer to such a charge. Faustus was the head of the Manicheans in Africa ; an able and polished man, but a most sophistical reasoner. As head of a nominal Christian sect he received the New Testament, but got rid of the troublesome passages by simply denying their authenticity. A favourite plan of his was to compare texts, find contradictions between them, and then reject as an interpolation the one opposed to his doctrines. He rejected the Old Testament altogether. He held the doctrine of inspiration, and even claimed it for the writings of Manes and for a number of apocryphal writings brought into his

---

[1] *De Doctrina Christ.*, ii. 8.   [2] *Life of St. Augustine*, ch. xxiv.

sect by the Gnostics. A Biblical discussion with such a man should exhibit the critical principles of the disputants ; and such a discussion we fortunately possess in St. Augustine's *contra Faustum*, from the close of which (B. xxxiii.) the present extract is taken :—

But what can I do with men so perversely deaf to the voice of Scripture, that when a passage is quoted against them they dare to assert that it was not said by an Apostle, but written in his name by some falsifier ? So manifestly opposed to Christian doctrine is that doctrine of demons which you preach, that you cannot possibly defend it as Christian except by denying the truth of the Apostolic Scriptures. Unhappy men, enemies of your own souls ! What writings can have any authority if the evangelical or apostolical writings have none ? What book is there of whose authorship we can be certain, if it be uncertain that the writings which the Church holds and asserts to be apostolical are really so ? and this Church propagated by the Apostles themselves, and so conspicuous throughout all nations. And we must, forsooth, hold for certain that other writings opposed to this same Church, were written by Apostles, although we have them only from heretics, bearing the names of founders, who came long after the Apostles. Have we not in secular literature undoubted authors in whose names many writings were afterwards published, but rejected as spurious, either because they did not agree with those which were certainly authentic, or because they had not been known at the time, or commended, or mentioned, or transmitted to posterity by the nearest friends of these authors ? To omit many others, have not certain books been published under the name of that most noble physician Hypocrates, which however have no authority among medical men ? A certain resemblance in matter and words has availed them nothing, since, on being compared with the genuine works, they are found to be quite inferior, to say nothing of the fact that they were never recognised as his from the time when his other writings were acknowledged. Now, as to those books by com- parison with which the others have been rejected, how are they proved to be the genuine works of Hypocrates, and so well- known that a doubter would not be argued with, but laughed at ? How is all this so certain, but because, from the very days of Hypocrates to our own times, there is a succession of evidence which only a madmen could question. How have men been able to authenticate the works of Plato, Aristotle, Cicero, Varro, and the rest, except by a similar unbroken succession of testimony. There are many ecclesiastical writings beside the Canonical Books. How do we make sure of their authors unless by ascertaining that each of them, in his own time, had communicated

and published his writings, and that they have been so transmitted
to us as to leave no room for doubt?   But why go so far back?
Take this work on which we are now engaged ; if, when we have
both passed away, some one should deny that this was written by
Faustus, and this other by Augustine, how is he to be convinced,
unless by the testimony of those now living and its continuation
through succeeding generations?   This being so, how can it be
asserted that the Church of the Apostles is unworthy to transmit
their writings to posterity? a Church so faithful, so numerous,
so fraternal? a Church which has preserved the very chairs of
these apostles through a most certain succession of bishops to
this day?   This being so as regards all writings, whether within
the Church or without, and their transmission being so easy, how
can anyone not blinded by satanic malice question the power of
the Church to transmit faithfully to posterity the writings of the
Apostles?   But, you say, they contradict each other.   Yes, in
your malignity you read them with a bad intention; in your folly
you do not understand them ; you are blind and do not see.
What great trouble would it have been to examine these writings,
and to discover their great and salutary harmony, if assisted by
piety and not perverted by the spirit of contention?   For what
man, reading two historians who treat of the same subject, would
accuse both or either of deceiving or being deceived, if one of
them should happen to mention something which the other had
omitted?   Or if one should have treated the matter compendiously
without affecting the sense, while the other enters into details,
and mentions not only what was done, but how it was done?
But Faustus calumniates the Gospels because Matthew says something which Luke omits ; as if Luke denied that Christ had said
what Matthew attributed to Him . . . .   Was the Scripture of
God to speak to us in language differing from that to which we
were accustomed?   This is my answer to obstinate and turbulent
men as regards the usage of language . . . .   I wish some one
of those who magnify these trifles against the Gospel would himself relate *twice* something of the same kind, with no intention to
deceive, but in all good faith ; and that his words be taken down,
and then recited to him.   Let him then see whether he has not
added or subtracted something; or changed the order not only of
the words, but even of the events ; or said something of his own
as if said by another, which, however, he had not actually heard
from his lips, but had known him to have felt and intended; or
compressed what he had more fully explained ; or if there be
anything else subject to the rules which explain how it may
happen that in two narrations of the same event we may find
diversity without opposition, variation without contradiction.

I submit that it is not good criticism to call the writer
of the above an incompetent critic.   But there are other

mistakes which it is no pleasant duty to point out in a
writer so conspicuous for his services against the 'destructive
critics.'

1. There was no 'enlarged Canon of Augustine.'
Dr. Westcott proves (p. 265) that the African Catholic Canon
was the same as that of the Donatists; now the Donatists
fell off from the Catholic Church in the year 311, that is just
forty-three years before St. Augustine was born. And in
his *History of New Testament Canon*,[2] he says that this Old
Testament Canon was the very one used by St. Cyprian,
who died in the year 258.

2. The words *consulatur Ecclesia transmarina* belong to
the Plenary Council of Hippo, A.D. 393, but were quoted by
the Council of 397, which composed a *Breviarium* of the
Canons of Hippo, the only record we now possess of that
celebrated council. The Canon of Scripture was promulgated
in 393, 397, and again in the Plenary Council of Carthage,
A.D. 419, *as received from our fathers*. This Council of 419
sent its acts to Rome in charge of the papal legates. It
is quite certain that in these African Councils *Ecclesia
transmarina* meant the Roman Church, as both Gallicans
and Anglicans insist when they think it adverse to Rome,
as in the question of appeals. The reason of these repeated
promulgations of the Canon was, probably, the prevalence,
often mentioned by St. Augustine, of apocryphal writings
circulated by the Manicheans. There may be also some
truth in Dr. Westcott's surmise, that the Donatists wished
to pose as the defenders of the old popular Canon. It was
only after its promulgation by the Councils of 393 and 397
that St. Augustine inserted the Canon in his work, *De
Doctrine Christiana*, ii. 8. Augustine was only a young
priest in 393, when the Council of Hippo was held. The
attempt to make him the author of the Canon, and at the
same time a bad critic, is evidently intended as a defence
of the Anglican dissent from the Catholic Canon.

3. Dr. Westcott lays great stress on St. Augustine's
little preface to the Canon, but omits altogether the following

words inserted immediately after it: *in his omnibus libris, timentes Deum et pietate mansueti quorunt voluntatem Dei.* From these words alone it is clear that Dr. Westcott has completely mistaken the meaning of this preface. He He says[1] that 'by this distinction he extended to others a certain freedom of judgment, and even exercised it himself.' Where did he exercise it himself? Where did he ever express a doubt about the inspiration of any of these Books? Does not Dr. Westcott tell us that he disregarded the distinction in practice? And, as to the liberty he allowed to others, take this specimen from his *contra Faustum*,[2] written about the same time: ' Such being the canonical eminence of the Sacred Scriptures, it is not lawful to doubt what has been said by a single Prophet, Apostle or Evangelist, once the fact has been declared and confirmed by the Canon.' St. Augustine's contemporaries raised no question about this preface, not even the Donatists, who were always on the watch. Its meaning was therefore understood, and could not possibly be what Dr. Westcott insinuates, viz., liberty to doubt of the *intrinsic* authority of the books now called *deuterocanonical*. As regards their *extrinsic* authority, he allowed the same liberty we use at present in not quoting them against Protestants. We must also remember that he was writing for Biblical students, who had to defend the *dogmatic* and authoritative Canon of Scripture, by proving that it coincided exactly with the *historical* Canon founded on sound critical principles. By following the rules laid down in this preface a student could construct critically such a Canon, just as students do at present.

Dr. Westcott cannot bear the thought of a dogmatic Canon, and denounces the decree of Trent on the Canon in almost the very words of Sarpi.[3] He is not content with the signatures of a pope, two cardinals, four legates, three patriarchs, twenty-five archbishops, one hundred and fifty-

---

[1] *Hist. New Testament Canon*, p. 454.
[2] Book xi., ch. 5.
[3] *Hist. N. T. Canon*, final ch.

eight bishops, seven abbots, seven generals of orders, and many procurators of absent bishops ;[1] while St. Augustine required only the signature of Pope Innocent, to say *causa finita est.*   Well Dr. Westcott has had his way ; for nearly half a century he and other distinguished men have expended splendid talents, great learning, and undoubted zeal in defence of the Bible.   But where are the results?   Is the Bible more respected ?   Do the masses believe more firmly in their Bible?   Do even the dignitaries and professors ?

St. Augustine knew the rules of criticism, and made good use of them at the proper time and place.   But it was not on them he relied when he said : ' I would not believe the Gospel were I not moved by the authority of the Catholic Church . . .   If I believe the Gospel, I must also believe the *Acts of the Apostles,* since both are equally commended to me by Catholic authority.' [2]

PHILIP BURTON, C.M.

---

[1] These are the final signatures, but of course they must be included in the charge of incompetence made against the fathers of the fourth Session.   The charge, that among all these and their theologians and advisers there was no critical ability, is so absurd that it refutes itself.   Pecock, who is quoted as a Catholic authority, figures in Fox's *Martyrology* at February 11.   He had got into trouble in Lollard times.   This whole chapter is unworthy of Dr. Westcott even as a critic.   Anglicans lose their heads whenever Rome is in question.

[2] *Epis. Fund.* 6

CATECHETICAL INSTRUCTION IN THE CHURCH

AMONGST his many glories St. Augustine counts that
of catechist; he was indeed the most distinguished
catechist of the most glorious period in this respect of the
Church. Heaven had gifted him with an almost universal
genius, and he possessed amongst other talents that of
instructing young intelligences. His brilliant imagination,
his enthusiasm, full of fire and sweetness; perhaps also the
errors of his youth and his marvellous return to virtue,
prepared him a favourable reception with his audience, and
gained their hearts. Rich in the experience of his predecessors, he analyzed their ideas, combined their methods,
and resumed in his works the discoveries of all the catechists
who preceded him in the east and west. His work, *De
Catechandis Rudibus*, is the outcome of the vast learning
and experience of St. Augustine, and is to catechetical
instruction what his work, *De Doctrina Christiana*, is to
sacred rhetoric.

It is not our intention to analyze the work of St. Augustine
more than to remark that he refers to *love* all the qualifi-
cations necessary to the catechist. If you do not love God
and your brethren, he says, how will you laboriously spell out
the first words of faith to instruct the ignorant? how will
you sustain the attention of an audience that shows signs of
fatigue? where will you find the secret of speaking of the
same truth again and again without repeating yourself?
where will you obtain the courage and industry necessary to
cultivate these barren lands which produce nothing but
briars and thorns? In this treatise the immortal Bishop
of Carthage gives advice that is invaluable to everyone
announcing the word of God, when he tells us to give
the light cheerfully, for God as well as man loves the
cheerful giver, to ever wear an appearance of happiness,
for happiness is a principal element of success, and

the love of God should give a joyous serenity to our language.

Perhaps [he says] you complain your discourse does not please you. Do you not know that the intelligence of the audience supplies the defects of your words, and that often the discourse that displeases its author, rejoices and improves the hearers? You have to do with people who do not understand the first word of your instructions! Then, like a tender mother who lisps the words to her children, distribute the crumbs of knowledge instead of seating yourself at a splendid banquet. They become tired of hearing you! Accommodate yourself to human infirmity and awaken their sleeping attention by ingenious devices. You must repeat and repeat the same things! Let the love which animates you give them an appearance of novelty. You would much prefer a different occupation! But would you do so much good in the work of your own choice as doing that which Providence has marked out for you. Scandals affect you! Eloquence is ordinarily the vibration of a stricken soul. You feel remorse, perhaps, for sins which you have committed! Be of good courage; redeem the evil by the best kind of alms, which is to break the bread of truth to poor intelligences.

Concerning the methods which one may follow, St. Augustine counsels the *logical* plan to the Deacon of Carthage, ' so that the catechumens in understanding may believe, in believing may hope, and in hoping may believe. In detached sermons, we find the Doctor of Africa, in order to follow the natural thread of ideas, treating of the Apostles' Creed and the Lord's Prayer. But he also loved the liturgical method. The festivals and sacred ceremonies offered subjects of instruction adapted to all. St. Augustine had the science and the taste for symbolism.

Yet, though he loved the liturgical method, his love was far from being exclusive. A part of his affection was reserved for the *historical* method. Thus when *Deo Gratias*, the Deacon of Carthage, asks how he is to teach the Christian Dogmas, he recommended him to teach them under the form of narrative. The books of Scripture composed before the birth of Christ foretel the coming of the Saviour, and the establishment of the Church which is His mystical Body. The Ancient Testament is a figure of the New; the reason of the coming of the Messiah is the showing forth of God's

love for men, especially in dying for them who were as yet
His enemies: the end of the precepts, and the perfection of
the law consist in charity.   And so we have the magnificent
theory of the Bishop of Hippo on Catechetical Instruction in
its *logical*, *liturgical*, and *historical* methods.

Every point of doctrine is based essentially on an *idea*,
and we may trace this idea to principles or attach it to
consequences.   Unity being universal, the idea of the
human mind on the simple enunciation of a proposition
of faith ascends and descends the entire scale of the
intellectual world.   This operation of the mind brings one
to the *logical* plan.   Again, Divine light falls, by the very fact,
into the domain of events.   When one relates what has
been, and when the progress and tendency of events are
shown; when one brings forward the supernatural effects
of the divine ideas, with their circumstances, their bearing,
and their order of generation, one is following the *historical*
plan.

But ideas and facts mark out a visible passage in the
universe.   Monuments attest to all ages phenomena of
the past.   The Church which is a monument, and by its
nature a necessary witness of the divine ideas and works
knows how to give a body to invisible things, and to lastingly
perpetuate them.   All in her speaks : persons, acts, prayers,
and ceremonies.   The Catechist who starts from the life
of the Church to ascend to God conforms to the *liturgical*
plan.

These three methods are not strangers one to the other;
there are, on the contrary, very strict bonds of relationship
between them.   We see history in science, and we perceive
science in history, and liturgy houses them in our
memory.

We will now exemplify the principles laid down in
former papers.[1]   As St. John Chrysostom was the most
perfect master of the 'homily' in the early ages of the
Church, the holy Curé of Ars seems to us to come nearest
perfection in modern times in this kind of preaching.   The

---

[1] See I. E. Record, May and July, 1897.

portions we possess of the venerable Curé's instructions and homilies are few and of a fragmentary nature, yet we can find in them sufficient to serve as models. As Michael Angelo studied the 'Torso,' and owned that his genius was the child of that mutilated fragment; so whoever studies the homilies and catechisms of the holy priest of Ars will find and acknowledge that he has seen the word of God clothed becomingly and sweetly in human expression. In his sermons and catechetical instructions M. Vianney was precise and exact in his theological statements, and the simplest words of these venerable lips possessed a singular majesty and an irresistible charm. As to his style, he always used the very simplest expression in which it was possible to clothe the idea which he wished to convey. He availed himself freely of images drawn from nature. His instructions were full of incidents from the lives of the saints, told with the life-like freshness of one who lived habitually in their company.

The Curé of Ars [says M. Monnin]. without ever suspecting it was a poet in the highest sense of the word; his heart was endowed in the highest degree with the gift of sensibility, and it opened only to give out the true note and the just accent.[1]

One Spring morning [said he] I was going to see a sick person ; the thickets were full of little birds, who were singing their hearts out. I took pleasure in hearing them, and I said to myself, ' poor little birds, you know not what you are singing ; but you are singing the praises of the good God ! '

We are here reminded of St. Francis of Assisi. The following may give an idea of his preaching :—

We see in to-day's Gospel, my brethren, that the master of the field having sown his seed in good ground the enemy came while he was asleep and sowed cockle in the midst of it. The meaning of this is, that God created men good and perfect, but that the enemy came and sowed sin in his heart. This is the fall of Adam,—a dreadful fall, which let in sin into the heart of man. This is the mixture of the good and the evil ; we find sin among virtues. Do you say, we must root up the cockle? ' No,' replies our Lord, ' lest with it you root up the wheat also. Wait till the harvest.' The heart of man must endure thus to the

---

[1] See *Life of the Cure of Ars*, by l'Abbe Monnin.

end—a mixture of good and evil, of vice and virtue, of light and darkness, of good seed and cockle. The good God has not been pleased to destroy this mixture, and make for us a new nature in which there should be nothing but good seed. We must struggle and labour to hinder the cockle from overgrowing the whole field. The devil will come, indeed, to sow temptations around our steps ; but by the help of Divine grace we shall be able to overcome them, and stifle the cockle. The cockle is impurity and pride. 'Without impurity and pride,' says, St. Augustine, ' there would be no merit in resisting temptation.' Three things are absolutely necessary as defences against temptation,—prayer to enlighten us, the sacraments to strengthen us, and vigilance to preserve us. Happy are the souls that are tempted ! It is when the devil foresees that a soul is tending to union with God, that he redoubles his rage. Oh, blessed union !

If the Curé of Ars is a model for preachers in the 'homily' he is yet a more perfect model of the catechist. Indeed he seems to have been raised up by God in this century of scientific unbelief to show forth the power of the word of truth in[1] Jesus Christ, not in the persuasive words of human wisdom. Nor am I forgetting the admirable catechists of St. Sulpice or ' la Madeleine,' with the great Dupanloup as their leader, but we are persuaded there is in the catechetical instructions of the Curé d'Ars that which like genius we fail to analyze, but which exerts a wonderful influence over us, and that something is not found in the works of others. The reader will judge. I will quote from that on the Holy Spirit, as M. Monnin gives it :—

Oh, how blessed is this, my children ! The Father is our Creator, the Son is our Redeemer, and the Holy Ghost our guide. Man is nothing by himself, but he is much with the Holy Spirit, the Holy Spirit alone can elevate his soul and lift it on high. Why were the saints so detached from earth ? because they suffered themselves to be led by the Holy Spirit. Those who are led by the Holy Spirit have a right judgment in all things. Therefore it is that there are so many ignorant souls who are far more keen-sighted than the learned. When we are led by a God of light and power we can never go wrong. The Holy Spirit is a light and power. It is He who makes us to discern between truth and falsehood, good and evil. Like those glasses which magnify the objects on which we look, the Holy Spirit shows us evil and good in all their magnitude. With the aid of the Holy

---

[1] Eph. Chap. 1.

Spirit we see all things on a large scale, we see the greatness of the smallest action done for God, and the greatness of the slightest fault. As a watchmaker discerns by the help of his magnifying glass the most minute wheels of his watch, so by the light of the Holy Ghost we discern the most secret details of our poor lives. Then do the slightest imperfections appear great, the lightest sins horrible. The Blessed Virgin, who never sinned, and to whom the Holy Spirit revealed the hideousness of evil, shuddered with horror at the slightest fault. Those in whom the Holy Spirit dwells cannot endure themselves, so conscious are they of their own misery. Worldly men have not the Holy Spirit; or, if they have, it is only at intervals. He does not dwell with them, the noise of the world drives Him away. A Christian who is led by the Holy Spirit feels no difficulty in leaving the good things of earth to pursue those of heaven. He can discern the difference between them. The eye of the world cannot see beyond this life as mine cannot see beyond that wall when the church door is shut. Without the Holy Spirit all is cold; thus, when we feel we are losing fervour, we must hasten to make a novena to the Holy Ghost to ask for faith and love. When we have made a retreat or a jubilee, we are full of good desires; these good desires are the breath of the Holy Ghost, which has passed over our soul and renewed all within it, like the warm wind which melts the ice and brings back the spring. You, even, who are not great saints, have moments in which you taste the sweetness of prayer and the presence of God. When we have the Holy Ghost, the heart dilates and bathes in divine love. The fish never complains of having too much water, so the good Christian never complains of being too long with God. There are some who find religion irksome, but it is because they have not the Holy Spirit. The Holy Spirit is a power. But for the Holy Spirit the martyrs would have fallen like the leaves from the trees. When the fires were kindled for them the Holy Ghost extinguished the flames by the fires of divine love. The Holy Ghost rests in the soul of the just like the dove in her nest. He hatches good desires in a pure soul, as the dove hatches her little ones. The Holy Ghost leads us as a mother leads a child of two years old by the hand— as one who can see leads a blind man. Our Lord said to His Apostles—'It is expedient for you that I go away; for if I go, not away, the Paraclete will not come to you.' The descent of the Holy Ghost was needed to render that harvest of grace fruitful. As with a grain of wheat, you cast it into the earth, but it needs the sun and the rain to make it spring up and bring forth the ear. We should say every morning: 'My God, send me Thy Holy Spirit to teach me what I am, and what Thou art.'

This is but a fragment of a fragment, yet the great lines are there;—lines of beauty, strength, and sweetness, by the study of which we may profit much.

We now come to the period when catechetical instruction
merges in great part into the 'teaching of catechism to
children,' and in Bossuet[1] it seems to us the transition was
made.

Bossuet has been called the last of the fathers of the
Church. There may be exaggeration in this praise, yet
everyone must admit the sublimity of his varied genius, and
that he has more than any other caught the style of the first
fathers of the Church ; Bossuet who spoke so nobly the
language of the most sublime theology knew how to lisp,
as it were, with children and prepare for them the milk
of doctrine until they should be able to partake of the food
of the strong. It is especially in his catechisms that we
admire the respect which this truly great genius had for our
sacred beginnings. St. Augustine was his model.

Wishing to spread the light in his diocese, the Bishop of
Meaux first published a catechism of questions and answers,
following the method of the catechism printed by order of
the Council of Trent, that is to say, on the *logical plan*.
That the instruction might be proportioned to the different
ages, he divided this first work into three parts : one for the
little children, which was to be learned at home; the second
was for those who already came to the church, attended
school, and were preparing for Confirmation ; the last for
those who were about to make their first Communion.
Bossuet himself marks for us the points on which it seemed
important to insist :—

We have judged it necessary [he says] to insist somewhat on
the creation of man, on the fall of our first parents, and on the
evil inheritance of sin, as also on the admirable mystery of our
redemption, on the Sacraments which apply its virtue to us,
in order that each one may know very distinctly the remedies
which God has furnished to our evils, and the dispositions with
which we ought to receive them.

The Bishop does not deny that certain parts of his

---

[1] St. Ignatius and other men of God had already brought into prominence
the teaching of the fundamental truths to the young, but we are not speaking
of it exactly in this relation.

instructions, though indeed very elementary, may seem beyond the capacity of children :—

> You ought not for that [he adds] to omit teaching them, because experience shows that, provided things are explained to children in short and precise terms, although these terms are not always understood at first, little by little, by thinking on them, they are at last understood. Moreover, looking to the salvation of all, we have preferred that the less advanced and the less capable should find things that they could not understand, than that those who are more intelligent should be deprived of anything.

Bossuet's intention was that history and liturgy should give a sensible form to the truths which the catechist was to explain to the children. Fleury at this time was after publishing his *Historical Catechism.* The Bishop approved of it for his diocese of Meaux, and recommended its usage. He himself wrote an abridgment of sacred history, and speaks thus in the preface :—

> At the commencement of this second catechism you will give the children, in an abridged form, the sacred history according to the method here employed. The parish priest will expand it and divide it into as many sermons or lessons as will seem good to his prudence. But by every kind of means he will endeavour to impress it deeply on the minds of the children by giving the lessons in the most vivid and pleasing manner, with the most characteristic and picturesque expressions, by repeating often, and making them repeat sometimes one part, sometimes another ; even making those who are capable to learn it by heart, remembering that nothing insinuates itself more quickly into the minds of children, and nothing makes more impression on them, than to insert the doctrine in their minds, as God did in the minds of Moses and the Evangelists.

After giving this important instruction, Bossuet shows in eight *tableaux* the most striking facts of history from the creation of the world to the establishment of the Church. Remark how the disciple of St. Augustine follows to the letter the instructions of the treatise '*De catechizandis rudibus.*'

Some time after Bossuet composed, for those who were more advanced, his *Catechism of the Festivals and other Solemnities and Observances of the Church ;* and here again he traces the method of catechetical instruction of the fathers of the Church, and notably of St. Augustine. He borrows also from them the enumeration of the duties of those who are obliged to instruct children. There are three sorts of persons, according to the Bishop, who are charged with the mission of the catechist—fathers and mothers, schoolmasters, and priests.

It had been our intention to speak of the *Teaching of Catechism to Children*, but, on consideration, the importance and difficulty of the subject have so grown upon us that we have given up the task in despair. Nor would we wish to seem what we are not ; and, therefore, we abstain from pronouncing on that which, on account of its gravity, can be done with becomingness only by the high dignitaries of the Church and those placed in responsible positions. We mean the strictness of this obligation on those to whom the souls of children are confided. Therefore, we will end these brief sketches by quoting the words of a distinguished Irish prelate in a remarkable book[1], many parts of which are of surpassing beauty and of the greatest interest to the priests of Ireland :—

I will remind you, venerable brethren [says Dr. Moriarty], that the most effectual of all preaching, and that without which all other preaching is nearly useless, is the teaching of the catechism to the young. I say it, brethren, advisedly. The priest who would neglect every other instruction, and teach the catechism to the children of his parish would have done a great deal. The priest who would discharge every other duty and neglect this, would have done nothing. The one will be preparing for his successor a generation, at least, of believing Christians, the other a generation of baptized pagans. Mind the decree of the Council of Trent, Sess. 24 chap. 4 : ' The bishops shall also take care that at least on the Lord's days and other festivals, the children in every parish be carefully taught the rudiments of the faith, and obedience towards God and their parents, by those whose duty it is, and who shall be constrained thereunto by their bishops, and, if need be, even by ecclesiastical censures.' Oh, brethren, I conjure you in the name of the living God to teach the catechism. Let it not be said that the little ones asked for bread, and that there was none to break it unto them (Lam. iv. 4).

JEROME O'CONNELL, O.D.C.

---

[1] *Allocations and Pastorals*, by the Right Rev. Dr. Moriarty, Bishop of Kerry.

Notes and Queries

THEOLOGY

DISPENSATION IN THE VOW OF CHASTITY

Rev. Dear Sir,—A penitent has taken a vow of perfect chastity *extra religionem*. Now, however, she wishes to be released from her obligation, and wants to know to whom she must apply for a dispensation. Have the bishops power to dispense?

Confessarius.

The bishop may, of course, have delegated faculties in virtue of which he can dispense in a vow of perfect and perpetual chastity. Without such special faculties, he can dispense in a case of urgent necessity *in quantum est necessarium*. But, *jure ordinario*, outside a case of necessity, bishops have no power to dispense in a vow of perfect and perpetual chastity. It should be observed, however, that the vow is reserved only when the following conditions are present: The vow must be—(1) perpetual, and (2) perfect; perfect (a) *ratione actus;* that is, the vow must be taken with full knowledge, deliberation, and freedom ; (b) *ratione materiae;* that is, it must prohibit, in the virtue of religion, *id omne contra castitatem quod illicitum est solutis;* (c) *ratione finis;* that is, the vow must be taken *ob amorem castitatis;* a vow of chastity taken from any other motive is not reserved; (d) *ratione formae*, that is, the vow must be absolute, not conditional, nor, as a rule, disjunctive—I will observe perfect chastity, or fast twice a week; if, however, both members of the disjunctive were reserved, the disjunctive vow would be reserved—I vow to enter religion or to observe perfect and perpetual chastity in the world; (e) *ratione obligationis;* that is, the vow must bind under a *grave* obligation; a vow of chastity, otherwise perfect, but binding only *sub veniale*, would not be reserved. Finally, we should add that if there be good and solid ground for thinking that the vow is imperfect, under any of the above-named five aspects, the bishop can dispense. For, the reservation is in that hypothesis doubtful, and here as elsewhere, *reservatio dubia est nulla.*

If the vow be unreserved, to whom must application be made for a dispensation? (1) To the bishop of the penitent's domicile or quasi-domicile; or (2) to the bishop of the place where the penitent happens to be, in case she is a *vaga*, or outside the diocese in which her home is situated.

CAN A CURATE DISPENSE IN THE LAW FORBIDDING SERVILE WORKS ON SUNDAY?

REV. DEAR SIR,—Can a curate dispense in the law forbidding servile works on Sundays and holidays? In the absence of the parish priest, I am sometimes asked to give permission to work at harvesting. May I do so, and by what authority?

C. C.

Custom has given parish priests the right to dispense in this and similar laws, but curates, as such, enjoy no similar privilege. A curate, therefore, can dispense only in virtue of jurisdiction from the parish priest or other superior. The power of dispensing in this and other laws over which the parish priest has power from custom, is, of course, delegated to the curate when, *v.g.*, the parish priest, about to absent himself, commissions the curate in a general way to attend to the parochial duties in his absence. In Ireland, as far as we know, the people who ask for permission to work at harvesting and the like are, as a rule, justified in working without any dispensation. A curate, though he cannot dispense, has, of course, a perfect right to declare that in given cases it is lawful to work on Sundays or holidays. This right will, probably, cover the cases that our correspondent is likely to meet.

INFORMAL WILLS AND PIOUS BEQUESTS

REV. DEAR SIR,—You will oblige by saying what should be my decision in the following case :—

A. B. has inherited considerable property from X. Y., recently deceased. The deceased had made a will distributing his property between A. B. and others. Among other bequests there were several for ecclesiastical and other charitable purposes. The will has been legally set aside as informal, and A. B. has come in for the whole property, as next-of-kin. He admits that as far as the pious bequests go, the will, though informal in the eyes of the law, represents X. Y.'s dying intention, and he is prepared to pay these pious bequests, if an obligation to do so be imposed on him. I have no doubt as to what the decision should be, but I should like to have an opinion in the next number of I. E. RECORD.

M.

A decision bearing on this case was rather recently obtained from one of the Roman Congregations. It is published, with an editorial note, in the I. E. RECORD of November, 1895.

We are at one with our correspondent in saying that the solution of this case presents no difficulty. A. B. is undoubtedly bound to pay these pious bequests according to the known will and intention of his deceased relative. Whatever may be said of the power of the state to invalidate, owing to legal informalities, bequests for secular purposes, the state has no power to make void bequests for pious purposes. A pious bequest that satisfies the requirements of the natural and ecclesiastical law remains valid despite the force of civil enactments. Such bequests and the conditions of their validity fall directly within the jurisdiction of the Church; and the claims of the Church and her legislation cannot be overridden by the inferior authority of the civil power. Our correspondent will find this to be the teaching of the decision to which we have above referred.

THE BULL 'APOSTOLICAE CURAE'

We deem it a duty to draw special attention to the brief addressed to the Cardinal Archbishop of Paris, and printed in the present number of the I. E. RECORD. This important pronouncement removes any doubt that may have remained regarding the scope and authority of the Bull *Apostolicae Curae,* in which the Holy Father established and defined the invalidity of Anglican orders.

In reply to several correspondents, we have already had occasion to assert the obligation of all Catholics to receive and assent to the teaching of the Bull *Apostolicae Curae ;* and that, not merely because of the proved invalidity of Anglican orders, but also in obedience to the teaching authority of the Holy See.

We recognised, too, that the condemnation of Anglican orders was a matter which fell within the domain of the Pope to decide absolutely and finally. The brief now published enables us to go a step farther. For it now appears, moreover, that the Holy Father *de facto* intended to define, absolutely and irrevocably, the invalidity of Anglican orders. *Consilium fuit,* we read, in the brief now published, *absolute judicare, penitusque dirimere . . . sententiam Nostram, Catholici, autem, omnes summo deberent obsequio amplecti tanquam perpetuo firmam, ratam, irrevocabilem.*

This clear pronouncement will be to many a welcome commentary on the teaching of the recent Bull, and will silence among Catholics, at all events, any dispute as to the import of the papal decision.

D. MANNIX.

CORRESPONDENCE

A QUESTION REGARDING THE COMMUNION OF THE FAITHFUL

REV. AND DEAR SIR,—Can you kindly throw some further light on the following question?

It not unfrequently happens in churches, where there is a large number of communicants at the early Masses on Sunday, that, in order not to inconvenience the congregation by delaying them too long in the church; and again, because the celebrant is infirm—immediately after his own communion, another priest vested in cotta and stole comes to the altar to distribute communion to the people. In this ministry, he either entirely replaces the celebrant, or he shares it with him, using a ciborium, which he takes from the tabernacle. In the former case the celebrant does not leave the altar, but goes on with his Mass. On his receiving the Precious Blood, the Minister at the Mass says the *Confiteor*, and very often it is the other priest who opens the door of the tabernacle, takes out the ciborium, says the *Misereatur*, &c., and the *Ecce Agnus Dei;* and the celebrant continues his Mass.

Now, is this the more proper course under the circumstances? My own opinion has always been that it is not; but that the celebrant should himself perform all these acts, which are prescribed to him by the rubrics of the Missal,[1] and as they are explained by all liturgical authors;[2] and, moreover, that he should himself begin the Communion of the people, by communicating, at least, some few; and that the other priest should at the altar-rails receive from his hands the sacred ciborium, and then continue the people's Communion. It might, indeed, be preferable that the celebrant should consecrate a ciborium in his Mass, and begin the Communion with it; meanwhile, the priest assisting would simply take the ciborium from the tabernacle

---

[1] Missale Rom. *Ritus serrandus in celebratione Missae*, x. 6. But here is contemplated a priest saying Mass at an altar where the Blessed Sacrament is not reserved in the tabernacle.

[2] Martinucci, tom. i., pp. 344-350., cap. xxiv., *De SS. Eucharistia Fidelibus administranda*, § 1., nn. 1-9. De Herdt, tom. i., P. ii., n. 292. S. Alph. Lig., *De Caeremoniis Missae*, Schober. Baldeschi, Part vi., ch. vi., n. 5.

and continue the Communion, and the celebrant might, at any time, go back to the altar to finish his Mass.

My reason for suggesting one or other of these courses, is that thereby there would be less violation of the letter of the rubrics prescribed to a celebrant of Mass in which there are communicants; and a greater conformity with the mind and spirit of the Church. For it always strikes me, in such a case, as an infraction of the prescribed integrity of Mass, for another priest, to take, so to say, out of the lips of the celebrant, words which it is his own duty to say, viz., *Misereatur*, &c., in response to the *Confiteor* which his own minister has just said in the name of the communicants; as also the *Ecce Agnus Dei*—Moreover, by giving communion to a few of them, he fulfils, so far, the rest of his duty, and prescribed integrity of the Mass, according to the rubrics of the Missal,[1] and the desire of the Church, as expressed in the Council of Trent.[2]

Liturgical writers treat of two modes only of giving Communion; the one *intra Missam*, at the hands of the Celebrant, and the other *extra Missam*;[3] but their prescriptions do not meet the case in point; and it is perhaps difficult to determine precisely to which of the two this belongs. To myself it seems decidedly to belong to the former mode, though attended by some exceptional circumstances for the avoidance of grave inconvenience, and that, consequently, all the rubrics prescribed for Communion *intra Missam*, have the first claim to observance.

I am not here venturing for a moment to question either the lawfulness or advisability of the practice itself; but am only inquiring how it may be best carried out, conformably with the rubrics, and the intention of the Church. I have known numerous cases, on the last Sunday of a Mission or of a Retreat to some Sodality, when the number of those at the General Communion amounted to many hundreds, and even greatly exceeded two thousand; when several priests were called to assist at the altar-rails, and, not unfrequently the Bishop of the Diocese was the celebrant at the Mass. From such obvious necessity the

---

[1] Missale Romanum, Ordo Missae, *Canon Missae.*

[2] 'Optaret quidem sacrosancta synodus, ut in singulis Missis fideles adstantes, non solum spirituali affectu, sed sacramenti etiam Eucharistiae perceptione communicarent, quo ad eos sanctissimi Sacrificii fructus uberior proveniret.'

Sess. xxii., *De Sacrificio Missae*, cap. vi. See De Herdt, tom. i., n. 204.

[3] Baldeschi, Part vi., ch. vi, n. 1-4.

practice has become more or less a custom, carried out under the eye of ecclesiastical authority, and meeting with, at least, its tacit sanction and approval.

Yet another mode of carrying out the practice under discussion may be considered preferable to those which I have suggested, as serving more to dissociate it from the Mass, and to render it rather a Communion *extra Missam*. It is this, that, where practicable, the Blessed Sacrament should be previously transferred from the Tabernacle at the High Altar where the Mass is celebrated, to one at another altar, and that the priest who assists in giving communion should go out with his own Minister to this altar and observe all the ceremonies prescribed for Communion *extra Missam ;* whilst the celebrant would fulfil what is enjoined on him by communicating some few with particles consecrated in his Mass. In the other modes suggested it seems to be a question, should the Communion still continue after the Mass is over, whether the priest on his return from the altar rails ought to pronounce the blessing, *Benedictio Dei Omnipotentis*, or not. It often happens, however, in the case of a very large General Communion, that two Masses are celebrated consecutively during the time of its ministration.

I am, Rev. Dear Sir,

Yours sincerely,

T. Livius, c.ss.r.

DOCUMENTS

THE BULL 'APOSTOLICAE CURAE'

EX ACTIS LEONIS XIII ET E SECRETAR. BREVIUM. SSMUS. ACRITER
REPREHENDIT LUTETIANAM EPHEMERIDEM 'REVUE ANGLO-
ROMAINE,' ILLAMQUE SILERE IUBET[1]

DILECTO FILIO NOSTRO FRANCISCO· MARIAE S. R. E. CARDINALI
RICHARD, ARCHIEPISCOPO PARISIENSI. PARISIOS

Dilecte Fili Noster, salutem et Apostolicam benedictionem.

Religioni apud Anglos aeternaeque animarum saluti pro
munere prospicientes, Constitutionem *Apostolicae curae*, ut nosti,
proxime edidimus. In ea causam gravissimam de ordinationibus
anglicanis, iure quidem a decessoribus Nostris multo antea
definitam indulgenter tamen a Nobis ex integro revocatam, consilium fuit absolute iudicare penitusque dirimere. Idque sane
perfecimus eo argumentorum pondere eaque formularum tum
perspicuitate tum auctoritate, ut sententiam Nostram nemo
prudens recteque animatus compellere in dubitationem posset,
catholici autem omnes omnino deberent obsequio amplecti, tanquam perpetuo firmam, ratam, irrevocabilem. At vero diffiteri
nequimus non ita a quibusdam catholicis esse responsum: id
quod haud levi nos aegritudine affecit. Hoc tecum, Dilecte Fili
Noster, communicare ideo placuit, quia ephemeridem *Revue
Anglo-romaine*, quae istic evulgatur, praecipue attingit. Sunt
namque in eius scriptoribus qui eiusdem Constitutionis virtutem
non ut par est tuentur atque illustrant, sed infirmant potius
tergiversando et disceptando. Quocirca evigilare oportet ut ex
tali ephemeride ne quid dimanet quod cum propositis Nostris
non plene conveniat ; certeque praestat eam desistere atque
omnino silere, ubi eisdem propositis ceptisque optimis difficultatem
sit allatura. Similiter, quando ex Anglis dissidentibus ii certi
homines qui veritatem rei de ordinationibus suis exquirere a
Nobis sincero animo videbantur, veritatem ipsam a Nobis coram
Deo significatam, animo longe alio acceperunt, plane consequitur
ut catholici quos supra commemoravimus, in eisque vir aliquis
religiosus, agnoscant officium suum. Iam nunc enim nec aequum

---

[1] Statim siluit, uti de iure et de facto omnino congruum reat.

fuerit nec decorum sibi, illorum hominum adiungi et quoquo modo suffragari consiliis, quod etiam optato religionis incremento possit non minime obesse.

De his igitur rebus quae magni momenti sunt, exploratae prudentiae ac sollertiae tuae, Dilecte Fili Noster, valde confidimus ; auspicemque divinorum munerum ac testem peculiaris Nostrae benevolentiae, Apostolicam tibi benedictionem peramanter impertimus.

Datum Romae apud Sanctum Petrum die v novembris, anno MDCCCXCVI, Pontificatus Nostri decimo nono.

LEO PP. XIII.

IT IS NOT EXPEDIENT TO CELEBRATE BY SPECIAL SOLEMNITIES THE 19th CENTENARY OF THE REDEMPTION

LITTERAE S. R. CONGREGATIONIS AD ILLUSTRISSIMUM COMITEM IONNEM ACQUADERNI : BONONIAM. DE CENTENARIA SOLEMNITATE CELEBRANDA REDEMPTIONIS HUMANAE

Romae, 14 Maii, 1895.

Illme Domine.

Iussu SSmi Dñi nostri Papae, Patrum Congregatio sacris Ritibus tuendis praeposita, in conventu die 7 huius eiusdem mensis, in Aedibus vaticanis habito, tum Literas Emo Cardinali, Pontificis primo Scribae ad extranea, die 24 Martii proxime elapsi a te datas, tum etiam his adnexum Programma de celebranda novies decies centenaria Redemptionis nostrae solemnitate, quae iuxta vulgarem computationem saeculo millesimo nongentesimo contingeret, diligenter expendenda suscepit.

Profecto laude et praemio apud Deum digna res est, ex qualibet temporum occasione ad excitandam Fidelium pietatem in Deum, devotionemque inflammandam erga hanc Apostolicam Sedem argumentum arripere ; quod procul dubio excogitatae solemnitatis Promotores et Programmatis auctores animo intendisse dicendi sunt. At vero et id probe agnoscens S. Congregatio, illico tamen animadvertit, omnino novum et inopportunum, imo etiam parum conveniens esse, morem qui iam ubique obtinuit, atque adeo frequenter exercetur, solemnitates saeculares celebrandi, praecipuis Religionis nostrae Mysteriis aptare. Prorsus existimari nec potest, nec debet, quod elapsis viginti quinque, aut quinquaginta, centum annis, illorum memoriam denuo excitare opus sit.

Qui haec Mysteria instar peculiarium solemnitatum habere et considerare velit, is ad proponendum consilium vel invitus trahitur, haud dissimile illi quod in Programmate proponitur, erigendi videlicet in perennem huius celebratae solemnitatis memoriam Redemptionis Sanctae Altare perpetuum; quasi vero in quolibet nostrorum templorum Altari Christus Cruci affixus, quod est omnium maxime visibile humanae Redemptionis signum, non adoretur; atque in omnibus nostris precibus non invocetur uti apud Deum Patrem intercessor idem noster Redemptor Christus.

Id profecto non advertit qui centenariam istam commemorationem excogitavit atque promovit, nec illi in mentem subiit decisio, ab eadem sacrorum Rituum Congregatione die 31 Maii Anno 1884 edita, qua postulationi plerorumque praeclarissimorum virorum, tum ex ecclesiasticis, tum vero etiam ex laicis respondebat; qui quidem sibi animo proposuerant centenarium commemorationem Nativitatis Mariae Virginis celebrare.[1] Huiusmodi decisio Eůo Cardinali Haynald per literas datas die 1 Iunii exhibita fuit, ac paulo post ab Ephemeridibus catholicis publicata.

In folio hic adnexo partem reperies, Illůe Domine, quae potiori admodum iure postulationi per te nuper admotae aptanda est, quae proinde aliud quam illa responsum expectare poterat, videlicet—non expedire—.

---

[1] En laciais litterarum, quae citantur :

Consuetudinem autem, quae invaluit, celebrandi sacras centenarias commemorationes, rei praesenti minus congruere deprehensum fuit. Quandoquidem, uti iidem centenarii fautores testantur, expetitum festum prima vice hoc decimonono saeculo foret inducendum, veluti quid novum in Dei Ecclesia, et cunctis retroactis sae. ulis ne cogitatum quidem ab eximia maiorum erga inclytam Dei Genitricem pietate et devotione, aut certe illis inusitatum. Profecto satis congrua theologica atque liturgica ratione inolevisse censendum est, ut saecularia solemnia, quae aliis sanctis cum Christo regnantibus non denegantur, ea de praecipuis sacratissimis Beatae Virginis vitae actis et mysteriis; scilicet de Nativitate, de Annuntiatione, de Assumptione, ac porro de ceteris. non celebrentur. Nam eminentiori veneratione supra ceteros Sanctos colit Ecclesia Coeli Reginam et Dominam Angelorum, cui *in quantum ipsa est mater Dei... debetur...non qualiscumque dulia, sed hyperdulia* (S. Thom. 3 part. quaest. 25, art. 5), Ideoque plusquam centenaria solemni commemoratione, eadem semper cultus praestantia, eodemque honoris tributo Ecclesia celebrat recurrentes eius mysteriorum solemnitates; cum de cetero cultus Deiparae in Ecclesia sit plane quot dianus, ac prope nulla temporis mensura limitatus.

Haec pauca, vel leviter tantum adumbrata, satis ostendunt prudentiam Sacrae Congregationis, quae proposito dubio: 'An recoli expediat anno proximo 1885 in toto Orbe centenaria commemoratio Nativitatis Beatae Mariae Virginis?' mature expensis omnibus, unanimi suffragio respondit: *non expedire.*

Dum hanc tibi S. Congregationis Decisionem, SSṁi Patris voluntati morem gerens, notam facio, meae erga te amplissimae observantiae testimonium mihi pergratum est tibi etiam atque etiam exhibere.

Tibi addictissimus servus

C. Card. Aloisi-Masella, S.R.C., *Praefectus*.

RESOLUTION OF DOUBTS REGARDING THE CELEBRATION OF REQUIEM MASSES

ROMANA. DUBIA QUOAD DECRETUM ' AUCTO ' CIRCA MISSAS PRIVATAS DE ' REQUIE '

Nonnulli Ecclesiarum Rectores sequentia Dubia super legitima interpretatione Decreti *Aucto*, die 8 Iunii anno nuper elapso 1896 editi, circa Missas privatas de Requie, die et pro die obitus indultas, Sacrae Rituum Congregationis resolvenda humiliter proposuerunt videlicet :

I. Privilegium circa Missas lectas de Requie ex praefato Decreto concessum sacellis sepulcreti, favet ne sive Ecclesiae vel Oratorio publico ac principali ipsius sepulcreti, sive aliis Ecclesiis vel Cappellis, extra coemeterium, subter quas ad legitimam distantiam alicuius defuncti cadaver quiescit ?

II. Missae privatae de Requie, quae sub expressis conditionibus celebrari possunt praesente cadavere, licitae ne erunt in quibuslibet Ecclesiis vel Oratoriis sive publicis sive privatis ?

III. Huiusmodi Missae privatae de Requie celebrarine poterunt sine applicatione pro Defuncto, cuius cadaver est vel censetur praesens ?

IV. Eaedem pariter Missae possuntne celebrari diebus non duplicibus, qui tamen festa duplicia I classis excludunt, uti ex. gr. feria IV. Cinerum ?

Et Sacra eadem Congregatio ad relationem subscripti Secretarii, exquisita sententia Commissionis Liturgicae, omnibusque mature perpensis, respondendum censuit :

Ad I. Negative ad utrumque.

Ad II. Affirmative, dummodo cadaver sit physice vel moraliter praesens ; sed, si agatur de Ecclesiis et Oratoriis publicis, fieri debet etiam funus cum Missa exequiali.

Ad III. et IV. Negative.

Atque ita rescripsit et servari mandavit, die 12 Januarii 1897.

C. Card. Aloisi-Masella, S. R. C., *Praefectus*.

L. ✠ S.

D. Panici, S. R. C., *Secretarius*.

CAN NUNS INHERIT PROPERTY WITHOUT A DISPENSATION OF THE HOLY SEE?

MONIALES NEQUEUNT ACCIPERE HAEREDITATEM, ETIAM IN BONUM
TOTIUS COMMUNITATIS, ABSQUE DISPENSATIONE S. SEDIS,—
QUAE, IN CASU, PRO URGENTIORIBUS NEGOTIIS EPUM ORATOREM
DELEGAT AD TRIENNIUM

BEATISSIME PATER :—Episcopus Zamorensis, in Hispania, ad
pedes S. V. provolutus, humillime exponit : N. N. Sanctimonialem
Ordinis Praemonstratensis in conventu civitatis N., huius dioecesis,
ex Constitutionibus, civilibus hispanicis ius habere ad haereditatem capiendam, quae eidem contigit ex morte fratris presbyteri
recens defuncti, Hinc quaeritur :

1. An praefata Sanctimonialis, posita solemni religiosa professione quam iamdiu emisit, licite in conscientia possit gestiones
agere, sive per se sive' per procuratorem, ut haereditatem capiat
proprio nomine coram saeculari iudice, in bonum tamen totius
Communitatis, ut par est ; vel potius egeat, ratione voti paupper-
tatis, legitima dispensatione ad praedictas gestiones iuridicas
agendas ad haereditatem adquirendam ?

2. Dato quod dispensatione egeat : an haec eidem tribui possit a
conventus Superiorissa, aut ab Episcopo cui conventus subest : vel
necessario, ratione solemnis voti, a Sede Apostolica obtineri debeat?—
Demum, posita necessitate recurrendi ad Apostolicam Sedem pro
praedicta dispensatione, Episcopus orator suppliciter postulat.

1. Ut praefatae Sanctimoniali facultas tribuatur ad iuridicas
gestiones per procuratorem instituendas ac perficiendas pro
haereditate sibi ac proprio nomine capienda, quae in bonum
cedat totius Communitatis.—

2. Ut eidem Episcopo oratori sufficiens facultas elargiatur ut
dispensare possit super vota paupertatis in casibus similibus ad id
ut providere valeat pro urgentia quae regulariter in iisdem
occurrit.—Et Deus...

Sacra Congregatio Emorum ac Rmorum S. R. E. Cardinalium
negotiis et consultationibus Episcoporum et Regularium praeposita, super, praemissis censuit respondendum prout respondet :

Ad 1ᵐ et 2ᵐ providebitur in Tertio.

Ad 3ᵐ Affirmative pro petita facultate ; ita tamen ut haereditas
acquiratur Monasterio.

Ad 4ᵐ Affirmative pro petita facultate ad triennium, pro
casibus dumtaxat urgentibus, in quibus nempe non suppetat
tempus recurrendi ad Sanctam Sedem.

Romae, 15 Ianuarii, 1897.

S. Card. VANNUTELLI, *Praef.*

NOTICES OF BOOKS

THE IMPERIAL HEALTH MANUAL. Being the Authorized English Edition of the Official Health Manual, issued by the Imperial Health Department of Germany. Edited by Anthony Roche, M.R.C.P.I., &c. Dublin: Fannin and Co., Ltd., 41, Grafton-street.

HANDBOOK OF HEALTH AND HYGIENE. By J. E. Dowling, M.D., Physician to St. Jarlath's College, Tuam, &c. Dublin: M. H. Gill & Son.

IN these countries we may, indeed, have more practical notions of sanitation and hygiene than our neighbours on the Continent; but it must be admitted that we are woefully behind the times in the matter of health manuals and popular handbooks which aim at bringing scientific notions of sanitation into every home in the land, no matter how remote the quarter may be in which it is situated. We have often heard it asked why the clergy do not exert themselves to impart proper notions of cleanliness to the people amongst whom their lot is cast in many wild and remote places in the country, and in some places which may be wild enough, but are certainly not remote. We have invariably replied that the clergy do far more in that respect than either gentry or the medical profession, notwithstanding the fact that it is much less their duty to do it than it is that of the other two classes mentioned. At all events, the task of those, whether lay or clerical, who seek to raise the standard of civilization amongst the people, will be much facilitated by such works as those we have here before us. We should like to see them both spread broadcast amongst the people. Indeed, we should like to see some manual of the kind placed in the hands of every boy and every girl attending our schools. If would be a matter for those who have charge of the department to say whether one or the other of these handbooks would be suitable for the young. We can only say that in both there is a vast amount of practical information to which all educated people should have access, and that a vast amount of time seems to us to be wasted in our schools on subjects that are not one-fifth as important or as practical as these for the average pupil. Whatever hesitation we might have in recommending one or other of these manuals for the school-room, we certainly can have none in recommending them both to the general public. Possibly a perfect manual might be constructed from both ; but, meantime, we gladly welcome such useful help towards perfect sanitation and practical knowledge of the rules of hygiene, as are contained in these two volumes.

J. F. H.

THE LIFE AND LETTERS OF JOHN MORRIS, S.J. By Father J. H. Pollen, S.J. London : Burns & Oates, Limited. Quarterly Series.

THOSE to whom the name of the late Father Morris, of the Society of Jesus, was familiar through his works and writings, and who still retain a vivid recollection of the suddeness of the death which put an end to his useful life four years ago, will read with interest these memoirs from the pen of a brother-Jesuit. With rare accomplishments for the task so lovingly undertaken, Father Pollen has succeeded in moulding out of the mass of material at his command, a highly attractive and most readable biography. In the lives of great men there is always much that charms, much that instructs, and much that edifies us. And it was a singularly happy thought that moved our author to familiarize his readers with these admirable qualities of head and heart that disposed the generous youth to make such noble sacrifices for conscience' sake, and that contributed to crown the life-work of the holy and humble priest with signal success. Born of Protestant parents, John Morris was sent to Harrow School, when he had completed his twelfth year. A short stay in this centre of culture was enough to destroy whatever germs of religious growth he had received in his boyhood, and he left Harrow without, as he himself avows, a single religious impression. To Dean Alford, under whose tutelage he was next placed, our pupil was indebted for the rekindling of his early faith, and for the awakening of that glow of religious enthusiasm which now fired him with the holy purpose of discovering which of the many churches throughout the world had strongest claims to be considered the one, true, divinely-appointed Church of Christ. In Cambridge, to which he next passed, the search was plied with unabated vigour, and after twelve months diligent and painstaking investigation, his doubts and difficulties were solved, and peace dawned upon his soul with the conviction that the house built upon the rock was the home of supernatural truth and the fortress of God's revelation. Like so many others who were irresistibly borne upon the waters of the strong current that had set in towards Rome about this time, John Morris, in his twentieth year, with wealth and luxury and social position in the world within his easy reach, exchanged all for the poor prospect offered by a life of penury, mortification, and retirement, and abandoned father and mother to follow Christ. This gift of faith, so dearly purchased—if we could regard the sacrifice from a worldly point of view—proved to be his most characteristic virtue, for ever afterwards, as he has assured us, he never seriously suffered from a temptation to religious doubts. He made his theological studies in Rome, and was ordained priest in 1849. Of his subsequent career in the Sacred Ministry, and in the Society of Jesus, which he entered in 1867, many interesting details will be gleaned from his own reminiscences of which Father Pollen's biography is extensively made up. His poetical philanthropy which prompted him to undertake many kind offices for the allevia- tion of the hard lot of the poor, his advocacy of the case for the canonization of the English martyrs, which succeeded to the length of getting a decree for their beatification, his volu- minous literary productions, and the widespread influence in calming the troubled souls who came to him for spiritual comfort, all these will contribute to make the memory of Father John Morris loved, reverved, and long-lived.

P. M.

PIUS VII., 1800-1823. By Mary H. Allies. London: Burns & Oates, Ltd. 1897.

We doubt if the history of the immortal Pope Pius VII. has ever been so successfully narrated in a brief monogram as it is in this volume. The work reflects the highest credit on the already illustrious name of Allies. It is, indeed, condensed history; and yet it presents to us a series of vivid pictures which are all the more impressive, as they are depicted mainly in outline. There is scarcely any period of history so rich in dramatic events and in the variety and originality of the personages who lived and moved through its various scenes as the first quarter of the century now dying out. France and Italy, Paris and Rome, were, as usual, the centres of greatest interest ; Napoleon and Pius VII., two of the characters who drew upon themselves most of the attention of the world. Miss Allies enters into the spirit of the times with all the tact and skill and discriminating judgment of the historian. Her power of presenting in outline the essential characteristics of a period and the details of some of its most striking events has, in our opinion, rarely been excelled. In a page or two the dying efforts of Jansenism and Gallicanism, the baneful influence of Joseph II. and his reign, the schemes of Kaunitz and Pombal, the last troubles of one who in the historical sense, at least, might justly be called ' the martyred Pontiff,' Pope Pius VI., are briefly sketched. Then come the election of Barnabas Chiaramonti, the intrigues of the Austrian Court ; the cruelty and brutality of Napoleon, Gonsalvi, Talleyrand, the ' Concordat,' the organic articles, Miss Patterson, Cardinal Fesch, all the well-known names and events are passed in review in a manner that will win for Miss Allies not only the gratitude of the general reader, but the special thanks of the students of ecclesiastical history. Indeed we do not think it would be possible for a student to find a more enjoyable and well-told narrative of the events of this period in a brief compass than may be had in this volume, for which we offer our most sincere congratulations to the author.   J. F. H.

CONFERENCES. By Fr. Dignam, S.J. With Retreats, Sermons, and Notes of Spiritual Direction. With a Preface, by Cardinal Mazzella, S.J. London : Burns & Oates, Ltd.

FOR the publication of this volume we are indebted to a desire on the part of some few of those to whom they were addressed, to rescue from oblivion the best among those thoughts and considerations which their good director gave expression to in the course of the retreats it was his wont to give them from time to time. It is the compilers' hope that as the holy priest's words carried consolation and comfort when uttered by the living voice, so they may still continue to exercise their salutary influences when echoed, as it were, from the grave. The work forms a sequel to another book, which has already been favourably noticed in these pages, ' Retreats, by Fr. Dignam, S.J.' The present volume contains much supplementary matter, comprising a six days' retreat given to young ladies, two triduums, conferences to nuns, and fragments of sermons on important subjects. The compilers do not profess to reproduce exactly the addresses of Fr. Dignam as they fell from his lips. What they attempt is to give us their recollections only of what he said. As a consequence, the various meditations and lectures are not so ample and complete as might be desired, neither is the style and arrangement everywhere eminently satisfactory. At the same time the ardent spirit of piety, and tender devotion to the Sacred Heart which characterized Fr. Dignam in life, are made to breathe through these pages, and we feel warranted in predicting for them a wide sphere of usefulness. They will supply excellent suggestions for private meditation, and much very suitable matter for embodying in an instruction to the faithful. The book has been prefaced by Cardinal Mazzella, and as it has been revised in Rome, its teaching and orthodoxy are necessarily irreproachable.   P. M.

THE IRISH MESSENGER OF THE SACRED HEART LIBRARY. Dublin: Irish Messenger Office, 5, Great Denmark-street.

WE beg to bring under the notice of priests and all whom it may concern, these excellent little tracts and booklets, which the zealous Father Cullen, S.J., has published in connection with the *Messenger of the Sacred Heart*. They bring pious literature, the lives of the saints and short treatises on the principal devotions of the Catholic Church, within reach of the poorest of the poor. The price of each booklet is only one penny. They will prove most useful to the poor who cannot afford the luxury of more expensive works.

THE CHAPLAIN'S SERMONS. By Rev. John Talbot Smith, LL.D. New York: William H. Young & Company.

WE plead guilty to a feeling of slightly hostile prejudice in undertaking the task of reviewing the *Chaplain's Sermons*. In common, we think, with host of others, we are inclined to disbelieve in the utility of the ready-made sermon as an aid to effective preaching. A ready-made garment does not always stand the test of excellence, or commend itself to the exigencies of taste. In like manner, the discourse that is served up in popular form, ready for immediate delivery, does not always fulfil the purpose intended by its author. No two men's thoughts run precisely in the same channel, and what suits the fancy of one does not ever fit in with the ideas of another. So long as instructions and discourses are not moulded on purely mathematical lines, there will ever be considerable room for discrepancy in tastes as to the plan and the selection and arrangement of matter. Above all, the sermons we find in books, being, as a rule, the outcome of a supreme effort for some extraordinary occasions are hopelessly above the heads of ordinary commonplace congregations, and though attractive and fascinating in their way, are often below the line of use-fulness in the instructing and influencing the minds of people. Now, these defects we were prepared to find, in some measure, at least, in Fr. Smith's volume. But we are happy to say that in this we were agreeably disappointed. For our author has produced a book of discourses on nearly all the important, moral, and dogmatic subjects, that cannot fail to please the most fastidious. The plan followed is most commendable. At the beginning of each subject he gives a number of suggestive points, which he then develops in the body of the discourse, following the three-fold formal division—a method which, we think, has its advan-tages as an aid to the memory, and a help to securing clearness. Thus, a person by looking over these headings will receive suggestions which he will be able to enlarge out of his own stock of knowledge into a sermon of fifteen or twenty minutes' duration. All the subjects touched on are beautifully treated. Father Smith wields a graceful and facile pen, and his book wants nothing of literary excellence. Perhaps we might deplore the paucity of Scriptural quotations, but we feel, as we are sure Father Smith also felt, that this is a want that may be easily supplied by a Testament at the elbow of the priest who is engaged in the work of preparing his Sunday sermon.

J. M.

ho

Ut Christiani ita et Romani sitis." "As you are children of Christ, so be you children of Rome."
Ex Dictis S. Patricii, In Libro Armacano, fol. 9.

The Irish
Ecclesiastical Record

𝔄 𝔐onthly 𝔍ournal, under 𝔈piscopal 𝔖anction.

𝔗hirtieth 𝔜ear]
No. 358.]
OCTOBER, 1897.
[𝔉ourth 𝔖eries
Vol. II.

Nihil Obstat.
GIRALDUS MOLLOY, S.T.D.
Censor Dep.

𝔍mprimatur.
✠ GULIELMUS,
Archiep. Dublin.,
Hiberniae Primas.

BROWNE & NOLAN, Limited

Publishers and Printers, 24 & 25

NASSAU STREET, DUBLIN.

. . **PRICE ONE SHILLING** . .
SUBSCRIPTION : Twelve Shillings per Annum. Post Free. payable in advance.

BREAD

··· AND ···

CONFECTIONERY

Finest

Quality

Only.

·-+·•·+-·

KENNEDY'S

127 & 128, GREAT BRITAIN STREET,

——DUBLIN.

THE KINETIC THEORY OF ACTIVITY[1]

I.

ACTIVITY is of two kinds. An agent is said to be active either because it is capable of acting or because it is actually in action. Thus, a man is capable of walking and of singing when he is sitting down in silence, and these capacities are real powers or activities ; they are completed by the action of walking or of singing, when either action takes place.

A mere capacity, such as those mentioned, is called by the Schoolmen an activity *in actu primo ;* there is a second kind of activity—the *actus secundus*—which is the action of walking or of singing, by which the capacity is completed and made to act.

Now, there are three classes of agents, each of which has its own peculiar form of activity ; they are, inorganic or dead bodies, living organs, and spirits. The actions peculiar to each in the order mentioned are, what are called purely mechanical motions, vital organic actions, and acts of intellect and of will. I do not propose in the present paper to deal with either vital or spiritual activities ; though, no doubt, much that is true of purely mechanical movements applies in its measure to those of a higher kind. I am about to propose some considerations with regard to the

---

[1] This paper was read at the International Catholic Scientific Congress, Fribourg, on the 18th August.

nature of purely mechanical actions, such as that of a cue on a billiard-ball, of the sun on the earth, or the mutual attractions and repulsions on which modern chemistry, physics, and astronomy, are based; and I limit the subject thus, chiefly because it is to discover the nature of these purely mechanical activities that modern scientific men have devoted so much attention.

It is well known that for some time a controversy has been going on in the schools as to the nature of purely mechanical activity, the disputants belonging principally to one or other of two parties, each with a well-defined theory of its own. One is called the Mechanical Theory,—though how it is a whit more mechanical than its rival I fail to see. The other theory has no name, but would be spoken of, I suppose, as the old opinion, the view that was almost universally accepted down to quite recent times. For reasons which will be apparent later on, I shall call this the Dynamic and its rival the Kinetic Theory;—the terms *dynamic* and *kinetic* expressing most aptly the nature of the opinion to which each term is applied.

II.

1. According, therefore, to the kinetic theory, the activity *in actu secundo*, or action, of inorganic or of dead bodies, consists entirely in and is formally identified with their motion;—action and motion being but two names for the same thing. And the activity *in actu primo* of the same agents,—that is, their capacity or power,—is nothing more than a capacity for *receiving* motions in the first instant, and then transferring to other agents, or to other portions of themselves, the motions thus received, and in which their actions formally consist. Hence the name *kinetic*,—the Greek word κινητικὸν meaning moving, movable, or producing motion.

By motion the modern advocates of the kinetic theory usually mean continuous change of place. Accordingly, their theory is, that a piece of inorganic or of dead matter cannot act unless by moving locally, and whenever it moves locally it acts. Moreover, it may pass its action on to another body by communicating to this the whole or part of its motion, in which case the action is said to be transient, or to pass from the first agent to the second ; and an effect is said to be produced in the second by the first. A motion or action is thus immanent or transient ; immanent, as long as it remains within the same moving body, as if a piece of matter were to revolve in pure space ; transient, when the motion passes from one body into another, or from one portion of the same body into another part.[1]

2. According to the dynamic theory, on the contrary, activity, *in actu secundo*, or action, consists not so much in motion itself as in something which produces motion,— something which is called ' force,' or the exertion of ' force ; ' and the *actus primus* or capacity for acting, which resides in agents before they begin to act, is this ' force ' existing in a latent manner within the agent.

The difference between the two theories is well illustrated by the explanations they give of what is called potential energy, such as resides in a stone raised up and resting on the hand. Dynamists contend that the stone has within itself ' forces ' of some kind, really different from motion, which are latent while the stone is at rest, but which are exerted or become operative when the support is removed. The advocates of the kinetic theory, on the contrary, maintain that when the hand is taken away the stone moves downwards, not by reason of any ' forces ' distinct from motions which may be communicated to the stone from without, but because something which is already in motion pushes the stone downwards, and so communicates to it the motion of gravitation with which it moves towards the earth's centre. According to the kinetic theory there is in inorganic or in dead matter no such thing as potential as distinct from kinetic energy, but every form of energy in such agents is essentially kinetic ; whereas dynamists

---

[1] According to the philosophy of the Schoolmen there is no action truly immanent which is not vital. If a piece of inorganic matter were made to revolve in pure space, without any change in the relative position of its parts, the action would be considered immanent only *per accidens* ; it is transient *per se* ; that is, it is of its nature such as must pass into another body should certain conditions occur. This is manifestly the correct view to take.

contend that there are ' forces ' where there is no motion,—
' forces' which will be exerted and produce motion when
certain conditions arise.

With regard to the term *force*, it should be borne in
mind that it is to be found in the writings of both parties,
but is not understood by both in the same sense. To a
dynamist ' force' is an entity of some kind exerted by the
substances or the faculties of bodies, capable of producing
motion, but differing really from the motion which it produces. The advocates of the kinetic theory are no less
strenuous in maintaining the existence of force—or, as they
prefer to call it, energy—as an objective reality; but to them
the mechanical energies of matter are not really different
from motions, and produce effects merely by passing from
subject to subject, or from one part or place of a subject into
another.

III.

Recent Catholic writers have represented the kinetic
theory as not only untrue but uncatholic ;—as being, in fact,
nothing less than a denial of efficient causality in material
agents ; and as a thinly-veiled Occasionalism, should the
perennial conservation of the motions of bodies be referred
to the First Cause. The object of this paper is to beg of
those Catholic writers and professors of the present day
who are interested in this department of science, to pause
before allowing the justice of these strictures, and especially
before repeating them. Think for a moment of what we
are asked to condemn.

It may be affirmed without hesitation that almost all
the great authorities in modern chemistry, physics, and
astronomy, have become convinced that it is only in
conformity with kinetic principles these sciences can be
ultimately explained.   I do not mean to insist that this,
if true, necessarily proves the truth of the kinetic theory ;
but only that a Catholic writer or professor should be cautious
before proceeding to hurl anathemas at those who maintain
a doctrine in physics which is based on so much scientific
authority.

As for the statement that almost all the great authorities

in the physical sciences are now advocates of the kinetic theory, it can be proved only by the testimony of experts. Dr. Mivart and Mr. J. B. Stallo shall serve my purpose; one a Catholic, the other a non-Catholic writer; each an authority of undoubted eminence in questions of this kind ; and both opponents of the theory in question. Dr. Mivart writes[1]:—

The tendency has arisen to consider all . . . forces as motion in some form or condition. Of late physicists have more or less discarded the term ' force ' in favour of the word ' energy.' . . . A further step was taken when the energy of the various physical forces acting in any substance came to be considered as being actually but different modes of motion of the molecules composing such substances. . . . A passion for considering nature as a mere mechanism of matter and motion, and all its actions as merely mechanical, is a tendency of our day. It is the scientific ideal of a very large school of thinkers, and is the goal towards which they strive.

In a note appended to these last words, Dr. Mivart remarks :—

Kirchenoff has said :—' The highest objects at which the natural sciences are constrained to aim, is the reduction of all the phenomena of nature to mechanics ;' and Helmholtz has declared :—' The aim of the natural sciences is to resolve themselves into mechanics.' Wundt observes :—' The problem of physiology is a reduction of vital phenomena to general physical laws, and ultimately to the fundamental laws of mechanics ;' while Haeckel tells us that ' all natural phenomena, without exception, from the motions of the celestial bodies to the growth of plants and the consciousness of men, are ultimately to be reduced to atomic mechanics.' Professor Huxley also speaks of ' that purely mechanical view towards which all modern physiology is striving;' and has said :—' If there be one thing clear about the progress of modern science, it is the tendency to reduce all scientific problems, except those which are purely mathematical, to questions of molecular physics ; that is to say, to the attractions, repulsions, motions, and co-ordinations, of the ultimate particles of matter.'

Mr. Stallo writes[2] :—

With few exceptions scientific men of the present day hold the proposition, that all physical action is mechanical, to be axiomatic, if not in the sense of being self-evident, at least in the sense of being an induction from all past scientific experience.

---

[1] *On Truth*, pp. 393-5.   [2] *Concepts of Modern Physics*, ch. i., p. 23.

Hence Professor Barker, of the University of Pennsylvania, who is, according to Mr. Stallo, one of the most noted physicists and chemists in the United States, tells us,[1]—what, indeed, is well known to everyone who dabbles even a little in these matters,—that ' attraction and potential energy are disappearing from the language of science.' [2]

This, of course, does not prove the truth of the mechanical, or as I prefer to call it, the kinetic theory ; but it seems to me to supply reason for very great caution before we condemn as uncatholic a doctrine backed by so much authority. I shall try to show later on that the doctrine is not without advocates among the very best of the old Catholic writers and theologians.

IV.

Coming to the intrinsic reasons on which the kinetic theory is based, I do not know that even scant justice can be done to them within the compass of a paper such as this. They are drawn from almost every part of physics, chemistry, and astronomy; nay even—I might say principally—from metaphysics and theology.

1. Let us take, in the first place, the phenomena of

---

[1] *Apud Stallo*, p. 29.

[2] I may now be permitted to add the following testimonies. In the address already cited Professor Barker goes on to say, that ' if we regard the aether as a gas, defined by the kinetic theory that its molecules move in straight lines, but with an enormous length of free path, it is obvious that this aether may be clearly conceived of as the source of the energy of all ordinary matter. It is an enormous storehouse of energy, which is continually passing to and from ordinary matter, precisely as we know it to do in the case of radiant transmission. Before so simple a conception as this both potential energy and action at a distance are easily given up. *All energy is kinetic, the energy of motion.*' ·

Of the kinetic theory of gases, now almost universally advocated by physicists, Lord Kelvin writes (*Popular Lectures*, p. 225), that it 'explains seemingly static properties of matter by motion ; so that it is scarcely possible to help anticipating in idea the arrival at a complete theory of matter, in which all its properties will be seen to be merely attributes of motion.'

In Ganot's *Physics* (English Trans. Ed., by Atkinson. 10th Ed., n. 6), I find the following, which may not be without interest, as that work is used as a text-book in Maynooth College :—

' In our attempts to ascend from a phenomenon to its cause, we assume the existence of physical agents, or natural forces, acting on matter; as examples of which we have gravitation, heat, light, magnetism, and electricity. Since these physical agents are disclosed to us only by their effects, their intimate nature is completely unknown. In the present state of science we cannot say whether they are properties inherent in matter, or whether they result from movements impressed on the mass of subtle and imponderable forms

attraction.   Everyone knows how fundamental are the facts and laws of attraction in all questions of natural science.   Volta, Newton, Dalton, and a hundred others, have immortalized themselves by analyzing these laws ; and it is to the progress made in this analysis that the advance of the natural sciences in modern times is mainly due.

What, then, is attraction in itself?   Take the simplest form of it, that of gravitation, and ask yourself how the sun attracts the earth, or the earth a stone thrown into the air. What is this pull on the earth and on the stone?   And to what precisely is it immediately and formally due?

Dynamists say that a 'force' goes out from the sun, approaches the earth, and pulls it ; that a similar 'force' proceeds from the earth to the stone and drags it down. But what is this 'force' in itself?   And how does it contrive to pull ?

'Force' is an accident, which must be supported by some substance in its passage between two bodies.   How is it supported in the cases proposed ?   In the ether ? Very well ; but then, being supported, how does it pull ?   For, if you wish to *pull* a thing to you, you must get behind it and

---

of matter diffused through the universe.   *The latter hypothesis is, however, generally admitted.* . . . All physical phenomena, referred thus to a single cause, *are but transformations of motion.*'

Professors Balfour Stewart and P. G. Tait write as follows in *The Unseen Universe* (p. 147) :—

'If Le Sage's theory, or anything of a similar nature, be at all a representation of the mechanism of gravitation, a fatal blow is dealt to the notion of the tranquil form of power we have called potential energy.   Not that there will cease to be a profound difference in kind between it and ordinary kinetic energy ; but that BOTH must come henceforth to be regarded as kinetic.'   BOTH is spelled with capitals in the original.

Finally, Herbert Spencer says (*First Principles*, 5th Ed., Appendix) :—

' I have, at considerable length, given reasons for regarding the conception of potential energy as an illegitimate one ; and have distinctly stated that I am at issue with scientific friends on the matter.   Let me add that my rejection of this doctrine is not without other warrant than my own. . . . Mr. James Croll, no mean authority as a mathematician and a physicist, has published in the *Philosophical Magazine* for Oct., 1876, page 241, a paper in which he shows, I think conclusively, that the commonly accepted view of potential energy cannot be sustained, but that energy invariably remains actual.'

Testimonies like these might be multiplied.   Indeed, who does not know that the term ' kinetic energy ' is now of universal use in treatises on Mechanics ? This very use is an admission of the principle for which I contend.—that activity may consist in the transfer of motion.   The universally accepted principle of the Conservation of Energy is intelligible only on this supposition.

push it on. A horse pulls a cart by pushing at a collar, which pushes a chain, every link of which gets behind another, pushing this on ; till we come to the last link, which gets behind and pushes some portion of the cart. When a little boy wishes to bring back to shore a toy boat that has floated beyond his reach, he throws stones into the water, pushing this against the boat, not at his own side but from behind, and thus brings the boat to land. And so, too, if the ' forces ' of the sun could get behind the earth and push it in towards the centre of the solar system, one could understand how the attraction of gravitation might take place in accordance with the principles of the dynamic theory. But how can these ' forces ' get behind the earth and not act before, with a prior and therefore a greater force, thus repelling rather than attracting the planet ? Here is a problem for the advocates of the dynamic theory, —a problem which recurs with regard to every form of attraction, chemical, magnetic, electric, adhesion, cohesion, or any other that may be. Since all take place between masses of which one is outside the other, how do the ' forces ' emanating from the masses not repel rather than attract ?

The great body of scientific men have made up their minds that every form of attraction is a mode of motion in some more or less elastic medium ; just as light and heat are now supposed to be nothing else than vibrations in ether. Accordingly, the sun and the earth would be said to attract each other, because each is beaten in towards the centre of the other by an indefinite number of tiny vibrations, which play freely on the rear of both bodies, but less freely in front, inasmuch as each mass acts as a breakwater to shelter the other from the tiny waves. This may not be true ; it is not without its difficulties ; but it is intelligible, and it is to some form or modification of this theory that men of science are looking for a solution of the mystery. Needless to say, the explanation, such as it is, harmonizes with the kinetic rather than the dynamic theory of activity.

2. Again, take resistance, which equally with attraction forms the basis of all science regarding material things ; and

ask yourself, what so few ask, in what does this resistance formally consist. I throw a ball against the ground ; it does not pass through the earth but rebounds. Why ? If ever there was a case for the existence of the 'force' of the dynamists, it is to be found here.

For, it is easy to say that when a body in motion comes into contact with another body, each gives out a 'force' which tends to repel the other. But why should 'forces' repel any more than substances ? What need is there of 'force' when the earth itself might throw back the ball ? This question has been asked by many philosophers since the time of Descartes, and it still calls for an answer from all who propound the dynamic theory of activity.

There is, however, a greater difficulty even than this, especially for those Catholics who look with veneration on the teaching of Aristotle, St. Thomas, and the Schoolmen. For, these all held that, when a ball rebounds, the object against which it was thrown remains inactive, in so far as it resists the motion of the ball ; it is active only in so far as it yields to the pressure of the missile and itself recoils. If a wall were made absolutely motionless, it would be absolutely inert or inactive ; in which case a ball would rebound from it without losing in the rebound the least portion of the motion which it previously possessed.

I beg you to attend most carefully to this. It is the teaching of all the moderns and of the best of the ancient philosophers, that the more immovable a body is, the less active it is ; yet it is the more capable of resistance. Its power of resistance is in inverse ratio to its activity. Resistance, therefore, is not activity. Can any dynamist explain or admit this doctrine ? Is it not of the essence of the dynamic theory that resistance is due to the exertion of 'force,' and that the exertion of 'force' and activity *in actu secundo* are the selfsame thing ?

I do not think it necessary to quote authorities to show what is the teaching of the moderns on this matter ; it will be evident to all who are even slightly acquainted with the scientific developments of recent times. But I am afraid many may be surprised to hear that the best of the ancients

were of the same opinion,—that resistance is not due to
activity but to the reverse. Yet, not only Aristotle and
St. Thomas, but even Suarez, distinctly affirm that resistance is due to inactivity rather than to activity ; and the
two former expressly state that, when a ball is thrown
against a wall and rebounds, the wall is inactive in so far
as it resists. In his famous treatise on Physics[1] Aristotle
says : ' When a ball rebounds, it is not moved by the wall
[against which it was thrown], but by him who threw it.' [1]

And St. Thomas comments on the passage as follows :—

If a ball rebound from a wall, it is moved, indeed, *per accidens*
by the wall, but not *per se ;* it is moved *per se* by whatever threw
it first. For, the wall has not given it any impulse to motion,
but only the thrower ; and it was *per accidens* that, when it was
prevented by the wall from being borne on according to its first
impulse, it [the ball] rebounded with a contrary motion.[2]

Suarez has a formal dissertation[3] on the nature of
resistance, in which he writes :—

One thing may resist another in two ways : first, formally, by
immediate repugnance ; secondly, radically, and, as it were, by a

---

[1] 'Η ἀνακλασθεῖσα σφαῖρα οὐκ ὑπὸ τοῦ τοίχου ἐκινήθη, ἀλλ' ὑπὸ τοῦ
βάλλοντος. Phys. L. 8, c. 4.

[2] ' Si sphaera, idest pila, repercutiatur a pariete, per accidens quidem
mota est a pariete, non autem per se ; sed a primo projiciente per se mota est.
Paries enim non dedit ei aliquem impetum ad motum, sed projiciens ; per
accidens autem fuit, quod dum a pariete impediretur ne secundum impetum
ferretur, eodem impetu manente, in contrarium motum resilivit.' In loc.

[3] 'Duobus modis contingit unam rem alteri resistere : primo, formaliter
per immediatam repugnantiam ; secundo, radicaliter et quasi per diminutionem
virtutis activae rei. Hoc posteriori modo . . . inter homines unus dicitur
resistere alteri si anticipato vulnere abscindit manum, aut alio modo diminuit
vires illius. Haec, ergo, resistentia revera non est nisi actio quaedam. Atvero
alius resistendi modus non consistit in actione . . . Unde non per se primo
nec consecutive provenit hic resistendi modus ex potentia activa, ut activa est
. . . De hoc ergo resistendi modo dicendum est non consistere in aliquo actu
positivo proveniente a virtute illa quae vis resistendi esse dicitur ; consistere
potius in privatione actus. Unde talis resistentia est potius impotentia, vel
incapacitas quaedam, quam propria potentia ; ideoque non debuit in divisione
potentiae adjungi . . . Consistit, ergo, in quadam formali incompossibilitate
seu repugnantia, a qua provenit ut actio contraria agentis vel impediatur
prorsus vel retardatur ac remissior fiat. Sic, ergo, haec resistentia actualis
non consistit in aliquo actu secundo positivo, proveniente a virtute resistiva,
sed potius in carentia, aut retardatione, seu remissione contrariae actionis.
Ideoque illa virtus resistendi non est facultas aliqua per se ordinata ad illam
carentiam vel retardationem actionis ; quia naturalis potentia non ordinatur
per se ad aliquam privationen ; et ideo dicimus hanc non tam esse potentiam
quam impotentiam et quasi incapacitatem.'—*Metaph.* D. 43, S. 1, nn. 8, &c.

diminution of the other's force. It is in this latter way . . . that amongst men one is said to resist another, when by anticipating his adversary, he inflicts a wound, cuts off his adversary's hand, or diminishes his power in any other manner. This kind of resistance is nothing else but an action.

The other kind of resistance, however, *does not consist in action* . . . Hence, neither of itself in the first instance, nor by any kind of consecutiveness, *does this kind of resistance proceed from an active power, inasmuch as it is active.* With regard, therefore, to this form of resistance, it is to be held that it does not *consist in any positive action proceeding from the power which is called the force of resistance ;* but [should be conceived] as consisting rather *in the privation of action.* Hence, *such resistance is rather impotence,* or an *incapacity of some kind,* than a power properly so called; wherefore, it should not be mentioned among the divisions of power.

. . . It consists, then, in a certain formal incompossibility or repugnance, from which it comes that the action of the contrary agent is either impeded altogether, or becomes more slow and remiss. Thus, therefore, *this actual resistance does not consist in any act of a positive character,* proceeding from the resisting power ; but rather *in the want,* or *the retardation,* or *abatement of the contrary action.* Hence, the power of resistance . . . is not so much a power as a want of power,—a kind of incapacity.

Here the Jesuit philosopher expands the teaching of Aristotle and St. Thomas. The resistance which a wall offers to a ball is manifestly of the second kind mentioned by Suarez ; it ' does not consist in action,' but rather in ' the privation of action;' not ' in any second act of a positive character, proceeding from the resisting power [in the wall] ; but rather in the want, or the retardation, or abatement of the contrary action. Hence, the power of resistance . . . is not so much a power as a want of power, a kind of incapacity.'

Will any honest man say that this is intelligible in accordance with the dynamic theory? If the wall resists by exerting a ' force,' does this exertion consist rather in the privation of activity than in action? Is it due to incapacity rather than to power?

V.

So far for the arguments drawn from the physical sciences; they might be multiplied, but that would require a volume rather than a paper such as this. I will pass on to some reasons of a metaphysical character, contenting myself with a few of the most obvious, and depending almost altogether on authority to prove the principles on which I base my contention.

One of the strongest arguments of the dynamists is to the effect, that if one agent were merely to pass on its motion to another, it would not thereby be really active *in actu secundo*, since action and motion are two different realities. Action is represented as the exertion of 'force,' and motion as an effect of this exertion.

1. Now, I find it laid down almost as axiomatic, not only by such writers as St. Thomas and Goudin, but even by Suarez, that action is precisely the same thing as motion, the two differing virtually but not really. Not only this, but it is equally an axiom in the Aristotelic philosophy, that action is really the same thing as being acted on (*passio*), and that both are really identified with motion. The philosophic axiom takes this form: *actio et passio sunt idem motus.*

In a formal dissertation on this very point Goudin writes:[1] 'Motion, action, and being acted on (*passio*), although they are the same in essence, seem, however, to be modally distinct: the conclusion is common, especially among the Thomists.'

And he goes on to explain and prove his statement:—

The first part, viz., that they are all three the same in essence, is manifest. For the very same entity, heating, for instance, as it is conceived to go out from the fire by way of diffusion of its heat, is the action of the fire; but as it is received in wood by way of change in the wood, it is called the *passio* of the same. Finally, in so far as it is a way or tendency to its

---

[1] 'Motus, actio, et passio, licet sint idem entitative, modaliter tamen videntur distingui: conclusio est communis, praecipue inter Thomistas.' Phys. P. 1. D. 3, a. 1.

term, that is, to [the quality of] heat, it is called motion. All three, therefore, are the same in essence; hence St. Thomas often says that action and being acted on (*passio*) are but the one motion.[1]

Here we have Goudin's testimony not only to the truth of the principle in question, but to its prevalence in the schools, 'especially among the Thomists;' and in particular, speaking of St. Thomas, with whose writings Goudin was more than usually familiar, even for a Dominican author, he expressly tells us, what indeed anyone at all conversant with the works of the Angelic Doctor must be acquainted with, that the saint 'often says that action and being acted on (*passio*) are but the one motion.' And lest it should be urged that Goudin had before his mind not so much local motions as alteration, increase, or diminution,[2] he illustrates his teaching not only by the motion of heat, but also by those of a traveller and of a ship.

So much for St. Thomas and his school. Suarez is no less emphatic. He also has a special dissertation[3] on the relation that subsists between motion, action, and *passio;* and in conformity with the traditional teaching of the disciples of Aristotle, he decides that the three are the very same reality under different concepts. Let anyone

---

[1] 'Prima pars, quod scil. sunt idem entitative, patet. Nam una et eadem entitas, v. g. calefactio, prout concipitur egredi ab igne tanquam diffusio ejus caloris, est actio ignis; prout vero recipitur in ligno tanquam immutatio ligni, dicitur ejus passio; prout demum est via et tendentia ad terminum, scil. ad calorem, dicitur motus; ergo ista omnia entitative sunt idem. Unde D. Thomas saepe dicit quod actio et passio sunt idem numero motus.' (*l. c.*)

[2] Three kinds of motion are recognised in the Aristotelic system;—change of place (*translation*), of quality (*alteration*), and of quantity (*increase* and *diminution*). Of the three, however, local motion is regarded as fundamental, inasmuch as without it neither of the other two 'could take place. 'Sine ipso [motu locali],' observes St. Thomas, 'non potest esse aliquis aliorum motuum, . . . neque alteratio potest esse nisi praeexistente loci mutatione' (Contra Gent. 3. c. 82). And again :—' Motus localis est principium et causa aliorum motuum' (Quod 1. 3, a. 6, ad of j.1. Once more :—' Quamvis in corporalibus sint plures motus, omnes tamen ordinantur ad motum localem coeli, qui est causa omnis motus corporalis; et ideo per motum corporalem tanguntur omnes' (1 D. 8, q. 3, ad 3). Extracts like these might be multiplied almost indefinitely; they remove altogether any possibility of doubt as to the nature of the motion which is identified with both action and *passio* in the Aristotelic philosophy.

[3] *Metaph.,* D. 49.

who may not be convinced of this, read the forty-ninth
Disputation of the *Metaphysics* for himself.

Here I will ask : Does any dynamist believe that action
and motion may be the same thing really ? Does he believe,
above all, that action is the same thing as being acted on ?
In the kinetic theory action is motion, and motion whilst
being received is called *passio*. This fits in precisely with
the metaphysics of the school; but how is a Catholic dynamist
to square his theory of activity with the traditional teaching
of our metaphysicians on this point ?

2. Again, take the definition of action given by St. Thomas :
' the essence of an action,' he affirms, ' consists in this, that
action denotes *a form in motion*, or in course of transmuta-
tion, as proceeding from an efficient cause.' And again :
' action and being acted on (*passio*) are quite the same thing,
which is *a form in flux* or in course of production.' Once
more : ' action and being acted on (*passio*) and motion are
quite the same thing.' And he goes on to illustrate his
meaning :—

> Hence *heating* is nothing else but *heat as it is in flux ;* inas-
> much, that is, as it is in the act of something in potentiality,
> *which is the same as motion.* For instance, when water is heated
> by fire, it is certain that there is some heat produced in the water
> by the heat of the fire. This heat, considered in its essence, is a
> form, which is a quality of the third species. Inasmuch, however,
> as it [the form or quality] *is in flux,* that is, *as it is more and more
> communicated to the water, it is called motion* . . . Inasmuch, again,
> as it has a relation to the fire as to an efficient cause, it [the same
> form] is action. . . . Hence, the essence of action, as a category,
> consists in this, that *action designates a form in motion*, or in
> course of transmutation, as proceeding from an efficient cause.[1]

---

[1] ' Ratio actionis, ut est praedicamentum, consistit in hoc, quod actio dicit
formam in motu vel mutatione, ut est a causa efficiente.' *Opusc.* 68, tr. 5, c. 7.
—' Actio et passio sunt una res et eadem, scil, forma quae est in fluxu vel in
fieri.' *Ibid.* c. 10.—' Actio et passio et motus sunt una et eadem res. Unde
calefactio nihil aliud est quam calor ut est in fluxu, prout scil. est actus
existentis in potentia, quod idem est quod motus. Verbi gratia, dato quod
aqua calefieret ab igne, certum est quod in ea esset aliquis calor causatus a
calore ignis, qui calor, quantum ad esse suum consideratus, est forma, quae est
qualitas in tertia specie qualitatis. Secundum autem quod est in fluxu, scil.
quod magis et magis participatur in aqua, dicitur motus. . . . Et secundum
quod habet respectum ad ignem ut ad causam efficientem, est actio. . . . Unde,
ratio actionis, prout est praedicamentum, consistit in hoc, quod actio dicit
formam in motu vel mutatione, ut est a causa efficiente.' (*Ibid.* c. 7.)

When you bend a bow, there is a continuous change of figure in the wood; you might stop an indefinite number of times in the course of the action, and at each stop the motion would terminate in a different figure, which would remain crystallized, so to speak, in the wood, as long as the bow remained in the same position. Any one of these figures would not be a motion or action of the bow; motion or action consisting rather in a flux, that is, a continuous flow from one form into another. So thought the Angelic Doctor; but can a dynamist agree in this? What, then, becomes of the 'exertion of " force " ' ?

3. Further, consider that special form of activity known as transient,—*actio transiens*. It is called transient to distinguish it from immanent actions; and from the very terms it is manifest that the distinction between the two kinds of activity consists in this, that in one case the action remains within its subject, whereas transient actions pass off into something else. Otherwise, why are they called *immanent* and *transient* ?

Now, it is almost a first principle of the dynamic theory that an action can never pass from subject to subject; rather, dynamists would say, an exertion of 'force' in one subject gives rise to another quite distinct exertion of ' force' in another. When, for instance, a billiard-ball is struck and moved by a cue, the exertion of 'force' in the cue does not pass into the ball, but rather produces in the ball a numerically distinct exertion of ' force' or action. This, I say, is almost a first principle in the dynamic theory,[1] the advocates of which do not condescend to explain how ' force ' can produce an effect outside its subject, unless by passing outside. Let that be, however.

But what, then, is a transient action ? One which does not itself pass into another subject, but merely produces a new and distinct action in the second subject while remaining within the first? Curious, nevertheless, that it—the

---

[1] See Sanseverino, *Phil. Christ. Comp. Ont.*, c. 9, n. 17; Pesch, *Inst. Phil. Nat.*, n. 61; Mivart, *Truth*, p. 412.

action, not the result—should be called transient. Curious also that St. Thomas and almost every other philosopher should define transient actions to be those 'which *pass* into something outside.'

So much was the Angelic Doctor convinced of the passage of activity from one subject into another, that he often repeats and emphasizes—what is surprising at first sight—that a transient action 'is from the agent as from its principle, and *in the recipient as in its subject.*'[1] This is but an application of the axiom of the Stagyrite, that 'movement is in the movable, for it is its act; and the act of the mover is not different.'[2] It is repeated in many forms in almost every one of the works of St. Thomas; as, for instance, when he says in the *Summa* :—[3]

Action is of two kinds; of which one proceeds from the agent into some exterior object, as in burning and cutting . . . An operation of this kind is not an act and perfection of the agent, but rather of the recipient. There is another kind of action which remains within the agent, as feeling, thinking, willing; and these are perfections and acts of the agent.

If, then, it is an essential part of the dynamic theory that an action never passes from one subject into another, what are we to think of this teaching of Aristotle and the Angelic Doctor? One kind of action 'proceeds from the agent into some exterior object.' So much so that it 'is not an act and perfection of the agent, but rather of the recipient.' It is so in the case of 'burning and cutting.' How can this be true if the action of burning or of cutting consists in the exertion of 'force' on the part of the fuel or of the knife?

---

[1] 'Idem actus est hujus, idest agentis, ut a quo; et tamen est in patiente ut receptus in eo. In Phys. Arist., l. 5. n. 9.

[2] Ἐστίν ἡ κίνησις ἐν τῷ κινητῷ, ἐντελέχεια γὰρ ἐστι τούτου, καὶ ὑπὸ τοῦ κινητικοῦ. Καὶ ἡ τοῦ κινητικοῦ δὲ ἐνέργεια οὐκ ἄλλη ἐστι. (Phys. c. 3.) Remark how all the energy of whatever is capable of producing motion, is made out to be kinetic. It is probable, that this is the first mention of kinetic energy in all philosophy.

[3] 'Duplex est actio. Una quae procedit ab operante in exteriorem materiam, sicut urere et senare . . . Talis operatio non est actus et perfectio agentis, sed magis patientis . . . Alia est actio manens in ipso agente, ut sentire, intelligere, et velle; et hujusmodi actio est perfectio et actus agentis.' 1, 2, q. 3, a. 2, ad. 3.

According to the kinetic theory it is easy to explain this seeming anomaly. Fire does not burn or a knife cut, until the motion of either has actually passed into the object cut or burnt. At that instant it is the motion or action of this object. So that action or motion truly passes from one subject into another, but may not with correctness be called transient until it has actually passed, when it resides in and is the action or motion of the second subject not the first.

4. Metaphysical arguments of this kind might be piled over one another almost indefinitely; I have space but for one more.

You will remember the definition of action given by St. Thomas; it is 'a form in motion or in flux.' Akin to this is the definition of efficient causality first given by Aristotle, as far as I am aware, adopted by the Angelic Doctor, and since his time traditional in the Catholic schools. An efficient cause is 'an extrinsic principle from which motion first flows.' [1]

Efficient causality consists in an *influxus* or flow from one thing into another, when the first is said to influence or have influence on the second. There is, therefore, a principle from which the flow takes place, a term into which it is received, and the flow itself. In that flow of something activity *in actu secundo* or action consists. What is the flow? It is a flow of motion: principium extrinsecum *a quo fluit motus*. Not one word of 'force,' which is so essential to activity according to the dynamic theory.

VI.

I can but touch very briefly on the theological side of the question, which has reference principally to the immediate production and perennial conservation of all things by God; a subject which ramifies all through theology, but comes out prominently in connection with the divine co-operation with the action of creatures.

It is an undoubted principle in the Catholic schools, that

---

[1] Principium extrinsecum a quo primum fluit motus.   *Vide* Zigliara, *Summa Phil. Ont.*, 44. ii. ; Suarez, *Metaph.*, D. 17, s. 1.

every reality in existence, substance or accident, from the greatest to the least, is produced by God immediately; that is, not by means of any other agent, substance or accident, 'force' or motion, which He may have produced already; but as the direct and immediate term of His own divine activity. This is true of every reality whatever; of accidents no less than substances; of actions, forces, exertions, entities of every kind; for all are true realities and must come equally from God.

Now, take the one thing on the existence of which dynamists insist so much,—the 'force' which the creature is supposed to give out in acting; and ask yourself is it produced by God immediately in the sense explained. And if its action or exertion is anything really different from the 'force' itself, is the action or exertion also produced immediately and perennially conserved—that is, continuously produced as at the beginning—directly by the divine activity?

Dynamists, I know, particularly those of a certain school, reply to the effect that there are two 'forces' acting concurrently,—the created and the uncreated,—whenever a finite agent is in action; and that the 'force' of the creature necessarily depends for its efficacy on that of the Creator. But I am not speaking of mere dependence, necessary or otherwise, but of immediate, continued production; and I ask again: are the created 'force' and its action—for this also is a reality—produced in the first instant and continuously kept in existence immediately and directly by the divine activity? If not, what becomes of the Catholic doctrine of the immediate divine production and conservation of all things? And if the force and the action of the creature are being continuously produced and infused into the created faculty by an immediate divine operation such as has been described, in what sense are they 'exerted' by the faculty of the creature, as the dynamists contend? That very 'exertion' is it not also a finite reality, and, as such, to be itself produced and conserved by God immediately? In what sense, then, is the 'exertion' due to the 'force' of the creature?

Here, again, St. Thomas comes to our assistance. According to the Angelic Doctor and his disciples, the Creator and His creatures co-operate immediately in the production of finite things; but the immediateness is not the same in the case of both the co-agents; in God it is an immediateness of virtue, whilst in the creature it is one of supposit.[1] In other words, God produces and infuses, and the created faculty supports, the virtue or power by which the effect is produced. If, in addition, you remember that the virtue—*in actu secundo*—of a creature, according to St. Thomas is a motion, you will have the whole kinetic theory in its essence. Effects are invariably produced by motions, which themselves are in every case the immediate results of the divine activity; so, however, that they truly reside in and belong to created things.

This is intelligible; it is consistent; it harmonizes perfectly with the Catholic doctrine of the immediate and continuous production of all things by the Creator. But if, as dynamists contend, there is a 'force' which emanates immediately and solely from the created faculty, and which co-operates with God in producing effects, how can this 'force' and its emanation,—not the effects produced, but the 'force' producing and its production,—how are these themselves produced immediately by God?

VII.

Here I must conclude. I do not pretend to have proved in this paper the truth of the kinetic theory of activity; and I readily acknowledge that the doctrine is not without its difficulties, and that it needs to be applied so as to fit in with the phenomena which are dealt with in the physical sciences. This is what is being attempted by the scientists of our time; and the object of this paper is, to beg

---

[1] 'Si considermus supposita agentis, quodlibet agens particulare est immediatum ad suum effectum. Si autem consideremus virtutem qua fit actio, sic virtus superioris causae erit immediatior effectui quam virtus inferioris.' *De Pot.* q. 3, a. 7, c. Cf.Ferrariensis :—' Deus immediate causat actum voluntatis inmediatione virtutis, non autem immediatione suppositi. . . . Voluntas autem causat ipsam volitionem immediate immediatione suppositi, non autem immediatione virtutis.' (L. 3. Contra Gent., c. 89.)

of Catholic students of philosophy and theology, not to interfere with their labours, nor to frighten Catholic physicists from taking their share in the toil, and participating in the glory of the consummation to which they look forward. The kinetic theory may not be true; it will certainly have to be modified in many ways before it can be got to fit in with all the phenomena of the universe; but it is not uncatholic; and no true son of the Church need hesitate, through fear of disobedience to ecclesiastical authority, to explain the activity of inorganic or of dead matter in accordance with the principles on which the theory is based.

WALTER McDONALD.

THE CATHOLIC MISSIONS IN ICELAND

ICELAND, or Ultima Thule, as it was once supposed to be, has of late years begun to compete with the 'Sunny South' for the tourist's favour. The hotel at Spitzbergen, which is now an accomplished fact, has shown that a northerly climate need not necessarily drive away the globe-roaming southerner, or debar him from enjoying the wild rough beauty of Iceland. A visit to these shores may teach all comers the lesson of simplicity, and if the voyage do no more than show us that three-quarters of our supposed necessities of life are fetters we ourselves have hung about our being, our toils, even across an ill-humoured Atlantic, may not be wholly profitless.

On hearing the name of Iceland, most people at once picture a land of nothing but glaciers. Certainly there are plenty of glaciers; just enough, however, to give every part of the land a variety entirely its own. Beauty, light, grandeur here feast the eyes; but the land is barren withal—rocks, and rocks again, and lava fields, where hot springs and boiling wells abound, and where, during the short summer time, there are only some patches of fresh green.   Sheep from these scant pastures, and fish from the sea are all on which the Icelander can rely.

Why, then, did people choose a land like this as a home for themselves and their descendants?   The question has often been put to me, and people may naturally be astonished. Why was it therefore?   Because the great families of Norway, the proud Norsemen, were too fierce to serve a king.   Why was it?   Because they themselves were strong and wild as the island is.   For poverty they had no fear.   Could they not help themselves to the treasures of Europe, and every year sally forth to return with the spoils of the mainland? The winter was long, but they had secured the means of feasting.

The first inhabitants went over towards the end of the ninth century.   Little more than a century later, all Icelanders were Christians.   How this was brought about is, perhaps, one of the strangest pages in the history of conversion.   After a while, a certain number of those who carried terror over Christian Europe went home with the Christian faith ; a greater number still with Christian slaves. And so the moment clearly came nearer and nearer when Iceland should have to determine upon what should be the religion of the Island.

It was the year of Grace 1000.   The people were gathered, as every year they were wont to gather, in the parliament valley (Thingvellir).   Christians and pagans stood face to face grasping their weapons, ready to fight the question out, when the voice of reason prevailed, and the proposal to choose an arbiter was unanimously accepted. The religion of the whole people should be that which their arbiter settled.   The man chosen was a pagan chief, and in the choice of him the Christians acquiesced.   He stretched himself out on the ground, covered himself with a bearskin, and so remained motionless for three days.   The Christians betook themselves to prayer.   The pagan arbiter at the end of the third day arose, and declared that henceforth all Icelanders were to be Christians; and in this they all agreed.

As time went on the people became Christians by more than law.   Comparatively numerous were the Christian establishments which arose and flourished all over the island. Two dioceses were founded, and ten monasteries; everywhere parish churches sprang up. The glorious ceremonies of the Catholic Church warmed the hearts under northern skies no less than in the ' Sunny South,' and her brilliant truths enlightened minds which nature had gifted with perspicacity and clearness.

Those were the palmy days of Iceland. Laymen and monks set to work, and wrote down the history of the country and of every family. Thus a series of ' sagas ' was issued, which has no equal in any literature. They soon became the property of high and low, and are so to this day. Nearly every Icelander knows his family from the day they came over, and the old sagas are known by heart. At the same time, a body of Icelandic poets were continually visiting the courts of all northern Europe, and drinking deeply at the best literary fountains. Much of the poetry these writers created still exists. Some of their poems are beautiful religious flowers grown on the tree of Catholic faith. The most celebrated is the ' Lily,' which consists of a hundred verses in honour of our Blessed Lady. It is in every respect a masterpiece. ' All poets would like to have sung the "Lily," ' is an Islandic proverb. It was the work of a monk, and, like the *Stabat Mater*, was written in prison. It opened the door to the poet, and was the beginning of a new life.

Much has changed since then. The blood of the people is still the same, but not the vigour. And how could it be? The Icelander's life is not rosy, and the isolation which has preserved his old rich language pure and his old customs intact, has also kept out the stirring impulses of other nations. Once Christians, the Icelanders had to live on the resources of their own land, and it is no wonder if the old pirate people was far richer than their honest descendants.

Most of all the conditions of eternal life have changed, and the way in which the people of the island regard it. It is a sad story to read how the Danish King forced Protestant faith upon them, reluctant as they were. The

last hero of faith and fatherland, and, at the same time, the
last Catholic bishop, and last poet of the Middle Ages
(Jon Arason), laid his old head on the block, and died a
martyr (1551).   Now they tell how his followers went to
bring back his body.   They killed the Danes, and brought
their beloved bishop home to his church.   Over the
mountains the funeral procession went six days' walk.   As
the corpse appeared in sight of the church, the bell, the
largest in Iceland, began to ring of itself, without being
moved by any man.   Wilder and wilder it rang until the
corpse had entered the church; when suddenly the bell
ceased, for it had burst, and fallen to pieces.

When I came over to Iceland this beautiful legend was
told me; and I could not but feel the symbolism of the
story.   How could the poor people have more touchingly
expressed their sorrowing fear, that the old truth which had
rung forth to their fathers had become silent, perhaps, for
ever.   I could not but listen to it as a welcome from the
very soul of the people to the faith of their fathers, and to
me as the one who came to bring it back again after
centuries.   I am sure nobody tells the legend and gives it
this meaning, but I am also sure I was right in understanding it in this sense.   I think a Catholic priest can
understand the language of the old Icelanders, and their
broken Catholic hearts.

When I speak about my coming to Iceland, I am referring to a time about two years ago.   Of course, God's Church
had not forgotten the people in the far North; but intolerant
laws, which the Icelanders had not made themselves, had
closed the door to the old church.   This was only changed
in 1874, when the land got a free constitution; but, even
then, circumstances did not permit the starting of the
Icelandic Mission.   Iceland belongs to Denmark, and
Denmark itself had need enough of men and means for
mission work at home, for it is itself a Protestant country,
where Catholic faith has but recently begun to spread.
Such considerations for a long time prevented the sending of
a priest, in spite of Rome's insisting that one should be sent.
At last, two years ago, Rome became so urgent that the

Danish Bishop could but regard it as Heaven's will, and, consequently, trust in Providence. The present writer had the good fortune to be chosen for the post, for which old predilection had disposed his mind. I started from Copenhagen on the 27th September, 1895. The steamer had to go round the whole island, and we had storm all the while, so that it was only after twenty-nine days of sailing that I found myself in Reykjavik, the capital of the island, and the site of the future mission.

When the Norwegians came over to Iceland they found a little colony of Irish monks established there, near one of the northern bays, called to this day St. Patrick's Bay. They had sought, as it seems, in Iceland the peace which the Normans would not let them enjoy at home, and they were sorely disappointed, when seeing their persecutors land on that very spot which they had thought so safe as a refuge. I have not the material at hand to form any opinion on what Irish authors relate of SS. Ernulf and Buo.

But the connection between Ireland and Iceland, or rather between Irishmen and Icelanders, has left deeper traces than old chronicles. The Icelandic blood is blended with Irish blood, and this fact is easily explained. Most of the Norwegian chiefs touched Ireland on their way to Iceland; from Ireland they carried people off to be their slaves. These generally had their own small household; and when Iceland had become Christian they became the free ancestors to a great number of the later population of Iceland. This fact can be easily demonstrated by the two quite different types which, to the present day, have been preserved in Iceland—the Scandinavian and Irish, kept distinctly marked by racial antipathies. Only recently they have begun to intermarry freely; but up to a very short time the two races would have nothing to do with each other.

One might expect to find some traces of Irish mixed up with the old Norse language. This, however, is not the case. The poor Irish, men and women, who were torn away from their own country, rich perhaps, and possibly princes' children, when reduced to be miserable slaves, were forced to adopt the language of their victorious masters. What untold form of sorrow, and despairing anger, and broken hearts! One example, old sagas tell us, of an Irishwoman, a king's daughter, if I remember rightly, carried off to Iceland. She was of uncommon beauty even among the fair daughters of her race, and her captor married her. She became the mother of one of the proudest families in Iceland; but never one word was heard to fall from her lips during the many years of her married life.

The language adopted in Iceland was the ancient Norse, or, as it was then called, the Danish tongue. Of all Teutonic languages this is, doubtless, the most perfect in structure, and the richest in words—certainly one of the finest languages in the world. It is spoken now as much as it was a thousand years ago; and the simple peasant of Iceland reads the sagas, and partially knows them by heart. In all Scandinavia, Iceland excepted, the old tongue has changed. In Iceland alone, therefore, can we hear the language of our fathers; the language used by King Canutes, and once well known in Northumberland.

The political bonds between Denmark and Iceland are rather loose. Up to the year 1874 Iceland was considered as a province, and like other Danish provinces had to suffer under absolute kings' misgovernment; less, however, than any other Danish province. I state this, because F. Baumgartner in his *Nordische Fahrten*, makes himself reporter of complaints which are not so much those of the people as of extreme radical politicans, and often mere oratorical flights. Neither I nor any Dane has any interest in whitewashing kings who ruined our country, our language, our people; but I, as every Dane, must protest against the charges brought by a German writer who knows little of northern history, and only knew Iceland by a summer trip to Reykjavik, and the coast.

Iceland at the present moment has a parliament of its own, its own finance department, a governor who is an Icelander by birth, as all other officials; Icelanders share all civil rights, as all other Danish subjects, while they are

free from all the latter's civil duties. Yet not all Icelanders
are satisfied, though those who know most are also those
who are generally best satisfied with the present state of
things. Discontent, however, has the merit of [providing
matter for discussion to the members of parliament, and
serves as pastime.

The place in which our present mission is established
had been chosen some thirty years before by a French
priest, who was, in fact, the first missionary in Iceland
after the Reformation. As we owe to him, not only the
good name he left in our favour, but also a beautiful
example of patient waiting for the time of God, his name
shall adorn these pages ; he was called Abbé Bandoin.
As above mentioned, there was no liberty of conscience in
those days, no possibility of public service, less of preaching.
Why then did he come over ? No doubt, also in the hope
of dawning freedom. But his first aim certainly was to offer
the loving care of the Church to the French fishermen, who
come over by thousands every summer. Eighteen years he
led a life practically as a hermit, studied the language and
the history of the people, whom he loved so intensely. Just
when he had mastered all difficulties, and the day of freedom
arose, a cancer brought him to his grave. Patience was the
service God craved of him, and patience has the promise of
eternal life.

As a visible souvenir of him, I found an old chapel, the
poorest I have ever seen. Between his death and my arrival
twenty years had elapsed, and the horror of desolation was
complete. A month after my advent I had the consolation
of getting a brother priest as my fellow-worker in this poor
ruined vineyard. I had meantime cleaned the wretched
little chapel as well as possible. We began preaching.
Would people come ? We had only one Catholic family.
Would they be the only attendants ? The wind blew through
the wooden walls, the rain streamed through the ceiling.
Would there come any Protestants ? Indeed they came,
came again the whole winter. They wondered to find
Catholicity such plain Christianity instead of all the super-
stition they had been told it was. At every sermon the

church was full. This was rather a surprise. Conversions we did not expect all at once; did not even wish them at once, preferring a solid ground to hasty building-up ; and it was no disappointment that we had to wait.

Another surprise, which looked like a disappointment, was to find the Icelandic winter much milder than we supposed. Of course, Iceland is no Andalusia ; but in Iceland, too, summer follows on winter. Summer brings to these shores a congregation of fellow-believers—viz., some four or five thousand sailors—the French fishermen already mentioned. Poor people they are, even when in health, leading a life which could scarcely be harder, and more devoid of every elementary comfort. But it is absolutely sad even to think of their condition when ill. In the whole island, to begin with, there was only a single hospital. One may easily understand how reluctant the captains were to leave their fishing-banks, perhaps for weeks, for a sick man's sake. And even when they came to the hospital, the doctor was the only man who understood them. The thought, therefore, forced itself upon us to try to get up two small hospitals, one on the western shore, and one in the east. Another thing necessary was the building of a new church.

Begging and the kind dispositions of Providence have made it possible to us to accomplish these works. Church and hospitals are built and partly paid for—partly only, but neither Providence nor charity will fail us, the rest will come. Catholic Sisters of Mercy have arrived to help us, and are nursing the sick in the hospitals and· in the homes. Sometimes they have to go on horseback over the mountains to the suffering. Charity has taught them to ride.

So we have not been without consolations. Also a conversion has been given us by heaven, and more are going on. A great comfort it is everytime either of us has the opportunity of administering the holy sacraments to dying fishermen, who might else have died as though they were not children of our warm-hearted mother the Catholic Church. However, such a death is sad enough, far away from wife and children, whose dear names we hear the poor fishermen call out in their delirium. Nothing is

more touching than to see the dead man's companions gather
in the church to the Requiem Mass. Their Sunday clothes
are in their far-off little homes, their thoughts also. The
tricolour covers the corpse, and the chant is better meant
than executed. The Mass ended, the funeral procession
goes to the churchyard, where the French have a corner of
their own. Their number is great, who like this man left
their home and beloved ones, hoping to see them again.
Heaven did not endorse his *au revoir.* There he lies under
a poor wooden cross. ' Marin Français ' is all the explanation you find.; and, perhaps, the relics of an artificial garland
sent the year after his death by his wife. The wife probably
was mad with grief when she got the news that the father
of her children had already reposed some months in the
barren cemetery of Reykjavik. But life was stronger than
love. The children need a father, and another fisherman
took the place at her side and in her heart, and the wooden
cross in the far-off churchyard moulders away. At last God
alone knows his tomb, and the resurrection-angel will find
it out. *Requiescat in pace.*

One may ask why a poor mission should charge itself
with the care of the French fishermen. The answer simply
is that they are poor helpless Catholics, and that the priest
has to take care of all the children of the Church. Catholic
means embracing all nations. Moreover, the French have
given all the means for the hospitals, and when we are
forced to appeal to the charity of other nations too, that is
for strictly missionary work.

There is another class of human beings in Iceland, who
are in a still more pitiful condition, the lepers. There are
at least two hundred of them in the island; that is to
say, out of a population of seventy-five thousand. As the
population is very scattered however, one may be long in
Iceland without seeing any lepers. Yet the very existence
of this awful plague must provoke the utmost pity. No
beings are more worthy of pity than these poor lepers. Year
after year they see their own body literally falling to pieces
while yet alive. Sense after sense goes, and death comes
upon them by slow and painful steps, until their existence

during the last year is well-nigh insupportable for dreadful pain. Here assuredly is a grand work of charity to be taken up; and please God, when we get over the first difficulties we are obliged to conquer, we shall make some day an appeal to Christian charity in favour of the poor Icelandic lepers. This very year the Icelandic parliament is deliberating about the establishment of a lepers' hospital outside Reykjavik, and no doubt it will be granted, as it is commanded by necessity. But there will only be provision for sixty out of the two hundred lepers, and no place at all for those whom it might, perhaps, be possible to save. The means of the country do not allow us to think about an asylum for them all, still less about a house of cure. Now this is exactly what we desire to establish later on, such a little hospital where leprosy in its earliest stages could be treated. Such an institution would certainly save some from years of suffering; for a cure is, if rare, still possible. At least such charitable provision would he a consolation for the poor stricken sufferer, preventing him from immediate despair. Hope for the hopeless, health for some already marked out by death—this seems to me a worthy aim, and I trust to God that in a short time it may be more than a dream.

JON L. FREDERIKSEN.

MODERN SCIENTIFIC MATERIALISM

Part II.—Life (continued).

SCIENCE tells us with certainty two things about life :—

I. In the past, there was a time when life was not on the earth.

II. In the present, life comes from antecedent life, and from that only.

I. There was a time when life was not on the earth.

(a) Geology and palæontology prove a condition of the earth when life did not, and could not exist—when in fact its surface was in a molten state, and necessarily at an enormously high temperature. Proof of this primitive condition is seen in the lower strata of rocks, which have evidently set from a state of fusion. Of course these rocks contain no trace of life.

(b) The leading materialists admit all this ; it is in fact part of their system.

Virchow :—

> There has been a beginning of life, since geology points to epochs in the formation of the earth when life was impossible, and when no vestige of it is to be found.

Huxley :—

> If the evolution hypothesis is true, living matter must have arisen from not-living matter ; for by the hypothesis the condition of the globe was at one time such that living matter could not have existed on it, life being entirely incompatible with the gaseous state.[1]

Tyndall :—

> There was a time when the earth was a red-hot molten globe, on which no life could exist. In the course of ages its surface cooled ; but, to quote the words of one of our greatest savants,

---

[1] *Ency. Brit. Biology.*

'when it first became fit for life, there was no living thing upon
it.'[1] . . . On its first detachment from the sun, life as we understand it could not have been present on the earth.[2]

The admitted truth of this first proposition throws on
materialists one of the heaviest of their tasks—to account
for *the origin of life*. We shall see immediately how
formidable a difficulty this is, and how vainly our 'advanced
philosophers' wrestle with it.

II. Life comes from life and from nothing else.

Lord Kelvin :—

This seems to me to be as sure a teaching of science as the
law of gravitation, that life proceeds from life, and from nothing
but life.[3]

Sir H. Roscoe :—

So far as science has progressed at present we are not able to
obtain any organism without the intervention of some sort of
previously existing germ.

Professors Stewart and Tait :—

As a matter of fact, we are led by science to receive the law of
biogenesis (*i.e.*, life from life) as expressing the present order of
the world. . . . As a matter of universal scientific experience a
living thing can only be produced from a living thing ; the
inorganic forces of the visible universe can by no means generate
life.[4]

Darwin :—

There must have been a time when inorganic elements alone
existed in our planet. . . . Now is there a fact, or a shadow of
a fact, supporting the belief that these elements, without the
presence of any organic compounds, and acted on only by known
forces, could produce a living creature? At present it is to us a
result absolutely inconceivable.[5]

Tyndall :—

If you ask me whether there exists the least evidence to
prove that any form of life can be developed out of matter
without demonstrable antecedent life, my reply is . . . men of
science frankly admit their inability to point to any satisfactory
experimental proof that life can be developed save from demonstrable antecedent life.[6]

[1] *Contemporary Review*, vol. xxix.
[2] *Scientific Use of the Imagination.*
[3] *Inaugural Address to the British Association.*
[4] *The Unseen Universe*, p. 244.
[5] *Athenæum*, 1863, p. 554.
[6] *Belfast Address.*

And again, and even more decidedly, four years later (1878) :—

· I affirm that no shred of trustworthy experimental testimony exists to prove that life in our day has ever appeared independently of antecedent life.[1]

Huxley :—

The chasm between the living and the not-living the present state of knowledge cannot bridge.[2] [And again, referring to the doctrine of life from life only, he says it is 'victorious along the whole line at the present day.'[3]]

Virchow :—

Never has a living being, or even a living element—let us say a living cell—been found, of which it could be predicated that it was the first of its species. Nor has any fossil remains ever been found of which it could ever be likely that it belonged to a being the first of its kind, or produced by spontaneous generation.[4]

One would think on reading these extracts that the proposition was fully and frankly conceded. There would seem to be no room left for a materialistic theory of life from dead matter. But needs must when the devil drives. We are dealing with men who *must* get life out of dead matter somehow, or fling their whole theory to the winds. According to Huxley—and he ought to know—

The *fundamental proposition* of evolution is that the whole world, living and not living, is the result of the mutual inter-action, according to definite laws, of the forces possessed by the molecules of which the primitive nebulosity of the universe was composed.[5]

How this result, as regards the *living* world, was produced, and what were the 'definite laws' capable of producing it, neither Huxley nor any other materialist can say.

---

[1] *Nineteenth Century*
[2] *Ency. Brit. Biology.* Compare this admission with his chemistry of living protoplasm, wherein he 'can see no break in the series of steps' by which it may be produced from lifeless elements.
[3] *Critiques and Addresses*, p. 239.
[4] *Address at Wiesbaden*, 1887. Of course this extract must be read in the light of the subject of the address, viz, the first beginnings of life on materialistic principles, and altogether prescinding from *creation*. It is in fact an absolute confession of the inability of materialism to account for the first living beings.
[5] *Critiques and Addresses*, p. 305.

MATERIALISTIC VIEWS OF THE ORIGIN OF LIFE

1. Many give it up as insoluble. Darwin again and again declares that he has nothing to do with the origin of life, and knows nothing about it :—

I have nothing to do with the origin of the primary mental powers, any more than I have with that of life itself [1] . . . Science as yet throws no light on the far higher problem of the essence or origin of life. [2] . . . Our ignorance is as profound on the origin of life as on the origin of force or matter. [3]

Huxley is equally explicit :—

Of the causes which have led to the origination of living matter, it may be said that we know absolutely nothing. . . . Science has no means to form an opinion on the commencement of life ; we can only make conjectures without any scientific value.

Again we ask ourselves in astonishment—What becomes of the chemistry of living protoplasm, which seemed so easy ?

Tyndall makes a similar confession of ignorance, though apparently with a reservation in favour of life in some other than ' our sense '—no doubt that extravagant sense set forth in next section. ' We are unable to trace the course of things from the nebula, when there was no life in our sense, to the present earth, where life abounds.' [4]

Continental materialism is in no better case. ' According to my opinion,' says the veteran Virchow, ' we should simply acknowledge that in reality we know nothing of the connection between the organic world and the inorganic.' Du Bois-Reymond, the famous Berlin scientist, places the origin of life among the seven riddles which seem to defy experimental science. Even Häckel has no cheering message to give. ' Most naturalists, even at the present day, are inclined to give up the attempt at a natural explanation [of the origin of life], and take refuge in the miracle or inconceivable creation.' [5] Ay, there's the rub ! There is

[1] *Origin of Species*, 1892, p. 191.   [4] *Fragments of Science*, p. 413.
[2] *Ibid.*, p. 369.   [5] *History of Creation*.
[3] *Athenæum*, April 25th, 1863.

no other alternative but ' inconceivable creation,' and of a'l ' unscientific ' things, next to the existence of God, creation is the most unscientific. ' The spirit and practice of science pronounce against the intrusion of an anthropomorphic creator.'[1]

Finally the ' advanced philosophy ' of the New World can only echo these disheartening admissions of the Old. Even the dauntless Professor Marsh—he of the limitless faith in science[2]—though he risks a mild guess as to the *nature* of life—(it *may* be a form of some other force, presumably physical !)—he has to confess utter ignorance of its origin.

2. Some hold continuous life throughout all nature, inorganic as well as organic. Häckel states that organic and inorganic substances are ' equally alive.'[3] Fiske asserts that ' the difference between a living and a not-living body is a difference of degree and not of kind.'

Tyndall, of course, following up his adoption of the ' double-faced ' theory of matter, gives his adhesion to this view :—

. Are the forces of organic matter different in kind from those of inorganic matter? The philosophy of the present day negatives the question. . . . The tendency of modern science is to break down the wall of partition between organic and inorganic, and to reduce both to the operation of forces which are the same in kind, but are differently compounded.[4] . . . The evidences as to *consciousness* in the vegetable world depend wholly upon our capacity to observe and weigh them. To a being with our capacities indefinitely multiplied I can imagine not only the vegetable, but the mineral world responsive to the proper irritants (*i.e.*, endowed with sensation !) . . . All three worlds constitute a unity, in which I picture life as the immanent throughout.[5]

What is any sane man to think of talk like this? If you scratch an oak tree or a granite boulder, it is really

---

[1] *Fragments of Science*, p. 413. Note how coolly ' science ' is appropriated as the private possession of the ' advanced philosophers.'

[2] I. E. Record, Fourth Series, vol. ii., p. 208, *note*.

[3] *History of Creation*.

[4] *Vitality*.

[5] *Fragments of Science*, p. 215.

'conscious' and 'responsive,' but you lack the 'capacity to observe' the fact! And for this you have the authority of 'the philosophy of the present day.' Tyndall challenges contradiction of this precious 'philosophy.' 'No man can say that the feelings of the animal are not represented by a drowsier consciousness in the vegetable.'[1] So 'no man can say' that the other side of the moon is not laid out by the occupant as a market garden. No doubt 'the capacity to observe it' is wanting; but to a being with our capacities so multiplied as to be able to see round a corner, we can imagine it quite visible. The reasoning is just as good in this case as in the other, the 'imagination' no more absurd, and the lunar garden as likely an entity as a 'drowsy' cabbage or a 'responsive' milestone. Such being 'the philosophy of the present day,' can anyone be surprised at the prevailing tendency—which Häckel laments—to 'take refuge in the miracle of inconceivable creation'?[2]

3. The theory of *spontaneous generation* was undoubtedly the most famous of all modes of accounting for the origin of life. It may be said to have held the field until it was finally disposed of by the researches of Pasteur and Tyndall. By these researches it was, to use Pasteur's words,[3] 'relegated to the region of chimeras.' Huxley terms Pasteur's experiments 'models of accurate experimentation and logical reasoning.'[4] 'At the present moment,' he says, 'there is not a shadow of trustworthy direct evidence that abiogenesis (*i.e.*, spontaneous generation) does take place, or has taken place within the period during which the existence of the globe is recorded.'[5] Similarly Virchow: 'Not a single positive fact is known which proves that an inorganic mass has transformed itself into an organic mass.'[6] And finally

[1] *Fragments of Science*, p. 244.
[2] As an illustration of the beautiful consistency of these philosophers, we find Tyndall elsewhere arguing thus :—' Does water think or feel when it rises into frost ferns on the window-pane?' We might very well answer him :—Perhaps it does, but we have not ' the capacity to observe it.'
[3] In 1875.
[4] *Critiques and Addresses*, p. 234.
[5] *Ency. Brit. Biology.*
[6] *Revue Scientifique*, Dec., 1877.

Tyndall : ' I hold with Virchow that the doctrine [of spontaneous generation] is utterly discredited.'[1]

4. The extracts just given might lead us to believe that
we were done with spontaneous generation in any and every
form.   But no; it has disappeared from the present only to
reappear in the remote past, when there were no inquisitive
Pasteurs to challenge it.   At some early epoch, it is assumed,
some protoplasm was produced from inorganic materials
either purely by accident, or by some happy, but altogether
extraordinary and unaccountable co-operation of the ordinary physical and chemical forces.   It is admitted that
this is contrary to all ascertained facts *in the present;*
and that therefore scientific analogy warrants the denial of
its having ever happened, unless it can be shown that the
physical and chemical forces possessed *specifically* different
powers in the past from what they do now.   Of this, as of the
main fact itself, there is not, as Huxley says, ' a shadow of
trustworthy direct evidence.'   The only *indirect* evidence is
supplied by the necessities of the evolution theory.   Huxley
has told us that ' the fundamental proposition of evolution '
is that the living as well as the not-living world resulted
from the mutual interaction of the forces of inorganic
matter.

I grant [says Virchow] that if anyone is determined to form
for himself an idea of how the first organic being came into
existence *of itself*, nothing further is left than to go back to
spontaneous generation. . . .   But whoever recalls to mind the
lamentable failure of all the attempts made very recently to discover
some decided support for it . . . will feel it doubly serious to
demand that this theory, so utterly discredited, should be in any
way accepted as the basis of all our views of life.[2]

Nevertheless this demand has to be made by our
' philosophers.'   There is for them no possible escape from
it.   The origination of life from dead matter is ' a necessary
implication of the evolution theory '; and so in spite of facts,
analogy, authority, and common sense—though without ' a
shadow of trustworthy direct evidence ' or ' a single positive

---

[1] *Fragments of Science,* p. 405.   [2] *Address at Munich,* 1877.

fact' to support it, though 'utterly discredited' and 'absolutely inconceivable,' still it *must* have happened. Otherwise, of course, 'inconceivable creation'—*quod absit !* The argument would stand thus—If the evolution theory is true, life originated from dead matter; but the evolution theory is true; therefore &c. If you demand proof of the minor proposition, you will learn from Tyndall that the theory is to be accepted chiefly on account of 'its general harmony with scientific thought.'[1]

Biologists in general agree [says Spencer] that in the present state of the world no such thing happens as the rise of a living creature out of non-living matter. They do not deny, however, that at a remote period in the past, when the temperature of the surface of the earth was much higher than at present, and other physical conditions were unlike those we know, inorganic matter, through successive complications, gave origin to organic matter.[2]

He assures us that 'men of science scarcely question the conclusion' that this happened; that it is 'a necessary implication of the hypothesis of evolution taken as a whole,' and therefore must, of course, be true. The 'biologists in general' and 'men of science' who agree on all this are solely the extreme evolutionary clique of which Spencer himself is such a shining light.

Häckel also declares some form of spontaneous generation to be 'a necessary part of the doctrine of evolution.'[3] Somehow and somewhere in the past a living cell originated just once from the fortuitous concourse of atoms. True, he admits that 'there is no experimental evidence in its favour ;' but that is of no consequence. The fact that it is 'a necessary part of the doctrine of evolution,' and the only refuge from 'inconceivable creation' is surely evidence enough.

Professor Weismann finds himself in the same dilemma as his countryman, and gets out of it in the same delightfully simple way. 'I admit that spontaneous generation, in spite

---

[1] *Belfast Address.*
[2] *Nineteenth Century,* May, 1886, p. 769.
[3] *History of Creation.* In fact he starts his famous pedigree of man (chap. xxii.) with the spontaneous generation of what he calls the *Monera.*

of all the failures to demonstrate it, remains for me *a logical necessity*.' As the Professor has not recanted his materialism, we must assume that he finds this 'logical necessity' a sufficient warrant for his belief. Apparently the 'logical necessity' of getting out of a difficulty is, for the 'advanced philosophers,' an all-sufficient reason for asserting anything.

Huxley, like his friend Spencer, shows a preference for the remote past. ' Were it given to me to look beyond the abyss of geologically recorded time, . . . I should expect to be a witness of the evolution of living protoplasm from not-living matter.'[1] It is a far cry to the other side of 'the abyss of geological time.' We thought he had only to go to his laboratory to witness all this. He admits indeed that this opinion of his is no more than 'an act of philosophic faith.'[2] But has he not told us elsewhere that in the scientific man 'the one unpardonable sin' is 'blind faith;' that such a man 'has learned to believe in justification, not by faith, but by verification'?[3]

Tyndall, disregarding a similar canon of his own,[4] propounds an equally practical solution. He would affirm that if a planet were 'carved from the sun, set spinning round an axis, and revolving round the sun at a distance from him equal to that of our earth,' one of the consequences of the refrigeration of the mass 'would be the development of organic forms.'[5] He states as 'the conclusion of science . . . that the molten earth contained within it elements of life, which grouped themselves into their present forms as the planet cooled.'[6] 'Who,' he demands, 'will set limits to the possible play of molecules in a cooling planet?'[7] Who indeed! Or to the 'possible play' of the scientific imagina-

---

[1] *Critiques and Addresses*, p. 239.
[2] *Ibid.*
[3] *Lay Sermons*, p. 16.
[4] 'Without verification a theoretic conception is a mere figment of the intellect.'
[5] *Vitality.*
[6] *Fragments of Science*, p. 246. Tyndall assures his readers that the only difficulty the human mind finds in accepting this 'conclusion' arises from theological prejudices—nothing else. The wild absurdity of the conception would form no obstacle. We had up to this thought better of the human mind!
[7] *Vitality*

tion! Surely Virchow's 'energetic protest' at Munich was not uncalled for!

This talk is about as sane as what we had higher up when we were invited to regard sticks and stones as sensitive and conscious—almost in fact as men and brothers. What is most astonishing about these 'advanced philosophers' is that, having confessed their utter inability to say what or whence is life, they still go on to give us a perfect *embarras* of theories on the subject. Not to speak of making it up in the laboratory *à la* Huxley, you have only to 'look beyond the abyss of geologically recorded time,' or take 'a planet carved from the sun,' and keep an eye on it while it is cooling, to 'witness the evolution of living protoplasm from not-living matter.' If you ask *how* this development of living from not-living matter took place even in the extraordinary circumstances here postulated, Professor Clifford will accurately explain to you that it was 'by continuous physical processes;'[1] Herbert Spencer will inform you that it was 'through successive complications;' Tyndall will blandly assure you that it was due to 'that potency of matter which finds expression in natural evolution'[2]—or if you like it better, 'by the operation of an insoluble mystery;'[3] finally, your enlightenment will be completed by Huxley's luminous statement that life 'was the result of the mutual interaction, according to definite laws, of the forces possessed by the molecules of which the primitive nebulosity of the universe was composed!' If you are not satisfied with all this you may consider yourself quite out of date.

A Sunday scholar once gave a definition of faith, with which Huxley was immensely pleased. 'Faith,' said the Sunday theologian, 'is the power of saying you believe things which are incredible.' This exactly describes the 'philosophic faith' we are here called upon to exercise—'the power of saying you believe things which are incredible.'

---

[1] *Fortnightly Review*, December, 1874.
[2] *Fragments*. p. 413.
[3] *Belfast Address*

5. What we call *vital force* is no more than a higher form of *crystalline* force ; and living beings originated pretty much like crystals. This is a favourite view with Tyndall, and he seldom misses an opportunity of urging it.

Men of science are intimately acquainted with the structural power of matter, as evidenced in the phenomena of crystallization. They can justify scientifically their belief in its potency, under the proper conditions, to produce organisms.[1] . . . Atoms and molecules are endowed with attractive and repellent poles, by the play of which definite forms of crystalline architecture are produced. Thus molecular force becomes *structural*. It required no great boldness of thought to extend its play into organic nature, and to recognise in molecular force the agency by which both plants and animals are built up[2] . . . In an amorphous drop of water lie latent all the marvels of crystalline force ; and who will set limits to the possible play of molecules in a cooling planet ? [3]

He speaks of crystallization as 'incipient life, manifesting itself throughout the whole of what we call inorganic nature.'[4] The argument may be stated thus :—The phenomena of crystallization show the existence of a wonderful *structural* power in matter—a power ' latent and potential ' in the liquid or vapour, but ready, under proper conditions, to build up forms as fair as any in the vegetable world. The fern of the woods is not more beautiful than the frost-ferns on your window-pane on a winter's morning. Yet for this no special force is postulated beyond the ordinary molecular attractions and repulsions conceded to all matter. Why then postulate a special *vital* force for the building up of plant or animal from seed or cell? The vegetable or animal germ is not less likely to contain the necessary formative force than was the drop of water. Why then deny the potentiality in one case, while you admit it in the other? The analogy between water-drop, seed, and germ speck, is complete. In each a *formative force* is certainly

[1] *Belfast Address.*
[2] *Ibid.*
[3] *Vitality.*
[4] *Scientific Materialism.* See this crystalline theory set forth at length, with great wealth and beauty of illustration, in his lecture on *Matter and Force;* also in a more advanced form in *Scientific Materialism.*

hidden. In each it springs into activity on the presence of suitable conditions. A *force* cannot be *seen;* so we must judge of its nature by its action. The structural work in all three cases is analogous, if not alike. In the simplest of the three cases you admit it to be no more than molecular force. It is therefore fair to conclude that in the more complex cases also we have only a more complex interaction of the same force.

The central fallacy in this argument lies in an assumption that might easily escape the unguarded reader—the assumption, namely, of the seed and the cell as analogues of the drop of water. Tyndall speaks of all three as if they came to hand in nature in pretty much the same way. But do they? Is it of no consequence that while the water-drop need not have aqueous ancestry, but may be flashed from its elemental oxygen and hydrogen, the vegetable or animal germ must come from a parent plant or animal? Does not this procession from living antecedents include the very point in discussion, namely, the intrusion of vital force into the physical processes compared? For the germ comes from the living parent endowed with a share of its vitality, and *this* is the force that lies latent until suitable conditions occur to render it active. To make the analogy complete we should have the crystallizable water-drop born of a grown up crystal, and procurable in no other way!

Tyndall is fond of describing—when it suits his argument—how men of science arrive at their conclusions about the far past. ' They prolong the method of nature from the present into the past. The observed uniformity of nature is their only guide.' Well, here ' the method of nature ' is that a fertile seed or cell comes from a living plant or animal, and from no other source. Therefore, 'the observed uniformity of nature ' authorizes us to conclude that the same was the case even among the playful molecules of a cooling planet.

Some years ago an ingenious Yankee manufactured eggs that could not be distinguished by experts from the genuine product of the poultry yard. Assuming that these eggs contained all the constituents of the real article, would

Tyndall maintain that with proper hatching they would produce chicks? Until something like that occurs, his pet analogy between crystallization and life is a broken chain.

Huxley over and over commits himself to the statement that *life is the cause of organization, not organization the cause of life;* and of course the cause must precede the effect. Now Tyndall's crystalline theory exactly reverses this order, requiring that organization should come first, as a result of the complex interaction of molecular forces ; and life second, as a result of the organization thus produced. The theory of the infidel physicist is overthrown by the infidel biologist, and in this biological region the latter knew his ground best. We remember his distinct and decisive statement that ' there is *no parallel* between the actions of matter in the mineral world and in living tissues.' We may also recall Dr. Beale's strong words when referring to this effort of ' scientific imagination : " The idea of a particle of muscular or nerve tissue being formed by a process akin to crystallization appears *ridiculous* to anyone who has studied the phenomena, or who is acquainted with the structure of these tissues." Add to these authoritative statements that of the great French naturalist, Quatrefages :—' It is inexplicable to me that some men whose merits I otherwise acknowledge should have recently compared crystals to the simplest living forms. . . . These forms are the antipodes of crystal from every point of view.'[1]

6. *Bathybius !*—The evolution theory derives much of its power for mischief from the argument of *authority*, as it is called—that is, from the eminence of the men who support it. Therefore, every opportunity should be taken to show how unreliable they are as leaders of thought, and how they

---

[1] *The Human Species*, p. 3. Several important differences may be pointed out between crystalline and organic structures. (*a*) Crystalline structures are mathematical, organic not in the least so. (*b*) Crystals grow by simple accretion on the outside, organic structures by absorption of nutriment and its conversion, first into protoplasm, and finally into organized tissue. (*c*) The formation of a crystal needs no germ from an antecedent crystal ; organic structures can only be developed from germs derived from antecedent organisms. (*d*) Crystals can usually be dissolved and recrystallized at will; organic structures once destroyed cannot be restored.

will not stop at asserting anything, however extraordinary, in support of their hypotheses. We have already had many instances of this, and sensible men will draw their own conclusions about 'philosophers' who calmly offer them theories founded on fiery clouds and cooling planets. But *Bathybius* supplies a crowning instance of folly. These gentlemen are fond of reminding us with what care and caution the 'scientific man'—meaning of course the materialist—proceeds. 'He guesses, and checks his guess; he conjectures, and confirms or explodes his conjecture.' This is how it should be, according to Tyndall.

Unfortunately, in the case of *Bathybius* the 'scientific men' chiefly concerned, viz. Huxley, who discovered it, and Häckel, Strauss, and others, who committed themselves unreservedly to belief in it, did not wait to 'check their guess,' or 'explode their conjecture;' and the consequence was that in a few years the whole scientific world 'exploded' with laughter at what Mivart well nicknamed 'Huxley's sea-mare's nest.'

Bathybius was the name given by Huxley to a sticky ooze found in the vessels containing deep-sea dredgings. He rushed to the conclusion that this gelatinous substance could be no other than Nature's grand store of *protoplasm*, and that here at last was the solution of the great life-puzzle! All this he proclaimed in a triumphant article in the *Microscopical Journal.*—'*Bathybius* is a vast sheet of living matter enveloping the whole earth beneath the seas.'

That was in 1868. In 1875 this is what he has to say about *Bathybius* :—

I fear the thing to which I gave that name is little more than sulphate of lime, precipitated in the flocculent state from the sea water by the strong alkali into which the specimens of the deep-sea soundings which I examined were preserved![1]

In his last work, *The Old Faith and the New*,[2] Strauss wrote :—

As long as the conception of a special vital force was retained there was no possibility of spanning the chasm [from the inorganic to the organic] without the aid of a miracle. By *Bathybius* the chasm may be said to be bridged.

---

[1] *Nature*, August, 19th.   [2] 1872.

When the bridge broke down would he have been prepared to admit the miracle?

Dr. John Murray of the *Challenger* writes :—

I have seen several *savants* losing their temper in my presence when I told them that a mistake had been made with regard to this subject, and that Huxley, Häckel, and others had been led into error.

Surely a very instructive side-light on the 'scientific man'!

'With the *Bathybius*,' sighed Virchow, 'disappeared our greatest hope of a demonstration (of the origin of life from matter).' Häckel had called it 'the main support of the modern theory of evolution'!

Perhaps we ought not to say that these six views exhaust the list of solutions. There is, for instance, what has been called the 'Colorado beetle' theory of the origin of life on the earth. Might not the first living germs have been brought hither from space on a meteorite? This would of course leave the origin of life still unexplained; but a good deal would be gained by shifting the discussion to the shadowy region from which meteorites come. Somebody gave concrete shape to the idea by figuring a Colorado beetle riding in on a meteoric stone to people the void earth! For picturesqueness this conception rivals Tyndall's 'cooling planet.' It is, moreover, subject to somewhat similar disabilities; for meteorites, as is well known, owing to the friction of our atmosphere, reach the earth *in a state of incandescence*—which would be uncomfortable even for a Colorado beetle. However, an incandescent meteorite is as safe a vehicle of life as an incandescent planet. No less an authority than Lord Kelvin declared, no doubt with a wink of the other eye, that whatever else might be said of this notion it had at least the merit of not being 'unscientific':— and that, we know, is everything.

Again, it is hardly fair to exclude Häckel's appeal to the possibilities of the future—what we may call the prophetic view. It is such a lovely specimen of the genesis of fact from fiction, that for that alone it would deserve a place :—

There is every probability that sooner or later we shall succeed in producing protoplasm artificially. *We may therefore assume* that in nature also there *may be* formed from inorganic substances, first some simpler carbon compounds, and from these protoplasm capable of life. *If this exists*, it only needs to individualize itself (!) in the same way as the mother liquor of crystals individualizes itself, and we have the *moneron*.

The present having utterly failed him, and the past proving somewhat unmanageable, Häckel tries the future. To escape miracle he has recourse to prophecy! What a picture of utter demoralization these various speculations about the origin of life afford. Driven from the present by Pasteur, the 'advanced philosophers' scatter in all directions. Huxley flies to the further side of ' the abyss of geological time,' where at a safe distance he 'would expect to be a witness of the evolution of living protoplasm from not-living matter.' Tyndall selects ' a cooling planet ' as his refuge, and with a tread-on-the-tail-of-my-coat air calls for the man who will presume to set limits to its powers. Häckel, 'individualizing' himself from the slime of *Bathybius*, makes for the open country of the future—the region of unknown possibilities. In which romantic situations we may for the present leave our philosophers.

And now for the second time we pause to take stock of our gains. What has this second instalment of ' advanced philosophy ' taught us, beyond showing us the utterly helpless and hopeless plight of knowledge without God ? We thought, perhaps, that we had sounded the lowest depths of absurity in the materialistic philosophy of matter. We have now beheld a deeper depth. Our ' philosophers ' are here more imperatively brought to book. The difficulty presents itself more clearly to the average man, and hence more insistently demands . solution. The question of the origin of matter out of void is so vast that it baffles the human mind to grasp it even as an unsolved difficulty. The nature of matter, too, with its metaphysical and mathematical surroundings, would obviously become a terror to ordinary inquirers—like Prout's Blarney-stone politician, 'an out-and-outer to be let alone.' But life is different. It resides in limited beings with which we are familiar. We see them come, and grow, and go. We trace this recurring cycle of life as far back as the memory of man. And beyond that the long memory of the old earth, fixed in her fossil shapes, takes up the tale and carries us back through ages that are little more to us than names. The structure of the Palæozoic leaf declares as clearly as structure can declare anything that it lived the life of the leaves of our woods,[1] and was just as inconceivable a product of inorganic force as an oak forest.

But the cycle of life had a beginning. Even our 'philosophers' have to admit that when we follow the stream of life backward to its source, we come at last to an absolute beginning—to a time when there was neither seed nor egg on the earth to produce a living thing in the ordinary way. In the forcible words of the Duke of Argyll :—

> We know, as certainly as we know anything in the physical sciences, that organic life must have had a beginning in time on this globe of ours. If so, then of course that beginning cannot possibly have been by way of ordinary generation. Some other process must have been employed, however little we are able to conceive what that process was . . . The facts of nature and the necessities of thought compel us to entertain the conception of an absolute beginning of organic life when as yet there were no parent forms to breed and multiply.[2]

Thus far we travel the same road with most of our 'philosophers,' but here we are forced to part company. We assert—they deny—that we here touch the limit of the powers of nature. They will have it that there are *not* more things in heaven and earth than are dreamt of in their philosophy. They will not admit into the calculation the only factor capable of solving the problem, thus rendering solution impossible. Hence all their difficulties, their verbal wrigglings, their fantastic fictions. Hence the 'logical necessity' of an 'utterly discredited' and 'absolutely

---

[1] See Sir J. W. Dawson's *Modern Ideas of Evolution.*
[2] *Nineteenth Century*, March, 1897.

inconceivable' spontaneous generation ; hence the reckless recourse to 'fiery clouds' and 'cooling planets' as primordial incubators of living germs ; hence 'double-faced' matter, 'sensitive' stones, and 'conscious' vegetables; hence all the other wild speculations about life, none of them a whit more credible than the adventurous voyage of the Colorado beetle, and all of them leaving their devisers still 'without an approach to a solution of the mighty question of the origin of life.'[1]

Science led our 'philosophers' unerringly to the great central fact of the universe, the ultimate solution of all puzzles, the supreme First Cause; but their eyes were blinded 'that seeing they might not see.' That peculiarly constituted organ, 'the eye of science,' has never, as we know, been able to discover 'any intrusion of purely creative power' in nature. But is that the fault of nature, or of 'the eye of science'? Surely it is only an eye wilfully shut that could fail to see an 'intrusion of purely creative power' in such a portent as the origin of life from dead matter. Jean Paul Richter could see 'two miracles or revelations' in 'the birth of finite being, and the birth of life within the hard wood of matter.' Scientific men as eminent as our 'philosophers' have similarly read the same signs. To them the origin of life is an effect for which the material universe supplies no adequate cause. They thus find themselves forced to seek such a cause in another region of thought—a cause unconditioned by material limitations. 'We have evidence in the commencement of life on earth,' says Sir G. G. Stokes, 'of the operation in time of a cause which, for anything we can see, or that appears probable, lies altogether outside the ken of science.'[2]

It is as certain as anything in human thought [says the Duke of Argyll] that when organic life was first introduced into the world, something was done—some process was employed differing from that by which those forms now simply reproduce and repeat themselves. . . . All our desperate attempts, therefore, to get rid

---

[1] Tyndall in the *Contemporary Review*, No. xxix.
[2] *Burnett Lectures on Light* (1892), p. 331.

of the idea of creation as distinguished from mere procreation are self-condemned as futile. [1]

We believe [write Professors Stewart and Tait] that an extension of purely scientific logic drives us to contemplate the occurrence of two events which are as incomprehensible as any miracle—these are the introduction of visible matter and of visible living things into the universe. . . . Furthermore we are led by scientific analogy to regard the agency in virtue of which these two astounding events were brought about as an intelligent agency, an agency whose choice of the time for action is determined by considerations similar in their nature to those which influence a human being when he chooses the proper moment for the accomplishment of his purpose. [2]

Dr. A. R. Wallace, Darwin's great rival, sees in the first introduction of life 'indications of a new power at work.' Darwin himself seemed to see that the origin of life was something beyond the reach of physical science to explain. His repeated assertions that it was no concern of his are very significant, as also his fundamental assumption of living types to begin with. He could get on if he had only ' a mud-fish with some vestiges of mind' but he should get his mud-fish *alive*, and he did not seem disposed to trust ' fiery clouds' or ' cooling planets' with its production. [3]

No less convincing than the direct testimony of all true science to the existence of a creative intelligence, is the utter failure of false science to find firm footing on matter alone.

No system of the universe [says Sir Joseph Dawson] can dispense with a First Cause, eternal and self-existent ; and this First Cause must necessarily be the living God, whose will is the ultimate force and the origin of natural law. [4]

So ' all roads lead to Rome,' and all the great highways

---

[1] *Nineteenth Century*, March, 1897.

[2] *The Unseen Universe*, p. 11.

[3] *Apropos* of Darwin's initial types someone may wish to ask *how* life first showed itself in answer to the *fiat* of creation—what sort of forms, vegetable and animal respectively, first arose ; and whether any of these primordial forms still survive, or whether all have been superseded. To such inquiries we can give no answer. The earliest geological specimens are highly organized types of many kinds. But do these represent the first forms of terrestrial life? We cannot tell. Science cannot carry the investigation beyond the metamorphic rocks, and revelation only states broad facts which show us the Creator starting the two great divisions of animated nature on the course they have ever since held.

[4] *Modern Ideas of Evolution.*

of knowledge to God. That which traverses the fair and fruitful region of physical science is no exception, provided the traveller, disregarding all will-o'-the-wisp gleams of 'scientific imagination,' keeps steadily to the firm ground of fact. The unerring certainty with which the pedigrees of matter and of life lead back through bewildering ages to the One First Cause reminds us of another pedigree, whose simple but sublime conclusion is—' who was of Seth, who was of Adam, *who was of God.*'

Just as we finish this paper the problem of life is once more, and positively for the last time, about to be solved. The ' undiscovered correlative' is at last about to be dragged from its hiding place into the light of day. A brand new speculation, hot from the brain of its author, appears in the *Strand Magazine* for March. At the close of an interesting account of Marconi's new system of telegraphy the writer seems suddenly seized by the prophetic *afflatus,* under the influence of which he gives us a specimen of the 'scientific use of the imagination.' Apparently electrified out of himself by the contemplation of the wonders of Röntgen rays, Marconi waves, Tesla circuits, and the rest, he bursts forth : ' The imagination abandons as a hopeless task the attempt to conceive what, in the use of electric waves, the immediate future holds in store. The air is full of promises of miracles.' We are bidden to look to the *ether* for the realization of these promises. This hypothetical substance is, alas ! itself ' one of the deepest of the scientific mysteries '—a name as inscrutable to the scientists of to-day as was the writing on the wall to Baltassar and his guests. The *Strand* writer cries aloud for the scientific Daniel who is to read meaning into it. He believes him to be at hand. When he comes we may expect ' a great epoch in knowledge, . . . a new light on all the great problems which are mysteries at present.' Considering the number of these problems this seems a large order, and will keep the coming Daniel quite as busy solving puzzles as his ancient prototype.

Among the 'great problems' which are to receive a special measure of illumination is, of course, ' the mystery of living matter.' ' The key to the mystery, if it ever comes (oh!), will come through the *ether*.' And if it should turn out to be true, as is strongly suspected, that the ether and electricity are one and the same—a sort of ethereal Jekyll and Hyde—then we shall have 'a great, a startling key to the now fathomless mystery of life.' It is a little discouraging to find such a battery of mysteries between us and the one in whose solution we are just now chiefly interested. The ether is 'one of the deepest of the scientific mysteries;' electricity is another. The identity of the one with the other is still purely imaginary. We begin to wish Daniel would hurry up and get to work.

Then the *Strand* writer's methods of deduction baffle our stupidity. The future solution of a mystery is necessarily something at present unknown. The future solutions of two mysteries do not increase the sum of present knowledge. How can it be seen that two such unknowns will solve a third and different unknown? 'I don't know what the ether is,' says, equivalently, the *Strand* oracle, 'and I don't know what electricity is, and I don't know what life is. But I do know that the solution of the first two will solve the third.' Verily he is himself the expected Daniel, and we knew it not! Looking at the matter from the point of view of real and reasonable science we are totally unable to see how the tracing of certain *physical* phenomena to one source instead of two must necessarily throw light on the source or principle of certain other quite different phenomena which all existing evidence shows to be *non-physical*.

Although not exactly connected with our present subject it would be a pity not to mention some of the other truly 'startling' revelations that are to follow the synthesis of the ether and electricity. 'The deeper and higher mysteries of *post-mortem* human conditions'—in other words, the secrets of the next world—are to be revealed. 'In the ether the secret lies.' Then 'the great concepts of religion,' though they 'are felt to be true,' stand much in need of demonstration 'by the ordinary methods of proof.' 'And the present prospect is that only from the study of the ether is this desired proof likely to come.' Undoubtedly, 'strange results are coming.' The four last things, we may expect,

will be shown on a screen—which will be certain to ' draw '
—while electric theology à la Marie Corelli will be hardly
less entertaining. ' Faith,' the *Strand* theologian informs
us, ' needs no facts to support it '—which is a most fortunate
dispensation, as otherwise the new creed might be somewhat
at a loss. Only one thing blocks the way, and its name is
ether. Let us all, therefore, attack it with one accord. Let
us get round it, or under it, or over it. On the other side
we shall be rewarded by finding ourselves on ' the old
Roman road of science, which leads no one knows whither '
—but presumably to the Millennium !

E. Gaynor, c.m.

HISTORY OF THE INSTITUTION OF THE SACRAMENT OF PENANCE

WHEN was the Sacrament of the Holy Eucharist
instituted ? No one with any pretence to a Catholic
education hesitates about the answer. On Holy Thursday,
the night before Jesus died.

When was the Sacrament of Penance instituted ? There
is reason to fear that this is a question rarely asked, and
still more rarely answered. Nevertheless it has been fully
examined and discussed by a host of Catholic writers and
scholars, whose opinion, though not solemnly endorsed by
the Catholic Church, it is quite safe to follow.

The great Sacrament of resurrection from sin was
instituted on the first Easter Sunday, the very day of the
resurrection of our Lord from the grave. The event took
place at one of the apparitions of the Risen Christ to His
disciples.

We cannot possibly discuss here the intricate and
almost interminable question of the place, time, and
manner of these many apparitions. Enough to say that
the order of the Easter Sunday apparitions, as laid down by

St. Augustine, and followed by the great Jesuit commentator, Maldonatus, is the most probable conjecture ever advanced on the subject.

FIVE APPARITIONS ON EASTER SUNDAY

According to this well-established view, our Lord appeared no fewer than five times on the day of His Resurrection :—[1]

1. In the early morning to Mary Magdalen, the penitent sinner, when He said, ' Mary,' and she said ' Rabboni,' or ' Master ' (John xx. 16). She was undoubtedly the first to arrive at the open tomb (Mark xvi. 9), and she had her reward.

2. The same morning early, to the holy women who had come with spices to anoint His body, and were returning heavy-hearted from the empty tomb, when they met Him alive, 'and took hold of His feet, and adored Him' (Matt. xxviii. 9).

3. The same day, He appeared to Simon Peter, as the disciples told the two late arrivals, ' The Lord hath truly risen and hath appeared to Simon ' (Luke xxiv. 34).

4. That afternoon to the two disciples on the Emmaus road, when their hearts burned within them at the words of the Stranger, till at length they recognised Him ' in the breaking of bread ' (Luke xxiv. 35).

5. Late that evening to all the Apostles, except St. Thomas, and to some other disciples who were gathered together like scared sheep, ' for fear of the Jews ' (John xx. 19).

This last is the apparition that concerns us, for it was on this occasion that the Holy Sacrament of Penance was instituted.

This is not the place to examine fully the question of the identity of the apparition in John xx. with the one recorded in Luke xxiv. Suffice it to say that the best authorities are satisfied that it is so.

---

[1] There is no need of any written record to confirm us in the pious belief that He appeared to His Mother. Those who entertain any doubt of it, are met by St. Ignatius of Loyola in his *Spiritual Exercises*, with, " Are ye also without understanding?" (Matt. xv. 16).

THE COMPANY AND CONVERSATION

The Apostles were huddled together in some out-of-the-way room, and had taken every precaution to conceal their place of retreat. They would seem not even to have laid in any store of provisions, for our Lord had occasion to ask if they had anything to eat in the house (Luke xxiv. 41), and all they could produce was a boiled fish and a honeycomb. Their hearts were full of the events of the past few days, and they had much to speak about in sad and solemn tones. The one engrossing topic was, of course, the Passion and Death of the Master, and the rumoured Resurrection, which they were far from believing. Their unbelief they excused to themselves, on the hollow plea that the first bearers of the news were women, and they were half-witted creatures (Luke xxiv. 11). But it would not be fair to say that *all* of them disbelieved. One at least did not, and that was Peter. Peter, whose mouth was ever near his heart, had been telling his sceptical companions òf his vision of the Risen Master, and no doubt he argued vehemently for the reality of the Resurrection, but the majority remained unconvinced.

There was another person present who could hardly have disbelieved at this stage. It was John. Like his Divine Master, the virgin-disciple loved the penitent Magdalen, and believed her story. When she ran back in breathless haste to tell of her discovery of the empty tomb, she made her way to Peter and John ; and John in his Gospel not only emphasizes the fact of the apparition to her, but lingers with loving minuteness on that scene, when Mary sat, her head buried in her lap, weeping bitterly, and Jesus disguised as a gardener, came noiselessly behind her, and asked her the cause of her grief (John xx. 15). On the strength of her word, Peter and John flew to the grave, but none of the rest stirred. And they were unbelieving still, as they sat together that Sunday night, especially Thomas, who seems to have left the room in a sullen mood and gone out.[1]

---

[1] St. Thomas made his act of faith, a week after, that is, on the first Low Sunday (John xx. 28).

Such was the company and such the frame of mind of these frightened and shepherdless sheep, when a stealthy knock was heard at the fast-closed door. Were they discovered? Was the Jewish police upon them? For a moment there was consternation and silence. But a friendly voice without soon re-assured them. Then, unbarring the door, they welcomed back the two disciples who had been that evening to Emmaus, and had had the unspeakable consolation of a long walk and conversation with their Risen Lord. Before they had time to recount their own experiences, the eleven and the rest told them of the apparition to Peter (Luke xxiv. 34). Then came the turn of the new-comers, and they told their story excitedly: how the Lord had joined them on the road, and spoken to them so sweetly, and tarried with them, and broken bread with them, and vanished (Luke xxiv. 35).

JESUS IN THEIR MIDST

At that moment—no one knew how, for the doors and windows were fast shut—Jesus Himself stood in their midst, and greeted them, saying, ' Peace be to you' (John xx. 19). Almost beside themselves with terror, they shrank from the sight, and thought it was a ghost (Luke xxiv. 37).

And here we may pause to note the loving condescension of our Lord. Just now the great danger for His Apostles was, that they should cease to think Him a man at all. In presence of this marvel of His power, when He passed inside, through the closed door, it was easier to believe Him God than man, and easiest of all to call Him a phantom or ghost. His whole efforts were now directed to prove to the startled company, that He was the very same Jesus they had known in the flesh, and going round from one to another, He said smilingly, at the sight of their dismay, ' Why are ye troubled, and why do thoughts arise in your hearts? See My hands and My feet, that it is I myself. Handle and see.' And He would seem to have stretched out His hands to be touched, and his feet to be viewed. Then calling attention to His very unghostly appearance,

He added, ' A spirit hath not flesh and bones, as ye see Me to have ' (Luke xxiv. 39).

Even this device of His love did not quite succeed. The disciples failed to draw the conclusion He wanted, and, we are told, they could hardly believe their eyes (Luke xxiv. 41). They were half distraught 'twixt joy and fear. So our Lord had recourse to another proof of the reality of His risen Humanity. He sat Him down in their midst, and complained half playfully, that they had offered Him no hospitality. Ghosts could not eat, but He could. Instantly they were on their feet to get Him all they had. It was only a bit of a fish and a honey-comb (Luke xxiv. 42). And sitting at table, with every troubled eye bent on Him, He was seen to eat of the frugal fare and to relish it. Then He bethought Him of their possible hunger, and perhaps—we do not know for certain—wrought once more the old familiar miracle of multiplying food, for He took what was left on the dish, and passed it round (Luke xxiv. 43).

BELIEF AND CALM

The little company was much calmer now. At last they believed.

Just before the institution of the Holy Eucharist, a similar calm had reigned, for Judas, the one disturbing element, had gone out,[1] and only friends were left. So now, the one unbelieving Apostle was away, and Jesus knew that He had none but believers before Him.

His first appearance in the room had given rise to a scene of wild confusion and panic. But for the barred door, the Apostles would have probably fled in abject terror from the ' ghost.' But now had he not *proved* that He was the selfsame Master they had known and loved so well, the same voice, the same face ; above all, the same tender compassion ? The word ' Peace be to you ' had not taken effect at once, but now it was bearing fruit, and the great Sacrament of Reconciliation was ushered in by a repetition of the soothing phrase (John xx. 21), and the tossing waves

---

[1] The more general opinion among the best modern commentators.

of doubt sank to rest, and the hearts of the listeners
became as a smooth sunlit sea, with the music of His words
floating over all.

SENT BY THE FATHER AND SENDING HIS APOSTLES

' As the Father hath sent Me, so send I you " (John
xx. 21). The intention the Father had in sending His Son,
was the same as Christ had in sending His Apostles. What
the Father intended is clear from the statement of Christ to
Nicodemus, ' God hath so loved the world as to give His
only-begotten Son, that whosoever believeth in Him may
not perish, but may have life everlasting ' (John iii. 16).
He was sent, and He came, ' not to judge the world, but that
the world might be saved by Him ' (John iii. 17). His
mission was ' to seek and to save that which was lost '
(Luke xix. 10). That work was done, as far as in Him lay,
and His Father was well pleased with it, and He now sent
for Him to return to His bosom with the glorified Humanity
He had taken up. In the strength of His Godhead, the
Man Christ Jesus had done the work God gave Him to do,
and it was now time to go back whence He came.

And was His work to vanish with Himself? He took
heed that it should not. Full well He knew the nature of
man, and saw that unless His work remained visible, it
would be practically lost on the world, and unless the power
to do that work were lodged in visible men, it would be
accounted by the world as badly done; that is, without
lasting fruit, that is, hardly done at all. So He cast about
for men, and He found them, and He, the God-Man, was
now about to commission men, mere men, to carry on
His work; not to add to the efficacy of His all-abounding
Redemption, but to apply its fruits, even to the end of the
world. And this they were to do, not in their own strength,
which was nought, but in His, and His strength is then
most enhanced and glorified, when the instruments it uses
are weakest.

Redemption is a rescue from something evil, and a
restoration to something good. The one evil that Christ

came to save us from, is sin; the one great good He gives us, is grace; and the Apostles now gathered round Him at table, are to be sent as He was sent, to save men from the yoke of sin and to re-instate them in grace.

THE BREATHING ON THE APOSTLES

Emboldened by gratified curiosity and growing comfort, they now clustered round Him, and began to find utterance for their thoughts. But they were soon hushed to silence. Rising from table and bending over them, He breathed upon them, saying: 'Receive ye the Holy Ghost: whose sins ye shall forgive, they are forgiven them, and whose sins ye shall retain they are retained' (John xx. 23). And the inspired words rise to the mind: 'And the Lord God breathed into his face the breath of life, and man became a living soul' (Gen. ii. 7).

Being in the state of grace, the Apostles were already in possession of the Holy Ghost. Where there is a soul in grace, there the Holy Ghost, Himself inseparable from His gift, abides. What then is the meaning of this new infusion of the Spirit by the mouth of the Eternal Son, from whom, as from the Father, the Holy Ghost proceeds? The Holy Spirit is given not only for purposes of personal sanctification, but for the profit of others. No doubt the Apostles at this solemn moment felt a stirring in the heart, and were endowed with a higher degree of sanctifying grace than before. But their own sanctification was not the primary object of our Lord in this sacred rite. The Holy Ghost was being given them, to have and to hold for a special use, in their ministrations to others. As on Pentecost, the Spirit was given, bearing with Him the gift of tongues, to help to the conversion of the babel-speaking world; so He was breathed now, that the recipients should breathe Him out on others, unto the remission of sins.

It was our Lord's design and will that these men should go about the world dispensing this gift in His name, and in the strength of the Spirit that filled them forgiving the sins of the children of men. They were to breathe the words

of absolution on the dead soul of the sinner, and the
Holy Ghost, who was in that breath, would raise the dead
to life.

THE HUMAN AGENTS OF DIVINE PARDON

But our Lord does not choose to dwell here on the inner
working of the Spirit. He is concerned just now only with
the human agents or instruments of justification, not with
its principal cause. The agents are denoted by the one
word *ye*. 'Whose sins *ye* shall forgive.' For the moment,
Christ keeps Himself and His Spirit in the background.
He does not say, 'I shall forgive or retain.' He does not
even introduce the word 'Heaven,' as He did in the great
foreshadowing of the institution of the Sacrament of Penance,
when he said to Peter, 'Whatsoever thou shalt bind upon
earth, it shall be bound in heaven; and whatsoever thou
shalt loose on earth, it shalt be loosed in heaven' (Matt.
xvi. 19); and again, 'Whatsoever ye shall bind upon earth,
shall be bound also in heaven, and whatsoever ye shall
loose upon earth, shall be loosed also in heaven' (Matt.
xviii. 18). But at this particular juncture our Lord is
thinking of earth and sinners on earth, and their treatment
by His ministers on earth. It is *their* action He wants to
emphasize, not His own. Though it is absolutely true to
say that without Him they can do nothing, He does not say
it, but rather, '*ye* are the ones to forgive.'

Catholics are constantly using a precisely similar expression, 'the priest forgives sin,' and they have the sanction
of Jesus Christ for it. We are forgiven by our confessor,
absolved by this or that man. We say so, and we say
so rightly. It is the height of churlishness and captiousness
and hair-splitting, to insist on our adding at every turn,
'And what he has done, he has done through Jesus Christ.'
Of course he has. Who ever doubted or questioned it?
We do not insist on a child saying parenthetically, whenever
it tells of its pastimes or pleasures, 'I owe it all, you know,
to father.' We know it, and we should not like the child
the better for talking so, and the teacher who taught it this
mode of speech, we should call a 'prig.'

So much for the human agents of the Divine pardon. A word must be added as to their action in

THE REMISSION AND RETENTION OF SIN

The two actions are obviously opposite, and cannot apply to the same sin. Consequently, there must be two sets of sins, or, rather, two classes of sinners, falling under the action of the ministers of pardon. The one class is to have its sins forgiven, the other is to be sent away with its sins not forgiven.

At this point we become straightway involved in the question of justice. These two classes are meant by the God of Justice to be treated justly. He gave no commission to the Apostles to forgive all sinners indiscriminately. This would be a travesty of justice. What would be thought of the judge on the bench, who held that he was authorized by English law to let all criminals off and sentence none? Still less does our Lord empower His Apostles to bind all sinners fast, and retain all sins, no matter what the sorrow or purpose of amendment. A principle like this would be a cruel outrage to the mercy of God.

We are thus compelled to infer that Christ intended the men He armed with this tremendous power, to use it by means of a careful and judicial discrimination and sifting of the two kinds of sinners. They are not to be mixed. They are not to be taken like so many balls, and thrown into the air ; those that fall on the right to have their sins forgiven, those on the left to depart unpardoned. The evidence must be gone into. Now, there is no one to give evidence as to the state and dispositions of the sinner's soul save the sinner himself. He must speak, and all others hold their peace. His statement made, it is for the presiding judge to determine if he is to be acquitted or remanded. If the former, he is absolved by the deputy of the Supreme Judge, Jesus Christ ; if the latter, he must be told to go away unabsolved, and begged to come again in a better frame of mind.

And this, very briefly, is *Confession.* ' Whose sins ye shall forgive, they are forgiven ; whose sins ye shall retain, they are retained.'

But fuller inquiry must be made about the class that has its sins *retained*. They fall naturally into two subdivisions. Thus we shall have in all three classes of sinners :— (1) Those who have received absolution or acquittal at the hands of the deputy judge ; (2) those who for some reason have been refused it ; (3) those who have never asked for it, nor presented themselves at all before the tribunal. This last class, or those who shun confession, call for special notice, not only because of the largeness of their numbers, but because an examination of their position will bring out clearly the great Catholic doctrine of the *necessity of confession* for the forgiveness of grievous sins committed after Baptism.

It will be observed that practically they hardly differ from the *second* class—a very small one—who have had their sins retained by a positive denial of absolution. A parallel suggests itself readily. I may refuse an alms to an undeserving beggar, or the beggar may never come near me, nor give me the chance of refusing him. On the first hypothesis there is a distinct refusal of alms; on the second, simply the omission of the act of almsgiving. But as far as the destitute man is concerned, it is all one. In either case he goes without the alms. A difference exists between the two cases, but it is in no sense fundamental.

The man who does not apply to the penitential court for absolution is no whit better off than the one who applied and had to be refused. See what has happened to each. The penitent whose sin was retained had nothing positive done him by the confessor. The whole was a negative process. The confessor did *not* give absolution. That is the whole essence of *retention*. The priest has not attacked this sinful soul, or thrown chains about it, or wound them round it, or drawn them tight, or rivetted them. Sin is the only bond wherewith it is bound. It is a chain of the sinner's own forging. No one has tied him up but himself. *Retention*, therefore, is no binding, or shackling, or hand-cuffing. It is only the negative of the positive act of *loosing* or absolving.

And what has befallen the sinner of the *third* class, who

never applied for priestly absolution? He is in precisely the same case as his companion, who came and went away unabsolved. Neither of them is *loosed.* To the man in bad dispositions, the judge in the tribunal of confession said, ' Owing to your lack of sorrow, or unwillingness to change your course of conduct, I cannot absolve you.' To the other the priest would say, could his voice be heard, ' You have laid no statement of your case before me. I am, therefore, powerless to acquit you. Your sin remains, by no positive act of mine, but by the fact that I do not absolve you.'

If anything, the advantage is on the side of the penitent, who is dismissed, for the time being, unabsolved. The chances are, that if kindly spoken to, he will return some day in better dispositions and ask and receive absolution. And if, as all are agreed, he is bound to return, are we going to allow the other, who never came near the appointed judge, to go scot-free and obtain forgiveness in some much easier way?

But is there another way, and if there is, what is it? The remission of sins is the goal to which all sinners must tend, if they hope to see salvation. The goal is none of our making. It is set up by our Lord Jesus Christ, the one Author of the grace of pardon. Only the Giver of grace can determine the conditions on which that grace is to be given. Plainly, one of these conditions is sorrow for sin ; the other is submission of our sins to the human and sinful judge of His choice. Whose sins ye men shall forgive, they are forgiven: whose sins ye men shall retain, that is, shall not forgive, they are retained, that is, not forgiven.

A hard saying this; but those who accept it and act upon it, know by experience that the hardness is all on the surface. They have struck the richest vein in the mine of God's mercy. They have felt the sweetest balm ever prepared by the Great Physician for the cure of the sin-stricken heart of man.

MATTHEW POWER, S.J.

THE EPISCOPAL CITY OF FERNS

FERNS is one of the most ancient sees in Ireland. The name signifies 'the place of the alder-trees,' although Colgan gave it a fanciful derivation, namely, from *Fearna*, son of Carroll, Prince of the Decies, who was slain at this place by Gall, the son of Morna. However, it really dates from the close of the sixth century. Traces of St. Patrick are met with at Gorey, Limerick, Kilpipe, Kilpatrick, Rathvilly, and Donoughmore. At Rathvilly, the Apostle of Ireland baptized Mell, the wife of Criffan, King of Leinster (who was buried in the church of Sletty, Co. Carlow), and her infant son Nathi, or Dathi, King of Leinster, who died in 496; St. Canoc of Kilmuckridge, died in 501; and King Cormac MacOilioll, after a reign of nine years, abdicated in 516.

In 598, Bran Dubh, 'Black Raven,' King of Leinster, opposed the invasion of Hugh II., son of Ainmire, King of Ireland, and St. Aidan (who is variously designated Edanus, Mo-Edan, Maidoc, Maedhog, Mogue, and Moses) prayed for the success of the Leinster monarch. In thanksgiving for the victory of Dunbolg, King Bran Dubh convened a Synod of the clergy of Leinster in 599, with the result that St. Aidan was made *Ardespoc*, or Archbishop of Leinster. The monarch assigned him *Fearna*, or Ferns, then a district celebrated for its alder trees, for the site of his future cathedral, 'which thus became the episcopal city of Ferns in Hy-Kinsellagh.'

Bran Dubh was slain at his royal residence in Ferns, in 605, by Saran Saebhderg, 'of the crooked, or evil, eye,' Erenach of Templeshanbo. This Saran, who was a relative of the King, experienced a terrible visitation in punishment of his crime, for we read that 'his hand was ever afterwards withered;' but he died, 'after the victory of penance, spending many years in sighs and tears at the grave of the murdered King.'

St. Aidan is said to have founded thirty churches in the County Wexford—his chief architect being the famous St. Gobban Saer—and he died at Ferns, January 31st, 632 The memory of the first bishop and patron of the diocese of Ferns is perpetuated in the names Tubber Mogue, Boola-vogue, Cromogue, Island Mogue, Coolatin, and Ballyedan, whilst his bell and shrine (*Breacc Maedoig*) are to be seen in the National Museum, Dublin. For four centuries and more, after his death, the place was known as *Fearna Mor Maedhog.*

Archdall made some surprising blunders in regard to several monasteries in County Wexford; but, perhaps, none more so than his brief reference to Clone, which was founded by St. Aidan. Clone is only a short distance from Ferns, of which it is still a prebend, and its architectural features have been frequently described. He writes as follows :—

The Abbey of DOWNE [of course this is a copyist's error for the ancient spelling *Clowne*, but Archdall was ignorant of the identity], six miles north of Enniscorthy. in the barony of Scara-walsh, and seated on the river Derrihy, which meeting the Boro [*sic*] falls into the Slaney, was founded for Regular Canons before the arrival of the English. It existed at the time of the general suppression, when by an Inquisition taken on the Feast of St. Katherine the Virgin, &c.

Anyone who knows the topography of County Wexford is aware that it is the river Bann, or Banna (so celebrated in the song, ' As down by Banna's banks I strayed,' by the Right Hon. George Ogle), which flows near Ferns, and joins the picturesque Slaney not far from Scarawalsh Bridge. And, in connection with this notice of Archdall, I may· add that the late Father Denis Murphy, S.J., was unable to identify *Downe*,[1] but an examination of the sixteenth century Inquisition settles the matter, as I shall explain in its proper place.

In 650, the Lord of Hy-Kinsellagh—that is, the district

---

[1] The little river Derry, a name I suspect to be a corruption of *Dearg*, the ruddy-coloured stream, in contrast with the name *Bau* = the fair river, flows by the ruined churchyard of Clone. In the succeeding ages, the old wattle church was replaced by a more substantial structure of stone and mortar.

which embraced the present Co. Wexford, as well as portions of Carlow and Wicklow—went the way of all flesh. St. Dachu, or Mochua Luachra, second Bishop of Ferns, departed this life June 22nd, 653, after whom came Bishop Tuenoc (653-662). Faelan, son of Colman, King of Leinster, died in 665; and the *obit* of Bishop Maeldoghar is chronicled in 677, followed by that of Bishop Diorath on July 27th, 690.

The great St. Moling Luachra entered on the episcopal office in 690, and ruled till his death, May 13th, 697.[1] To the antiquarian, among the greatest art treasures of Ireland is the venerable book shrine of the Gospels of St. Moling, which has been fully described by Cardinal Moran, Miss Stokes, and others. The *Yellow Book of St. Moling*, referred to by the learned Dr. Geoffrey Keating, has unfortunately disappeared. To the historian, the principal event of this period is the remission of the Boromean tribute by King Finnachta ' the Hospitable,' at the request of our saint in 692. The place-names Timoling (Co. Kildare), St. Mullin's (correctly *Teach-Moling*, Co. Carlow), Camolin, Monamoling, &c., still survive; and, until recently there were some fragments of the ruins of St. Moling's monastery on the Norrismount Estate, near Camolin.

After the death of Cillene, seventh Bishop of Ferns, in 714, Aireachtagh MacCuana succeeded to the vacant see, and, in a few years later Feargall, King of Ireland, claimed the Boromean tribute. This monarch invaded Leinster, then governed by Murchadh MacBran, and a great battle was fought at Allen, Co. Kildare, in which the Ard Righ was completely routed, December 13th, 722. Faelan O'Byrne, eighteenth king of Leinster, died in 737, ' after a well-spent life.'

The ancient monastery of Ferns included a number of cells or oratories, and the Cathedral was built in the Irish style. Under date of 745 we read of the death of Seachnasach, Lord of Hy Kinsellagh. Bishop MacCuana died in 741, and his successor, Breasil MacColgan, in 748,

---

[1] The festival of St. Moling is celebrated on June 17th.

whereupon Ksoddaidh was elected, who ruled till 763. At the Battle of Ferns in 768 Dubhchalgach, son of Lynam, was slain.

Under date of 773 we find recorded the death of Imraiteach of *Gleann-Cloitigh*, anchorite, *i. e.*, of the Valley of the Clody, near Bunclody, now known as Newtownbarry. In 778 Edersgel, son of Aedh, Lord of Hy-Kinsellagh died ; and in the same year Clonmore Maedhog near Rathvilly, was burned. Among the *obits* for the year 781 are those of Dubhinracht MacFergus, Bishop of Ferns, and the Abbot of Inch, near Gorey. Bishop Cronin departed this life in 789, and the episcopate of his successor, Finnachta, lasted till 799.

Finsneachta, King of Leinster, died at Kildare, in 808, and in the following year a faction fight took place in Hy-Kinsellagh, in which Ceallach MacDonnghall was slain. The demise of Cillene, Bishop of Ferns, occurred in 815 ; and, in 816, a battle was fought between the people of Taghmon, led by Cathal MacDunlaing, Lord of Hy-Kinsellagh, and those of Ferns, in which four hundred of the laity, and some of the clergy, were slain. In 826 the Danes were defeated by Cairbre MacCathal, Lord of Hy-Kinsellagh, and the men of Tagmon ; but in 834 the Norsemen plundered Ferns. On Christmas night of the year 835, ' the foreigners burned Clonmore Maedhog, killing many of the monks, and bringing away many captives.' The Danes again plundered Ferns in 836, and they burned it in 838.

Cairbre MacCathal, Lord of Hy-Kinsellagh, died in 842 ; and his successor, Echtighern, ' was treacherously slain by the foreigners ' in 851 ; but, a week later, his death was avenged by his own people. The next occupant of the Lordship, Ceallach MacGuire, died in 856. On the demise of Finncallagh, Bishop of Ferns, in 860, Dermot succeeded and ruled till 869.[1]

In 864 Tadhg, son of Dermot, Lord of Hy-Kinsellagh,

[1] Lewis says that after the year 814, there was an interregnum in the see or a hundred years, after which ' it was governed by Laidgnen, under the title of *Comorban*, who died in 937.' This statement is truly ludicrous, inasmuch as the regular successions of bishops was maintained, and the title *Comorban* means simply ' the successor ' of St. Mogue, generally written Coarb.

was slain by his own brethren, a fate which, four years later was shared by his successor, Donegan.   Under date of 875 the Irish Annals chronicle the death of ' Lachtnan, son of Moichtighearn, Bishop of Kildare, and Abbot of Ferns ;' and, in 876, Cairbre MacDermot, Lord of Hy-Kinsellagh, was slain by his own brethren.'

Fearghal, Bishop of Ferns, died in 882; and ten years later we read of the death of Riagan MacEchtighern, Lord of Hy-Kinsellagh.   In 904 died Lachtnan, Bishop of Ferns, and he was succeeded by Lynam.   From the *Four Masters* we learn that, in 905, ' Ciarodhar, son of Crunnmhael, Lord of Hy-Felimy [the present barony of Ballaghkeene] was slain.'   In 908 Cormac MacCullenan, Archbishop of Cashel and King of Munster, declared war against the province of Leinster, and the battle was fought at Ballaghmoon, near Old Leighlin, on August 16th, the Archbishop, as also Carroll, son of Muiregan, King of Leinster, being amongst the slain.   This Carroll was the last monarch who resided at Naas, Co Kildare.

Aedh, son of Dubhgilla, Lord of Idrone and Tanist of Hy-Kinsellagh, was slain in 910, and was interred at Ferns. The city of St. Mogue was devastated by the Danes, in 917, and again in 920, 928, and 930.   Cinaedh, son of Cairbre, Lord of Hy-Kinsellagh, was slain by the Danes of Wexford, in 935.   Ferns was burned in 937, and in the following year died Lynam, ' Bishop of Ferns and Abbot of Tallaght.' His successor, Flathghus, ruled from 938 to 945.   Under date of 947 we read that ' Bran MacMaelmurry, King of Leinster, and Ceallach MacKenny, Lord of Hy-Kinsellagh, were slain by the Ossorians.

In 953 King O'Toole joined Aulaf *Cuaran*, or the Crooked, in plundering Inis Damhle (Inch, near Gorey), and Inis Uladh (near Donard, Co. Wicklow) ; and, in 956 he defeated the forces of Hy-Kinsellagh.   Dunlaing O'Donegan, Abbot of Inch and Taghmon, died in 954; and in 957 the demise is chronicled of Finnachta, son of Lachtnan, Erenach of Ferns.   Under date of 966 we find the *obit* of Cairbre, son of Lynam, Abbot of Ferns and Timoling (St. Mullin's).   In 977 Conaing, son of Cathan, Bishop of Ferns, went the way of all flesh ; and in 980 Donald *Claen*, King of Leinster, was ransomed from the Danes.   Conn O'Lynam who entered on the episcopal rule of Ferns in 977, died ' after a well-spent life ' in 996.

At this epoch, and for fifty years subsequently, various Celtic crosses were erected in Ferns ; but, owing to a piece of vandalism that cannot be too strongly deprecated, many of them were used in the construction of the boundary wall near the town where they are still to be seen.   Two, at least, of those sculptural crosses seem to date from the early portion of the seventh century.   There were also ancient crosses ot Clone ; but, alas ! they have disappeared within the present century.

The Four Masters, under date of 1003, chronicle the fact that ' Aedh [Hugh], son of Echtighern, was slain in the monastery of Ferns, by Donnchadh, surnamed Mael-na-mbo, King of Leinster ;" and, in 1005, Mael-na-mbo, Lord of Hy-Kinsellagh was killed by his own people.   As a set-off to this, there is an agreeable entry for the year 1030, which is as follows :—' Tadhg, son of Lorcan, Lord of Hy-Kinsellagh, died on his pilgrimage at Glendalough.'

Donnchadh, son of Brian, sacked Clonmore Maedhog in 1040, and Ferns in 1042 ; but those deeds were avenged by Dermot, son of Maelnambo, King of Leinster. This monarch, in 1042, gave a charter by which the Abbey of Taghmon, so famed for its university, was constituted a cell to the Abbey of Ferns, and at the same time he bestowed on the monks ' the chapel of St. Mary, together with the land of Ballygeary and all its fisheries.'

Conor O'Lynam, Bishop of Ferns, died in 1043, and was succeeded by Dermot O'Rodachain, whose demise is chronicled in 1050. In 1051 the two Saxon princes, Harold and Leofwin, sons of Earl Godwin of Kent, fled to Ireland, and remained during the winter at Ferns Castle, as the guests of King Dermot.   There is an entry in the *Four Masters*, under date of 1052, to the effect that Bran MacMaelmordha, the deposed King of Leinster (whose eyes had been put out by Sitric, the Dane, in 1019), ' died in religion at Cologne.'

St. Peter's Church, Ferns, dates from about the year 1055, as may be judged by the chancel arch. It is of the Hiberno-Romanesque style, and was built by Bishop Murchadh O'Lynam, who 'slept in the Lord' in the year 1062. The reader who is anxious to learn of its architectural features may well peruse an interesting article on the subject which appeared in the *New Ireland Review* from the pen of the Rev. J. M. F. ffrench.[1]

King Dermot became supreme monarch of Ireland in 1064; but, at length, was killed at the battle of Odhbha, 'on Tuesday, the 7th of the Ides of February,' 1072. The great fair of Wexford was celebrated by Conor O'Conor Faly, in 1079, to prove his claim to the sovereignty of Leinster. In 1085 Ugaire O'Lynam, Erenach of Ferns died; and in 1089 O'Conor Faly killed Donnchadh O'Murphy, Lord of the Hy-Kinsellagh. Two years later his successor, Enda, was slain by his own people.

Cairbre O'Kearney, 'the noble Bishop of Ferns,' died of the plague, in 1095. The next local entry of importance is in 1106, when Donnchadh, Lord of Hy-Kinsellagh, was slain in battle. In 1117 died Ceallach O'Colman, Bishop of Ferns; and, under date of 1125, we find recorded the death of his successor, Maeleoinn O'Donegan, who is described as 'a paragon of wisdom, and Bishop of Wexford.'

MacMuirgheasa, Lector of Ferns, departed this life in 1129; and, in 1135, Bishop O'Cathan, who is designated 'Archbishop of Hy-Kinsellagh,' was gathered to his fathers. Dermot MacMurrough, King of Leinster, who, after the death of his wife, Cacht O'More, married Mor, sister of St. Laurence O'Toole, founded various religious houses between the years 1146 and 1152, including the Cistercian Abbey of Baltinglass, the Nunneries of St. Mary le Hogges, Dublin; Kilclehin, or *de Bello Portu*, near Waterford; and Athaddy, Co. Carlow, for canonesses of the Order of Aroaise. Yet, notwithstanding this apparent zeal for religion, we find the Leinster monarch plundering various churches in 1151 and 1152; and, in 1154, he burned the monasteries

---

[1] Vol. iii., No. 1, March, 1895.

and city of Ferns. In the latter year, through jealousy of the growing power of Tiernan O'Rourke, Prince of Breffni, and meeting with no opposition from the Princess herself, he carried off the mature Dervorgilla [2] from her husband's roof, and brought her to his fortress in Ferns. Soon after, King Turlogh O'Connor came and destroyed Ferns Castle, bringing back with him the Princess, whom he left as a lady boarder in the Convent of St. Bridget at Kildare.

Turlogh O'Connor died in 1156, and was succeeded by Murty O'Loughlin, to whom Dermot submitted, and was restored to his rightful sovereignty. O'Loughlin was slain in 1159, whereupon Roderic O'Connor ascended the throne of Ireland. In 1161 'a victory was gained by Donal *Kavanagh* [so called from having been fostered in *Cill-Coemhgen*, now Kilcavan, near Gorey], son of MacMurrogh, and the people of Hy-Kinsellagh, against the foreigners of Wexford, where many were slain, together with O'Donnell.'

Dermot re-founded the venerable monastery of Ferns at the close of 1160, or early in 1161, for Regular Canons of St. Augustine, and it was dedicated to the Blessed Virgin. Archdall incorrectly gives 1166 as the year of this foundation, but a glance at the names of the subscribing witnesses to the charter confirms the fact that we must date it as 1160, or certainly not later than 1161. Ware and Harris say 1158, but this cannot be so, inasmuch as one of those names appended to the charter is Malachy O'Byrne, Bishop of Kildare, who only began to rule in 1160; whilst another is Laurence, Abbot of Glendalough, who was elevated to the see of Dublin in 1162.

By the terms of the foundation charter, the monks were endowed—

With so much lands of Ballysisin and Ballilacussa as would form the site of a village; Borin, Roshena, and Kilbridy for two

---

[1] Dervorgilla was then in her forty-fifth year, whilst Dermot was about sixty-four. In accordance with the enactments of the Brehon Code of Laws, this 'Helen of Ireland' brought with her to Ferns 'her cattle, her furniture, and the valuables which constituted her dowry.' At the consecration of the grand Cistercian Abbey Church of Mellifont, in 1157, she gave an offering of pure gold, as also 'a gold chalice for the Lady Altar, sacred vestments, and other ecclesiastial furniture for each of the nine other altars that were in the church.' She died at Mellifont, in 1193, aged eighty-four.

villages ; and the lands of Ballyfislan, in Fotherth, near Wexford, and those of Munemothe in Ferneghenal ; also a cell at Thamoling, being the chapel of St. Mary ; the lands of Ballygery, with all its fisheries, and his own chapelry, together with the tithes and first-fruits of the demesne of Perhukensilich, and a scaith or flaggon out of every brewing of ale in Ferns ; the cell of Finnachta in Ferns aforesaid, and the lands of Balliculum and Balinafusin, with three acres adjoining the said cell.

In fulfilment of a vow made during a severe illness, Dermot founded the Priory of All Hallows, College-green, Dublin, early in 1166. Enna Kinsellagh, the only legitimate son of the Leinster monarch, was blinded by MacGillapatrick, Prince of Ossory, at the close of the same year. MacMurrough sailed for Bristol in August, 1167, where having tarried for some days he crossed to France to solicit the aid of Henry II. The English King had already obtained, by a base lie, a Bull from Pope Adrian IV. authorizing him to look after the interests of religion in Ireland, and he issued letters patent to all his liege subjects to further the cause of the Leinster sovereign.

King Dermot, accompanied by his secretary, Maurice Regan, and a pioneer force of Galls, or foreigners, arrived at Glascarrig, Co. Wexford, at the close of the year 1168, and remained shut up in the monastery of Ferns during the Christmas and Spring. In February, 1169, Roderic O'Connor and Tiernan O'Rourke marched to Ferns, upon which Dermot fled. After a few skirmishes, the King of Leinster made complete submission to the Irish monarch, in March, only asking for permission to hold ten cantreds of land in Ferns, and offering seven hostages to Roderic, as also 100 ounces of gold to O'Rourke. The two kings then departed, but, almost immediately, Dermot despatched Maurice Regan to Wales, to hasten the coming of the Welsh Knights.

On May 11th, 1169, Robert FitzStephen and Maurice Prendergast, with an army of three hundred archers, thirty knights, and sixty men-at-arms, landed at Bannow, Co. Wexford; and a second contingent arrived the day following, headed by Maurice FitzGerald, accompanied by Hervey de Monte-marisco, Meyler FitzHenry, Milo de Cogan, David

Barry, and other adventurers. On May 15th, Dermot joined his new allies, and, on the following day, the combined troops marched to Wexford. ' On their way they were joined by Dermot's illegitimate son, Donald Kavanagh, with 500 Irishmen.' The Wexford inhabitants, aided by the Danes, repulsed the enemy ; but, three days afterwards, offered to surrender, promising to renew their allegiance to Dermot. The Leinster sovereign then granted the lordship of the city, with the adjoining cantreds of Forth and Bargy, to FitzStephen and FitzGerald, whilst he gave Hervey de Montemarisco two cantreds lying between Wexford and Waterford. ' Dermot then led his allies to his city of Ferns, where the soldiers were rested, and the knights feasted for three weeks.'

After a successful raid on Ossory, Dermot again retired to Ferns, where he spent the Christmas of the year 1169. Raymond *le Gros* landed near Waterford, May 1st, 1170, with a force of one hundred and thirty knights and archers ; and, on August 23rd, the celebrated Richard de Clare, Earl of Pembroke, better known as Strongbow, disembarked at Waterford with about two thousand men. The old city by the Suir was taken on August 25th, and immediately afterwards the nuptials were celebrated between the Norman widower de Clare and Eva, the beautiful young daughter of Dermot MacMurrough. The newly-married pair then proceeded to Ferns, where they spent the honeymoon. Dublin was captured on September 21st, but was retaken by the Anglo-Irish during the Whitsuntide of 1171. An old Norman chronicler tells us that Donald Kavanagh, in command of the Co. Wexford troops, ably seconded the efforts of Raymond le Gros on this occasion, ' who continually invoked his patron St. David, highly venerated by the Wexford allies as the instructor of St. Mogue.'

In October, 1170, Roderic O'Connor, who, by the Treaty of Ferns, had been given Conor and Art na n Gall, the son and grandson of the King of Leinster, and the son of his foster brother, O'Kelly, as hostages, remonstrated with Dermot for his flagrant violation of the conditions agreed on, and threatened to execute the princes in case of non-compliance. The Leinster monarch laughed at the royal message, and the result was that the three hostages were put to death at Athlone. Keating, however, and others say that Roderic did not put his threat into execution.

Dermot MacMurrough[1] died under the most revolting circumstances at the monastery of Ferns on May 14th, 1171, and was buried 'near the shrines of St. Mogue and St. Moling.' His monument may still be seen in the grave-yard attached to the Cathedral, though some silly legend has it that he was interred at Baltinglass.

Henry II. landed at Passage, near Waterford, October 18th, 1171, with a large force, and having remained during the winter in Dublin, spent the six weeks of Lent at Selskar (St. Sepulchre) Abbey, Wexford, and sailed from Wexford Haven on Easter Monday, April 17th, 1172. After the departure of the English king, Strongbow retired to Ferns ; and in June was celebrated the marriage of the Earl's natural daughter to Robert de Quincey, Constable and Standard-Bearer of Leinster, who was assigned by his father-in-law the district known as the Duffrey—so familiar to the denizens of Enniscorthy.

The Irish Annals, under date of 1172, chronicle the death of Brighdian O'Cathan, Abbot of Ferns.[2] In October, 1174, Raymond le Gros was married to Basilia, sister of Strongbow, at Selskar Abbey, and was assigned the lands of Fethard, Idrone, and Glascarrig. Richard de Clare died June 1st, 1176 ; and in the following year we read that William FitzAdelm de Burgo[3] seized on the Castle of Wicklow, which belonged to Maurice FitzGerald. This De Burgo had been given Ferns by Henry II., and, as a set-off for said annexation, he gave the three sons of that first Geraldine, namely, William, Gerald, and Alexander, the Cathedral City of Ferns. 'These brothers, wishing to

---

[1] Murty MacMurrough, nephew of King Dermot, Lord of Hy-Kinsellagh, and ancestor of the MacDamores, died in 1193.

[2] Lanigan says that he was Bishop of Ferns, but resigned the see in 1150, whereupon Joseph O'Hea succeeded.

[3] De Burgo died January 8th, 1205.

render their new establishment secure, began to build a castle, which was immediately demolished by Walter Allemand [FitzAdelm's nephew, and a man of obscure origin], who has become conspicuous through the influence of his uncle, who committed to him the government of Wexford.'

In 1178, Robert le Poer, Lord of Waterford, sent troops to pillage the territory north of Ferns, 'whence they returned to Wexford loaded with booty, having assassinated Dunlaing O'Toole, Lord of Imayle.' We are told that Walter Allemand, who was Seneschal of Wexford in 1178, 'received bribes from the Murrahoos [Murphys] of Hy-Kinsellagh to prejudice the FitzGeralds;' but in the summer of 1179, Raymond le Gros was restored to his old position as Governor of Wexford town and castle.

The Venerable Joseph O'Hea, Bishop of Ferns, whose name appears as witness to the foundation charter of Dunbrody Abbey, died, full of years, in 1184, after a rule of sixty years. His memory has been traduced by writers who follow the calumnious statement of Harris in regard to the siege of Wexford; but, as Lanigan rightly observes, the honest Ware does not mention the fable. The see of Ferns was then offered to Giraldus Cambrensis, the Munchausen of the Barry family; but that astute cleric, having more ambitious views in his mind, declined it. At the close of the year 1185, Albin O'Molloy, Cistercian Abbot of Baltinglass, was appointed bishop; and most readers are familiar with the scathing rebuke he administered to the aforesaid Archdeacon Gerald Barry (at the Provincial Council of Dublin, held during the Lent of 1187), who presumed to asperse the character of the Irish clergy. Bishop O'Molloy was present at the coronation of Richard I., September 3rd, 1189. On April 3rd, 1206, King John signified his wish for the promotion of this worthy prelate to the Archbishopric of Cashel; but the Pope declined to ratify the appointment. In the same year the King confirmed Philip Prendergast in the lordship of Enniscorthy and the barony of Daffryn, or of the district called 'the Duffry,' ' the black, turfy land.'

Bishop O'Molloy, on September 15th, 1215, received letters of protection from King John, *en route* for the fourth General Council of Lateran, at which he assisted.   In 1218 the see of Ferns was forcibly deprived of two manors by William Marshall, Earl of Pembroke, who, as a consequence, was excommunicated by the Bishop. He died under anathema, and was buried in the Temple Church, London, on Ascension Thursday, 1219. Three years later Bishop O'Molloy passed to his eternal reward, after a rule of over thirty-four years.

John St. John, Treasurer of Ireland, who, in 1217, had been given a royal grant of the Manor of Newcastle Lyons, at an annual rental of 100 marks, was appointed to the see of Ferns at the close of the year 1222, and was assigned a pension of £40 yearly out of the said lands. The present Castle of Ferns was built about this time (some say by William Marshall, in 1216), and the Bishop took up his residence therein. On July 7th, 1225, the King sent him an order concerning fairs and markets.

Bishop St. John assigned the manor of Enniscorthy to Philip Prendergast and his wife, Maude de Quincey, on April 8th, 1227, 'in exchange for six ploughlands for ever to the Bishop and Chapter of Ferns, so that the said Philip and his wife might hold the said town of Enniscorthy as a lay fee for ever to them and their heirs.' Five of these ploughlands were situated in Ballyregan, and one near Clone, which had been held by the FitzHenrys. From official records we learn that, on September 6th, 1232, Henry III. granted the office of Treasurer of Ireland to Peter de Rievaulx, and ordered the Bishop of Ferns to deliver up the said office to him.

On the 1st of April, 1234, Richard Marshall, Earl of Pembroke, was basely set upon in an ambuscade on the Curragh of Kildare by some of the Anglo-Norman nobles,

---

[1] William Marshall founded Tintern Abbey, Co. Wexford, in fulfilment of a vow, in 1200, and peopled it with Cistercians from Tintern, Monmouthshire, with John Torrell as first abbot. The name ' John Torellus' appears in a deed of 1248. William, second Earl Marshall, who did much for the commerce of New Ross, was appointed Lord Justice of Ireland in 1224, but was replaced by Geoffrey de Marisco on July 4th, 1226.

'and he died on Palm Sunday, the sixteenth day after he had been mortally wounded,' being interred in the Black Abbey, Kilkenny.   He was succeeded in the title and estates by his brother Gilbert, in reference to whom we find a letter, printed in Theiner's *Vetera Monumenta*, dated June 18th, 1235, wherein Pope Gregory IX. places all the property of the Pembroke family in Ireland and Wales under the special protection of the Holy See.   This Earl died childless, in 1241, and was succeeded by his brother Walter.

Bishop St. John held a Synod in the Priory of SS. Peter and Paul (Selskar Abbey), Wexford, in 1240, and his death is chronicled three years later.   Walter Marshall died without issue in November, 1245, and was succeeded by his fifth and youngest brother, Anselm, who died 'on the Nones of December, after enjoying the family honours eighteen days.' In 1246 the Palatinate of Leinster was partitioned among the five sisters of Earl Anselm, in which most of the present County Wexford fell to the lot of Joan or Johanna, the daughter of Maud Marshall, who had married Warren de Monte Caniso, better known as William, 6th Earl of Warren and Surrey.   This Joan married William de Valence, who in her right, became Earl of Pembroke and Lord of Wexford. From the Patent Rolls we learn that the Wexford estates were at this date valued at £341 10s. 4d. per annum, Ferns being estimated at £91 15s., Wexford Borough at £42 1s. 5d., and Rosslare at £68 19s. 11d.

In a succeeding paper I shall treat of the varying fortunes of the city and prelates of Ferns until the sad period of the Reformation, after which the diocese became one of the poorest in Ireland.

WILLIAM H. GRATTAN FLOOD.

Notes and Queries

THEOLOGY

AN ARCHBISHOP ASSISTING AT THE MARRIAGE OF A SUBJECT OF HIS SUFFRAGAN

REV. DEAR SIR,—Can an archbishop validly assist at the marriage of parties who belong to a suffragan diocese? It has been asserted to me that he can, but I was not aware that archbishops retain any such power.

INQUIRER.

As a rule, the archbishop, as such, cannot assist at the marriage of persons belonging to the diocese of one of his suffragans. Like any bishop, the archbishop can, of course, assist at the marriage of his own subjects, but, in ordinary cases, his power ends there. In two cases, however, an archbishop gets from Canon Law the right to assist at the marriage of the subjects of his suffragan.

Matrimonio subditi suffraganeorum [Archiepiscopus assistere potest]:—(a) Quando visitat diocesim suffraganeam in casibus a jure determinatis; (b) in casu appellationis.[1]

The case brought under our correspondent's notice, was, very probably, a case of appeal. If the bishop of the parties had forbidden their marriage, and if, on appeal, the archbishop, had reversed the decision of his suffragan, the archbishop might then validly assist at the marriage, or he might delegate any priest to do so. It should be noted, however, that in the case supposed, the archbishop's power to assist at the marriage would begin only when he *had already pronounced* his sentence, and that his power would lapse, if the bishop, or one of the parties duly lodged a further appeal to the Holy See.

---

[1] *Vid.* Gasparri, ii., n. 935.

DOES DELEGATION TO ASSIST AT A MARRIAGE CEASE ON THE DEATH OF THE DELEGANS?

REV. DEAR SIR,—I was delegated by my parish priest to assist at the marriage of a parishioner, The parish priest died before the marriage came off. Would I have been justified in assisting at the marriage, as the delegate of the deceased parish priest ?

COADJUTOR.

The delegation expired with the death of the parish priest: you would not, therefore, have been justified in assisting at the marriage.

Morte parochi aut ordinarii delegantis, vel amissione officii qua cumque de causa cessat licentia [assistendi]; si mors aut amissio communiter ignoratur, delegatus [vi tituli colorati] valide assistit ; secus matrimonium est nullum.[1]

CLANDESTINE MARRIAGES WHERE THE LAW OF TRENT HAS NOT BEEN PROMULGATED

REV. DEAR SIR,—Where the law of Trent is not binding is a marriage celebrated without the presence of priest or witness lawful as well as valid ?

A. B.

A marriage contracted without the blessing of a priest and in the absence of any witness was, before the Council of Trent, and now is, where the Tridentine law has not been promulgated, valid but *per se* unlawful. For, there is, independently of the law of Trent, an obligation to have marriage blessed by a priest. If the marriage, however, be celebrated publicly, and blessed by a priest, the presence of other formal witnesses does not seem to be strictly obligatory, unless where the Tridentine law is in force.

It may be, that this question is meant to refer to the case in which, owing to public necessity, the law of Trent is said to be suspended, so that persons can validly marry without the presence of the parish priest, or of the ordinary. If so, we should reply that the marriage is, in such a case,

[1] Gasparri, ii., n. 951. Rosset, iv., n. 2242, *et seq.*

valid, and lawful in the absence of the parish priest. But it would still be obligatory to have the marriage blessed, if possible, by some priest. It would be not merely obligatory, but necessary under pain of nullity, to have the marriage celebrated, if possible, in the presence of, at least, two witnesses.[1]

D. MANNIX.

LITURGY

THE CALENDAR TO BE FOLLOWED IN THE CHAPEL OF A CONVENT, &c.

REV. DEAR SIR,—May a religious follow his own *Ordo,* when saying Mass, as chaplain or otherwise, in the private chapels of convents or hospitals?

A RELIGIOUS.

A certain ambiguity lurks in our correspondent's phrase ' private chapels.' It is not clear whether he means the principal chapels of convents and such like institutions, or other chapels, distinct and apart from the principal chapels. For the former, the principal chapels, may be called ' private chapels,' inasmuch as they are not in the full and strict sense public chapels or oratories. But so far as regard the application of the decree of December, 1895, the principal chapels of the institution which our correspondent contemplates must be regarded as public oratories. Hence the phrase ' private chapel ' when applied to a chapel of one of these institutions, means a chapel other than the principal chapel. But as we cannot be certain in which signification the phrase is understood by our correspondent, we will answer the question for both significations.

1. In strictly private chapels of convents, &c., that is, in chapels distinct from, and forming no part of, the principal chapels, every priest whether regular or secular, not only may, but must follow his own calendar. This follows from a decree of the Congregation of Rites dated May 22, 1896. The Congregation was asked if the decree of December 9,

---

[1] Rosset, *De Sacramento Martimonii,* iv. 2138, 2139.

1895, declaring that Mass should be said in conformity with the Directory of the place wherein Mass is celebrated, extended to the chapels of colleges, convents, &c. The Congregation replied in the affirmative, *dummodo agatur de capella principali quae instar oratorii publici ad effectum memorati decreti habenda est.* Hence the change introduced by the decree of December 9, 1895, regards only the principal chapels of these institutions; and consequently the rubrics regarding the Mass to be said in the other, and strictly private chapels, are the same as before the issue of this decree. But the universal rule formerly was, that in private oratories every celebrant should say Mass in conformity with his own calendar. This, then, still remains the rule for private chapels in convents and such like institutions.

2. The decree of May 22, 1896, from which we have just quoted, declares that the principal chapels in institutions, such as those about which the present question is concerned, come within the operation of the decree of December 9, 1895. Consequently all priests celebrating in one of these chapels must follow the calendar of that chapel. Whether the celebrant be a secular or a regular, he must celebrate Mass in accordance with the calendar of that chapel, and must, moreover, use the Missal used in that chapel, provided it contains a special Mass of the saint not contained in the Missal used in his own church or Order. To this rule there is only one exception. When the rite of the feast celebrated in the chapel in question is less than double, the celebrant is free to say his own Mass—a Requiem Mass or other Votive Mass. What then is the calendar for those chapels about which our correspondent inquires? With regard to the calendar to be followed in convent chapels an obvious distinction must be made. Either the nuns are bound to recite the Divine Office, or they are not. In the former case, the calendar followed by the nuns is the calendar of their chapel, and must consequently be followed by all priests celebrating Mass in their principal chapels. In the latter case, as well as in the case of the other institutions included in our correspondent's question, the chaplain's calendar is the calendar of the principal chapel—the

calendar of the institution.   Hence, if a secular priest be
the duly appointed chaplain to a convent, hospital, work-
house, &c., the calendar followed by the secular priests of
the place must be followed by all priests celebrating in the
principal chapel of the institution.   Similarly, if the chaplain
be a member of a religious Order, then the proper calendar
of the Order to which he belongs becomes the calendar of
the principal chapel, and must be followed by all priests,
whether regular or secular, celebrating therein.   These
conclusions are fully established by a reply of the Congregation of Rites, bearing date June 27, 1896.   We give
the question and reply :—

Ubi unus tantum saceredos quoad missae celebrationem addictus sit oratoriis competenti auctoritate erectis in Gymnasiis,
hospitalibus ac domibus quarumcumque piarum communitatum ;
hic si saecularis teneturne sequi calendarium diocesis in qua
extat oratorium, et si regularis calendarium ordinis si proprium
gaudet; et si aliquando celebrent extranei, hi debentne se
conformare calendario sacerdotis ejusmodi oratoriis addicti ?

Resp. Affirmative in omnibus si oratoria habenda sint ut
publica ; secus negative.

To give effect to the chaplaincy of a member of a
religious Order it is not necessary that a certain individual of the Order should be appointed by the bishop ; it
is sufficient if the duty of supplying a chaplain to the
institution be committed to the head of a religious house.

As we have travelled somewhat beyond the scope of our
correspondent's question, it will make for clearness if we
append a summary of the conclusions at which we have
arrived :—

1. A priest celebrating Mass in a private chapel of a
convent, or such like institution, should follow his own
calendar.

2. A priest celebrating in the principal chapel should
follow the calendar of the institution.

3. The calendar of the institution is the calendar of the
chaplain to the institution.

4. When the chaplain is a secular priest, all priests
celebrating in the principal chapel must follow the secular

calendar; when the chaplain is a regular, all priests must follow, in the principal chapel, the calendar of the Order to which the chaplain belongs.

THE REVERENCE TO BE MADE AT THE FOOT OF THE ALTAR AFTER THE LAST GOSPEL
THE MASS TO BE SAID AT A DEFERRED MONTH'S MEMORY

REV. DEAR SIR,—(1) A priest, having celebrated Mass, finished the last Gospel, comes to the foot of the altar to say the *De Profundis;* what rubric is to be observed by him? Is he to genuflect—the Blessed Sacrament being in the tabernacle—to make a profound reverence, or no reverence at all? The present practice, as far as I know, is to genuflect.

2. A Month's Memory Office and Mass are to be said for a deceased person; not an exact month after the death or burial, but perhaps five weeks afterwards. What Mass is to be celebrated? Is it a *Missa Cantata?* An answer will oblige yours respectfully.

C. C.

1. The best and most general practice is to make no reverence whatever at the foot of the altar before saying the *De Profundis.* Neither positive law nor custom requires a reverence on this occasion, and analogy is opposed to it. The celebrant comes to the foot of the altar after the last Gospel, not to commence a new function, but to complete that in which he has been engaged. Theoretically, he has only come from the Gospel side to the centre of the altar; for his descending *in planum* is a mere accidental circumstance, since he might recite the psalm on the predella. Hence there is no more reason from analogy for his making a reverence before beginning the *De Profundis* than for his making one before beginning the Creed, or saying *Dominus vobiscum* after the first Gospel. We do not, of course, mean to assert that the *De Profundis* is, strictly speaking, a part of the liturgy of the Mass; but we do say that custom in this country has so welded it to the Mass that we are justified in regarding it as a part of the Mass, in so far as external rites are concerned.

2. The Mass to be said is the *Missa Quotidiana*, with the proper prayer for the deceased, not from the Mass of the thirtieth day, but from the *Orationes diversae*.

THE PRAYER TO BE SAID FOR THE COMMEMORATION OF ST. LELIA, WHEN IN CONCURRENCE WITH ST. CLARE

Rev. Dear Sir,—From the *Ordo* you will see that the feast was of St. Lelia on the 18th, and of St. Clare on the 19th inst., and that the Vespers of the 18th were 'a cap. de seq. comm. praed. et Oct.'

Now the question I wish to ask you is, how is this commemoration to be made? Or, more particularly, what prayer is to be said in this commemoration?

Doubtless, you will have observed that there is only one prayer—'Exaudi nos,' given in the breviary, as peculiar to a ' Virg. non Mart.'

If the question is not too small and insignificant for notice in the I. E. Record, may I hope for an answer to it in the October number or some succeeding issue?

Yours very truly.
C.C.

It is a general law of the liturgy that a prayer should not be repeated in the same function, or same part of the Divine Office. Hence, when the feasts of two saints of the same Order, each having the same prayer from the common, concur in Vespers, this prayer is said for that saint for whom the whole Vespers, or from the *capitulum*, are recited; while for the saint who is commemorated, another prayer from the same common is taken. But in the common of doctors, abbots, and virgins, not martyrs, only one prayer is found; what, then, is to be done when two feasts of any one of these classes of saints concur? The answer is almost obvious. For a doctor the prayer is taken from the common of bishops, or of confessors, according as the doctor was, or was not a bishop; for an abbot, from the common of confessors; and for a virgin not a martyr, the prayer *Indulgentiam* for a virgin martyr, omitting the title *et martyr.* In the case proposed by our correspondent the prayer *Exaudi* should have been said for St. Clare, and for the commemoration of St. Lelia, the prayer *Indulgentiam*, with the omission just mentioned.

THE PROPAGANDA FACULTIES AND DOLOUR BEADS

REV. DEAR SIR.—Do the Propaganda faculties for blessing and indulgencing beads &c., give priests enjoying them power to bless and indulgence the ' Seven Dolours ' beads with the same indulgences as the Servites attach to them? An answer would greatly oblige.

NEO-CONFESSARIUS.

We have great pleasure in giving an affirmative reply to our correspondent's question.

D. O'LOAN.

DOCUMENTS

ENCYCLICAL OF OUR HOLY FATHER LEO XIII. ON THE ROSARY OF MARY

SANCTISSIMI DOMINI NOSTRI LEONIS DIVINA PROVIDENTIA PAPAE XIII. EPISTOLA ENCYCLICA AD PATRIARCHAS, PRIMATES, ARCHIE-PISCOPOS, EPISCOPOS, ALIOSQUE LOCORUM ORDINARIOS PACEM ET COMMUNIONEM CUM APOSTOLICA SEDE HABENTES.

DE ROSARIO MARIALI

VENERABILIBUS FRATRIBUS PATRIARCHIS, PRIMATIBUS, ARCHIEPIS-COPIS, EPISCOPIS, ALIISQUE LOCORUM ORDINARIIS PACEM ET COMMUNIONEM CUM APOSTOLICA SEDE HABENTIBUS

LEO PP. XIII.

VENERABILES FRATRES SALUTEM ET APOSTOLICAM BENEDICTIONEM

Augustissimae Virginis Mariae foveri assidue cultum et contentiore quotidie studio promoveri quantum privatim publiceque intersit, facile quisque perspiciet, qui secum reputaverit, quam excelso dignitatis et gloriae fastigio Deus ipsam collocarit. Eam enim ab aeterno ordinavit ut Mater Verbi fieret humanam carnem assumpturi ; ideoque inter omnia, quae essent in triplici ordine naturae, gratiae, gloriaeque pulcherrima, ita distinxit, ut merito eidem Ecclesia verba illa tribuerit : 'Ego ex ore Altissimi prodivi primogenita ante omnem creaturam.'[1] Ubi autem volvi primum coepere saecula, lapsis in culpam humani generis auctoribus infectisque eadem labe posteris universis, quasi pignus constituta est instaurandae pacis atque salutis. Nec dubiis honoris significationibus Unigenitus Dei Filius sanctissimam matrem est prosequutus. Nam et dum privatam in terris vitam egit, ipsam adscivit utriusque prodigii administram, quae tunc primum patravit ; alterum gratiae, quo ad Mariae salutationem exultavit infans in utero Elisabeth ; alterum naturae, quo aquam in vinum convertit ad Canae nuptias : et quum supremo vitae suae publicae tempore novum conderet Testamentum divino sanguine obsignandum, eamdem dilecto Apostolo commisit verbis illis dulcissimis : 'Ecce mater tua.'[2] Nos igitur qui, licet indigni,

[1] Eccli. xxiv. v.   [2] *Id.*, xix. 27.

vices ac personam gerimus in terris Iesu Christi Filii Dei, tantae
Matris persequi laudes nunquam desistemus, dum hac lucis usura
fruemur. Quam quia sentimus haud futuram Nobis, ingraves-
cente aetate, diuturnam, facere non possumus quiñ omnibus et
singulis in (hristo filiis Nostris Ipsius cruce pendentis extrema
verba, quasi testamento relicta, iteremus : ' Ecce mater tua.' Ac
praeclare quidem Nobiscum actum esse censebimus, si id Nostrae
commendationes effecerint, ut unusquisque fidelis Mariali cultu
nihil habeat antiquius, nihil carius,liceatque de singulis usurpare
verba Ioannis, quae de se scripsit : ' Accepit eam discipulus in
sua.' [1]   Adventante igitur mense Octobri, ne hoc quidem anno
patimur, Venerabiles Fratres, carere vos Litteris Nostris, rursus
adhortantes sollicitudine qua possumus maxima ut Rosarii
recitatione studeat sibi quisque ac laboranti Ecclesiae demereri.
Quod quidem precandi genus divina providentia videtur sub
huius saeculi exitum mire invaluisse, ut languescens fidelium
excitaretur pietas ; idque maxime testantur insignia templa ac
sacraria Deiparae cultu celeberrima.—Huic divinae Matri, cui
flores dedimus mense Maio, velimus omnes fructiferum quoque
Octobrem singulari pietatis affectu esse dicatum.   Decet enim
utrumque hoc anni tempus ei consecrari, quae de se dixit :
' Flores mei fructus honoris et honestatis.' [2]

   Vitae societas atque coniunctio, ad quam homines natura
feruntur, nulla aetate fortasse arctior effecta est, aut tanto studio
tamque communi expetita, quam nostrâ.   Nec quisquam sane id
reprehendat, nisi vis haec naturae nobilissima ad prava saepe
consilia detorqueretur, convenientibus in unum atque in varii
generis societates coeuntibus impiis hominibus 'adversus Dominum
et adversus Christumeius.' [3]   Cernere tamen est, idque profecto,
accidit iucundissimum, inter catholicos etiam adamari magis
coeptos pios coetus ; eos haberi confertissimos ; iis quasi com-
munibus domiciliis christianae vinculo dilectionis ita adstringi
cunctos et quasi coalescere, ut vere fratres et dici posse et esse
videantur.   Neque enim, Christi caritate sublata, fraterna societate
et nomine gloriari quisquam potest ; quod acriter olim Tertullianus
hisce verbis persequebatur : ' Fratres vestri sumus iure naturae
matris unius, etsi vos parum homines, quia mali fratres.   At
quanto dignius fratres et dicuntur et habentur qui unum patrem
Deum agnoscunt, qui unum spiritum biberunt sanctitatis, qui de

---

[1] *Ib.*   [2] Eccli. xxiv. 23.   [3] Ps. ii. 2.

uno utero ignorantiae eiusdem ad unam lucem expaverint veritatis?'[1] Multiplex autem ratio est, qua catholici homines societates huiusmodi saluberrimas inire solent. Huc enim et circuli, ut aiunt, et rustica aeraria pertinent, itemque conventus animis per dies festos relaxandis, et secessus pueritiae advigilandae, et sodalitia, et coetus alii optimis consiliis instituti complures. Profecto haec omnia, etsi nomine, forma, aut suo quaeque peculiari ac proximo fine, recens inventa esse videantur, re tamen ipsa sunt antiquissima. Constat enim, in ipsis christianae religionis exordiis eius generis societatum vestigia reperiri. Serius autem legibus confirmatae, suis distinctae signis, privilegiis donatae, divinum ad cultum in templis adhibitae, aut animis corporibusve sublevandis destinatae, variis nominibus, pro varia temporum ratione, appellatae sunt. Quarum numerus in dies ita percrebuit, ut, in Italia maxime, nulla civitas, oppidum nullum, nulla ferme paroecia sit, ubi non illae aut complures, aut aliquae certe habeantur.

In his minime dubitamus praeclarum dignitatis locum assignare sodalitati, quae a sanctissimo Rosario nuncupatur. Nam sive eius spectetur origo, e primis pollet antiquitate, quod eiusmodi institutionis auctor fuisse feratur ipse Dominicus pater ; sive privilegia aestimentur, quamplurimis ipsa ornata est, Decessorum Nostrorum munificentia.—Eius institutionis forma et quasi anima est Mariale Rosarium, cuius de virtute fuse alias loquuti sumus. Verumtamen ipsius Rosarii vis atque efficacitas, prout est officium Sodalitati, quae ab ipso nomen mutuatur, adiunctum, longe etiam maior apparet. Neminem enim latet, quae sit omnibus orandi necessitas, non quod immutari possint divina decreta, sed, ex Gregorii sententia, 'ut homines postulando mereantur accipere quod eis Deus omnipotens ante saecula disposuit donare.'[2] Ex Augustino autem: 'qui recte novit orare, recte novit vivere.'[3] At preces tunc maxime robur assumunt ad caelestem opem impetrandam, quum et publice et constanter et concorditer funduntur a multis, ita ut velut unus efficiatur precantium chorus : quod quidem illa aperte declarant Actuum Apostolicorum, ubi Christi discipuli, expectantes promissum Spiritum Sanctum, fuisse dicuntur 'perseverantes unanimiter in oratione.'[4] Hunc orandi modum qui sectentur certissimo fructu carere poterunt nunquam.

[1] *Apolog.*, c. xxxix.
[2] *Dialog.*, I. i. c. 8.
[3] In Ps. cxviii.
[4] Act. i. 14.

Iam id plane accidit inter sodales a sacro Rosario. Nam, sicut a sacerdotibus, divini Officii recitatione, publice iugiterque supplicatur, ideoque validissime ; ita, publica quodammodo, iugis, communis est supplicatio sodalium, quae fit recitatione Rosarii, vel ' Psalterii Virginis, ' ut a nonnullis etiam Romanis Pontificibus appellatum est.

Quod autem, uti diximus, preces publice adhibitae multo iis praestent, quae privatim fundantur, vimque habeant impetrandi maiorem, factum est ut Sodalitati a sacro Rosario nomen ab Ecclesiae scriptoribus inditum fuerit ' militiae precantis, a Dominico Patre sub divinae Matris vexillo conscriptae,' quam scilicet divinam Matrem sacrae litterae et Ecclesiae fasti salutant daemonis errorumque omnium debellatricem. Enimvero Mariale Rosarium omnes, qui eius religionis petant societatem, communi vinculo adstringit tamquam fraterni aut militaris contubernii, unde validissima quaedam acies conflatur, ad hostium impetus repellendos, sive intrinsecus illis sive extrinsecus urgeamur, rite instructa atque ordinata. Quamorbem merito iis huius instituti sodales usurpare sibi possunt verba ill S. Cypriani : ' Publica est nobis et communis oratio, et quando oramus, non pro uno, sed pro toto populo oramus, quia totus populus unum sumus.[1] Ceterum eiusmodi precationis vim atque efficaciam annales Ecclesiae testantur, quum memorant et fractas navali proelio ad Echinadas insulas Turcarum copias, et relatas de iisdem superiore saeculo ad Temesvariam in Pannonia et ad Corcyram insulam victorias nobilissimas. Prioris rei gestae memoriam perennem exstare voluit Gregorius XIII. die festo instituto Mariae victricis honori ; quem diem postea Clemens XI Decessor Noster titulo Rosarii consecravit, et quotannis celebrandum in universa Ecclesia decrevit.

Ex eo autem quod precans haec militia sit ' sub divinae Matris vexillo conscripta,' nova eidem virtus novus honor accedit. Huc maxime spectat repetita crebro, in Rosarii ritu, post orationem dominicam angelica salutatio. Tantum vero abest ut hoc dignitati Numinis quodammodo adversetur, quasi saudere videatur maiorem nobis in Mariae patrocinio fiduciam esse collocandam quam in divina potentia, ut potius nihil Ipsum facilius permoveat propitiumque nobis efficiat. Catholica enim fide docemur, non ipsum modo Deum esse precibus exorandum, sed beatos quoque caelites,[2] licet

---

[1] *De orat domin.* [2] Conc. Trid., sess. xxv.

ratione dissimili, quod a Deo, tamquam a bonorum omnium fonte, ab his, tamquam ab intercessoribus, petendum sit. 'Oratio,' inquit S. Thomas, 'porrigitur alicui dupliciter, uno modo quasi per ipsum implenda, alio modo, sicut per ipsum impetranda. Primo quidem modo soli Deo orationem porrigimus, quia omnes orationes nostrae ordinari debent ad gratiam et ad gloriam consequendam, quae solus Deus dat, secundum illud Psalmi lxxxiii. 12 : "gratiam et gloriam dabit Dominus." Sed secundo modo orationem porrigimus sanctis Angelis et hominibus, non ut per eos Deus nostras petitiones cognoscat, sed ut eorum precibus et meritis orationes nostrae sortiantur effectum. Et ideo dicitur Apoc. viii. 4, quod ascendit fumus incensorum de orationibus sanctorum de manu Angeli coram Deo.'[1] Iam quis omnium, quotquot beatorum incolunt sedes, audeat cum augusta Dei Matre in certamen demerendae gratiae venire? Ecquis in Verbo aeterno clarius intuetur, quibus angustiis premamur, quibus rebus indigeamus? Cui maius arbitrium permissum est permovendi Numinis? Quis maternae pietatis sensibus aequari cum ipsa queat? Id scilicet causae est cur beatos quidem caelites non eadem ratione precemur ac Deum 'nam a sancta Trinitate petimus ut nostri misereatur, ab aliis autem sanctis quibuscumque petimus ut orent pro nobis;'[2] implorandae vero Virginis ritus aliquid habeat cum Dei cultu commune, adeo ut Ecclesia his vocibus ipsam compellet, quibus exoratur Deus : 'Peccatorum miserere.' Rem igitur optimam praestant sodales a sacro Rosario, tot salutationes et Mariales preces quasi serta rosarum contexentes. Tanta enim Mariae est magnitudo, tanta, qua apud Deum pollet, gratia, ut qui opis egens non ad illam confugiat, is optet nullo alarum remigio volare.

Alia etiam Sodalitatis, de qua loquimur, laus est, nec prae-tereunda silentio. Quoties enim Marialis recitatione Rosarii salutis nostrae mysteria commentamur, toties officia sanctissima, caelesti quondam Angelorum militiae commissa, similitudine quadam aemulamur. Ea ipsi, suo quaeque tempore mysteria revelarunt, eorum fuere pars magna, iisdem adfuere seduli, vultu modo ad gaudium composito, modo ad dolorem, modo ad triumphalis gloriae exultationem. Gabriel ad Virginem mittitur nuntiatum Verbi aeterni Incarnationem. Betlemico in antro, Salvatoris in lucem editi gloriam Angeli cantibus prosequuntur. Angelus Iosepho auctor est fugae arripiendae, seque in Aegyptum

---

[1] S. th. 2ᵃ 2ᵃᵉ , lxxxiii. a. iv.　　[2] Ib.

recipiendi cum puero. Iesum in horto prae moerore sanguine
exsudantem Angelus pio alloquio solatur. Eumdem, devicta
morte, sepulchro excitatum, Angeli mulieribus indicant. Evectum
ad caelum Angeli referunt atque inde reversurum praedicant
angelicis comitatum catervis, quibus electorum animas admisceat
secumque rapiat ad aetherios choros, super quos 'exaltata est
sancta Dei Genitrix.' Piissima igitur Rosarii prece inter sodales
utentibus ea maxime convenire possunt, quibus Paulus Apostolus
novos Christi asseclas alloquebatur : ' Accessistis ad Sion montem, et civitatem Dei viventis, Ierusalem caelestem, et multorum
millium Angelorum frequentiam.'[1] Quid autem divinius quidve
suavius, quam contemplari cum Angelis cum iisque precari ?
Quanta niti spe liceat atque fiducia, fruituros olim in caelo beatis-
sima Angelorum societate eos, qui in terris eorum ministerio sese
quodammodo addiderunt ?

His de causis Romani Pontifices eximiis usque praeconiis
Marianam huiusmodi Sodalitatem extulerunt, in quibus eam
Innocentius VIII. 'devotissimam Confraternitatem [2] appellat ;
Pius V. affirmat, eiusdem virtute haec consequuta ; 'Coeperunt
Christi fideles in alios viros repente mutari, haeresum tenebrae
remitti et lux catholicae fidei aperiri '; [3] Sixtus V. attendens
quam fuerit haec institutio religioni frugifera, eiusdem se studiosis-
simum profitetur ; alii denique multi, aut praecipuis eam indulgentiis, iisque uberrimis auxere, aut in peculiarem sui tutelam,
dato nomine variisque editis benevolentiae testimoniis, receperunt
Eiusmodi Decessorum Nostrorum exemplis permoti, Nos etiam,
Venerabiles Fratres, vehementer hortamur vos atque obsecramus,
quod saepe iam fecimus, ut sacrae huius militiae singularem
curam adhibeatis, atque ita quidem, ut, vobis adnitentibus, novae
in dies evocentur undique copiae atque scribantur. Vestra opera
et eorum, qui e clero subdito vobis curam gerunt animarum,
noscant ceteri e populo, atque ex veritate aestiment, quantum in
ea Sodalitate virtutis sit, quantum utilitatis ad aeternam hominum
salutem. Hoc autem contentione poscimus eo maiore, quod
proximo hoc tempore iterum viguit pulcherrima in sanctissimam
Matrem pietatis manifestatio per Rosarium quod 'perpetuum'
appellant. Huic Nos instituto libenti animo benediximus ; eius
ut incrementis seddulo vos naviterque studeatis, magnopere

[1] Heb. xii. 22.
[2] *Splendor paternae gloriae*, die 26 Februarii, 1491.
[3] *Consueverunt RR. PP.*, die 17 Septembris, 1569.

optamus. Spem enim optimam concipimus, laudes precesque
fore validissimas, quae, ex ingenti multitudinis ore ac pectore
expressae, nunquam conticescant ; et per varias terrarum orbis
regiones dies noctesque alternando, conspirantium vocum concentum cum rerum divinarum meditatione coniungant. Quam
quidem laudationum supplicationumque perennitatem, multis
abhinc saeculis, divinae illae significarunt voces, quibus Oziae
cantu compellabatur Iudith : ' Benedicta es tu filia a Domino
Deo excelso prae omnibus mulieribus super terram . . . quia
hodie nomen tuum ita magnificavit, ut non recedat laus tua de
ore hominum.' Iisque vocibus universus populus Israel accla-
mabat : ' Fiat, fiat.' [1]

Interea, caelestium beneficiorum auspicem paternaeque Nostrae
benevolentiae testem, vobis, Venerabiles Fratres, et clero populoque universo, vestrae fidei vigilantiaeque commisso, Apostolicam
benedictionem peramanter in Domino impertimus.

Datum Romae apud S. Petrum die XII. Septembris MDCCCXCVII.,
Pontificatus Nostri anno vicesimo.

LEO PP. XIII.

SOME DIFFICULTIES ABOUT THE ORDINATION OF PRIESTS

I.

ORDINANDUS AD PRESBYTERATUM TETIGERAT CALICEM ANTEQUAM
PRONUNCIARET FORMAM : *acquiescat.*

BME. PATER,

Sempronius Sacerdos Regularis, ad S. V. pedes provolutus,
humili prece petit solutionem dubii cuiusdam, quo iam a
plurimo tempore, circa validitatem suae ordinationis sacerdotalis,
exagitatur. Quum enim in tactu instrumentorum adhibuisset
non quidem indices et medios digitos, sed indices et pollices,
prius tetigit cuppam calicis ; sed postea, quum Episcopus
formulam pronunciavit, tetigit tantummodo patenam cum super-
posita hostia super calicem. Itaque, quum res non adamussim
processerit iuxta praescriptiones Pontificalis, Theologorumque
doctrinam, Orator pro conscientiae tranquillitate suae, petit quid:
tenendum de validitate suae ordinationis ?

Feria IV., 17 Martii, 1897.

In Congne Gen, S. R. et U. Inquisitionis habita ab Emis ac
Rmis DD. Card. in Republica christiana adversus haereticam

---

[1] *Iud.* xiii. 23 *et seqq.*

pravitatem Generalibus Inquisitoribus, proposito suprascripto
dubio praehabitoque RR. DD. Consultorum voto, iidem Emi ac
Rmi Dni respondendum mandarunt:

Orator acquiescat.

Sequenti vero die ac feria, de praedictis relatione SS. D. N. D.
Leoni Div. Prov. Papae XIII in solita audientia R. P. D.
Adsessori S. O. impertita, Sanctitas Sua Emorum Patrum
resolutionem adprobavit.

I. Can. MANNCINI, *S. R. et U. I. Not.*

II.

ORDINANDUS AD PRESBYTERATUM, AD CALICEM TANGENDUM, SED
INCASSUM, CONNISUS FUERAT : *acquiescat*

BEATISSIME PATER,

Caius Sacerdos, ad S. V. pedes provolutus, humiliter petit,
ut conscientiae suae tranquillitati provideatur, solutionem dubii
cuiusdam a quo vexatur, circa valorem sacerdotalis ordinationis.
Ex hoc profluit tale dubium, quod in traditione instrumentorum,
non omnia processerunt exacte secundum praescriptiones Pontificalis, quum tetigerit tantum patenam et hostiam super calice
positam, non autem ipsum calicem etsi ad istum cum digitis
tangendum connisus fuisset.

Feria IV., 17 Martii, 1897.

In Congne Gen. S. R. et U. Inquisitionis habita ab Emis ac
Rmis DD. Cardinalibus in rebus fidei Generalibus Inquisitoribus,
proposito suprascripto dubio praehabitoque Rrum DD. Consultorum voto, iidem Emi ac Rmi Dni respondendum mandarunt:

Orator acquiescat.

Sequenti vero die ac feria, facta de praedictis relatione SS.
D. N. D. Leoni Div. Prov. Papae XIII in solita audientia
R. P. D. Adsessori S. O. impertita, Sanctitas Sua Emorum
Patrum resolutionem adprobavit.

I. Can. MANCINI, *S. R. et U. I. Not.*

NOTICES OF BOOKS

COMMENTARIUM IN FACULTATES APOSTOLICAS PER MODUM
FORMULARUM CONCEDI SOLITAS. Auctore Joseph
Putzer, C.SS.R. New York, Cincinnati, Chicago:
Benziger Brothers.

THERE frequently arises in every parish the necessity of
applying for dispensations. The clergyman interested often finds
it difficult to obtain reliable information on the many intricate
questions that occur to him. To whom must he apply for the
dispensation? What form must the application take? What is
it necessary to mention in the form? How are the faculties,
when received, to be used? These and many other inconvenient
difficulties disturb his equanimity. The best thanks of all
concerned are due to anyone who helps to smooth the way.
Fr. Putzer has done his part, and has done it well. Hence he
deserves our thanks for his work.

Fr. Konings, a name to be held in veneration, began the
work of explaining the faculties which the American bishops
received from Rome. His treatise was published soon after
his death, which occurred in 1884. The book quickly reached
a second edition. Fr. Putzer then improved the work in many
ways, and issued it in a third edition, in 1893. It was received
with such favour that soon a new edition was called for, and it is
this edition which we have before us.

The title of the work explains its subject-matter. It is a
commentary on the Apostolic Faculties given to bishops, &c., in
the different formulæ. The book has two parts. In the first
part the author gives a general explanation of Apostolic Faculties
—their nature, the rules for their interpretation, their communication and subdelegation, their cessation and expiration,
their application and use. All these subjects are discussed with
sufficient fulness and clearness of style. To this portion of the
work is affixed a chapter on the manner of applying for faculties,
which contains some model applications that must be of great
service to many priests.

In the second part there is a detailed exposition of the faculties
granted in Formula I., which the American bishops have received

from Propaganda. In the appendices there are copies of the
Formulæ given to the bishops of other countries, including the
Formula VI., which is given to the Irish Hierarchy. In these
appendices references for explanation are given to the corresponding portions of Formula I. The author seems not to be perfectly
certain about the extension of Art. 3 of Formula VI., which
Pius IX. granted the Irish bishops in 1854. A glance into the
I. E. RECORD 1872-3, p. 240, to which he refers, ought to satisfy
the author of its authenticity.

Though the work has been primarily written for American
ecclesiastics it can be gleaned from what we have said that it is
of immense use to Irish ecclesiastics also. We venture to hope
that as soon as they are acquainted with its existence and utility
many of them will purchase the little volume.

J. M. H.

MELLIFONT ABBEY, COUNTY LOUTH: ITS RUINS AND
ASSOCIATIONS. A Guide and Popular History. Permissu
Superiorum. James Duffy & Co., Ltd., Dublin, for the
Cistercians, Mount St. Joseph Abbey, Roscrea, 1897.

HISTORICALLY there is in Ireland no more interesting ruin
than Mellifont Abbey, and few, indeed, are the Irish ruins which
from any point of view approach it in interest. Founded largely
through the co-operation of the great St. Malachy, the bosom
friend of St. Bernard, by a colony of monks sent thither from
Clairvaux, it was the parent house of the Cistercian Order in
Ireland. Before it had been nine years in existence it could
reckon six important filiations in various parts of the country—
Bective, Newry, Boyle, Athlone, Baltinglass, and Manister. In
later times the number of Cistercian houses founded from
Mellifont, or from its early filiations, were very numerous. Its
abbots took precedence of all other Irish abbots of the order;
were lords of Parliament; wielded enormous power in Church and
State; and were many of them men of exalted sanctity and great
learning. Of their number, four became bishops of Irish sees —
Lismore, Emly, Clogher, and Achonry. The first abbot, who
became Bishop of Lismore, was also Papal Legate in Ireland, and
is honoured in the Church's calendar as St. Christian. Within the
cloisters of Mellifont were interred the earthly remains of many
princes and other notabilities; and there, too, the faithless but

penitent Dervorgilla, ' life's fitful fever over,' found a last resting-place.

Clearly, then, the story of Mellifont Abbey deserved to be told, and with all possible completeness. Told it is most interestingly and exhaustively in the unpretending, but important, work under review. This work we strongly and unreservedly recommend to our readers, and to all who take even a slight interest in Irish historical or antiquarian studies. We are convinced that no more satisfactory work dealing with any of our ruins has made its appearance for many a day. Henceforth it will be an indispensable *vade mecum* to all visitors to Mellifont.

The first chapter is descriptive. It deals with the ruins as they are at present, and tells with a completeness which leaves nothing to be desired how the abbey looked in the days of its greatness and prosperity. The remaining seven chapters are mainly historical. They deal exhaustively with the rise, progress, vicissitudes, and decline of the famous abbey. Subjoined are three appendices. The first contains a list of the abbots of Mellifont, not absolutely complete, but as nearly so as it is now possible to make it. The second consists of a copy of the charter of Newry, taken from the original in the British Museum. In the third is given an inventory of the estates of Mellifont.

The work is published anonymously ; but we consider ourselves at liberty to state that the author is a well-known member of the community of Mount St. Joseph, Roscrea. That he has been at extraordinary pains to make the work as complete as possible is quite obvious. Not only has he drawn largely upon the voluminous literature of his Order, but he has laid under contribution all the sources of information on Irish history, Annals, Monasticons, State papers, &c. In the preface is given a list of authorities, the most cursory glance at which is sufficient to show that no work at all likely to contain information suited to the author's purpose was left unconsulted. There are eight fairly good illustrations. In addition, are given two folding plans—one of Clairvaux, after which Mellifont was modelled, another of Mellifont itself ; and these add much to the value of the work. The book is sold at the very low price of one shilling. We augur for it a large sale ; its sale, if commensurate with its merits, will indeed be large. It were well if other notable Irish ruins—our ruined abbeys and monasteries especially—should be dealt with at no distant day in works of even a much less satisfactory character. M. P. H.

THE WICKED WOODS.   By Rosa Mulholland (Lady Gilbert)
London : Burns and Oates, Limited.

WE have read through this fascinating story with unwearied
and unflagging interest.   The charm of narrative, and the grace
of style that have popularized so widely her earlier works are not
missed in the latest effort of our gifted authoress.   Lady Gilbert
possesses one of those touches that makes the whole world kin.
She has an intimate knowledge of the various phases of peasant
life she describes; she has a thorough insight into the springs of
action by which her heroes and heroines are actuated in their
varying moods, and she has the art of delineation in a very highly
cultured degree.   Her characters, therefore, are no overdrawn
creatures of the imagination, but simple, honest, God-fearing
country folk, such as are to be met with in the realities of Irish
life.   Moreover, there is a vein of purity and wholesomeness
permeating all her writings, which places them in severe contrast
with the morbid productions of latter-day novelists, and makes
it not only safe but desirable to have them placed in the hands
of the young.

The plot of the present story is well laid and skilfully developed.   To stimulate the interest of the reader in this beautiful
tale, we abstain designedly from hinting at the plan, even in outline, preferring to leave him to follow the guidance of our authoress
through the thrilling and touching incidents of the 'Wicked
Woods,' and promising him a most delightful experience.

P. M.

THE NEW EXPLICIT ALGEBRA IN THEORY AND PRACTICE.
By James J. O'Dea.   London : Longmans, Green & Co.

WE have great pleasure in drawing the attention of the heads
of Intermediate Colleges and Schools to the above work.   It is
the most successful attempt we have yet seen at simplifying the
teaching of algebra.   Not merely is the solution of typical
problems and examples indicated, but these are worked out
exactly as the student should present his answering at a written
examination.   Then the selection of examples is most judicious.
The algebra papers, set in past years at the Intermediate, Royal
University, London University, and other similar public examinations have yielded up their choicest exercises to furnish Professor
O'Dea's *thesaurus* of algebraic difficulties and peculiarities.   We
cannot find language more suitable than the author's own to set

forth the merits of his treatise:—'The leading features [he writes in his preface] of the *Explicit Algebra* are fulness of detail, without being uselessly exhaustive ; lucidity and conciseness of statement ; brevity and neatness in the manipulation of examples, which are numerous and varied ; together with copiousness and variety of exercises methodically arranged ; while the disposition of the various portions of the work, considered as a whole, is in strict logical sequence.'

The very favourable reception which has been accorded to the author's *Explicit Arithmetic* is sufficient testimony to Professor O'Dea's ability as a mathematician.

T. P. G.

THE CREED EXPLAINED : OR AN EXPOSITION OF CATHOLIC DOCTRINE ACCORDING TO THE CREEDS OF FAITH AND THE CONSTITUTIONS AND DEFINITIONS OF THE CHURCH. By Rev. A. Devine (Passionist). Dublin : M. H. Gill & Son. New York : Benziger Bros.

THE author of this book scarcely needs an introduction to our readers. His previous labours in the domain of ascetical literature have already stamped him as a ripe theologian and a scholar of high attainments. He and his learned brother, Father Pius Devine, have by their prolific pens shed renown on the illustrious Order to which they both belong, and contributed to vastly increase our stores of Scriptural knowledge.

In the opening chapters of the present work we have a concise little treatise on Faith, in which everything necessary to be known about this divine virtue is accurately explained. Each article of the Creed is then taken up and treated in exhaustive detail. Nothing of importance to the thorough understanding of the truths comprised in these articles is omitted, and the method of treatment followed is very satisfactory. Proofs of dogma are given at great length from the Scriptures, fathers and councils of the Church, and we feel confident that everyone who reads these carefully will be able to render a solid ' reason for the faith that is in him.'

That the book has a wide range of usefulness is manifest from the fact that a second edition has been demanded and published.

P. M.

"Ut Christiani ita et Romani sitis." *"As you are children of Christ, so be you children of Rome."*
Ex Dictis S. Patricii, In Libro Armacano, fol. 9.

The Irish
Ecclesiastical Record

A Monthly Journal, under Episcopal Sanction.

Thirtieth Year]
No. 359.

NOVEMBER, 1897.

[Fourth Series
Vol. II.

Nihil Obstat.
GERALDUS MOLLOY, S.T.D.
Censor Dep.

Imprimatur.
✠ GULIELMUS,
Archiep. Dublin.,
Hiberniae Primas.

BROWNE & NOLAN, Limited

Publishers and Printers, 24 & 25

NASSAU STREET, DUBLIN.

BREAD

AND

CONFECTIONERY

Finest

Quality

Only.

KENNEDY'S

127 & 128, GREAT BRITAIN STREET,

DUBLIN.

THE ABERDEEN ROMANCE

THERE were few men pleasanter to know, or more delightful to chat with, than the late Sir Bernard Burke, Ulster King-of-Arms. He was a thorough gentleman, somewhat. of the old school, of high culture and kindly tongue, who made the most of what was good, and the least of what was bad in his fellow-man ; brimful, too, of the most interesting information, which he imparted freely in a genial and bright way. He once recounted to a person, who enjoyed and prized his friendship, the strange resolve, and still stranger action of a Scotch nobleman, giving him, at the same time, his own book, *Reminiscences, Ancestral and Anecdotal*, in which anyone may read of both under the title, *The Aberdeen Romance*. Romance it reads like ; but romance it is not, but a history of hard and clearly-proved facts.

This romance, for let us call it such, interested and edified the friend who first heard of, and then carefully studied it. But more, he became convinced that this nobleman, in his truly extraordinary action, was influenced by a different motive, sought a different end, and was sustained by a different power from those suggested by Sir Bernard, or likely, perhaps, to occur to many. But, first of all, it is necessary to consider well the facts ; this done, each may draw from them his own conclusion, or adopt his own theory, if he cannot accept mine. For these facts I have no authority, nor have I sought any save Sir Bernard's; but this rests on letters written by the nobleman himself, and on well-authenticated sworn evidence obtained, after his death, by the Rev. William Alexander, who was sent twice to America by his family to seek it.

The hero, for I at least will call him so, of this romance, was George Gordon, sixth Earl of Aberdeen in the peerage of Scotland, and third Viscount in the peerage of the United Kingdom. He was born on the 10th of December, 1841, and, being the eldest son, succeeded his father on the 22nd of March, 1864, being then a few months over twenty-three. Gordon is a noble and historic name, linked, with honour, courage, and loyalty. Miss Strickland, in her life of Mary Queen of Scots, states that the reason why her enemies forced her to marry Bothwell was, that conduct so disgraceful might disgust the Gordons and the Maxwells, who had never wavered in their devotion to her, and that, notwithstanding this wretched act, both were the first to stand at her side, and place their swords at her service.

Earl of Aberdeen meant large landed property, stately mansions, and great influence. Still, within two years of coming into possession he practically renounced all, and left his country never to see it again. In January, 1866, he embarked at Liverpool on board a sailing vessel, the ' Pomona,' bound for St. John's, New Brunswick, where he stayed for a short time with his uncle, the Hon. Arthur Gordon, who was Governor of the Colony. Towards the end of April he was residing in a hotel at Boston, ' the Revere House,' under his own name and title; but these he laid aside about May 22nd, as the hotel register shows, and assumed that of George H. Osborne, under which he passed till his death. In the month of June he took service as a *common sailor*, in the brig ' R. Wylie,' and made a voyage to Palmas Grand Canary Island. In the years 1867, '68, '69, he sailed, in the same capacity, on board different merchant-vessels, to Vera Cruz, Mexico, Florida, Texas, and New York. In 1870 he was engaged as mate on board the ship ' Hera,' which left Boston on the 21st January bound for Melbourne. During this voyage the Earl, when engaged in lowering the mainsail, was washed overboard and drowned. The captain gave the following account of this sad event :—

When I heard the alarm, ' A man overboard,' I came at once on deck to find that this man was Osborne. Everything was done to save him, ropes and planks were thrown, the boat was cleared away, but being very heavy, it was impossible to launch her in time to do any good. In any case the waves were so high, she could scarcely have got free of the vessel or lived. When I came first on deck I saw him struggling in the water, and heard him cry, but this ceased before it was possible to lower the boat. The water was very cold, and even a good swimmer must have perished very soon. I am quite sure he must have been drowned.

Such are the facts. Now for the reasoning conclusions or theories which they may suggest. But that these may have fair play we must bear well in mind, and give full weight to some remarkable circumstances of the case.

The Earl freely, of his own accord, renounced title, position, the wealth, pride, and pomp of this world—·things dear to the heart of man, and adopted a sailor's life, selecting a *poor class of merchant-trading vessels*, making voyages on dangerous coasts to uninteresting places, bearing all the privations, hardships, and sufferings incidental to such a life—things naturally most disliked by man'; leading, in a word, a life of common-place drudgery, devoid of that love of adventure or of wild and daring feats which have an attraction for some. Moreover, he remained almost to the end a common sailor, doing, as mate, a common sailor's work, although he had studied navigation in Boston Nautical College, and had a certificate of full fitness to take the command of any merchant vessel. In the words of one who knew him well, and had sailed with him, ' he was a first-rate navigator, and no calculation puzzled him.' He could have changed all this at any moment; could have taken himself away from a most severe and trying life, and gone back to one of comfort, ease, and enjoyment, but did not. For four years he lived his freely-chosen hard life, and we are not without some reasons for believing that he purposed living it to the end. His careful study of nautical affairs seems to suggest this intention on his part.

We learn all the above-mentioned circumstances from
his own letters, and from several persons who sailed with
him.   In a letter to his mother, with whom he kept up the
most affectionate relations, he writes: ' When in a small
leaky vessel a furious storm arose, I, with others, was
working at the pumps for seventeen hours, each moment
thinking it would be the last.'   In another: ' To-morrow we
sail for the coast of Florida, famous for its tales of piracy,
wreckage, and murder.'   In another: ' I have been all this
time on a barren coast with nothing interesting but the
wrecks of other vessels which had ventured on this
inhospitable and dangerous coast, and paid dearly for their
rashness.'   He writes, in the same letter, of a danger shared
by him and others, who had to man a boat in order to lay
out the bower anchor :—

The boat was so low in the water that every wave washed
over, and threatened to swamp her. We succeeded at last, and
were glad to get back to the vessel, for the sea was full of sharks.
We remained for some time on this howling coast, where sandflies,
horseflies, and mosquitos abound, and where at night can be
heard the savage roar of the tiger and wild beasts that inhabit
the impervious tropical jungle, which lines this coast down to the
beach.

In another he describes a storm which lasted for three
days with the ' heaviest rain and the darkest darkness,'
during which he was at one moment in great danger, ' out
on the main boom, swinging backward and forward.'   A
fellow-sailor named Small stated :—

At Vera Cruz we were employed for four days discharging a
cargo of corn. I observed that Osborne, in doing his work, did
not appear like a man used to it ; his hands looked soft, blistered
easily, his legs tottered under him when carrying the sacks ; but
he never gave in.

Now, for a little reasoning on the facts and circumstances
of the case.   Imagine for a moment a large hall, and in it two
tables; one beautifully decorated with the rarest flowers, and
on plates of silver and gold every viand and delicacy which
could satisfy the appetite and please the palate of man; on the
other, a plain board, nothing but bread and water.   Let us
suppose a crowd admitted, perfectly free to partake of one or

the other. If all rushed to the first, most attractive table, we certainly would not be surprised, nor would we stop for a moment to seek a reason for their doing so. But if we saw one or two turn away and go to the second, most repelling one, we should be at once forced to the conclusion that they were actuated in their strange conduct by some extraordinary, unnatural, or supernatural motive. Now, let us substitute for the two tables the life freely given up, and the life freely chosen by the Earl, and our wonder must be greater; nor can we help speculating as to the reasons which influenced him.

Some men, no doubt, have fallen from high positions, and taken to low employments, low companionship, and unworthy ways; but this, as a rule, could not be called freely chosen—it was the consequence of extravagance which brought on poverty, or of scandalous living, which ostracized them from the society of their equals, or of both. This theory could not be held for a second by any sane man, as the Earl—and it is necessary to bear this well in mind—was a noble, not only of unblemished fame and irreproachable morality, but a man of high-toned Christian and religious character. Sir Bernard gives three reasons for his strange resolve and action. Firstly, 'a passion for seafaring life, which had taken hold of his mind from early boyhood;' secondly, 'a strong democratic element in his character;' thirdly, 'eccentricity.' I do not believe these theories tenable, if we bear in mind the hardships and sufferings of his sailor life to one reared and educated as he was. It is true that boys have often shown a strong passion for the sea, and gratified it against the will of their parents, sometimes by running away. These were, however, generally the wild boys of the family, and were very glad, not unfrequently, to get back to the home-nest after one or two trials of such a life. Now, the Earl was not a wild boy; he did not adopt this career when a boy; and, presuming he had this passion, could he not have indulged it to his heart's content in his own yacht, or by sailing around the world, and where he liked, as a passenger, or, if you will, as a sailor in ships of the first class.

As to. 'the democratic element in his character,' we may consider it for the moment under two aspects. Firstly, that it would prompt him to become a propagandist of democratic or radical principles; secondly, that it was simply personal, and inclined him to seek companionship with persons of a lower position, and, by doing so, to assert the principle that there should be no class distinction, and that all ought to be on the same level. With reference to the first, there is no evidence that he had any such desire; but, if he had, he could have gratified it in his own country, where the spread of such principles would seem more needed than in America, and where he could have done so in an open, honourable, and popular way by identifying himself with the Radical party, and using his great influence for its advancement. As to the second, he could have indulged a mere personal inclination to mix with the masses in many ways, devoid of the toil, hardships, sufferings, and dangers which were a matter of course in the sailor life he freely selected. Indulging a passion generally, if not necessarily, supposes pleasure, enjoyment, delight of some kind. When, therefore, we find a man freely embrace a life which entailed much naturally hard and distasteful to man's nature, we must, I think, seek some reason or motive other than the wish to give full scope to mere passion.

The above theories become still more untenable when we consider the sort of man the Earl was, and the life he led during those sailor years. He was, first of all, an educated gentleman, and though remarkable for his friendly and kindly ways with his seafaring companions, he never put off this character. They knew from his bearing that he was not one of themselves, or used to their work, and they talked of this amongst themselves. They spoke of him as a 'shy and modest man, who did his hard work with great care, and was obliging and charitable to others.' A carpenter, in whose house he lodged, in Boston, stated that—

He drew beautifully; was fond of music and reading; often played on the piano for us; was very good to children; he took a good deal of notice of a child four or five years old in my house, and often brought her presents.

A man named Pearson, in whose house he lived for some time, gave him the following letter of character, the reading of which may well cause a smile :—

To whom it may concern : this is to certify that Mr. George Osborne has lived in my house for the last four months, and I can cheerfully recommend him as a young man of good habits and kind disposition.

The following is still more amusing. Small, who had been intimate with Osborne on board the ' Yeyla,' made the following patronizing statement :—

When I became mate it was my duty to select a sailor to be in my watch. I selected George Osborne, because I knew that I could chat freely with him, though I was an officer ; he would not take advantage of it as other fellows would.

He was most kind-hearted and helpful to all, using the needle at times, and when an accident happened he was physician and nurse. On one occasion, when a sailor had his leg broken, it was he who made the splints, applied them, and tended him till the bones knitted, and the limb was straight, and as long as the other. But he was more than all this ; he was a truly religious and pious man. Many who sailed or lived with him for the four years spoke of him as a man ' whose morality was irreproachable.'

Who used all his influence with his companions to fix their minds on God and religious subjects. He read portions of Holy Scripture every day, and on Sundays when the captain failed, as sometimes happened, he assembled all for religious service, and used to read prayers out of an old Catholic prayer book.

Without bringing forth argument or proof for the following proposition, I have no fear of asserting it. There are few, if any, better signs of a good man than his being a good son to a widowed mother. Now, this trait of character comes out in letters which he wrote to his mother; letters so refined, tender, and affectionate, that a stranger can scarcely read them unmoved. In one, dated August 12th, 1867, he says :

Dearest Mother, I hope you are keeping well. I am now with a very good man ; it is good for me to be here. I hope you will get this letter, and that it will cheer your heart ; it tells you of my undiminished love

Again, in 1869:—

I must come and see you soon. It is so long since I heard of you, that a sort of vague dread fills my mind, and I seem rather to go on in doubt than to learn what would kill me—I mean, were I to return and not find you. Many weary times has this thought come to me in the dark and cheerless night-watches, but I have driven it away as too terrible to think of. I wonder where you are now, and what you are doing. I know you are doing something good, and a blessing to all around.

He ends another as follows :—' Give my love to all dear ones, and believe in the undying affection of your son George.' In a letter written from Texas to his brother, the Hon. James Gordon, he says :—

I have never seen an approach to a double of you and mother. I know that there cannot be a double of her in the world ; she has not an equal. My best love to her. I think of her only ; she is always in my mind.

When off Palmas Grand Canary Island he writes to his mother :—

I saw a magnificent spectacle in passing the far-famed Teneriffe. It was a grand sight, and one which called up in my mind solemn thoughts and good resolves.

In another he writes :—

When making a voyage in a small vessel, heavily laden and very leaky, a furious gale came on ; the water gained on us, and the storm increased. We carried an awful press of canvas, but the poor water-logged schooner lay on her beam-ends. We were toiling at the pumps, and throwing over our deck-load ; already there were five feet of water in the hold: nothing could have saved us but a miracle or change of wind. But at 9.0 a.m., God, in His mercy, sent a sudden change of wind, with floods of rain, which beat down the sea, and in half an hour the danger passed away.

We must give one other extract. Sir Bernard states that the Earl had resolved to practise a rigid economy, in order to be able to live on his wages, and to put by a little. In the month of February, 1867, however, he drew two cheques for one hundred pounds each on his banker, in Glasgow, payable in New York.   In the following March he wrote as follows :—

I never had any self-respect since I found means to get that money in New York ; I have never-had any pleasure in life since. I despise myself for my foolish weakness; I shall never again hold up my head.

I attach a certain importance to the above words as supporting my theory. They express strongly, and in a very penitential spirit, the regret and remorse an honourable and upright man should feel for having broken a solemn resolution or vow to support himself by labour, 'to which man is born,' and ' in the sweat of his face.'

A word now on the third reason thrown out by Sir Bernard, ' eccentricity.'   That the Earl was singular, exceptional, eccentric, in the fact that he did what perhaps no other man in the world would, is evident. Men, no doubt, have given up freely all things of earth, but they did this believing that God called them to do so, not committing themselves, however, freely or as a consequence of their vocation, to the low companionship and hard life selected by him.   It must be said, also that outside his strange resolve there is not, in his general character, a shadow of that eccentricity which is often akin to insanity, or a dogged form of self-will, obstinacy, and selfishness.   Many, whose lives his would have shamed, most probably spoke of him as a fool or a madman.   Yet, I think, even these, having fairly studied the whole case, must admit that, apart from his strange action, there was no look of one or the other about him.   Moreover, it appears very improbable that his, or any other man's, eccentricity would seek its indulgence in a hard life, filled in with things most distasteful to human nature, particularly to a man born to comfort, ease, and luxury ; a life persevered in for four years.

It appears also unlikely, that so good, so intelligent, so sensible, so religious a man, of such refined feeling, of so high a sense of duty, so affectionately fond of his mother and relatives, would have allowed mere eccentricity to keep him away so long from them, from home and country, not without anxiety and suffering to himself, and to those

most dear to him. Besides, to attribute an action or a line
of conduct to eccentricity because it is very exceptional or
extraordinary, would strike at and disfigure some of the
grandest and most heroic events of history ; events in which
men, under no pressure of strict duty, have sacrificed all,
even life itself, from some high principle or motive. To do
so would be to stamp as eccentric martyrs to faith, to charity
or to country, as well as those glorified by the Divine
Teacher, for doing exactly what the Earl did, ' who hath
left house, or brethren, or father, or wife, or children, or
lands for His Name's sake.' Although Sir Bernard suggested the motives already discussed, I cannot but think
that he unconsciously believed in some higher influence.
If not, how could he have closed the sad scene of the Earl's
death with the following words, ' so perished one of the
most excellent men that ever graced the peerage of Scotland
or any other country '?

I cannot help being convinced that we must seek, and
can find, a theory more tenable than those put forward by
Sir Bernard. Are there not reasons for presuming, if not
believing, that the Earl's strange conduct was dictated by
some supernatural motive, was planned according to some
divine truths, and upheld by some superhuman power? Is
it possible that any merely human motives could have
prompted such a resolve, or that any merely human power
could have kept and sustained him, *the good man he was*,
during the years of his freely-chosen, hard, and suffering life ?

With all Catholics I, of course, hold—first, that God's
greatest grace and gift is to be born, or in time to become,
a child of the one, true, Catholic Church, which our Lord
founded, into which He poured all truth, and which is to
last ' till the consummation of ages,' the visible, infallible
organ and exponent of the dogmas to be believed, and the
moral code to be observed ; second, that this Church is the
only *ordinary* means settled and fixed by God for the salvation of man ; third, that outside of it there is no salvation
for anyone who perseveringly rejects the grace of a call to it ;
for anyone who is not at the moment of death united with it
by actual membership, or by a spiritual union with what

theologians call 'the soul of the Church.' Still, we know
from God's own inspired words, that 'He enlightened every
man that cometh into this world ;' 'that he willeth not the
death of the sinner,' but 'that all men be saved, and come
to the knowledge of the truth.' God also proved how real
and sincere this saving will was, by sending His only-begotten
Son, 'to seek the perishing and the lost, not to judge the
world but to save it.' And our Lord proved in the clearest
and strongest way He well could, that He was one in will with
His Father, by dying for all men. Holy Scripture overflows
with proofs of this most consoling truth—Christ died for all
men because He died for all whose nature He took. He
died for all those 'against whom stood the handwriting of
the decree.' He gave Himself 'a redemption for all;' 'He
came into this world to save sinners, even the worst.' So
reasons and writes St. Paul. St. John tells us that 'Christ is
a propitiation for our sins, and not for our sins only, but also
for those of the whole world.' We have this great truth
proclaimed in the Nicene Creed, and in the name 'Saviour
of the world,' given by excellence to our Lord.

Without entering into the question of what is strictly
defined dogma, we can have no doubt as to the mind of the
Church on this point. We find it formulated by theologians
as follows :—First, God really and sincerely wills the salvation of all men ; second, Christ died for all men ; third, grace
is given to all men with a view to their salvation. But
someone may fairly ask, If all this be true, how can anyone
be lost ? Well, the answer to this question is simple enough.
God never acts violently. He always respects His gift of
free will; He never coerces it ; He gives grace, but He
does not necessitate co-operation with it. Hence, a man can
neglect or refuse to use grace, can even abuse it, and by
doing so suffer the loss of his soul. The Council of Arles
expresses this truth as follows :—'That some are saved, is
the gift of the Saviour; that some are lost, is their own
fault.' And another Council says :—

As there is, was, and will be, no man whose nature Christ
did not take, so there is, was, and never will be, a man for whom
He did not die, though all may not be saved by the mystery of
the Incarnation.

Pope Pius IX. of holy memory, treats the two sides of this question in an Allocution given on the 9th of December, 1854. He condemns, as 'impious and fatal,' the opinion of those who hold ' that we may well hope for the salvation of all who were never members of the Church of Christ, and that the way of salvation may be found in any religion.' He then adds :—

God forbid that we should dare to place limits to the divine mercy, which is infinite. God forbid that we should wish to scrutinize the secret councils and judgments of God, which are a 'great deep,' and cannot be penetrated by human reason. The dogmas of Catholic faith touching the justice and mercy of God are not opposed one to the other. It is to be held, as of faith, that no one can be saved outside the Apostolic Roman Church. This is the one ark of salvation, and he who enters not into it shall perish in the flood. At the same time it is to be held as certain that they who are ignorant of the true religion, if their ignorance be invincible, are not guilty of fault on this head before God. Moreover, charity demands that we pour forth assiduous prayers that all nations may be converted to Christ, that we labour with all our strength for the conversion of all men, for the hand of God is not shortened, and the gifts of heavenly grace are never wanting to those who wish and ask with sincere mind to be refreshed with His light.

With reference to this question of exclusive salvation, we may say, that no one is forbidden to hold as probable, or even more probable, that the majority of mankind will in the end be saved ; still we should be well on our guard against making too little of God's greatest grace, the priceless pearl of true faith and of membership of the Apostolic Roman Church, and making too much of the chances of salvation outside her pale.

That a person can be invincibly ignorant of her claims is admitted by all, and is quite intelligible. We may fairly suppose that there are some, many perhaps, who, owing to their position and surroundings at home, at school, college, &c., are confirmed in the religion of their birth and family, and protected against any doubt concerning it. Every individual with whom they come in contact, every book placed in their hand or within their reach, every fact and view touching religion keep them in unquestioning good faith with reference to their own position, and too often in dislike, if not horror, of the true Church of Christ. It is, moreover, probable that such persons may have been validly baptized, or if not, may still be firm believers in the fundamental truths of Christianity, in the Holy Scriptures being the word of God, in prayer, charitable works for their neighbour, and other supernatural helps; 'wishing and asking with sincere mind to be refreshed with heavenly grace,' and to do God's holy will. Persons who never sinned against the light given to them, but, who, in God's mysterious providence, died before they came to its full glory. His Eminence Cardinal Vaughan, in his inaugural address at the late Augustine Centenary, speaking of such persons, said : ' Of those who have sickened and died in good faith on the way, how many have been saved by prayer.' To such souls, deprived without fault of their own of the ordinary means of salvation, God can and does give grace which, if corresponded with, will in an extraordinary way unite them with Himself.

I cannot resist the temptation to take a sentence or two from Lady Herbert's charming narrative, *How I Came Home*, because it expresses better than I could what I should wish to say, and because the words have that authoritative approbation which is given to those interesting and instructive tracts published by the Catholic Truth Society:—

The Catholic belief is, that no penitent soul can perish, and that one who really loves God cannot be lost, and there are holy and penitent and loving souls in the most erroneous systems.

I have no doubt [writes an eminent Catholic ecclesiastic] that through imperfect ministries and irregular systems, God shows His mercy on every soul which has the right dispositions. Therefore, no doubt could be cast on the reality of the work of grace in human souls in the Church of England or any other Church, by being convinced that its position is schismatical and its acts irregular. When convinced of this, however, it is a vital duty to submit to the law of unity and authority in the Church of God. I believe all sincere souls receive grace according to the measure in which they act up to their own light and convictions.

Now my theory places the noble Earl in this class. We

have undoubted testimony that he was a man of irreproachable life; an apostle amongst his sailor companions, doing
his best to fix their thoughts on God and holy things; a
man of reverent mind and religious dispositions, who loved
Holy Scripture, particularly the New Testament, portions
of which he read every day : a man, I believe, of good faith
and will, who wished and prayed to be refreshed with the
light of heavenly grace, and who corresponded with the
grace given.   A man of this mould would naturally take a
serious view of life, present and future ; would desire to
know the state or manner of life safest for his own salvation
and most pleasing to God, and would seek for light and
direction, in this all-important matter, according to his own
religious principles.   God's inspired word would be his first
study.   This would tell him that ' man was born to labour
as the bird to fly,' born ' to toil and eat bread in the sweat
of his face.' Also, that the things of earth are vain, unprofit-
able, uncertain, unsatisfying, shortlived, and, therefore, not
to be loved by one ' who has not here a lasting city, but seeks
one which is above.'   Nay more, that things of earth, especially those to which he was born, are a danger and a snare
in the path of man, and are often so abused as to become
the cause or occasion, not only of unhappiness in this world,
but of spiritual and eternal ruin in the next.

Reading religiously and thoughtfully every day portions
of the New Testament, he would hear of that ' wide gate and
broad way which leadeth to destruction in which the many
enter,' and resolve not to be of their number; of that
' narrow gate and strait way which leadeth to life,' and
resolve to be of them.   He would also learn that they who
ambition this life 'of the narrow gate and strait way' should
not set their hearts on what he had in abundance, namely,
earthly treasures, which rust and moths and thieves destroy,
but on heavenly treasures which these cannot touch: that
they should not only fly sin, but everything which would
really endanger sin, even though to do so were as painful
and as harmful as cutting off the right arm or plucking out
the right eye: that they should labour to acquire and
practise humility, poverty of spirit, meekness, patience,

charity, purity, unworldliness, trust in God and His fatherly
providence :—all which the Divine Teacher preaches so
powerfully and beautifully in His sermon on the Mount.
In his daily readings he would come across texts in which
the Divine Teacher speaks in very striking, if not startling,
terms, of the higher life which our Lord not only preached
but lived : ' Everyone of you that doth not renounce all
that he possesseth cannot be My disciple ;' ' He that loveth
father and mother more than Me is not worthy of Me ; '
'If anyone come to Me, and hate not his father and mother,
and wife and children, and brothers and sisters, yea, and his
own life also, he cannot be My disciple.' He would also
get some idea of the value of this higher life, and be attracted
to it by the magnificent rewards promised in this world and
in the next to all who would embrace and be true to it:
' For everyone that hath left house or brethren, or sisters, or
father and mother, or wife or children for My Name's sake
shall receive one hundred-fold, and shall possess life everlasting.' It is not difficult to imagine a man so deeply
religious as the Earl was, a true believer also in our Lord
as the Divine Teacher and Model, meditating on those words,
desiring to make them practical in this life, and praying for
heavenly grace to do so. I am inclined to think that the
Earl acted after this manner. Attracted by the life and
teaching of our Lord, he resolved to lead a life as like to
His as possible.

But how was this to be done ? The noble Earl had not
that authoritative divine key to the right interpretation of
Holy Scripture which the Catholic Church alone holds ; nor
had he the advantages of that safe guidance and direction in
spiritual affairs which is her gift also. If he had been one
of her children, she would have given him the full true
meaning of those texts. She would not only have directed
him, but also have given him the opportunity and means of
embracing and living this higher life. She would also have
encouraged him by calling his attention to the fact that
many of her children, under her guidance, had given up all,
even more than he possessed, to make these texts a reality
in their lives, and this without doing the strange things

which he did. The Earl, deprived, without fault of his own, of such help, had to use the only means in his power—prayer and private interpretation; and these resulted in selecting a state of life the most in keeping with our Lord's words and life, as he understood them. A life of self-denial, of renunciation of all things, of labour and toil and suffering, and of contact with the poor and lowly, a life which would lift him far above the best life he could lead in the state and position to which he was born. He believed his call to be personal, and that nothing of this world should be allowed to stand in its way : settling any scruples he may have had concerning his duties to others by the conviction that these were of minor importance dispensed with by Him who had given him a higher call, and that they would be discharged by others of his blood and name, as well or better than by himself.

Many may have, and likely did, call him a fool or a madman, or spoke of him as a man who made a big mistake. And yet, must not even they admit that there was a self-sacrificing heroism in his foolishness and mistake which they themselves would shrink from. I would answer such persons by asking them a question : Could you imagine yourself, or anyone you know, or ever knew, doing or equal to doing what he did ? If the answer be negative, it almost, if it does not really, prove that the Earl must have been under influences of a higher order and of a greater power than those which belong to our common nature.

Someone may, perhaps, say, if he were so religiously disposed, why did he not give himself to the ministry of his own Church, and work for the good of others. This may be answered: first, by saying that it was to the goodness and perfection of his own life he seemed to look; and that,although he edified those he came in contact with, he never showed any inclination to what I may call the missionary career. Secondly, taking him to be the man he was, according to my theory, he would see little or no difference between the Earl of Aberdeen and the Rev., Very Rev., or Right Rev. the Earl of Aberdeen. But, supposing for a moment that he did make a mistake in not becoming an apostle of his own Church, we may find the reason of this mistake in this Church itself, according to a view of Lord Macaulay in his review of Ranke's *History of the Popes*. He glorifies the Catholic Church because of certain extraordinary characteristics special to her and not found in any other human institution. He endeavours, weakly enough we must admit, to account for these on purely human grounds. Amongst them he places as an important item in the policy of Rome that 'she thoroughly understands what *no other Church* has ever understood, how to deal with enthusiasts.' ' In some sects, particularly in infant sects, enthusiasm is supposed to be rampant, in other sects, particularly in sects long established and richly endowed, it is regarded with aversion; the Catholic Church neither submits to enthusiasm nor prescribes it, but uses it.' He develops his opinion at some length. I give merely the substance of it. ' The Catholic Church knows that a religious enthusiast is no object of contempt. She accordingly enlists him in her service, assigns to him some forlorn hope, and sends him forth with her benediction and applause.' ' But for such a man there is no place within the pale of the Establishment ; ' he is cast off or deserts her, takes many with him, and ' in a few weeks the Church has lost for ever a hundred families, not one of which entertained the least scruple about her Articles, her liturgy, or her ceremonies.' ' Place Ignatius Loyola at Oxford, he is certain to become head of a formidable secession; place John Wesley at Rome, he is certain to be the first general of a new society devoted to the interests and honour of the Church.' Place the Earl of Aberdeen at Rome, and he would most probably have become a contemplative like Bruno, or a contemplative and missioner like Bernard. But being a member of a Church 'which has no place for such a man' he became of himself what he was, not, however, without some extraordinary supernatural help and power. Nothing merely human could have suggested to such a man so strange a life, and kept him, the good man he was, so long faithful to it. It is not in our corrupt nature, when unaided by divine grace, to restrain, crush, and crucify itself in things most dear to and loved by it. In any case, the Earl's career, view it as we like, contrasts favourably with the lives of many, and the world would not be the worse if all men, particularly of his class, no matter of what religion, lived more according to the spirit of his heroic and edifying life.

N. WALSH, s.j.

THE ANCIENT IRISH CHURCH

I HAVE read Dr. MacCarthy's attack on my *Ancient Irish Church as a Witness to Catholic Doctrine.* It appears in the August number of the I. E. RECORD (pp. 166-170), which I have only now had an opportunity of seeing, and forms, certainly, a notable contrast to the high, perhaps I should say too high, encomium passed upon that book, by the liberality of a learned reviewer, in the April number. Visibly, Dr. MacCarthy has no liking for the volume to which he devotes four and a-half querulous pages. He may be said, adapting the poet's language, to wave all his banners and charge with all his chivalry against it. However, with permission of the Editor, he shall not have everything his own way. I will reply, or endeavour to reply, to his somewhat Scioppian strictures.

Taking his remarks in their order, Dr. MacCarthy, in the first place, objects (pp. 166-167) to the use which I have made of the ancient Bobbio Missal. I have included this document among my sources of evidence on the doctrine professed by the early Christian Irish; I have referred to it on several primary points, and my quotations from it are numerous. 'They total pretty large,' as Dr. MacCarthy elegantly says (p. 167), in a parenthetic piece of jargon, that sounds like pigeon English, or some other foreign attempt at expression in the language. But let us pass away from that. My critic contends (p. 167) that the Missal in question ' was drawn up for a church in France, most probably in

Burgundy.' Be it so. I am sure I have nothing to say to the
contrary. I am so far of his opinion, as my *Appendix* shows.[1]
On the other hand, the MS. is allowed by Dr. MacCarthy to
be of Irish execution. In his monograph *On the Stowe
Missal*, he says :[2]—' The Bobio [*sic*]' Missal, in transcription,
was the work of an Irishman.' Now, this is quite enough
for me, and will be for most people. The script of the
Bobbio Missal being ours, by Dr. MacCarthy's own confession, its dogma may, fairly and justly, be adduced as ours
also, unless he holds, or means to maintain, as I am satisfied
he does not, that Irish monastic scribes, at home or abroad,
were in the habit of copying and preserving liturgies, and
other religious writings, *from the characteristic theology of
which they dissented.* If, like Todd or Warren, Dr. MacCarthy
denied the Irish nature of the penmanship exemplified in the
Bobbio Missal, now a settled point with most palæographers,
his objection to the use that this document is put to by me
would then have at least the force of consistent logic to
recommend it ; but, as things are, it is not for my present
critic to lecture me on ' due discrimination of the material,'
and bid me omit, as he does, all my citations from the Bobbio
Missal as ' irrelevant.' I have proved nothing, from the
Bobbio Missal, which is not equally proved by me, or
provable, from documents that were in undoubted employment in Ireland ; and if I allow that the Bobbio Missal was
not actually employed over here, Dr. MacCarthy will surely
not assert that it was not in daily use and requisition in the
seventh and following centuries at the monastery of Bobbio
itself, where, for a long period, there were always Irish
monks in more or less numbers, whom reason will accept as
types of their fellow-countrymen at home, in what regarded
the national faith.

The foregoing remarks, which justify me in appealing to

---

[1] *The Ancient Irish Church as a Witness to Catholic Doctrine*, p. 227.
Dublin: M. H. Gill & Son, 1897.
[2] *Transactions of the Royal Irish Academy*, xxvii., p. 151; Dublin, 1877-86.
[3] Would Dr. MacCarthy consider whether ' Bobio ' for ' Bobbio '—the
orthography which he adopts throughout the whole of his paper *On the Stowe
Missal*—has the sanction of Italian writers, who are surely the proper judges of
what it ought to be ?

the Bobbio Missal, will equally justify me in appealing to the Penitential at the end of it. *I*, however, have little concern in Dr. MacCarthy's paragraph on this Penitential. *I* have not quoted Cardinal Moran for what Dr. MacCarthy produces from him. If the Cardinal has ever 'transformed an *old woman* into a *village*,' *I* have not. 'Thou canst not say I did it,' as Macbeth exclaims. I cheerfully leave all such feats of legerdemain to the Herr Döblers, the Professor Andersons, and the Dr. Lynns.

We come, next, to Cummian's Penitential. This, it should seem, or at least portions of this, I ought not to have cited, as casting any light on early Irish dogmatic or disciplinary history. And for what reason? Because, forsooth, 'every indication denotes decisively that Cummian wrote his work not in his native but in another land, and drew from Irish, Anglo-Saxon, and Frankish Penitentials.' 'This being so,' Dr. MacCarthy continues (p. 167), 'ordinary prudence would suggest what has, unfortunately, not been done here, to verify the origin before adopting the citation.' Just as if, in tracing the current of Irish religious sentiment, it mattered a jot whether Cummian compiled his Penitential at home or on the continent! Just as if Anglo-Saxon and Frankish Penitentials were not consonant to the spirit of his native training, when we have the fact that he embodied some of their provisions in his work, and so made them his own!

Dr. MacCarthy is apparently much displeased that, by extracting fifteen *capitula* from Cummian's Penitential, I should imply the existence of such a thing as heresy in Ireland in the early Christian ages; whereas, he says (p. 167', 'St. Columbanus boasts that Ireland produced no heretic.' True; but that does not settle the matter. St. Columbanus died in 615, and, of the three Cummians to whom the authorship of the Penitential has been variously assigned, two did not depart this life till some half a century after that great missionary abbot, and the third flourished, at the very least, another half a century, or more, after either of his namesakes. It would be possible for heresy, and even much heresy, to spring up in any country, the Island of

Saints not excepted, in fifty or a hundred and odd years, and the testimony of St. Columbanus is not to be strained beyond his personal knowledge. Pelagianism made its appearance among our forefathers during the lifetime of St. Cummian the Tall, and that of his contemporary St. Cummian the Fair, to both of whom the Penitential, which deals with heresy, has been attributed; but to what extent this poison prevailed is not precisely known. At any rate, the fact is alluded to in 640, only twenty-five years after the death of St. Columbanus, by John, pope-elect, and three others of the dignified Roman clergy, in their joint letter to certain Irish bishops and priests on the Easter observance.[1] A little later on, a suspicion of at least some partial prevalence of heresy may be inferred from the *Hibernensis*, which, as Dr. MacCarthy says, in his paper *On the Stowe Missal*, 'was admittedly compiled for the Irish Church.'[2] The fifty-seventh book of this Collection of Canons has six *capitula* on heretics (*De hereticis*), the fourth containing an extract from a Synod in which it was decreed that heretics should be avoided.[3] This, more or less, supposes their existence amongst us. We need not stop, however, at generalities. Irish heretics are not unknown to history even by name. Here and there, one can be picked out. In 745, St. Boniface, the Apostle of Germany, complains to Pope Zachary of two heretical blasphemers—Aldebert (sometimes called Adalbert), a native of Gaul, and Clemens, a *Scotus* or Irishman, who, like so many of his race, had travelled to the continent.[4] Both were condemned at

---

[1] They say :—' Et hoc quoque cognovimus, quod virus Pelagianæ hæreseos apud vos denuo reviviscit ; quod omni[n]o hortamur, ut a vestris mentibus hujusmodi venenatum superstitionis facinus auferatur.' See Beda, *Historia Ecclesiastica Gentis Anglorum*, lib. ii., c. 19, p. 150 ; London, 1838.

[2] *Transactions of the Royal Irish Academy*, xxvii., p. 152 : Dublin, 1877-86.

[3] ' *Sinodus* ait : Definimus, hereticum esse vitandum, sicut enim cancer serpit per membra, ita doctrina ejus serpit in animas.' See Wasserschleben, *Die irische Kanonensammlung*, p. 223 : Leipzig, 1885.

[4] St. Boniface writes :—' Maximus tamen mihi labor fuit contra duos hæreticos pessimos, et publicos, et blasphemos contra Deum, et contra Catholicam fidem. Unus qui dicitur Aldebert, natione generis Gallus est ; alter qui dicitur Clemens, genere Scotus est : specie quidem diversi, sed pondere peccatorum pares.' See Ussher, *Veterum Epistolarum Hibernicarum Sylloge* (*Works*, iv., p. 457 : Dublin, 1847-64).

Further on (*ib.*, p. 459), St. Boniface gives the opinions of Clemens : — 'Alter autem hæreticus, qui dicitur Clemens, contra Catholicam contendit

Soissons in 744, and at Rome in the following year.[1] No branch of the early Christian Church, perhaps, can rival— none certainly can excel—the doctrinal purity of the ages of faith in our island ; but to suggest, or seem to suggest, that the whole nation was ' one entire and perfect chrysolite' of orthodoxy, or that heretics never by any chance had their origin or their abode amongst us, is not going the right or reasonable way about to be historical. It even ' strains credulity' worse than anything that I have attempted. The above remark applies equally to the state of morals ; and this brings me to Dr. MacCarthy's next accusation.

'To the same lack of discrimination,' he says (p. 168), ' is due a still more aggravated libel on the morality of the ancient Irish Church.' And what is that? Just this : that I have fetched forward from the Irish MSS. at St. Gall a musty *Ordo* of Penance, in which the confessor is directed to inquire whether or not his penitent is living in incest. I might have added that there is another copy of this *Ordo* among the Irish MSS. at Basle.[2]

> The very head and front of my offending
> Hath this extent, no more.

But Dr. MacCarthy is patriotic. He is a champion of champions. He will not have an *Ordo*, alluding to such a crime as incest, to be Irish. He casts about to deposit the shame of it elsewhere. The natural enemy must sustain it. The *Ordo* is to be—'purely Anglo-Saxon.' ·It is too bad, though, that the Anglo-Saxons should have all the odium. The obnoxious interrogatory was formerly not an uncommon

Ecclesiam : canones Ecclesiarum Christi abnegat, et refutat tractatus ; et intellectus sanctorum patrum, Hieronymi, Augustini, Gregorii recusat, synod- alia jura spernens, proprio sensu affirmat, sc, post duos filios sibi in adulterio natos [sub nomine episcopi] esse posse legis Christianæ episcopum. Judaismum inducens, judicat justum esse Christiano, ut, si voluerit, viduam, fratris defuncti accipiat uxorem. Ipse etiam contra fidem sanctorum patrum contendit, dicens : quod Christus filius Dei descendens ad inferos, omnes quos inferni carcer detinuit, inde liberasset, credulos et incredulos, laudatores Dei simul et cultores idolorum : et multa alia horribilia de prædestinatione Dei contraria fidei Catholicæ affirmat.'

[1] Peltier, *Dictionnaire Universel et Complet des Conciles*, ii., cols. 626, 893 : Paris, 1847. Alzog, *Universalgeschichte der christlichen Kirche*, p. 400 : Mainz, 1844.

[2] *Irish Ecclesiastical Record*, 1st series, i., p. 480 : Dublin, 1864-65.

one in the circumstances. Dr. MacCarthy, while his hand was
in, might just as well have shifted it on as far as France and
Germany, for it is found in *Ordines* of those countries too
of the ninth or tenth century. 'Possibly, therefore,' as
Warren says, 'the question was a necessity of the times
rather than indicative of any special degradation in the
morality of Ireland. I t should also be remembered that
marriages with persons occupying positions of spiritual
affinity as well as with near kindred fell under the designation
of incest.'[1] There is no use in closing one's eyes to facts.
There is as little in crying 'Libel!' where no libel has been
perpetrated. Marriage, with all its purity in the era of our
saints, was not without its occasional abuse. The pro-
hibited degrees were sometimes not sufficiently observed,
and sometimes a man wedded the widow of his deceased
brother. A *Synodus S. Patricii*, so called, though of a later
age than our apostle, condemns this Jewish custom in its
twenty-fifth canon, reciting the decree of an early Council
of the Church.[2] It is also condemned in the ancient
Hibernensis Collection.[3] Marriage with a deceased brother's
widow was favoured by Clemens, the Irish heretic before
mentioned, as St. Boniface notes,[4] and the practice maintained some hold here as late, at least, as the twelfth
century.[5] It was, however, generally reprobated, and in
the seventh century we have St. Kilian losing his life
in Franconia, through female vengeance, for his efforts to
break such a union between Duke Gozbert and Geilana.
So much on matters matrimonial.

Dr. MacCarthy then descends to trifles, and I am constrained to follow his bad example.

---

[1] Warren, *Liturgy and Ritual of the Celtic Church*, pp. 151-152: Oxford, 1881.
    [2] 'Audi decreta synodi: "Superstes frater thorum defuncti fratris non
ascendat, Domino dicente: Erunt duo in carne una." Ergo uxor fratris tui
soror tua est.' See Villanueva, *Sancti Patricii Ibernorum Apostoli Synodi, Canones,
Opuscula*, &c., p. 108: Dublin, 1835.
    [3] Wasserschleben, *Die irische Kanonensammlung*, p. 194: Leipzig, 1885.
    [4] See note 4., pp. 405-406.
    [5] Giraldus Cambrensis, *Topographia Hiberniæ*, dist. iii., c. 19, *apud* Camden,
Anglica, Normannica, Hibernica, Cambrica a Veteribus Scripta, pp. 742-743:
Frankfort, 1603.
    [6] O'Hanlon, *Lives of the Irish Saints*, vii., pp. 130-131: Dublin, n.d.
Alzog, *Universalgeschichte der christlichen Kirche*, p. 368: Mainz, 1844.

In the Memento of the Living, in the *Stowe Missal*, the Mass is stated to be offered, among other purposes, *pro . . . actuum emendatione eorum*, and construction shows that *eorum* is an error demanding correction. I amend it by [? *nostrorum*]: Dr. MacCarthy by [*r*]*eorum*. His emendation has the advantage of requiring only one letter: mine, *nostrorum*, makes the clause in question run in verbal consonance with the one in the preceding line, *pro remisione pecatorum nostrorum*. I keep to the orthography of the MS. The Holy Sacrifice is offered 'for the amendment of *guilty* actions' in Dr. MacCarthy's reading: 'for the amendment of *our* actions' in mine. Where is the difference in sense? Surely it is not *so* extreme that my conjecture should be made a fault. But Dr. MacCarthy has another hair to split. The Memento also has *uti eos in aeterna summae lucis quietae pietas diuina suscipiat*, translated by me, 'that the divine piety may receive them into the eternal regions of sovereign light and peace.' Dr. MacCarthy suggests a construction which would translate, 'that the divine piety may receive them into the eternal rest of sovereign light.' Is the difference in sense between us worth all this quarrelling? It is a pity to see the I. E. RECORD space so wasted. The suggestion that I failed to recognise the *e* sound denoted by *ae* in *quietae* is not correct. I was well aware of it, but translated the clause as I did, for the sake of a little more roundness of expression than could be got from it by servilely observing the strict grammatical construction; and this without any injury to the general meaning. I have good translators on my side for such harmless departures from literality.[1] But to proceed. The *Stowe* Offertory has: *Sacrificium tibi domine celebrandum placatus intende quod et nos a uitiis nostrae condicionis emundet, &c.,* which I translate: 'O Lord, graciously dispose the Sacrifice to be celebrated to Thee, that it may cleanse us from the

---

[1] Dr. Rock translates 'pro spe salutis et incolumitatis suae' in the Commemoration of the Living, in the Ordinary of the Mass, 'for the health and salvation they hope for.' See his *Hierurgia*, i., p. 39: London, 1833. The construction is here entirely disregarded; yet, who will say that he has not given the true sense?

vices of our condition, &c.'[1] Dr. MacCarthy tells us (p. 169), that he 'must play the pedagogue,' and that the meaning is: 'Graciously regard the Sacrifice,' &c. I have examined a number of Latin Dictionaries, but none of them have 'regard,' or any synonym of 'regard,' among the significations of *intendere*. They give 'design,' 'direct,' 'apply,' &c. Substitute any of these for 'dispose,' and what is the amount of my error? Tried by the Dictionaries, I may claim an acquittal.

As to my emendation of a passage in the *Tripartite Life* of St. Patrick, as we now have that *Life*, it is true that it has the *Book of Armagh* against it. It is no less true that there is nothing forced about the emendation, so simply is it made, as any reader will see who will consult my book;[2] and, remarkably enough, it brings the passage, so far, in accord with the *Tripartite* as possessed by Colgan, in very old MSS., not now known, and perhaps utterly lost. As far as my chain of argument is concerned, my suggested emendation may go by the board, if necessary. I have adduced facts enough, without its aid, to show that there were three bishops at our episcopal consecrations, and, if there were only two at Cairell's, perhaps Cairell was only made a *chorepiscopus*. In that case one bishop was sufficient. The other may, of course, have assisted at the ceremony.

As regards the testimonies given in Irish, Dr. MacCarthy is not ordinarily reasonable when he selects ' the arbitrary scribal joining and disjoining of words,' to take exception to (p. 169), as a matter that 'will scarcely afford "special satisfaction" (p. xiii.) to scholars.' In quoting venerable writings, edited by Zimmer or Whitley Stokes, I am justified in adhering to their text, just as they themselves are in keeping to the well-known agglutination of words characteristic of the original MSS. which they edit. In this way the individuality of old literature is preserved and placed before the student; and many would have thought better of Dr. MacCarthy himself, if, in his edition of the *Stowe Missal*,

---

[1] *The Ancient Irish Church as a Witness to Catholic Doctrine*, p. 89: Dublin, 1897.
[2] *Ibid.*, p. 118.

he had refrained from modernizing the orthography (though he does append clues to the state of the words in the original, on each page, in a host of notes), and had set forth the text of the MS. just as it stands, with all its quaint peculiarities, as in the edition given by Warren.

I come now to faults of the press. Man composes one thing: compositors sometimes compose another. Few books, especially learned books, are published without printers' errors. Dr. MacCarthy, *On the Stowe Missal*, contains a number. There are even some in his article in the I. E. Record. Distressing circumstances prevented me, during part of the time that my work was at the printer's, from giving that last attention to the press that I otherwise should have done. I know what it is to have marked errors for correction, and to have afterwards found the sheet, in one instance, to have passed to the machine uncorrected. Still, the work was most carefully proofed, as a whole. Dr. MacCarthy pitches upon the weakest spot; but page 231 is no fair or honest criterion of the remainder, and candour ought to have made him say so. It is not here a case of *Ex uno disce omnes.* In the other 230 pages, combined, there are not half as many errors of the press as there are in that one page. A Dr. MacCarthy is well able to correct page 231 for himself; to most persons, the page, though it were as free from *errata* as a page of a Bagster's Bible, would have to remain a dead letter. In over eleven hundred references, spread through some seven hundred and forty notes, there are not three figures astray. I have verified them, with the works before me, since the book came out. The printers' errors have been corrected in a number of the fifteen hundred copies sold since Patrick's Day, the date of publication. They are not of such a nature as to incommode any well-disposed or generous-minded reader. Only one is in any way unfortunate. In a note to page 22 it is said, of the Quartodecimans, that they kept Easter 'on the 14th March, no matter what day of the week it fell upon;' and, in another note, page 230, it is said : ' In strictness the Irish were not Quartodecimans. They did not celebrate Easter on the 14th March unless that date fell on a

Sunday.' In both cases my manuscript contains '14th moon,' not '14th March.' I suppose, as this seemed a kind of date, the compositor jumped at the erroneous reading.

I am next twitted (p. 169) for referring to 'an ancient treatise, in Irish, preserved in the *Leabhar Breac.*' The original, Dr. MacCarthy says, is Latin. But if, as he also says, 'the sentences of this Latin original are respectively followed by versions, sometimes literal, sometimes paraphrastic, in the native tongue,' assuredly these versions constitute 'an ancient treatise, in Irish, preserved in the *Leabhar Breac;*' and then wherein am I to be blamed ?

In sense there is no shadow of difference between Dr. MacCarthy's translation of the passage pointed at, the Irish in this case forming the better illustration, and my gathering of its import; not represented, be it observed, as a quotation, as I have not marked it with inverted commas in my book ; and I even find that a scholar like the Rev. Sylvester Malone makes a very similar collection from the same passage.[1] It is matter for regret that Dr. MacCarthy's criticism should so often resemble what lawyers call vexatious proceedings.

We arrive now at the last of his strictures as yet unnoticed. It has as little pith as its predecessors.

At pages 134-135 I deal, in connection with clerical celibacy, with an entry in the *Annals of Ulster*, in which it is stated that Archbishop O'Murray, who died in 1185, was 'buried at the feet of his father Bishop O'Coffey. I point to the dissimilarity of surnames, and remark, from this, that Bishop O'Coffey was apparently Archbishop O'Murray's 'father' only in the metaphorical sense. Dr. MacCarthy will have him to have been the 'father' in the natural sense. 'The most elementary knowledge of Irish,' he says, 'shows that the word was employed with the primary meaning.' Now there is nothing in the word itself to indicate this. Words, in all languages, remain the

---

[1] Malone, *Church History of Ireland*, i., p. 145 : Dublin, 1880.

same—they undergo no change in themselves—whether
employed in the primary or the metaphorical sense. Therefore, the passage itself will not enlighten us. True, Hennessy,
the editor of the *Annals of Loch Cé*, suggests that the Archbishop's mother ' may ' have been of the family of O'Murray,
and that the Archbishop 'may' have adopted her name;[1]
and true, also, Dr. MacCarthy takes these 'mays' to his
bosom, in a short note on the *Annals of Ulster*.[2] But
I challenge some proof that, in the Ireland of the twelfth
century, children, especially sons, ever received, or took, their
mother's name in preference to their father's; and until that
is forthcoming, I claim to have given a not unreasonable
solution of the difficulty. O'Donovan himself never thought
of saying that Archbishop O'Murray was named after his
mother. There is no evidence who his mother was. There
is none that she was an O'Murray. All that O'Donovan
could state, in explanation of a Bishop O'Coffey being an
Archbishop O'Murray's 'father,' was, that it was 'very odd.'[3]
To him there would have been no ' oddity ' in it had he
known of any such practice as the one inferentially
suggested, but supported by no proof, by Hennessy and
Dr. MacCarthy.

A word now, in conclusion, on the tone of Dr. MacCarthy's
article. It makes no compensating acknowledgments. From
first to last he is all censure. He is not a critic with any
art. My book, whatever its defects may be, is obviously
one that cost much trouble. For the research and the
patient toil which it represents it has received the kindest
possible notices, even from the adverse Protestant press.
It cannot evoke, however, a single genial word from
Dr. MacCarthy. Its intention is laudable; it is not unlikely
to do good; it is published with episcopal sanction; but all
this cannot move him to a syllable of toleration. He is even
quoted in it himself for the valuable information contained
in his treatise, *On the Stowe Missal*, and opportunity is

[1] *Annals of Loch Cé*, i., p. 170: London, 1871.
[2] *Annals of Ulster*, ii., p. 205: Dublin, 1887-95.
[3] *Annals of the Four Masters*, iii., p. 69: Dublin, 1856.

taken in the text to preface the mention of his name with
an epithet of respect for his attainments; yet, courtesy and
good taste dictate to Dr. MacCarthy to be the first Catholic
to fall foul of my book, and to have no name for its author
at all, but to refer to him throughout by the one monotonous
expression, ' the compiler,' which is evidently used in the
spirit of depreciation and contempt, and from which he
might have varied occasionally if only for the improvement
of his style; while he winds up his ungracious remarks
with a sentence, in which Horace is cited for my benefit,
and I am curtly advised to defer the appearance of my
proposed enlarged edition for nine years.

Should Dr. MacCarthy decide to rally his dissipated
forces, and advance once more at the head of his Anglo-
Saxons, Franks, and Burgundians, with the other as yet
unemployed levies hinted at by him in italics, I am not
indisposed to encounter his motley hordes again, and may,
perhaps, send them back to Youghal in the company of
defeat.

JOHN SALMON.

DR. TROY, AS BISHOP OF OSSORY, 1776-1786

THE POLICY OF 'RALLY' AND CONCILIATION

A HISTORY of the episcopacy of Archbishop Troy would include a history of the Catholic Church of Ireland for almost half a century of one of the most eventful periods of her existence. The present writer cannot claim to have access to the documents which would be required in order to do justice to the long and memorable episcopacy of this illustrious Irish prelate. Still, it may not be amiss to make some effort to supply information which might be useful to historical students, almost a century after some of the most important events which rendered his episcopal rule one of the most momentous in Irish ecclesiastical history. John Thomas Troy was born of respectable parents near Lucan or Porterstown, Co. Dublin, May 10, 1739.[1] In his diary, published in the I. E. RECORD, May and June, 1872, he writes : 'While yet very young, I was removed to Smithfield, and sent to school in Liffey-street. I was received into the Order of the Most Holy Rosary, at Dublin, July 5, 1755.' The same diary informs us that he sailed from Dublin for Leghorn, on his way to Rome, February 18, 1756 ; and that he arrived in the City of the Popes, and commenced his ecclesiastical studies at the Dominican Convent of SS. Sixtus and Clement, April 11, of the same year. There he was ordained priest by Dominic Gindane, Patriarch of Antioch. There also he acted as Master of Novices, as Regent of Studies, and as Prior from 1763 to 1776. In the years 1768 and 1769, Father Troy was employed by his illustrious predecessor in the see of Ossory, Bishop Burke, to procure for him many important documents from the archives of the Vatican and other Roman

---

[1] The name Troy must have been formerly one of considerable importance in the neighbourhood of Kilkenny. The still surviving appellations Troy's Wood and Troy's Gate attest this. A beautiful antique embroidered silk escutcheon, bearing the Nolan-Troy arms, is in the possession of E. Nolan, Esq., Parliament-street.

libraries for the *Hibernia Dominicana*.   Father Troy was
then a bachelor o ftheology.   Dr. Burke refers to him as—
' Troio isto bacculareo, non minus religioso, quam docto.'

Bishop Burke (De Burgo) having died, September 26,
1776, great efforts were made by influential personages in
favour of a very distinguished and popular priest of Ossory,
Dean Mulloy.   In a letter written from Rome at this time
by Mr. Stonor to Lord Fingall, he informed him that neither
Mr. Mulloy ' nor the principal candidate opposed to him will
be appointed, but a Mr. Troy, who, I am persuaded, had no
such views, and who, from what I know of his piety, learning,
and prudence, will give satisfaction to the clergy and people
of Ossory.'

The Archbishop of Cashel, Dr. Butler, having written to
the Propaganda in favour of Dean Mulloy, was informed by
the Cardinal Prefect, Castelli, that the Prior of St. Clement's
had been already appointed, ' Vir pietate, doctrina, caeterisque
optimo pastore dignis virtutibus commendatissimus.'

The Archbishop and his suffragans were at the same time
exhorted to exercise their influence in favour of the new
bishop, in order that he should be received by his subjects
with becoming filial love and reverence.   It is on record that
Dr. Troy was the last episcopal nomination made by the
' Pretender.'   If so, it brought very little advantage to the
Stuarts, and it may have been one of the reasons why
Dr. Troy was so little uneasy about granting the veto to
the House of Brunswick.   A record of his appointment and
consecration, in his own handwriting, is preserved in the
Ossory diocesan register.

It records that John Thomas Troy, Prior of the Convent
of SS. Sixtus and Clement, Rome, and for about twenty-
one years successively employed in all the offices of that
community, was nominated to be Bishop of Ossory in a
congregation of the Propaganda, held on the 26th November,
1776, at which Cardinals Castelli, Corsini, Visconti,
Antonelli, Orsini, and the Secretary Borgia were present.
The nomination was approved of and confirmed by Pope
Pius VI., on Sunday, the 1st of December, and the Apostolic
letter of the appointment stamped with the seal of the

Fisherman on the 16th of the same month. Dr. Troy did not leave Rome on his homeward journey until March 21, 1777. Probably he was receiving full instructions relating to the settlement of the Armagh controversy.

From his diary we learn that at Pistoja he paid a visit to General O'Reilly, formerly governor of that city, and that at Leghorn he was often hospitably entertained by Messrs. Cosgrave, M'Carthy, and Brennan, a ship-chandler from Kilkenny. At Paris he met the Nuncio, who talked of the Test Oath ; and at Versailles he met the King and Queen in their private way. Dr. Troy was consecrated on the 8th of June by His Excellency Ignatius Busca, Archbishop of Emessa, Nuncio of Flanders, assisted by two mitred abbots of the Premonstratensian Order—Joseph De Rondeau, Abbot of Grimberg, and Francis Genere, Abbot of Park, near Louvain, where the ceremony took place.

In order to counteract all feelings of opposition, the Bishop elect addressed his first pastoral to the chapter, clergy, and people of Ossory, Feb. 2, 1777. It was dated from outside the gates of Rome, and opens with a declaration that it had pleased the Almighty, the author of consolation and peace, whose ways are unsearchable, and judgments inscrutable, to summon such an insignificant, unprepared, and weak individual, and one not dreaming of any such dignity, from the secure harbour of the religious life to face the perils of the deep, and to undertake the guidance of the Church of Ossory.

He consoles himself with the reflection, that, according to the teaching of his Angelic Master, St. Thomas, God never elects any person to any special office or dignity without endowing that person with suitable and proportional graces. He refers to his immediate predecessor, Bishop Burke, as one whose life and episcopal rule was a bright example, and one calculated to reflect great lustre on the entire hierarchy, his own religious family—the Friars Preachers, and the Irish nation. For all the circumstances relating to himself, ' quae circa me sunt qui agam,' he refers them to his illustrious metropolitan, Archbishop Carpenter. He concludes with a most earnest appeal for the assistance

of the prayers, in the first place, of the chapter, his crown
and his joy ; of the secular clergy called on to share in his
pastoral solicitude ; and of the regulars, ' Ecclesiae divitae,
et episcoporum coadjutores, quos in perfectionis spiritu
ambulantes impense colo.'

Dr. Troy took possession of his diocese, by procurator, on
the 1st day of March. He reached Ireland, July 21, and
arrived in Kilkenny on the 14th August, 1777. His residence
during the time of his sojourn in the ' Marble City ' was a
very humble one-story cottage, on the north side of Dean-
street, somewhat apart from the main thoroughfare, and
under the shadow of the venerable Cathedral of St. Canice.
It is now in ruins, but in its best days it could not have
been a desirable residence.

The new Bishop pontificated for the first time in his
diocese, August 17, in the parish church of St. Canice ;
and, by a special brief from Pius VI., was empowered to
grant a plenary indulgence to all the faithful assisting at
the ceremony.

Dr. Troy was honoured with the full confidence of the
Holy See from the time of his arrival in Ireland. And he
succeeded in retaining this confidence against very powerful
undermining influences to the end of his career.

His first important employment was, when as Delegate
Apostolic he restored his primatial jurisdiction to Archbishop
Blake, and endeavoured to compose the unhappy differences
that had arisen between the Primate and an influential
section of the clergy of Armagh. As we learn from the
Renehan MSS., p. 113, Dr. Troy's conduct in the whole
course of this affair was ' applauded in the highest strain of
panegyric by his superiors,' notwithstanding the misrepresentations made against him at Rome, by a considerable
number of his episcopal brethren.

October 25, 1777, there was a communication to the
clergy of Ossory, written from Dublin, notifying to them
that they were in future to make use of the Directory
published there by Rev. Mr. J. Kelly.

His first Lenten Pastoral, dated Kilkenny, Feb. 7, 1778,
prescribes the fast of Lent to be strictly observed ; people

who might require a dispensation, from infirmity or feeble
old age, were allowed the use of flesh meat on certain days,
provided that they ' had it boiled, and the broth given to
the poor.'

Dr. Troy came to Ireland with the intention of giving a
strenuous support to the policy of ' rally' in favour of the
house of Brunswick, and of their representatives in the Irish
Government.   This policy appears to have been inaugurated by Bishop Burke as early as 1760, in a pastoral in
which he exhorted his people to behave themselves with all
that respect and submission which becometh pious Christians
and peaceable subjects, not giving the least shadow of offence
to the Government; but, on the contrary, let your words and
actions be such as deserve a continuance of that moderation
and lenity which we experience these many years.   Furthermore, we earnestly desire you to join us in offering most
fervent prayers to the all-merciful God, beseeching His
Divine Majesty to preserve this kingdom from intestine
war, or any other national calamity.   A similar exhortation
was read from the altars of the archdiocese of Dublin,
Oct. 2, 1757.   The above was repeated on the occasion of
the fast ordered by the Government in 1762; and the people
were exhorted to avoid ' all tumults, especially when soldiers
were being enlisted for His Majesty's service.'   In the
pastoral published against the Whiteboys, Nov., 1764,
Bishop Burke reminds them, that, if they think themselves grieved in any respect, they might seek redress by
lawful ways and means :—

They ought to be amenable to the laws of the nation, and not
to provoke the Government, which is mild beyond expression.
Hence, in the name of the Roman Catholic Church, I abhor and
detest their doings, and I declare that their combination oath
does not bind them.   Wherefore I command them to behave
as peaceable subjects, and so deserve a continuance of that lenity
and moderation we have experienced these many years past.
Otherwise, I will punish them to the utmost of the power I have
from God and the Church.   I am not only encouraged, but
likewise requested to do so by personages in power.   To be
read in an audible voice, and to be explained in Irish from the
altar for three Sundays.

. In the Ossory register, a note is appended to the above stating, that it was published in Faulkner's *Dublin Journal*, *The Dublin Gazette*, in the News Occurrences, *The Dublin Gazetteer*, *The Universal Advertiser*, *The Dublin Courier*, *Freeman's Journal*, *The London Chronicle*, and many other newspapers. In 1771, under the viceroyalty of Lord Townsend, an Act was passed enabling Catholics to lease and reclaim fifty acres of bog, and one-half an acre of arable land adjoining thereto, as a site for a house, but it should not be within a mile of any city or town.

This policy of conciliation and loyalty to the King and Government, was taken up and urged on the Catholics of Ireland by Dr. James Butler of Cashel, Dr. Moylan of Cork, but above all by Dr. Troy. It has been the means of saving our national Church in trying times from terrible perils, if not from destruction, and of raising her to her present position of prosperity, and of world-wide renown and beneficence. In the stress of the war with the American colonies, a proclamation was issued by the Viceroy, Lord Buckingham, for a general fast. As on a previous occasion, in 1762, copies were forwarded to all the Catholic bishops. Dr. Troy, in a letter written to Archbishop Carpenter of Dublin, Feb. 18, 1878, gives his reasons for publishing the Government fast :—

Your opinion on the propriety of publishing the Government fast coincides with mine. Our neighbours of Munster deserve no compliment, and their example is no rule for me. Other circumstances, however, make me apprehend that my silence on the occasion would be misinterpreted, perhaps to the disadvantage of the clergy of this diocese in general; the spirit of Whiteboyism is not yet extinct in this county, and jurors, and non-jurors equally wish for opportunities to show their abhorrence of every combination against Government.

The following pastoral was accordingly published on Sunday, Feb. 22. It is remarkable for its reference to the war with the American colonies, and as introducing for the first time, in prayers publicly offered up by Irish

Catholics, the names of a Protestant king, queen, and viceroy:—

DEAR CHRISTIANS,—You have been frequently reminded of the obedience you owe to the powers whom the Almighty has appointed to rule over us. Your pastors and teachers have not ceased to inculcate and enforce that indispensable duty after the example of our Divine Redeemer, who commands us to 'give unto Cæsar what belongeth to Cæsar, and unto God what belongeth to God.'

You have experienced the lenity of Government in the execution of penal laws which continue to distinguish you from other subjects, notwithstanding your irreproachable demeanour in times of temptation and trial.

Impressed, as I know you are, with these considerations of duty and gratitude, I cannot doubt of your persevering endeavours to merit an increase of indulgence from His Majesty, and every other branch of the legislature. A cheerful compliance with this important obligation is particularly requisite in these days of discord and calamity. . . .   And whereas it has pleased His Excellency the Lord Lieutenant and Council to order a general fast on Friday next, the 27th inst., I desire you will observe the same with that religious decency and exactness which are expressive of compunction and a lively feeling of our present situation. Offer up your most fervent prayers on that occasion for the spiritual and temporal happiness of our Most Gracious Lord and Sovereign King George the Third, his Royal Consort and Family, approach with confidence the Supreme Ruler of Empires and States, by whom kings reign and legislators determine what is first, humbly imploring Him to direct His Majesty's Councils and render him the happy instrument of a speedy, honourable, and lasting reconciliation between Great Britain and all her once flourishing colonies in America, without further effusion of blood.

Your love for your native country will induce you to recommend this poor kingdom in your prayers, and also His Excellency the Lord Lieutenant and Chief Governor thereof, who like his Royal Master has nothing more at heart than the happiness of all His Majesty's subjects, without distinction. I wish you all every blessing, and am, &c., &c.,

JOHN T. TROY.

The above was printed in Finn's *Leinster Journal*, Kilkenny, and in all the Dublin newspapers. Writing to Dr. Sweetman of Ferns, September 24, same year, Dr. Troy refers to 'the alarmed Protestant strictures on my pastoral letter, and the different replies.'

In a letter to Dr. Carpenter, written from Kilkenny, March 13, he informs him that his letter publishing the Government fast 'pleased everyone here, particularly the non-jurors.' The non-jurors were those who did not wish to take the test or oath of allegiance, which was then a source of so much controversy amongst Irish Catholics.

Dr. Troy informs the Bishop of Ferns, December 23, 1778, that he had long reconciled his mind to the formulary, and that he had declared his opinion and resolution to his clergy without an injunction on any person to adopt them ; and in a letter to the same prelate, dated Kilkenny, April 1, 1779, he states, ' Last Monday I took and subscribed the famous test oath in the court-house of this city before the Attorney-General Scott (afterwards Lord Clonmell); the major part of my clergy and a prodigious number of the laity went through the same ceremony. I fancy you will think this an odd preparation for Easter.'

Dr. Troy also wrote a letter on the same subject to his Metropolitan, Dr. Carpenter of Dublin, October 28, 1778, which had the effect of removing his hesitation, as after much consultation he also subscribed the oath in open court. The advantage to be gained by subscribing this oath was the Catholics might thereby, from the Act of the Irish Parliament passed the previous year, take, enjoy, and dispose of a lease for 999 years certain, or determinable on the dropping of five lives, and that the lands then seised by Catholics should in future be descendable, devisable, or alienable, as fully as if they were in the seisin of any other subject of His Majesty. It was no longer in the power of a child to dispossess his parents by pretending to become a Protestant. Catholic priests were allowed to celebrate Mass, and their flocks to assist at Mass without incurring the penalties previously exacted.

This was the first important breach made in the fortress of the penal enactments, and Archbishop Butler and Dr. Troy are entitled to their full share of credit for their part in such a successful and far-reaching effort. The eulogium passed by Mr. Burke on another Co. Kilkenny man, Sir Hercules Langrishe, who was one of the warmest supporters

THE IRISH ECCLESIASTICAL RECORD

of the Emancipation Bill in the Irish House of Commons may be applied to his fellow-county-man, Dr. Butler, and to the Bishop of Ossory, Dr. Troy:—

My opinion ever was (in which I heartily agreed with those that admired the old penal code) that it was so constructed, that if there was once a breach in any essential part of it, the ruin of the whole, or nearly of the whole, was, at some time or other, a certainty. For that reason I honour, and shall for ever honour and love you, who first caused it to stagger, crack, and gape. Others may finish; the beginners have the glory; and take what part you please at this hour, your first service should never be forgotten by a grateful country.

We have on record a striking effect of the policy of 'rally' and of the loyalty of Dr. Troy and of the Irish Catholic Bishops. Theobald M'Kenna relates that:—

In 1780, when the French Court made preparations to invade Ireland, very high offers were held out to any *Irish Priest*, who would embark in the expedition. There were above two hundred on the foundation of the Irish College at Paris. I recollect that the proposal was made and rejected unanimously and indignantly. I understand it was repeated through the entire French dominions with the same effect.[1]

On the 27th January, 1779, another pastoral was published for the purpose of further impressing on the faithful the duty of loyalty and submission to their temporal rulers:—

As to the fast ordered by the Government, on Wednesday, the 10th of next month, I require you to exhort your several congregations to the observance thereof, and to join all other good subjects in fervent prayers for success to His Majesty's arms by sea and land; and a speedy, honourable, and lasting reconciliation and peace with all the enemies of these kingdoms. On that occasion, you will not fail to inculcate the sentiments of loyalty, respect, and gratitude to Government, expressed in my circular letters of the 20th February, and the 10th September, 1778.

This pastoral concludes with a repetition of the sentence of excommunication, fulminated against the Whiteboys, by Bishop Burke, in September, 1775. The same censure was again fulminated in a more solemn and impressive form by Dr. Troy, October, 1779.

[1] *Thoughts on the Civil Condition, &c., of the Roman Catholic Clergy*, p. 52.

The following notice has reference to a celebrated abduction case, fully described in all the magazines of the closing years of the last century :—

On Saturday, December 2nd, 1780, Messrs. Garrett Byrne, James and Patrick Strange, were executed in Kilkenny for forcibly carrying away Catherine and Anne Kennedy. It was afterwards rumoured about the city that the High Sheriff refused the Roman Catholic clergy admittance into the jail during the confinement of said Byrne and the Stranges. Therefore, it was thought proper to publish the following lines from the different altars of Kilkenny: ' Whereas it has been reported through this city and neighbourhood that John Warren, Esq., High Sheriff of this County, refused the Roman Catholic clergy admittance into the jail upon a late occasion, we think it incumbent on us to declare in this solemn and public manner that said report is entirely groundless, as we had access to the prisoners whenever we required it.'

A new Catholic Relief Bill had been introduced, January, 1782, into the Irish House of Commons, by Mr. Gardiner (afterwards Lord Mountjoy, killed at the battle of New Ross). Its progress was slow and very much disputed, although advocated by some of the ablest and most eloquent members of the House, viz.:—Sir H. Langrish, Mr. Connolly, Mr. Ponsonby, Kilkenny county; Mr. Hussey Burgh, the Provost of Trinity; Sir Boyle Roche, Gowran; Mr. Mossom, Kilkenny city; the Attorney-General, Mr. Scott, Sir Lucius O'Brien, and Mr. Grattan. In the meantime the Volunteers held their Convention at Dungannon, February 15, and passed the following (14th) resolution :—' Resolved, that as men and as Irishmen, as Christians and as Protestants, we rejoice in the relaxation of the penal laws against our Roman Catholic fellow-subjects; and we conceive the measure to be fraught with the happiest consequences to the Union and prosperity of the inhabitants of Ireland.'

Within five days after the passing of this resolution, Mr. Gardiner, the sponsor of the Bill, declared to the House that 'he was happy to find that the liberal spirit of toleration which had originated in that House, had so universally diffused itself through the whole kingdom ; and he rejoiced that in the north, where ill-nature had supposed that prejudice would prevail, benevolence was seen to flourish.'

Mr. Grattan, in giving his constant support to the

measure, bore the following testimony in favour of his
Catholic countrymen :—

When this country had resolved no longer to crouch beneath
the burden of oppression that England had laid upon her ; when
she armed in defence of her rights, and a high-spirited people
demanded a free trade, did the Roman Catholics desert their
countrymen ? No ; they were found amongst the foremost.
When it was afterwards thought necessary to assert a free
constitution, the Roman Catholics displayed their public virtue :
they did not endeavour to take advantage of your situation ; they
did not endeavour to make terms for themselves, but they entered
frankly and heartily into the cause of the country, judging by
their own virtue that they might depend on your generosity for
their reward.

The Act, when passed, enabled Catholics to take, sell,
and dispose of lands and hereditaments in the same manner
as Protestants, except advowsons and manors, or boroughs
returning members for Parliament. It removed several
penalties from such of the secular clergy as shall have taken
the oath and been registered, and from the regular clergy
then within the kingdom. Officiating in a church or chapel
with a steeple or bell would deprive them of the benefit of
the Act. It repealed several of the most obnoxious parts of
the Acts of Anne and George I. and II.—such as the power
given to a magistrate to fine and imprison every Papist
refusing to appear and declare upon oath when and where
he heard Mass, who celebrated and assisted at it, and the
residence of any Popish ecclesiastic, prohibiting a Papist to
have a horse of the value of £5 under certain penalties, or
to take or purchase a house in Limerick or Galway, or the
suburbs thereof, giving power to grand juries to compel
Catholics to make good the depredations committed by
robbers in the country in which they resided. The Act also
enabled Catholics, except ecclesiastics, to be guardians to their
own or any other Popish child. It did not enable them to
take any, even the lowest, office of trust of profit, to vote at
an election, to be freemen in a corporation, to serve on a grand
jury, to become barristers, solicitors, &c. But Catholic
schoolmasters, on taking the oath of allegiance, and with
the license of the Protestant Bishop of the diocese, were
permitted to instruct Catholic scholars in their own (Catholic)

schools.   One of the first of the Irish bishops to take
advantage of this Act was Dr. Troy.

Writing to Dr. Fallon, Bishop of Elphin, September 23,
and November 9, 1782, he informs him that :—

The Education Act does not regard the clergy as such, but
is confined to schoolmasters, who can teach in future with
impunity on taking the oath of allegiance, and obtaining a
license from the respective Protestant Bishops.   I have intimated
a Diocesan Synod for next year, and ordered my clergy to provide
themselves with soutanes, surplices, and caps, to be made use of
within the precincts of our places of worship.   The enclosed
printed paper will explain the nature and design of an academy
now erecting here.   I have the pleasure to assure you it meets
with general approbation and encouragement.

In the Diocesan Register, under date September 4,
1783, the following entry appears in the handwriting of
Dr. Troy :—' The Rev. John Dunne, Con-Rector of the
Kilkenny Academy, is appointed Canon of Tasscoffin;
Rev. James Lanigan, Con-Rector of the Kilkenny Academy
becomes Canon of Killamery.'

These two distinguished clergymen became the immediate
successors of Dr. Troy.   Dr. Dunne ruled the see of Ossory
from 1787 to 1789, and Dr. Lanigan from 1789 to 1812.   In
the letter of Cardinal Antonelli to Dr. Lanigan, intimating
his appointment as bishop, the school is mentioned in the
most flattering terms.   The site of the old Kilkenny
Catholic Academy had been at one time occupied by a
member of the Clifden family, and the occupation of such a
house by Catholics for a Catholic school was then considered
an immense progress for the Papist Church.   The Academy
was at that time chosen for the education of the children
of the most respectable Catholic families of Ireland.   It
numbered amongst its pupils Shee and Clarke, who rose to
great honours in the French army, under the Republic and
Napoleon.   The learned Dr. Milner, in a letter written to
Edmund Burke, mentions that he visited the old Catholic
Academy of Kilkenny whilst the public examinations were
being held, and that—' The Established Bishop, who was
formerly Provost of Trinity College, Dublin, frequently
honours the examinations there with his presence, and was
expected the morning when I attended.'

It appears that the custom of wearing garlands and other decorations, generally known as May Balls, because given by young married people, and carried about on the 1st day of May, was at one time very prevalent in different parts of Ireland, and a cause of much scandal. Dr. Troy published an order, December 12, 1782, commanding his priests not to administer Sacraments to any person or persons who shall hereafter demand or give said May Balls, or call for money, liquor, or anything else in place of them, till such transgressors declare their repentance and promise amendment before the assembled congregation. The first child of any couple giving May Balls was to be baptized in the parish chapel!

In 1784 the disunion amongst the Volunteers upon the question of granting the Parliamentary franchise to the Catholics had a most injurious effect. The bond of union was in some measure broken, and the divisions were encouraged by the Government. In the Munster diocese, and from thence to Ossory and Ferns, there was a revival of the Whiteboys, now calling themselves "Right Boys," led by an imaginary "Captain Right." These not only committed outrages against the tithe-proctors, agents, and middlemen, but even went so far as to prohibit the usual offerings to their own clergy.

Archbishop Butler and the Munster Prelates, as we learn from the Renehan MSS., pp. 346 and 347, not content with denouncing the members of this illegal and sinful confederacy, made strict regulations against any unreasonable or rigorous exaction of dues. Dr. Troy acted in like manner. His ordinance regulating the amount and manner of collecting dues was published in the parish of Camross, Queen's County, and is so lenient in favour of the laity that one cannot imagine by what contrivances the unfortunate clergy were able to keep themselves alive and in working order. This ordinance is only to be found in the old parochial registry of Castletown, Queen's County, and is dated August 29, 1786. The clergy of Ossory were amongst the most determined opponents of the veto, and were almost unanimous in supporting the celebrated declaration or address of Dean O'Donnell, of Kilkenny, which started such a strong wave of public opinion contra, as eventually submerged that ill-starred measure.

February 1, 1783, a circular letter was read from all the altars of the diocese, announcing the glad tidings of the peace lately concluded between the contending powers, and inviting the faithful to join in fervent thanksgiving for this long-wished-for blessing; and, likewise, 'for the religious toleration and freedom of trade which they then enjoyed.'

A Pastoral which attracted much public notice, and is dated, November 12, 1784, concludes as follows :—

We condemn these deluded offenders (White or Right Boys), who call themselves Roman Catholics, as scandalous and rotten members of our Holy Church, from which they have been already cut off by sentence of excommunication, solemnly fulminated against them in all the chapels of the diocese. We cannot conclude without beseeching you, dearest Christians, to join us in fervent and constant prayer for the speedy conversion of these unthinking creatures. Their condition is truly deplorable in this life, exposed by their nocturnal excursions and wanton depredations, to sickness, loathsome imprisonment, and an infamous death ; whilst in the next their obstinacy will be punished with endless torture. May our gracious God, by His efficacious grace avert this greatest of all evils, and thereby prevent the bitter recollection of their having disregarded our timely and pastoral admonitions.

We shudder at the very apprehension of the manifold evils which must necessarily ensue to themselves, to their families, and to their country, from a continuation of their unwarrantable proceedings.

It being equally our wish and duty to promote the happiness of mankind in general, and that of our country and flock in particular, we shall invariably conduct ourselves in a manner becoming ministers of the Gospel, and members of society ; uninfluenced by fear, or any worldly consideration, we are determined to adopt such further means as shall be found conducive to the above-mentioned and other great objects of our vocation.

The Duke of Rutland, who was then Lord Lieutenant, had the following acknowledgment of the merits of the Pastoral conveyed to the Bishop of Ossory :—

DUBLIN CASTLE,
20th November, 1784.

SIR,—I read with pleasure your forcible and well-timed exhortation to the Roman Catholics of the Diocese of Ossory upon the re-appearance in the County of Kilkenny of these execrable rioters, formerly called Whiteboys. I thought it a justice to you to lay it before the Lord Lieutenant, and I have his commands to assure you of the great satisfaction he feels on the part you have taken for the preservation of the peace, and preventing the unhappy consequences which must follow from those wicked and deluded people persisting in such outrageous violation of the law.

I trust your endeavours will have that success which they merit,[1] and which claim the esteem of all good men.

I have the honour to be, sir,
Your most obedient humble servant,
THOMAS ORDE.

It was during the time of Dr. Troy's sojourn in Ossory, that an important and prolonged discussion was started as to the reception of, and the advisability of publishing the law of clandestinity, and its effect on the validity of mixed marriages in Ireland. Dr. Troy was in favour of the receipt and publication of the law, but he wished that the marriage of a Protestant and a Catholic should be regarded as valid in Ireland without observing the form of the Council of Trent, if no other impediment intervened.

His letters on this subject may be seen in the Renehan MSS., pp. 441 to 451. They are masterpieces of reasoning and judgment, and prove that their author must have been deeply versed in the knowledge of theology and canon law. Although he was at this time only Bishop of Ossory, he succeeded in bringing over to his views the entire Irish Church, together with the Roman Propaganda. The question was finally discussed in the presence of Pius VI., March the 3rd, 1785, and a decree, signed by Cardinal Antonelli, given in favour of the opinion advocated with so much ability by Dr. Troy, from the year 1777.

N. MURPHY, P.P.

---

[1] They may not have had any immediate visible success, but it is remarkable how comparatively free Ossory and the Munster dioceses were from the '98 movement. How was such a change brought about ?

WINGED WORDS OF FATHER KNEIPP

In the matter of eating and drinking we should think rather of our stomach than of our palate.

* * *

The finest children are to be found amongst the poorest people, who live on potatoes and bread soup.

* * *

I was brought up on potatoes and bread, and at eighteen years of age I was a powerful fellow.

* * *

My native home was an old cabin. There was a little window in it, which stood wide open, winter and summer; under that window I slept.

* * *

The night air is in no wise poisonous; if it were, all the birds would die.

* * *

The Kur-guests are always in too great a hurry. When they have been doctored for years elsewhere, they come to Wörishofen, and ask for instructions how to treat themselves at home, and want to be off by the next train.

* * *

People think they have only to come to Wörishofen and produce their diseases; then the old Pfarrer blows on them and they are well.

* * *

Put a fashionable boot on the floor beside your foot, and just see how far the work of the bootmaker corresponds to the work of the Creator.

* * *

Who walks barefoot will never have a headache.

* * *

For the healthy, cold water is an excellent means of preserving health and strength; for the infirm, it is the most natural, the simplest, the cheapest, and, if rightly applied, the surest means of cure.

* * *

Madame Influenza has no more dreaded enemy than cold water.

* * *

I say it to you in all truth, whatever is curable can be cured by water.

* * *

You must not think that I invented the water-cure, or that I got it out of books; I simply learned it from experience.

* * *

I should like to teach the whole world what they ought to do;—if I had only time enough.

* * *

When a man is seventy years old, as I am, he is like a soldier on furlough, who knows not the moment he may be called back.

G. M.

THE PRESENT POSITION OF ANGLICANISM

WHEN the great religious revolt of the sixteenth century began to take shape, it alarmed those who believed in an indestructible Catholic Church: When in later centuries, the Bible and English dominion went hand in hand, and when, together with her losses on the Continent, the Catholic Church had lost her hold on the English throne and the English people : it seemed, for a time, as if the Church which Jesus Christ established was about to be superseded, or rivalled, by the institutions of men. But, as was natural to expect, the spiritual kingdom could not prosper in the keeping of the temporal monarch. And the Church of England, divorced from her spouse by the monarch who had divorced his wives, pined, as in bondage, in the hands of his successors. And after three hundred years we find that, even in England, the boasted conquest of the Reformation, the cloud is breaking, and the 'city on the mountain' begins to appear in her ancient comeliness.

If the diminishing proportions, and waning influences, of the Church of England indicated a corresponding growth of the Catholic Church, then indeed would the harvest be great. But this is not so. For although we see small, perhaps increasing, numbers of converts, and greater numbers who by conviction, or by the fear of coming danger, are drawn to the threshold of the Vatican ; the tendency of the vast majority is to the broad ways of indifference, or infidelity, or of creeds whose definite teaching retains scarcely a vestige of Christianity.

This tendency is manifest from the way in which parents choose to have their children educated. There are two systems of primary education in the country: one established and endowed, the other tolerated and inadequately assisted. The former may be said to be purely secular, the latter combines religious with secular instruction. In the former, known as the Board School system, all dogmatic teaching is excluded. The doctrines of the Blessed Trinity and the

Incarnation would be irregular, because they may be offensive to the consciences of Unitarians or others. And the moral teaching is scarcely nominally religious. And, even if it were in accordance with the moral laws of the Gospel, there is nothing to give it a hold on the minds of the children ; it is put before them on no authority that can command their respect. Perhaps an example would best explain my meaning. A correspondent from one of the London newspapers, some short time ago, visited various schools, and gave a description of the religious instructions he had heard. In a Board school the teacher was explaining the Parable of the Ten Virgins, and his explanation was to this effect. Several boys were invited to a wedding ; but were first sent on errands. Some went directly and brought their messages, and went to the wedding; while others delayed, looking in at shop windows, and were late ; and he gravely informed the children that these latter boys were not asked to any more weddings. The moral he drew from the parable was punctuality. And this is the divine teaching confided by Jesus Christ to His Apostles, and by His Apostles to the nations ! Surely this is not religion, even in its broadest sense. Would it not be better if the very name of religion were excluded? For it might then be brought to the knowledge of those children, in after years, that there was a treasure of sacred truth they had not heard of. But when religion is first profaned, and then offered to them; they will grow up, thinking that they have as children learned Christianity, which as men they cannot respect ; since it was put before them with the same authority, and the same worth, as Æsop's Fables.

And if we apply the wise test of the Gospel, judge the tree by the fruit, we arrive at the same conclusion. For those who have been educated in Board schools practise no religion. They believe in the Christian law as far as it coincides with the civil law. By their duty as Christians they understand their duty as citizens. And for the future, they have a vague doubtful trust in some undefined providence. It is only twenty-five years since this system of secularism was adopted, and now half the children of

England are educated in it. Take then from the schools, where religion is taught, the Catholics and Jews; and the remnant represents the numbers of the rising generation, in the once powerful, prosperous, Anglican Church. And a large proportion of those who are trained in Anglican schools, and profess membership of that communion, grow out of the practice of their religion, as they grow out of their boyhood; and think no more of the Church, when they have left the school. This is true, especially of the cities, and large towns; for in the country districts the old subserviency still exists, and the people are found at church, for the service of God, or to catch the eye, and gain the graces of the squire and parson. It was estimated last year, by some of the news-papers, that four-fifths of the population of London never enter a place of worship, and unfortunately the number is not exaggerated. And when the Non-conformists, and Catholics whose proportionate attendance is much the largest of any denomination, are subtracted, we can form some idea of the practical strength of the Anglican Church, in the metropolis of more than four millions. Nor is this the worst, for we must bear in mind that the Church of England, besides her decay, and her losses, has still to reckon the difficulty of reconciling the many jarring sections that dwell within her fold. There are High Church, and Low Church, and elements of dissension breeding in each of those, which have no bond of sympathy between them, except the golden bond of endowment, while they remain within the broad lines of the Established Church. All this goes to show how much those were mistaken, who thought that by a reunion with the most advanced High Church Anglicans, they could bring about the conversion of the whole, or the majority of the English people.

But I would here caution my readers lest they may conclude from what has been said, that the Church of England has already passed away; that there remains but some ruined gable of the great imposing edifice that was raised on the sands of human power. For she still comprises many millions of subjects, who are heart and soul devoted to, or at least in sympathy with, her welfare. And the millions whom she can no longer reckon as hers are, to a great extent, the poor, or those who are in the lower grade of the social scale; so that she still possesses her wealthy patrons, and, endowed at home, can disburse her thousands of pounds to those, who go as missionaries to the heathens, and practise the charity which begins at home, by providing themselves with temporal, and promising themselves eternal, welfare. And other thousands of charities endowed, or charities subscribed, are in her hands, for the pious use of encouraging worshippers to attend her churches at home. The visiting lady goes her rounds with the Bible in one hand, and a shilling in the other, to pay for the privilege of reading to those who will hear and receive. The excursion, or the free holiday in the country, or by the seaside, is held out to the denizens of the city, as an inducement to attend the services in the churches. And need I say that even yet the Catholic, who has faith to sell, can find a market for it, and sell it at a premium. The pieces of silver are ever ready for the purchase of a betrayal. And the pious Protestants think it a most godly use for their Church's wealth to purchase the hated, the jealously-dreaded Roman faith. But it must be said that the spirit of proselytism, which inspired their ancestors, has much diminished; perhaps, because the needs of their own household are sufficient to occupy their energy.

It is evident from what has been said that the Church of England is not what she used to be, in power or influence, and like all things human, time has brought about the beginning of her dismemberment. But will she be won back to the fold of salvation, and how? Or will she drift into that broad Christianity which differs but little from infidelity, and what then? Two ways of bringing her back to her place in the true Church have been suggested; reunion, and reconversion. The reunion movement has deceived many. It began in the Anglican community, or rather in that portion of it known as Ritualists, and it does not seem as if it were destined to bring about any appreciable results. When they had adopted almost every paragraph of the Catholic Ritual, when the parson sat down to act as minister in the much-abused confessional, and vested as the Catholic priest attempted to celebrate the Sacrifice of the Mass, which his ancestors since the Reformation had declared idolatrous ; when Protestants invoked the Virgin Mary, and declared the Pope the first bishop in Christendom ; then it might be said, there was needed only to arrange a few details of discipline, and call them Catholics once more. But, narrow as the space which separates truth from error may seem, still a vast deep chasm heaves between them. Those were only advanced outposts of the Anglican communion, and those who would follow them would be comparatively few. And even the most advanced would still regard England as a national branch of a Universal Church, as a branch establishing in itself, laws and customs, and discipline, not in keeping with, or contrary to, those observed in the Catholic Church. In a word, they would be with us, not of us ; they would claim to be a sister, rather than a child ; a self-sufficient Church which did not need the spiritual waters from the spiritual rock.

Reunion of this sort would be impossible, or undesirable ; and therefore, the two methods are reduced to one reunion by reconversion. And we can expect to see the Church of England brought back to Catholic unity, only when individually, or bodily, her members renounce the faith they hold, and embrace that which their ancestors, some few centuries ago, renounced. There are many difficulties which bar the way to this reunion, the difficulty of prejudice, the difficulty of the position in which the Anglican clergy find themselves, and the difficulty of renouncing the laxity of conscience which Protestantism permits. Those are human, is there a higher difficulty between God and the nation that renounced His truth ? The depths of His wisdom are too great for us. And in reviewing those difficulties it seems as if the first were likely soon to become the least.

The day has passed, or soon shall have, when the Protestant threw up his hands in pious horror, and raised his indignant voice against the imaginary abominations of ' Popery.' In sermons, in prints, in conversation, the gospel promulgated as the religion of Protestant England used to be : trust in God, hate the Pope, and glory in the

liberty and enlightenment of the national Church; and
then all was heaven, no matter how often God's Commandments might be violated.   This bigotry against Catholics
has, to a great extent, disappeared; and when Leo XIII.
declared Anglican orders invalid, we no longer see the
tide of indignation which burst over the country when,
nearly half a century ago, Pius IX. re-established a
Catholic hierarchy.   Nevertheless there exists, here and
there through the country, much latent prejudice against
us, which may fester anew into violence at any moment.
There is still much of the old bitterness against Rome
handed down from father and son, and the decline of
prejudice corresponds with the decline of Protestant faith.
Liberty and tolerance for Catholics have been warmly
supported by, and owe much to those who had little, if
any, faith themselves; and cared but little what others
professed.   And they have contributed to form the public
opinion which forbids too greedy a display of public
bigotry.   But even yet, where Protestant faith is strong, there
lurks much prejudice against the spiritual sovereignty of
the Roman Pontiff, and it is a difficulty in the way of
conversion.

But, apart from this prejudice, this fear of the Pope's
jurisdiction, real or simulated, there are many ties which
bind the Anglicans fast to the position they occupy.   The
people, as far as they follow religion, are naturally guided by
their clergy, and for the clergy change of faith will lead in
many instances to destitution.   They cannot fulful the
office of priests in the Catholic Church, for they are men of
wives and families.   And the sacrifice of celibacy in Catholic
clergy, even for a limited time, and under extraordinary
circumstances, would strike a blow at the noblest endowment,
and most attractive feature of Latin Christendom; and would
lower the Church to such an extent in the eyes of her
children, and in the eyes of the world, that it would take
very many conversions to compensate her loss.   And it is
to be feared that this is a serious obstacle in the way of
many ministers, who feel themselves drawn towards the
Catholic Church.   It is to be feared that the cry of the

children for bread, and of the wife for comfort, has stifled
the cry of many a conscience seeking greater certainty and
security of faith.

The day the Church of England submitted to force, and
placed herself under the patronage of, and bargained servitude
to, the state, for a state endowment, she was bound by a
golden chain to the throne of the monarch, and that chain
is still strong and hard to break.   The day she acknowledged
the monarch as her head, she gave to Cæsar the things that
were God's, and she has ever since remained the servant
of Cæsar, and not the servant of God.   And how far the
way, how trying the journey, to Rome must seem to the
Archbishop of Canterbury, when it would cost him £15,000 a
year.   If the conscience points there, as in many instances
it does, the cost is a sordid motive to bar the way to rewards
a hundredfold ; but man is not all soul, his motives are not
all spiritual ; a doubtful conscience, and a comfortable home
are often weighed against, and preferred before, what seems
the securer, but rougher, way to heaven.   ' The young man
went away sad, for he had great possessions.'

Would it not then be a benefit to the Church of England
if she were disestablished by the state? would it not instil
new life into her if she were thrown on her own efforts for
maintenance?   Disestablishment might have had this effect
before the Church had lost, as she now has, her high place
in the esteem of the people; but now it is too late ; she has
grown fat, and morbid, and feeble, in the luxury of her state
alliance.   And besides the English people are not yet prepared
for disestablishment.   Ever since their heresy of the sixteenth
century a national Church has been part of their national
pride.   When an Englishman sees qualities he admires in
those of other nationalities, he says how like an Englishman.
In his own mind he himself is the model of what man should
be, and his nation the model of perfect nations ; and he
claims not only a model kingdom of earth, but also a model
kingdom of heaven.   He will have no religious jurisdiction unless its source and administration are English.   He
regards the Pope as a foreign prelate ever plotting for the
destruction of his liberty.   And he forgets that in the kingdom

of salvation there is neither Gentile nor Jew, circumcision nor uncircumcision, barbarian nor Scythian, bond nor free. He forgets that the human nature of Jesus Christ was Galilean, and that the Apostles He appointed teachers and rulers in His kingdom were also many of them Galileans, and none of them Englishmen. He forgets that the Popes so hated were, like their Master, enduring prisons and death for the Christian Gospel, while yet Englishmen were searching the heavens and the earth to find an idol for their worship.   It is true, however, that the position of the Church of England is due more to statesmen than to church-men.   The state is the keeper of the will of the Church, and requires that the Church should sway the consciences of the people according to the purposes, religious or otherwise, of the state; and when she can no longer do this she shall have served her political purpose, and disestablishment may come ; and one difficulty, at least, to England's conversion shall be removed.

But I do believe that one of the greatest hindrances to England's conversion is generally overlooked.   The fall of the country into heresy has been followed by the lapse of great and increasing numbers into indifference, if we may not call it infidelity. The loss of faith, however, was followed by the loss of moral virtues ; so that we see a tendency to the repetition of cause and effect, as described by St. Paul in his Epistle to the Romans, where he treats of the religion of the heathens. And England having lost the moral virtues with her ancient faith, both obstacles have to be overcome, she must ascend the steps she has descended, before the Church, without spot or wrinkle, can regain her lost dominions. Liberty of conscience was the watchword of England's apostacy; and it meant liberty from the law of God, liberty for every excess, while the Saviour was called upon to remain on Calvary, and bleed and die, that a fallen people may trust in Him, and go from a life of sin to the life in heaven. This religion was bound to fail; it was the offspring of private judgment, and the gates of hell were too strong for private judgment. And the result was that God was driven from the people's hearts; then He left their national Church. Will those who threw off His yoke renounce their false liberty, pay homage to His law, and to His Church? and when? The answer will decide the question of England's future religion.

But beneath the superficial indifference, which seems spreading fast amongst the English people, there lies a strong Christian respect for the supernatural, and a yearning for the knowledge of it. They will have a religion; every people must be compelled by the conviction of their own conscience; and England will soon want a religion. For the Anglican Church is doomed; losing in numbers, losing in influence, she is passing slowly, but steadily, to the end of all things human. With contending elements within her, High Church, Broad Church, and Evangelicals, she may at any moment, be divided into many so-called Churches; she is, in reality, only a name embracing many sects. Divided against herself she cannot stand. Dissensions within her, and the contempt rather than the hostility of her enemies, will decide her fate. The fingers are beginning to trace the fatal *Mane* on her walls. And Nonconformity—thus the beliefs of dissenters from the Church of England are named—will never be, in any of its forms, the religion of the nation. It cannot convince the intellect; it does not appeal to the heart; it is too thin, too cold; its seeds are too near the surface; and beneath the sun of unbelief, which is testing every seed, they will be scorched, and because they have not root they will wither away.

But when all those have failed, when the absence of a Church, the want of a religion for the nation will lead to the desire of it, who will be there to give it? Where else can we look save to that nursery of true religion, from which an Augustine was sent, in far back ages, to lay the foundation of a noble Church in England? We must look to the Catholic Church, who had seen and fearlessly weathered the roughest storms before the heresiarchs who seduced England from her were born. She had seen many years before the Anglican Church began, and she is still fresh and strong, still growing and maturing, while the Anglican Communion is feeble with old age. And the divine hand that guided and supported her when the nations raged against her, can give her victory alike over those who rebelled against her authority, and those whom she has never numbered in her fold. But will it? Will God give the grace sufficient to draw back reluctant England through the sins of her fathers and the prejudices she has inherited to the communion of His Church? The secret is locked infinitely deep in the bosom of the Lord, and who hath known His mind?

Nevertheless we may be permitted to conjecture according to human light. What then is the status of the Catholic Church in England? And what are her prospects? In numbers she is comparatively small, her power and influence are growing far beyond her numbers. She is losing some, but she more than compensates her losses by those she is winning back to the fold. Her progress is not as rapid as we could wish, although perhaps as great as we could, humanly speaking, expect it. She is holding her own, and gaining somewhat, while the tide of religion is ebbing from the country, and the life and strength of other denominations are floating on it. It is true that the neglect, and indifference, which are knawing to the vitals of the Church of England, and the dissenting sects, have also left a passing mark on the Catholic Church. When all around them have lapsed into apathy, the contagion has spread amongst the Catholics, and they too in great numbers live in neglect of their religion; but with this difference: they preserve their faith. They respect their Church; they respect their priest, and will die for the religion they do not practise. Their children by their own desire are educated as Catholics, and they anxiously ask for the sacraments when they are about to die. No wonder that neglect, the dust of the decaying edifices around her, should fall upon the Catholic Church as well; but it lies upon the surface, and beneath the rock of faith remains unmoved, unbroken.

Therefore the Catholic Church in England is not, like the Anglican communion, betrayed or denied by those whom she has fostered in her own bosom; but only forgotten for a while, by some who still love her dearly in their hearts.

And I believe that if much of the energy which is expended in trying to bring Protestants back to the true faith, were exerted in bringing Catholics who already profess that faith to the practice of it, there would be more fruitful results; for the Catholic Church, freed from the scandals which her own children bring upon her, would draw all things to herself. And the example of the early Christians, more than the eloquence of their preachers, was used by God as an external grace to draw the nations to that Church. But looking at her as she is there can be little doubt that, when the other religions, which usurped her birthright, have failed, and they are failing fast, to satisfy the English people, the Church, which for more than three centuries lay bleeding beneath the persecutor's lash, and could not die, will come back to the full possession of her own again. The stone which the builders, in the sixteenth century, rejected under false pretences, shall be made the head of the corner again. But when? God knows; but do the angels in heaven? Four thousand years the world waited for a promised Saviour. It is not yet two thousand since He came. Will the periods of the New Testament exceed those of the Old? And if so, how short the period, not yet four hundred years, in the eyes of God, since England threw off His yoke. How long He may leave her in error as a punishment for her sin, we cannot tell; but the ways of heaven, and the ways of men, point to the conclusion that, after their years of religious wanderings, the sons will come back to rest in the bosom of the Church their fathers left.

M. RYAN.

HISTORY OF TRIM, AS TOLD IN HER RUINS

ON the banks of the Boyne about seven miles from the chief seat of royalty, on the Hill of Tara, and twenty from the City of Dublin, stands the town of Trim, the capital of Royal Meath. There are few places in Ireland, rich as she is in historic reminiscences, more worthy of notice. The majestic ruins of ancient buildings, civil and ecclesiastical, that meet the eye on every side open up a wide field for reflection. Standing out in all their rugged grandeur the many time-worn monuments of by-gone days that are to be seen scattered around arrest the attention of all who pass by the way, and awaken in their minds a multiplicity of thoughts regarding the many battles, sieges, forays, and skirmishes formerly witnessed within the hoary walls of this stronghold of the Pale. The old Church of St. Patrick, with its ivy-clad tower, the stately form of the 'yellow steeple,' and the other remnants of ecclesiastical structures, are even more suggestive than the frowning walls, and the jutting battlements of 'King John's Castle,' and speak to the soul more eloquently than words.

> Here you stand,
> Adore and worship when you know it,
> Pious beyond the intention of your thought,
> Devout above the meaning of your will.[1]

Like many other places in Ireland, Trim is an historic spot that deserves to be better known. Within its gates there are treasures enough to woo the footsteps of the student and the stranger, and full of the deepest interest to the scholar and the antiquarian. Here, undoubtedly, all lovers of ancient lore can make themselves at home. They can come close, and feast their eyes on every precious remnant of the past. They can gaze intently on the massive walls so imposing even in their ruins, and scan the delicate moulding

---

[1] Wilde's *Beauties of the Boyne*, p. 79.

and tracery of the finely-chiselled windows; they can pace
to and fro, and gauge the proportions and symmetry of the
entire building, and think of the genius that devised the
plan, and the hands that executed the work, and of the voices
long silent that once resounded within the walls.   In a word,
they can carry away with them a whole host of historic
memories that 'round them, like visions of yesterday,
throng,' and that fill the imagination with pictures of real
though undefined pleasure.   A man of refined archæological
tastes, a careful gleaner in the field of antiquarian research,
one, ' who finds tongues in trees, books in the running
brooks, sermons in stones, and good in everything,' tells us
the impressions made upon him on the occasion of his visit
to this classic locality :—

To see Trim aright [says this competent authority] the tourist
must approach it by the Blackbull-road from Dublin, when all
the glorious ruins which crowd this historic locality, and which
extend over a space of above a mile burst suddenly upon him.
    The remains of St. John's Friary and castellated buildings at
the bridge of Newtown, a little further on the stately Abbey of
SS. Peter and Paul, raising aloft its tall light and ivy-mantled
windows, the neighbouring chapel with its sculptured tombs and
monumental tablets, the broad green laws through which the
Boyne winds between that and Trim, the silver stream itself
gliding smoothly onward with unbroken surface, the grey massive
towers of King John's Castle, with its outward walls and barbican,
the gates and towers, and bastions, the fosse, and moat, and
chapel, the Sheep-gate, and portions of the town wall, and towering above all, the tall commanding form of the Yellow Steeple,
which seems the guardian genius of them all. All these beauteous
objects, with the ancient church tower of St. Patrick, the town
itself, the Wellington monument, and the modern public buildings,
form a combination of scenery and an architectural diorama such
as we have rarely witnessed.[1]

Though every one of these 'beauteous objects,' so
graphically depicted by Sir William Wilde, has its own
peculiar history, I shall pass them over for the present, and
in this paper draw attention to a very curious fact of which
little or no notice is ever taken, e$_{ven}$ by the close student

---

[1] Wilde's *Beauties of the Boyne*, p. 79.

of sacred history, viz., that Trim is the *oldest* Church in Ireland, being established by St. Patrick, at least twelve years before the foundation of the Church at Armagh, and consigned to the care of Loman, who accompanied our saint into Ireland, and was constituted first Bishop of Trim.

Before entering on the evidence which goes to show that Trim is the oldest Irish episcopal see, it may be well to remind our readers that the ancient name of which the present is only an abbreviated form, was ' Ath-Truim,' or ' Ford of the Elder Trees.' About the meaning of the first part of the patronymic there is no controversy or doubt. The ford to this day is still quite discernible, and young folk, especially in Summer time, not unfrequently amuse themselves by running across barefoot from one bank to the other. The ford is only a few perches above the Town bridge, and quite close to the mill in possession of Mr. Kennedy, the present Chairman of the Town Commissioners. Above and below the ' Ford ' the river itself is deep, and the current rather rapid. As an illustration of this I may be permitted to put on record a remarkable and melancholy incident that occurred at this very place last year. On the night of the 11th of April, a poor man living in the neighbourhood, named Goggins, was missed by his friends at Galtrim. He had been in Trim during the day, and in such company as begot in the minds of his friends a strong suspicion of foul play. The services of the police were accordingly requisitioned, scouts were despatched in all directions, but all to no purpose. After a fruitless search of several days, on the evening of the 22nd of April, a little boy espied on the north side of the river something in the shape of a human being. When the officers of the law came upon the scene, they found it was the body of the missing man. At the inquest it transpired the poor creature was seen going late at night down a lane leading to the 'Ford' or shallow. Some persons stated that when they were retiring to rest about eleven o'clock on the 11th of April, they heard something like a sudden splash, and a shrill cry of a swan whose favourite resort is near the ford at the mill, and so the jury came to the conclusion that the poor man missed his footing, and fell into the deep water beside the 'ford' and was drowned. The body was not found in the spot where it fell, but was borne down by the rapidity of the current below the bridge, where it was discovered after eleven days, with the hands clasped upon the muddy sedge caught up by the drowning man in his efforts to save himself. The second portion of the name owes its origin very probably to the profusion of the 'elder trees' found growing in former times along the banks on this part of the river, or, according to another authority, to the formation of the bank itself, which here assumes the form of a long low hill, and hence the name ' Ath-Druim ' the ' Ford of the Ridge.' [1]

But whether the latter derivation of Dr. Todd, or the other more commonly adopted, be the correct one, is a matter of little consequence, compared with the proposition with which this paper proposes to deal, viz., whether there is sufficient historic evidence for the statement, that Trim is the *oldest* Irish episcopal see, older by at least twelve years, than the primatial see of Armagh.

The statement, on the face of it, seems to be a rather bold one, the fabrication of some fiery enthusiast, of some one unduly anxious to put ' Ath-Truim ' in a position of prominence to which she can lay no claim. At all events, one cannot be expected to accept the assertion without proof; and the interesting question then arises for discussion, is that proof forthcoming. Let us see. In the first place, we have the very valuable evidence of Tirechan, who flourished in the early part of the seventh century. He was a pupil of the renowned and saintly B.shop of Ardbraccan, St. Ultan, and subsequently his successor in that see. This eminent scholar, whose collections of Church History are found embodied in the famous *Book of Armagh*, wrote a life of St. Patrick, the particulars of which, he ' learned from the mouth of his master, Bishop Ultan.' It may be well to remember that Ultan was an uncle on the mother's side to St. Brigid, and may be said therefore to belong to the

---

[1] Dr. Todd's *Life of St. Patrick*, p. 160.

Patrician era.[1] He died at a very advanced age, in the year
656. Now the testimony of such an ancient writer as
Tirechan, brought up in the school of such a master, who
had such opportunities of knowing the truth, is manifestly of
supreme importance. What account does he give us of the
foundation of Trim? We quote from the Primordium of
Ussher:—[2]

In the year 433, when Patrick, in his holy navigation, came to
Ireland, he left St. Loman at the mouth of the Boyne, to take
care of his boat forty days and forty nights; and then he (Loman)
waited another forty out of obedience to Patrick. Then, according to the order of his Master (the Lord being his pilot), he came
in his boat against the stream, *ad vadum Truim*, as far as the
ford of Trim, near the fort of Feidilmid, son of Loiguire.

And when it was morning Fortchern, son of Feidilmid, found
him reciting the Gospel, and, admiring the Gospel and his doctrine,
immediately believed; and a well being opened in that place, he
was baptized by Loman in Christ, and remained with him until
his mother came to look for him; and she was made glad at his
sight, because she was a British woman.

But she likewise believed, and returned to her house, and told
her husband all that had happened to her and her son. And then
Feidilmid was glad at the coming of the priest, because he had
his mother from the Britons, the daughter of the King of the
Britons, Scothnoessa. And Feidilmid saluted Loman in the
British tongue, asking him in order of his faith and kindred; and
he answered: 'I am Loman, a Briton, a Christian, a disciple of
Bishop Patrick, who is sent from the Lord to baptize the people
of the Irish, and to convert them to the faith of Christ, who sent
me here according to the will of God.'

And immediately Feidilmid believed, with all his family, and
dedicated, *immolavit*, to him and St. Patrick his country, with his
possessions and with all his family; all these he dedicated to
Patrick and Loman, with his son Fortchern, till the Day of
Judgment.

But Feidilmid crossed the Boyne, and Loman remained
with Fortchern in Trim until Patrick came to them, and built a
church with them twelve years before the foundation of the
church of Armagh.[1]

Stripped of its quaint style and cumbrous Irish names,
so difficult in appearance to one not acquainted with the
language, we find on a brief analysis of the above narrative,
four events very circumstantially detailed:—(1) Patrick's

---

[1] *Ireland's Ancient Schools and Scholars*, p. 115.		[2] *Prim. Uss.*, p. 853.

boat left in charge of Loman at the mouth of the Boyne, probably near the River Nanny, where our saint landed and met his future coadjutor in the person of the boy Benignus. (2) The launching of the boat by order of St. Patrick, after a stay of eighty days at the river's mouth, and its coming up against the stream, *Deo gubernante*, as far as the ford of Trim, *Usque ad vadum Truim.* (3) The preaching of the Gospel the morning after the arrival, when God opened the hearts of Fortchern, his royal mother, and father, and the whole household, to listen to the words of Loman, to accept his teaching, and to receive the great grace of faith and of baptism. (4) Supernaturally enlightened by faith, and filled with sentiments similar to St. Paul, who said of himself, *Omnia detrimentum esse et arbitror ut stercora ut Christum lucrifaciam*,[1] -'I esteem all things to be but loss, and count them but as dung that I may gain Christ,'—Felim gave up, *immolavit,* his possessions around Trim to Patrick and Loman, together with his son Fortchern, till the Day of Judgment; and there on that royal site granted by Felim, Patrick with them, built a church twelve years before the foundation of Armagh.

Another Roman character, x, is inserted in the text, as I suspect, through an error of the copyist, which would make the foundation of Trim twenty-two years previous to Armagh.

Having consulted the best authorities on the subject, I find Armagh was founded A.D. 445, when the site of a cathedral was granted by Daire to Patrick on ' Macha's Height,' and Trim was founded the first year of St. Patrick's arrival in Ireland, A.D. 433, leaving a difference between the foundation of both of twelve years, as stated above. Bishop Ussher examined the foregoing narrative of Tirechan in all its details with the eye ·of a critic, and, whilst passing no encomium on the venerable author for his language or his style, '*licet minus eleganter explicata*,' he can find no reason whatever to question the accuracy of the account itself.

The next authority in favour of the antiquity of the Trim Church is Jocelyn, a celebrated monk of Furness, in

---

[1] Epist. Pauli ad Philipp, c. 3, v. 8.

Lancashire, who flourished in the twelfth century, and was placed in Iniscourcey, in Down, by John de Courcey, Prince of Ulster. At the request of Thomas O'Connor (Archbishop of Armagh), Malachy (Bishop of Down), and John de Courcey, he wrote a life of St. Patrick. His selection for such a work by a trio of such eminent men was, in truth, a very high compliment paid to Jocelyn, as well as a strong proof of his special fitness for the task assigned him.

Now, this learned monk thoroughly endorses Tirechan's account regarding Trim, and gives even fuller details of the manner in which Loman's boat came up as far as the ford of Trim, together with the other important events that took place the morning after his arrival.

Again, in the *Annals of the Four Masters*, marked at the year 432, we read : ' Ath-Truim was founded by Patrick, it having been granted by Fedhlim, son of Laighaire, son of Niall, to God and to him, Loman, and Fortchern.'

It would exceed the limits of space allowed in the pages of the I. E. RECORD, if I were to proceed and make separate quotations from the Bollandists, the Tripartite, Dean Butler, Colgan, and Cogan. Suffice it to say, that these and the other authors whom I consulted, with the single exception of Dr. Lanigan, are *all at one* in conceding to Ath-Truim the singular distinction of being the *oldest* Irish see, the first established in our midst by our national apostle, and presided over by St. Loman, Patrick's nephew.

The *Book of Armagh* gives a list of eight abbots of Trim previous to 741, and of these it observes : *Hi omnes episcopi fuerunt et principes venerantes Sanctum Patricium et successores ejus.*

Before closing this preliminary sketch, I may be permitted to add, that Colgan quotes from the Martyrology of Tallaght a very interesting passage in reference to Ath-Truim :—

Lomain Athrumensis cum sociissuis id est, Patricio, ' hostiario' Lurecho filio Cuanach, Fortcherno, et Coelo.   Ochtra Aido, Acdo Cormaco Episcopo Lacteno Sacerdoti Ossano Sarano Conallo Colmano Luctano Episcopo et Finnescha Virgine.   Hi omnes Athrumiae requiescunt.[1]

---

[1] *Dean Butler*, p. 139.

Here the Martyrology tells us where the hallowed bones of Loman and his companions are laid to rest. The Cormac mentioned in the above list of saints, nephew of King Laighaire (being the son of his brother Enda), was in the year 482 transferred from Trim to Armagh as Coadjutor to Patrick, who was then very old, and wholly intent on Divine contemplation. Having governed the Church of Armagh fifteen years, he (Cormac) died on the 17th of February, 497. His saintly remains, I presume at his own request, were brought back to Trim, and laid by the side of Loman, and within sight of his ancestral home at Tara.

This quotation of Colgan's, and indeed all the accounts given by historians, ancient and modern, relating to Trim, are assailed by Dr. Lanigan with a virulence quite unintelligible, and hardly consistent with his eminent position. But with the kind permission of the Editor of the I. E. RECORD, I shall, in a subsequent paper, endeavour to reply to the objections raised by that learned, but hypercritical writer, and to remove the aspersions which he strives to cast upon the antiquity of the Church of Ath-Truim.

PHILIP CALLARY, P.P., V.F

Notes and Queries

THEOLOGY

A CASE OF CLANDESTINITY

Rev. Dear Sir,—Would you kindly state in next issue of I. E. Record, if a marriage contracted in the following circumstances is valid :—

A man and woman living in Ireland wished to be married. The parents of both parties objected, and so they came to Scotland. On arrival here, their intention was to settle down, wherever they could secure work, and to remain until such time as their parents should request them to return to Ireland. They had, therefore, the intention of returning to Ireland in the event of their parents asking them to do so; but if not asked, and, at all events, until such time as they should be asked, they intended to stay wherever they got work in Scotland. Having secured a promise of work, there was a probability of their settling down in a certain parish, the priest in charge of which assisted at their marriage a few days after their arrival in the country.

As a matter of fact, they did stay a few months after their marriage; but the pardon then came, and they returned to Ireland rejoicing.

Was the marriage valid?

Sacerdos.

In various forms, the points involved in this case, or closely connected with it, have been repeatedly submitted to us. Perhaps, therefore, the most satisfactory way of replying to this question will be found to be by enumerating briefly the various hypotheses bearing on this matter, in which two persons may be conceived to cross over from Ireland—where the Tridentine law of clandestinity is in force—to contract marriage in Scotland—where the same law has not been promulgated. In each hypothesis we shall, as we proceed, indicate the validity or invalidity of the marriage, in so far as the law of clandestinity is concerned.

I. And first, we may distinguish between (A) those who, on arriving in Scotland, acquire there a domicile or quasi-domicile; and (B) those who do not.

(A) If either of the contracting parties has acquired a domicile or quasi-domicile in Scotland, they may *validly*, though not lawfully, contract in Scotland without any witness whatever—priest or other. It may be useful to note explicitly, (1) that this power to contract validly dates from the moment that the person has taken up his residence in Scotland with the intention of dwelling there permanently, or, as the case may be, for the greater part of a year; (2) that the power to contract is independent of the fact, whether or not the parties had or retain a domicile or quasi-domicile in Ireland; and (3) that it is unaffected by the intention with which the new domicile has been acquired. It may be that the domicile in Scotland has been acquired for the express and sole purpose of evading the Tridentine law, as it affected the parties in Ireland; still their marriage will be valid.

(B) If neither of them acquired a domicile or quasi-domicile in Scotland, we must further distinguish various cases. (1) Both parties may retain a domicile or quasi-domicile in Ireland, or (2) one, at least, may be a *vagus*.

In the latter hypothesis, (B 2) they may contract validly in Scotland without priest or witnesses. If the man, for example, be a *vagus*, he is himself, while in Scotland, in no wise affected by the Tridentine law, and he communicates his own privilege to the other contracting party—even though she may have a domicile in Ireland, may have come to Scotland precisely in order to evade the law of Trent, and may intend to return to her home immediately after the marriage. Where, therefore, one or both contracting parties are *vagi*, no question of invalidity can arise, when their marriage is celebrated in a place where the law of Trent is not in force.

(B 1) If, however, both the contracting parties retain a domicile or quasi-domicile in Ireland, while neither acquires, even a quasi-domicile in Scotland, a further distinction is necessary. (a) Both may be Catholics, or (b) one, at least may be a baptized non-Catholic. We pass by the case in which both are unbaptized, because ecclesiastical impediments do not affect such persons; also, the case in which one is baptized, the other unbaptized, because, there we should have the distinct impediment of *disparitas cultus*.

Now (b) if either of the parties be a baptized non-Catholic, their marriage in Scotland would be valid, even though they intended, as far as they could, to act in *fraudem legis*. The reason is, that the Tridentine law of clandestinity does not, in Ireland, affect heretics marrying *inter se* or with Catholics. A mixed marriage in Ireland between persons domiciled in Ireland is not invalidated by clandestinity. And, manifestly, an Irish Protestant, for example, does not lose his privilege or dispensation by crossing over to Scotland. The non-Catholic party, then, being capable of contracting a clandestine valid marriage, communicates this privilege to the other party to the contract.

(a) Finally, if both parties are Catholics, both domiciled in Ireland, neither in Scotland, they can, of course, contract in Scotland before the *proprius parochus* of either, or before any priest delegated by the *proprius parochus*. But, without the *parochus proprius* or his delegate, can they validly contract in Scotland? We make three cases :

(1) If they go to Scotland solely or mainly for the purpose of evading the Tridentine law of clandestinity, *i.e.*, for the purpose of dispensing with the presence of their *proprius parochus*, their marriage will be certainly invalid. Theologians are agreed that to this extent, at all events, the law of Trent is personal. The law follows those who, being bound to it territorially, leave the place of their domicile or quasi-domicile *in fraudem legis*, for the purpose of evading the law. So far there is no room for controversy. A marriage contracted *in fraudem legis* is, as all admit, invalid; all recognise *fraus legis* in the case just made.

(2) If, however, the parties seek the exempt territory for the purpose, indeed, of getting married there, but not for the purpose of evading the jurisdiction of their *proprius*

parochus, can they without delegation contract validly? We can conceive, for instance, persons going over from Ireland to Scotland to get married there rather than at home for some reason, who would be quite willing to contract before their own parish priest if he were to accompany them. Are they to be considered as acting *in fraudem legis?* If so, their marriage will, as in the previous case, be invalid. Or is there *fraus legis* only when they go to Scotland for the purpose of evading the jurisdiction of their parish priest? Undoubtedly, the law is often stated, by theologians, as if nothing else than an intention of evading the jurisdiction of the *proprius parochus* would constitute the fraud that entails invalidity. Such a position, however, cannot be maintained. We refrain from enumerating a list of theologians that can be quoted for our interpretation of the law. With D'Annibale, we are content to base our opinion on repeated decisions of the Roman Congregation. According to a decision of the S. C. of the Council, 26th August, 1873, the marriage of persons who were ignorant of the very existence of the law of clandestinity, and could not, therefore, have fraudulently intended to evade it, was declared invalid, because, though they contracted in an exempt territory, they belonged to a place where the law of clandestinity was in force. Again the same Congregation decided, 3rd April, 1841, against the validity of a marriage contracted in similar circumstances, where the parties left their home and sought the exempt territory, not by any means to elude the jurisdiction of their own pastor, but merely to evade the opposition of their parents and the consequent impediments of the civil law. A further decision, given 16th June, 1866, declared a marriage invalid where the object of the parties in leaving their own territory and contracting in a place exempt was that they wished to have the marriage blessed there by a priest who was a relative of one of the parties.

In view of these decisions, it appears to us abundantly clear, that an *intention of evading the law of clandestinity* is not necessary in order to make a marriage contracted in an exempt place fraudulent in the sense of the Canon Law ; at *the very least*, these decisions seem to show that, when a man subject (*i.e.*, by reason of, at least, a quasi-domicile) to the law of clandestinity seeks an exempt place for *the purpose of getting married*, no matter what his motive may be for wishing to marry *in loco exempto*, he goes *in fraudem legis*, and his marriage will be invalid. The assumption, of course, is that not even a quasi-domicile is acquired in the exempt territory.

(3) Lastly, we can conceive a case in which the parties leave home for some reason wholly unconnected with marriage. At home, they were bound by the law of clandestinity. Now, however, they happen to be in an exempt place. Are they free to contract there without the Tridentine formalities? Two persons having domiciles in Ireland become acquainted for the first time, let us suppose, during a holiday in Scotland. Assuming that both are Catholics, and that neither has a domicile or quasi-domicile in Scotland, can they validly contract there without reference to their parish priests in Ireland?

The more common opinion, certainly, seems to be that there is, in this case, no *fraus legis*, and that such persons are free, therefore, from the law of clandestinity. This is the opinion of Sanchez, Lugo, Reiffenstuel, Viva, Schmalzgrueber, Billuart, Gury, Ballerini, and others. On the other side we find Sylvius, Roncaglia, Benedict XIV., St. Alphonsus, Carriere, Gasparri, Rosset, holding that a marriage in these circumstances is invalid.[1] Apart from the great authority on which the first opinion rests, we should have no difficulty in asserting that the second is the only tenable opinion.

We incline to the second opinion, for the following reasons :—

(1) The Council of Trent makes those who have a domicile or quasi-domicile, where the law of clandestinity is promulgated, incapable of validly contracting marriage without the presence of the *proprius parochus*, and, at least, two other witnesses. Nothing in the law restricts the inhability to the case in which the marriage is contracted where the law of clandestinity is in force. But we need not

---

[1] *Vid.* Rosset, iv., n. 2092.

delay in enforcing our interpretation of the law. We find
that this interpretation rests on, what appears to us, unim-
peachable authority. We proceed to adduce our evidence.

(2) The following question was proposed by the Archbishop of Cologne, and the reply given 5th Sept., 1626 :—

(1) An incolae tam masculi quam foeminae loci in quo Conc.
Trid. in puncto matrimonii est promulgatum, transeuntes per
locum in quo dictum Concilium non est promulgatum, retinentes
idem domicilium, valide possint in isto loco matrimonium sine
parocho et testibus contrahere? (2) Quid si eo praedicti incolae
tam masculi quam foeminae solo animo sine parocho et testibus
contrahendi se transferant, habitationem non mutantes? (3) Quid
si iidem incolae tam masculi quam foeminae eo transferant habitationem illo solo animo ut absque parocho et testibus contrahant?

There can be no ambiguity about these questions. The
third makes the case, where two persons domiciled in
Ireland, for example, would go to Scotland, and acquire a
domicile[1] there for the express purpose of dispensing with
the presence of their Irish parish priest. The second puts
the case, in which the same persons might go to Scotland
for the purpose again of evading the law of clandestinity,
but without acquiring a new domicile in Scotland. The
first question, which, of course, must arise from distinct
hypothesis, can regard no other than that case precisely
which we are discussing, where, *e.g.*, the same two persons
are merely passing through Scotland, or sojourning there.
The only difference, manifestly, between the second hypothesis and the first is in the intention with which the parties
left their homes. The second question supposes on the part
of the persons concerned an intention of evading the law of
clandestinity; the first, by necessary implication, excludes
such intention.

The reply must seem equally clear:—*Ad primum et
secundum non esse legitimum matrimonium inter sic se trans-
ferentes et transeuntes cum fraude. Ad tertium, si domicilium
vere transferatur matrimonium esse validum.* In the first
case, therefore, as in the second, the marriage is invalid.

---

[1] Or quasi-domicile. It will be understood throughout that in the matter
of clandestinity, a domicile and a quasi-domicile have precisely the same effect.

In both cases there is fraud, or an infringement of the rights of the *proprius parochus.*

If these same questions were put to those who differ from us, assuredly they would give an affirmative reply to the first question. Not so the Congregation. According to the Congregation, in the only legitimate sense of the reply, the answer to the first and to the second question is the same, viz., as long as persons retain a domicile, where the law is promulgated, and do not acquire one in a place exempt, their marriage in an exempt place will be invalid,— whether they have, as the second hypothesis, or have not, as in the first, an intention of evading the Tridentine law.

(8) The reply of the Congregation of the Council just quoted was confirmed by Urban VIII. And Benedict XIV. in the Constitution, *Paucis ab hinc* refers to the reply and to the confirmation.

Both Pontiffs interpreted the law of Trent and the reply of the Congregation as we have done. We shall only quote the words of Benedict XIV. from the Constitution *Paucis ab hinc.* Commenting with approval on the opinion of Sylvius—the same that we adopt—Benedict XIV. writes :—

Sapienter animadvertens, matrimonium esse validum, si quis, admissa etiam fraude patriam suam deserens ubi Tridentinum Concilium promulgatum fuit illud contrahit in loco ubi non est promulgatum, postquam tamen ibidem verum quasi domicilium acquisierit ; ex eo infert, nullum esse matrimonium, quoties cumque ille, qui contrahit regreditur illico ad locum unde decessit, quin speciem quandam domicilii adeptus fuerit in loco ubi matrimonium contraxit.

Altogether, irrespective of a man's intention, he will, therefore, according to Benedict XIV., contract invalidly in the circumstances named. And, further on, referring to the decision of the S. Congregation, 5th Sept., 1626, already quoted, he says :—

Hujus vero definitionis contextu bene perpenso, facile intelligitur, matrimonia primo ac secundo loco exposita, irrita ac nulla ab eadem Congregatione decerni, eo quia fraus intercessit.

Benedict XIV., therefore, (1) distinguishes the first case from the second, (2) he discovers *fraus* in the first case, as well as in the second. Yet, as we have already shown, the hypothesis in the first question necessarily excludes the intention of evading the Tridentine law. Evidently Benedict XIV. required no intention of evading the law.

All extant decisions and instructions from the Roman Congregations have been consistently, as far as they can tell one way or the other, in favour of this opinion of Benedict XIV.

In recent times, a case has been decided by the Congregation of the Council which seems to us to end, as far as an authoritative decision can, the controversy with which we are dealing, and to place the opinion for which we contend beyond reasonable dispute. We take the account of this case from Gasparri.[1]

Albertus L. an 1867 illicitis amoribus sese implicuit cum Armanda R. muliere perditissimis moribus. Aegro animo parentes hanc Alberti calamitatem ferebant, et nihil intentatum reliquerunt, ut a pessima consuetudine juvenem abducerent. Tandem indignatione parentum, bonorum interdictione ac vitae turpitudine defatigatus, Albertus melioris consilii propositum amplecti visus est, atque, ejus matre suadente, in Americam profectus, eo appulit die 10 Mart, 1868. Hoc animo iter suscepit, ut peregrinatione distractus, obscoenum amorem deponeret, et revera in America continuo huc illuc vagatus est. Interim Armanda juvenem litteris tentare coepit ; deinde, die 11 Augusti, in Neo-Eboracensem civitatem pervenit ; et triduo post in eadem civitate, in qua decretum Tridentinum pro Catholicis publicatum non fuit, coram sacerdoti rectore ecclesiae Catholicae S.Vincentii de Paulo ac duobus testibus matrimonium initum fuit. S. Cong. edixit nullum hoc matrimonium, Jan. 25, 1873.

Now, in this case, Albert left his home without any intention of evading the Tridentine law. He simply found himself *in loco exempto* solely for quite another purpose. It was not even contended that, being already in New York, he expressly conceived the idea of evading the Tridentine law, by marrying before his return home. According to the opinion against which we are arguing, Albert was, on his part, perfectly capable of contracting validly before the New York rector. And if Albert himself were free, his marriage with Armanda would, by universal consent, be valid, no

---

[1] *Vid.* ii., n. 989.

matter what her intention may have been in going to New
York ; the marriage would, therefore, be valid. But, unfortunately, the Congregation judged otherwise, and pronounced
this marriage invalid ; the only assignable reason, of course,
being that the parties, while they retained their former
domicile, and had not acquired one in New York, were bound
by the law of clandestinity, were necessarily infringing—
whether intentionally or not—the rights of the *proprius
parochus*, and attempting to marry *in fraudem legis*. The
force of this decision did not escape the decision of those
whose opinion, as we think, it overturns. A writer in the
Acta S. Sedis virtually confesses the difficulty raised against
his opinion to be insurmountable, by having recourse to the
arbitrary hypothesis that this marriage was declared invalid,
not because of *fraus contra legem clandestinitatis*, but for
some other reason not alleged during the process of trial.
Decisions are valueless as an authentic source of legal interpretation, if it is open to anyone and everyone to maintain
that they may be based on some unassigned reasons.

Before concluding these arguments, it is worthy of note
that, as late as 1867, the Congregation of the Holy Office,
with the nature of this controversy before it, simply repeats,
without qualification, in an Instruction to the English and
American bishops, the old doctrine of Benedict XIV. and
Urban VIII. :—

[Lex clandestinitatis] quatenus localis afficit territorium
eosque qui ibi matrimonio jungendi sunt obligat ; quatenus
vero, personalis eos obligat qui domicilium vel quasi-domicilium
habentes in loco ubi Tridentinum decretum promulgatum est et
viget, in altero, ubi illud non viget contrahere vellent.

Unless, therefore, we introduce into this Instruction a
distinction which the Instruction itself does not make or
insinuate, we must conclude that the Tridentine decree, *qua
personale*, affects not merely those who seek an exempt
territory *for the purpose of evading the law*, but also those
—and *all* those—who *retain a domicile where the law exists*
and *have not acquired one in a place exempt* from the operation of the law.

In view of the reasons we have advanced, and of the

authority by which our opinion is supported, we agree with Gasparri, when he concludes his discussion of this question as follows :—

In praxi si agitur de matrimonio ineundo [a partibus Catholicis domicilium in Hibernia retinentibus nec domicilium in Scotia habentibus] in [Scotia] fieri non debere nisi coram parocho aut ordinario proprio aut coram alio sacerdote de eorum licentia et duobus saltem testibus; sed etiam si agitur de matrimonio contrasto et ad forum contentiosum deducto, officialis debet ni fallimur, ob auctoritatem SS.CC. pro nullitate pronuntiare.[1]

And, now, we reply, in a few words, to the question proposed to us. Applying the principles laid down above, we say :—

(1) That if either of the parties were a *vagus* or a heretic their marriage was valid ; at all events, it was not invalidated by the Tridentine law of clandestinity.

(2) If both were Catholics, and retained their domiciles in Ireland, their marriage would still be valid if either had antecedently to the marriage acquired a domicile or quasi-domicile in Scotland. But, did they acquire, at least, a quasi-domicile? We are merely told that there was 'a probability of their settling down,' and that they intended to remain until such time as their parents may relent. Of course, 'a mere probability of settling down' where they had got a promise of work, would not be sufficient to constitute a quasi-domicile ; you require *habitatio actualis jam incoepta*. But, we take it, the meaning is that they had actually taken up their residence in a certain place, and that there was a probability of their remaining in that place. There was *habitatio incoepta*, therefore. Had they, moreover, the requisite intention of remaining for the greater part of a year? The priest who assisted at the marriage might put a different complexion on the facts, if we had his statement, and the change may affect our opinion. But as the facts have been presented to us, we should not undertake to say that the intention of these persons was sufficient for the acquisition of a quasi-domicile.

(3) In default of a domicile or quasi-domicile, may the

[1] *Vid.* ii. 985.

marriage have been valid, without delegation from a *proprius parochus* in Ireland? In our opinion, the marriage would be invalid. For (a) if they went to Scotland, solely or mainly, with the intention of evading the law of clandestinity, the marriage would, as all admit, be invalid; (b) if they went, at all events, with the primary intention of getting married—as they undoubtedly did—it is, we think, equally certain that the marriage would be invalid; (c) and lastly, even if they had gone to Scotland merely for a holiday, and while there decided on getting married, their marriage would, in our opinion, be invalid. *Ante factum* the Scotch priest should not, we think, assist at their marriage without delegation. *Post factum*, no individual priest or theologian should take the responsibility of declaring the marriage certainly null; he is quite free to hold, and—until the Roman decisions and Instructions are explained away or modified—we think ought to hold, that the marriage is invalid, and that if the matter comes before the Roman authorities, the decision will be, as in like cases already decided, against the validity of the marriage.

ARE RELIGIOUS IN A PROTRACTED ILLNESS EXEMPT FROM THE FAST BEFORE COMMUNION?

Rev. Dear Sir,—Kindly answer the following question, and oblige a subscriber.

Is it true that Rome has granted a concession in favour of religious, exempting them from the Communion fast in cases of protracted illness? If so, does the concession carry with it the privilege of receiving Holy Communion whenever the community does?

Sacerdos Americanus.

The obligation to be fasting when receiving Communion, being a matter of ecclesiastical law merely, might, of course, be removed by the Holy See. As a matter of fact, dispensations have been granted from time to time, though rarely. Konings (n. 1309) says: ' S. Pontifex raro et gravi tantum de causa, attamen etiam cum privatis (quemadmodum ex casu particulari ipse nosco) et non tantum, sicut olim fere, cum publicis, ceu publica de causa, ut semel, ter, aut etiam pluries in anno communicare possint, dispensare solet.'

It is, therefore, quite possible that individual members of religious communities have got this Papal dispensation. It is possible—though we have no reason to think it the fact--that certain orders or congregations have a privilege in this matter. But religious, as such, have no general dispensation exempting them from the Communion fast, even in the case of protracted illness.

Needless to say, a religious, like anybody else, may in a protracted illness in which there is danger of death receive Communion repeatedly and frequently *per modum viatici.*

ECCLESIASTICAL TRIALS

REV. DEAR SIR,—Will you kindly answer the following question in your next issue ? In these countries we have not all the ordinary ecclesiastical courts. To whom then are we to have recourse for the settlement of a case assigned by Canon Law to the adjudication of such a court? A case in point, the separation of husband from wife for sufficient reasons. Theology directs that, as a general rule, recourse must be had to the ecclesiastical judge in such a case. Does the bishop take the place of this court contemplated by Canon Law for us? Are we bound in the same way to have recourse to him for the settlement of such a case? Or are we free to regard it as a matter of prudence to consult the bishop in the circumstances?

SACERDOS.

The bishop is the official to whom the cases contemplated by our correspondent should be submitted. Nor is it ever competent for parish priests or confessors to look upon reference to the ordinary in such cases as a mere matter of prudence, and to constitute themselves judges. When the case is stated to the bishop he will, as the case may admit or require, constitute a court for the trial or take steps to have the matter sent on to the proper tribunal.

D. MANNIX.

462 THE IRISH ECCLESIASTICAL RECORD

LITURGY

METHOD OF EXPOSING THE MOST HOLY SACRAMENT

REV. DEAR SIR,—There is a slight diversity of procedure in exposing the Blessed Sacrament in connection with the Rosary, &c., during the month of October; and as the authors generally at hand do not distinctly provide for this new development of devotion, may I ask your direction in the matter?

It is supposed that the Blessed Sacrament is exposed for adoration during the recitation of the Rosary, &c., and that, in a particular church, the priest who has performed the ceremony of exposition finds it necessary to retire from the altar in order to lead the recitation of the Rosary, &c., from the pulpit.

Now, in this case, is it the correct course for the priest, when proceeding from the sacristy to perform the ceremony of exposition, to wear a cope with the stole, &c., as for the ceremony of ordinary benediction; and, having incensed the Blessed Sacrament on the throne, to lay aside cope and stole and proceed to the pulpit, resuming these vestments to give benediction?

Or is it correct to proceed from the sacristy without cope but with stole over surplice, and thus to expose the Blessed Sacrament; then, having performed the incensation as in the last case, to lay aside the stole, and proceed to the pulpit, taking stole and cope on his returning to give benediction?

The latter course is suggested by Hughes on the *Ceremonies of High Mass*, pp. 134-135, and to some degree by a response of the Sacred Congregation given in the *Manuale Sacerdotum* (Ed. nona), pp. 730-731, note 2.   C. C.

The use of the cope while merely exposing the Blessed Sacrament is not prescribed,[1] and, though recommended,[2] is not, we think, common. The following general directions for exposing the Blessed Sacrament, taken from *The Ceremonies of some Ecclesiastical Functions*,[3] will be a guide to our correspondent in the particular case to which he refers:—

If the Blessed Sacrament is to be exposed before the clergy enter choir, the priest who is to perform the ceremony, vested in

[1] S.R.C. 22 Jan. 1701. 3426-3575., De Carpo, Par. 3., n. 186.
[2] De Herdt, *S. Lit. Prax.*, tom. 2, n. 26.
[3] Part 2, chap. 2, p. 148.

surplice and white stole, and wearing his biretta, goes to the altar preceded by a thurifer with the censer, and by two or more acolytes with lighted torches. Arrived at the foot of the altar he gives his biretta to one of the assistants, genuflects *in plano*, and kneels on the first step to say a short prayer. He then mounts the altar, spreads the corporal, and takes the biretta containing the Blessed Sacrament from the tabernacle, and places it in the monstrance, observing the proper reverences. Having placed the monstrance on the throne he genuflects on the predella, and having descended to the foot of the altar kneels on the lowest step, inclines his head profoundly to the Blessed Sacrament, and then rises to put incense into the censer. Having replenished the censer, without blessing the incense, he again kneels on the lowest step and incenses the Blessed Sacrament, making a profound inclination of the head before and after. He then hands the censer to the thurifer, rises, and having genuflected on both knees, as those who accompany him also do, returns to the sacristy.

The only modification in these directions which the case in question calls for is the following : Having handed his censer to the thurifer, and while still kneeling he removes the stole, rises, genuflects on both knees, and goes to the pulpit to recite the prayers.

THE PRAYER IN THE OFFICE AND MASS FOR THE ANNIVERSARY OF THE DEDICATION OF A CHURCH.

REV. DEAR SIR,—The following additional question suggests itself to me.

On the anniversary of the dedication of the churches of Ireland, should a priest, in saying the prayer of the feast in the Office and Mass, say it with reference to all the churches of Ireland, and therefore always in the plural form ? Or, should he say it with reference only to the church or churches of his own parish, or to which he is attached, and therefore in the singular or plural form, according to the circumstances of the case ?

C. C.

The kernal of this question is : Should the prayer in the Office for the Anniversary of the Dedication of a Church ever be said in the plural ? For if we must give a negative reply to this question, it matters little what we say regarding the other part of the question. And to this question as we have stated it, a negative reply must be given. For, in the first place, no rubric, either general or particular, of either missal or breviary prescribes the use of the plural form when the anniversary of the dedication of more than one church is commemorated. But, it may be objected, the rubrics do not contemplate the commemoration on the same day of the anniversary of more than one dedication. In reply to this we have only to point to the anniversary of the dedication of the basilicas of SS. Peter and Paul, which is commemorated on November 18th. Here we have the anniversary of the dedication of two churches commemorated on the same day and by the same Office and Mass. And two is a plural number. Yet the only directions given in the missal for the Mass of this feast, are :—*Missa Terribilis de Comm. Dedicat. Ecclesiae.* The directions in the breviary correspond with those in the missal. Now if the prayer should be said in the plural when the anniversary of more than one dedication is commemorated, both missal and breviary should indicate the change in their directions for this feast. But since no indication of this change is contained in either, we are not at liberty to make; we must follow the directions given, and say 'all from the common,' including the prayer, just as we find it in the 'common.'

We have employed this argument taken from the anniversary of the dedication of the two basilicas, because this feast is to be found in all breviaries and missals, and each one, consequently, can verify for himself the accuracy of our statements. But in recent breviaries and missals, especially those for use in France, the feast of the dedication of all the churches — a feast similar in every respect to our own — is put down for the first Sunday after the Octave of All Saints. And here, again, the only directions given in the special rubrics are the same as those given in the special rubrics for the feast of the dedication of the two basilicas: *Omne. de Comm. Dedicat. Ecclesiae.* We have now said more than enough in reply to a question for the solution of which the authority of the *Ordo* might have sufficed. If the prayer should be said in the plural on the feast of the dedication of the churches of Ireland, surely the compiler of the *Ordo* should call attention to this change; he calls attention to many things much less obvious; and since the *Ordo* is silent about the matter, it should follow that the change is not to be made.

Now, what is the object to which the prayer is to be referred? In replying to this question we do not intend to enter on a grammatical or metaphysical disquisition as to how the *veritas verborum—hujus sancti templi*, &c.—can be preserved when the prayer is said in commemoration of the dedication of more than one church. We consider it a sufficient reply to say that the prayer should be referred to the object for which the feast was instituted.

SHOULD THE BLESSED SACRAMENT ALREADY EXPOSED BE INCENSED IMMEDIATELY AFTER THE OFFICIALS COME TO THE ALTAR?

REV. DEAR SIR,—Kindly inform me, is it correct on a day of Exposition *not* to incense the Blessed Sacrament when the priest goes on to the altar for Benediction in the evening? May he recite the Rosary, Litany of B. V. M., and prayer to St. Joseph —though these prayers take up fifteen or twenty minutes— before the *Tantum Ergo* is sung, and the Blessed Sacrament incensed?

Any reference to the point that I can find supposes that the *Tantum Ergo* is begun immediately the priest goes on the altar.

C. G.

Our correspondent's question contemplates a case which must frequently occur. The Blessed Sacrament has been exposed during the day, and the adoration is to be brought to a close with Benediction. The officiant, vested for Benediction, and accompanied by the required ministers, comes to the altar. But before the actual ceremony of Benediction begins, certain prayers are to be recited or sung, such as the prayers prescribed for the month of October, which are referred to in our correspondent's question; the Litany of the Saints, which is sung at the close of the Forty Hours' Adoration, when exposition of the Blessed Sacrament takes place in the evening; or the Litany of the Blessed Virgin, which may be sung on ordinary occasions. Our correspondent, then, wishes to know whether, in such circumstances, the officiant should not incense the Blessed Sacrament immediately after coming to the altar, instead of waiting until the choir begins to sing the *Tantum Ergo*.

We reply that he should not incense the Blessed Sacrament immediately after coming to the· altar, but should wait until the *Genitori Genitoque* of the *Tantum Ergo*. The following extract from De Carpo[1] will serve both to explain and confirm what has just been said :—

Ad reponendum SS. Sacramentum quod spectat . . . celebrans erit semper pluviali indutus quum impertire debeat benedictionem cum SS. Sacramento. Ipse porro ac sacri ministri simul atque in conspectum venerint SS. Sacramenti caput detegunt, et in plano ante altare utrumque flectunt genu, ac profunde se inclinant . . . Mox celebrans, sacri ministri ac caeremoniarius erecti genua flectunt in infimo altaris gradu. . . . *Deinde incohantur preces*, si quae sunt dicendae, dummodo sint ex approbatis, alioquin *Tantum Ergo* dumtaxat concinetur, atque *ad hymnum hunc SS. Sacramentum thure adolebitur.*

D. O'LOAN.

---

[1] Par. 3, n. 190.

CORRESPONDENCE

THE BLOODY SWEAT ON THE PICTURE OF OUR LADY IN
JAURIN RAAB, ST. PATRICK'S DAY, 1697[1]

REV. DEAR SIR,—In his very interesting letter on this
wonderful event, Dr. Healy says :—

(1) Haec *una tantum* fuit sed omnium ferocissima legum
quae in hoc Parliamento contra Religionem Catholicam sunt
latae ? (2) Quo *die* lex illa infamis regium placitum obtinuerit
reperire adhuc non potui.

And, again,.Father Ryan, in his able paper of March, admits
that he ' *cannot fix the day this enactment became law.*'
These two queries are answered very clearly in (Irish) *Journals
of the House of Commons*, vol. ii., p. 939.

Monday, 25th September, 1697.
A message by the Gentleman Usher of the Black Rod.
That their Excellencies the Lords Justices commanded this
House to attend them in the House of Peers immediately.
Whereupon this House, with their Speaker, attended their
Excellencies the Lord Justices accordingly ; and being returned,
Mr. Speaker reported that this House, with their Speaker,
had attended their Excellencies the Lords Justices in the House
of Lords, and that their Excellencies had given the Royal assent
to the bills following :—
1. An Act for banishing all Papists exercising ecclesiastical
jurisdiction, and all Regulars of the Popish religion.
2. An Act for the confirmation of articles made at the
surrender of the City of Limerick.
3. An Act to prevent Protestants from intermarrying with
Papists.

The two last were as injurious to the Catholic laity as the
first was to the clergy. The second was constitutionally more
unjust and illegal, as it deliberately and avowedly violated almost
the whole of the stipulations contained in the articles of the
Treaty of Limerick, which were solemnly signed and ratified by
the King and his commanding officers. It was, in one way,
more injurious to religion than the first Act ; for as long as the

---

[1] See I. E. RECORD (Fourth Series), vol. i., p. 178 ; and *ibid.*, p. 193.

articles of the Treaty remained in force, the first Act could not
be put into execution.   Hence, the Orange faction in that Protestant Parliament passed it *unanimously*, as we see here, in the
diary of *Journals of the Commons*.   They, however, met with an
unexpected and vigorous resistance in the House of Lords.   To
their eternal honour, a protest was signed against it by Lords
Duncannon, Londonderry, and Tyrone, the Barons of Limerick,
Howth, Ossory, Killaloe, Kerry, Strabane, and Kingston, and
also by the Bishops of Derry, Elphin, Clonfert, Kildare, and
Killala.

It gave the following reasons :—

1. Because the title did not agree with the body of the bill ;
the title being ' An Act for the Confirmation of Irish Articles,'
whereas no one of said articles was therein fully confirmed.
2. Because the articles were to be confirmed to them to whom they
were granted ; but the *confirmation of them by that bill was such
that it put them in a worse condition than they were before.*
3. *Because the bill omitted the material words,* ' *And all such as are
under their protection in the said country,*' which were, by his
Majesty's titles patent, declared to be part of the second article ;
and several persons had been adjudged within said articles who
would, if the bill passed into law, be entirely barred and excluded,
so that the words omitted being so very material, and confirmed
by his Majesty after a solemn debate in council, some express
reason ought to be assigned in the bill in order to satisfy the
world of that omission.   4. Because several words were inserted
in the bill which were not in the articles.

The same *Journals* give us the following petition of ' Robert
Cusack, Captain Francis Segrave, and Captain Maurice Eustace,
in behalf of themselves and others, comprised under the Articles
of Limerick, setting forth, that in the said bill there were several
clauses that would frustrate the petitioners of the benefit of the
same, and if it passed into law would turn to the ruin of some,
and the prejudice of all persons entitled to the benefit of the
said articles ; and praying to be heard by counsel to said matters.
It was unanimously resolved that the said petition be rejected.'

This was in direct contradiction with the promises made in
the Treaty of Limerick, which said :—' Their Majesties, as soon
as their affairs will permit them to summon a Parliament in this
kingdom, will endeavour to procure the said Roman Catholics
such further security in that particular as may preserve them
from any disturbance upon the account of their said religion.'

And this was duly ratified by their Majesties' letters patent. So that, to use the words of Canon O'Rourke :—' It was beyond the power of King or Parliament to curtail or alter such a treaty. . . If the Parliament did not like the terms of the Treaty, they had no power to set them aside, without putting the other contracting parties in the same position which they held before the Treaty was made. This could not be done, and there was, therefore, no course open but to fulfil the terms of the Treaty.'[1]

The 'opening' of this Parliament took place on the 16th March, 1697, the day before this miraculous sweat of blood on this picture of the Blessed Virgin in Hungary. It is quite certain that these three infamous penal Acts were a foregone conclusion, and were already prepared by the Orange members of that Parliament on that memorable 16th March, now two hundred years ago. No wonder, then, that our Blessed Lady should show her sorrow and sympathy for the faithful children of St. Patrick, on his feast day, the 17th March, as the Queen of Heaven already knew the bloody enactments drafted against Irish Catholics, and the dreadful persecutions and cruel spoliations of their properties they were about to endure. We are sure your readers will be glad to see a summary of these nefarious statutes, which we here subjoin. It will show them that, if there is a vestige of faith or religion remaining in Ireland—and where is there such faith and practical religion ?—it is owing to a higher Power than the vain efforts of man. Never, perhaps, since the first persecutions of the Church were there such Machiavellian laws enacted to destroy the religion of a country than those passed in this and the subsequent Irish Parliaments. Hell and earth seemed to have combined in this fatal year of 1697 to crush out the very name of Catholic from our faithful people. ' But He that dwelleth in heaven has laughed at them . . . and He has broke them in pieces like a potter's vessel.' To-day there is no nationality in the world which shows its gratitude to the Mother of God, and proclaims her glory, like the children of St. Patrick, over whose sorrows and persecutions she showed such sympathy in this Sweat of Blood two hundred years ago. And well may they do so, for without her all-powerful aid with God, and her loving care of our poor martyred forefathers, religion and the Catholic faith would have passed away from our country, as has happened to England

---

[1] *Battle of the Faith*, p. 499.

and all the Northern nations of Europe. That sympathy shown
by the Queen of Heaven two hundred years ago is still continued
by her, not only in Ireland, but in every clime watered by the
blood and hallowed by the sufferings of the Irish race, as we
priests have good reason to know. May she now, in our present
disturbed state, bring back peace and union to our land, and
save us, as she has often done in the past, from the effects
of the worldliness and materialistic spirit of this nineteenth
century.

Friday, 3rd September, 1697, p. 892.

A message from the Lords by the Lord Chief Justice Pyne
and the Lord Chief Justice Hely.

That their Lordships have passed a bill, entituled [entitled]
an Act for banishing all Papists exercising any ecclesiastical jurisdiction, and all regulars of the Popish clergy, out of this kingdom,
to which they desire the concurrence of this House.

Then the said bill was read a first time, and ordered to be
read a second time to-morrow morning.

Saturday, 4th September, 1697, p. 895.

An engrossed bill from the Lords, entituled an Act for banishing all Papists exercising any ecclesiastical jurisdiction, and all
regulars of the Popish clergy, out of this kingdom, was read a
second time, and committed to a Committee of the whole House
on Monday.

Monday, 6th September, 1697.

They postpone this Committee till the 7th, and on the
7th they put it off till the Thursday morning after ; *i.e.,*
9th September.

Thursday, 9th September, 1697, p. 897.

Then the House, according to the order for the day, resolved
itself into a Committee of the whole House to consider of an
engrossed bill from the Lords, entituled an Act for banishing all
Papists exercising any ecclesiastical jurisdiction, and all regulars
of the Popish clergy, out of this kingdom, and, after some time
spent therein, Mr. Speaker resumed the chair.

Mr. Weaver reported from the said Committee that they had
gone through the said bill, and agreed to the same, *without any
amendment.* [This was worthy of the miscreants who framed
these and all the other diabolical penal laws of Ireland.]

Ordered—That the bill be read a third time to-morrow
morning.

Friday, 10*th September*, 1697, p. 897.

An engrossed bill from the Lords, entituled an Act for banishing all Papists exercising any ecclesiastical jurisdiction, and all regulars of the Popish clergy, out of the kingdom, was read a third time, and passed.

A SUMMARY OF THE THREE[1] ACTS AGAINST CATHOLICS SANCTIONED BY WILLIAM, SEP. 25, 1697.

II.

An Act for the Confirmation of Articles made at the surrender of the City of Limerick.

In reference to this Act it must be remarked—1. The title omits the word ' the ' before 'Articles.' 2. The preamble of the Act shows the intention of its authors was to evade what ought to have been its proper object. It runs thus : ' That the said Articles or so much of them as may consist with the safety and welfare of your Majesty's subjects of this kingdom may be confirmed.' 3. The first Article of the treaty, which guaranteed to the Catholics the free exercise of their religion, and an exemption from all disturbance on account of it, is wholly omitted. 4. In the second Article, the following words, ' and all such as are under their protection in the said counties ' followed after the words, ' any of them,' in the original draft of the treaty which was signed by both parties. Through inadvertence they were omitted by the scribe, but later, attention being called to the omission, the king when ratifying the treaty, ordered them to be inserted and to be part of the said article, ' and ratified and confirmed the said omitted words.' By the omission of them now, the benefit of the treaty was confined to the Irish army, the inhabitants of the city of Limerick, and of a few other garrison towns, the rest of the Catholics of the counties of Limerick, Clare, Kerry, Cork, and Mayo being excluded, though in the preamble of the treaty, it is stated that the Irish Generals acted on behalf ' of the Irish inhabitants of these counties.' 5. After the words ' freehold and inheritance, a semicolon was substituted for a comma; and after the words, ' privileges, and immunities,' the words ' to the said estates.' were inserted, and in this way ' the rights, privileges, and immunities,' is made to refer only to the estates of the Catholics, and not to their persons and liberties also, to which the original Article referred. 6. The whole of that part of the second

---

[1] As the full text of the first of these three Acts was printed in the April Number of the I. E. RECORD (p. 370 *et seq.*) we omit F. Jarlath's summary of it. [Ed. I.E.R.]

Article which guaranteed to Catholics the exercise of their several respective trades, professions, and callings is omitted. The 9th article is omitted.

III.

An Act to prevent Protestants intermarrying with Papists.

1. If any Protestant woman possessed of lands, &c., to the value of £500 or more, shall after January 1st, 1698, marry any person without having first obtained a certificate, under the hand of the minister of the parish, or bishop, or some justice of the peace, that he is a known Protestant, such Protestant person so marrying, and the person she shall so marry, shall be for ever afterwards rendered incapable of having any of the aforesaid estates, but they shall go to the next Protestant of the kin, to whom such estate would descend by law, were such Protestant woman, and all other intervening popish heirs, &c., really dead and intestate at the time of such marriage. And any Protestant minister or Popish priest, who shall after January 1st, 1698, join in marriage any Protestant woman having any of said estates, &c., without having certificate as aforesaid, being convicted thereof, shall suffer one year's imprisonment, and forfeit the sum of £20.

2. In case any Protestant shall marry any woman without a certificate of his being a known Protestant, such person shall be deemed to all intents and purposes, a popish recusant, and shall afterwards be rendered incapable of being executor or guardian, or being heir to any person whatever, and disabled to sit in either house of Parliament, and of having any civil or military employment whatever, unless within a year after such marriage, he procures such wife to be converted to the Protestant religion, and shall procure a certificate under the hand of the Bishop of the diocese that she is so converted.

3. Any popish priest or Protestant minister that shall marry any soldier enlisted in his Majesty's army to any wife, without such certificate, shall forfeit £20 for every such offence, or in default of goods, &c., be committed to the county jail till he shall pay the said sum, one moiety to such person as shall give information, the other to the Treasurer of the county.

F. JARLATH, O.S.F.

---

[1] See Parnell, *History of the Penal Laws*, p. 30. Mitchel, *History of Ireland*, p. 26. Canon O'Rourke, *Battle for the Faith*, p. 499. *Our Martyrs*, p. 51. *Haverty* (who evidently did not consult the original authorities, as he gives the year 1695), p. 677.

The extracts from the Journals and Statutes are from the copies in the library of the Friary, Killarney.

DOCUMENTS

AT the October meeting of the Archbishops and Bishops of Ireland, held at Maynooth College, the following Resolution was unanimously adopted :—

We, the Archbishops and Bishops of Ireland, deem it our duty to submit to the Government of the country the statement of our conviction, founded on the personal knowledge of several members of our body, that the failure of the potatoe and cereal crops in many districts of the country, particularly on the Western and Southern coasts, must lead during the coming winter and spring to very acute distress amongst large numbers of the population, and, unless well-conceived measures of relief are taken in good time, may result in disastrous consequences.

✠ MICHAEL CARDINAL LOGUE, Archbishop of Armagh, and Primate of All Ireland, *Chairman.*

✠ FRANCIS J. MacCORMACK, Bishop of Galway and Kilmacduagh, } *Secretaries to the Meeting.*
✠ JOHN HEALY, Bishop of Clonfert,

The following Resolution in reference to the annual payments under the Glebe Loan Acts was also unanimously adopted :—

The Bishops warmly sympathize with the efforts of borrowers under the Glebe Loans Acts to get a reduction of the annual instalments payable to the Board of Works, and recommend that, with a view to procure concerted action in the matter, a priest should be named in each diocese to organize the borrowers and urge the question on the attention of the Government.

✠ MICHAEL CARDINAL LOGUE, Archbishop of Armagh, and Primate of All Ireland, *Chairman.*

✠ FRANCIS J. MacCORMACK, Bishop of Galway and Kilmacduagh, } *Secretaries to the Meeting.*
✠ JOHN HEALY, Bishop of Clonfert,

ABSOLUTION IN CASES RESERVED TO THE POPE

THE Holy Office recently arrived at an important decision with regard to cases reserved to the Holy Father, and the decision has been ratified by His Holiness. The following is the text of this decision, which is in the form of a reply to an inquiry by a bishop :—

Ex decreto S. Inquisitionis 23 junii 1886 cuilibet confessario directe absolvere licet a censuris etiam speciali modo S. Pontifici reservatis in casibus vere urgentioribus, in quibus absolutio differri nequit absque periculo gravis scandali vel infamiae, injunctis de jure injungendis, sub poena tamen reincidentiae in easdem censuras, nisi saltem infra mensem per epistolam et per medium confessarii absolutus recurrat ad S. Sedem.

Dubium tamen oritur, pro casu quo nec scandalum nec infamia est in absolutionis dilatione; sed poenitens censuris palpalibus innodatus in mortali diu permanere debet, nempe per tempus requisitum ad petitionem et concessionem facultatis absolvendi a reservatis ; praesertim quum theologi cum S. Alphonso de Ligorio ut quid durissimum habeant pro aliquo per unam vel alteram diem in mortali culpa permanere.

Hinc, post decretum 23 junii 1886, deficiente hac in quæstione theologorum solutione, quaeritur :

I. Utrum in casu quo nec infamia, nec scandalum est in absolutionis dilatione, sed durum valde est pro poenitente in gravi peccato permanere per tempus necessarium ad petitionem et concessionem facultatis absolvendi a reservatis, simplici confessario liceat a censuris, S. Pontifici reservatis directe absolvere, iniunctis de iure iniungendie, sub poena tamen reincidentiae in easdem censuras, nisi saltem infra mensem per epistolam et per medium confessarrii recurrat ad S. Sedem ?

II. Et quatenus negative, utrum simplex confessarius eumdem poenitentem indirecte absolvere debeat, eum monens ut a censuris directe in posterum a superiore absolvi curet vel apud ipsum revertatur, postquam obtinuerit facultatem absolvendi ?

Feria IV., 16 Junii, 1897.

In Congregatione generali S. R. et U. Inquisitionis habita ab Emis ac Rmis DD. cardinalibus in rebus fidei generalibus inquisitoribus, proposito supra scripto dubio praehabitoque RR. DD. consultorum S. Officii voto, iidem Emi ac Rmi DD. respondendum censuerunt.

Ad I. affirmative, facto verbo cum SS. mo.

Ad II. provisum in primo.

Insequenti vero feria VI. die 18 ejusdem mensis et anni in solita audientia R. P. D. Adsessori S. O. impertita, facta de omnibus SS. mo D. N. Leoni PP. XIII. relatione idem SS. Dominus Emorum Patrum resolutionem adprobavit.

J. WAGNER.

SOME DIFFICULTIES ABOUT THE ORDINATION OF PRIESTS

ORDINANDUS QUI A MANIBUS COORDINANDORUM IMPEDITUS EST NE
TANGERET INSTRUMENTA : *acquiescat.*

BEATISSIME PATER,

Gaspar Sacerdos ut suae conscientiae consulatur, humiliter postulat sequentis dubii solutionem. Quum Orator sacrum suscepit presbyteratus ordinem, quatuor vel quinque insimul erant ordinandi qui omnes certatim instrumenta tangere connitebantur. Meminit se prius talia tetigisse, sed quando prolata est formula, etsi conaretur illa denuo tangere, impeditus fuit a manibus caeterorum: inde timores agitationesque circa suae ordinationis validitatem.

Feria IV., 17 Martii, 1897.

In Congne Gen. S. R. et U. Inquisitionis habita ab Emis ac Rmis DD. Cardinalibus in rebus fidei Generalibus Inquisitoribus, proposito suprascripto dubio, praehabitoque RR. DD. Consultorum voto, iidem Emi ac Rmi Dni respondendum mandarunt :

Orator acquiescat.

Sequenti vero die et feria facta de praedictis relatione SS. D. N. D. Leoni Div. Prov. Papae XIII in solita audientia R. P. D. Adsessori S. O. impertita, Sanctitas Sua Emorum Patrum resolutionem adprobavit.

I. Can. MANCINI, *S. R. et U. I. Not.*

NOTICES OF BOOKS

TENNYSON : A MEMOIR.   By Hallam Lord Tennyson.
2 vols.   London : Macmillan & Co.

How difficult a task it is to portray with detailed accuracy
the life of a great man, and at the same time to produce a volume
the attractions of whose style will rivet popular attention, may be
inferred from the very small number of biographies that have
become lasting memorials of those whom they were intended
to commemorate. The difficulty that primarily besets the
biographer is to arrive at a true estimate of the character and
guiding principles of him whose life he writes ; to enter into his
mind, and trace his actions to their source ; as the late Laureate
himself expressed it in an unpublished preface to *Becket* : —

> For whatsoever knows us truly, knows
> That none can truly write his single day,
> And none can write it for him upon earth.

Moreover, where special facilities for knowledge of the
subject's inner life are had, not always are the graces of style at
the command of the biographer. These difficulties, however, are
largely surmounted in the volumes before us, for, while we are
admitted into as close communion with the life of the great poet
as the most eager can desire, the work evinces also a high degree
of literary and artistic merit.

In his biographer Tennyson has been singularly favoured.
His life is written by one who knew him better than anyone else
on earth, who had been the constant companion of his later man-
hood and declining years, who had watched him with solicitude
—affectionate even for a son—and who had treasured up his
utterances with a jealous care that might outrival Boswell. The
writer of the memoir had at his command the knowledge derived
from the unconstrained intercourse of years ; he has utilized, in
addition, the diary of his mother, in which the conversations and
actions of 'A' are minutely recorded, the letters and manuscripts of the Laureate himself, and the poems, with every line of
which he shows thorough acquaintance, and in which long
familiarity has taught him to see a perfect reflex of his father's
spirit.

All these poems it has been his privilege to hear his father read and explain ; nay, in many cases he has himself been the witness of their conception and elaboration. Nor with this large store of materials has he been content, for he has supplemented the recollections of the domestic circle by those of many learned men who have been the intimate friends of the great poet. Reminiscences furnished by Jowett, Froude, Gladstone, Tyndall, Palgrave, the Duke of Argyll, and Aubrey de Vere, find a place in the volumes, and contribute much to their interest.

The history of the literary life of the poet is given in his own riddle of Merlin and the Gleam, and explained by his son as he himself read it. The story of his birth, boyhood, homes, school, college, friendships, and travels is very exhaustive, and though containing many things of slight importance in themselves, will be read with avidity owing to the lustre which the subsequent eminence of the poet reflects upon them. For his later life the compiler's difficulty has been to choose from the abundance of materials at his disposal what was most suitable for the work in hand. For instance, with the assistance of Professors Palgrave and Sidgwick, he has made a selection for publication from upwards of 40,000 letters.

He has aimed throughout at letting his own hand appear in the biography as little as possible, supplying merely the setting and the connection for the whole. While the authentic value of the work is thus perhaps enhanced, its unity and continuity is somewhat marred. Many poems or fragments, rejected from his publications by the author, are inserted by the biographer. These show us what a rigid critic the poet was of his own work. Interesting notes also detail his manner of collecting materials, the incidents, often accidents, that led to the conception of his poems, and the history of their production and reception.

Full of interest, too, are the notices of Arthur Hallam that appear in the work, and the testimony of many of his learned college contemporaries silences for ever the cavil that Tennyson had exaggerated the merits of his companion, and that Hallam was not really worthy of such sorrow as his poet friend's, or of such a lament as ' In Memoriam.'

To the student of Tennyson the work is invaluable, as it gives the poet's own interpretation of many difficult parts of his poems. Thus, a manuscript note of its author gives the key to

' In Memoriam,' tells the circumstances in which it was written and the divisions of the poem ; the poet's MSS. also furnishes an explanation and a lengthy analysis written to remove the many misconceptions of reviewers and commentators of the structure and idea of Maud.   The Memoir, too, sets forth the poet's own conception of the Allegory in the Idylls—how far it is to be sought for and insisted on—and the scheme of Epic Unity in the poem.   These are but a few of the obvious advantages to the student from the poet's own commentary on his work.   Most of the Idylls were originally written in prose ; the perusal of the prose version of Balin and Balan under the title of ' The Dolorous Stroke,' makes us regret that further specimens of these interesting compositions are not found in the volumes.

In an Appendix are published the letters of Tennyson and the Queen ; the former largely characterized by their effusive loyalty, the latter progressing with time from the cold formalities of stately courtesy to affectionate condescension for an old friend. The Memoir is dedicated by permission to the Queen, the title page bearing an unpublished ode to Her Majesty the Queen, by the Laureate.

The volumes are beautifully illustrated.   There are ten photographs of Tennyson, besides those of Mrs. Tennyson, of their children Hallam and Lionel, views of their homes at Aldworth and Farringford, and facsimiles of many of the poet's manuscripts.

We are informed by Messrs. Macmillan that the first edition of 5,000 copies is already exhausted, and that a second edition has just been issued.   We are not surprised at this rapid sale.   No genuine student of English literature, and no true admirer of Tennyson, as a poet, can afford to dispense with these beautiful volumes. ·

C. M.

THE ENGLISH BLACK MONKS OF ST. BENEDICT. By Rev. Ethelred L. Taunton. 2 vols. London: John C. Nimmo.

THESE two volumes are full of interest from many points of view.   The author has evidently laboured long and hard in collecting and collating materials for his work.   He has consulted many authorities, and gone to the sources of genuine history, making use of the materials placed at his disposal with a courage and spirit that relieve the monotony of history. If it be true that the civilization and supremacy of Europe are due to the Popes and Bishops and monasteries of the middle ages, it is no less clear that England's power and domination at the present day can be traced without much difficulty to the great and liberty-loving prelates, and to the powerful religious bodies that directed and moulded its civil and religious life during the eventful centuries that witnessed the evolution and definite establishment of its institutions. In that great development the Black Monks of St. Benedict undoubtedly played a leading, if not a preponderating, part.

The first of these volumes deals with their achievements up to the time of Henry VIII.; the second, with their restoration and growth in modern days.

As we are struck by the fact that so few great names stand out in the whole history of the Order in England, we feel bound to attribute the great influence of the Benedictines much more to the system and organizations of monastic life than to any great master-mind, of native origin, that directed and guided them. With a few well-known names in the early days of the Order in England, the first volume is practically exhausted. It is no wonder, therefore, that the author devotes so much of his space to an exposition of the mode of life and methods of work which led to the vast influence of the Black Monks in England.

The second volume is mainly dominated by the personality of Dom Leander, who may justly be called the second founder of the Benedictine Order in England.

A considerable amount of space is given in this second volume to the rivalries and bickerings of different religious bodies, lay and clerical, secular and regular, and weighty indictments are drawn up against illustrious personages whom Catholics had hitherto regarded with a certain amount of veneration. These charges are, in our opinion, not unlikely to call for protest. Whether any good may result, either from the charges or their refutation, is another question. The different policies and the rival intrigues of zealous men did a great deal, in critical times, to weaken the action of the Catholic body in England. Anything like a revival of these buried ghosts would serve no good purpose at the present day. History, however, has its lessons and its warnings, and an honest and impartial historian cannot afford to keep them in the background.

J. F. H.

CATHOLIC DOCTRINES EXPLAINED AND PROVED.   By
    Rev. P. Ryan.   London: Washbourne.   Dublin: James
    Duffy & Co., Ltd.

In this little volume many questions are treated of that are of
special interest to converts.   Many difficulties that they labour
under are solved.   There is, first of all, the difficulty of learning
what exactly is the teaching of the Catholic Church.   This is often
the greatest obstacle to the conversion of souls.   In the little
book before us the author explains the truths of faith, and thus
removes to a great extent this impediment.   Another difficulty
of non-Catholics is to realize that the Catholic Church is the
Church of early Christianity, the Church of the fathers.   A
perusal of this work will help to remove some of the doubts that
may exist on this point; for many extracts from the writings of the
fathers are given to bear out the truth of Catholic doctrines.

If often happens that it is not the books which display the
grandest style, the most correct punctuation, and the best
grammar that do the greatest good.   We hope it may be so with
this work.   Though the arguments are sometimes not sufficiently
developed, and though some improvement might be made in the
grammatical construction of sentences, still we hope that the
zeal displayed by the author will gain for those who read his
work the grace of accepting the truths of Catholic faith such as
they are presented.

                                                    J. M. H.

"*Ut Christiani ita et Romani sitis.*" " As you are children of Christ, so be you children of Rome."
Ex Dictis S. Patricii, In Libro Armacano, fol. 9.

The Irish
Ecclesiastical Record

A Monthly Journal, under Episcopal Sanction.

Thirtieth Year] No. 360.	DECEMBER, 1897.	[Fourth Series Vol. II.

Nihil Obstat.
GIRALDUS MOLLOY, s.t.d.,
Censor Dep.
Imprimatur.
✠ GULIELMUS,
*Archiep. Dublin.,
Hiberniae Primas.*

BROWNE & NOLAN, Limited
Publishers and Printers, 24 & 25
NASSAU STREET, DUBLIN.

. . PRICE ONE SHILLING . .

BREAD

··· AND ···

CONFECTIONERY

Finest

Quality

Only.

KENNEDY'S

127 & 128, GREAT BRITAIN STREET,

DUBLIN.

THE TEACHING OF MUSIC IN IRISH SCHOOLS

A T their meeting in October, 1895, their Lordships
the Trustees of Maynooth College passed a
resolution, asking the Scholastic Council of the
College to report to them ' on any measures they
may think it desirable to take with a view to improve,
strengthen, and complete the teaching department of the
College.' In accordance with this resolution, a large
number of meetings were held, during the academic year,
by the Scholastic Council, the condition of the various
studies of the College was discussed, and suggestions as to
improvements were formulated. At one of these meetings
I submitted a memorandum on my own department, the
Class of Church Music. This memorandum was favourably
received by the members of the Council, and ordered to be
submitted to the Trustees for consideration. At subsequent
meetings of their Lordships the Trustees, the various
proposals of the Council were considered, and some very
important alterations, such as the establishment of two
new chairs, were decreed. At the last October meeting,
then, my memorandum was brought under the notice of
the Trustees. Their Lordships did not see their way to
granting at once the institution of an Entrance Examination
in Music, as proposed in my memorandum, but they passed
the following resolution :—

Resolved, that Father Bewerunge is requested by the bishops
to publish in the I. E. RECORD the useful suggestions he has made

in his letter to the Council of Studies, in reference to the improvement of the work of his department. It is considered that, in this way, the suggestions will at once be brought under the notice of the Managers of Primary Schools, and the Presidents of Intermediate Schools and of Diocesan Seminaries, throughout the country ; a necessary preliminary to their adoption in reference to the examination of students entering the College.

In accordance with this resolution I here publish the text of my memorandum, to which I will add some further considerations :—

GENTLEMEN, I beg to submit to your consideration, the fact, that the class of Church Music is at present in an unsatisfactory condition, and to suggest a means which, in my opinion, would go far to remedy the defect.

The object of the teaching of music in a college like this must be twofold : first. to enable the students to sing in a becoming manner all the chants which the liturgy assigns to the celebrant and the sacred ministers ; secondly, to place the future parish priests in a position to control the music in their churches to such an extent that they may be able to judge whether that music is in accordance with the laws of the Church, and the dignity of Divine Worship.

As to the first point, the proper state of things would require that all the students, or at least the large majority of them, should be able to sing the Prayers, Gospels, Prefaces, *Ite Missa est's*, &c., correctly and with a well-trained, agreeable voice. As to the second point, the theoretical instruction ought to comprise subjects like the following :—The Legislation of the Church concerning Church Music ; a History of Gregorian Chant and the Elements of its Theory (tonality, rhythm, forms) ; a History of Church Music in general, as far as necessary to understand the various styles and forms of harmonized Church Music ; the Aesthetic Principles of Church Music.

As things are at present, both these aims can but very imperfectly be attained. Only a small number of students are. at the end of their course, able to sing the melodies prescribed by the Church for the *Ite Missa est* and *Benedicamus Domino*. A considerable number are not even able to sing the Gospels and prayers correctly ; and as to voice training, very little can be done to enable the sudents to render the Sacred words with that dignity and beauty that befit the Divine Worship and save the ears of the congregation from offence.   The theoretical instructions, too, can be imparted only to a very insufficient extent.

This condition of things, however, is not due to inadequate arrangements being made in the teaching plan of this College.

As much time is given now to instruction in singing, as can be spared from the other studies, and as would be amply sufficient, if the students on entering had the qualification which ought to be expected from them. The one reason for the defects complained of is that most of the students enter here with their voices and ears absolutely untrained. Most of the time, then, allotted to Gregorian Chant, has to be spent in teaching the very rudiments of music, awakening the first sensations of musical intervals, and trying to get some musical sound out of the rough and uncultured voices.

This occupation is not only unworthy of a professor of this College, and unworthy of students engaged in, or immediately preparing for, theological studies, it is also a great waste of time. The students enter here at a period of their life when it is too late to begin musical study with good results. Singing, that is to say, the perception of the harmonic relations of tones, and the emission of pleasing vocal sound, can best be taught in earlier years, when the organs are pliable, and the brain is susceptible of new impressions. It then is very easy and satisfactory work. But, as Mr. Goodman, Examiner of Music to the Board of National Education, says in his report for 1894 : ' No one who has not had experience of it can form an idea of what a painful, laborious, and all but hopeless task it is to have to teach singing to adults who never had " voice " or " ear " developed in early youth.'

Hence the task of teaching the elements of singing must be assigned to the Primary and Intermediate Schools, and an essential change in the results of the musical teaching of this College can be expected only if the Primary and Intermediate schools begin to recognise their obligation of imparting the elementary instruction in singing.

It is my opinion, then, that we ought to do all in our power to secure this end. For if the subject in question is important enough to justify the appointment of a special professor for it, it also justly claims that everything necessary should be done in order to secure the efficiency of his teaching. As the best means to this end, I beg to suggest that an examination in music should be made part of the Entrance Examination for this College. The requirements need not, for the present, be put at a very high level. A great advantage could, be gained, if, for instance, every student on entering were required to be able to imitate a given tone. I remain, &c.

As is easily seen, the burden of this paper is an appeal to the managers of schools and the presidents of colleges and seminaries. It was in order forcibly to draw their attention to the necessity of musical teaching in their schools that I suggested the entrance examination in music. Their Lordships the bishops have taken a more moderate course; they simply wish to bring the matter under the notice of the managers and presidents. Their policy may be the wiser one, and I am not wanting in confidence that it will prove successful. No one who, with an unprejudiced eye, examines the progress made by the Irish schools during the comparatively short period they have been allowed to exist, can withhold his unbounded admiration. The work that has been accomplished is enormous and worthy of the highest praise. And, in no small degree, to the wisdom and energy of the managers and presidents of schools this gratifying state of things is due. There is every reason to hope, therefore, that since the necessity of musical training has been put before them, not for the first time, indeed, but under a new aspect and with episcopal recommendation, they will do their part to bring about the required improvement.

No doubt there are difficulties in the way. One difficulty, for primary schools at least, is the scarcity of competent teachers. In the training colleges, indeed, good work is being done. But they are labouring under the same difficulty as Maynooth College—the backward state of the candidates on entering. I have already, in the above memorandum, quoted from a report of Mr. Goodman, Examiner of Music to the Board of National Education. I cannot refrain from quoting, at some length, from the same gentleman's report for the year 1896. He says:—

Musical work continues to proceed steadily in the Training Colleges. No other subject is studied with more zeal, or taught with more earnestness. If greater results are not obtained, the cause is to be found, not in any want of efficiency on the part of the professors, but in the conditions under which they have to teach. So long as the great majority of the students continue to come up to the Training Colleges without any previous training or practice in vocal music, so long will the work of the music teachers in the colleges be one of labour and of difficulty. The first thing required, therefore, in my opinion, is to improve, from a musical point of view, the material coming into the colleges. This, I feel convinced, could be very effectually done by placing practical vocal music among the requirements of the examination of candidates for entrance. Such an examination need not be a very strict one; it might be, indeed, in the beginning simply a test of voice and ear rather than of musical knowledge. But the great result of placing vocal music among the subjects for examination at entrance would be to direct the attention, from an early period, of all intending candidates to the necessity of preparing themselves in this as well as in the other ordinary subjects of examination. And it would be very much to the advantage of the students themselves if they would only secure this preliminary training in singing. . . . If a student be utterly unpractised in singing at the time of his entrance into training, he will in all probability never be in a position to teach it. Skill in all musical matters is best acquired in early youth. Proficiency in singing especially, is rarely obtained by anyone beginning in adult age ; while in very early life singing is as easy as it is delightful. Hence the necessity of very early training in music, above all to those who are to teach it.

We find, in this extract, the same complaint that I gave expression to in my memorandum : the want of musical training in early youth. This, indeed, is the *circulus vitiosus* under which we labour. There are no teachers competent to teach music ; consequently, the aspiring teachers have no chance of learning music while at school ; in the Training College they cannot acquire a sufficient knowledge of music, and therefore go out as teachers incompetent to teach music. This is a very serious difficulty indeed, and one that cannot be overcome in a few years. But it is all the more desirable that a vigorous effort should be made to accelerate progress in this matter. Managers of schools have a great influence here. By applying for teachers capable of teaching music, they will encourage the study of music among the aspirant teachers ; by giving their own pupil teachers an opportunity of being taught in music, and by directing their attention to the necessity of such preparatory study, they will facilitate the work of the Training Colleges in this department.

It may be well to mention here, that the certificates issued to teachers regarding the teaching of music are no guarantee that the owner of such a certificate is a good teacher of music. They only enable the teacher to earn result fees in music ; they secure that if he teaches pupils so that they will pass the examination, he will be paid for his work; but they are no proof that his teaching really will have this effect. It is advisable, therefore, that managers desirous of getting teachers for instruction in music, should make special inquiries as to their capability of teaching it.

As to the Intermediate schools, I am not aware that the same difficulty of obtaining a competent teacher exists. There the great obstacle is the pressure of other studies, and the fact that no payment is given for the teaching of singing. The best remedy here would be a complete change of the system of Intermediate examinations—a measure now advocated, we believe, from many quarters, and for many reasons. But in the meantime we trust that the merits of the case itself will induce enlightened presidents of colleges and seminaries to bestow due attention to this subject. In Germany, at the intermediate schools, in the lower classes at least, two hours a week are devoted to class-singing, while the members of the choir have two additional hours' practice. Perhaps it would be too much to expect so much time to be given to singing in this country, for the present at least. But I imagine that an hour every week could easily be spared for class-singing, and a great deal of good work could be done during this hour. The teaching, however, should be given to *all*, and in a scientific manner.

A good effect could also be produced without any additional loss of time, if congregational singing were employed at the various college devotions, at Mass, Benediction, perhaps even at night prayer, and the like. The introduction of this practice might cause some difficulty; but, if it were once well established, it would work quite easily. The simpler melodies of Gregorian chant, such as the *Tantum Ergo, Veni Creator, Salve Regina, Te Deum*, and the *Ordinarium Missae*, together with simple devotional hymns, would furnish the proper material for this congregational singing.

The reasons I have given for the teaching of singing apply only in the case of students intended for the priesthood. It might, therefore, appear desirable that I should say a word about the advantage of singing lessons for boys preparing for other avocations. These advantages are claimed to be many and great. But they have been explained before me in a much better way than I could do it. I, therefore, confine myself to mentioning the benefit derived from singing lessons for public speaking. It is clear that if such an advantage can be derived, it is of great importance to every educated man. But I may refer here particularly to the case of teachers, Primary as well as Intermediate. It is a well-known fact that teachers, to a great extent, are suffering from throat affections, resulting from an overstrain of the voice in speaking. Now, it is maintained by the best authorities that these evils could be avoided, if the voice were used in a proper and scientific manner. This being so, I should like to point out that the practice of singing, in as far as it concerns itself with voice production, is the very best means of learning the proper use of the voice even for speaking purposes. The pronunciation of the consonants is the same, of course, in singing and in speaking, while the formation of the vowel sounds, the ' placing of the voice,' is also best learnt by singing, because the prolonged tones of singing enable the student to become conscious of the way he produces his voice, and to find out, while listening to himself, the means of improving his tones. For this reason declamation masters actually make the pupil *sing* the vowel sounds to learn the proper way of emitting them. If, therefore, a singing lesson is properly conducted by the teacher, and carefully attended to by the pupils, it cannot fail to produce the beneficial results alluded to.

I have been informed that since my above memorandum was brought under the notice of their Lordships, in one seminary a special class for singing Gregorian chant has been instituted. This is very gratifying to learn. *Vivant sequentes.*

H. BEWERUNGE.

PHOENICIA AND ISRAEL

TO the Biblical student every name occurring in the pages
of the Sacred Text has a peculiar interest. It recalls,
perhaps, some incident in the lives of the patriarchs or some
event in the troublous days of the kings—it may be a
victory, it may be a defeat, it may be some deed of valour,
or even a deed of treachery and shame. Or, perhaps, it
reminds us of some striking intervention of Divine Power
in favour of the chosen people, and brings before us once
again the venerable figure of the aged patriarch or roughly-
clad prophet—mysterious, awe-inspiring figures upon which
our fancy loves to dwell. We never read of Bersabee but
we think of the league between Abraham and Abimelech,
or later, between Isaac and Abimelech ; while Mambre and
Hebron, Bethel and Gerara, are names which make us live
over again the great patriarch's life. Gelboe calls to mind
David's lament over Saul and Jonathan ; Moab tells us
of the passage of the Arnon and the disputes about
the boundary. If we listen to the tale of Sennacherib,
or the story of the Exodus, we instinctively contrast the
present state of Assyria and Egypt with their former
insolence and rapacity. They were the oppressors of God's
people—where are they now ? And so it is with any name
we choose [to mention ; be it town or village, hill or dale,
stream or well, they all carry with them the most vivid
associations ; they are relics of the past, telling their story
to every passer-by.

It is this, perhaps, which, apart from all considerations,
gives so great a charm to the merely historical side of the
New Testament. We meet the same people, and come to
the same places ; the same venerable names occur again and
again ; we mingle amid the same familiar scenes as before ;
and yet there is no change. The people are still children
of Abraham, still Israelites as of yore ; but Pharisee and
Sadducee contrast strangely with the idolatrous Jews of the

Captivity: here are the same Levitical Priests, yet how different from the lax and dissolute body of whom we have so dark a picture presented to us in the sons of Eli. Then they disregarded the law, both spirit and letter; now, if they know not its spirit, they yet cling tenaciously to its letter. And even where the light of the New Covenant shines most brightly, where the change is an unmixed blessing and fills our hearts with joy, we yet derive a new pleasure from the thought of the contrast afforded by the old associations with which the spot is inseparably linked. We read of the desert, and it is 'no longer Moses and the stiff-necked Jews who people it, but a solitary figure wanders there clad in camel's hair. We come to Jacob's well: the white tents of the patriarch with the far-spreading flocks do not meet our gaze, but we see instead a weary figure seated there while a woman with her vessel in her hand listens spell-bound to His words.

So too, Tyre and Sidon, one phase of whose history forms the subject of this present paper, awaken in our minds a long train of thought as we read about them in the New Testament. They seem from the casual way in which our Saviour, the Evangelists, and St. Paul speak of them, to have been poor and insignificant then, but we cannot help recalling those marvellously poetical chapters in Ezechiel wherein the prophet depicts in such glowing terms their power and beauty : 'O Tyre, thou hast said : I am of perfect beauty, and situated in the heart of the sea. Thy neighbours that built thee have perfected thy beauty.' And again : 'The Persians, and Lydians, and the Lybians, were the soldiers in thy army. . . . The men of Arad were with thy army upon the walls round about. . . . The Carthaginians thy merchants. . . . Greece, Tubal, and Mosoch, they were thy merchants : they brought to thy people slaves and vessels of brass.'[2] How sad a contrast is this picture of far-reaching power, of a sovereignty which extended as far as the limits of the then known world, with the woeful spectacle which these same cities present to the

---

[1] Ezech. xxvii. 3, 4.   [2] Ezech. xxvii. 10-13.

readers of the Acts of the Apostles! ' And he (Herod) was
angry with the Tyrians and the Sidonians. . . . And he
made an oration to them, and the people made acclamation
saying: It is the voice of a god and not of a man!'[1]   And
this was the city which had resisted the besieging army of
Nabuchodonnosor for fifteen years, this the city whose king
had said in his heart: ' I am God, and I sit in the chair of
God, in the heart of the sea!'[2]

A knowledge of the past history of these famous cities
renders still more striking the sad contrast between these
two pictures. It is a history which cannot rival that of
Greece or Rome in the stirring excitement of constant warfare, nor can Tyre and Sidon boast a long line of kings of
heroic mould such as were the leaders of the Grecian and
Trojan hosts. Neither were the Tyrians famous for their
cultivation of literature and the muses ; no Homer or Virgil
told their history in an epic, no Horace or Ovid graced the
courts of their kings. Their fame and their right to
perpetual honour rests on a very different foundation, such
as, perhaps, would have merited for them but scanty praise
from the brusque and haughty Roman or polished Greek.

From a mere cursory reading of the Bible we might
be tempted to rank the Phœnicians among those numerous
peoples whose names occur very frequently in the sacred
page, but who have had to all appearances little or no
material influence upon the chosen people. We say, to all
appearances, because we would not for one moment assert
that 'any of the nations with whose names we become so
familiar as we read the Bible, had no influence upon the
Israelites ; the more carefully and thoughtfully we read,
the more wonderfully do the designs of Providence with
regard to these same peoples, manifest themselves to us.
We see how each one of them had its appointed part to play,
and when we are enabled, as now, to throw the light of the
inscriptions discovered in such numbers in late years, upon
the Bible records, passages which up to now had meant
little or nothing to us, assume a new importance and put

---

[1] Acts xii. 20, 21.   [2] Ezech. xxviii. 2.

us in possession of facts of which we had hitherto never dreamed. Thus it has been with the Hittites, that mysterious people of whom till recent years we knew next to nothing, but who, as Professor Sayce so clearly shows in his history of this 'forgotten empire,' by their long and arduous contest with Egypt, prepared Palestine for its occupation by the Israelites. But to the cursory reader, as we have said, these things are not so apparent, and it is only when some accident has, so to speak, put us upon the scent, that we enter upon a series of investigations and comparisons which at the same time that they open up to us a new and deeply interesting bye-path in history, also establish the accuracy of the Bible narrative in a most convincing manner. The history of the relations between Phœnicia and Israel form one of the most interesting subjects which the Biblical student can investigate, and it is a history which only patient investigation will unravel. The Bible is a history of the Jewish people, but as it goes along it drops hints and suggestions regarding the history of the surrounding nations, and these when woven together form a long and connected skein of marvellous consistency. Like the geologist at work in the quarry or the cutting, we pick up inch by inch the particular stratum of which we are in search. At one time it runs clearly along, standing out in bold relief on the face of the cliff, at another time only minute traces of its presence are to be found ; now we are to be guided by some peculiar fossil, now by the characteristic colouring of the rock, while occasionally all signs of its presence are lost to us, and we have to dig deeper in search of the vein which has come to an unexpected ' fault.' The first step then in our investigations is to find out who the Phœnicians were, and as their history is not familiar to everyone, it may be of interest to many, and we will therefore give it at some length.

When we first learnt to spell, we were probably told by our spelling-book or by our teacher, that the alphabet was invented by the Phœnicians. If we pressed our instructor further, there was probably a silence, which we in our innocence attributed to an unwillingess to burden our too youthful minds, but which, had we known it—and well for us we did not so much as dream it—was in all likelihood due to ignorance. Who were the Phœnicians? As years slipped by, and we conned our Virgil in lower forms at school, the old familiar name which had aroused our childish curiosity, cropped up again in its Latin garb of *Poeni*. They were fearful men those Poeni. Their portraits, as drawn for us by Roman writers, cling to us now, and we fancy we see Regulus, hero-like, suffering those cruel tortures, even as we write. And yet we little thought as we read on, that the Romans were much the same: quite as fierce, quite as superstitious, and not one half so civilized even, if more humane; though they were, perhaps, less gloomy in their beliefs, and with higher ideals, higher instincts and pursuits. Then the same old question recurred: who were these mysterious Poeni? and we were told that they were the sailors of the ancient world, the pioneers of civilization, the fathers of trade and commerce, founders of cities, and colonisers of distant lands; their chief town was Carthage, and they were said to have come there from Tyre in the Holy Land. And now, when our school days are over, and we read and ponder over our Bible, the same old question meets us once again: Who were the Tyrians, and where did they come from?

This is a question which has been much discussed by ethnologists, and various opinions, into which it would be foreign to our purpose to enter, are upheld. The account given us by the Bible tallies admirably with all that profane history can tell us on the point, except in one particular, and that regards the language of the Phœnicians; for while the Bible makes them the sons of Canaan, who was the son of Cham, there seems to be little doubt that their language was Semitic. After describing the flood, the sacred writer gives us the geneological tree of the sons of Noe: 'And the sons of Cham: Chus, and Mesraim, and Phuth, and Chanaan.'[1] 'And Chanaan begot Sidon his first-born, the Hethite, and the Jebusite, and the Amorrhite, and the

---

[1] Gen. x. 6.

Gergesite, . . . '[1] And the rest of the nations whom the
Israelites were bidden drive out of the land. He then adds :
' And afterwards the families of the Chanaanites were
spread abroad,'[2] that is, from the mountainous district of
Armenia, where the Ark had settled. For some years then
these tribes dwelt in the land which lies between Armenia
and Arabia; they peopled those vast plains watered by the
Tigris and the Euphrates, and many of them wandered even
as far as the Indus, passing through Susiana, Elam,
Carmania, and Gedrosia keeping close to the shores of the
Persian and Arabian Gulfs. As years went by, the land
grew too narrow for the immense hordes which rapidly
sprang into existence, while vast masses poured into it from
the east and north, thus driving the Chanaanites towards
the west, where they peopled Africa and Palestine, which
latter country was called after them, the land of Chanaan.
This, in the main, is the view generally accepted. But a
difficulty still remains regarding the name Phœnicians.
The clue to this difficulty seems to be found in the testimony
of Herodotus and Strabo, the former of whom avers that the
Phœnicians, whom he questioned, traced their origin to a
migration from the shores of the Erythraean Sea. The
locality of this sea is a matter of dispute, geographers being
undecided whether to refer it to the Persian or the Arabian
Gulf; but its locality is not so important for us as the
meaning of the name. In Greek, φοῖνξ means red, and
so does Ἐρύθρος. May we not, therefore, suppose that
the name Phœnician was one which the Chanaanite tribes,
who for a long time after the flood had dwelt on the shores
of the Erythraean Sea, appropriated to themselves, throwing
round it a mythical glamour which made them the descendants of the mythical Phœnix, son of the still more mythical
Antenor. This, of course, is a theory, and a theory only.
Still it has the advantage of according with the Biblical
narrative, at the same time, that it does not, as far as we know,
fall foul of the witness of modern discovery. In confirmation
of the statement of Herodotus, it may be mentioned, that

---

[1] Gen. x. 15, 16.   [2] Gen. x. 16.

severel of the islands in the Persian Gulf bear Phœnician names ; while the Syrians of the time of Herodotus pointed as a proof of their story, to temples and buildings still existing on those islands.   The date of their emigration from the Erythraean Sea cannot, of course, be so definitively settled. Lenormant assigns it to 2400 or 2300, B.C.

The new arrivals would not find the land empty when they came, for Palestine was far too luxuriantly beautiful, and, at least in parts, far too lazily fertile to be long unoccupied. Many of the aboriginal inhabitants seem to have been of abnormal size and strength, and tales of their formidable appearance so terrified the Israelites that they determined to go back to Egypt. ' The people that we beheld are of a tall stature ; there we saw certain monsters of the sons of Enoc, of the giant kind, in comparison of whom we seemed like locusts.'[1] We have no notice of the wars which the Chanaanites must have waged against those monsters ; but at the time of the exodus they do not seem to have existed in very great numbers, and it is noticeable that they are nearly all collected on the desert side of the Jordan.

From the Bible narrative we gather, that the Chanaanite tribes which now occupied the Holy Land, were divided by the localities in which they had established themselves into two main bodies: 'And the limits of Chanaan were from Sidon as one comes to Gerara, even to Gaza, until thou enter Sodom and Gomorrha, and Adama, and Seboim, even to Lesa.'[1] One body then seems to have taken up its abode in the neighbourhood of the Dead Sea, the other to have occupied the long strip of coast-land which we now know as Phœnicia. It is with this latter body that we are chiefly concerned ; the former appears to have gradually disappeared before the impetuous advance of the Israelites, who in time reduced them to a state of servitude.   Phœnicia, some two hundred miles in length, with a maximum breadth of perhaps twenty, was in every sense a favoured nook, and one well suited to a tribe which had, if we are to believe

---

[1] Numb. xiii. 33, 34.   [2] Gen. x. 19.

their own account, been reared upon the sea-shore. At their backs lay the 'everlasting hills' of Palestine; before them stretched the Mediterranean. The hills sheltered them from the marauding tribes of the interior, and from the Egyptian hosts, which under Thothmes III. and Ramses II. spread desolation throughout Palestine and Syria, in their efforts to overcome the redoubtable Hittites. The mountain slopes yielded pines and cedars, cypresses and firs, for their huge fleets; while their flocks roamed the hillside, which was a veritable garden of Eden in its profusion of oriental flowers and fruits. Citrons and melons, almonds and peaches, vied with plantations of olives, spices and pomegranates in loading the air with their rich perfume. Lebanon has been justly called 'the glory of Phœnicia.' This world-renowned range of mountains rose to a height of six thousand feet and more, and was covered with immense groves of cedars and pines. How glorious they must have looked, clothed to within a few hundred feet of their summits, with those magnificent trees which stood out in clear startling contrast with the everlasting snow crowning the topmost peaks! Well-nigh numberless are the similes and allusions which the inspired Hebrew poets drew from those royal trees: 'Behold the Assyrian like a cedar in Lebanon, with fair branches and full of leaves . . . the cedars in the paradise of God were not higher than he.'[1] But few, alas! now remain, the hand of the spoiler has come upon them. Hiram and Solomon we may suppose to have exercised discretion in felling the timber, but not so Sennacherib and the vandals who succeeded him in stripping the mountains of their pride and glory: 'With the multitude of my chariots, I have gone up to the height of the mountains, to the top of Lebanus; and I will cut down its tall cedars, and its choice fir-trees.'[2] In the year 1875, but three hundred and seventy-seven were to be counted, and few of these were of real antiquity. We who have rarely had the chance of seeing more than a few cedars together, can hardly imagine what an entire grove of them can have been like.

---

[1] Ez. xxx. 3-8.   [2] Is. xxxvii. 24.

The tree looks ill-adapted to growth in company since the expanse of its boughs is often greater than its height, and great numbers of men with their flocks can find shelter beneath the huge limbs. They were specially suited to a country where rain ceases to fall from May to October, and where the sun has a power which we can only faintly appreciate.

Of the towns of Phœnicia the most important were Aradus, Sidon, Tyre, Gebal, and Byblus. There were others such as Tripolis and Acco, the modern Acre, but they do not seem to have played so prominent a part in the commercial world of Phœnicia as the afore-mentioned, which formed a strong confederacy among themselves, and made their power felt far inland, though they never seem to have aimed at acquiring large territorial possessions in their own immediate neighbourhood. 'They dwelt without any fear according to the custom of the Sidonians, secure and easy,'[1] devoting themselves to the acquirement of immense wealth and far-reaching power by means of trade and the cultivation of the mechanical arts. The early history of these towns is shrouded in the mist of ages. In the Bible, Sidon is called the first-born of Chanaan, but at the same time it is certain that Berytus and Byblus were of a far greater antiquity; they may have been founded by the aboriginal inhabitants who were afterwards dispossessed by the Phœnicians, and in this case Sidon's title of the eldest born of Chanaan, if applied to the town at all, and not merely to its founder, would mean that it was the first Chanaanite town founded in Phœnicia, or perhaps that it was the first to assume the hegemony over the others. Sidon was a double city, one part lying inland, the other on the shore of the Mediterranean; she could boast two harbours, one for winter, and the other for summer. Her trade was early developed, and she showed her colonizing tendencies by establishing both in Cyprus and the isles of the Aegean sea commercial centres which served as the nuclei of future towns. Similar settlements soon dotted the littoral of Asia

---

[1] Jud. xviii. 7.

Minor and the North Coast of Africa. But of these colonies one of the earliest was the partial cause of the mother city's fall. Tyre, some distance to the south of Sidon, was for many years little more than an insignificant second-rate town, but the misfortunes of the parent city proved Tyre's gain, and she rapidly rose to a supremacy which she retained for many a long year. The Philistines, that free-booting, war-loving people, who were so perpetual a thorn in the sides of the Israelites, had for some time been at feud with the Sidonians; open war does not seem to have been declared, and anything like systematic offensive or defensive tactics was quite unthought of, when one morning in the year 1209 B.C., the Philistine fleet sailed boldly into the open and unguarded harbours of the Sidonians, stormed the defenceless city, put great numbers of the unresisting inhabitants to the sword, and loaded their vessels with a rich booty. The calamity was almost as complete as it was sudden, and the Philistines can have little suspected as they manned their vessels for the piratical expedition, how complete would be the downfall of the city they were going to attack. Sidon lay a heap of smoking ruins, and her fortunes seemed scattered to the winds. What could her merchant-princes do? Whither could they betake themselves? The rising town Tyre lay near and afforded a safe shelter from the Philistine swords. The crowd of fugitives both rich and poor fled in the direction of Tyre, who willingly opened her gates to receive them. From that hour her fortunes were established; her augmented population required room, and building was carried on apace; the city grew rapidly, and with increased numbers gained influence year by year.

As Renan has well remarked, it is hardly correct to call Phœnicia a country; it is rather a string of islands clinging close to the shore, and so adapted that while a great part of the town lay on the mainland, the remainder occupied the adjoining island, and the sea lying between the two portions of the town formed a convenient road for the shipping. The liability to predatory incursions by the marauding tribes beyond Lebanon was the probable cause of this unique arrangement, which, however, proved so convenient that it endured till long after all fear of invasion had died away. Aradus, Tyre, and, to all intents, Sidon also, were thus really double cities; and indeed Island-Tyre at one time consisted of three islands over which the city was spread ; two of these were afterwards joined together by Hiram, the most famous of the Tyrian monarchs ; the third supported the temple of Melkarth, the tutelary god of the city. That portion of the city which lay on the mainland was known as Palae-Tyrus, or Old Tyre ; its exact site is difficult to determine, but recent investigations by Major Conder of the Palestine Exploration Fund Society have enabled him to dentify a spot called Ras-el-Ain with ancient Tyre. Ras-el-Ain means ' The Fountain Head,' and there yet remain large cisterns, some of them even now in good repair, which testify to the existence of extensive waterworks at this spot. This agrees well with what we know to have been the case at Tyre, and combined with other circumstances renders the identification almost certain. Major Conder has also pointed out one feature of these historical towns, which, though it ought not to astonish us upon reflection, yet at first comes upon us with somewhat of a shock ; we refer to their small size. Renan imagines Palae-Tyrus to have been a vast suburb spreading over the plains in the neigh-bourhood, and he would have us picture to ourselves a town one-fourth of the size of London. But if this were really the case, it is certainly strange that no remains of this vast city should be forthcoming ; no Palestinian town that we know of attained to anything like these dimensions, and the island-city of Tyre would almost fit into Hyde Park. Thus Jerusalem, Samaria, and Joppa, were all small towns, and quite out of proportion to the power they wielded or to the fame which clings to them. The harbour of Sidon was famous, and yet we are amazed when we look at it now, it is a mere fishing-harbour such as one sees round our English coasts, and quite unable to afford anchorage for our modern large vessels.

The island city is commonly known as the metropolis. This term is rather misleading : it was the metropolis, if by this word we understand seat of power, but the island-city

was in no sense the mother city; indeed the early inhabitants
of Palae-Tyrus seems to have disregarded the island, and to
have looked upon it merely as a refuge, for until the time of
Hiram it was only partly built over. But after the improvements which this monarch set on foot, the relative positions
of the two parts of the town were reversed, and the island,
now improved and enlarged in surface by its connection
with a hitherto neglected islet lying close to, was covered
in a short time with houses and public buildings, besides
being strongly fortified. The water-supply of these island-
towns was a difficulty which it required various ingenious
contrivances to overcome. Aradus owed its fresh-water
supply to a really novel source. It was somehow discovered
that at the bottom of the sea off the island a fountain of
fresh-water came bubbling up. Divers were accordingly
sent down, who succeeded in fastening a bell-mounted tube
over the orifice from which the water flowed, and the
imprisoned stream was then brought safely to the surface,
and conducted into the city by conduits and pipes. Maspero
has asserted that Island-Tyre had no such supply of water;
and such, indeed, seems to have been the case for a time,
and water was conveyed in pipes from the mainland, a fact
which explains the large cisterns which still exist at Res-el-
Ain; but it is certain that later some source of fresh-water
must have been discovered within the island, as it is
impossible otherwise to explain how the beleagured
inhabitants withstood the lengthy sieges for which the
city afterwards became famous.

To be concluded in our January number.   HUGH POPE, O.P.

THE ECONOMIC ASPECT OF SOCIALISM

I.

THE limited aspect under which I shall review the social
problem needs no apology. The ethics of socialism
is too well known to the readers of the I. E. RECORD to need
repetition. Its history I shall touch on briefly, and only *en
passant* while assigning economic theories to their authors
and locating them relatively to each other. I am now
directly concerned only with the economic bearings of
socialism, and shall be quite content if I can indicate the
lines on which controversy on this matter ought to run,
should it be incumbent on us to enter it. Hence I shall say
nothing new, but shall merely state afresh old doctrines and
criticisms, with whatever light more recent literature can
supply.

Now, what is socialism? The number of schools that
claim the name and the variety of their theories make the
word difficult to define. For us Catholics, however, the
word has but one meaning, since socialism has recently been
condemned by name at Rome. 'To remedy these evils,' says
Leo XIII. in his Encyclical of May, 1891, 'the socialists,
working on the poor man's envy of the rich, endeavour
to destroy private property, and maintain that individual
possessions should become the common property of all to be
administered by the State or by municipal bodies.'

Thus socialism is identified with collectivism, and in
this sense we shall henceforth understand it.

Dr. Schaeffle, in his *Quintessence of Socialism*, thus
describes the tenor of the socialistic programme and its
aim as an international movement:—

To replace the system of private capital (*i.e.*, the speculative
method of production, regulated on behalf of society only by the
free competition of private enterprises) by a system of collective
capital, that is by a method of production which would introduce
'unified' (social or 'collective') organization of national labour
on the basis of collective or common ownership of the means of

production by all the members of society. This collective method of production would remove the present competitive system by placing under official administration such departments of production as can be managed collectively (socially or co-operatively), as well as the distribution among all of the common produce of all, according to the amount and social utility of the productive labour of each.

These are the aims of socialism in its real sense. I shall now briefly mention some other schemes that are usually known as socialistic.

Conservative Socialism has been pithily defined by Professor Rae as the faith of those ' in whom the most obstinately conservative interests in the country go to meet the social democrats half-way, and promise to give them better wages if they will but go to church again, and pray for the Kaiser.'

Certain forms of anarchy too, like that of Bakunin have merited the name, and more especially that more sweeping form, the Nihilism of Belinsky and Petracheffsky, ' which,' Herzen tells us, ' would have nothing to do with mind or God, state or country . . . but somehow manages to shift its hue, with whatever ground it happens to occupy.'

The ' Socialists of the Chair,' as Oppenheim denominated the group of young Hegelians who, in 1872, ' socialized ' the Chairs of Economic Science in the best of the German universities, differ from the socialists with whom we are acquainted—Blatchford, Kirkup, Bernard Shaw, &c., only in the intellectual groundwork of their theory.

A form more prevalent than all these is that which is known as State Socialism ; a species of quite recent growth, which has indeed little in common with the collectivism, it shall be my task to criticize, being little more than an exaggerated protest, which the evils of modern economic enterprise have evoked against the system of *laissez faire !*

Le socialisme d'état [says M. Chailley] est l'introduction des idées de reforme sociale dans l'organization de l'état sans ébranler et sans changer à fond les institutions legales et politiques du statu quo.

Then there is what is known as Christian socialism.   Of

this I wish to speak at some little length before I come to discuss the principles and aims of the Collectivist programme. I shall not again have an opportunity for doing so, as these articles are in the main critical. Were they constructive I should afterwards have to spend much time on the detailed schemes for social amelioration, which the Christian economists of our day have formulated.

It is often thought that the Christian schemes for social reform are nothing more than the Christian protest against sin; that they are based mainly on sentiment; that they alleviate all evils with 'cheques on heaven'; and, whilst deploring the tyranny of capitalism, have little better to offer to the proletarian than 'transcendental yearnings' after a future recompense. This, I think, is the view that many entertain of the Christian efforts at reform. Catholics are, perhaps, more ignorant than Protestants, of what we may repute the keenest, deepest, and most vital action that has occupied the social stage of Europe for many years, an action fraught with interest for us all, from the issues it entails.

More than thirty years ago an ecclesiastic arose in Germany, who, we may almost say, put Church energies into new channels, and faced the social problem with a bearing Churchmen had seldom hitherto assumed. This was Monsignor Von Ketteler, Archbishop of Mayence. Before his ordination, Monsignor Von Kettler had served in the army, as a non-commissioned officer, and had also occupied important posts in the public administration. He was thirty-nine years of age when he became Archbishop of Mayence, and during the twenty-seven years that he occupied that see, he vindicated, with all his might, the rights and liberties of labour. He vigorously attacked the attitude of liberalism in its selfish schemes at social reform. He endorsed Lassalle's destructive criticism of the Manchester economists, but opposed for the most part his constructive theory. But we must admit that what was positive in the Archbishop's schemes, though morally right, was not quite practical. He had little confidence in State interference in industrial relations, and little hope of subsidy from it. But human charity, he thought, would certainly provide for the relief of the poor, and supply what capital was required for the establishment of a national co-operative industry. His schemes fell through, but the principle of his labours and his life lived with his followers.

The programme for reform proposed and passed at the Congress of Fulda, formulated a detailed and exhaustive scheme for the amelioration of the poor. This, and the protests of Canon Moufang, Von Ketteler's disciple, are a happy contrast, in their practical cognizance of detail, to the vague formulas of socialism. Whatever was good in the socialistic ideal, the Christian reformers made their own. 'The best means,' said Canon Hitze, at the Catholic Congress of Frieburg, 'for defeating democratic socialism, is to take up its truths, eliminating from them what is erroneous;' and, 'fortunately,' says Professor Nitti, 'what was erroneous in it, was also impracticable.' We too can ignore the extravagances to which the energy of their too keen charity sometimes drove the Catholic economists— extravagances which the logic of consistency did not postulate. Their principles were sound; and everything that is practical in the socialistic programme, we find in theirs, and very much more besides.

Count Losewitz and Baron Von Vogelsang, both converts to Catholicity, whilst bitterly opposing the 'Byzantine smothering up of every liberty in the absolutism of the State,' have practical remedies and large-minded principles for the evils wrought by liberalism.

Switzerland, even more than Germany and Austria, has had its Catholic reformers. So searching and detailed were the plans and principles of M. Gaspard Decurtins, that the bitterest enemies of the Church could not withstand their power; and in the Social Congress of Berlin, the young Radical party, though it had previously proclaimed its severance from the Church, stood to him, under Favon, to a man. That which followed—the establishment of the Swiss *Secretariat Ouvrier*—M. Drage has reckoned one of the crying wants in the industrial life of Great Britain.

In France, too, the two schools of economic reform, under

Perin and Count de Mun, have done much for the abolition
of social wrongs, and have won from the democrats much
of their vantage-ground.

I mention these things that the reader may see how
practical these Catholic reformers have been. The wide
range and vast depths of their programmes, into the details
of which I should like to enter, but cannot here ; their
subtlety in abstracting from the minute and complex centres
of industrial life the germs of disease that time has fostered
there, are a remarkable contrast to the vague formulae of
the socialists. Let us dwell on this a while, before we
criticize the principles of socialism.

The socialistic programme has this one end—the
abolition of private capital. To throw the whole industrial
machinery of the nation upon one centre, and let its produce
flow out from that, in equal quantities, to the labourers at
its periphery, is the socialistic grand ideal. How this,
however, may be brought about, or how maintained, if once
begun, we are not informed. Surely the overthrow of the
springs and hinges of our present industrial life, stocks,
shares, partnerships, mortgages, loans, rent, &c., and the
substitution of another, centralized or federal, necessarily
more delicate than our own, would demand a previous, perfectly adjusted plan and a programme of infinite detail.
But on detail the socialists are silent. ' Le socialisme,'
says M. de Laveleye, ' ni est une science ni un art, il est une
critique, parfois une attaque violente, et il est une aspiration.'

The socialistic theory has never been seriously constructive. I say seriously, because we have had much in
in the way of poetry and romance and toy states, in anti-
cipation of the socialistic era.

We can scarcely take Mr. Bellamy's vision, *Looking
Backward*, as a responsible item in the literature of socialism,
whilst the toy states that Robert Owen established at New
Lanark, New Harmony, Otbarton, and Nashoba, proved
only the *reductio ad absurdum* of the socialistic principle.[1]

---

[1] M. Louis Reybaud in his *Etudes sur les Reformateurs*, and Mr. Dale Owen
in his interesting autobiography, *Threading My Way*, give interesting accounts

Socialism, then, has been up to this merely 'une critique, une attaque violente' on existing systems. The Socialistic attack is two-fold in its character; either it is directed against real evils—and these we shall see can be remedied without socialism—or it is directed against the original and essential groundwork of society—and that, we hold, requires no remedy. I should like to adduce a few examples of the 'critique socialiste.' Many of them are amusing to a degree, particularly in their onslaught on the exclusiveness of class. I shall quote just one from Mr. Belfort Bax's vituperative attack on the 'bourgeoisie' in his *Religion of Socialism*. If I mistake not, Mr. Belfort Bax is one of the leaders of the Fabian economists, who, Mr. Sidney Webb tells us, 'best represent the socialist ideal in its latest and maturest forms.'

Socialism [says Mr. Belfort Bax] is the great modern protest against unreality, against the delusive shams that now masquerade as verities. We defy anybody to point out a single reality, good or bad, in the composition of the Bourgeois family. It has the merit of being the most perfect specimen of the most complete sham that history has presented to the world.

The Bourgeois hearth dreads honesty as the cat dreads cold water. The literary classics that are reprinted for its behoof it demands shall be vigorously Bowdlerised, even at the expense of their point.

Topics of social importance are tabooed from rational discussion, with the inevitable result that erotic instances of middle-class womanhood are glad of the excuse afforded by good intentions, honest fanaticism, and the like things, supposed to be associated with 'Contagious Diseases' Act and 'Criminal Law

---

of the life led by the inhabitants of these miniature states. They were founded by Robert Owen to prove the possibility of the socialistic state and the justice of its promises. But they soon broke up, for they never paid, and the forced peace that reigned in them was quickly proved chimerical. But their life was interesting, such as it was. At evening the children of New Lanark filed out into the square, and sang their hymn, 'When first this humble roof I knew.' Men and women wore good-conduct badges, and on their heads they carried an indicator with four sides, coloured respectively white, yellow, blue, and black. White signified 'very good;' yellow, 'good;' blue, 'middling,' and black, 'bad.' The colour, seen from the front, interpreted the wearer's conduct for the week; and so, when visitors arrived, these pretty children of forty, fifty, or sixty years of age, filed out smiling into the square, for commendation or reproach; and, M. Reybaud remarks: 'Il était rare que tous les indicateurs ne fussent pas tournés du coté de la marque blanche; à pene on apercevait-on quelques unes de jaunes, moins encore de bleues, de noires point.'

Amendment' agitation, to surfeit themselves on obscenity. . . .
Then, again, the attitude of the 'family' to the word 'damn.'
Indeed, if there is an honest, straightforward word in the English
language, a word which the Briton utters in the fulness of his
heart, it is that word 'damn.' . . . Then there is that other
fraud of middle-class family life—the family party. The principle of the family party is this, that a body of persons having
nothing in common but ties of kinship, that such a motley crew
should meet together in exclusive conclave, and spend several
mortal hours in simulated interest of each other. Now, a cousin,
let us say, may be an interesting fellow; but very often he is not.
If he is not, why should one be expected every twenty-fifth of
December, or other similar occasion, to make a point of spending
one's leisure with a man who is a cousin but not interesting,
rather than with another who is interesting but not a cousin? . . .

On the same principle, the symbolic black of mourning is
graduated by the tailor and milliner in mathematically accurate
ratio, according to the amount, not of affection, but of relationship. The utter and ghastly rottenness of the Bourgeois family
sentiment is in nothing more clearly evinced than in this. To a
person of sensibility, the notion that, the moment he enters on his
last sleep, his relatives will 'see about the mourning,' may
impart to death a terror it had not before, and thus act as an
incentive to carefully-concealed suicide.

THE PRINCIPLES OF SOCIALISM

The two great principles on which socialism is based,
are the labour theory of Karl Marx, and the *loi d'airain*,
the 'iron law of wages' of Lassalle. Let us discuss them
separately.

The *Das Kapital* of Karl Marx was the first great
literary effort of the socialistic body. In it is expounded
the celebrated doctrine, that has made socialism a popular
creed: the doctrine, namely, that the source and standard of
economic value, in the industrial world, is labour. Capital
is only accumulated labour, congealed 'labour-jelly.' This
view was not original with Marx. It was taught and
defended by Adam Smith, Quesnay, Ricardo, Tracey, Bastiat,
Carey, and other economists of the classical school. In the
development of his theory, Karl Marx distinguished between
the 'use,' and 'exchange' value of saleable commodities.
'Use value,' he says, is nothing more than the intrinsic
use of an article to men. 'Exchange value' is the ratio in

amount, in which one commodity exchanges with another.
'Value in use,' and 'value in exchange' are distinct, co-ordinate, perfectly independent, and often even utterly opposed.
The 'use value' of air, is very great. Its value in exchange
is absolutely nothing. The 'use value,' of a diamond is
practically *nil*. Its value in exchange is fabulous. Value
in exchange, though distinct from utility, is not determined
by caprice or covenant. It necessarily depends on some
one quality common to the commodities exchanged : something which may supply us with a ground of comparison
between the heterogeneous kinds of articles on sale. Utility
is evidently no such ground. The use value of bread bears
no comparison to the use value of music, or books, or scenery.
What, then, is the common attribute of commodities ?
Karl Marx replies : 'the labour used in their production.'
But labour itself is not homogeneous. 'Planing' and
'filing' are not 'healing' and 'instructing,' and the labour
metre must apply to all. Well, even here there is a common
element, a point of juncture between all kinds of labour,
namely, the time occupied by the work. Thus labour time
is the source and standard of value in exchange. But
Karl Marx narrows his criterion further. Energy and
skill vary with persons, places, and times. If labour-
periods be the source of value, will value not fluctuate with
the varying and unstable humours, tastes, capabilities, and
designs of the workman momentarily employed ? No, there
is a permanent factor in the labour period, independent of
the transitory conditions of work : that is, the 'socially
useful time of labour,' the time an artisan need not exceed
in the production of an article. This is the celebrated labour-
gauge of socialism—the 'socially useful time of labour.'

Following these principles, Marx now proceeds to account
for a strange economic fact : the existence, namely, and
increase of capital. Production like products, labour like
commodities, has it own value in exchange. The value of
labour is precisely that which is necessary for its support.
The value of a day's labour is just what sustains the labourer
for a day, what compensates him for decay of tissue, and
renews spent energies. But labour is cumulative whilst

products are not. Five pounds of bread may compensate the labourer for five hours' work; but five hours' labour will produce a hundred or more pounds of bread. A labourer produces in one hour what his master pays him for the day. The other twelve or fourteen hours he works for nothing, storing up capital for his master. This is the origin of increase of capital—the 'surplus-time' of labour—the sweat that the labourer pours out gratis.

Now what are we to think of this? Is labour the sole source of value; and, if not, how shall we answer Marx's difficulties? Let us suppose that A and B till each a piece of land. Their energies, talents, implements, and opportunities are exactly alike. When the harvest comes, it will be found, that the produce taken from one piece of land is double that given by the other. Will anyone doubt that the value of one is exactly double that of the other. If labour were the source of value, the values of the two should exactly coincide. What, then, is the source of the difference in value (for the source of the difference will be the source of the whole)? The source of the difference is intrinsic to the land; the difference, viz., in the qualities of the soil. If anyone were to prophesy the market price by the expenditure of labour alone, he would learn to his cost that market laws were different from his own.

Labour, no doubt, is often a factor in the determination of value and price; but only in so far as it bears on the relation of supply and demand in the market sale; and we shall afterwards see, that supply and demand are efficient principles in the determination of price, just in so far as they are a token or condition of 'value in use.'

The difficulties incident to Marx's theory are obvious enough. We must admit, however, that he faces them boldly, though his solutions are neither creditable nor ingenious. Thus:—(1) If the Marxian theory of value be true, then nothing which labour has not produced should possess a value in exchange; and (2) nothing which cost labour should ever be valueless. Thus virgin soil, uncultivated fruits, fish, birds, minerals like coal and oil, trees of spontaneous growth, &c., on Marx's principles should have no value. On the other hand, bad fruits, decaying vegetables, botched and useless products should have a value equal to the labour spent in their production.

Marx answers : Commodities which have cost no labour like coal, oil, and uncultivated fruits, though valueless, may have a price. As to spoiled products, we must remember that the labour that is at all recognisable in exchange is only the 'socially useful labour,' and not the mere output of energy.

'Un vrai casse-tête,' exclaimed M. de Laveleye, when he was caught in the intricacies of *Das Kapital.* 'A valueless article may have its price,' says Marx. The question arises,— and what is price? Fortunately, Karl Marx himself defines it : 'Price is the money-form of value.' Price, therefore, without value, is a contradiction in terms. We need not say that the absurdity of the reply could not, when pressed to its logical issues, result in anything but a paradox. To the second difficulty he replies : 'No labour, but that which is socially useful, can impart a value to products and effects.' The reply is not happy for Karl Marx's theory, for it hands him over to the very doctrine it was the aim of his efforts to refute. For what is the socially useful labour? It is that which produces useful objects. Thus, labour is not the source of value, but the utility of its products.

The discussion of this theory leads me to a point of much importance in 'Economic Science.' I put it in the form of a difficulty, thus : 'If supply and demand are the main condition of the value of commodities in an open market, how can it be said that value depends on the intrinsic use-fulness of the goods on sale?' The obvious answer to such a difficulty will probably be such as this : 'Demand is always proportioned to utility.' But what shall we say of utility and supply? I answer,—supply as well as demand is a source of value, just in so far as it affects utility. But let me here indicate an ambiguity which may prove a likely source of error. 'The useful' and 'the beneficial' are not quite the same, in the language and usages of 'Political Economy.' 'The utility,' says Professor Walker, 'which the economist recognises is not that of the physiologist.'

'Utility' is the capacity an object possesses of satisfying
a human want; whether that want be virtuous or vicious,
and whether the commodity be beneficial or pernicious.
The case now may be stated thus:—I go to market to
purchase fruit. One pound would satisfy my necessities
for the moment; a second pound would satisfy my tastes;
a third would be superfluous and waste. It is evident that
I would pay more for the first pound than for the second,
and for the second than for the third, for that is their order
in utility. In the purchase, however, I do not pay a separate
price for each separate pound. I pay one price for all. The
greater the supply which *must* be sold, the less is the
average utility of the lot, and the less is paid for each
separate pound. This is what is called 'the law of
diminution in marginal utility.' The final price realized
by the sale will rest at the point, where it is more useful
for the buyer to pay out his money and receive the article,
than keep his money in his pocket. And by what is the
price regulated in the case? By the utility of the marginally
useful pound. Supply, therefore, as a determinant of value,
is such only as the determinant of marginal or final utility.
Thus, according to Ricardo, 'the rent of any particular land
is the difference between its productiveness and the productiveness of the worst land in cultivation which pays no
rent,' *i.e.*, the land on the margin of cultivation.

The law, therefore, of supply and demand, though an
axiom, is not primary. It is secondary and derivative.

The second principle, on which socialism is based, is the
'loi d'airain' of Lassalle. Lassalle himself thus states the
law:—'The iron economic law, which in our day under the
rule of supply and demand, determines the wages of the
labourer, is as follows:—The average wages is always confined to the necessary sustenance, which, according to the
custom of a nation, is necessary to insure the possibility of
existence and propagation. This is the point around which
the actual wages oscillates like the swing of a pendulum,
without ever remaining long either above or below this
standard. Wages cannot persistently rise above this average;
otherwise there would result from the easier and better con-

dition of the labourers, an increase of the labouring population and a supply of hands which would again reduce the wages to, or even below, the average point. Nor can the wages permanently fall below the average of the necessary sustenance of life, for this would give rise to emigration, celibacy, prevention of propagation, and, finally, to the diminution of the labouring population by want, which consequently would reduce the supply of hands, and again raise wages to a former or even a higher rate. . . . Thus, labourers and wages continually revolve in a circle, the circumference of which can at most reach the margin of what is barely sufficient to satisfy the wants of human subsistence.'

This is the 'iron law of wages' received from Ricardo, Adam Smith, Malthus, and Bastiat, and the other classical economists. I would ask the reader to bear this statement of the law in mind whilst he glances over the following figures. The law states that the wages of labour cannot rise above, nor fall below, the point at which sustenance and propagation is possible.

The following tables have been compiled or taken from reliable authorities on the statistics of finance. First I shall examine the state of wages for the last half century in England alone; then I shall briefly refer to the progress of labour on the Continent and in America. Mr. Giffen gives us the following figures in his *Essays on Finance* :—

WAGES IN ENGLAND

		Wages fifty years ago, in Shillings per Week		Wages now, in Shillings per Week		Increase in wages for the fifty years
		s.	*d.*	*s.*	*d.*	
Carpenters at	Glasgow	14	0	26	0	85 per cent.
,,	,, Manchester	24	0	34	0	42 ,,
Bricklayers ,,	Glasgow	15	0	27	0	80 ,,
,,	,, Manchester	24	0	36	0	50 ,,
Masons	,, Glasgow	14	0	23	0	69 ,,
,,	,, Manchester	24	0	29	0	10 ,,
Weavers	,, Huddersfield	12	0	26	0	115 ,,
,,	,, Bradford	8	3	20	6	150 ,,

On the other hand, the hours of labour for these same

men have decreased in the time fully 20 per cent. In
round numbers, we may say the wages of labour have
increased from 70 per cent. to 120 per cent. in fifty
years in money return. The reader may object that, if
wages have increased during the period in question, the
prices of food and other commodities may have increased
in proportion, which would only confirm the ' iron law '
and make clear its meaning and its drift. On the contrary,
I say that articles, as a rule, are cheaper now. The sovereign
goes farther than it did fifty years ago. Mr. Giffen tells
us that wheat is cheaper than it ever was, even in the era of
free trade. And I find that his remark holds good, not only
of the English, but also of the German, Russian, Austrian,
and American markets. But we must remember that
averages in this matter are deceptive rules ; for often they
are struck between extremes, one term of which must have
played havoc at times with the health of the people. Thus
in the thirties and forties of this century, the extremes in
the market price of wheat, meant famine almost for the
labourer. Most articles of food have come down, like bread,
for the last half century. Clothing and utensils are very
much cheaper. In two commodities alone has there been
any rise in price. Beef has gone up in most of our markets.
In some of them, however, the difference is so slight, that
we need scarcely take account of it. But we must remember
that if the rise in beef is any burden on the labouring class,
it is so, because the wages of labour have so risen that beef
is a common article at their tables. Fifty years ago, this
was not the case. And if we may be allowed to go back
farther, we find that very few workmen ever ate beef. King,
in his *Natural and Political Conclusions*, tells us that at the
end of the seventeenth century, not half the poor people
ever ate meat. And we know that the meat they more
commonly ate was bacon, and not beef. But the price of
bacon has decreased since then. House rent, no doubt,
stands higher now than it did half-a-century ago, but the
houses are more elaborately built. It is not, therefore, that
rent is higher, but that the labourer occupies a better house.
But, now, even if we regard the rise in beef, and the rise in

rent as purely an unmixed loss to the labourer, and discarding for a moment the fall elsewhere, which more than compensates for these two, the workman's labour is paid in the net as much as twice what it formerly was.

So much for England. In America wages have quadrupled in this century. They have doubled in France, Germany, Belgium, and Italy, in almost every stable trade.

I am not suggesting that labourers are paid too much, or enough. I think they have a right to some share, at least, in the great increase that industrial progress has given to profits. I am only showing that the iron law as stated by Lassalle is not in accordance with stubborn fact. No doubt, the rich would try to keep the wages of labour at its lowest point. But such a course would not make for the interest of capital or of profits, and would seriously interfere with the life of trade. The increase of wages that has accrued to labour must have some cause, beside the charity of capitalist or entrepreneur. That canon of induction, treated of in our schools, the 'canon of concomitant variations' will indicate, if it does not prove, that increase of wages follows as a rule, the increased efficiency of manual labour. According to Cairnes, a day's labour in America produces as much as a day and a third in England, a day and a half in Belgium, a day and three-quarters or two days in France, and five days in India; and remarkably enough, the relative wages in these five countries, is exactly the same in any particular branch of industry.

Supposing now that the iron law has any validity as an economic principle, we fail to see why socialists should adduce it, as an apology or a plea or in justification of their system. If it may serve as a protest at all, it ought to be directed against the system from which it springs. And what is the source of the 'iron law'? It is indicated by Macaulay in his *History of England*, in a remarkable chapter on the wages of manufactures.

Sixpence a day was now [1] all that could be earned, by hard labour at the loom. If the poor complained that they could not

---

[1] He is speaking of the end of the seventeenth century.

live on such a pittance, they were told that they were free to take
it or leave it. For so miserable a recompense, were the pro-
ducers of wealth compelled to toil, rising early, and lying down
late ; while the master clothier, eating, sleeping, and idling,
became rich by their exertions.

This is the system which explains and originates the law
in question. The iron law, if it exists at all, originates with
the system of iron competition. Put capital and labour in
an open market, without the restrictions of State interference,
and capital must have its way. This is the system of *laissez
faire* which the growth of charity, and the demands of labour,
and the denunciations of the Church, have been staggering
of late. The remedy for the evils it has wrought amongst
us must be sought in the dissolution of the system itself,
and in the substitution of effective State protection, not of
commodities, but of industry.

We must remember too that the 'reserve army of
industry' which now cramps labour, is not likely to decrease
in the socialistic state ; and that the industrial decay which
the extinction of private Capital will induce, may heighten
instead of lessen the evils of competition. For if twenty
per cent. of the population be idle, through causes for
which they are not responsible, the State could not fairly
refuse to employ those that will work for diminished wages.
If the obligations of the State towards A and B be perfectly alike in all respects, why should it employ one of two,
to the exclusion of the other, who will work for less ? Here, I
think, is a defect, that the critics of Socialism have neglected
or overlooked, that the evils of an absolutely competitive
industry, against which socialism is the 'great modern
protest,' are necessarily incident to socialism itself; and
that 'the eager eyes at the work-yard gate ' will have more
power, and a juster influence, in the search for work, and
the distribution of profits, when the State has made itself
the father of us all, the universal employer, paymaster, and
provider.

Let it not be thought that pauperism will vanish with
the destruction of private competitive enterprise; for every
incentive that now quickens trade will cease with its

absorption by the State, and employment is not likely to increase in the rapid industry that must necessarily ensue. Individual enterprise has been sufficient at times to reduce pauperism to its lowest ebb. Only seven years ago, 1890, the unemployed in England did not reach a maximum of one per cent. of the entire population. Whether this might be realized permanently, it would be difficult to affirm; but anyone who has read Mr. Drage's book on *The Unemployed*, will not hesitate to say that much might be done that is not yet done to relieve the nation of the weight of pauperism that presses on it so heavily.

Nor need anyone think that in the socialistic state pauperism will be made light by a large share in the national profits. Mrs. Annie Besant, a well-known socialist, in assigning the stimuli to industrial exertion, in the Collectivist State, thus speaks of pauperism :—

The stimulus to exertion will be the starvation that would follow the cessation of labour. Until we discover the country in which jam-rolls grow on bushes, and roasted sucking pigs run about, crying, 'Come, eat me,' we are under the imperious necessity to produce. We shall work, because on the whole we prefer work to starvation. In the transition to socialism, when the organization of labour by the Communal Council begins, the performance of work will be the condition of employment.

And Mr. Bernard Shaw asserts that 'the last (*i.e.*, wages for the unemployed) is not to be thought of. Anything is better than *panem et circenses.*'

It comes, therefore, to this, that in the socialistic state, if the unemployed are to live at all, it must be like the *ateliers nationaux* of France, after the revolution of 1848; or by some wise scheme of Poor Law support, on the basis of our own. The first, history has taught us to fear. For the second, socialism is not necessary. But whichever we adopt, the burden shall be heavier, than now it is, or has yet been.

I shall next treat of the outlook for labour in the socialistic state.

M. CRONIN, D.D., M.A.

OUR VISION OR KNOWLEDGE OF GOD

THE word vision, in a derived sense, signifies intellectual knowledge or understanding. Our knowledge of God may be acquired through the intellect aided by sense, through the natural power of the intellect unaided by sense, through the supernatural light of faith, and through the intellect assisted by the light of glory. Knowledge of God obtained by sense and intellect is abstract; whereas that acquired through faith is called supernatural *obscure* knowledge, to distinguish it from intuitive vision which implies clear and immediate perception of the divine essence.

That God can be known through the intellect aided by sense is a truth both of revelation and philosophy. St. Paul, in his Epistle to the Romans, chapter i., v. 20, tells us that the 'invisible things of Him from the creation of the world, are clearly seen, being understood by the things that are made.' Effects convince us of the existence of a cause; every particular object in nature, even the whole universe, has impressed upon it the essentials of an effect. In every essence abstracted from singular things, we find after examination by the eye of the soul, the idea of essential dependence, we know such essences cannot exist of themselves, nor give existence to one another, all necessarily presuppose an absolute being, essentially perfect under every aspect. Therefore the intellect through sensible phenomena arises to the existence of God; and as a consequence, knowledge of God through the understanding aided by sense is an evident truth. Again the intellect by its own natural power unaided by sense can know God. We freely confess this is not admitted by all philosophers. Some, however, maintain it on the authority of St. Thomas. Let us hear the Angelic Doctor :—

Utrum potentiae rationales sint semper in actu, respectu objectorum in quibus attenditur imago. Respondeo quod secundum Augustinum (lib. de util. credendi ch. XI.) differunt cogitare, discernere, et intelligere. Discernere est cognoscere rem per

differontiam sui ab aliis. Cogitaro autem est considerare rem
secundum partes et proprietates suas. Intelligere autem nihil
aliud quam simplicem intuitum intellectus in id quod sibi est
pracseus intelligibile. Dico ergo quod anima non semper cogitat
et discernit de deo, nec de se ; quia sic quilibet sciret naturaliter
totam naturam animae suae ; ad quod vix magno studio per-
venitur. Ad talem enim cognitionem non sufficit praesentia
objecti quo libet modo, sed oportet ut sit ibi in ratione objecti, ct
exigitur intentio cognoscentis. Sed secundum quod intelligere
nihil aliud dicit quam simplicem intuitem (qui nihil aliud est quam
praesentia intelligibilis ad intellectum quocumque modo) sic
anima semper se intelligit et Deum indeterminate.[1]

Hence according to St. Thomas the soul *ab initio* had
some knowledge of God and of itself; and that too independently of sense : as it had both objects *ever* present to
itself. We now propose to develop this doctrine. Can
we argue from the fact, that we know God in this indeterminate manner; that He is an *actual reality* existing
outside the mind itself ? Certainly; if we call in the aid of
sense. Before we proceed to prove this theory, a few remarks
must be made about the mind. The character of the mind
is ontological, that is, just as the sense of sight is ordained to
some coloured thing outside itself : so is the mind to an
entity independent and distinct from itself; moreover the
object of the mind is real entity : and were we to say that
unreal being was its object we would be destroying all knowledge. To know a thing is to know that it is true, for
nothing but truth is or can be an object of knowledge. To
say you know a thing, and yet do not know whether it be
true or false, is only saying you do not know it at all. No
man does or can know falsehood, for falsehood is nothing, a
nullity, and therefore is no intelligible object.

Falsehood is intelligible only in the truth it denies, and
is known only in knowing that truth, hence *real* being is the
direct and proper object of the understanding. Again, the
mind in its primary operations or analytical judgments is
infallible. If we were to deny this we become sceptics.
Now, having established two facts—namely, the objectivity
and infallibility of the mind, we proceed to reply to the
point at issue. According to the article of St. Thomas just
quoted, there has *ever* been present to the intellect some

---

[1] Lib. i., Sent. Dist. iii., Quaes iv., Art v.

ındeterminate knowledge of God, which clearly enters into
our very essence ; a knowledge we cannot put aside. The
question arises, is the object of this knowledge a reality?
What criterion have we for distinguishing real from unreal
being? First, our concepts are real when they represent
something actually or possibly existing, and by possibility
we mean that the concept of existence is not *essentially*
contained in the concept of the nature we conceive ; but can
be *actually* joined to it by some cause. Secondly, our
concepts are unreal when they are mere relations of reason
that do not or cannot exist outside the mind. The mind
itself, therefore, separates the *real* from the *unreal*. God,
as we have already seen, is always present to the intellect ;
and from the remarks just made it is evident He is present
as a reality. Now, are we logical in concluding that He is
also an *actual reality* outside the mind? Is not the mind
objective? Is it not also infallible in its analytical judgments? If we know *aliunde* (as we do), that existence
is essentialy contained in the divine essence, is not the
judgment *God exists* analytical? Consequently, as God is
ever present to us as a reality, we logically conclude from
sound premises that he also actually exists outside the
mind, *as actual* and not *possible* existence must be predicated of *ens quo majus et melius cogitari non potest.*

As we said in the beginning, the knowledge of God
through the intellect aided by sense is abstract, since
determined intuitive knowledge of God is, in the natural
order, absolutely impossible. Natural knowledge is, as such,
proportioned to him who knows, and not to the object
known ; otherwise it would transcend the power of the
faculty, and as a consequence would cease to be natural.
The mode of action always follows the mode of being.
Operatio sequitur esse, and everything we know is in us
according to the mode of our being. *Quidquid recipiter ad
modum recipientis recipiter ; Cognitum est in cognoscente
secundum modum ejus.* Every intellect, therefore, whatever
it understands, necessarily does so in accordance with the
mode of being proper to that intellect. The human intellect,
as long as it exists in the body has the essence of material

being for its direct and proper object; and again, *determinate* knowledge cannot be acquired unless by species abstracted from the phantasia. God, as He is in Himself, is a pure spirit transcending all created nature; species cannot represent Him as He is in Himself, and what is seen through species is not seen immediately. No human intellect, therefore, as long as its knowledge is in proportion to its nature, can know God as He is in Himself, nor can He be to it the object of intuition. What we have said of the human intellect is equally true of the angelic. The angels are in potentia to their existence; hence they are not absolutely simple; consequently, God as He is in Himself is not the object of intuition to the unaided angelic understanding. The Divine intellect alone has the Divine essence as an object in proportion with it, and so God as He is in Himself is present to Himself intuitively. Again, we may know God through the supernatural light of faith. Faith, taken in the general sense of the word, is our belief in any truth founded on the testimony of others. Our faith may be human or divine. Human faith is when we believe anything we learn from the testimony of man. It is divine when we believe in the testimony of God. Now the certainty of what we learn from the testimony of others depends on the authority of those who give the testimony. In other words, it depends on their knowledge and veracity; hence, since human creatures are liable to be deceived and to deceive, it follows as a necessary consequence that human faith does not carry with it absolute certainty. On the contrary, God cannot deceive nor be deceived; hence, everything we know from the testimony of God we know with the most absolute certainty. Divine revelation teaches many mysteries about God; the human understanding left to itself staggers before them; they seem to be impossibilities. To assent to them is out of the question. This is the position of the person without divine faith, and under the circumstances we must not wonder at it. The supernatural light of faith, however, removes the difficulties, and though it does not manifest to us the nexus between the predicate and subject of the given mystery, yet we assent easily and intellectually.

Therefore the human intellect through faith learns and assents to many truths about God which left to itself it could never have discovered. 'But the things that are in heaven who shall search?'[1]

Fourthly, we can know God through the light of glory. The Holy Spirit, speaking through the Prophets and Evangelists, tells us that the clear vision of God will be the reward in the next life for those who have been faithful here. 'Everyone that calleth upon My name I have created him for My own glory.' The glory of God, in the life to come, consists in manifesting to the blessed the treasures of His infinite goodness, so that the end God had in creating us was primarily His own eternal glory; and secondly, our eternal happiness. Again, our Blessed Lord says, to the good servant, 'I will set thee over many things; enter thou into the joy of the Lord.' That joy by which God is, and by which He is essentially happy, is the joy which He communicated to His saints, which must necessarily have for its efficient cause the clear vision of the divine essence. Now St. Paul in his First Epistle to the Corinthians, chap. xiii., contrasts this intuitive vision with the knowledge we have of God through faith. The latter, he says, shall be destroyed in the next life. 'But when that which is perfect has come, that which is in part shall be done away.' Our faith, however, will not be completely destroyed, according to St. Thomas 'aliquid fidei remaneat in patria,' eo quod eadem est in genere ac visio clara.'[2] Again the Apostle tells us that our present knowledge of God, whether it be natural or supernatural, is through a glass; in a dark manner, that is, it is not an immediate knowledge of things in themselves, but a mediate knowledge by means of other things. On the other hand, St. Paul speaks of the vision of God promised to us in the life to come as intuitive immediate: 'Then I shall know face to face. I shall know even as I am known.'

We have already seen that this clear vision of God transcends the natural powers of every created understand-

---

[1] Wisd. ix. 16.   [2] Ia IIae Quaes. lxvii., Art. v.

ing ; hence a supernatural aid is necessary by which the created intellect should be raised to this intuitive or beatific vision.   This supernatural aid or force is called the light of glory, and it is according to the more probable opinion a permanent quality by which the understanding is informed supernaturally and disposed to elicit the beatific vision. Understanding is a vital act produced by one's own intellect. The blessed, therefore, by their own vital act see God, and by this act they are made eternally happy.   Whether they produce by this act of intelligence a species *expressa* or not is disputed by theologians.   Some maintain that a species *expressa* corresponding to the act of vision which each of the blessed possess is possible, and we think some solid arguments are adduced to support this theory.   Before we dwell on the knowledge of the saints in heaven it may be well to refute here the opinion of Master Bonae Spei and Valentia, who say that the glorified bodily eye can see God as He is in Himself.   Origin, arguing against Celsus, says, on this point, ' Falsely, therefore, does Celsus attribute to us the hope that we are to see God with our bodily eyes ;' and St. Cyril of Jerusalem tells us God cannot be seen by the eye of the flesh, for what is incorporeal cannot fall within the range of the corporeal eye.   St. Athanasius, too, says that God is altogether invisible in everything which is proper to the Divine Nature except in so far as He can be perceived by the intelligence.   The opinion of those fathers was evidently not that of Bona Spei and Valentia.   Again, God as He is a pure spirit, is not an object proportioned to the glorified bodily eye ; and a corporeal sense, even if it were glorified, is not, on that account, raised to the level of an operation which is intrinsically and essentially intellectual, such as the vision of a pure spirit.   This reason is, in itself, sufficient to prove that the doctrine of the aforesaid theologians is false.

But what do the blessed now see in virtue of the beatific vision ?   They, seeing God as He is, behold everything formally and necessarily contained in Him, namely, essence, absolute, attributes, or perfections, and the Three Divine

---

¹ Catech. 9.   ² Apud S. Aug., Epis. iii.

Persons. The object of faith now will be the object of
vision then. Whatever, at present, we believe in, whether
it be connected with the essence, attributes, or persons, or
whether it be something outside God, shall then be clearly
seen. All the blessed, seeing God as He is, must necessarily
see the divine attributes, essence, and persons. The justice
of God is His mercy, and His mercy is His goodness ; His
goodness is identical with all His other perfections. All
again are identified in and with the simple essence of God ;
consequently, seeing God as He is, the blessed also see all
His absolute perfections. So also the Three Divine Persons
are clearly seen. They are really distinct from one another ;
but they are identified with the divine essence. The essence
of the Father is the essence of the Son, and the essence of
the Son is the essence of the Holy Ghost. The divine
essence then cannot be seen without seeing the Persons, as
the knowledge of the blessed is intuitive and quiddative. As
regards the vision of other things in God which are outside
God, and not God, the intellect of the blessed understands
those things in accordance with the degree of the light of
glory it posesses, and also in accordance with the particular
state of each, or again they may be seen by means of infused
species, or by a special revelation of God. Each of the
blessed can be considered, first, as elevated to the order of
grace ; secondly, as a part of the universe ; and, thirdly, as
a public or private person. If we consider the blessed as
elevated to the order of grace, then we must grant to them
clear vision of the truths of revelation, a clear insight of the
mysteries of the Incarnation, Resurrection, and Redemption
of our Lord ; also the mysteries of grace and predestination ;
in a word, whatever belongs to the object of faith now will
be the object of intuition then. Each of the blessed as a
part of the universe beholds all creation, heavens, elements,
and stars, and whatever belongs to the integrity of the world,
all the essences and species of things, and all the angels.
They see everything in which God has manifested His
creative power ; however they do not see everything which
is the object of that power, as this would imply compre-
hension if these things were seen in the word of God ; and

we cannot find any sufficient reason to justify us in saying
that God by a special revelation communicates such a knowledge to the blessed.   Finally, the blessed do not lose the
knowledge they have acquired in this life: ' And Abraham
said to the rich man in hell, Son remember that thou didst
receive good things in thy life time.' Neither do they lose
their knowledge of human affairs, nor their relations with
mankind. It is natural that the Popes who have passed
away would be specially interested in the work of the
Church militant; natural too, that kings and princes would
feel an interest in their earthly kingdoms or principalities,
and how desirous parents must be to know everything in
connection with the children they have left behind.   Such
a knowledge must be attributed to the blessed as every just
and reasonable desire is satisfied in heaven.

The vision the blessed have of God depends for its clearness and intensity on the degree of the glory communicated
to the created understanding : and this communication is
made in accordance with the merits each one has acquired
in this life.   Some of the blessed, consequently, know God
more perfectly than others as the merits of all are not equal.
' Beatos intueri Deum sicuti est, pro meritorum tamen
diversitate alium alio perfectius.   Concil. Florentinum Sess.
ultima.'   Though all see God clearly, nevertheless He is
incomprehensible to the angelic and human understanding.
He alone comprehends Himself.   His vision is infinite, just
as His essence is infinite.   So, as He is to Himself infinitely
knowable, so He understands Himself in an infinite manner:
in other words, He comprehends Himself, ' For the Spirit
searcheth all things, yea the deep things of God.' [1]

LOUIS M. RYAN, O.P., S.T.L.

---

[1] 1 Cor. ii. 10.

HISTORY OF TRIM AS TOLD IN HER RUINS

IN the last number of the I. E. RECORD, a paper appeared treating of the antiquity of the Church of Trim. It alluded to the origin of the ancient name 'Ath-Truim,' and referred to the many remarkable ruins with which this classic locality is studded, and which ' extending for the space of above a mile, form, in the striking description of Sir William Wilde, a combination of beauty and an architectectural diorama rarely ever seen in any other part of Ireland.' These many interesting monuments of the past abounding in Trim and its surroundings, unquestionably furnish a standing palpable proof of the civil and ecclesiastical importance of the place in former times. But the principal portion of the paper was devoted to the discussion of the curious question, whether Trim is the *oldest* Irish episcopal see founded by St. Patrick—twelve years before the primatial see of Armagh—and placed by our saint under the care of his nephew Loman who was constituted its first bishop. Tirechan, Ussher, Jocelin, the *Annals of the Four Masters*, the *Tripartite*, the Bollandists, Colgan, Cogan, and Dean Butler—doubtless a formidable array of eminent authorities—were produced in support of the statement, that Trim is certainly the oldest Irish episcopal see.

There is only one author, as far as we have seen, who strikes a discordant note, and disdains to travel by the old path, or walk in the footsteps of any of those who have gone before him. He says, in effect, to the historians, ancient and modern : you are all wrong, and the sooner you see the error of your ways, and retrace your steps, the better it will be for the cause of truth. As a matter of fact, there was no such man as Loman, a contemporary of St. Patrick ; no such person accompanied Patrick into Ireland ; and the long preamble about his being left in charge of his uncle's boat at the mouth of the Boyne ; its subsequent sail up to Trim against the stream; the conversion and baptism of Fortchern, of his mother, father, and royal household ; the donation of the lands around Trim as a site for the church, and other spiritual purposes; all these alleged events so circumstantially detailed, are nothing more nor less than pure fiction, a story started by Tirecham, improved upon by Jocelin, and blindly adopted by Ussher, the Bollandists, and all subsequent writers of Church history.

Lest we should do Doctor Lanigan the least injustice by misquoting him, we shall give his own precise words, for they reveal his sentiments, and put forth his ideas with a pungency and force that few could attempt to rival, and in language plain and unmistakable.   He says :—

The *Tripartite* introduces on this occasion, viz., on the occasion of the arrival of St. Patrick, Luman or Loman (whom it makes a nephew of St. Patrick) as left to take charge of the boat, and adds, that in consequence of an order from the saint, he sailed up against the current of the river as far as Trim.   This was too good a story to be passed over by Jocelin, who, to make it still more marvellous subjoins that, the sails being hoisted the vessel went up without the assistance of oars ; notwithstanding furious blasts of wind in the direction straight opposite to its course.   He might as well have said that it had been carried in the air, for as Ussher has remarked, the channel of the Boyne is so unfit for navigation, that it would be impossible for a boat to proceed as far as Trim, even were both the current and the wind favourable.   Tirechan as quoted by Ussher, has a part of this story as given in the *Tripartite*, but instead of calling Loman a nephew of St. Patrick, he makes him only a disciple of his.

Connected with this fable is what we read in the tracts referred to, concerning his having been placed at Trim (Jocelin makes him a bishop), and the antiquity of that church which Tirechan says was founded the twenty-second year before that of Armagh.   The donations of town and lands spoken of in the above tracts, do not by any means agree with the times of St. Patrick.   Tirechan, or rather the person who assumed his name, and who was a Meath man, represents the possessions as annexed for ever to the see of Trim, but it seems they were claimed by the Archbishop of Armagh ; and hence Jocelin, one of whose patrons was the Primate Thomas O'Connor, mentions a disposal of these lands made not long after, in virtue of which the right of them was transferred to St. Patrick and the see of Armagh.   The *Tripartite* also, a compilation apparently patched up at Armagh, has something to the same purpose.   Thus we have a key to the whole business.   While it was pretended that these possessions belonged to St. Patrick, that is to Armagh and not to Trim (the name of St. Patrick was mistaken for the saint considered personally), and thus he and Loman were made contemporaries.   Whence flowed other allegations.

Had Ussher and the Bollandists reflected on these circumstances, they would not have laid down that Loman was the first bishop consecrated in Ireland, and Trim the oldest Irish see.[1]

There is no possibility of mistaking the meaning of the foregoing words.   They prove, beyond doubt, that the evidence of Tirechan and the *Tripartite*, and the authority of Colgan, Ussher, and the Bollandists, are entirely brushed aside, and the history of the events narrated by them boldly impeached on intrinsic grounds.   The objections urged with such remarkable ingenuity, and such pointed language by Dr. Lanigan, are :—

(*a*) The bed of the river Boyne was so unfit for navigation that it would be impossible for a boat to come to Trim, even if the current and the wind were both favourable.

(*b*) The donations of land mentioned in the various tracts do not at all agree with the times of St. Patrick.

(*c*) The accounts are contradictory.   The *Tripartite* makes Loman a nephew, and Tirechan only a disciple of Patrick.

(*d*) There is an incidental remark made by Dr. Lanigan about Fortchern, to the effect that, ' notwithstanding his royal descent, I find Fortchern set down in the *Tripartite* as St. Patrick's blacksmith.

You can easily perceive how every little point, no matter how trifling, every little seeming contradiction, is seized on by our learned but hypercritical friend to discredit the accounts given by all other historians, and to prop up his own pet theory, that Loman was no contemporary of St. Patrick's, but belonged to the seventh century.   Even at the risk of being tedious I must take up the objections one by one.

1. The bed of the river Boyne was so unfit for navigation as to preclude the possibility of a boat proceeding as far as

---

[1] Lanigan, vol. i., p. 222,

Trim. In reply to that objection, my first impulse would be to say simply, *Quod gratis asseritur gratis negatur.* Dr. Lanigan has not given us a particle of solid proof to show that it was impossible in *olden* times for a boat to be got up as far as Trim. No doubt he quotes Ussher; but, curiously enough, Ussher entirely disagrees with Dr. Lanigan, and accepts the history of the sailing of Loman's boat from Drogheda to Trim, as quite accurate and authentic. Ussher speaks of the bed of the river at *the present day* being such that it would be very difficult to bring a vessel through from Drogheda to Trim; but does not go so far as to say, that it was utterly impossible. It is quite true, the bed of the Boyne is not of uniform depth. In parts there are sharps and shallows, and these together with the numerous mill and fish weirs to be encountered on the way would, undoubtedly, at present prove to be almost insuperable barriers to the progress of any boat of considerable dimensions.[1]

Of course, in any circumstances, it would be a matter of more or less difficulty for a boat to be got up against the current; but in estimating the extent of the difficulty, it would be well to bear in mind, that the boat in which Loman in all probability sailed was not of that cumbrous build and massive construction to which we are accustomed nowadays. In the fifth and sixth centuries, we know, the sons of Erin sailed not merely on the placid waters of a river like the Boyne, but braved even the perils of the deep in fragile barks formed of ribs of osier, covered with hides, commonly called currachs, and that skimmed like swallows over the surface of the waters. Ware, in his *History of Ireland*, speaks of such boats being in use amongst the early Irish.[2]

In such a vessel we are told St. Cormac sailed from Iona, to seek some solitary island in the ocean, and was fourteen days out of sight of land. A few years ago the writer of these pages saw near Drogheda Bridge a wicker currach with its horse skin covering, somewhat similar, perhaps, in

---

[1] Ussher, p. 412, vol. vi,: Alveus fluvii Boyne ita augustus et scopulosus *hodie* dicatur, quod nullus pateat a ditus ab ejus ostio ad urbem Trimmenseu.

[2] Ware, vol. i., p. 178.

design and execution to the one that carried Loman and his companions more than fourteen centuries ago, from the mouth of the river Nanny up the Boyne to Trim. In dealing with this point I may be permitted to call attention to a very interesting old document which I happened to come across, and which will serve to throw light on the subject-matter under consideration, as well as show what was the condition and appearance presented by Trim a little over three hundred years ago. It is a memorial from Robert Draper, parson of Trim, and afterwards promoted to the important position of Bishop over the two dioceses of Kilmore and Ardagh. It was addressed to the Right Honourable the Lord Burghley, Lord High Treasurer of England :—[1]

Most humble besecheth your honour Robert Draper, parson of Trim, in Irelande, that yr. Lordshipp wolde vouchesafe to take vewe of the convenyences and comodyties being in and about the said towne of Trym, for the foundation of an unyversitie, and that yf yr. lordship shall like of them, it wold please the same (both in consideration of the fytness of the place, and also in respecte that yr. said suppliant hath been a long suter, to his greate charge, thoughe not for an unyversytie, yet for a grammar schoole to be erected there), to graunte yr. honours letters to the Lord Deputie and Councell of Irelande, that when that matter shall come in consultation there, they will have (the rather at yr. honour's request) regard and respect to that pore towne, being a place both for the fytness of it for that purpose, and for the extreme poverty that it is brought to, especially to be regarded and relieved. First ; It is situate in a most fresh and wholesome ayre, xxti. myles from Dublin, and xv. from Droghedaghe an haven towne. The towne itself is full of very faire castles and stone houses buylded after the Englishe fashyon, and devyded into five faire streetes, and hath in it the fairest and most stately castle that her Majestie hath in all Irelaund, almost decayed. It hath also one greate and large abbey nothing thereof defaced but the church, and therein greate store of goodly roomes, in meetely good repair, the howse is put to no use, and will (I think) be easily boughte of the owner, Edward Cusack of Lesmollen. The said Edward hath also a fryary in the said towne, a very fit place for a college, which also may be easily gotten of him ; further, your suppliant hath a friery havinge staunche and good walls,

---

[1] State Paper Office, Ireland, 15th May, 1584.

for an hall, for four or five lodginges, a cellar, a kitchen, a place
for lectures, with a pleasante backside conteyning three acres at
leaste; all which your said suppliante will freely give to the
furtherance of this goode work.

Through the myddest of the towne runneth the most pure
and clere ryver of the Boyne; *up this ryver might all provision
come from Droghedaghe to Trym by boate*, yf the statute to that
purpose made in Sir Henry Sydneis' time were executed.

Harde by the towne is an excellent good quarry if they should
need any stone, lyme stone, enough hard at the gate, slates
within vi. myles, and timber enough within three myles.   The
conntry round aboute verie fruitful of corne and cattel, yielding
besides plentifull store of firewood and turfe a verie good and
sweet fewel and yf the statute aforesaid for the setting open of
weares and fishing places in the Boyne were executed, the fewel
in greate quantitie for smale pryce *might be broughte down by
boate.*

Lastly, which is a matter of great importance, the towne is in
the myddest of the Englishe Pale, and is well and strongly walled
about, a thinge that will be a meane to draw learned men thither,
and be greate safety to the whole company of students there;
for your honour knoweth that wheresoever the universytie be
founded the towne must of necessitie have a good wall elles will
no learned men goe from hence or any other place thither neither
they of the country send their sounes to any place that is not
defensible and safe from the invasion of the Irish.   The buylding
of a wall will coste as muche as the colleges which charge (yf your
honour and they by your procurement shall like of this place)
will be saved.

Endorsed: 15th of May, 1584.

ROBRET DRAPER,

Parson of Trym in Irelande.

For a Unyversitie or Free School to be erocted here.

The writer of the above important letter was manifestly
a shrewd man of business, with a sound head upon his
shoulders.   If he failed to get from Her Majesty, Queen
Elizabeth, a university founded in Trim instead of in Dublin,
it was not from any lack of ability in putting his case.

In his petition no point is overlooked. He draws
attention to the situation of the place, to the number of
friaries and religious houses that could be procured at small
cost and utilized for class halls; to the castle and the strong
walls round about the town; and, though last, not least, to

the ' pure and clere ryver of the Boyne running through the midst of the town, and which affords over and above the good supply of water, this additional advantage, *that up the ryver might provisions be broughte from Drogheda to Trim,* if the statute of Sir Henry Sydney for setting open the weirs were executed.'

The italics are mine, and I have used them in order to emphasize the fact that Robert Draper, who knew well what he was writing about, had no such ideas as Dr. Lanigan about the impossibility of getting up a boat from Drogheda to Trim. In fact, he considered it quite feasible and actually set it down as one of the advantages to be attained by the establishment of a university at Trim, that provisions could ' be brought up by boate from Drogheda an havan town to Trim where the petitioner resided.' The first objection then raised by Dr. Lanigan about the impossibility of navigating the Boyne is sufficiently disposed of by the simple reply that he has not adduced a single solid proof in support of his assertion ; and, furthermore, even if it were proved to demonstration that it would be impossible by human agency to bring up a boat from Drogheda to Trim on the waters of the river Boyne, still that fact would not of itself be sufficient to warrant us in rejecting forthwith a narrative that has such an over-whelming weight of historic evidence in its favour.

Surely, Dr. Lanigan is not arguing with rationalists who deny even the possibility of miracles, and in their blind folly refuse to recognise the Divine hand of the All-Wise and Omnipotent Ruler, Who created the universe and controls its laws. Should sufficient testimony, therefore, be produced to show that a certain event took place, one cannot straight-way pooh-pooh it on the sole ground that it is not in accordance with the laws of nature ; or, in other words, that it is miraculous. If that were so, to take a familiar instance, the history of the transfer of the holy house of Loretto would not stand long under such a canon of criticism. For without a moment's hesitation, and without the slightest examination of the evidence, the cynic would at once exclaim, ' oh, it is sheer nonsence to suppose a house could fly through the air ; such a thing would be utterly at variance with the laws of gravitation; and, therefore, no such event could or did take place, no matter what historians tell us to the contrary.'

In the instance under consideration the manner in which Loman came up to Trim was, beyond doubt, miraculous, for without chart or compass, without the assistance of oars or sails, the boat conveyed himself and his companions *usque ad vadum Truim*, though the current and wind were both unfavourable. Ussher looked on the event as miraculous, so too did Jocelin, who says :—

Oh, Signum hactenus inauditum et incompertum Navis nemine gubernante contra fluvium et ventum ad vocem viri Dei velificavit, et ab ostio Boyni fluminus usque ad Ath-Trym cursu prospero illum transvexit ?[1]

And the original text of Tirechan also clearly conveys the idea that Loman came to Trim in the boat, under a *special interposition* of Divine Providence, ' Deo ipso gubernante, the Lord being his pilot.'[2]

The second objection of Dr. Lanigan has in it no greater weight than the first. The donations of lands, he says, mentioned in the various tracts do not correspond with the times of St. Patrick; and in proof of this assertion, he quotes the *Confessions* of St. Patrick himself. Now, what does the saint really say—' Forte autem, quando baptizavi tot millia hominum, speraverim ab aliquo illorum vel dimidium scriptulae Dicite mihi et reddam vobis.'[3] In other words, the saint challenged anyone to say that he accepted presents or donations for his own personal use or for the labour connected with any of his many ministrations, as the author of *Ireland's Ancient Schools and Scholars* puts it in his singularly able and fascinating book :—

Patrick, like St. Paul, refers to the perils by which he was encompassed, and the many toilsome duties of his episcopacy. He then vindicates his own disinterestedness, and challenges his accusers to show that he ever received a single farthing for preaching the Gospel and administering baptism to so many thousand persons even in the remotest parts of the country where the Word of God was never heard before ; not that the people

---

[1] Jocelin, cap. 54.   [2] *Prim.*, p. 853.   [3] *Confess.*, p. 79.

were not generous, for they offered him many gifts and cast their ornaments upon the altar ; but he returned them all, lest even in the smallest point the unbelievers might have cause to defame his ministry or question the purity of his motives.

But, whilst refusing to accept gifts for himself, ' ne vituperetur ministerium nostrum,' our saint *did not refuse* sites for the various churches which he founded, and which he dedicated to God and set apart as places of public worship. Hence in the case of his first convert, Dicho, the Irish annalists inform us that in gratitude to God for the great gift of faith, the northern chief offered our saint a portion of ground on which to erect a church, which, when completed, received the name of Sabhal Padruic or Patrick's barn. This Sabhal or Saul was ever afterwards a favourite retreat of the apostle ; and, when in process of time, he erected a monastery there, he often came to seek repôse from his labours, and within its hallowed walls he breathed his last. ' Dichus credidit ei primus prae omnibus toto corde ; et baptizatus obtulit Deo et S. Patricio agrum in quo stabant.' [1]

It is related also in the *Tripartite* life of St. Patrick, and published by Colgan in the *Trias Thaumaturga*, that Conall the brother of King Laighaire, who resided at Teltown, did not imitate the bad example of his two brothers, Laighaire and Carbre, by rejecting the teaching of the apostle and refusing to believe ; but, on the contrary, received him with great joy, was baptized by him, and *gave him his house or rath* on which to erect a church ; and the outline of this very rath can still be discerned in the present graveyard at Donaghpatrick.[2]

Baptigavit S. Patricius Conallum, et obtulit ei Conallus omne Castellum Suum diceus ei : Fac tibi hic monasterium et civita tem et ego faciam mihi aliud habitaculum prope.   Et fecit ibi S. Patricius monasterium et designavit civitatem quae dicitur Domnach-Padraig. [3]

And, not to speak of other cases, we have a remarkable

---

[1] *Tripartite.*
[2] Wilde's *Beauties of the Boyne*, p. 155.
[3] *Tripartite*, as quoted by Usaher, vol. vi., p. 412.

instance, recorded in history,[1] where Daire resolved to give
Patrick the Ridge of the Willows, that he might build a
church unto his God. St. Patrick and Daire, with his queen
and the clerics and warriors of Daire, ascended the slope,
and on the crown of that sacred hill, Patrick, book in
hand, marked out the site of the church of (Ard-Macha) and
consecrated it to God for ever.

In the face of these and other facts that might be adduced,
it is absurd to state with Dr. Lanigan, 'that donations of
land do not agree with the times of St. Patrick.'

With all respect to this eminent man, I will go farther,
and say that donations of land and other forms of property
for pious uses agree with all times since the very dawn of
Christianity. In fact, exceptional generosity, in one shape
or another, is the natural and necessary outcome of divine
faith. Hence, when Zacheus received the divine gift, he
not only came down with haste, and received our Lord with
joy, but he stood, and, in the hearing of all who murmured,
cried out, and said : ' Behold, Lord, the half of my goods I
give to the poor ; and if I have wronged any man of anything
I restore him fourfold.'[2] So too when the wise men came
from the far East to pay their homage to the new-born
King, they did not come empty-handed. For we read, when
they found the object of their search, that going in, enlightened by faith, they bowed down before Him, 'and opening
their treasures they offered to Him gifts, gold, frankincense,
and myrrh.'[3] And on a solemn occasion when Magdalen
would give a tangible testimony of love for her Master, at
Bethania, she ' took a pound of ointment of right spikenard,
of great value, and anointed the feet of Jesus, and wiped His
feet with her hair ; and the house was filled with the odour
of the ointment.'[4] In St. Luke we read that our Lord, looking on at the rich men casting their gifts into the treasury,
and seeing also a certain poor widow casting in two brass
mites, said : ' Verily, I say to you that this poor widow hath
cast in more than they all. For all these have of their

---

[1] *Ireland's Ancient Schools and Scholars.*   [3] Matt. ii. 11.
[2] Luke xix. 8.   [4] John xii. 3.

abundance cast into the offerings of God, but she of her
want hath cast in all her living that she hath.'[1] There is no
use in multiplying instances, for these already given are
more than sufficient to show that there is nothing at all
extraordinary or incredible in the fact that Feidilmid at the
preaching of Loman, and supernaturally enlightened by faith,
despised all earthly things, ' and gave up, as historians tell
us, all his possessions, together with his son Fortchern, to
Patrick and Loman till the day of judgment.'

The two other objections raised by Dr. Lanigan are
hardly worthy of serious notice, and the man must be hard
pressed when he was forced to make them.

There is no contradiction whatsoever between the
authorities who give an account of Loman and the antiquity
of the Trim foundations. It is quite true, the *Tripartite* calls
Loman a nephew of St. Patrick, Tirechan a disciple, Jocelin
a bishop. Where is the contradiction? Could he not be all
three—disciple, bishop, and nephew, of St. Patrick. How
many were taught, tonsured, ordained priests, and consecrated
bishops by our saint. Not to go farther, have we not a
striking instance in the case of the boy Benignus, who was
baptized by Patrick, trained by him in all divine and human
knowledge, his disciple therefore, and afterwards made by
him the heir to his kingdom, for he consecrated him bishop,
and placed him as his helper in the primatial see of Armagh.

If one author called *him* a disciple, another a bishop, a
third ' the heir of St. Patrick,' where is the contradiction?
One simply gives a piece of information not given by the
others ; and hence there is not any conflicting evidence
between them. If so, Dr. Lanigan would make short work
of the concordance of the Gospel history as given by the four
Evangelists.

Lastly, there is a statement made by the learned Doctor
that sounds like a sneer, and hardly dignified enough for one
in his position. ' I find Fortchern (successor of Loman)
notwithstanding his royal descent set down in the *Tripartite*
as St. Patrick's blacksmith.' Be it so. In this there is

---

[1] Luke xxi. 3.

nothing at all inconsistent with his royal descent, nor
derogatory to his position as monk or bishop, or calculated
to throw discredit as an historian on the venerable author
of the *Tripartite*. In Montalembert's *Monks of the West*
we read of Dega or Dagan, who flourished about the year
586; that he was a monk, a bishop, and, at the same
time, an artificer in iron and brass, a very useful blacksmith
indeed. He passed his nights in transcribing manuscripts,
and his days in reading and in carving in iron and copper.
So laborious was he, that the construction of three hundred
croziers for bishops and abbots is attributed to him: 'Hic
Dagaeus fuit faber tam in ferro quam in aere et scriba
insignis.' [1]

St. Patrick was a practical man of business, and utilized
for the building up of the infant Church all the talents of
those around him on his missionary staff. Hence we find
Benignus described by historians as his psalmist, or, as we
would say, leader of his choir, and we have Bishop 'Asicus,
of Elphin, an expert in metal work, who employed part of
his time in making altars, and quadrangular tables called
miassa, which probably were metal altar-flags used on the
rude altars of the churches in those days, during the
celebration of the holy mysteries.' [2] There is no sense,
therefore, in levelling a sneer at Fortchern, the successor of
Loman, but only for a few days in the see of Trim. One
other remark, and I am done with the objections which I
undertook to answer. The man who has a case to make is,
as a rule, one to be pitied. For, like the lawyer with a bad
case, he is obliged to have recourse to special pleading, to
attribute motives, and to end, in heaping abuse on his
opponents. So it is with Dr. Lanigan, who with all his
cleverness puts himself into a false position by assuming
that Loman belonged to the seventh century. He hits hard at
every historian, no matter how respectable, who says anything that tends to upset his favourite theory. I am not
surprised, therefore, to find the Doctor waxing warm, and
pouring the vials of his wrath on Tirechan, Jocelin, the

---

[1] Bolland, vol. iii., p. 657.   [2] *Ancient Schools and Scholars*, p. 142.

Tripartite, and all the other venerable authorities who go against him.

The *Tripartite*, whose authorship is generally ascribed to St. Evin, of Monasterevan, and of which the learned Bishop of Clonfert, says that ' it is, on the whole, the most valuable document concerning St. Patrick that has come down to our time,'[1] in the eyes of Dr. Lanigan is nothing more than a ' compilation apparently patched up at Armagh.' Jocelin, who was selected for the work of writing St. Patrick's life by three of the greatest men of the time—Thomas O'Connor, Archbishop of Armagh ; Malachy, Bishop of Down ; and John de Courcey, Prince of Ulster ; is, in the opinion of Dr. Lanigan, a man only too eager to jump at a story, to improve upon it, and then pawn it off as genuine history. ' The story of Tirechan was too good a one to be passed over by Jocelin, who, to make it still more marvellous, subjoins that the boat came up against the stream, though the current and wind were both unfavourable.'

Finally, when the learned doctor undertakes to give what he calls the key to the solution of the difficulty in which all historians before him were involved, he really runs amuck. There was a squabble, he says, between Armagh and Trim about some pretended possessions of land around Trim, purported to be given by Felim to Patrick and Loman. Tirechan, who was a Meath man, maintained the rights of Trim ; whereas Jocelin, who was a patron of Dr. O'Connor, was equally strong in claiming them for Armagh. But, strange enough—and this is a point overlooked by the learned Doctor —both Tirechan and Jocelin agree that Loman was a contemporary of St. Patrick ; and the history given by both, of all the subsequent events, is precisely identical in every particular. Furthermore, the possessions were not *pretended* ones ; if so it would hardly be worth while fighting about them. As a matter of fact, part of the lands of Crowpark, adjoining the town, are still the property of the see of Armagh. In 1614 an inquisition found that the Archbishop of Armagh was seized, in right of his see, of one tenement

---

[1] *Ancient Schools and Scholars*, p. 90.

and three acres of land, within the parish of Trim. The
Bishop of Meath receives rent from the Crown for the manor
of Trim. And in the time of Henry IV. the Archbishop of
Armagh had a charge upon the Crown of £8 16s. 7½d. for the
site of the castle, town, and bridge of Trim. The church and
glebe, and the land belonging to the see of Armagh, are
on the north side, and the castle is on the south side of the
Boyne.

Having now gone over the whole ground traversed by
Dr. Lanigan, and having endeavoured to reply to the
objections raised by him against the commonly received
history given by ancient and modern writers regarding the
antiquity of the Trim Church and See, I think the intelligent
and dispassionate reader will have little difficulty in fully
endorsing the mild and dignified rebuke of the liberal-minded
and large-hearted Dean Butler, who says :—

Doctor Lanigan was a Roman Catholic, and had been Professor
of Hebrew, the Sacred Scriptures, and Ecclesiastical History in
the University of Pavia.   His *Ecclesiastical History of Ireland* is
a work of great labour and learning ; but *here* we cannot forgive
this vain attempt to degrade the Church and bishops of Trim
against the evidence of Tirechan and the *Tripartite*, and the
authority of Colgan, Ussher, and the Bollandists.[1]

It is scarcely necessary to remind our readers, that Trim
has long since ceased to be a distinct episcopal see. The
episcopal sees in Ireland have undergone many changes,
and were at first exceedingly numerous. In Meath alone
were the sees of Clonard, Duleek, Skryne, Kells, Trim,
Ardbraccan, Dunshaughlin, Slane, and some also add Foure.
But in the famous Synod of Kells, presided over by Cardinal
Paparo, the Papal Legate, the sees of Meath were reduced to
the sees of Clonard, Kells, and Duleek. Clonard, I presume,
for the western portion of the diocese ; Kells and Duleek for
North and South Meath.

At another synod held in Trim, in the year 1216, in the
Cathedral Church of St. Peter and St. Paul, Newtown-Trim
built by Simon Rochfort, the first Englishman that wore the

---

[1] Butler's *Trim*, p. 138.

mitre of Meath, it was ordered that the Churches of Trim, Kells, Slane, Skryne, and Dunshaughlin, being heretofore bishops' sees, shall hereafter be the heads of rural deaneries, with archprestyters personally resident therein.[1]

The first bishop who assumed the title of Bishop of Meath was Eugene, who died about the year 1194, and was the immediate predecessor of Simon Rochfort, who transferred his seat from Clonard to Trim, which at this time became the great central town and stronghold of the Pale.

Meath, at the present day, consisting, as it does, of a whole cluster of dioceses, is in area the largest diocese in Ireland. It extends from the Shannon to the sea, and is almost commensurate with the ancient principality of the Melaghlins and De Lacies. It comprised at one time within its boundaries the diocese of Clonmacnoise. On the 29th of September, 1725, we find that Dr. Stephen Mac Egan, an illustrious member of the Dominican Order, and one of the most celebrated preachers in Ireland, was nominated and elected to the see of Clonmacnoise, and consecrated by Pope Benedict XIII. Four years afterwards, in 1729, Dr. Mac Egan was transferred by the Pope to the see of Ferns, and, in the same year, to that of Meath, as successor to Dr. Luke Fagan, who was promoted to the archiepiscopal see of Dublin. On his appointment to Meath, the Holy See granted him the parish of Navan *in commendam*, and the administration of the diocese of Clonmacnoise. In his old days, when unable, through infirmity, to go through his visitations in that district, he requested Dr. Chevers, then in Ardagh, to supply his deficiencies, and this induced Dr. Chevers to petition the Holy See for the union of Clonmacnoise with Ardagh. He assigned as his principal reasons the vast extent of Meath as more than enough to tax the energies of one bishop, the poverty of Ardagh, its proximity to Clonmacnoise, and the fact that he had the labour of it. Five years later Dr. Chevers was translated to Meath, and then found, to his

---

[1] Wilkin's *Concilia*, vol. i., p. 547.

mortification, that his reasons had induced the Holy See to
incorporate Clonmacnoise with Ardagh. He petitioned, it is
said, for the administration of Clonmacnoise, on the ground
of being able to attend to it, and received for answer a copy
of his reasons why Clonmacnoise should be united with
Ardagh.[1]

The bishops of Meath, from time immemorial, were
entitled at all official meetings to rank next to the archbishops, and claimed an appellation similar to theirs of
' Most Reverend.' ' Episcopus Midensis primus semper est
Provinciae Armacanae Suffraganeus, quanquam Enim inter
coeteros Hiberniae Episcopos esset consecratione Junior eos
nihilominus loco praecederet.'[2] Up to the disestablishment
of the Irish Church by Mr. Gladstone, the bishops of Meath
had a seat, by virtue of their office, on the Irish Privy
Council, and all communications between the Crown and the
bench of bishops passed through the hands of the bishop of
the premier diocese of Meath.

It is scarcely necessary to add, that all these titles
and privileges attaching to the see of Royal Meath, were
quietly assumed by the Protestant bishops of the so-called
Reformation, and availed of by them as coolly as if they were
the real lawful heirs, coming down in a direct and unbroken
line from the days of Loman, the first bishop who wore the
mitre of Trim.

Although this paper has run on to a pretty considerable
length, we feel it would be incomplete if we neglected to
mention that there is one townland, in the parish of
Mullingar, called after our saint, Port-Loman.   Here a
monastery was founded by him, on the western bank of
Lough Owel, and his festival was kept in the Church on
the 7th of February. In the *Martyrology of Donegal*
(Dr. Todd's edition), we read :—

The Feast of St. Lomman, bishop-nephew of St. Patrick by
his sister, is celebrated in his church in Port-Loman, diocese
of Meath. His buchall (crozier) is *extant*, being in possession of

---

[1] Dean Cogan's *Meath*, vol. ii., p. 164.
[2] *Hib. Dom.*, by De Burgo.

Walter Mac Edward, in Port-Lommain. Temple Lommain is on the brink of Loch-Uail. The parish has a holiday. There are two rivers flowing out, and no river going into the lake.

We shall conclude this sketch by one other quotation from Dean Cogan's *Diocese of Meath :*—

> The ruins of St. Loman's church are situated on the very margin of Lough Owel, about three and a-half miles to the north-west of Mullingar, and measure seventy-seven feet by twenty feet four inches. A stone, shaped like the lid of a coffin, having a cross inscribed, was found some years ago deeply embedded in the clay, and was disentombed. It seems to have marked the grave of some distinguished ecclesiastic. The tourist or pilgrim who visits Port-Loman will linger long before he can withdraw himself from the enchanting scenery which meets him on all sides, and, above all, from the venerable consecrated walls, endeared by so many associations of religious worship, and now sacred and solemn for being the resting-place of the dead . . . [1]

In that resting-place of the dead, close by the monastery founded by Loman, many of his followers are sleeping, but as we observed in a former sketch, the hallowed bones of the founder himself, are laid in another place with Fortchern, Cormac, and his other companions in the ministry—viz., in the ancient church of Ath-Truim, the seat of his episcopal see.

PHILIP CALLARY, P.P., V.F.

---

[1] *Diocese of Meath*, vol. iii., p. 601.

Notes and Queries

THEOLOGY

CLANDESTINITY AS IT AFFECTS IRISH PROTESTANTS

REV. DEAR SIR,—In your paper on Clandestinity, in last month's I. E. RECORD, at page 452, in Section (B) you say, ' And, manifestly, an Irish Protestant, for example, does not lose his privilege or dispensation by crossing over to Scotland.' Is this so clear or certain? The exemption or dispensation from the law of Clandestinity in favour of heretics in Ireland is local or territorial. Can they enjoy this exemption when they leave the country? Could they, *qua* Irish Protestants, marry validly and clandestinely in France? I am not certain on the point, but wish to see the questioned raised and settled.

AN INQUIRER.

Our correspondent rightly understands us to have asserted (1) that heretics domiciled in Ireland are not affected by the law of clandestinity (at all events, as long as they remain in Ireland); and, (2) that in the event of their going to a place such as Scotland, where the decree *Tametsi* has not been promulgated, they will still be unaffected by the law, and that even though they retain their domicile in Ireland. Our correspondent hesitates to accept the second assertion just mentioned. We may venture to assure him that his special difficulty has no foundation, either in law or theology.

As we understand it, his line of reasoning is this: ' An Irish Protestant while travelling in France does not enjoy exemption from the law of clandestinity. Therefore, *a pari*, an Irish Protestant travelling in Scotland is not exempt.' This we take to be the argument; and our answer will be very brief. It is true—and we should have said so in our last paper, if it had not been irrelevant to the subject discussed—that the Irish Protestant travelling in France is, while in that country, bound by the law of clandestinity.

The fact, however, as we *now* learn, admits of two explanations ; (1) the Irish Protestant in France is bound by the decree *Tametsi, because he is out of Ireland ;* or, (2), because the decree has been promulgated in France, and is there binding on Catholics and heretics alike, whether residents or non-residents. The latter is the explanation hitherto accepted by all theologians and canonists. Our correspondent, however, prefers the first explanation. And then, logically enough, he infers that, if an Irish Protestant loses his privilege by merely leaving Ireland, he has certainly lost it when he has arrived in Scotland.

MASSES FOR THE DEAD

DEAR SIR,—In many parishes just before All Souls Day, an announcement is made to the congregation in something like the following terms : —' Masses will be offered once a month for the repose of those souls whose names are entered on the List of the Dead. Persons wishing to give in names may do so during the coming week.'

The faithful then give in names, accompanied with an offering.

(*a*) What are these offerings? Are they dues? (*b*) If they are dues, is there any obligation to offer Mass? (*c*) Would a second Mass on Sunday suffice? (*d*) Do the faithful regard the matter as a contract—*do ut des ?*

SACERDOS.

(*a*) The offerings made in the circumstances in question could scarcely be called ' dues' in any sense of the word with which we are acquainted. They are purely voluntary offerings made for the purpose of having Masses celebrated for deceased friends. (*b*) There is a strict obligation to have the Masses offered according to the terms of the express announcement or implicit understanding. (*c*) A priest who duplicates on Sunday cannot satisfy his obligation to say one of the Masses thus promised, and on the same day take a honorarium for his second Mass. (*d*) The faithful will rightly regard the contract to be of the nature we have indicated.

D. MANNIX.

LITURGY

A CORRECTION.

IN replying to the question of a correspondent regarding the calendar to be followed by a religious in the chapels of convents and analogous institutions, we stated in the October number of the I. E. RECORD[1] that a religious, if chaplain to one of the institutions in question, should follow his own calendar as well in the principal as in the private chapels. And furthermore, we stated that in the case in which a religious is chaplain, his calendar becomes the proper calendar of the principal chapel of the institution, so that all priests celebrating in the principal chapel should follow his calendar. These conclusions were based on a decree of the Congregation of Rites issued in June, 1896. The meaning of this decree was quite plain, and the conclusions we drew from it were little more than a free translation of its terms. We copied the decree from a journal published in Rome, which we have always found to be most accurate. Consequently we were quite certain of the correctness of the statements made in the reply above referred to. A few days ago, however, we took up a recent number of the Roman journal from which the decree had been copied, and were much chagrined to find in it a note in which the editor apologized for the omission of an important word from the decree as first published in his journal. The omission of the word completely changed the meaning of the decree as far as religious are concerned. Without the omitted word it made, as we have seen, the calendar of a religious chaplain to a convent, &c., the calendar of the institution, which not only the chaplain himself, but all priests celebrating in the principal chapel should follow. With the omitted word, the decree declares, that the religious chaplain must abandon his own calendar, and follow the secular calendar of the place in which the institution of which he is chaplain is situated.

---

[1] Page 366.

No matter, then, who is chaplain, whether he is a religious or a secular priest, the calendar of the place must be followed by him and by all priests celebrating in the principal chapel; in private chapels every priest must follow his own calendar.

We are aware that religious chaplains were in the habit of following their own calendar without insisting, however, that it should be regarded as the calendar of the institution. Doubtless such chaplains heard with satisfaction that their practice had been approved by the Congregation of Rites itself. We are sorry, therefore, to be obliged to say that, so far from the practice having received the sanction of the Congregation of Rites, it has been *expressly* forbidden by this Congregation since June, 1896.

As the matter is of considerable practical importance, we again print the decree; but this time in its correct form :—

Ubi unus tantum sacerdos quoad missae celebrationem addictus sit oratoriis competenti auctoritate erectis in gymnasiis, hospitalibus ac domibus quarumcumque piarum communitatum ; hic si saecularis teneturne sequi calendarium diocesis in qua extat oratorium ; et si regularis calendarium ordinis si proprio gaudeat [*relinquere*] ; et si aliquando celebrent extranei hi debentne se conformare calendario sacerdotis ejusmodi oratoriis addicti ?

Resp. Affirmative in omnibus si oratoria habenda sint ut publica ; secus negative.

The word *relinquere* to which we have called attention in the text of the decree, is the word originally omitted. A glance at the context will show how profoundly the exclusion or addition of this word affects the meaning of the question, and also, how correct were the conclusions drawn in these pages ftom the mutilated decree. For if *relinquere* be omitted, *sequi* from the preceding clause must be understood, and the question is to this effect: If the chaplain [to a convent, &c.] be a secular, is he bound to follow the calendar of the diocese in which the convent is situated ? if a regular, is he bound to follow the calendar of his Order, if it has a proper calendar ? The reply of the Congregation, *Affirmative in omnibus*, made it quite certain so far as the terms of the decree were concerned that the regular was to

follow his own calendar ; while the remaining part of the
question regarding externs, made it also clear that these
should follow the calendar of the regular when celebrating in
the principal chapel. But when *relinquere* is added, the
question must be read thus : If the chaplain be a secular, is
he bound to follow the calendar of the diocese . . . and
if a regular, to abandon the calendar of his Order? It
was to the question in this form that the Congregation replied
in the affirmative. Hence there can be no longer any doubt
as to the practice to be adopted by chaplains, whether secular
or regular. They should follow—in the principal chapels of
course—the calendar of the diocese in which the institution
is situated, unless in so far as the diocesan calendar may
have been modified by the grant of special feasts, or of
special solemnities to certain communities of nuns.

We quote the following extract from the apology of the
Roman editor for the omission of the word *relinquere* from
the decree as first published by him. It will form a sufficient
apology for the share we may have had in confirming a
practice not in conformity with the decrees of the
Congregation of Rites, and will, at the same time, confirm
and accentuate the true meaning of the decree :—

In x^{mo} vol., Anno 1896, p. 520, vulgatum fuit decretum . . .
septem constans dubiis, totidemque, ut par est, relativis responsis.
Ex iis dubium iv. . . . aliquo defectu laborat, vel typographico,
vel amanuensis. Defectus in hoc consistit quod in ultima linea
post vertum '*gaudeat*,' omissum fuit verbum '*relinquere*' ; per
quod verbum additum totus mutatur sensus dubii, proinde que
et responsi, uti perpendenti facile patebit Additio verbi
' *relinquere*' necessaria et authentica est ; et certa scientia nobis
constat de omissione illius verbi illiusque addendi necessitatem
monitum fuisse oratorem, qui dubia volvenda proposuerat. Con-
sequenter venerabiles lectores certiores facimus dictum decreti
dubium cum praefato verbo ' *relinquere*' legendum et intelligendum
esse.

Hinc sequitur sacerdotem sive saecularem sive regularem.
quoad missae celebrationem alicui oratorio addictum . . . teneri
ad calendarium ejusdem Oratorii, si sit publicum : *et regularem
proinde debere sui Ordinis calendarium in dicta celebratione
negligere ut dioecesis sequatur.*

1. WHEN A PRIEST DUPLICATES IN THE SAME PLACE HOW
SHOULD THE UNPURIFIED CHALICE BE COVERED?

2. WHERE SHOULD THE UNPURIFIED CHALICE REMAIN
BETWEEN THE TWO MASSES?

REV. DEAR SIR,—When the same chalice is used at second
Mass, as in first Mass in the same church, would it not be
better to cover it during the interval, with the pall, rather
than with the patena for the purification of which there is no
provision? It is covered with the pall during the communion
of the faithful, and is unpurified. It is also covered with the
pall in the second Mass from the Offertory, and from the consecration to the end of Mass, so to say. I think this is very practical,
and I would ask you to say if there is not room for improvement
in the rules laid down for us in the matter; namely, of covering
the chalice with the patena, somewhat the same as on Good
Friday. (2) Is it not better to leave the unpurified chalice on the
altar, if it may be so left with security, rather than be brought into
a sacristy, or put into the tabernacle as some do, but which
O'Callaghan does not seem to contemplate?

M.

1. The pall alone is used, as our correspondent points out,
to cover the chalice, from the consecration to the communion,
when it contains the most Precious Blood, and during the
communion of the faithful while it is still unpurified.
Why then should not the pall alone be used to cover the
chalice left unpurified at his first Mass by a priest who
has to celebrate two Masses on the same day in the same
church? It cannot be because the pall should not come
into contact with the unpurified chalice. The instances
brought forward by our correspondent dispose of this
contention. Indeed even the purificator may come into
immediate contact with an unpurified chalice, as we learn
from the instructions issued by the Congregation of Rites
in 1857, regarding the celebration of two Masses in different
places on the same day. We must, then, seek some other
reason why in the directions for celebrating three
Masses on Christmas day, as for celebrating two Masses
on the same day in the same place, the celebrant is told to

cover the chalice, after he has consumed the Precious
Blood, first with the paten, then with the pall and veil.
We have not found anywhere a reason for this, but we can
probably infer one from the directions given by Martinucci
for the celebration of three Masses on Christmas day. The
celebrant, according to Martinucci should cover the chalice
with the pall after he has consumed the Precious Blood, as
is done when communion has to be distributed ; say the
usual prayers, and purify his fingers ; and having done this,
he should remove the pall from the chalice, replace it with
the paten, *on which he should place a host for the next Mass*
and cover the paten and host with the pall and veil. Hence
it would appear, that one reason for placing the paten and
not the pall next the chalice in the case contemplated by
our correspondent, is that in the second Mass .the paten,
host, and pall may have from the beginning of Mass their
proper places. It would be contrary to all custom to have
the chalice on the altar during the early part of the Mass
without either host or paten ; yet if the chalice is to be
covered first with the pall, the host and paten should
necessarily be absent.

Having shown that the common teaching, and the
common practice have some reason to justify them, we
come to our correspondent's inquiry ; whether a change
might not be an improvement. We frankly confess, we
do not think any change would be an improvement ; and,
moreover, the common practice is so firmly established
that we would consider it wrong to advocate any other in
opposition to it. It is mentioned in a decree of the
Congregation of Rites regarding the celebration of two
Masses in the same place, on the same day. The words of
the reference are :—

. . . Calici autem statim (*i.e.*, immediate post Sumptum
SS. Sanguinem) imponit patenem et pallam, dein calicem et
patenam cooperiat velo.[1]

These words do not, we believe, strictly speaking, impose

---

[1] S.R.C., Sept. 16, 1815.

an obligation; but, taken in conjunction with the directions given by all writers who refer to the matter, they constitute a precedent from which it would be rash to depart.

2. The chief thing to be looked to is the reverence due to the unpurified chalice. Hence if it is certainly safe from irreverence on the altar, it may be allowed to remain on the altar. Otherwise it should be placed on a corporal in a secure place in the sacristy, or it may even be put into the tabernacle.[1]

D. O'LOAN.

---

[1] S.R.C., loc. cit.

CORRESPONDENCE

THE ANCIENT IRISH CHURCH

Rev. Dear Sir,—In the I. E. Record for August, typical examples were set forth to show the radical defects of the little compilation, *The Ancient Irish Church as a Witness to Catholic Doctrine*. As a result, the November number contains a long-drawn and heated (not to say intemperate) ' endeavour to reply,'—fresh proof that equanimity under criticism is not easy to find.

As regards the Bobbio Missal, the admission that it is Irish in script is enough for the compiler, 'and will be,' he adds, 'for most people.' He had better, perhaps, have answered for himself ; 'most people,' he has some reason to fear, may demur somewhat decidedly when they learn that he has not alone suppressed, but given no indication of, what his critic wrote in the very next paragraph to that quoted from :—' But it does not follow, because the writing is Irish, that a MS. was written in Ireland ; much less, upon Irish subjects. In the present case, the Mass of St. Martin and the names introduced into the Canon tell as plainly as the most explicit Colophon that the Missal was drawn up for a church in Gaul.' (*Stowe Missal*, Trans. R. I. A., xxvii. 151.)

The compiler next formulates a canon to suit the occasion. When the writing is Irish, the dogma is Irish too, unless (which is absurd) you mean to hold that scribes copied liturgies and kindred matter, from the characteristic theology of which they dissented. To apply the principle to the subject in hand. The scribe of the Bobbio MS. was demonstrably ignorant, very ignorant, of Latin. Nevertheless, we are to hold that he never put pen to parchment until he satisfied himself that the theology of Missal and Penitential was such as he could assent to !

Behold a miracle, instead of wit.

Again, when Eustasius, abbot of Luxeuil, was charged, in the Synod of Macon (623), with differing from others in the celebration of Mass, his objection, it was stated and conceded, lay not to the theology, but to the comparative brevity, of the local liturgies. So much for the new criterion.

Finally, the assurance about his critic not asserting that the

Missal was not in daily use at Bobbio was somewhat premature. ' Of a certainty,' the discoverer of the Missal asserted, ' this codex was not for use of the Bobio monks. For there is nothing in it of Bobio, of Columbanus, or his disciples ; nothing likewise of matters monastic.' [1] Mabillon, however, it must be admitted, made the assertion more than two centuries ago.

As to the Penitential of Cummian, no amount of declamation will conceal the fact that the compiler has evaded the proofs of Wasserschleben that the work was continental in origin and application. One cannot but smile at the grasp of the subject and the logic that put forward a solitary authority (for the second given, belongs to the eighth century ; the third refers to an Irishman who lived, and most probably became a heretic, on the continent, in the same century) to prove that Ireland had in the seventh century what Cummian dealt with,—heresy professed by congregations and priests ; heresy favoured by bishops and abbots ; heresy glorified in its saints. For the rest, the fifteen items, the compiler has again to be reminded, have all been traced to the sources :—the Penitential of Columbanus, a work not drawn up for Ireland, which contains the first ; and the Penitential of Theodore, archbishop of Canterbury (ob. 690), of which the other fourteen, section for section, compose the fifth chapter of the first book.

The St. Gall *Ordo*, it was shown by original proof from a work long acknowledged as classic, was Irish only in writing. In return, the compiler derides the demonstration, and fails to see that he has perpetrated a libel !

To better *eorum* by *nostrorum* ' keeps to the orthography of the MS.' It never dawned upon the Belfast Bentley that the problem was to find a word ending in *eorum* that would keep to the sense.

Sacrificium Tibi celebrandum intende. ' Tried by the Dictionaries ' the translation, *dispose the sacrifice to be celebrated to Thee*, ' may claim an acquittal.' Quite so ; it takes some knowledge to discern wherein one is confuted. The blunder lies in taking *sacrificium celebrandum* [*esse*] to be an infinite clause depending on, instead of two accusatives governed by, *intende*. And, to obviate the objection (not likely, it is true, to be made

---

[1] Certe hic codex non fuit ad usum monachorum Bobiensium. Nihil enim in eo de sanctis Bobiensibus, Columbano, ejusve discipulis ; nihil item de rebus monasticis. (*Museum Italicum* I. 276.) Note the single *b* ; never *bb*. See also Bobienais, Bobiensibus, in Muratori (*Antiq. Ital. Med. Aevi*, III. 680). Cf. *Borio* (= *Bobio*) in Cummian's epitaph (*ib.*).

by the compiler) to *Intende quas fundunt preces*, that the object of *intende* is placed in the relative clause and consequently in the accusative, owing to the metre not admitting *precibus*, another Offertory may be quoted. Intende, quaesumus, Domine, sacrificium singulare, ut . . . exspectata sumamus (Gregorian Sacramentary, Migne, *P. L.* 78, col. 190).

Comparatively numerous errors of the press appeared, it was said, in the Irish testimonies. This is taken to apply generally, and made the pretext to impute unfairness and hostility. The other 230 pages, it is vaunted, do not contain 15 such errors. But, to mention only one instance, p. 230 presents no less than 26 !

Again, all the references, it is boasted, have not three figures astray. The compiler has verified them with the books before him. Now, mark how limp the verification emerges : (1) p. 72, note 16, *for* p. 258, *read* p. 257 ; (2) p. 96, note 66, line 5, *for* p. 237, *read* p. 257 ; (3) p. 122, note 22, *for* p. 120, *read* p. 220 ! And if you complain that these so-called references to a lithographed Irish MS., with two columns of from 75 to 90 lines each to the page, incommode you, why that proves you are neither 'well-disposed,' nor 'generous' to the compiler who supplied them for your 'special satisfaction.'

As the compiler demurs to the proof that his 'simile' from the *Speckled Book* is not found in the original, let him give the text and literal translation of the Irish referred to at p. 72. In addition, he will know whether it is to be found on 'p. 258.' It remains to say that, had the *Annals of Ulster* intended to convey that O'Coffey was O'Murray's fosterer or tutor, not father, they would have employed (not *athair*, but) *aite*, a word which it is superfluous to establish from the written, as it lives (under the form *oide*) in the spoken, language.

Here one would willingly have closed (for, as to the other 'endeavours to reply,' *valeant quantum*); but the bravado of the concluding paragraph must not pass with impunity. Critical discrimination is further illustrated in the following :—Arreum anni triduanus in ecclesia sine. . . . vestitu, sine sede, etc. (p. 104). *Triduanus*, to begin with, is a vox nihili in this place ; read *triduum* and translate: *Commutation of a year's penance* [is to have the penitent] *to stand three days in a church without clothing ! ! !* One has heard of gods and goddesses standing naked in the open air ; but to read of Christian men and women in that condition in a church somewhat strains one's trust in the informant.   A copy of the *Commutations* (which the compiler had under his eyes) containing Irish glosses reads *triduum* and (for *sine vestitu*) *cum vestimento circa se*, with a garment around him (*Bussordnungen*, p. 139, n. 12).

The textual recension and grammatical knowledge appear in the opening words of the Memento of the Dead as given in the Bobbio Missal. Memento etiam, Domine, et eorum nomina qui, etc. It requires no great acumen to see that *nomina* is a rubric; eorum (*nomina*); meaning that the celebrant was to (mentally) particularize those whom he wished to pray for. But the compiler renders it by 'Remember also, O Lord, the names of those who have gone before us,' etc. (p. 149)!

Similar to the *memento nomina* and equally indicative of intimate acquaintance with the meaning of the Canon of the Mass is 'Quorum meritis precibusque concedas, *to* whose merits and prayers grant' (p. 157). Now, the *compilers* of prayer-books took *quorum meritis precibusque* to mean *by* whose merits and prayers, and it will be time enough to quote Menard in support of them, when their rendering is seriously questioned. At the same time, it is but fair to remark that the books in question were issued before 'St. Patrick's Day,' the date of publication of *The Ancient Irish Church*.

The compiler says the Irish were not in strictness Quarto-decimans. But unwittingly he proves that they were. According to his rendering of *die dominica octavarum Pasche* of the *Navigation of Brendan*, the Irish kept the 'Sunday within the octave of Easter' (p. 220). Such an incidence could happen only when Easter was held on a day other than Sunday,—which was a strict result of the Quartodeciman heresy.   The meaning is, Sunday, the Octave of Easter ; in other words, Low Sunday. (The plural, *Octav*[*a*]*e*, is usual in mediæval Calendars.)

Of a piece with this is the statement that the 'mode of computing Easter is an astronomical . . . question' (p. 41). But Ideler was an eminent astronomer, and so little did he clear up the Paschal Question, that he took a well-authenticated Table to be a forgery (*Handbuch*, ii. 275). 'The Easter Term,' he had already said with the accuracy of a master, 'is not computed by the aid of astronomical tables, the use of which not everyone can understand, but *by cycles*, in a manner which even a non-expert is easily able to master.' [1]

---

[1] Die Ostergrenze wird nicht mit Hülfe astronomischer Tafeln, deren Handhabung nicht jedermann's Sache ist, sondern cyklisch auf eine Weise berechnet, die auch der Laie leicht zu begreifen im Stande ist (*Hand'uc*), ii. 192).

Having regard to the confused chronology found in his authorities, it were unfair perhaps to hold the compiler to blame for erroneous dates. But two instances admit of no valid excuse.

(1) ' Under the same date [664], there is the following entry in certain Annals in the *Book of Leinster* :—'Voyage of Bishop Columbanus to Inisboffin, with relics of Saints ' (p. 197). 'See the *Book of Leinster* (p. 25a),' and you will see the whole column without a single date ! The annalistic items referred to have, however, been published by Stokes in his *Tripartite Life*. On a left-hand page (518), he gives the text in question, *but without date ;* on the right hand (p. 517), the translation. To the latter he prefixed [664] (erroneously, *more suo ;* for the true year, given in Tigernach and the *Annals of Ulster*, is 668). Yet the gatherer who collects at second-hand in this way will not have you dub him compiler !

(2) Diarmait, we learn (p. 106), was 'king of Ireland, A.D. 538-588).' Accuracy is of first importance here. This king and his immediate predecessor, every tyro knows, were synchronous with the early saints of the second order. Hic Ordo duravit . . . ab extremis Tuathai 1 et per totum Diarmata regis regnum, etc. A minimum of industry would have discovered in the *Tripartite* version (p. 515) of the *Leinster* ' Annals,' that Tuatha 1 fell in [544] and Diarmait in [565]. The New Chronology, by stroke of pen, expands the reign, *hinc inde*, from twenty-one to fifty years !

Finally, to show how a text can be made to bear two meanings. Kannanus . . . portavit secum ignem . . . benedictum. ' It would seem from the context . . . that the '' blessed fire" . . . was incense' (p. 98). But the doubt disappeared in the progress of compiling. At p. 220 the quotation is repeated, with an addition containing (*inter alia*) ut accenderet fumum benedictum, to prove that incense is alluded to by Tirechan (in the *Book of Armagh*). And, to remove all doubt, there is a note that ' nothing could be clearer than this reference to the " blessed fire " and the " blessed smoke " ' !

The foregoing, *which is not exhaustive*, will, it is submitted, be held to furnish ample proof of the soundness of another Horatian counsel :—

> Sumite materiam vestris qui scribitis aequam
> Viribus.

B. Mac Carthy.

DOCUMENTS

APOSTOLIC CONSTITUTION OF FRIARS MINORS

SANCTISSIMI DOMINI NOSTRI LEONIS DIVINA PROVIDENTIA PAPAE XIII.

CONSTITUTIO APOSTOLICA DE UNITATE ORDINIS FRATRUM MINORUM INSTAURANDA

LEO EPISCOPUS

SERVUS SERVORUM DEI AD PERPETUAM REI MEMORIAM

Felicitate quadam nec sane fortuito factum putamus, ut Nobis olim, in episcopatu gerendo, ex omnibus Italiae provinciis una Francisci Assisiensis parens atque altrix Umbria contingeret. Assuevimus enim acrius et attentius de patre seraphico locorum admonitu cogitare : cumque indicia eius permulta, ac velut impressa vestigia passim intueremur, quae non memoriam eius solum Nobis afferebant, sed ipsum videbantur in conspectu Nostro ponere : cum Alverniae iuga semel atque iterum ascensu superavimus : cum ob oculos ea loca versarentur, ubi editus ac susceptus in lucem, ubi corporis exsolutus vinclis, unde ipso auctore tanta vis bonorum, tanta salus in omnes orientis atque obeuntis solis partes influxit, licuit profecto plenius ac melius cognoscere quanto viro quantum munus assignatum a Deo. Mire cepit Nos franciscana species atque forma : quoniamque intimam franciscalium institutorum virtutem magnopere ad christianam vitae rationem videbamus conduxisse, neque eam esse huiusmodi ut consenescere votustate possit, propterea in ipso episcopatu Perusino, ad christianam pietatem augendam tuendosque in multitudine mores probos Ordinem Tertium, quem Nosmetipsi viginti quinque iam annos profitemur, dedita opera restituere ac propagare studuimus. Eumdem animum in hoc apostolici muneris fastigium eamdemque voluntatem ex eo tempore susceptam attulimus. Ob eamque caussam cum non circumscripte, sed ubique gentium eum ipsum Ordinem florere in spem beneficiorum veterum cuperemus, praescripta legum quibus regeretur, quatenus opus esse visum est, temperavimus, ut quemvis o populo christiano invitaret atque alliceret effecta mollior et accommodatior temporibus disciplina. Expectationem desiderii ac spei Nostrae sat implevit exitus.

Verumtamen Noster erga magnum Franciscum et erga res ab

eo institutas singularis amor omnino quiddam adhuc postulabat : idque efficere Deo aspirante decrevimus. Animum videlicet studiumque Nostrum nunc convertit ad sese franciscanus Ordo princeps : nec sane facile reperiatur in quo evigilare enixius atque amantius curas cogitationesque Nostras oporteat. Insignis est enim et benevolentia studioque Sedis Apostolicae dignissima ea, quae Fratrum Minorum familia nominatur, beati Francisci frequens ac mansura soboles. Ei quidem parens suus, quas leges, quae praecepta vivendi ipse dedisset, ea omnia imperavit ut religiosissime custodiret in perpetuitate consequentium temporum : nec frustra imperavit. Vix enim societas hominum est ulla, quae tot virtuti rigidos custodes eduxerit, vel tot nomini christiano praecones, Christo martyres, caelo cives ediderit : aut in qua tantus virorum proventus, qui iis artibus, quibus qui excellunt praestare ceteris iudicantur, rem christianam remque ipsam civilem illustrarint, adiuverint.

Horum quidem bonorum non est dubitandum maiorem et constantiorem futuram ubertatem fuisse, si arctissimum coniunctionis concordiaeque vinculum, quale in prima Ordinis aetate viguit, perpetuo mansisset : quia ' virtus quanto est magis unita, tanto est fortior, et per separationem minuitur '.[1] Quod optime viderat et caverat mens provida Francisci, quippe qui suorum societatem praeclare finxit fundavitque ut corpus unum non solubili compage aptum et connexum. Quid revera voluit, quid egit aliud cum unicam proposuit vivendi regulam, quam omnes sine ulla nec temporum nec locorum exceptione servarent, vel cum unius rectoris maximi potestati subesse atque otemperare iussit universos ? Eiusmodi tuendae concordiae praecipuum et constans in eo studium fuisse, perspicue discipulus eius confirmat Thomas a Celano, qui ' assiduum,' inquit, ' votum vigilque studium in eo fuit custodire inter fratres vinculum pacis, ut quos idem spiritus traxerat, idemque genuerat pater, unius matris gremio pacifice foverentur.'[2]

Verum satis in comperto sunt posteriores casus. Nimirum sive quod flexibiles hominum sunt voluntates et varia solent esse ingenia in congregatione plurimorum, sive quod communium temporum cursus sensim ac pedetentim alio flexisset, hoc certo usu venit franciscanis ut de instituenda vita communi aliud placeret aliis. Concordissimam illam communionem quam

---

[1] S. Thom. 2, 2^{ae}, quaest. xxxvii., n. 2 ad 3^{m}.
[2] *Vita secunda*, P. iii., c. cxxi.

Franciscus spectarat et secutus erat, quamque sanctam esse apud suos voluerat, quae res potissimum continebant: studium voluntariae paupertatis, atque ipsius imitatio exemplorum in reliquarum exercitatione virtutum. Haec franciscani instituti insignia, haec eius fundamenta incolumitatis. At vero summam rerum inopiam, quam vir sanctissimus in omni vita adamavit unice, ex alumnis eius optavere nonnulli simillimam: nonnulli, quibus ea visa gravior, modice temperatam maluerunt. Quare aliorum ab aliis secessione facta, hinc *Observantes* orti, illinc *Conventuales*. Similiter rigidam innocentiam, altas magnificasque virtutes, quibus ille ad miraculum eluxerat, alii quidem imitari animose ac severe, alii lenius ac remissius velle. Ex prioribus iis fratrum. *Capulatorum* familiâ coalitâ, divisio tripartita consecuta est. Non idcirco tamen exaruit Ordo: nemo est enim quin sciat, sodales singularum, quas memoravimus, disciplinarum praeclaris in Ecclesiam meritis praestitisse et fama virtutum.

De Ordine Conventualium, item de Capulatorum nihil omnino decernimus novi. Legitimum disciplinae suae ius, uti possident, ita possideant utrique in posterum. Eos tantummodo hae litterae Nostrae spectant, qui concessu Sedis Apostolicae antecedunt loco et honore ceteros, quique *Fratrum Minorum* merum nomen, a Leone X. acceptum,[1] retinent. Horum quoque in aliqua parte non est omnium vita consentiens. Quandoquidem communium iussa legum universi observare studuerunt, sed aliis alii severius. Quae res quatuor genera, ut cognitum est, effecit: 'Observantes, Reformatos, Excalciatos' sue 'Alcantarinos, Recollectos:' et tamen non sustulit funditus societatem. Quamvis enim privilegiis, statuits, varioque more altera familia ab altera differret, et cum provincias, tum domos tironum unaquaeque proprias obtineret, constanter tamen omnes, ne principium prioris coagmentationis interiret, obtemperationem uni atque eidem antistiti retinuerunt, quem 'Ministrum generalem totius Ordinis Minorum,' uti ius est, vocant.[2] Utcumque sit, quadripartita istaec distributio, si maiorum spem bonorum, quam perfecta communitas attulisset, intercepit, non fregit vitae disciplinam. Quin etiam cum singulae auctores adiutoresque habuerint studiosos alienae salutis et praestanti virtute sapientiaque viros, dignae sunt habitae, quas romanorum Pontificum benevolentia complecteretur et gratia. Hoc ex capite vi et fecunditate hausta, ad fructus efferendos salutares et ad prisca franciscalium exempla renovanda valuerunt.

---

[1] Const. *Ite et vos* iv. kal. Iun., 1517   [2] Leon. X., Const. cit. *Ite et vos*.

Sed ullumne ex humanis institutis est, cui non obrepat aliquando senectus?

Certe quidem usus docet, studium virtutis perfectae, quod in ortu adolescentiaque Ordinum religiosorum tam solet esse severum, paullatim relaxari, atque animi ardorem pristinum plerumque succumbere vetustati. Ad hanc senescendi colla-bendique caussam, quam afferre consuevit aetas, quaeque omnibus est coetipus hominum natura insita, altera nunc ab inimica vi accessit extrinsecus. Scilicet atrox procella temporum, quae centum amplius annis rem catholicam exagitat, in ipsas Ecclesiae auxiliares copias, Ordines virorum religiosorum dicimus, naturali itinere redundavit. Despoliatos, pulsos, extorres, hostiliter habitos quae regio, quae ora Europae non vidit? Permagnum ac divino tribuendum muneri, quod non excisos penitus vidimus. Iamvero duabus istis coniunctis caussis plagam accepere nec sane levem: fieri enim non potuit quin duplicato fessa incommodo compago fatisceret, quin vis disciplinae vetus, tamquam in affecto corpore vita, debilitaretur.

Hinc instaurationis orta necessitas. Nec sane defuere in Ordinibus religiosis qui ea velut vulnera, quae diximus, sanare, et in pristinum statum restituere se sua sponte ac laudabili alacritate conati sint Id Minores, etsi magnopere vellent, assequi tamen aut aegre aut nullo modo possunt, quia desideratur in eis conspirantium virium cumulata possessio. Revera praefecturam Ordinis gerenti non est in omnes familias perfecta atque absoluta potestas: certa quaedam eius acta et iussa repudiari privatae nonnullarum leges sinunt: ex quo perspicuum est, perpetuo patere aditum repugnantium dimicationi voluntatum. Praeterea variae sodalitates, quamquam in unum Ordinem confluunt et unum quiddam aliqua ratione efficiunt ex pluribus, tamen quia propriis provinciis differunt, domibusque ad tirocinia invicem distinguuntur, nimis est proclive factu, ut suis unaquaeque rebus moveatur, seque magis ipsa quam universitatem diligat, ita ut, singulis pro se contendentibus, facile impediantur magnae utilitates communes. Denique vix attinet controversias con-certationesque memorare, quas sodalitiorum varietas, dissimili-tudo statutorum, disparia studia, tam saepe genuerunt, quasque caussae manentes, eaedem renovare easdem in singulos prope-modum dies queant. Quid autem perniciosius discordia? quae quidem ubi semel inveteravit, praecipuos vitae nervos elidit, ac res etiam florentissimas ad occasum impellit.

Igitur confirmari et corroborari Ordinem Minorem necesse est, virium dissipatione sublata : eo vel magis quod populari ingenio popularibusque moribus volvitur aetas ; proptereaque expectationem sui non vulgarem sodalitium facit virorum religiosorum ortu, victu, institutis populare. Qui populares enim habentur, multo commodius et aspirare et applicare se ad multitudinem, agendo, navando pro salute communi, possunt. Hac sibi oblata bene merendi facultate Minores quidem studiose atque utiliter usuros certo scimus, si validos, si ordine dispositos, si instructos, uti par est, tempus offenderit.

Quae omnia cum apud Nos multum agitaremus animo, decessorum Nostrorum veniebat in mentem, qui incolumitati prosperitatique communi alumnorum franciscalium succurrere convenienter tempori, quoties oportuit, consuevere. Idem Nos ut simili studio ac pari benevolentia vellemus, non solum conscientia officii, sed illae quoque caussae, quas initio diximus, impulere. Atqui omnino postulare tempus intelleximus, ut ad coniunctionem communionemque vitae priscam Ordo revocetur. Ita, amotis dissidiorum et contentionum caussis, voluntates omnes unius nutu ductuque invicem colligatae tenebuntur, et, quod consequens est, erit ipsa illa, quam parens legifer intuebatur, constitutionis forma restituta.

Duas ad res cogitationem adiecimus, dignas illas quidem consideratione, quas tamen non tanti esse vidimus ut consilii Nostri retardare cursum ulla ratione possent, nimirum privilegia singulorum coetuum aboleri, et omnes quotquot ubique essent Minores, de quibus agimus, unius disciplinae legibus aeque adstringi oportere. Nam privilegia tunc certe opportuna ac frugifera cum quaesita sunt, nunc commutatis temporibus, tantum abest ut quicquam prosint religiosae legum observantiae, ut obesse videantur. Simili modo leges imponere unas universalis incommodum atque intempestivum tamdiu futurum fuit, quoad varia Minorum sodalitia multum distarent interioris dissimilitudine disciplinae : contra nunc, cum non nisi pertenui discrimine invicem differant.

Nihilominus instituti et moris decessorum Nostrorum memores, quia res vertebatur gravioris momenti, lumen consilii et prudentiam iudicii ab iis maxime, qui eadem de re iudicare recte possent, exquisivimus. Primum quidem cum totius Ordinis Minorum legati an. MDCCCLXXXV Assisium in consilium convenissent, cui praeerat auctoritate Nostra b. m. Aegidius Mauri S. R. E.

Cardinalis, Archiepiscopus Ferrariensis, perrogari in consilio sententias iussimus, de proposita familiarum omnium coniunctione quid singuli censerent. Faciendam frequentissimi censuerunt. Imo etiam lectis ab se ex ipso illo coetu viris hoc negotium dedere ut Constitutionum codicem perscriberent, utique communem omnibus, si communionem Sedes Apostolica sanxisset, futurum. Praeterea. S. R. E. Cardinales e sacro Consilio Episcoporum atque Ordinum religiosorum negotiis praeposito, qui pariter cum S. R. E. Cardinalibus e sacro Consilio christiano nomini propagando Nobis de toto hoc negotio vehementer assenserant, acta Conventus Assisiensis et omnia rationum momento ponderanda diligentissime curaverunt, exploratisque et emandatis, sicubi visum est, Constitutionibus novissimis, testati sunt, petere se ut Ordo, sublato familiarum discrimine, unus rite constituator. Id igitur omnino expedire atque utile esse, idemque cum proposito conditoris sanctissimi cumque ipsa Numinis voluntate congruere sine ulla dubitatione perspeximus.

Quae cum ita sint, auctoritate Nostra apostolica, harum virtute litterarum, Ordinem Minorum, variis ad hanc diem sodalitiis distinctum, ad unitatem communitatemque vitae plene cumulateque perfectam, ita ut unum atque unicum corpus efficiat familiarum distinctione omni deleta, revocamus, revocatumque esse declaramus.

I. Is, extinctis nominibus *Observantium, Reformatorum, Excalciatorum*, seu *Alcantarinorum, Recollectorum*, ORDO FRATRUM MINORUM sine ullo apposito, ex instituto Francisci patris appelletur : ab uno regatur : eisdem legibus pareat : eadem administratione utatur, ad normam Constitutionum novissimarum, quas summa fide constantiaque ab omnibus ubique servari iubemus.

II. Statuta singularia, item privilegia iuraque singularia, quibus familiae singulae privatim utebantur fruebantur, ac prorsus omnia quae differentiam aut distinctionem quoquo modo sapiant, nulla sunto : exceptis iuribus ac privilegiis adversus *tertias personas :* quae privilegia, quaeque iura firma, ut iustitia et aequitas postulaverit, rataque sunto.

III. Vestitum cultumque eádem omnes formâ induunto.

IV. In gubernatione Ordinis universi, quemadmodum unus Minister generalis, ita Procurator unus esto : itam Scriba ab actis unus : honorum caelestibus habendorum Curator unus.

V. Quicumque ex hoc die minoriticas vestes rite sumpserint ;

quicumque maiore minoreve ritu vota nuncupaverint, eos omnes
sub Constitutionibus novas esse subiectos, officiisque universis,
quae inde consequuntur, adstringi ius esto. Si qui Constitutionibus novis abnuat subesse, ei habitu religioso, nuncupatione
votorum, professione interdictum esto·

VI. Si qua Provincia his praeceptis legibusque Nostris non
paruerit, in ea nec tirocinia ponere quemquam, nec profiteri rite
Ordinem liceat.

VII. Altioris perfectionis vitaeque, ut loquuntur, contempla-
tivae cupidioribus praesto esse in provinciis singulis domum unam
vel alteram in id addictam, fas esto. Eiusmodi domus iure Constitutionum novarum regantur.

VIII. Si qui e sodalibus solemni ritu professis addicere se
constitutae per has litteras disciplinae iustis de caussis recusarint
eos in domos Ordinis sui certas secedere auctoritate nutuque
Antistitum liceat.

IX. Provinciarum cum mutare fines, tum minuere numerum,
si necessitas coegerit, Ministro generali coniuncte cum Definitori-
bus generalibus liceat, perrogata tamem Definitorum Provinciarum de quibus agatur, sententia.

X. Cum Minister generalis ceterique viri Ordini universo
regundo ad hanc diem praepositi magistratu se quisque suo abdi-
carint, Ministrum generalem dicere auctoritatis Nostrae in caussa
praesenti esse volumus. Definitores generales, ceterosque
munera maiora gesturos, qui scilicet in conventu Ordinis
maximo designari solent, designet in praesenti caussa sacrum
Consilium Episcoporum atque Ordinum religiosorum negotiis
praepositum, exquisita prius ab iis ipsis sententia, qui potestatem
Definitorum generalium hodie gerunt. Interea loci Minister
generalis Definitoresque generales in munere quisque versari suo
pergant.

Gestit animus, quod Nostram in beatum Franciscum pietatem
religionemque veterem consecrare mansuro providentiae monu-
mento licuit : agimusque benignitati divinae gratias singulares,
quod Nobis in summa senectute id solatii, percupientibus, reser-
vavit. Quotquot autem ex Ordine Minorum sodales numerantur,
pleni bonae spei hortamur obsecramusque, ut exemplorum magni
parentis sui memores, ex his rebus ipsis, quas ad commune eorum
bonum decrevimus, sumant alacritatem animi atque incitamenta
virtutum, ut digne ambulent ' vocatione, qua vocati' sunt, 'cum
omni humilitate, et mansuetidine, cum patientia, supportantes

invincem in caritate, solliciti servare unitatem spiritus in vinculo pacis.'[1]

Praesentes vero litteras et quaecumque in ipsis habentur nullo unquam tempore de subreptionis aut obreptionis sive intentionis Nostrae vitio aliove quovis defectu notari vel impugnari posse ; sed semper validas et in suo robore fore et esse, atque ab omnibus cuiusvis gradus et praeeminentiae inviolabiliter in iudicio et extra observari debere, decernimus : irritum quoque et inane si secus super his a quoquam, quavis auctoritate vel praetextu, scienter vel ignoranter contigerit attentari declarantes : contrariis non obstantibus quibuscumque, etiam speciali mentiono dignis, quibus omnibus ex plenitudine potestatis, certa scientia et motu proprio quoad praemissa expresse derogamus, et derogatum esse declaramus.

Volumus autem ut harum litterarum exemplis etiam impressis, manu tamen Notarii subscriptis et per constitutum in ecclesiastica dignitate virum sigillo munitis, eadem habeatur fides, quae Nostrae voluntatis significationi, his praesentibus ostensis, haberetur.

Nulli ergo hominum liceat hanc paginam Nostrae constitutionis, ordinationis, unionis, limitationis, derogationis, voluntatis infringere, vel ei ausu temerario contraire.—Si quis autem hoc attentare praesumpserit, indignationem omnipotentis Dei et beatorum Petri et Pauli apostolorum eius se noverit incursurum

Datum Romae apud S. Petrum Quarto Nonas Octobris Anno Incarnationis Dominicae Millesimo octogesimo nonagesimo septimo, Pontificatus Nostri anno Vicesimo.

C. CARD. ALOISI-MASELLA, *Pro-Datarius.*

A. CARD. MACCHI.

VISA.

DE CURIA I. DE AQUILA E VICECOMITIBUS.

Loco ✠ *Plumbi*

Reg. in Secret. Brevium.

I. CUGNONIUS.

---

[1] Ephes. iv. 1-3.

NOTICES OF BOOKS

COMMENTARII DE SACRAMENTIS. IN GENERE AC DE
S. S. EUCHARISTA, AD USUM ALUMNORUM COLLEGII
HIBERNORUM PARISIENSIS. Parisiis : 5, Via Dicta,
' Des Irlandais,' 5.

WHEN expressing an opinion on the merits of a work, we may
look on it absolutely or relatively to the end for which it was
written. The book before us looked on absolutely does not
profess to be a mine of theological learning. It professes to
contain nothing that the great theologians have not already fully
discussed. It does not profess even to treat its subject-matter so
fully as many theologians are accustomed to do. But if we look
at the work relatively to the end for which it was intended, it is
of great value. The author wished to place in the hands of
theological students a handy text-book which, under the guidance
of a professor, would serve as a foundation for their theological
knowledge. As a text-book of this nature it is admirable. The
order is logical. The explanations are usually clear. The proofs
are generally cogent. For these reasons we say that the work is
of great value—in the first place, to the college for which it was
primarily intended, and, in the second place, to other colleges
where students must be content with a substantial, yet brief
training in theology.

We consider the work useful also for priests on the mission
who cannot spare time to open larger volumes for the solution of
every little question that may arise. The practical nature of the
questions discussed, especially in the Blessed Eucharist, will
relieve them from that necessity to a great extent. For them,
too, as indeed for students of sacramental theology generally, it is
useful to have dogma and moral treated side by side. This is the
method adopted by the author.

With the subject-matter of the work we can find no reasonable fault. No doubt there are little things, such as the cogency
of certain proofs, the relative importance given to certain subjects,
in which we do not agree with the author ; but this does not arise
from any defect in the work, but from a reasonable diversity of
opinion. There is one matter on which we are not so sure such

a diversity of opinion may exist. It is the manner in which the author gives quotations from other authors. When a man writes a book we expect to see the ideas expressed in his own words. If there be a question of great importance or great difficulty, it is useful to give extracts from theologians to bear out or make clear what the author wishes to inculcate. These extracts should, we think, be taken, as far as possible, from first-class theologians. Now, the author before us quotes extracts too often from theologians who are by no means first class. This he does not merely in more important or difficult questions, but even in things of minor importance, and of no special difficulty. Sometimes even he does not express the matter in his own words at all, but at once gives a quotation from those authors.

This, however, does not lessen the value of the book, so we can recommend it as a useful text-book for colleges in which a very extended course of theology is not read, and also for priests on the mission who desire to have practical matter in a convenient form.

J. M. H.

LIFE OF ST. JOHN OF THE CROSS. By David Lewis, M.A. London : Thomas Baker, Soho-square. 1897.

THIS is a very simple and readable narrative of the trials and triumphs of a remarkable saint. Although the perusal of a saint's life must make a serious reader feel how far he is from the summit of perfection, and even see that this level is practically beyond his reach, yet he will, we think, derive no small encouragement, direction, and consolation, from a study of the life and character presented to us in those pages. St. John made a great distinction between himself and the rest of men. On himself he imposed extraordinary penances, and he bore extreme trials with heroic fortitude. He renounced the mitigated rule of the Carmelites, and under the direction of St. Teresa became one of the first friars of the reform. Under his poor habit he wore a penitential shirt. Barefooted during the day in all weathers, his couch at night was ordinarily the hard ground. For his body generally he had no anxiety except in the direction of devising modes of annihilating the inferior appetite. But towards others, whether religious or secular, he was as indulgent as their state in life would permit. In his direction of religious he insisted on the penance of obedience, and was very cautious in allowing his penitents to undertake novel experiments in mortification. Here are some of his views about beginners in the spiritual life :—

'Allured by the sweetness they find therein, some of them kill themselves by penance, and others weaken themselves by fasting, taking upon themselves without rule or advice more than their weakness can bear ; they try to hide their doings from those whom they are bound to obey in the matter, and some even dare to practise austerities expressly forbidden them. These are full of imperfection, people without reason who put aside descretion and submission and obedience, which is the penance of reason, and therefore a sacrifice more sweet and acceptable to God than all the other acts of bodily penance. Bodily penance is full of imperfections if that of the rule be neglected.' [1]

It was his determination to enforce ordinary monastic discipline that occasioned some of his bitterest trials.

'While the saint was living in Penuela, his brethren were preparing another cross for him, which is one of the hardest to bear—the contradiction of good men. His good name and spotless life were made the sport of idle tongues, and one of the members of the Council went from monastery to monastery gathering materials in order to bring grave charges against him. . . . The source of this trouble was Fra Diego of the Evangelist, who when he was a friar at Seville had to bear, and bore ungraciously, the correction which the saint, then his superior, administered to him, for his non-observance of the discipline of Carmel. The servant of God, elected Vicar-Provincial in the Chapter of Pestrana, in 1585, found in the discharge of his duties that strict observance, according to the rule, was not kept in the monastery of Seville. In that house were two friars, great preachers, wise and discreet in the estimation of people who could never see them too often in their houses. The friars were certainly men of zeal, and very readily gave themselves up to good works with which they had nothing to do. They were continually busy, absent from choir, refectory, and recreation, scarcely ever in their cells, and, the more effectually to do good, dressed themselves not quite like the other friars of Carmel of the Reform.'

St. John, it appears, had the hard-heartedness only to recall those two excellent and presentable friars to the good works with *which they had to do*. He paid the penalty of his temerity — a usual experience of reformers. One of them, Fra Diego, later on, even when he became a superior of some kind himself, wasted

---

[1] Page 134.

much of his time and powers of research in proving the saint to
have been all through life a hypocrite ; the other, Fra Francis of
St. Chrysostom, used his position as superior of the house in
which the saint died, to mortify his former superior.   In the
course of his investigations Fra Diego died, and it is only just to
add that towards the close of St. John's last illness Fra Francis
relented, and left nothing undone to atone for his uncharitableness.

In a very short preface the author mentions the sources from
which he compiled his book, but one could wish for more references in the body of the work.   The most extraordinary
events are narrated with the same *naivete* as characterizes his
record, say, of the holding of a chapter or the election of a prior.
We are told, for example, that to accomplish the ruin of a nun
to whom St. John had given direction, the devil assumed the
guise of the saint, went into the confessional, sent for the nun,
and there ' plied her with deadly teaching ; ' that Satan wrote a
letter to the same nun in the handwriting of the saint.   We are
told that the tempter failed ; but, in my opinion, it is desirable
that an author should at least say expressly if he had satisfied
his own mind about the historical accuracy of such preternatural
phenomena, and, furthermore, that he should append references
for the benefit of the incredulous.

This fault does not, however, detract much from the ascetic
value of a work which unfolds with ample fulness of detail and
simplicity of style the career of a man who, born and bred in
poverty, voluntarily embraced the Cross while yet a youth, advanced daily in sanctity by means of sorrow, prayer, humiliation,
and patience, until, at the early age of 50, he succumbed to the
weight of accumulated sufferings, not without signs visible to the
multitude that the soul of a very mean-looking, bare-footed friar,
known to many of them as Fra John of the Cross, passed from
earth to heaven.

T. P. G.

LAYS OF THE RED BRANCH.   By Sir Samuel Ferguson.
With an Introduction by Lady Ferguson.   New Irish
Library Series.   London : T. F. Unwin.   Dublin :
Sealy, Bryers & Walker.   1897.

To all Irishmen who love good literature, and who are
anxious to spread a knowledge of it amongst the people, we most
cordially recommend this handsome little volume.   It is, in our

opinion, decidedly one of the best in the new series published by
Sir Charles Gavan Duffy. The interesting and valuable introduction of Lady Ferguson enables us to trace with little effort
the outlines of the plan followed by her illustrious husband in his
treatment of the legends of Ireland's heroic age. Every note in
the lays themselves proves to us how thoroughly Sir Samuel
Ferguson entered into the spirit of these shadowy times, and
sympathized with every movement of those epic cycles which
fired his heart and his intellect as well as his imagination. No
one but a genuine Celtic bard, worthy representative, as his name
implies, of Fergus and of Sanchan, of Murgen and Eimena, and
Ilan Finn, with all the love of cadence and of song that
distinguished these early singers of Erin, 'could have penned
those stanzas of the Tain-Quest, uttered by Murgen over the
grave of Fergus. The claims of gratitude, of kindred, and of
love, were powerless to awaken Fergus from the ' deaf heaps '
of death, and induce him to recount the tale of the great
cow-foray, of which he had been the witness and the bard.
Another appeal, however, is made, and it is not made in
vain :—

> Thou the first in rythmic cadence dressing life's discordant tale,
> Wars of chiefs and loves of maidens, gavest the poem to the Gael,
> Now they've lost their noblest measure, and in dark days hard at hand,
> Song shall be the only treasure left them in their native land.

> Not for selfish gauds or baubles dares my soul disturb the graves
> Love consoles but song ennobles ; songless men are meet for slaves,
> Fergus ! for the Gael's sake waken ; never let the scornful Gauls,
> 'Mongst our land's reproaches reckon lack of song within our halls."

Even the bonds of death respond to this appeal. Fergus rose
and in all the solemnity of night communicated to Murgen the
heroic episodes of the foray of Queen Meav :—

> All night long by mist surrounded, Murgen lay in vapoury bars ;
> All night long the deep voice sounded 'neath the keen enlarging stars,
> But when, on the orient verges, stars grew dim and mists retired,
> Rising by the stone of Fergus, Murgen stood a man inspired.

The poems of this volume, however, belong mainly to the
cycle of King Conor MacNessa, and deal with the deeds of the
king himself or of the heroes that surrounded his throne. How
faithfully Sir Samuel Ferguson depicts the various moods of the
Celtic nature, the intensity of its sorrow, the fulness of its joy,
the moral or intellectual ideals that it invariably follows, the
principles of mutual trust and natural honesty by which primitive

society was held together in Ireland, must be left to be appreciated by the readers of his poems. We cannot, however, refrain from quoting an example. Take, for instance, that wierd lament of Deirdre for the sons of Usnach. What could be more penetrating than these accents of grief? Those of Hecuba,

When she her own Polyxena saw dead,

are not more intense or more faithfully attuned to the spirit of her race and time : —

The lions of the hill are gone
And I am left alone—alone—
Dig the grave both wide and deep,
For I am sick, and fain would sleep.

The falcons of the wood are flown ;
And I am left alone—alone—
Dig the grave both deep and wide;
And let us slumber side by side.

.   .   .   .   .

Stag, exult on glen and mountain—
Salmon, leap from loch to fountain—
Heron in the free air warm ye—
Usnach's sons no more will harm ye !

It was, we believe, a famous French academician who said, that the old Celtic harp gives out its fullest melody and its sweetest notes, only when it is touched by pure hands. The hands of Sir Samuel Fergus n are pure ; his theme is always a noble one ; his verses are the clearest reflection of a sound and manly nature. This modern bard required no golden ' cicada ' such as the Athenians of ancient days were accustomed to fix in their head-gear to prove that they were Ἀυτόχθονοι. He was, on the contrary, native of the native. He felt satisfied that the far-off voice of those early ages of his country would yet be heard high up in Olympus. He had absolute faith in the fruitfulness of those old Celtic stores through which he loved to roam. He had faith too in the future as well as in the past of the Celt. When the sword of King Arthur was cast into the mere, an arm rose out of the waters, and, as Tennyson puts it :--

Clothed in white samite, mystic, wonderful,
Caught him by the hilt and brandished him
Three times, and drew him under in the mere.

To Ferguson, as to all his countrymen, that arm rising out of the waters was an emblem of the hope of the Celtic race, just as the lance of Percival typified the war which Celtic nations were to wage against strangers and invaders. The poet was,

unfortuately, taken from us too soon. No one in these days
could have modulated the great voices of the past with a finer
result than he. He did however a man's part, and felt confident
that others would follow.

Such a man deserves the fullest recognition from his
countrymen ; and we trust that even the poorest will show their
appreciation of his genius and patriotism by purchasing, at least,
this small volume.

J. F. H.

PRAELECTIONES JURIS CANONICI QUAS JUXTA ORDINEM
DECRETALIUM GREGORII IX., TRADEBAT IN SCHOLIS
POTIF, SEM. ROMANI. Franciscus Santi, Professor Tertia
Editio emendata et recentissimis Decretis accomodata
cura Martini Leitner, Dr. Jur. Can. Vice Rectoris in
Seminario Clericorum Ratisbonae. Ratisbonae, Neo-
Eboracae et Cincinnati, Sumptibus et Typis Friderici
Pustet S. Sedis Apostolicae Typographi, MDCCCXCVIII.

THE work of the learned Father Santi on the Decretals of
Gregory IX. has already made its way in the schools and in the
estimation of canonists all over the world. It is, without doubt,
one of the best works on Canon Law that has appeared in recent
times. It is full, without being diffuse ; it is accurate and
concise in expression, and where there is room for doubt or
disagreement of authorities, it steers an even course and gives a
good account of itself.

This is the third edition which is now being issued from the
press of the great establishment of Frederick Pustet, at Ratisbon.
Father Santi is at present, we hope, enjoying the reward of his
labours in heaven; but this third edition of his work is edited by
one of his pupils, now professor and vice-rector of the seminary
at Ratisbon.

In this first volume now before us the treatment of various
questions in connection with the ordination of priests is very full
and satisfactory. So are the chapters ' De Judiciis,' ' De Foro,'
' De Dolo et Contumacia,' ' De Testibus et Attestationibus,' ' De
Appellationibus.' As a practical treatise on some of the most
important questions of Canon Law, we cordially recommend this
work to students and priests.

J. P.

NOTES ON CHRISTIAN DOCTRINE. By the Right Rev. Edward Bagshawe, D.D., Bishop of Nottingham. Kegan Paul, Trench, Trübner & Co.

THOSE notes, it appears, were put together some forty years ago, when the author was lecturer on Christian Doctrine at Hammersmith Training College. The title of the book is an accurate description of its contents. Under such headings as Faith, Hope, Charity, God, Jesus Christ, &c., the salient points of Catholic theology are arranged in logical sequence, and numbered one, two, three, four, &c. Too condensed to be suitable for popular reading, and too meagre in details to be called a treatise, it is still by no means a useless book. It will help a busy priest to prepare a dogmatic discourse, and presents an excellent programme of catechetical instructions. It is written in a clear didactic style, and although heavily weighted with theology, its perusal will, we think, prove entertaining and useful even to those who cannot fully comprehend the significance of doctrinal terminology.

T. P. G.

MANUALE PRECUM IN USUM THEOLOGORUM CUM APPROBA-TIONE. Rev. Vic. Cap. Friburgansis. Friburgi, Brisgovia : Herder.

HERE is a very neat collection of prayers, litanies, meditations, and hymns (without the music), specially, it would seem, selected for theologians. An introductory chapter contains ' S. Coroli Monitiones ad Clerum,' and ' S. Coroli Institutiones ad Clericos Seminarii,' and an appendix gives an extract from the Pontifical ' De Ornibus Conferendis.' No critic could fail to recommend such a book to all priests and theological students.

THE FORMATION OF CHRISTENDOM. By T. W. Allies, K.C.S.G. Three volumes. London : Burns & Oates, Limited. New York, Cincinnati, Chicago : Benziger Brothers. 1897.

As ' good wine needs no bush,' the work now under review needs no eulogy at our hands. Whilst not a new work, it is a new and cheap edition of a work of great value, and of rare and abiding interest. To the Catholic student of history and of the philosophy of history, what subject can approach in interest

the subject with which Mr. Allies' volumes deal? The author
approaches it not so much from the historical as from the philo-
sophico-historical standpoint, This lends all the more interest
and fascination to his treatment of it. In the first volume he
deals with ' The Christian Faith and the Individual ;' in the
second with ' The Christian Faith and Society ;' and in the third
and concluding volume with 'The Christian Faith and Philosophy.'
It were difficult to say which branch of the subject possesses
most interest, or which is most satisfactorily treated. All its
branches are of absorbing interest, and the treatment of all
alike reveals the hand of the master.

In the Press of these countries and of the United States, the
work when first published was warmly eulogized, and all
thoughtful and scholarly Catholic readers, both clerical and lay,
gratefully welcomed it as a masterpiece of its kind. To the
new edition, with which we are at present more immediately
concerned, a reception more cordial still has been extended.
In a letter which forms a preface to the first volume, Cardinal
Vaughan leads the chorus of eulogy.

' It is [writes His Eminence] one of the noblest historical works
I have ever read. Now that its price has placed it within the
reach of all, I earnestly pray that it may become widely and
appeciatively studied. We have nothing like it in the English
language. It meets a need which becomes greater daily with
the increase of mental culture and the spread of education. . . .
If any man desires to ennoble his own estimate of the Catholic
Church, let him read this book. . . . I used to urge, even while
none but the expensive first edition was accessible, that it ought
to be made a text-book for every ecclesiastical student, whether
destined for the home or foreign missions, for a Religious house
or for the world.'

This is high, but not, we maintain, exaggerated praise;
and we believe that every reader of the work will share our view.

Nowhere that we know of is the evolution of the Church
dealt with so satisfactorily, so comprehensively, so discriminat-
ingly, with such historical insight and literary skill, as in the
pages of the work under review. The story of the struggle
between Christianity and Pagan philosophy, between the Church
and the Empire, between Christian morality and the corrupt but
powerful civilization of the Rome of the Cæsars is graphically
and entrancingly told. Scattered up and down through the work

we have literary portraits, in all cases skilfully and firmly drawn, of Cicero, St. Augustine, and many others of the rival champions of the new and old civilization and beliefs, and these form a particularly interesting feature of a most interesting work. Another most interesting feature, is a remarkably fine appreciation of Greek philosophy. Its salient points are seized upon, and are so presented, that one is likely to carry away from a moderately careful reading of the lectures devoted to this subject a clearer, more accurate, and more durable idea of what it was, of what precisely its exponents taught, and of its influence on the human intellect, than is generally obtained from even the best manuals treating expressly of the History of Philosophy. In fact, every lecture of the twenty-two which these volumes contain, is full of good things, set forth in masterly and attractive form, and never before for a moment is the reader's interest allowed to flag.

For Irish readers the work has a peculiar interest. Dr. (afterwards Cardinal) Newman, the first Rector, appointed the author Lecturer on the Philosophy of History in the Catholic University, and this work was the outcome of that appointment. The introductory lecture alone was delivered, it is true. But all the lectures included in the first volume were prepared with a view to their delivery before the same audience ; and the appointment, doubtless, introduced the venerable and distinguished author to the careful, exact, and systematic study of the subject with which the volumes deal. That the lectures would have been eminently worthy of any Catholic University, no one who reads them can for a moment doubt.

We heartily recommend the work to our readers. It would, we are satisfied, be a valuable acquisition to the library of every priest. We should like to see it in the hands of all educated Catholics, and notably in the hands of ecclesiastical students. Nor do we confine our recommendation to the work at present under review. We recommend just as strongly the author's other works on kindred subjects : they are, in the main, a continuation of the work which now lies before us. We doubt if it is feasible to make *The Formation of Christendom*, as Cardinal Vaughan suggests, a class-book in our ecclesiastical seminaries ; but we are entirely at one with an American reviewer who urges that it ought to be frequently read in the refectories of all such institutions. It is unquestionably a great and luminous work on a great

subject. With the *Mores Catholici* and the immortal works of
Newman, it undoubtedly deserves to rank amongst the most
valuable gifts for which English Catholic literature stands indebted
to that brilliant company—now for the most part departed to
' the better land '—who led by the Holy Spirit and answering to
a very special divine call (or, as is sometimes said, through the
memorable Tractarian Movement), nobly sacrificed so much
which the world holds dear for conscience' sake, and ' the faith
of their fathers.'

M. P. H.

THE ST. COLUMBA COMMEMORATION AT IONA, June 9th,
1897. Edinburgh : William Blackwood & Sons.

WE are indebted to the courtesy of Messrs. Blackwood and
Sons, of Edinburgh, for this interesting and handsome little
pamphlet. It contains an account of the Presbyterian pilgrimage
of Scotchmen to the tomb of the great Abbot of Iona and
apostle of Scotland in commemoration of the thirteen hundredth
anniversary of his death. The pamphlet is interesting from
many points of view ; but the portion of it that naturally attracts
our attention most is the eloquent panegyric of the saint that
was delivered on the occasion by the Very Rev. Dr. M'Gregor.

In this sermon Dr. M'Gregor undoubtedly pays a very
sincere and eloquent tribute to the memory of our great countryman. As might be expected, however, there were features of
St. Columba's life and teaching which do not meet with his
approval. The gospel of this great saint which rescued Scotland
from pagan barbarism is not pure enough for the ' General
Assembly.' It was John Knox and Henry VIII. who purified it.
Whilst giving full credit to St. Columba and his monks for the
measure of Christian belief which they held according to their
lights, they were, nevertheless, much behind the Reformation
apostles in this respect.

' We must not, however, conceal the fact [says Dr. M'Gregor]
that, though free from many of the corruptions of later days,
they had departed not so much in doctrine as in worship, from
the purity of apostolic and sub-apostolic times. Fasting, penance,
and auricular confession were practised. They believed in the
intercession of departed saints. They offered prayers for the
dead. They made free use of the sign of the cross not only on
their persons but on their domestic vessels and agricultural

implements. They came perilously near to a belief in transubstantiation, the root-error of Rome. They called the Holy Table the Altar, and the Sacrament of the Lord's Supper the Mass.'

Dr. M'Gregor forgives them, however, for these deviations from the modern standard on account of the splendid work they achieved in the conversion of Scotland; and we, on our part, are inclined to pass rather lightly over Dr. M'Gregor's absurdities and corruptions of doctrine on account of the unconscious testimony he thus clearly bears to the doctrines and teaching of the early Celtic Church as well as for the sake of the noble tribute he otherwise pays to the character and labours of St. Columba.

'Familiar as we too well are [says Dr. M'Gregor] with the difficulties which beset all missionary enterprise among a pagan and barbarous people, we cannot but marvel at the well-authenticated success which crowned the efforts of St. Columba and his Muintir Iae—his family of Iona, and must attribute it at once to his own marvellous powers, to his magnetic influence, and to an abundant outpouring of the grace of God.

'From Banff and Buchan, the Moray Firth and Sutherland, and remoter still, from Orkney to Dumfries and Galloway; in the western islands back to far and fertile Tiree, the granary of Iona; in green Lismore, Loch Awe, and the Island of Bute; in central Scotland, in Abernethy on the Tay, and Dumblane, founded by King Aidan's son; in Kilrimont or St. Andrews on the east—over this vast area—as well as in various parts of Ireland, we have satisfactory evidence that churches and monasteries were founded directly by Columba himself or by his disciples. In brief, the whole of Celtic Scotland occupied by the Irish Scots and by the Northern, the Southern, and the Nidauri Picts, came more or less under his influence.'

He quotes with much effect Adamnan's description of the great Abbot:—

'From his boyhood he had been brought up in Christian training, in the study of wisdom, and by the grace of God had so preserved the integrity of his body and the purity of his soul, that, though dwelling on earth, he appeared to live like the saints in heaven. For he was angelic in appearance, graceful in speech, holy in work, with talents of the highest order and consummate prudence. He lived during thirty-four years an island soldier—*insulanus miles*. He never could spend the space even of one hour without study, or prayer, or writing, or some other holy occupation. So incessantly was he engaged, night and day, in

the unwearied exercise of fasting and watching, that the burden
of each of these austerities would seem beyond the power of all
human endurance; and still, in all these, he was beloved by all.
For a holy joy, ever beaming on his face, revealed the joy and
gladness with which the Holy Spirit filled his inmost soul.'

And Dr. M'Gregor, after speaking of his masterful strength
of character and great abilities, adds :—' He comes before us as
one who won not merely the reverence but the love of his age, a
man who was as meek and unselfish and kind even to the dumb
creatures as he was true and strong and brave. His own people
spoke of him as their ' soul's light.' He was called ' God's
messenger '—' a harp without a base chord '—' a shelter to the
naked '—' a consolation to the poor.' ' There went not from
the world one who was more continual for the remembrance of
the Cross.'

Let us hope that Dr. M'Gregor may come one day to recognise
that St. Columba's interest in Scotland is not yet at an end ;
and that, if duly invoked, he may still do much to restore the
true faith both north and south of the Tweed.

J. F. H.

DE VERA RELIGIONE.   By Gust. Lahousse, S.J.   Lovanii :
         Car. Peeters.
DE RELIGIONE REVELATA. By G.Wilmers, S.J. Ratisbonae:
         Pustet.

FEW portions of theology can boast the careful study that, in
these days of increasing infidelity, ' True Religion' claims for
itself from the learned. We cannot believe unless we accept
divine revelation. We cannot accept divine revelation unless we
examine the motives that convince us of its existence. This
examination is scientifically made in the tract *De Vera Religione.*
Hence, it is the constant aim of Rationalism to minimize the
arguments that are there found for a revealed religion. All
Christians there stand side by side defending the foundations
of their faith. All must welcome the works that tend to impress
on the mind of the world the principles that are of use in this
battle of faith with infidelity. We, accordingly, bid welcome to
the two able works that we have before us.

Father Lahousse is to be congratulated in a special way on
the admirable work of which he is the author. As a class-book
for students of theological colleges it has special value. Without
being diffuse it discusses fully the many interesting questions that

arise in connection with 'True Religion.' Though philosophical, as the name of Father Lahousse will indicate, it is simple—its depth does not destroy its clearness. We are particularly pleased with the treatment it gives to the authenticity of the books of Sacred Scripture. We cannot consider that a work on Revealed Religion which passes lightly over this most fundamental question on Revelation, can have any pretensions to completeness. Father Lahousse sees this necessity, and acts up to his convictions.

There are a few little points in which Father Lahousse scarcely does himself justice. For example, we may take his explanation of the definition of a miracle. The definition itself is perfect, but the explanation given would lead us to think that every work, which is so above natural powers that God alone can perform it, is a miracle. This, of course, is not the case. Other conditions are required which an author would do well to mention.

The work of Fr. Wilmers possesses many qualities that must recommend it to the theological student. Catholic doctrines are explained and proved with much learning and force of argument. As to the substance of the work we can utter nothing but praise. There are a few points, however, on which we consider Fr. Wilmers to have erred. In the first place, we consider it an error on his part to treat so briefly the authenticity of the sacred books. No doubt he asserts in excuse that this subject is treated of sufficiently in other portions of a theological course. This we do not consider a reasonable apology for discussing lightly, in a work on Revealed Religion, so fundamental a question. In truth the same reason ought compel Fr. Wilmers to leave practically untouched some other questions that he treats at greater length. We may mention the Divinity of Christ, as an example. In the second place, the author is too desirous to overcrowd his book with matter. Many things may be left out without interfering with the utility of the work. The result of this superfluous matter is, that, while the work cannot pretend to be a mere book of reference, it is too long for the ordinary student of theology. Then again the type in which the work is printed detracts from the utility of so learned a volume. In size there are three classes of type generally employed in the book. The subject matter is distributed among these three classes in a way that we cannot altogether approve of. We frequently find most important matter in the smallest type. As a rule, the explanations of doctrine are in this type. Apart from the question of appearance, which, no doubt, is something, this is hardly logical. As is evident, these mistakes are principally in form. They do not touch the substance of the work directly. Notwithstanding these extrinsic defects the intrinsic merit of the book will well repay any student for the time he may devote to a careful study of its many interesting and intricate discussions.   J. M. H.

THE CATHOLIC HOME ANNUAL.   New York: Benziger Brothers.

The Catholic Home Annual of Benziger Brothers, which made its first appearance fifteen years ago, has just been issued for 1898, and will, we are sure, meet with a hearty welcome from its ever-increasing army of friends. The present number is unusually interesting, and in its pages will be found contributions from the foremost Catholic writers.

A glance at the number shows a delightful choice of reading: there are stories by Maurice Francis Egan, Walter Lecky, Rosa Mulholland (Lady Gilbert), Katharine Tynan Hinkson, Marion Ames Taggart, and Margaret M. Trainer; more serious articles by Right Rev. Mgr. Conaty, of the Washington University, and Very Rev. Father Girardey, Provincial of the Redemptorists in the Western Province; the history of a famous pilgrimage, told by Very Rev. Dean Lings; an interesting sketch of Nassau, by a resident priest; and a brief biography of the Apostolic Delegate, Archbishop Martinelli, by Rev. Joseph F. McGowan, O.S.A., and of St. Vincent de Paul, by Ella McMahon.

From the start this Annual has been a success, and every year has seen an increase in its circulation. Nor is this surprising, for it is intended for the many rather than the few, and it is so made as to insure its popularity, and both in the quality and the variety of its reading and its illustrations, is the best of its kind.

We can heartily recommend it for family reading; and he will be hard to suit, indeed, who cannot find in it much to his taste.

[All Communications for the Editor should be addressed to the Rev. J. F. Hogan, D.D., Maynooth College, and authenticated by the name and address of the writer, not necessarily for publication. Anonymous communications receive no attention.—ED. I. E. R.]